Trisha Telep is the editor of, among other books, the best-selling Mammoth romance titles, including *The Mammoth Book of Vampire Romance, Love Bites, The Mammoth Book of Paranormal Romance* and *The Mammoth Book of Time Travel Romance*.

GHOST

THE MAMMOTH BOOK OF

ROMANCE

Edited by

TRISHA TELEP

ROBINSON

RUNNING PRESS
PHILADELPHIA · LONDON

Constable & Robinson Ltd
55–56 Russell Square
London WC1B 4HP
www.constablerobinson.com

First published in the UK by Robinson,
an imprint of Constable & Robinson Ltd, 2012

A copy of the British Library Cataloguing in Publication
Data is available from the British Library

UK ISBN: 978-1-84901-468-7 (paperback)
UK ISBN: 978-1-84901-770-1 (ebook)

1 3 5 7 9 10 8 6 4 2

First published in the United States in 2012 by Running Press Book Publishers,
A Member of the Perseus Books Group

Books published by Running Press are available at special discounts for bulk purchases
in the United States by corporations, institutions, and other organizations. For
more information, please contact the Special Markets Department at the Perseus
Books Group, 2300 Chestnut Street, Suite 200, Philadelphia, PA 19103, or call
(800) 810-4145, ext. 5000, or e-mail special.markets@perseusbooks.com.

US ISBN: 978-0-7624-4269-0
US Library of Congress Control Number: 2011938678

9 8 7 6 5 4 3 2 1
Digit on the right indicates the number of this printing

Running Press Book Publishers
2300 Chestnut Street
Philadelphia, PA 19103-4371

Visit us on the web!
www.runningpress.com

Printed and bound in the UK

Contents

Copyright   vii

Introduction   ix

THE CHINESE BED   1
Anna Campbell

OLD SALT   37
Carolyn Crane

HAINTS AND HOBWEBS   73
Jennifer Estep

HAT-TRICK   101
Gwyn Cready

GHOST OF BLACKSTONE MANOR   123
Donna Fletcher

SEVENTEEN COPPERS   149
Jeannie Holmes

YOURS IN ETERNITY   184
C. T. Adams

THE LOVERS 194
Julia London

A SINGLE GIRL'S GUIDE TO GETTING AHEAD 222
Liz Maverick

JONQUILS IN THE SNOW 241
Annette Blair

THE HEART THIEF 285
Cindy Miles

GHOST IN THE MACHINE 312
Dru Pagliassotti

THREE LITTLE WORDS 345
Christie Ridgway

GHOST OF A CHANCE 374
Caridad Piñeiro

IN HIS HANDS 405
Sara Reinke

CAN YOU HEAR ME NOW? 440
Sharon Shinn

THE STORM 464
Linda Wisdom

>>>--4EVR---> 481
Holly Lisle

Author Biographies 513

Copyright

Introduction

If popular movies are anything to go by, love after death is hardly unusual. Sexy, romantic ghosts like Patrick Swayze (*Ghost*) and Alan Rickman (*Truly Madly Deeply*) give us hope that the afterlife is not a total downer. Sexy men make sexy ghosts, of course, and what hopeless romantic in her right mind would turn down the opportunity to be whisked off her feet by invisible hands? The stories in this collection are a perfect mix of ghostly stories, from spooky to funny to wistful, and all hopelessly romantic.

Ghosts have all sorts of reasons for sticking around, it seems: wrongs that must be righted, evil deeds that must be avenged, loves that must be won. Sometimes ghosts linger to fulfil destinies, to bring together great loves here on Earth. Sometimes they are the suitors themselves, wooing living lovers across the ages. For all the ghosts that sit around flicking the lights off and on or hiding your car keys, there are many more who aren't content just to rattle their chains and moan – they want another chance at life and love. And they're looking right at *you*.

So if your next hot crush happens to be missing a head, or a whole body, for that matter, don't let it worry you. Death doesn't mean much when love is at stake, as you'll find out in this big book of fun, fresh stories from some of your favourite romantics writing today. It takes more than just a pulse to raise a girl's temperature.

Trisha Telep

The Chinese Bed

Anna Campbell

Marston Hall, Norfolk, 1818

Josiah woke to thick darkness.

He knew immediately where he was. Sprawled across the great Chinese bed at Marston Hall. His glorious, extravagant marriage bed. The King's gift to his dear friend, Lord Stansfield, upon the Earl's nuptials. Josiah had expressed suitable gratitude for the royal generosity, but he couldn't avoid thinking the bed was a rum sort of present.

Thick hangings enclosed him, hangings cut from robes sewn for a Chinese princess's wedding. A wedding that never took place. The princess's lover had betrayed her and she'd poisoned herself, cursing all marriages.

Or so the legend went.

Josiah's hand slid across the silk counterpane, feeling the raised patterns of embroidery under his palm. But he already knew his beloved wasn't here beside him.

Hell, he must have been half seas over before he tumbled onto the cream cover with its thickly twining peonies and fragile pagodas. By God, he was still wearing his wedding clothes. He hadn't been sober enough to undress. No wonder Isabella had left him to sleep it off. His darling had a temper. He'd hear about his excesses soon enough. He deserved to.

He didn't even remember crawling into bed.

Which now he thought about it, struck him as rather odd.

This couldn't be right. On his wedding day, he'd been drunk

on love, not liquor. And he certainly didn't recall imbibing so deep that he'd collapsed insensible.

If only he could remember.

He frowned into the stillness, struggling to bring events into focus. He'd spent the day in a lather of wanting Isabella. He'd been so hungry to have his bride to himself, he'd dragged her away from the wedding breakfast with scandalous impetuosity. Lord Fenburgh, her drier-than-dust father, had frowned disapproval, but Isabella's black eyes had sparkled with excitement. Josiah had claimed a lusty wife, thank the angels. She'd been as eager as he to consummate their chaste wooing at last.

He remembered her delicious, husky little moan as he'd kissed her ravenously, passionately, behind one of the man-size Japanese jars in the hall, barely out of sight of the guests. He remembered fondling the sweet curve of her breast before towing her willy-nilly toward the carved oak staircase. She'd scurried to keep up, running with a rustle of silk skirts and a patter of delicate heels across parquetry flooring. He'd swept his laughing bride into his arms and carried her up the stairs, golden light spilling over them from the high mullioned windows.

And then . . .

Something was badly amiss. He hadn't been drunk on his wedding day. His head remained clear and his mouth wasn't stale with alcohol. When he married Isabella, he hadn't needed intoxicants. He'd been delirious with happiness and itching to possess his bride. A glass of champagne to toast her bright eyes and a lifetime of happiness. That was all.

So why was he lying all alone in the darkness?

Where the hell was Isabella? She should be here. With him.

Isabella was dead.

Crippling grief thickened his blood like grey sea-ice. His memory remained disturbingly blank about details, but he knew without question that she was dead. Of course he knew. They'd been so close in life, they'd shared a heartbeat.

Isabella was dead. And so was he.

"Kiss me, Calista."

Austerely intellectual Lady Calista Aston giggled in an extremely unintellectual manner and allowed the handsome young man to tug her from the empty hallway into the shadowy bedroom. "Miles, I haven't got time," she said without sounding in the least convincing.

"I'll be quick."

Through dimness created by drawn curtains, she shot him a disbelieving look. "That's what you always say."

As ever when she regarded the man she was to marry, her heart twisted in an agony of love. A tide of self-doubt threatened to drown her, in spite of her appearance of light-heartedness. She still couldn't believe this superb creature had chosen her from all the women in the world to become his wife.

She was a devotee of logic, of scientific process. Miles Hartley's partiality for a bluestocking Long Meg like her seemed completely nonsensical. She'd imagine he was mad if she wasn't herself victim to a madness impervious to research or reason or cold, hard reality. But while she recognized her affliction as permanent, how long would his madness last? Until tomorrow? Next year?

From the moment she'd seen him across her father's drawing room, she'd fallen under Miles's spell. She still recalled her incredulity when he'd proposed six weeks later. Desperately, she'd hoped she'd become more secure in his love as time passed, but with every day of the last three months, her uncertainties had grown. Now, the afternoon before her wedding, they gnawed at her like starving rats on a loaf of stale bread.

She told herself a thousand times she was a silly goose. Miles said he loved her. But at her deepest level, nothing convinced her she was worthy of his regard. He was elegant and brilliant and gifted with a vivid masculine beauty. He should choose a wife who was equally beautiful, a toast of society, instead of a drab wallflower like her. Calista was bitterly aware that she was no beauty, with her straight brown hair and long, thin body and strong features.

With his usual careless grace, Miles kicked the door shut behind him and drew her inexorably into his arms. Another shudder of love ran through her. It was dangerous to love a man as much as she loved Miles.

"It's your fault." He smiled at her as though she were as bright and lovely as a rainbow. "If you weren't so delicious, I'd be happy with a mere peck on the cheek."

"You're a sweet-tongued devil." The grim tenor of her thoughts lent the remark a sharp edge.

His smile turned wicked. "Let me show you."

He kissed her and she melted into his arms. She was helpless against this passion. It terrified her even as she flung herself into the blaze. From the first, he'd made her feel almost painfully alive. If he ever left her, she had a bleak premonition she'd never feel alive again.

Reluctantly they drew apart. Tomorrow . . . Tomorrow when he kissed her, they wouldn't need to worry about proprieties. Tomorrow they'd share the carved bed that loomed behind her. The bed that was much closer than it had been. While kissing her, Miles had nudged her backward.

"We shouldn't be here alone," she whispered, resting her hands on his shoulders. She didn't know why she lowered her voice. Something in this hushed, close room always made her want to tiptoe. Nobody else loitered on this floor of her father's hitherto neglected mansion on the Norfolk Broads. The servants were too busy preparing for the festivities and trying to ready a long-empty house to welcome the onslaught of visitors.

Miles stroked his hand down her cheek with a tenderness that she felt to her toes. Clawing doubt receded. "Of course we should."

"Tomorrow . . ." she said on a fading protest as he gently pushed her back onto the mattress. It sagged under their weight when Miles kneeled above her. For all her pleasure in his touch, something in her didn't want to be on this bed – and not just because Miles tempted her to impropriety. She'd believed herself immune to the house's dark legends, but apparently she wasn't quite as level-headed as she thought.

"I'm not sure I can wait until then." He rose above her, supporting his weight on his arms.

She struggled to shore up the crumbling remnants of common sense. "It's only one more day."

"How cruelly you say that, as if my torment doesn't signify."

"Of course it matters," she said unsteadily, panting with delicious fear.

The amusement ebbed from his face and she couldn't quite interpret his assessing look. "I wish I believed that."

She frowned. The gravity in his voice seemed out of kilter with their flirting. "What do you mean?"

"I mean that sometimes I feel . . . my passion for you outweighs your passion for me."

"No!" Shocked, she stared up into the perfect planes of his face. Her eyes had adjusted to the dull light so she saw the uncertainty that flickered in his eyes. Miles Hartley, Viscount Kendall, wasn't by nature an uncertain man. "No, Miles. You know I love you."

"Then prove it." His voice was harder than she'd ever heard it.

"This time tomorrow, we'll be married."

"Yes."

"You can't tumble me here with the house full of people."

"So you say."

Calista grabbed his arms, feeling the tensile strength under the dark-blue riding jacket. "Miles, what is it?"

He shook his dark head and his gaze slid away from hers. Disquiet filled her. She hadn't been sure if he was joking when he'd started this game. Now she sensed something was wrong. Something more than male frustration.

"Miles?"

He stared directly at her, his hazel eyes dark and somber as she'd never seen them. "It's just . . ."

He paused, searching for words, he who never lacked a ready quip or a witty riposte. Her disquiet transformed into a coiling mass of adders hissing and squirming in her belly. She'd known this day would come. She'd known he'd recover from whatever whim had made him want her. She braced herself for him to reject her, to send her back to the lonely prison her life had been until he'd miraculously fallen in love with her.

Miles spoke in a rush. "I feel you're holding yourself back from me."

"I don't understand."

But she did, oh, she did.

She'd never trusted this happiness. Self-preservation insisted she reserved a fraction of her soul from him. So that when the inevitable happened and he decided he didn't love her after all, she'd survive.

He kissed her again but the entrancing sweetness had leached away. Sorrow weighed her heart even as she kissed him back. This was how it would be in years to come, she knew. Little by

little, he'd realize what a poor bargain he'd made in marrying the
Earl of Stansfield's awkward daughter. With every day, the glow
that lit his eyes when he looked at her would fade until nothing
remained.

If she were brave, she'd end the engagement now and face
down the scandal. She should make the break sharp and hard
before he hurt her as he would undoubtedly hurt her. But she
was too weak. She wanted all she could get of him. She wanted
to cling to the memory of the short while when he loved her.
Even if only a little.

Fighting the tears that would betray her misery, she stared up
past Miles toward the tester. Once or twice, she'd come close to
confiding her doubts to him. Every time, she'd stopped herself
from speaking. If he took her seriously, he'd think she was
appallingly poor-spirited. Most of the time, *she* thought she
was appallingly poor-spirited. If he didn't take her seriously,
he'd try to cajole her fears away as childish fancies. She couldn't
bear that.

Unlike the counterpane, the tester above her was decorated
not only with flowers and fanciful Chinese buildings, but also
with faces. A wizened mandarin glowered down at her. His
devilish black eyebrows arched over eyes strangely stitched in
red. In her imagination, the face's smile turned demonic, as if
mocking her futile yen for Miles to love her as she loved him.

"We can't." With a trembling hand, she reached up to brush
the fall of soft dark hair back from Miles's forehead. "You know
we can't. Someone would catch us and Papa would have an
apoplexy."

His smile became less strained. "They wouldn't catch us
tonight."

"T-tonight?"

"Yes, tonight."

He'd always been gentle with her. This hint of arrogance filled
her with unwelcome excitement. "Where?"

He raised his head and cast a telling look around the room.
"Why here, of course."

Something other than excitement at the prospect of Miles
tumbling her made her heart skip a beat. "In the haunted bed?"

"I thought you didn't believe the legend. That's why you had
the bed brought up from the cellars and put back together. You

said a woman who believed in science would never fall victim to ludicrous superstition."

"I did say that, didn't I?"

His unfamiliar ruthlessness faded into the affection that always warmed her in his presence. "In fact, you insisted this would be our marital bed, curse be damned. That was about the same time you said you didn't believe Marston Hall was haunted, and the aspect was so pleasant you wanted to live here instead of in one of my houses. You said even if the doomed Chinese princess's robes formed the bed's hangings, her spirit was long gone. She had no influence over the living."

"I didn't say 'damn'," Calista prevaricated.

He laughed softly. She loved his laugh. Just the sound of it made the world a better place. Oh, she was so overwhelmingly in love with him. He'd destroy her before he was done, however she battled to protect herself. "Perhaps not. But you definitely said that even if wicked Josiah Aston was dragged from the bed on his fatal wedding day, the bed can't curse all newlyweds in this house."

"I know it sounds absurd." She'd always dismissed the tale of the Chinese princess drinking hemlock after her lover deserted her. Somehow, today, as she lay on the bed and contemplated her own wedding, the tale gained fresh sway. "But I'd like formalities out of the way before I test the legend's falsehood."

"And I'd like to banish any lingering specters with good earthy lust before I make an honest woman of you on the morrow, my love." He paused, inadvertently giving her a chance to relish the endearment. "The specters in this room, who I don't believe in at all. And the specters in your heart, who wield far too much power over you."

Miles rolled away and lay stretched out upon the heavy silk, his thoughtful gaze never shifting from her. She was surprised he saw so much of her turmoil. Most people found her hard to read. For a moment, the temptation to confide her fears hovered. Then, like a coward, she avoided the questions in his eyes.

"You're a barbarian, Miles, putting your boots on that cover. The embroidery is priceless."

His lips curved in a lazy smile. "If you're going to nag like a wife, beloved, at least offer me some husbandly privileges to sweeten the pill."

"Miles . . ."

"Please." He extended his hand toward her, palm upward.

Dear heaven, she was a hopeless case. She couldn't resist him. She could never resist him. Which of course was a large measure of the problem.

Hesitantly she placed her hand in his and felt immediate warmth when his fingers closed hard and secure around hers. At moments like this, she could almost believe that the love in his eyes would endure.

"You're as wicked as Josiah Aston." She hoped he wouldn't hear the revealing huskiness in her voice.

His smile indicated he recognized his triumph over his bride's scruples. "Only with you, Calista."

"If we're discovered, we'll be the talk of the county."

"I'll make it worthwhile."

"You're very sure of yourself."

Actually, she had no doubts he was a wonderful lover. His kisses sent her flying toward heaven. She'd spent the last months wandering in a daze of sensual hunger for more than the frustrating caresses they'd sneaked under the watchful gaze of parents and society. Her doubts, as ever, centered on her ability to satisfy him.

"And of you." It was as if he read her mind. He sat up and pressed a fervent kiss to her palm. "Midnight."

"Midnight," she echoed, wondering just what she promised.

From the shadows, Josiah watched as the lovers kissed for a few minutes more before the young man swept the tall, slender girl from the chamber. Their games inevitably reminded him of his wife. It seemed a grotesque, malicious jest that he was dead. And alone.

Josiah's mind worked furiously. So little of what he'd heard made sense. What the hell had happened here?

A poisonous brew of grief and frustrated anger swirled in his gut. He'd had a whole life ahead of him, a life of love and achievement and purpose. A life with Isabella at his side. A life with children and hope and happiness. A life he'd been denied.

He must say he admired the fellow's spirit in luring his lady into sharing his bed before the wedding. Josiah had tried to seduce Isabella, but for a girl famously indifferent to society's strictures, she'd surprised him with her prudishness. Strange, because when he met her the tattle had been that Isabella Verney was no virgin.

Who were these two people who embraced on his bed and kissed and bickered, just as he and Isabella had kissed and bickered? Although, Isabella had been a queenly creature; this girl's eyes betrayed a vulnerability that was foreign to his darling.

Calista's clothing was outlandish to his eyes. Too light and simple to adorn a gentlewoman. Like a night-rail rather than a garment a decent woman displayed in public. Where were her hoops? She wore no stomacher and her dress was belted high under her breasts. Nor was her chestnut hair dressed with proper care, just a simple knot half tumbled down her back after her tryst on the bed.

Yet her voice, her manner, her sense of ownership of this house – *his house* – indicated she must belong here. More, the way that too serious face warmed into radiance when she smiled reminded him of his mother.

The man was a complete stranger. But Josiah was familiar enough with the demeanor of a fellow desperately in love to recognize his plight. He was a handsome devil, the sort women made fools of themselves over. But the intensity in his eyes suggested intelligence and a discomfiting level of perception.

The girl was something different. Plain and almost forbidding with her severe Aston bone structure, always more suited to masculine members of the family than females. Until she smiled, when she became almost as beautiful as Isabella Verney.

Wicked Josiah Aston?

The description seemed far too damning. Like any sprig with gold in his pockets, he'd been wild in his youth. But from the moment he'd seen Isabella the day after his twenty-eighth birthday, he'd known what he wanted. The beautiful heiress Isabella Verney had been headstrong and, at twenty-six, late to choose a husband. No matter. He recognized his destiny. He'd courted her for a year, seen off a crowd of rivals, many of greater estate than he. Then, praise God, she'd admitted her love and consented to become his wife.

According to the couple, people had dragged him from the Chinese bed on his wedding day. They hadn't mentioned his wife. Had she been there? What on earth had he done to deserve such a despicable reputation?

Had he possessed sweet Isabella before everything went wrong? They'd married. He remembered that distinctly. Surely he wouldn't take her to wife without seeking his delightful reward. Yet something about the straining, bristling energy in his body indicated he hadn't had her. And he couldn't imagine he'd forget holding her in his arms.

The damnable thing was, although he was dead his body continued to experience sensation, however false the perception. He recognized the day as warm for May. He was aware of the weight of his braided blue velvet coat, newly tailored for his great day. His non-existent blood still pulsed with desire for his absent bride.

So, no, he doubted he'd claimed her before he . . . died.

Before he died.

Time had passed since his wedding day in 1749.

A long time.

Time seemed determined to play nasty tricks on him. The space between waking and now, late afternoon, had passed in moments. He felt like he'd only stirred within the last hour, yet the tiny ormolu clock on the carved chest indicated a whole day had gone by.

What the hell had he done? He desperately needed to find out.

More than that, he needed to find Isabella. He couldn't endure being here on his own. An eternity without her was too cruel a punishment for any crime, however heinous.

He turned toward the door, left ajar after the lovers' departure. Neither had had an inkling he observed them. He could see everything around him while it seemed that nobody could see him.

Moving provided yet another odd sensation. Although he recognized he had no physical existence, he felt he walked like a living man, covered distances like a living man. Yet he kept tumbling into gaps in time when he was . . . nowhere. He felt battered by confusion, questions, contradictions.

Wicked Josiah Aston?

The bedroom was full of unfamiliar furniture, apart from the ostentatious bed. Little in the corridor was familiar either, apart from the faded wallpaper and the window at the end of the hall. He drifted through a few rooms, noting the occasional painting or table that remained from his time in the house. The decorations weren't nearly so elaborate as they'd been in his day. Had the family come down in the world since his demise? Or was he just observing a change in fashion?

Slowly, carefully, he made his way through the house, seeking Isabella and some clue to his fate. Nothing provided any indication, unless absence of evidence was indication enough. The double portrait he'd commissioned from Allan Ramsay for his wedding was nowhere to be seen. At times, in spite of his urgency to see his wife, he'd find himself transfixed by something. A painting. The library. The view across the park, which had changed remarkably little. He'd stir to continue his exploration, check one of the household clocks, and find that an hour, two hours had passed. Time moved differently for him. A second could spin into an hour yet continue to seem a second. And still he had no idea what had happened to him. Or his darling.

All the bedrooms were readied for wedding guests but he couldn't miss the house's barely concealed signs of neglect. Many of the rooms reeked of disuse, dust, stale air, in spite of windows opened wide to the late spring afternoon.

Occasionally he encountered a servant or a wedding guest. They paid him no attention, confirming his suspicion that they couldn't see him. In one bedroom, he found a half-finished letter, dated at the top. In horrified shock, he'd stared at the page.

It was nearly seventy years since his wedding. Since, presumably, his . . . death.

How could he have no recollection of anything between that day and now? Where had he been all these years? Was he somehow attached as a spirit to the bed? The young man – Miles, the girl had called him – had said it was only recently reassembled. Did that wake him from oblivion?

Only another question among so many.

Afternoon faded into evening and still he searched. His eyes remained sharp as a cat's, whether the room was dark or lit with candles. Finally as night deepened toward midnight, he opened the door to the tower chamber. The room Isabella had chosen as hers the night before the wedding. On the last occasion he'd seen this room, stealing a few forbidden moments to kiss his bride, it had been an untidy jumble of silks and brocades and feminine gewgaws. Isabella had an uncanny ability to make any space uniquely hers.

A woman still slept here, he immediately realized. But a woman very different from coquettish, worldly Isabella. Even before he noticed the beautiful pink silk gown spread across the bed, he guessed this room, with its lovely outlook over the gardens, now belonged to his descendant Calista.

No, if he'd died – the idea still struck a discordant note like a hammer hitting brass – his brother George must have inherited. Calista must be George's great-granddaughter.

Calista wasn't here. She must have accepted her lover's entreaty to anticipate their wedding vows. He wished to God he and Isabella had done the same. He wandered over to lift a book from one of the tottering piles that littered every flat surface. And only then realized that while he was invisible to all living beings, he could apparently move physical objects. Of course he could, he'd been opening doors throughout the house. In his lather to find Isabella, he just hadn't noticed.

Isabella wasn't here.

Was she anywhere? Or had her spirit ascended on high while his lingered to atone for some unidentified but clearly hideous sin?

He glanced at the book. It was something serious and scientific and botanical. Definitely nothing Isabella would read. Her taste had veered toward the sensational and romantic. And the room, apart from the massing books and papers, was much tidier than any space Isabella ever inhabited. Even the set of scientific apparatus with scales and vials and microscopes on the desk in the corner was neat.

He heard the door open behind him. Odd how his senses remained so attuned to the world when he no longer existed as a physical entity. Then all thoughts but one fled his mind.

Isabella stared at him from the doorway.

"My love . . ." he choked out, stepping forward and reaching for her.

During their courtship, he'd inundated her with extravagant endearments. It had been a laughing game, how wildly he could compliment this woman he loved more than his life. He'd called her his treasure of Trebizond, his glorious angel of heaven, his exquisite diamond of Ind, his shining pearl of the Orient.

But all his playful words had meant only one thing. She was his love and he'd lay down his life for her.

Joy exploded with painful force. Surely he could touch her. If he could lift a book or open a door, surely he could touch this woman who turned his world to sunlight.

"Isabella . . ."

Still she didn't speak.

He stepped closer, wondering at her silence, at her lack of movement toward him. She'd so rarely been still. It was part of the quicksilver brilliance of her character. She'd been endlessly fascinating, flashing like a jewel, his darling Isabella.

His darling Isabella who stared at him as though she beheld a monster.

Her expression made him pause before he reached for her. "Isabella?"

She was trembling and pale as she'd never been in life. He couldn't mistake the terror in her beautiful black eyes. "Stay . . . stay away from me."

Of all the shocks, this was the worst. What the hell had happened on his wedding day? *What the hell had he done?*

"I don't understand," he said dully, lowering his hands to his sides.

"Don't come near me."

She sounded so frightened, his lovely girl who had never been frightened of anything in her whole life. This was the woman who galloped hell for leather at the most dangerous fences. This was the woman who faced down her ambitious father and insisted she'd marry no man but the Earl of Stansfield.

The Earl of Stansfield who apparently she now loathed.

Questions jammed in his throat. Very carefully he stepped back, giving her space. He had to find out what was going on, but first he had to banish the dread from her expression. Her quivering fear struck him with painful force. He abhorred seeing it.

"I won't touch you." The words cut at him like razors. "Trust me, Isabella."

A disbelieving huff of laughter escaped her as she retreated, preparing to flee.

"No . . ." He surged toward her again before he remembered she didn't want him to touch her. Quickly he lowered his arm, but not before he caught another flash of terror in her eyes.

Whatever he'd done, it set his intrepid bride quaking with fear. Good God, what was going on here?

She lifted her chin, a poignant echo of the woman who had led him such a dance. She still wore the beautiful dress of blue French silk she'd had made for the wedding. Delicate pearls and summer flowers twined in her coils of shining black hair. "You can't hurt me anymore."

He frowned. "Hurt you? I don't want to hurt you."

"Don't lie to me, Josiah." She backed off surreptitiously as if afraid he'd pounce on her if he guessed she was trying to escape.

"I'd never lie to you."

Bitter cynicism tightened her expression, although at least she stopped edging away. "Of course you would."

With every moment, he understood less. Foolishly he'd imagined he'd understand everything if he could just find Isabella. Well, he'd found her and the mysteries had become more bewildering than ever. "Tell me what I did, Isabella."

Something in his tone must have convinced her to take his question seriously. A series of emotions crossed her face, fugitive as summer lightning. Puzzlement. Anger. Then a deep sadness that matched the stabbing grief he'd felt waking without her and realizing he and his beloved were both dead.

Grim premonition gripped him. "Isabella?"

Her black gaze settled upon him, somber and lightless as he'd never seen it. "You murdered me, Josiah."

Gingerly, Calista inched inside the Chinese bedroom, feeling her way ahead with trembling hands. There was a full moon tonight so sneaking down from her eyrie in the east tower hadn't posed a problem. Unless she counted her bleak conviction that this was a mistake and once Miles discovered how inadequate she truly was, he'd cry off, never mind the promises he'd made.

This room was pitch black. The curtains remained drawn, blocking out the moonlight. With every step through Stygian darkness, the temptation to turn and run grew.

"Miles?" she whispered, although there was little chance of anyone hearing her. Everyone in the house was asleep and this entire floor had been left empty for guests who arrived tomorrow.

No answer.

Dear Lord, had he decided even before he had her that he was no longer interested? She told herself it was no more than she'd expected, but even so, an agony of pain cramped her belly.

"Miles?" she hissed more loudly, wishing to heaven she had a candle, even if it increased the risk of discovery. Then instead of stumbling around like a blind woman, she could check the room, confirm he wasn't here and leave.

To cry herself to sleep up in her lonely room.

Too pathetic to contemplate. She straightened, although nobody was present to witness her revival of spirit, and reached in front of her.

She'd sit on the cursed bed and wait a few minutes – at least that proved her courage: the bed was said to promise tragic death to any bride who lay in it. Easy to scoff at ridiculous super-stitions in the light of day; less easy when she stood in a closed room, listening for anyone else breathing in here. Since last century's grisly murder of Isabella Verney, there had been numerous accounts of specters in the house. Calista was too modern to believe in ghosts. Or at least she'd thought that was the case until she'd entered the room where they seized Josiah Aston after he killed his wife.

Opening this beautiful, neglected house for her wedding had seemed a brave, positive act. Right now, she reconsidered the whim as rash and stupid. She counted herself the most rational of creatures, but something in this room wasn't right. Even someone as insensitive to the occult as she was could sense deep sadness here. The atmosphere's heaviness was more obvious now she couldn't see and she felt air that should be still, but wasn't, moving on her bare arms.

She ventured another step and slammed into something big and warm and strong.

Like a stupid ninny, she screamed.

"Calista, you goose, hush now. You'll have us discovered. And if we're going to face down a scandal, I damn well want the pleas-ure first."

Of course it was Miles. Living, breathing, provoking Miles.

Nothing unearthly from the other side of the grave. Sternly she reminded herself she didn't believe in ghosts.

"Why didn't you answer me?"

He laughed softly and put his arms around her. Until the first time Miles held her, she'd never felt she had a place in the world. She closed her eyes and relished the heat of his body even as her heart kicked into a gallop at the prospect of that strong male body naked against hers.

"I wanted to tease you."

"By scaring me and risking discovery," she said crossly, although, in his embrace, it was difficult to cling to her temper. Nerves and excitement churned in her stomach.

As if by common consent, they stood a few seconds without speaking, waiting to hear if anyone would investigate the cry in the night. The house around them remained silent.

"Actually I wasn't sure you'd come." Miles drew away and led her toward the bed. Or at least she assumed he led her toward the bed. The darkness disoriented her. The darkness and the dizzy pleasure of being alone with Miles.

"I nearly didn't," she admitted in a low voice, following without resistance.

"Let me open the curtains. We can't risk a light but the moon is bright."

She shivered with the trepidation his embrace had briefly vanquished. "I'd rather do this in the dark."

He laughed again. "How do you know?"

He seemed to take this encounter so lightly. She admired the way he always responded to life with a smile, but something in her resented that he didn't recognize her surrender as the huge concession it was.

"I don't."

"Then trust me. I'd prefer to do this in a blaze of light so I see every expression on your lovely face. Moonlight will have to suffice."

She almost missed a step. He frequently called her "pretty" and "his darling" and other such nonsense. The problem was he sounded so sincere, if she wasn't careful, she might start to believe him, in spite of the damning evidence of her looking glass. But something about this casual reference to her beauty cut straight to her yearning heart.

She wanted to be beautiful for him. As he was beautiful for her.

"Miles . . ." she said helplessly. He raised her hand to his lips and placed a kiss on her palm. She felt the caress to her bones.

"Stay there," he murmured.

She listened to him prowl around the room. He seemed to have an unerring instinct for where he went. With a swish of the curtains, moonlight flooded the chamber, turning black to molten silver.

She poised, trembling, trapped between a craven urge to flee and a powerful, intoxicating desire that kept her feet fixed to the floor. For a moment, she watched Miles at the window. He was limned in light like something from another world. The sight made the breath catch in her throat. He wore a loose white shirt and breeches and she'd never been so aware of his height or the lean strength of his body.

He turned and at last she saw the smile that tilted his mouth. Then his eyes focused on her and the smile faded, replaced by an expression that looked like awe. He became quiveringly still as he surveyed her from her loosened hair to her bare toes peeping beneath the white hem of her night-rail.

The light was so bright, she saw his Adam's apple bob when he swallowed. As though he found her as breathtaking as she found him. Some of her uncertainty ebbed and the babble of thoughts in her head quietened to a low hum of need.

"You're undressed," he said huskily.

It seemed foolish to blush when they both knew she was about to offer herself to him, but heat flushed her cheeks. "I wasn't sure what to wear."

His joyous smile made her toes curl against the Turkish rug at her feet. "Or not, as the case may be."

"Or not."

She waited in an agony of pleasurable suspense for him to seize her, but he approached slowly, as though afraid if he moved too suddenly, she might disappear. By the time he stopped in front of her, she trembled with fear and desire. Her body felt too small to contain the storm of emotions raging inside her.

He reached out to smooth her hair away from her face. His touch always turned her knees to custard. Now, when the bed and all it promised filled the shadows behind him, the glance of his hand set her burning. If such a seemingly innocent touch had this effect, she'd most likely combust into ashes before they were done.

Calista bit her lip to contain her unruly reactions and stood in shaking stillness as he trailed his hand across her neck and shoulders. His touch felt like a discovery rather than a seduction. Although of course she was seduced. Her heart thundered and her breasts tightened against the lawn of her nightdress. He glanced down and her blush heightened as she realized he saw her beaded nipples pressing against the fine white material.

"Beautiful," he whispered, running his hand down her side then up again.

A tremulous sigh escaped her. This tender wooing lured her deeper and deeper into the stormy waters of desire. She should move, do something to encourage him. But his touch was so delicious, she found herself unable to do anything beyond accept this worship.

Through the haze of intoxicated pleasure enveloping her, she managed to send up a silent prayer. That the reverence she read in his face would last. That he'd still love her after he'd taken her to bed.

Finally after what felt like an eon of teasing touches, he cupped her breast. His thumb brushed her nipple and she sagged as sensation roared through her. At last, he bent his head and kissed her with a ravenous hunger that outstripped anything she'd experienced before. She sighed and gave herself up to pleasure. The doubts that tortured her faded under desperate passion.

Clumsily, trying not to break the kiss, he tugged off his shirt. They both laughed breathlessly. Then laughter died and heat shuddered through her as she flattened her hand on the bare skin of his chest. They'd snatched occasional moments of privacy, but never before had she been free to learn the mysteries of his body.

She moved closer, pressing her hips into his. He was hard and throbbing against her. She wasn't so innocent that she didn't know that, whatever the future brought, right now he wanted her. She had the evidence of his erection against the softness of her belly. There was his ragged, rasping breath and the craving she felt in his touch as he fondled her through the thin nightgown. Soon even that barrier became unbearable and he roughly tugged it over her head and flung it away.

For the first time she was naked with a man. Self-consciousness rose like a tide of icy water. The night wasn't cold but the air chilled her skin. Awkwardly she broke away, but Miles caught her hand and stopped her escaping. Gently but inexorably, he turned her toward the moonlight flooding through the window.

"Exquisite," he breathed.

She wanted to argue. To tell him she was too tall, too thin, and that her breasts were too small. But the veneration in his face held her silent.

He reached out to trace the shape of her body, the subtle curves and lines. This time there was nothing between her skin and the seeking, gliding touch of his fingers. This time when he kissed her, she sensed a new wildness. As though now he'd seen her nakedness, some wall between them had crumbled.

She became lost in a dark forest of sensation. Of soft sighs and caressing hands and pleasure she'd never imagined in all her twenty-five years. When he stroked her between the legs, she jerked on a strangled moan of shocked delight. Desire was a molten weight in the pit of her belly. She clung to his shoulders and instinct made her lean forward and bite him on the chest. She heard surprised appreciation in his gasp, then the world whirled as he swung her up in his arms and took the few steps to the Chinese bed.

For the first time in her life, she heard a man undressing. The whispering slide of fabric on skin was almost unbearably erotic. She snatched at another breath. Silly woman she was, she kept forgetting to breathe. This new world left her floundering. How she wanted to be brave, spirited, reckless, but shyness overcame her and she closed her eyes against his nakedness.

When she opened her eyes, he came down over her, blocking the silver moonlight. He supported himself on his arms and he seemed large and powerful and resonating with an alien masculinity. For the space of a second, the haze of arousal faded and fear revived.

"You make me feel too much," she whispered. "It frightens me."

"Trust me," he murmured. So often during their courtship, he'd said those exact words. "I love you."

Calista wanted to tell him she loved him too but the declaration jammed in her throat. She was too conscious of his nakedness, of his barely leashed passion. While she loved his passion, it daunted her too.

A low keening sound emerged from her throat and she stroked his hair with a trembling hand. The overflowing tenderness in her heart made it impossible to hide her quaking uncertainty.

The shadows and his position poised over her meant she could no longer see his expression. But as she trailed her hand down his face, she felt him smile. He sucked in a deep, shuddering breath and bent to kiss her, with a return of reverence.

"You drive me mad, Calista. But I love you too much to hurt you."

Her nervousness drifted away and she arched toward him in unmistakable invitation. Her voice was steadier than it had been since she'd entered the room. "Make me yours, Miles."

He was careful with her, but still she suffered an instant of sharp pain. She dug her fingernails deep into his back as her body braced for more discomfort. But then he started to move within her. All her love for him focused on this act, this union, this gift they both shared. The sweet intimacy extended beyond anything she'd ever imagined and at the height of her pleasure, she broke on a cry of rapture. As she drifted down from the golden realms, held safe in Miles's arms, she basked in a peace unlike anything she'd ever known.

He'd murdered Isabella?

Josiah staggered back to escape the accusation. Horrified denial kept him silent as he stared aghast at Isabella. But even while everything in him rejected what she'd said, the day's hints and confusions slammed into him.

Over and over. Until he wanted to scream "Enough."

"No." The word emerged as a croak.

The unwavering certainty in Isabella's eyes. The certainty combined with fear in a woman who had never been frightened in her life. These, these almost convinced him.

Almost . . .

He could never have killed her. Never. Never. Never.

Nothing she did would stir him to violence. There must be some mistake, some misunderstanding.

He clung to that one fading hope even as all other hope seeped away.

As though he bit down on a cracked tooth, he tested the truth of her assertion against what he knew of himself. If he'd killed her, he'd feel it in his bones, in his blood.

No, on his honor, no.

"I don't believe you," he said, still in that artificial voice that didn't sound like the man who had sworn to Isabella that he loved her and he'd devote the rest of his life to her.

"Don't you remember?" She regarded him with horror as if his denial were worse than the act itself.

"I don't remember because there's nothing to remember." In his desperation, he rushed toward her but came up short when she jerked away.

"Don't touch me."

The loathing in her voice made him feel ill. He spread his hands in a gesture of non-aggression and stepped back. "I can't hurt you now," he said with a hint of snap. "You and I are beyond the reach of physical injury."

"I don't . . . I don't want to see you. Can't you go back to where you came from?"

"My love . . ."

"Don't call me that," she demanded with some of her old imperiousness. He was glad to see something remained of her other than just a timorous girl.

"Why not? That's what you are. Seventy years haven't changed how I love you. An eternity won't change that."

"You don't love me," she said sulkily. "If you loved me, you wouldn't have killed me."

He fought back the urge to rage, to tell her she knew him better than this. Temper wouldn't bring him through this disaster. She still looked like she might run at the slightest sign of danger from him. *From him?* The thought beggared belief.

He fought to keep his voice steady. "Tell me what you remember."

She straightened and cast him a disdainful look familiar from life. She'd always been haughty and headstrong. "Surely you know."

He slumped against the wall, folding his arms to stop himself reaching for her. It was torture to be so close to her without touching. "The last thing I remember is stealing you away from the wedding feast."

"And then you murdered me." She looked less likely to take to her heels. He wasn't sure how these things worked, but if he lost her now, it was possible he might never find her again.

"Just like that?" He arched his eyebrows in disbelief. "I went from kissing you in the hall to pricking you with my pocket knife? Or did I come into possession of a loaded pistol somewhere between vowing a lifetime's devotion and getting you into bed?"

"You have no right to mock me." Anger sparked in her black eyes. The push and pull between them was familiar, no matter how much time had passed. Although the ridiculous truth was he felt like he'd only seen her an hour ago, when they were both alive and in love.

He shook his head in bewilderment. "It seems so unreal, my darling. That we're dead and here and it's seventy years since I held you in my arms. And that you claim I killed you."

"You did," she said sullenly, stepping into the room. His heart lurched with relief. "Now you think it's funny."

"Anything but." His tone was grim and he didn't make the mistake of interpreting her approach as an invitation to touch her.

What would it be like to touch her? Could he even touch her?

He could touch inanimate objects, but what about someone formed from the same indefinable material that he was?

"You pushed me down the stairs in a fit of jealous rage." She spoke as though her impossible statement ended all argument between them.

Shock held him motionless. Could he have done that? *Could he have done that and forgotten?*

Their courtship hadn't been undiluted harmony. He'd loved her to distraction and she, knowing that, hadn't been above teasing him. From the first, he'd been unsure of her chastity. Even so, he couldn't imagine killing her. She could lie under every man in the Royal Navy and he'd still want her.

With difficulty, he kept his voice even. "Why? Had you betrayed me?"

She didn't meet his eyes. "Of course not. I loved you."

"And I love you." Foreboding filled him. Her unease was

visible. Nor did he miss the significance of the past tense in her statement. "Whatever you did, my beloved, I wouldn't hurt you."

"Stop it, stop it, stop it!" She raised her hands to her ears and turned away in a fury. "I told you what happened. Now go away and never come near me again."

Her distress lashed at his heart, convincing him further that he could never hurt her. "Isabella, tell me what you remember," he said urgently.

Her shoulders trembled. Damn it, he'd made her cry. His voice softened and he fought the urge to take her in his arms and reassure her. The edge had come off her terror, but he knew she'd scarper if he pushed her too far. "Sweetest love, tell me."

She turned. "I . . ."

She raised a shaking hand to her lips as though afraid to say the words. But when she spoke, her voice was surprisingly steady, for all that her cheeks glistened with tears. "I was on the landing at the top of the grand staircase. All the wedding guests were crowded around something below me. I bent over the banister to see and realized that it was me. Lying on the tiles. I . . . I tried to say something, to tell them I wasn't dead at all, I was here alive. But even though I cried and screamed and shouted and pleaded, nobody paid a moment's attention. Then my father gathered the men and they rushed upstairs and grabbed you. The family story is you were hauled out of the Chinese bed but it's not true. You were in the corridor near the staircase. I tried to call out to you but you didn't hear me either."

He frowned. "But do you remember me pushing you?"

She shook her head. "No. But everyone says you did. They carried you off to London in chains and tried you in the House of Lords. Then they hanged you."

Her matter-of-fact tone confirmed her complete faith in what she said. He felt like all the blood drained from his body. Which was absurd. He had neither blood nor body.

Dear God, what an appalling fate. For anyone. Perhaps it was a mercy he remembered nothing.

She was still speaking. "After that, they closed up the house and dismantled the bed saying it brought bad luck. I've been here alone for seventy years, barring the few servants who acted as caretakers." In spite of the misery in her face, her lips twisted in a wry smile. "You'd think, given I was the innocent party, I'd waft up to heaven and you'd linger to expiate your sins down here. Where have you been?"

There was so much he wanted to say, so much he wanted to disagree with in her tragic story. But his resistance to what she'd told him was purely emotional. He had no facts to go on. Nothing she said stirred a shred of memory in him. His history remained a blank from the moment he'd swept Isabella into his arms, the happiest man in the world.

He forced himself to answer, although where he'd been was one of the least important issues between them. "I don't know. I woke up in the Chinese bed last night. I remember kissing you behind the vase then carrying you up the stairs. That was seventy years ago and there's been nothing in between."

"There's a wedding in this house tomorrow. Perhaps that conjured you from hell." She didn't sound like she was joking.

He frowned. "I don't think I've been in hell. Or if I have, I don't remember it. It was like no time had passed since we wed. When I woke up, I thought I was still alive. That you were still my wife."

Her lips twisted in an unamused smile. "I suppose I still am. Although we vowed to stay together till death us do part, and death did indeed part us. It's quite a conundrum. One for the ecclesiastical courts, I'm sure."

It was his turn to find her mockery grating. She seemed to accept without question that he'd murdered her. When she'd known how steadfastly he'd loved her. But then she'd had seventy years to come to terms with what had happened. He'd only been extant for one bewildering day.

"Don't," he couldn't help saying.

She cast him an unimpressed glance under her thick dark eyelashes. "Perhaps your spirit is attached in some way to the bed. It's been in pieces in the cellar since they closed the house. They only finished reassembling it yesterday."

The theory made as much sense as anything else in this topsy-turvy world. So many mysteries. So many puzzles. But just one was important. Had he killed this beautiful bright woman whom he adored?

He forced himself to ask the question. "If you don't remember, how can you be sure?"

Her eyes held a wary light. "We quarreled in the Chinese bedroom. The servants heard us."

"We were always quarreling. That was nothing new." Their wooing had been a tempestuous affair, marked by passionate clashes and even more passionate reconciliations.

She shrugged, but he didn't find her nonchalance convincing. "Well, apparently this time, your temper attained such a pitch that you shoved me down the stairs."

The story still seemed wrong. But Isabella believed he'd killed her. Family history confirmed he'd killed her. What was the revulsion in his soul compared to all these hard facts?

"I cannot believe it. I *will* not believe it," he said in a flat voice, even as bleak reality battered him, insisted he accept the completely unacceptable.

She regarded him sadly. "No, you don't *want* to believe it. Neither did I." She paused. "But you will, over time. Anything is possible over time."

When she slipped out of the room, he didn't have the heart to stop her.

Calista opened her eyes. She lay atop the lavishly embroidered cover of the Chinese bed. The room was still dark. If she'd slept after discovering such astonishing pleasure in Miles's arms, it hadn't been for long.

She shifted carefully. Her body ached with unfamiliar twinges. But what did fleeting discomfort matter when Miles had opened a whole new world of joy to her? Miles slept at her side, curled around her as if he couldn't bear to let her go, even in sleep. The closed room was redolent of heat and the scents of sex and sated male.

As she stared up into the darkness, she wondered if she could endure such happiness. If she could endure the possibility of losing such happiness.

Better to die now . . .

She frowned. What prompted that bleak thought? When she reached her peak in Miles's embrace, she'd believed she'd never doubt his love again.

She stared up at the tester and saw two tiny pinpoints of bright red above her. Two tiny pinpoints of red that focused on her in a way that both frightened and fascinated. She realized with a shiver that the lights were the eyes of that malevolent face she'd noticed this afternoon.

No, this wasn't happening. She was a devotee of scientific process. She didn't believe in disembodied voices or curses or spirits.

Except she'd heard that voice most distinctly . . .

Perhaps she was dreaming. Everything else in the room was black and silent. But she was too aware of Miles beside her, the possessive weight of his arm across her breasts, the soft sigh of his breathing, the heat of his body along her side.

She was undoubtedly awake.

And unable to break the hold of those two burning red eyes. They pierced her to the soul. They saw all her faults and inadequacies. All her unrequited longing to have Miles love her for ever.

The eyes mocked. They knew her wishes would never come true.

"I don't believe in ghosts," she whispered. "This is all imagination."

Beside her, Miles stirred but didn't wake. The eyes didn't waver. The steady red glow was uncomfortable, unwelcome, but still she couldn't look away. Suddenly, in spite of the warmth of Miles's body against hers, she was deathly cold.

A whisper came to her. Hissing. Caustic. Knowing.

You'll never be enough for him.

The voice's cruel assurance sliced through her. Closing her eyes, she insisted again she didn't believe in ghosts. She'd never been a fanciful woman. She'd been hostile to anything she couldn't measure with her own senses, scornful of weaker minds that credited influences beyond the here and now.

She felt neither hostile nor scornful now. She felt scared and alone and defenseless. And helpless to combat the truth of what she heard.

Let him go, Calista. Let him go. He'll tire of you before long. Perhaps even now he dreams of leaving you.

To escape the taunting voice, she turned her head away. Uncannily, the voice said everything she'd told herself over and over since she'd fallen in love with Miles. The voice caught her doubts and turned them into excruciating reality.

"You're not real," she whispered. "You're not real."

The voice didn't even bother contradicting her desperate denial. Instead Calista heard a laugh. Low and full of such evil that the hairs rose on her arms.

You've had your measure of joy. More than you deserve. Give up and leave Miles free to find someone who will make him happy.

She knew that the voice, the eyes, wanted her to leave Miles's side. "No," she said almost soundlessly. She squeezed her eyes shut, although some preternatural element knew the red lights still burned down at her.

You know this happiness won't last. Come with me. I'll give you peace.

"I've found peace."

Again, that low, derisive laugh. The voice obviously considered her answer completely fatuous. Unfortunately, so did she.

Still she fought back. When Miles had held her in his arms and touched her, she'd felt his love. He hadn't lied when he said he loved her. He'd been so tender, so passionate, so eager to show her pleasure. Of course he loved her. He loved her.

He loves you now. But for how long?

"For ever," she whispered, but both she and the voice knew she lied.

For long minutes, she and whatever malign spirit inhabited the room conducted a silent battle. And all the while, doubts scuttled through her heart like cockroaches.

She resisted until the pull became too strong to withstand.

Slowly she sat up. Miles's arm fell away from her. She immediately felt the absence of his protective embrace.

Even as her mind insisted she was being ridiculous, that she still possessed an independent will, she tugged her nightdress over her head.

Come. Come with me . . .

Now it had her cooperation, the voice was no longer evil. Instead it was sweet. The sweetest sound she'd ever heard, apart from Miles telling her he loved her.

Would she ever hear him say that again?

Come with me, Calista. Come to a place where you'll never be sad again.

She could no more ignore the voice than she could tell herself not to love Miles.

As she rose from the bed, she heard Miles stir, but some force prevented her from speaking to him or looking back. Instead she drifted toward the door, already open, although she knew it had been firmly shut when she and Miles lay together.

Purpose gripped her as she turned down the corridor toward the staircase. The moon floated behind the huge mullioned window, showing her way. Brighter than the moon were those two red lights luring her further along the hallway.

"Calista?" Miles's voice behind her was thick with sleep.

She struggled to answer but her trance-like state robbed her of speech.

"Calista, where are you going?" Through her daze, she registered that he sounded concerned, loving. She heard the bed creak as he shifted.

He doesn't really love you. You know that.

The voice no longer taunted, even when its words cut her to the quick. The words only cut her so sharply because they were true. Miles might believe he loved her now. Even she believed he loved her now. But she was too awkward, too plain, too adoring, too clever. Too . . . Calista Aston for him to love her forever.

That's right. That's right. Better to save yourself a lifetime of pain. You know it's what you want.

The voice promised rest, an end to the spiteful chatter in her mind. She thought she'd found rest in Miles's arms but she'd been deceived. She turned toward the twin red lights almost in relief, ignoring Miles calling for her.

Her mind knew it was dark, the middle of the night. But she could see as clearly as at midday. Ahead loomed the staircase, winding steeply to the black and white tiles in the hall below.

The same black and white tiles where seventy years ago they'd found Isabella Verney with her neck broken. A woman betrayed by her lover. That lover had paid with a humiliating execution and a pauper's grave.

Miles will betray you too. You know that.

"But he hasn't betrayed me yet," she whispered, even as she took another reluctant step toward the top of the stairs. Her feet felt weighted with bricks, but still she couldn't cease her forward momentum.

He will.

"Calista? Calista, what is it? Did I hurt you?"

As if through a mist, she heard the slap of running feet behind her. Miles grabbed her arm. After what they'd just done, his touch was heartbreakingly familiar.

"Calista, speak to me." The bewildered concern in his voice pierced her daze. "Are you sleepwalking?"

She turned to him, blinking slowly. It was odd. A strong light shone on him although she couldn't discern its source. It was brighter than the moonlight. He looked handsome, ruffled, worried. He'd tugged his breeches on. Her wondering gaze traced his body, as though she saw him for the first time. The powerful, lean torso, the long legs, the elegant bare feet planted on the polished boards of the floor. Even his feet were beautiful.

All of him was beautiful. Too beautiful for her.

Yes, too beautiful for you.

Her rational mind insisted she question what was happening, resist. But it was easier, almost pleasant to accept the voice's dictates and float at its command. Without speaking, she faced toward the stairs, edging closer to the void. The eyes hovered ahead of her now. Chips of burning ruby.

"Calista!" She heard genuine panic in Miles's voice. "You're too close to the edge. Be careful, darling, it's dangerous." His hand tightened on her arm and he wrenched her back.

"No . . ." she moaned, straining toward the stairs. The one word shattered whatever spell held her mute. She turned to stare at him and said what she'd always believed but never been brave enough to say aloud. "You will stop loving me."

Astonishment made him drop his hand and shift back. "What bloody nonsense is this?"

"It's true." She spoke almost indifferently. With every inch closer to the stairs, the pain of her endless longing receded.

Temper darkened his eyes. "After what just happened between us, how dare you say that? Don't tell me it's because you don't love me. The woman who lay in my arms tonight was incandescent with love."

An eerie calm had descended upon her soul. She summoned a regretful smile. Didn't he understand this was for the best? "Of course I was. I love you. And I know you believe you love me. But it won't last."

"Like hell it won't." He sounded angry and confused. "We're getting married tomorrow. I'll swear my life to you."

"And you'll regret it."

"Rot."

He was so brave and honorable. Her heart overflowed with love, love without the bitter edge that so often accompanied her recognition of how vulnerable he made her. In a few moments, she'd never be vulnerable again. "Goodbye, Miles. I have loved you so dearly."

"Damn it, Calista, answer me. What's happening?" He dashed forward and his grip closed hard and strong around her arm as if confirming he'd never betray her. "This isn't you. You're a fighter. It's one of the things I love about you."

He kept insisting he loved her. A moment's doubt pierced her certainty that no good could come of their marriage tomorrow.

He's lying. You know what you have to do.

Of course he was lying. She turned to the voice as though to an old friend. The voice knew she couldn't survive the loss of Miles's love.

"Let me go, Miles," she said evenly.

"Never."

"You have to." With a strength she didn't know she possessed, she managed to tug free. She made no conscious effort to move, but suddenly she was several paces away, standing near the carved post at the far corner of the staircase. In the bright, eerie light, she read the denial, the disbelief, the confusion in his beautiful eyes.

"Farewell, my beloved," she whispered and turned toward the stairs.

Josiah lurched forward to wrench Calista to safety but his grip slid uselessly away. His dead man's hands gained no purchase on living flesh. Her eyes were dazed as she stared ahead, listening to voices he couldn't hear. A fusillade of sparking red lights darted angrily around her.

Some disturbance in the air had drawn him to the landing, as though the encroaching evil demanded that he witness its triumph. He glanced up in despairing frustration and met Isabella's anguished gaze. She stood just behind Miles and the furious sorrow in her expression scored Josiah's heart.

Miles hadn't moved since Calista had dragged herself free. "Calista, look at me."

When something in his commanding tone compelled the girl's attention, the lights burst into a storm of flying vermillion. Jerkily, as though some force resisted her action, she turned to face him. In her loose white nightgown, she looked like she already hovered on the edge of the spirit world.

"This is best. You know it is." She didn't sound nearly as tranquil as she had before, and Josiah read something in her blank eyes that looked like terror.

Miles was pale and a muscle jerked in his cheek, but he didn't shift toward her. It was as if he recognized any reckless move would prompt disaster. "Do you love me, my darling?"

Her face was ashen with sorrow and regret. Her throat moved as she swallowed. "I'm doing this because I love you."

The participants in this drama were lit as brightly as if they stood on stage at the Theatre Royal. Calista looked torn and distraught. Miles's jaw set with a stubbornness that indicated he intended to fight whatever forces captured his beloved – and prevail. But his eyes were dark with torment and his hands opened and closed at his sides as though he struggled against grabbing Calista and defying the powers that possessed her.

"No, you're not," Miles said with absolute certainty.

The girl cast a longing glance down the stairs but, thank God, moved no closer to the edge. "All right, I'm doing this because you don't love me."

"You know that's not true. You're doing this because you don't trust me."

"Yes, I do."

"Then you're doing this because you don't trust yourself."

"Why wouldn't I trust myself?" she asked with a hint of irritation.

"Because you never have. You don't think you're worthy of my love."

She licked lips reddened with kisses, or Josiah was no judge of women. "I'm not."

"Yes, you are. I'll spend the rest of my life proving how wonderful you are, if only you'll give me the chance." Miles paused and Josiah could see he frantically scrambled for words to convince Calista to stay with him, to resist the dark forces hunting her. He stared straight at her and his voice rang out.

"Prove you are worthy. Come to me, my darling. Break away from whatever holds you and come to me."

She faltered toward him before she stopped, trembling. "I . . . I can't."

"Yes, you can."

"I'm not free."

"You'll be free if you trust me."

He sounded so sure. Josiah wondered how he could be so sure. For one piercing moment, he envied Miles. Much as he'd adored Isabella, he'd never been so sure of her, even when she pledged her life to him.

After a fraught instant of silence, Miles chanced a step in Calista's direction.

But he was too eager. She jerked back. For one horrifying moment, she teetered on the lip of the stair. She cried out and grabbed the banister, but it was a near thing.

Josiah released the breath he hadn't realized he held. Dear God, tonight mustn't end in tragedy as his own wedding seventy years ago had ended in tragedy. Yet he could do nothing to prevent calamity. Frustration was a rusty taste in his mouth.

"Trust yourself. Trust me. Trust our love." Miles's voice cracked with emotion. "For God's sake, Calista, don't throw away what we have because you're frightened."

"Trust myself . . ."

The girl hovered on the top step. Josiah poised in sick dread for her to lean a few inches backward and topple to her death. The red lights performed a stately minuet around her, as though they knew they'd won.

"Yes, trust yourself." Miles's voice lowered to vibrating intensity and his gaze burned into Calista's as if sheer force of will could convince her to return to him. "I love you. If you destroy yourself, you destroy me too."

For a moment, it was as if she hadn't heard. Josiah braced himself for her to fall. Hope and wretchedness warred in her eyes before, at last, she ventured one shaky step toward her lover.

Again she wavered in trembling indecision. The red lights blazed in a frenzy around her. Whatever held her was strong, it was malevolent, and it wanted her dead.

For an endless moment, red fire meshed the girl, threatened to devour her. Calista moved no closer to Miles and with her surrender to its promptings, the light grew brighter until it hurt to stare into it.

"For God's sake, Calista, run!" Josiah shouted at her but she didn't hear. The glaze in her eyes hinted she couldn't even see Miles anymore.

"Calista, don't leave me," Miles whispered, reaching for her without touching her. The red lights' power seemed stronger than mortal flesh.

Still Calista didn't move. The girl's eyes were stark with longing and doubt and fear. Her gaze didn't waver from her lover's.

Then Josiah saw her suck in a deep breath. Purpose, courage, life flooded her features. She straightened and raised her chin with fresh defiance.

Her voice emerged with steady confidence. "I trust you, Miles. I trust you and I love you and I want to be your wife."

The red lights ruptured into a blinding cascade of flame, but this time she proved herself immune to their promptings. She smiled at Miles with the radiance Josiah had noticed the first time he saw her. She wasn't beautiful, but when she smiled, she seemed beautiful.

With a stumble, she burst free of the cloud of red. Her lover groaned and dragged her into his arms, muttering an incoherent litany of love and relief. Calista sagged against him in exhaustion and started to cry.

Around her, the red lights circled in confusion then, one by one, winked out to nothing. The air suddenly seemed cleaner, cooler, untinged by the low buzz of malevolence.

Josiah glanced up to see Isabella approaching him, a smile transfiguring her face too. At last she looked like the woman he'd kissed so passionately behind the Japanese vase.

She reached for his hand. It was the first time she'd touched him.

"Isabella . . ." he stammered. Turbulent hope crammed his throat, making a wreck of eloquence.

She was trembling. So was he. Her touch contained magic. It always had. Now she made him feel alive, as if he was once again that joyful bridegroom of so long ago. His fingers closed hard around hers in a silent claiming that he defied her to deny.

How fiercely he'd loved her, loved her still. And staring into her beautiful black eyes, he could almost imagine she remembered just how she'd loved him in return.

He could never have killed her. Never. Whatever she'd done. Whatever she believed. He'd rip his beating heart from his chest before he'd hurt her.

She raised a finger to her lips and turned to watch as Miles and Calista drew apart. Calista stared across at Josiah and Isabella, and one of her beautiful smiles lit her expression, almost as if . . .

"Do you see them?" she whispered to Miles.

The young man kept his arm around his bride's shoulders. "I do."

Astonished, Josiah realized he and Isabella had become visible to the couple. He raised his hand in a heartfelt gesture of blessing and Miles bowed in acknowledgement. Isabella curtsied with flirtatious grace, her wide skirts swaying into a graceful bell.

"It must be Josiah Aston and Isabella Verney," Calista said breathlessly. "You know, he doesn't look . . . wicked."

"No, he looks like a man besotted. Believe me, I know the signs." Miles pressed his lips to Calista's hair in a caress that expressed adoration and gratitude in equal measure.

"Calista and Miles, I want to wish—" Josiah began, but Isabella squeezed his hand and shook her head.

"They can't hear us."

"But they can see us."

"No longer," she said softly.

Calista turned to Miles. "They're gone," she said regretfully.

"Yes." Miles drew her closer into his body. "Do you believe in ghosts now?"

The girl responded with a choked laugh. "I don't know. I suppose I must." She tilted her chin so she met her lover's eyes. "Whatever I believe, we're going to burn that bed."

Miles smiled down at her as if he beheld a priceless treasure. "We are indeed, my love. Now kiss me before I go mad."

"With pleasure," she sighed and stretched up to press her lips to his with a sensual confidence that gladdened Josiah's heart.

Josiah blinked to clear his vision as a strange wall of grey descended. He blinked again, but still the fog enveloped the lovers, made them seem strangely distant for all that they embraced only a few feet away. The grey encroached on everything around him except Isabella who still burned as brightly as a candle in his vision.

Isabella's regard was open and trusting as he'd longed to see it. "Do you remember everything, Josiah?"

And just like that, he did.

Memory crashed through him with the force of a towering wave. Reeling under the onslaught of recollection, his clasp tightened on Isabella's hand. "When you told me you weren't a virgin, I acted like an ass and lost my temper. We were in the Chinese bedroom."

"Standing near the bed." She released his hand and turned to face him, her regard searching as if she remained unsure of him, even now.

He'd acted like an ass but he hadn't killed her. Astonished relief thundered in his head. "You remember too?"

"Yes. At last." Her voice broke and her eyes glittered with tears. "Oh, my love, how could I have doubted you? Can you ever forgive me?"

Josiah smiled down into her lovely face and reached out to cup her cheek. "I'm the one who should ask forgiveness."

With breathless speed, long ago events slammed into order. He'd carried his bride into the Chinese room and started to kiss and undress her. He'd never been so happy in his life – he'd never imagined such happiness was possible – until she'd abruptly pulled away and whispered a shaken confession that she wasn't a virgin.

Like an arrogant blockhead, Josiah hadn't told her that her previous lover didn't matter a tinker's damn, that she'd married him and he'd love her forever. Instead, he'd succumbed to masculine pride and lost his temper. Isabella's guilt had soon transformed into characteristic defiance.

Then with an eerie abruptness that made sense to him now he'd witnessed the malign forces stalking Calista, Isabella had fallen silent. She'd cast him one last look as though her heart had shattered into a thousand pieces, then whirled away and fled the room as if devils pursued her.

Devils indeed.

Panicked by her incomprehensible actions, he'd abandoned his pique and his pompous insistence on a full confession. He'd raced after her into the corridor, but not fast enough to save her from throwing herself down the stairs. Barely had her terrified scream echoed through the great hall before she lay broken on the tiles below.

After that, the world went mad. Nobody ever questioned that he'd killed his wife and he'd been too numb with grief to mount a convincing defense. And part of him, a large part, had believed that the trial in London, the disgrace, the hanging, were just punishment for failing to protect his beloved.

His beloved . . .

"And now, my sweet Isabella, we have eternity," he said gently, extending his arm with a formal gesture, as if they were guests at a court ball and he invited her to dance.

"I can't wait," she whispered, accepting his arm and turning toward the stairs with an elegant flick of her skirts.

His heart finally at ease, Josiah escorted Isabella down the curved staircase and into the light.

Old Salt

Carolyn Crane

Cassie Nolan addressed the tourists in a solemn tone. "Ready?"

They nodded and murmured their *yes*es. It was a small group tonight – six adults and two kids, standing out on the porch of the Old Salt Tavern in the growing dusk.

She raised her eyebrows as the town clock rang eight chimes, scrutinizing their faces, as though she wasn't convinced they could handle Old Salt's nightly haunting . . . as though it might be too frightening, too horrifying, too shocking.

Not.

Old Salt William McHenry was the most pathetic haunter ever. Clearly he was a real ghost, that's what frustrated Cassie. Could he not come up with something cooler and scarier than dragging an invisible chain around on a dock? Maybe throw stuff around? Smash something?

The tourists would stand there in awe of Old Salt's ghostly clanking, and she would stand there in awe of his ghostly ineptitude, thinking, *A chain? Really? That's what you came up with?*

Of course, she kept her opinions to herself. These people were paying to witness Old Salt, but more than that, they were paying for the experience of wonder and mystery. As tour guide, Cassie set the tone for that. This was a family business, after all.

Cassie sipped her caramel latte, acting mysteriously hesitant a few beats longer, then she turned and headed down the steps and out across the expanse of sand and sea oats toward the haunted pier. The tourists followed. It was a pleasantly warm and still September evening, and she told the story of how the

Gertie Gail sank in a hurricane just offshore at precisely eight o'clock back in 1879.

It was young William McHenry's first voyage as captain. He had made sure his crew escaped, but he went down with the ship and died. He was a man in love, however, desperate to get to shore to his beloved and enigmatic Nell.

In fact, poor, dying William McHenry's passion was so strong that his ghost rose from his body and swam to shore, hook hand and all, and climbed onto the pier, dragging his chain along, calling her name: *Nelllll!* But she wasn't there. So he turned around and dragged his chain back to the far end of the pier. From there, he floated away or disappeared – nobody knew what happened to him after the clanking ceased.

"But there is one thing we do know," she said. They'd reached the shore's edge; they would stay there, just shy of the pier. "He's back here every night, at about a quarter past eight, dragging his chain. It's as if he relives the sinking of his ship and his own death every night at eight. And every night he comes back to this pier, searching for his beloved Nell, calling out her name on the wind."

Cassie had never heard Old Salt McHenry call Nell's name on the wind, but it was part of the legend, and a lot of people thought they heard it.

Whatever.

She put a finger to her lips; it was important to enforce absolute silence during Old Salt's visits.

Captain William McHenry stood against the raging cyclone, clinging to the ship's mast as the last of his men escaped in lifeboats. Though he couldn't see the shore, he'd heard the town clock chime eight o'clock. Land lay near.

McHenry shut his eyes and said a prayer for his crew as spray lashed his face; everything seemed strangely dreamlike. Tremors in the deck, wood cracked all around him, and a dark form blotted out the sky – a rogue wave. The ship slid sideways; the hull heaved, ropes and pulleys took flight like startled birds. William began to slide. He grabbed hold of a wooden rail just as the anchor chain came loose and flew toward him. He tried to pull himself from its path but it caught him, wrapped twice around his ankle, and yanked him down through the icy depths.

Next thing he knew, he was on the rocky sea floor. Frantically he kicked, trying to free his ankle from the chain. He pulled at the chain, attempting to loosen it, but his hook kept catching in the links. He cursed his useless hand.

He thought of Nell. So close. She said she'd watch for his ship's return and be waiting on the pier. He'd spent ten months at sea, reliving his time with her, remembering the way she'd made him feel, longing to see her again.

Despair jolted through him. With his good hand, he grabbed the anchor from the ocean floor and heaved it up, amazed when it lifted – he'd never been able to hoist the anchor before. Perhaps he could still get to her! He swam upward, anchor in tow, stunned at his own strength . . . yet somehow not.

When he reached the surface, he kicked and thrashed through the icy water, toward the Clancyville pier, amazed how the waves had calmed. Many a fire blazed in the distance. He reached the pier and hauled himself and the anchor onto it.

A handful of people had gathered at the shore, but none came out to meet him. Why?

"*Nellllllllll!*"

He waited, tired, disoriented. Why would they not come out to greet him? They acted as if they didn't see him, didn't hear him.

"*Nelllllll!*" He'd been at sea since the age of twelve and hadn't known many womenfolk. He was twenty-six now, and Nell was the first woman he'd ever felt easy with. She looked beyond his hook and his rough sailor manners and made him feel happy, in a way he'd never known.

"*Nelllllll!*" Still the people ignored him.

It struck him that he'd been here before, sitting with his anchor, chilled by the water, yet not wet.

Slowly he stood, feeling as if he were waking from a dream; this was Clancyville to be sure, but there were many more buildings. So foreign, yet familiar. And the contraptions, the colorful gaslights, the people in their strange garb.

Anguish gripped his heart. He knew this place. He knew it to be a lonely place.

"*Nellllll!*" Some of the gathered cocked their heads, as if they'd heard a distant sound.

He grabbed the chain and lifted the anchor; the metal clanked and the people gasped as one, all eyes turned to him.

"Hallo there!" He carried his anchor up the pier, dragging the chain, which still wound round his ankle. The people gaped. Had they never seen a chain before? Nor boots? Up the pier he trudged and the people just watched his feet, daft with wonder.

"Hallo! Can you not hear me?"

No response. Dread settled over him like a cold mist.

And he remembered. Again.

It always took him a while – he would forget during the storm, the way a man forgot himself during a nightmare. He would think only of Nell, but then he would come face to face with the people. This was Clancyville, but 1879 was long past. And these people couldn't see him, nor hear his voice. By some mystery, they were aware only of the sound of his chain.

He was dead.

Not only dead, but a ghost, doomed to be insulted and mocked by the townspeople and their kith and kin. Except for those spells when he was back in the storm, he was trapped in this town. Torment knifed into his heart. His Nell was lost, gone years and years ago. He was alone. Never again would he experience that happy feeling, that belonging, that connection.

He stared at the crowd, and it was then he saw her – the worst one of them all, the redheaded girl they called Cassie. She stood there, smirking.

He had to get away. He turned and trudged back to the other end of the pier. But there was only the sea. Then he remembered – when he closed his eyes and thought hard enough of other places in Clancyville, he could travel there. He closed his eyes and thought of the old barn on Garvey's farm where some kittens had recently been born.

Cassie Nolan took another sip of her latte and put her finger to her lips, reminding the tourists not to speak until she gave the sign.

The six of them had gone through what she termed to her friend Belinda as "the stupid look of wonder phase", where they'd stand at the foot of the pier, hearing the chain drag and clank, wearing stupid expressions. Then, as Old Salt got maybe halfway to them, they would go into the "sharing looks of wonder with their neighbor" phase, to be closely followed by "turn your idiotic look of wonder to the tour guide" phase. Cassie, at this time, would clap a perfectly neutral expression onto her face. These phases would cycle around as Old Salt dragged his chain the other way, back to the sea. Then would come the silence.

Sometimes she wished she could disappear off the end of the pier, too. She couldn't believe she was back in Clancyville. God, she'd worked so hard to escape! She wanted to be anywhere else.

And it was all Old Salt's fault. Indirectly, OK, but still!

Every evening as he clanked along the pier, it was all she could do not to yell, *Give it up, dude! Your old Nell isn't here! She will never be here!*

She didn't know how he came to be called Old Salt, since he was supposedly a strapping young man in the prime of his life when he died, and she doubted he'd looked anything like the Old Salt caricature that seemed to be everywhere in Clancyville – some 1920s commercial artist had seen fit to do him as a kind of piratey Popeye, hook hoisted menacingly. The image was on souvenirs, storefronts, T-shirts, signs, often with the caption "Never give up on love". If she had made the souvenirs, they'd have a different caption – possibly, "The ultimate stalker". Or, "Hey Old Salt McHenry, buy a clue!"

She knew she should be grateful to Old Salt. Half of the economy of Clancyville, North Carolina came from his ghostly visits, and her family had the luck to own the land nearest the haunted pier. Her great-greats had built the Old Salt Tavern there nearly a century ago, once they realized people were interested in the ghost, and it had been their living ever since.

Right next to the start of the pier, a thick steel pole rose out of the ground, high up into the air. On top of it sat a giant circular sign with lights all around, featuring – of course – the Old Salt image smack in the middle, like a two-story high Old Salt lollipop.

"There he goes," she told the tourists. "Back to the sea. But mark my words; he'll return just after the town clock chimes eight tomorrow, rain or shine. We'll hear his call on the wind, and his chain on the dock. He'll defy the elements, he'll defy time, he'll defy the very laws of physics to seek out his lady love."

She watched them contemplate this last bit, waiting for the "asshole verification" phase to start up. And indeed, it did, courtesy of a dad and his teenaged daughter, who decided Old Salt was a ruse, and asked to inspect the pier. Cassie smiled and waved them on, reminding them that there were seven affidavits posted on the wall of the Old Salt Tavern from various scientific institutions, including one from a group of scientists from UNC, stating that after thorough inspection above and below the waterline, it had been determined that no known mechanical device could be producing those sounds and vibrations, and its source was "deemed inconclusive".

Old Salt, forever searching for his Nell.

If he was corporeal, she'd walk right up to him and grab his sailor-suit collar and shake the bejesus out of him. *"If you've done something twenty thousand times over with a poor result, it means it's not working, dude!"*

She sighed. If he were a real man, she could only imagine how much it would suck to sleep with him. Obviously his Nell had the right idea.

A few minutes later the father and daughter gave up on their inspection, having found nothing but wooden planking, boat bumpers and lifesaving rings.

Now the "walk back to the bar excitedly baffled and wondering mildly about the meaning of life" phase could begin, to be followed by the "stuff yourself with burgers and French fries and a beer served by your waitress Cassie" phase.

Two hours later she pulled off her apron and collapsed on a bar stool. The rush at Old Salt Tavern was finally over. Cassie's dad put a napkin in front of her.

Like everything, the napkin had Old Salt's picture. As a child, she'd deface his image every chance she got – monocle, Martian antennae, pimples – much to the chagrin of her parents.

"Yup," she said, meaning, the usual. The usual was a shot of tequila and a black and tan. Not like she had to be chipper in the morning.

Just over a year ago, Cassie was out in LA, screenwriting degree in hand, working on a fun comedy entitled *Blue Sorbet* with her writing partner, Alice. She'd gotten a sitcom staff-writer job offer she was planning to accept, too. In other words, she was on her way. Going places. If there was one thing she was good at, it was going places.

And then her mother had broken her hip. At first, her worries focused on her mother's health; hip breaks were serious business. Once she got back out to Clancyville, however, it became clear that her parents were on the brink of losing the tavern. Thanks to the economy, they couldn't hire help, and they couldn't sell or retire. She called her rebellious older brother, Kenny, and begged him to come help out. Kenny moved from city to city, waiting tables and carving tiny wooden birds – he could just as easily do that in Clancyville. But Kenny hadn't spoken to their parents for seven years and he wasn't about to start. Kenny's rift with her parents had begun with his refusal to go to college and his wild partying ways, and gotten worse with her parents' insane ultimatums, and then it went completely downhill with both sides saying hurtful, damaging things. She visited Kenny now and then, but his absence made a big hole in their family.

Reluctantly, she turned down the sitcom job to help her folks out for the tourist season. There'd be other offers, she told herself, and she could work with Alice by Skype for now.

But there was so much to do at the tavern. Leaks in the tall peaked roof, staffing nightmares, refrigeration problems, and general decay that her parents wouldn't have tolerated even five years ago. Just another month or two, she kept thinking. Tourist season bled into the winter. Spring. And another tourist season was ending.

Stupid Old Salt. She'd actually tried to pitch the idea to a TV show on paranormal phenomena – she'd thought if the place got more popular, there'd be more tourist business year round, and her folks could sell. But no, as she'd feared, Old Salt's method of haunting wasn't visual enough. And certainly not very exciting.

Yeah, thanks to Old Salt McHenry's shitty haunting ways, the ghost wharf of Clancyville, North Carolina was just a rung above the nearby llama show and below the pirate museum. If it wasn't for Old Salt's feeble hauntings, the town would've died a natural death decades ago and her parents would have carved out a different living – an alternate life that might have allowed them to retire.

Her dad set down her drinks. "One of these days you oughta write a movie about the legend of Old Salt!" This was the third time that year he'd suggested it. And he wasn't the only one; lots of people liked to tell her she should write a movie about Old Salt William McHenry.

She drained the tequila shot. "The only problem with that is, if I started writing a screenplay about Old Salt, I'd have to gnaw off my own hands to keep myself from scratching out my eyes."

"Oh, Cassie." Her father laughed and walked off to the other end of the bar.

"Hey babe." Daryl slid in next to her. His blues band, the C-sides, played the Old Salt Tavern on weekends; Daryl was the drummer and the singer. He called for a tap beer. The band got taps and soda free.

He turned to her. "Wanna blow on my stick for good luck?"

"Hell no." He'd been a jerk in high school, and he was a jerk now. In fact, she was 98 per cent sure he'd swiped a tip off one of her tables, but she hadn't directly seen it, so she couldn't do anything. Other waitresses suspected it too, but he'd expertly eluded being seen. Swiping tips was a sin against waitpersons of the world, and they all watched Daryl covertly now. Operation Jackass, they called it.

This was what her life had come to. She stared up at the beams, criss-crossing all the way up to the peaked ceiling, with old shipping implements hanging down like Christmas tree ornaments. She was as trapped as Old Salt, with the tavern as her personal wrecked ship.

She got up and walked outside and into the adjoining house – extended in a hodgepodge way over the years – that hugged the tavern like a bulky crust of barnacles.

In some ways, growing up in a house built around a bar had been great. Her parents were never far, and there was always the sense of being at the center of activity, a feeling she still prized.

There were downsides, though. Cassie and Kenny and their friends had to be quiet in the rooms abutting the bar, because the sounds of children playing made the daytime drinkers self-conscious. And the toilet in the far bathroom was off limits during bar hours unless the music was loud, because the throaty sound of the flush would reverberate through the whole place. And there was always the faint smell of fry grease, even in her princess bedroom. Still, she was lucky. It was a happy home, especially back when Kenny was part of the family. Pig-headed as they were, her parents were good parents, and she considered them to be two of her best friends these days. She wouldn't dream of leaving them high and dry.

Still, she couldn't shake the sense that real life was being lived elsewhere, and she was missing out. She stretched out on the couch, fired up her laptop and played Jungle Jewel, her favorite game, to the thumping beat of the C-Sides next door. Later she Skyped Alice to tell her about an idea she had for a scene they'd been fighting over. But Alice didn't want to talk about the scene. She had news. The writing-partners-over-Skype wasn't working out for her.

"Alice, no!" Cassie pleaded. "We're the best team ever!"

It turned out Alice had somebody new. They had a new project. Cassie could have *Blue Sorbet*. But Cassie wasn't sure she wanted it without Alice.

She shut her laptop and stared at the wall, devastated. She needed Alice. The project needed Alice. Her friend, her creative partner. She had to get out of Clancyville!

Just then, the C-Sides started up with their most popular tune, "Rooster Bay", a funky song that she hated, but it always got people up and dancing. At the pinnacle moment, there would be a ten-beat silence where people would freeze in vogue poses. After that, Daryl would tap his sticks together, once, twice, and then he'd launch into a drum solo. If there was one thing you could say about "Rooster Bay", it certainly showcased Daryl's drumming talents.

She sighed. She wasn't thrilled about going back over while the C-Sides were playing, but she didn't want to be alone. She headed back to help close.

She got there just as vogue pose silence had begun. She slipped onto a bar stool and smiled when her dad saw her. He got her another black and tan and a tequila. She set it on an Old Salt napkin so that it bisected Old Salt's face in a way that made him look like he was frowning, and chatted with her dad about nothing. He was always so happy to see her; it sometimes made her feel bad that she wanted to be anywhere but Clancyville.

She had another shot of tequila and, when the C-sides started their next set, she went into the kitchen to help Corky, the hippie dishwasher, rack up the last of the beer mugs and ketchup-smeared plates.

An hour later her dad sent her out to turn off Old Salt's face.

She nearly fell over one of the chairs on the bar's empty porch, and had to hold tight to the rail on the rickety steps to the beach. Shit! She shouldn't have had that last tequila.

Old Salt McHenry lorded over her from on high like an evil, grinning doofus of a seafarer. She picked up a rock, wanting to hurl it right into his face as she'd done so often in her youth, but she might break the tiny light bulbs that surrounded it. And Corky would have to go up on a ladder and replace them. She turned her attention to the sea, choppy tonight. It was getting on storm season, just a month off the anniversary of the sinking of the *Gertie Gail*.

"Old Salt, you dumbfuck!" she yelled into the wind. She leaped onto the pier, got a running start, and hurled the stone out to sea. You could hardly see its splash among the waves. "Take a hint!" She backed up, tripping on a coiled rope. She cried out, flailing to avoid a collision with a post. A blinding pain seared through her head.

The next thing she knew, people were crowded around the beach, down the shore, and the wharf was awash in flashing red lights.

She wandered over and caught sight of her friend Belinda. "Hey! What's going on?"

Belinda just sobbed.

Cassie grabbed at Belinda's sleeve, but missed. Yow, was she *that* drunk? "Belinda! What's wrong?" She grabbed at her sleeve again, but it was like she couldn't grasp it.

Corky was there, black hair in a long ponytail. Police. People in wetsuits. Then she spotted her parents.

"Dad! Mom!" Cassie rushed over. Her mother was crying. "Mom!" Cassie tried and failed to touch her.

"What the hell!" she yelled. "Hello!" Was she dreaming? There was something dreamlike about the whole scene.

That's when she spotted the body washed up on shore. A woman face down, wearing the same shoes as her – black patent leather with a strap over the top, and thick black soles. The red tights and black skirt and apron were the same as hers, too . . . and the grey hoodie jacket over a white blouse. The girl lying on shore wore her exact same outfit! She might even have the same hair, weirdly, except it was wet . . . but it was long like hers, and it did look reddish, and it covered the side of her face. Did they think it was her?

"You guys! I'm right here!" She ran from one person to the other, trying to shake them, push them. "Hello! This isn't funny!" She knew what she was supposed to think here – she'd seen this sort of scene in movies enough, where a character dies, but doesn't know they're dead.

Was this a lucid dream? Probably. She'd heard about those, dreams where you are aware you are dreaming, but you can't wake up. The whole thing felt so weird, like she was a cut-out figure, laid over a photograph, so that she was *in* the photograph, but not *of* it. Like she was on a different layer of reality. Even her feet sank deeper into the sand than normal. Like she wasn't really walking on it. She wasn't even making tracks! "Fuck!" She looked around wildly. "Hello!"

A lone figure sat on the side of the pier, just a few yards away, big boots dangling over the water, arm draped on something next to him; he seemed to be watching her. At least somebody saw her!

"Hey!" She ran over. "What's going on?"

"Well, well, well." He adjusted his brown seaman's cap over dark curly hair, which was half in and half out of a little ponytail. Several days' growth of dark whiskers covered his tanned, weathered face, just below his cheekbones. And what the hell was he wearing? A long tattered coat with lots of buttons. A white shirt, open at the neck, with a scarf hanging around it. "If it ain't Miss Filthy Mouth herself."

"You can hear me."

He tilted his head and scrutinized her face. "Always have, though I can't rightly say it's been my pleasure."

Had he been on one of her tours? She'd remember a guy this hot. He had an arm draped over . . . an anchor, of all things. A lacy shirt cuff covered his hand.

Beep-beep-beep. Over on shore, an ambulance backed toward the crowd.

"See all those people over there? Can you get their attention or, I don't know . . ." If this was a dream, what good would that even do? It was all very confusing.

"Folks never see me neither."

"Well, can you try?"

The guy gave her a look, then put a hand to the side of his

mouth and, in a loud, deep voice, he shouted, "Ahoy there! Hey scalawags! Look at us here!"

Nobody noticed.

"What the hell is going on?" she demanded. "It doesn't make sense that I can talk to you, but not them."

"Well, if you ask me nice-like, I might see my way clear to telling you."

"If I ask you *nice-like*? What if I don't feel like asking nice-like?"

"Then I don't reckon I'll tell you."

Scalawags? "Who are you supposed to be? A Civil War re-enactor? Uh!" She slapped at her own cheek. "I have to wake up."

The man smiled.

"What's so funny?"

He said nothing. Even his lips looked rough, like they'd been chapped and healed dozens of times, but still, his smile was, well, beautiful. She'd put him at maybe thirty, though it was sort of hard to tell, because he seemed so masculine, in a larger-than-life way.

"I don't have time for this." She stormed back over to where they were loading the body into the ambulance now. "You guys!" Her mother was hysterical. And now Cassie saw why.

The girl was her, right down to her freckled face. "Mom! I'm here! I'm right here!" She touched her mom's back, but her hand went right through, like her mom wasn't there.

No way.

She was breathing, walking. Her heart beat. The night air felt cool on her skin. She was not dead.

The doors of the ambulance shut. Corky held Belinda's arm and they trudged up the sand beach toward the parking lot. Dimly, she noticed dawn was breaking. How did it get to be dawn? Corky unlocked his station wagon and her parents got in with Belinda. Corky was driving them all somewhere.

She thought back . . . she remembered a few tequilas. Daryl the jerk. Going out to turn off Old Salt's face. She'd thrown a rock and slipped on the pier. She touched her head. A bump.

Everyone was leaving in cars except for a few cops.

"All manner of contraption y'all have." The Civil War re-enactor was back.

"You going to tell me what the hell's going on?"

"That's your version of asking nice-like?"

"Jesus Christ, come on!"

He crossed his arms, shirt cuffs flopping, and fixed her with a tiny grin, eyes sparkling merrily. She didn't know this guy from Adam, but she'd seen that kind of grin, that kind of sparkle. It was the look that said, *I've got a zinger to tell you.*

"What? You obviously have something to say."

"I was just thinking that my Nell would never use such language."

Shivers rained down over her body. "What?"

"My Nell. You haven't by chance seen her now, have you?"

Cassie backed away. "This isn't funny." It was here she noticed the hook hand under one of his floppy shirt cuffs. Her heart dropped like a stone. "You get away from me."

"With pleasure, Miss Cassie. I got enough troubles without a devil-tongued girl who sees fit to call me names and pelt me with stones every night." With that he walked off, carrying his anchor, which was connected to a chain that seemed to be tied to his boot. A bit of the chain dragged behind him.

Cassie stared after him, chilled to the bone. It wasn't a dream. She had died. That had been *her* body on the beach.

When the clock struck eight, William was back there again, clinging to the mast with his good hand, trying to see through the blinding rain and wind to the lifeboats that carried his crew. He said his prayer, and then the rogue wave hit. The deck lurched and splintered under him, pulleys snapped and the mast toppled with a loud groan. McHenry went sliding, flailing and the anchor chain caught his ankle.

Over he went, a stone into the icy depths.

It was all so dreamlike – yet real. The one thing he knew was that his Nell would be waiting on shore. The thought gave him the strength to hoist the anchor and swim up toward the surface with it. She was close – he was sure of it!

Some time later – Was it minutes? Years? – he was on the pier, calling out to Nell. She was so close! He could almost feel her. "*Nelllll!*" Up the pier he went, with the growing sense that he'd been here before. That something bad would happen.

He called more loudly, "*Nelllll!*"

He stopped, anchor in hand. He was waking into the reality of this realm now, as he always did. He *had* been here before. This was the point where he usually realized she was lost to him. But something was different.

He looked around. Where were the strange folk that usually gathered? They hadn't been there the day before, or before that, he now recalled. And the lights around that blasted sign were off, though he could still see the face, unfortunately. How he hated that image, the way it highlighted his hook and made a joke of his search for Nell. The whole town, it seemed, was bent on mocking him, and the worst one of all was that gangly redhead with the filthy tongue. Bad enough when she was a child, adding spots and scars and whatnot to the caricature of him, hurling stones and insults like he was the town fool. But now she'd come back to lead the groups who stood witness to his agony each and every evening. He hated how she smirked when she spoke of his love for Nell, as if it were all a joke.

And then it came it to him – she was dead. The redhead was dead, to her family, her friends, and all of that realm, but alive to him. She'd spoken to him. The one woman he'd never cared to meet. What had she called him the day she died? *Dumbfuck*, yes.

A few souls had spent time as ghosts in Clancyville over the years, but none as long as him. They usually got their fill of being ghosts and moved on, but he hadn't gotten his fill of it yet. He wouldn't give up on Nell that easily.

Was it yesterday Cassie died? The day before?

Lights were on in the tavern. People in there, but no music. A funeral?

He turned around and trudged back down to the end of the pier, as he always did, and he stood there remembering Cassie's lost look. He'd felt lost at first, too. Still did, at times.

She'd be around family and friends in there – would that make it better or worse? His kith and kin had fled Clancyville, worried his ghost was after them. In the years right after the wreck, all of Clancyville avoided the dock, frightened of him and his chain. Unlike now.

Had Miss Cassie thought to go through walls yet? Did she get called away to other realms, the way he got called to his sinking ship? He'd been confused by that at first, but it seemed rather simple now. The sound of the clock tugged so hard at his memory that it thrust him back there, and it was his reality for a spell, and he'd forget everything else, much in the way a dream felt like the only reality, but it was more than a dream – he was sure of that. He was back in that time and place during those moments.

He could explain it all to her – or would, if she wasn't so very unpleasant to him.

Still, he was curious as to how she was faring. He picked up his anchor and chain and floated up the beach, across the porch and through the wall. It tickled his cheeks as most walls did.

A great many people had gathered inside. Up front, a large likeness of Miss Cassie showed her lying in a patch of green grass and daisies, red hair splayed around her smiling face. The likeness was so very real, he knew it wasn't a painting – it was photography. They had a lot of that in the future, both moving and still.

"Mischievous as they come, our Cassie," her mother said, tears streaming down her cheeks. "She loved to surprise, shock, entertain. She had big dreams to be a screenwriter in LA, and she would've been a wonder at it, because she was clever, and had a big heart."

He moved to the front, careful not to drag the chain, and studied the likeness up close. This Cassie looked happy, whereas the Cassie he'd observed over the years was ornery, standing out there on the pier, hurling her insults and stones.

"She put all her dreams on hold to help us here," the mother went on, "missing out on starting her young life, but she never complained." Her mother blotted her eyes, and whispered, "Never complained."

A voice sounded behind him. "Just what I need. A visit from Old Salt."

He turned and was about to make a quip about her never complaining, but he stopped when he saw her eyes, swollen from crying. Hair a bit wild. Dreary and sweetly sad.

"How you faring?"

She motioned toward the photograph. "I was faring a fuck of a lot better on that day." Her voice sounded hoarse to his ears. She'd been yelling and carrying on, trying to get people to hear her. He'd done the same thing.

He turned back to the picture. "Reckon so."

She came up beside him. They stood together, listening. A young man with red hair and freckles, just like Cassie's, took the stage and told stories about Cassie as a girl, always exploring and stirring up trouble. The brother. William remembered a boy like that from years back. The brother read something Cassie had written, a pretty little passage about the wharf.

"You were some manner of writer then?"

"Fuck." She began to cry. "Yeah." She sniffled. "Everybody said I should write a thing about you. Write a movie about Old Salt."

"Well, I sure am glad you didn't go and do that."

She smiled through her tears. "There's one thing we can agree on."

He was struck by how pretty she was when she wasn't being ornery. "You woulda gotten everything wrong."

Cassie snorted. "I think I would've gotten plenty right."

"Nah. You don't know anything."

"I know I'm not going to be like you, haunting around this stupid town."

"Oh yeah?"

"Yeah," she said.

"Well, then tell me, what do you reckon you're doing right now?"

"I'm watching my funeral."

"And how is it that you're able to see your own funeral?"

She frowned.

"Could it be you're haunting around this stupid town just like me?"

"This is temporary."

"It's all temporary, Miss Cassie."

"Well . . ." She twisted up her lips, as though unsure how to respond. "Anyway, I can already move around however I want. Like, if I think hard about the laundromat, I can just appear there. Or if I think hard about the historical Hyde House – you know, the old mayor's mansion? – suddenly I'm there. On the good side of the velvet ropes. Eventually I'll be out of here."

"Tried yet?"

She shrugged.

Of course she'd tried. He'd tried to travel other places numerous times – Charleston, Newark, Bangor. Even tried to go to

New York City. But he was trapped in Clancyville. Even when he was reliving the cyclone, that was in the vicinity of Clancyville.

"I'll get there," she said. "Powers grow."

"Says who?"

"All movies, comic books and video games."

"Phhft."

Cassie watched a young boy and girl come onto the stage. An older woman fussed with their chairs. "We're not the only ghosts here, are we?" she asked. "There must be others."

"Nah, just us. In these parts, anyway. Been five or six others come and gone through the years, but most who die don't stick around at all."

"But I did? That doesn't make any sense. I would be the last person to stick around. I didn't even want to be here in life."

William watched the stage; the boy started strumming his guitar and the little girl sang. "Well, I got a theory on that," he said. And she wasn't going to like it much.

"Oh yeah? Let's hear it."

William bit back a smile. "In sailing, when you fix your eyes real hard on something, you will tend to go toward that thing. Even with aid of a chronometer, I'd always fix on a point on the horizon and use it in my navigation. That's why they always say don't fix your eyes too firmly on a thing you want to avoid. Many a sailor has focused so hard on some rocky shoal they fear to hit, fixing their gaze so fiercely, that they end up driving their ship right onto it."

"You think I've fixated on this town? Is that it?"

He bit his lip. No, she wasn't going to like his theory at all.

"What?" she demanded.

"I don't reckon it was specifically *this town* you fixated on."

"What do you mean?"

"I think you fixated on *somebody* in this town, and you have all your life."

Her jaw hung open. "You think I'm fixated on you? *That's* what you think?"

"It sure is what I think."

"No way." She watched the musical children, but William felt sure she was looking back. "Oh my God," she said. "Oh my God." Then she glared at him. "What? You think it's funny?"

He paused. "I wouldn't say it's *funny* exactly . . ."

"You do think it's funny!"

He smiled.

"Screw you! It's not funny at all." With that she floated up to the rafters.

It was a good steady upwards float, her being so new. And it was impressive that she'd figured out that she could appear in local places by putting them topmost in her thoughts. It had taken him some time to get that.

Too bad ghost Cassie was every bit as unpleasant as the mocking, stone-throwing girl she'd been. Pretty or not, he'd had more than enough lip from her for a lifetime. He closed his eyes and tried concentrating on the underwater wreckage of the *Gertie Gail*, hoping to appear there. He'd begun going there at first because it was comforting, but these days, he enjoyed the fish that lived there. One of the good things about being a ghost was that you could stay underwater as long as you pleased. The old laws didn't apply.

He knew before he opened his eyes that he was still in the tavern. Fine.

He shut his eyes and tried with the tavern sign. He could appear up there and see how the seagull family was faring. People couldn't see him or interact with him, but the animals could. They seemed to have gotten used to his quiet presence. Back when he was first a ghost, the animals made him feel less alone. He was more a part of the animals' families than any family he'd ever had in Clancyville. He and his kin never had much use for each other, and he'd shipped out so young.

When he opened his eyes he was still in the tavern, which meant the tavern was topmost in his thoughts. Fine. He'd take the long way – he'd float. He drifted out through the wall, out to the shore, and up to the top of the still unlit sign.

The baby gulls were sleeping, or so he thought until he noticed a wee open eye looking right at him.

He set his anchor on his lap. "Hey, bird."

The eye closed. The sky had darkened, and the night birds were coming out to hunt skeeters and other critters. He watched them for a good long spell, wondering if Cassie liked animals. He could show her some pretty interesting things.

His thoughts kept turning back to the two of them, him and Cassie, standing quietly together, listening to the talk. Unpleasant as she was, it comforted him to know another had arrived. And the people seemed to like her. They'd described the type of person he'd have wanted to know. Had he given her a fair shake?

He got to thinking about her and, eventually, he was thinking about her hard enough that he was back at the bar.

Noise. The musicians that played nightly had taken the stage. He sure didn't fancy their kind of racket.

Cassie was still up in the rafters, looking doleful. He glanced back over at her photograph, her so happy in the field of daisies. There were lots of flowers all around the tavern, too, mostly roses and lilies, but the daisies struck him as a proper flower for her. Why hadn't people brought her daisies? Then he spied a few little ones, tucked deep into one of the arrangements. It was a bit risky, but he snuck over and plucked a daisy and floated up over the crowd, anchor and all, floated up to where she perched. He thrust it at her.

"For you."

She rubbed her eyes. "What?"

"This here's for you."

She stared at the daisy.

"I know I haven't been much of a help to you."

She held out her hand to take the daisy. "Thanks, McHenry," she said, just as it fell through her fingers, floated down toward the crowd. "Fuck!"

William dived down to get it and floated it back up.

Her pretty eyes widened. "How are you carrying that? It went right through my hand."

"Concentration. You'll be able to do as much in time. This here's a realm of thought. You're setting on that rafter, right?"

She stared down, dumbfounded. "Right. How come I don't go through?"

He sat down next to her and settled his anchor in his lap. "Just the way of the place. You can set on things. You'll be able to hold things soon. I'll hold it for you for now, how 'bout that?"

"Thanks," she whispered, staring back out. They sat in companionable silence.

Her cheeks were pinker now that she'd been crying, and it made her freckles look burnt-butter brown – all the prettier, really.

"My poor parents," she said after a while.

"People find their way," he said.

Down below the music bellowed on. There was no clue in her thoughtful expression as to whether she believed this or not.

"Daisies are my favorite flower," she said later.

He felt a bit of a fool for how his heart swelled at that. "Well, I'm glad." He was seized with the urge to lay his hand over her pretty freckled cheek, to slide his fingertips over the soft spatter of freckles. Or maybe to kiss her.

"Wait a minute—" She stared at the daisy, baffled. "So, all this time, you could've been making stuff float through the air?"

"I don't want to frighten folks."

She laughed. "You're a ghost. You're supposed to frighten folks."

"I spent a good deal of my life frightening folks. I'd frighten my crew at times. This frightened and repelled some folks." He held up his hook. "And sometimes I played it up, angry I didn't have my hand. Frightening people, it doesn't feel good in a man's heart." He was also thinking about the portrait they had of him everywhere, how menacing they made him look. "Some men'll tell you different, but no man wants it truly."

He paused. What did he want? *That sense of connection. To feel loved.* He'd felt it only that one time, with Nell.

He turned to find Cassie's full attention on him. Intelligence shone through her eyes; he'd never noticed that before. "You think you frighten people?" she asked.

"Don't try to tell me different. I see all those portraits you folks put around."

"Dude, those portraits don't look like you at all."

"It's how folks feel about me."

"That picture was just some dumb thing a no-talent artist scribbled out, and it kind of stuck, it's not how people feel about you. It's sensationalism. This is a tourist trap. If anything all of Clancyville is grateful for the tourists you attract. And you give tourists a sense of something larger than themselves that comforts them in a weird way – I see it all the time. And God, if people knew how hot you are, I bet we'd get more women tourists."

He studied her face, bemused.

"Hot means handsome."

"I know what it means." He smiled. "Hell, if I'da known you'da turned nice for a daisy, I'da given you one years ago."

Her cheeks had grown pink. "I'm just telling you the truth." She shrugged. "So. You shipped off at what age, twelve?"

"How did you know I shipped off at twelve?"

"We all know about you. Shipped off at twelve. Got your hand shot off in a barroom brawl in Barbados at twenty, but you stuck it out and eventually became captain. That first voyage of yours as captain was your last. You got your crew into boats and they all got back, but you went down with your ship and missed meeting your Nell. You were talking about her the whole trip back, though none of your crew knew who she was."

Because she was a whore, but he didn't say that. He'd suspected Nell wasn't her real name. He'd only known her a night.

Cassie turned her attention down to the stage where one of the musicians was speaking. "No way," she said, pink lips plumped into a frown, freckles just a shade darker. "No fucking way."

"This was her favorite song," continued the musician – a slouchy fellow holding drumsticks. "I'd like to play it in remembrance . . ."

"Fuck! Don't you dare play 'Rooster Bay'! Don't you dare!"

"I'd like to play 'Rooster Bay' in honor of Cassie Nolan."

"No!" She yelled. "I hate that song, you asshole!"

William suppressed a grin. Seemed Cassie wasn't pleasant to much of anyone.

"He just wants to play his drum solo! At *my funeral*. God!"

The tune started up. He couldn't blame her for disliking it.

She looked at the daisy, at him. "You could manipulate physical objects all this time?"

"Sure thing. You can, too, with practice."

"You can carry things. That means you can probably push on things."

"Depends."

"Can you do this huge favor for me?"

He eyed her suspiciously. "I'm not going to scare these people, Miss Cassie."

"We won't scare them, but—" She tried to grab his sleeve but her hand went through. She paused, looked dismayed. "If you could just do this one thing? Please?" She floated down toward the band, stopped in mid-air and turned. "Please?"

William lifted off and followed her over the stage where the fellows were making their musical ruckus, and through the wall behind. They ended in a tiny water closet full of shiny plumbing fixtures. A framed child's drawing of a horse vibrated to the thump of the music.

"What do you have in mind here, Miss Cassie?"

"You think you can flush a toilet?"

He tilted his head. "I never worked a flush toilet."

She pointed to the silver lever. "You just push down on this thing."

William set down his anchor and reached out with his good hand.

"No! Wait! You have to wait until I say. There's a ten-beat silence in the song, and it has to be then."

"Don't like scaring folks."

"It'll be hilarious." The music stopped. "Now."

William gave her a suspicious smile. It was improper in most every way he could think of.

Cassie raised her eyebrows. "Come on!" She smiled excitedly, rubbing her hands, and that's when he saw it – her as that girl in the photograph. He liked that girl. He liked *this* girl. He put two fingers on the lever and concentrated until he felt it forming under his touch, then he pushed. Cassie widened her eyes as a loud, deep whoosh broke the silence.

"Come on!" She flew back through the walls and he followed. People gaped at one another. Some amused, some not. Laughter started up.

Cassie clapped her hands. "That was perfect, William."

Her parents made their way through the crowd, looking slightly baffled. Her mother clutched hands with the redheaded fellow. Her father walked next to them.

"They're going to check that water closet now," he said as the drummer began to bang.

She watched them, her expression hopeful. "They'll know it's me. I would only flush that toilet during bar time at my most naughty, and I'd get in so much trouble. I think it was good we did that. I think they'll know I'm OK." She nodded. "That's my brother with them. He'll figure it out if they don't."

William thought about this. It seemed harmless enough. "Can't say the musicians much liked it."

A grin lit up her face. "Can't say they did, McHenry."

Together they floated back to the rafters.

"I'm doing that from now on," Cassie said. "As soon as I learn to manipulate objects, that's going to be my thing. I'm flushing that toilet during that song."

"You can't do that, Cassie."

"Why? What's wrong with it?"

"It will disturb people's minds."

"It was hilarious."

"They're going to wait in that water closet to see."

"What do I care? I think they'll like it."

"They won't like it, Cassie – they'll come to hate it. And it's an uncouth style of haunting. It ain't right."

"It's the first thing that has given me pleasure since I died, and you're going to be all judgemental now?"

"It just ain't right." It was all coming out wrong. He wanted something better for her than a mocking flush toilet joke; he wanted her to have a shining hope, like his shining hope to find Nell, to experience that belonging once again. And hadn't the parents just bemoaned the fact that she'd been stuck in Clancyville? They wouldn't like to think of her haunting the toilet.

Her eyes shone. Was she about to cry? "Look here, Miss Cassie, I don't mean—"

"I don't care what you mean. At least my haunting thing accomplishes something." She crossed her arms. "I'm not dragging around a chain, which is, by the way, totally unoriginal."

"It's doing something hopeful."

"Dragging around a chain and calling out to somebody who is never going to be there is not hopeful. It's stupid and useless."

He could barely breathe. She'd said it to injure him. He knew it. And it did injure him. He had a hole in him, a hole made up of loneliness, and . . . calling out, it's just what he did. It seemed as natural as breathing. He felt so hopeless, suddenly, and filled with shame. Was it really so ridiculous? Those times when he called out, Nell was near, he was sure of it! He grit his teeth. "You don't know anything about this here place," he said. "Anything could happen."

"Why, because it's a realm of thought?"

"I could get to her."

"You've only attempted it like a hundred thousand nights. With zero success. But yeah, maybe next time."

William grit his teeth. "When the town clock chimes eight, I'm alive on that ship, in the same time and place as my Nell. There's always hope and I don't mean to give up."

"It doesn't make sense, if you're in a realm of *thought* and she's not."

"You listen here – it's real, *and* it's thought, and if I got to shore faster, maybe I would reach her . . . there is a slice of possibility—" He felt deeply upset. During his darkest days, he too sometimes wondered if it was all for naught.

She sat up straight, seeming to sense his shift in mood. "Shit, I'm sorry, William—"

"Save it." He didn't need her pity, and he was past sorry with her now. She had no idea how it felt, hoping so dearly to find someone, and having those hopes dashed and broken, only to hope again the next time. The hope felt good in his heart for those moments; it warmed him when he swam through the icy sea and, someday, he'd feel that connection again. Being in the water closet with Cassie, having that moment of fun with her, it only hurt because it made him crave that good feeling all the more. Had she been sent by the devil to torment him?

"William—" She reached out but he let her pass through. He would not meet her touch.

"You stay here with your flush toilet. I hope you're both real happy together."

"Fine." She crossed her arms. "We will be."

"You and your precious flush toilet." He floated off.

Cassie lay on the couch in the parlor of the historic Hyde House, surrounded by antiques, dreading the coming night. The night before had been hard. Long. Dark.

She stared at the velvet ropes. As a girl, she'd loved taking the free tour on Wednesdays. She'd stare into the lavish room arrangements full of rich draperies and shiny lamps, imagining the old-fashioned people living their lives on the other side. How wonderful it must have been. Even then she was looking to be somewhere else.

And here she was, on the other side of the rope. Great.

She hugged her knees, feeling more cold and alone and afraid than she ever had. She'd thought a lot about what would happen next, and she didn't know what she dreaded more – that she might pass to some unknown after-after-death place, or that she'd stay here for an eternity. William said others had come and gone. Was he right about the fixation thing? Did a ghost leave once they stopped fixating? Maybe she needed to stop fixating on McHenry.

She floated over the fireplace and tried to pick up a match off the tiles in front of the hearth, but her fingers went through. She'd managed – she didn't know how – to dump the matches out there. Now she just needed to grab one, strike it and light the wood. The flue was open, the chimney was clear; she'd checked the whole thing out. She wanted a fire in the fireplace so badly. Today she'd really enjoyed the warmth of the sun. It had made her feel more real, and not so alone. But now it was almost night, and she felt so blue.

Uncouth, he'd called the toilet joke. *You and your precious flush toilet*. She laughed softly. Old-fashioned as he was, he had a point about the toilet thing. He'd said people would come to hate it, and they would. Particularly her parents – the thought that she was stuck there in Clancyville would torment them.

Yes, William McHenry was downright perceptive. Gruff, but perceptive. Thoughtful. Of all the flowers, he'd sought out a daisy for her.

And she'd been such a bitch to him! Not just lately, but forever, making him feel mocked. It had never occurred to her to treat him as human – he was just a ghost, after all. But even a ghost felt despair, joy. A ghost could cry, or feel heart-pounding excitement. Sure, maybe it was just a ghostly heart pounding away, but it felt real.

She smiled in spite of herself – she never thought she'd meet somebody who hated that Old Salt caricature more than she did, and now she had – McHenry himself. And it was so wrong! Who knew Old Salt was super hunky in big black boots and beat-up mariner clothes? And that little smile when she told him to flush the toilet. *Uncouth*. He was a Southern man of his time. She liked that, too. Could she touch him if she concentrated?

Not that he'd want her to.

She'd gone down the pier at eight a day or so ago, just to see him. She'd stayed hidden as he searched the tourists' faces, and then he'd yelled out for his Nell so mournfully. He was like a lost animal, baying for his mate. And what had the people of

Clancyville done for him all these years? They'd made him feel like a sideshow freak. Even the saying "Never give up on love" trivialized what William McHenry was going through. His devotion wasn't something to be made fun of. It was amazing, and powerful, and so sexy. McHenry was a rare kind of man. And that Nell was a lucky woman.

She tried again to touch a match, concentrating hard, like William had said, even just to move it a hair.

She floated back to the sofa, frustrated, feeling the tears come. Ghost tears. But they felt wet and hot all the same.

How many nights had she been floating about? Time was weird, but things around the tavern seemed to have returned to normal. She guessed it was three days past her memorial, maybe four.

Sitting up there on the rafters during her funeral, there had been this one moment when she'd felt such peace, just *being* there with McHenry. She thought about his big sad eyes, his quiet calm. She'd always been so busy hating where she was or trying to get somewhere else, she'd never known what it was to just *be*. So weird.

It was just dusk outside, but the room had grown fully dark thanks to the heavy draperies. And the cosy lamps weren't lit as they were during the tours. Cassie fell into a gloomy reverie – for how long, she didn't know.

Some time later, she was startled to alertness by the whooshing roar of a fire. A figure stood before her; thanks to the bright flames behind him, she couldn't see his face, but his hook hand glinted. And she could see the outline of his cap, and the anchor and the chain he carried.

"William!" Cassie sat up, grateful for the warmth and light. "Thank you."

One shoulder lifted. "It's nothing."

"How'd you know?"

"Wasn't me that made a mess of the matches." He sat next to her and set the anchor on the floor. The firelight gave his skin an amber glow. There was a tiny white scar above one of his thick dark brows that look etched. Like a drawing. Gold twinkles danced in his dark curly hair. "I used to come here, too. Used to love it here. And I made a fire for myself a few times. A fire's cosy. Feels like life."

"Feels *like* . . ." she whispered.

He nodded. "And cuts the aloneness."

"You used to come here, but you don't anymore?"

"Nah . . . it's a family home. Made me feel more like I was on the outside looking in than the people they have parading through here."

God, how had he endured all this alone for so long? Could she have? And he seemed to care about the feelings of people, even though they mocked and feared him. "I'm so sorry for how I've been to you, William," she said. "I had no idea . . ."

"It's OK, Miss Cassie."

"Just let me apologize," she said. "I was pretty awful to you."

He nodded. "That you were."

She gave him a playful look of warning that made him smile his beautiful smile.

"Apology accepted," he added.

"Good."

He watched the firelight. There was something deep and ancient in his big eyes, his quiet beauty, and she was glad it was him with her. She felt happy suddenly. They were just sitting there, and she felt happy. Was that a ghost thing? After a while, she said, "It's all I could do to knock the stupid matches over."

"It's a start."

"I tried to pick them up, to concentrate on grabbing them."

"That there's your problem. You shouldn't think about how you move; you should think about how you touch. The point of contact."

"What do you mean?"

He turned to her and lifted his hand up near her cheek.

Her heart beat like crazy. She wanted more than anything for him to touch her.

"You mind?"

"No," she whispered.

He moved his hand, but if he was touching her, she couldn't tell.

"You lay a hand best you can," he said, "and then concentrate on feeling it form under your touch."

Suddenly she felt it. His hand was warm. She wanted to cry. She hadn't touched or been touched in days, and now this. His hand on her cheek. A fire in the fireplace. He drew his fingers down to her jaw.

"Don't," she said, lifting her hand.

He took it away. "Don't?"

"Don't take it away. Keep it there, I mean."

"You sure are bossy."

She smiled. He laid his hand back on her cheek and she placed her hand over his, trying not to go through it. She could feel nothing.

He said, "Imagine a tiny layer between your hand and mine. Tiny as metal shavings. Touching something big or small, don't matter, there's always just that thin plane under your fingers – it's that you must feel."

"I can't."

"Where skin meets skin—"

Suddenly it was there. "I feel it! I feel your hand now. Like it appeared."

"It appeared to your touch is all." He smiled. "Now you'll do it easy."

He kept his hand there on her cheek, under her hand. Slowly she slid her hand up and down over his weathered knuckles, his warm skin. And then she slid her fingers down to his wrist, and she wrapped her fingers around it, much as she could. Just this little bit of touch – there was something so real about it. So human.

So erotic.

His grey eyes looked light, like a cloudy sky. She was in this pretty place on the good side of the velvet ropes with this man she'd despised and belittled all her life. But now she wanted to kiss him.

His gaze fell to her lips. He'd thought the same thing. A kiss was thick in the air now.

"William," she said, sliding her hand back up to his, curling her fingers around his, bending them, feeling his fist form under her touch. She closed her eyes and turned her head, concentrating, dragging her lips across his knuckles. She could *feel*.

"Cassie—" A slight tug. He took back his hand.

"Oh, I'm sorry. Your Nell."

"No apologies needed." He went over and knelt in front of the fire, pushed on the logs with his hook hand. The flames blazed.

"No, I should respect that. You and Nell."

He settled back onto the couch. "We'll have to put in some new wood in the morning and clean out the ashes. They can't see the smoke what with the trees and terrain, but they'll sure see this."

"Right." She crossed her legs. "I'd always meant to finish *Anna Karenina*, and I noticed a copy of it here. Now that I can turn pages . . . yay."

"They got a good library here." They sat in silence for a while, and then he glanced at her, like he had an idea. Or a question.

"What?"

He touched the brown scarf that hung around his neck. "You think you could tie my kerchief?"

Of course. He hadn't been able to tie it all those years because of his hook hand. "How does it go?"

He pointed at an old-fashioned engraving on the wall. A president? "Some manner of knot like that."

Carefully, she lifted her fingers to his neck, felt the cloth form and, after three tries, she had it looking like the picture, a floppy bow.

"So I fixated on you, and now I've run aground on you."

"Just a theory."

"And you've run aground on Nell."

"Well, she ain't here, is she?"

She pictured McHenry on the pier, his look of hurt when he snapped to and realized he wasn't in the same time or place with his Nell. "I'm sorry," she said.

He shrugged.

"Maybe you'll find her tomorrow."

"You don't believe that now, do you?"

"Not really," Cassie said.

"Sometimes I think . . ." He got a faraway look. "Sometimes I think it's not her I ran aground on, but the idea that she might not be there. Maybe that's my rocky shoal. Nothingness. I think that sometimes."

She felt so sad for him, calling out, so lost. "I bet she was pretty."

"Yup."

"What did she look like?"

McHenry didn't reply.

"Did she have brown hair? Blue eyes? You know, did she wear pretty dresses?"

"I can't recall her face. Nor her looks . . ."

"What do you miss most about her?"

"I miss being with her. The way she made me feel."

"You must've really loved her."

"I didn't know her long enough for that. I did want to see her something fierce, though."

"How long did you know her?"

He traced a finger around the curve of his hook, stopping at the point. "A night. Before I shipped off."

Cassie sat up. "Seriously? All this for a woman you knew a night?"

He gave her a warning glance. "I don't want you casting aspersions on her now." The town clock started its *bong bong*.

Cassie bit her lip.

"I know what you're thinking. Sure, I been with a lot of whores, but she was different. Fallen on hard times is all. And she was kind – the best sort in all of Clancyville. When she looked at you, it made your heart glad."

A prostitute?

William sat up straight as the clock ceased its *bong bong*. "Eight chimes!"

Cassie widened her eyes. "Right! It's eight." The tourists would be there.

"Why am I still here? Eight chimes always put my mind back to the ship's deck, the cyclone." He closed his eyes. "I have to get back."

"William."

"Hush."

"Even if she was waiting, William, how would you recognize her if you don't even remember what she looks like?"

"By the way she looked at me."

"William—" She touched his arm.

"Stop it."

She let him alone, and finally William opened his eyes. "Tarnation." He rose up and floated through the wall.

He'd called his hope for finding his Nell the one shining thing in his life. A hope he clung to. Was she messing it up? Obviously she was. She should probably feel guilty, but instead she was . . . relieved. Excited.

She was jealous of Nell.

She floated through the wall and over the hill and joined

the tourists crowded down at the foot of the pier. Kenny was leading the group. She was glad; she'd worried he'd leave after the funeral. He looked good, and she hadn't seen him drink once. He was smoothing back his hair, a nervous habit. "Can't quite set your watch by Old Salt, but the man usually turns up by half past. Nobody knows where he comes from. Some say he sails upon a ghost ship in the sky."

The sky? Kenny was making that up. Nervous because Old Salt William McHenry was late.

Then she spotted a figure sitting way down on the end of the pier. McHenry. She ran out there. If he heard her coming, he made no sign.

"William!"

He stared out to sea, anchor nestled in his lap. "You were right. It's stupid what I been doing."

"It's never stupid to hope."

"It is if your hopes are cock-eyed. She's long gone. Just a whore who I paid."

"It didn't mean the whole thing was nothing. Doesn't mean you didn't feel connected."

"I felt connected all right."

"I didn't mean that in a dirty way." She'd meant in life. In a human way. "Hey, since they're all here, you should still maybe drag that chain around for them."

He glowered at her. "I should?"

She regretted the request intensely.

"I should be that fool dragging the chain and wailing her name?" He lifted his anchor and started dragging it. The sound rang out. The people stilled, eyes widened. "Happy?" he yelled over his shoulder. "This what you want?"

She stood helplessly, watching him drag the chain up the pier and come face to face with the crowd of people who could neither see nor hear him. "You like that, people?"

Cassie trailed behind, unsure what to do.

He picked up the anchor and let it go; it smashed onto the dock, creating a large crater. Everyone jumped. William stilled, let loose the chain. He hung his head low. "All this time, moaning for a feeling that wasn't even real. A woman who likely forgot me the second I walked out."

"If it was real for you, then it was real enough," Cassie said.

"What kind of man am I?"

Cassie placed a hand on his shoulder, felt his strength, his solidity. She squeezed. "You're the best kind of man." She meant it. She hoped he could tell. "You're the best kind."

Silence. The people waited expectantly for the part where Old Salt dragged his chain back to the end of the pier.

"It's heroic that you never gave up. You wanted to feel connected to one other person. It's what everybody wants." Suddenly she realized something. *Hello!* She knelt down and worked at the chain around his ankle, trying to loosen it.

"What are you doing?"

"Getting this stupid chain off your ankle so you don't have to carry that anchor all over." She pulled at a stubborn knot, twisted and yanked. "Now that I can touch stuff. I'm feeling this chain form under my fingers and . . ." Why hadn't she thought of it before? She pulled one section under another, feeling his gaze on her. "No wonder you couldn't get this thing off," she said. "Hard enough with ten fingers." She finally liberated a section, undid a loop and unwound the rest. His ankle was free.

He stared, incredulous. "Thank you."

She smiled. "Least I could do. Let me finish this show now. I can't stand to see them waiting like that." She hoisted the anchor, surprised at her strength. Maybe ghost things weighed differently. She grabbed the chain with the other hand and dragged it down the pier toward the sea, mimicking the sound she'd heard for so many years.

Halfway down William was there, blocking her way. "Don't do it. You've been telling me all these years to stop." He grabbed the chain. "Throw it over. The anchor, the chain. Let's just throw it over."

"That's not how the Old Salt legend goes. I have to get it to the end."

"So now you want Old Salt to keep on? Your hated legend?"

"They depend on it."

He was back in front of her, holding her arm. "I won't let you."

She jerked it away. "This is my new thing. You didn't like my toilet flush thing, and now you'll stop me from this?" She kept dragging.

He grabbed the anchor. "It's my ship's property. I'll say what happens with it."

"Finders keepers." She pulled at it. Soon they were in a tug of war, chain clanking. The people looked startled. Kenny improvised some explanation involving vortexes. Cassie laughed, pulling. "Goddamn it!" She got it away and rushed onward.

Strong arms came around her shoulders from behind. "No you don't."

She twisted. "Let me go!"

"You're not doing it."

She stilled, felt his whiskers on her cheek, his breath in her ear. It felt so good. *He* felt so good, and she had the strangest thought: she could stay right here. Just right here with him.

"We'll throw it over," he whispered. "I'm done with this folly."

"You are so stubborn!" She pulled out of his hold and finally got to the end of the pier. He caught up again and tried to take the anchor from her, but Cassie pushed him in. "Hah!"

He gasped and laughed. Then he surged up out of the water, grabbed the anchor and yanked her in with it.

She screamed, letting go of it. The water was cold, but it felt good. Like life.

She splashed William. With a serious look, he threw the anchor aside and came for her. She laughed and swam toward shore – she'd always been a strong, fast swimmer. As she neared shore, she could see her brother leading the tourists away, unaware of their splashing and screaming.

A hand grabbed her ankle and she screamed. He pulled her to him. She flailed and laughed, and then she came to him and put her arms on his shoulder and wrapped her legs around him. He felt cool and solid and strong.

"I thought you wanted to be done with Old Salt."

She pulled back and looked at him. She felt good in his arms, but more than good – OK, yes, she felt lust, stronger and wilder than anything she'd ever felt out in the world, but she also felt a sense of epiphany, as though she'd uncovered a secret. There were so many places in the world to be, so many things to do. And then there was this – this man who never gave up on a dream of connection. It was as if the planet had finally stopped spinning, to reveal worlds and mysteries eons deep, right here in Clancyville.

"What I want is this." With one light finger, she traced over his cheekbone and down his cheek. All her writing, all her wandering, was she looking for the same thing William was searching for? A sense of human connection, of belonging? And right here she'd found this Southern sailor with sky-grey eyes – she couldn't think of anybody more beautiful. Anybody she'd rather be with. Any feeling greater than this.

Old Salt McHenry. It was the damnedest thing.

His gaze changed – she didn't know really what he saw – something in the way she looked at him, maybe, but with an inhale he pulled her tight, kissed her all over her face. Then he just held her close, like a precious thing. She turned her ear to his chest. She could hear his heart. The water lapped around their shoulders. She felt its coolness, but no wetness came through.

"We left that fire burning," she said.

"So we did." He pulled away, looked into her eyes. "You know what I'd like to do? I'd like to fixate on you some, Miss Cassie."

She smiled. "Oh, I'd like that."

"Let's us go home," he said.

They must have formed the thought at the same time – *home* – and there they were, in the parlor with the fire blazing. He pulled her to the sofa with him. Shadows danced in his eyes as he touched her cheek, her neck. His touch felt electric. Slowly he unbuttoned her blouse. One button, then another. "You have freckles here all down."

"I have freckles almost everywhere, McHenry."

"That's good, Miss Cassie," he said.

She took off his kerchief and, eventually, the rest of his clothes, all funny loops and clasps. She enjoyed watching his sky-grey eyes as she touched him this first time, enjoyed his gentlemanly surprise at her forwardness, enjoyed the feel of his cock, heavy and warm in her hand.

And when he pushed her down and made love to her, it was with the same passion that had kept him forever in this place, forever back in that cyclone, forever searching.

Epilogue

William dragged his chain along the wooden planks, very nearly to the beginning of the pier, where wide-eyed tourists waited. He gazed over them, and down along the crowded shore. Buses glinted in the setting sun, and then he locked eyes with Cassie, who stood just over on the beach, long hair wild in the wind. She placed her hands on her hips and tilted her head, jokingly, as if to say, "Get on with it."

"Caaaaaaaaaa-ssieeeeeee!" he shouted, though nobody would hear but one. "I love you!" She blushed. He couldn't see her freckles from that distance, but they'd look all pretty and brown on her pink cheeks. He loved her – he did! Sometimes he wondered if it was her he'd been seeking all those years.

He turned and dragged his chain back to the sea. "Caaaaaaaaaaa-ssieeeeeee!" And then he jumped in.

By the time he swam to shore, she'd chosen her piece of driftwood – tourists had been bringing their own pieces, throwing them on the sand, hoping their wood would be used by the Sandwriter Ghost. She'd begun humbly last year, writing "Nelll!!" or "I'm awaiting!" in the sand, pretending to be him. She'd switched to other things later: "Home" or "Love" or "Never give up". The people couldn't see her, of course. All they would see was the piece of driftwood, floating through the air, making letters in the sand. TV crews had filmed it – Cassie had explained to William how it all worked. Her brother, Kenny, was running the tavern and the tours now. He and his parents had grown close, much to Cassie's relief. She'd visit them often, and come back to William feeling hopeful.

She was so smart and funny and beautiful. He was so proud of her. And they had so much fun fixating on each other, a word that had increasingly dirty connotations. Sometimes he thought maybe they might stay forever, anchored there by each other, and that would be fine with him.

Today, like many days, she'd written "I love you!" She threw down the driftwood and smiled over at him. The tourists clapped and cheered.

He went to her, careful not to make tracks, and wrapped his arms around her from behind.

"You know what I wanted to write?" she said, grabbing on to

his hook hand, and nuzzling the back of her head underneath his chin. "I wanted to write, 'Happy'."

"Why didn't you?"

"I didn't want to make them feel bad. We have so much."

"That we do." He kissed her cheek. And they floated off home to their lovely parlor behind the velvet ropes, the finest and happiest home in Clancyville.

Haints and Hobwebs

An Elemental Assassin story

Jennifer Estep

The first time I saw the haint was in the cemetery.

Shocking, I know, a ghost hanging out in a graveyard, but the pale, wispy figure still caught my eye, if only for the fact it was the first one I'd ever seen.

You'd think that I would have been visited by more haints in my time, given the fact that I was a semi-retired assassin – and I'd helped a lot of people move on from this life to the next with a slice or two of my silverstone knives.

I'd come to Blue Ridge Cemetery to place some forget-me-nots on the grave of Fletcher Lane, my murdered mentor. The old man had taken me in off the streets when I was thirteen, trained me to be an assassin like him, dubbed me the Spider, and then set me loose on the greedy, corrupt citizens of the southern metropolis of Ashland.

Good times.

I'd been crouched over Fletcher's grave for about ten minutes, brushing the dry, withered remains of the autumn leaves off his granite gravestone and arranging the forget-me-nots in an empty soda bottle that I'd brought along for the purpose. The slick green glass was the same color that Fletcher's eyes had been.

It was January and bitter cold. The sun looked like it was submerged under dingy dishwater clouds rather than hanging in the sky, and its weak rays didn't even come close to melting the

thin patches of crusty snow that littered the ground like shreds
of tissue paper.

But I didn't pay much attention to the cold – I was too busy
talking to Fletcher. I'd been catching the old man up on everything that was happening in my life, from the reappearance of
my baby sister Bria back in Ashland to my ongoing war against
Mab Monroe, the Fire elemental who'd murdered my family
when I was thirteen.

Fletcher's grave was my own private confessional, a place
where all my whispered secrets and worrisome weaknesses
would be whipped away by the biting winds that whizzed across
this particular ridge of the Appalachian Mountains.

Weaknesses that I had to hide as Gin Blanco, and most especially as my alter-ego – the Spider.

I'd just finished telling Fletcher about my deepening feelings
for my lover Owen Grayson when a flash of movement caught
my eye. I immediately palmed one of my silverstone knives. I
might be mostly retired from being the Spider these days,
but I still had plenty of enemies who wanted me dead, namely
Mab, now that I was openly gunning for her.

My fingers curled around the knife's hilt, and a small symbol
stamped into the metal there pressed into a larger matching scar
embedded in my palm. Both of them spider runes – a small
circle surrounded by eight thin rays. The symbol for patience.
The same rune, the same scar, that had been branded into my
other palm. It was my assassin name, and so much a part of who
and what I was.

Knife in hand, I turned my head, ready to face whatever
danger might be lurking in the cemetery – and put it down, if
necessary, in the bloody, permanent fashion I was fond of and so
very good at.

And that's when I first saw the haint.

She hovered over a gravestone about twenty feet away from
the slab Fletcher was buried under. I'd never given much thought
to ghosts before. They were dead, after all. It was the living you
had to watch out for – the people who could still fuck you over
six ways from Sunday the second they got the chance.

Still, it surprised me how translucent she was, like a shadow
cast out by the moon. Everything about her was a pale silver,
from the sweet old-fashioned gingham dress that she wore to the

wild, wavy hair that cascaded down her back like a waterfall. Her features were sharp, though, painfully so. Big eyes, full lips, a crook of a nose. She wasn't what I would consider to be pretty – her features were too hard for that – but there was something in her face that made you take a second look at her.

All put together, she looked like an old-timey mountain girl, someone who had once lived up in one of the hundreds of forested hollers that clutched around the city of Ashland like thin, green grasping fingers.

Besides, haints or not, only mountain girls went around barefoot in the winter. Like Jo-Jo Deveraux, the Air elemental who healed me whenever I needed patching up. I eyed the ghost's bare toes, which rested on a patch of snow. I wondered if she could even feel the cold in whatever half-life she was so obviously clinging to.

I'd told Fletcher everything that was troubling me, at least for today, so I slid my knife back up my sleeve and focused on the ghost. It took me a minute to realize that she was trying to clean off the gravestone, just like I'd done with Fletcher's. I didn't know if she could really brush aside the glittering hobwebs – that swooped from one side of the gravestone to the other – with her silvery fingers, but the tight set of her mouth told me that she was sure determined to try.

I got to my feet and walked over to the grave she was cleaning. The haint didn't stop her phantom brushing, much less look at me. I supposed that she was used to being ignored. So was I. As the Spider, I'd spent a good part of my life creeping through the shadows and being as invisible as possible – until the moment I chose to strike.

I watched the haint work for a while. Maybe it was just my imagination, but the silky strings of the thick, sticky hobwebs seemed to quiver, shiver, and slowly break apart one thread at a time under her relentless touch. Maybe she really *could* brush them away if she focused hard and long enough. And what was time to a haint?

My grey eyes traced over the faint markings on the smooth stone. *Thomas Kirkwood, beloved son, 1908–1929.* Maybe it was because I'd been thinking about Owen so much lately and trying to come to terms with my feelings for him, but I didn't think the long-dead Thomas was the haint's son. No, I thought, only a lover could inspire that kind of devotion, even among ghosts and, most tellingly, almost a hundred years later.

Curiosity was one emotion that Fletcher had instilled in me above all others, so I crouched down in front of the gravestone, then reached forward and ran my fingers across the weather-worn words.

The stone radiated sorrow.

People's actions and feelings sink into their surroundings over time, especially into stone. As a Stone elemental, I could sense those psychic vibrations in whatever form the element took around me, from the proud whispers of a beautiful gemstone to the harsh cries of a concrete floor spattered with blood.

The gravestone's sad murmurs filled my mind, along with soft whistling notes that told of the crumbling passage of time and how the sun, wind, rain and snow had slowly worn away the hard pointed edges of the marker. Not unusual emotions in a cemetery. The same feelings would eventually sink into Fletcher's gravestone as the years rolled on by.

What surprised me was the rage.

It pulsed through the stone like a cold, black, beating heart – slow, steady and unending. *Thump-thump-thump.*

Somehow, I knew it was the haint's rage. After all, if she'd died around the same time as Thomas had, then she'd probably been haunting the cemetery since the late twenties, which meant that she'd had almost a century for her feelings to sink into the gravestone. But who was the haint so angry at? Thomas? Had their love affair somehow gone wrong?

I concentrated on the rage, listening to the harsh mutters buried deep, deep down in the stone. I got the sense that the ghost's anger was directed at someone else – someone who'd taken Thomas away from her. Sharp, anguished shrieks of help-lessness also trilled through the stone, punctuating the rage and mixing with faint whispers of guilt.

Whatever had happened to Thomas, there was nothing the haint could do about it now –and it was eating her up on the inside. If she even had an inside anymore. Maybe that's why she hadn't faded away into the afterlife just yet. Maybe she couldn't until things were set right. At least, that's what always seemed to happen in the stories I read for the various literature classes I took in my spare time over at Ashland Community College.

Guilt, rage, helplessness – they were all emotions that I could relate to, that I'd felt every single day since Mab Monroe had murdered my mother and older sister. Really, they were the driving forces of my life – and would probably be the death of me when I finally went up against the Fire elemental.

So I took pity on the ghostly mountain girl. I leaned forward and spent the next few minutes brushing off all the hobwebs that decorated the gravestone, as well as dusting off the dried leaves and snapped twigs that the wind had carried that way as well.

When I was finally done, I turned to look at the haint. "There," I said. "Better now?"

I must have surprised her because, for a moment, she zipped around me like moonlit lightning. I blinked, and there she was, shimmering a few feet away. The mountain girl's eyes met mine. When she realized that I was actually looking at her, that I could actually *see* her, her mouth rounded into a perfect O. After a moment, she crept forward and waved her hand in front of my face.

"What?" I asked, brushing away her cool, ghostly fingers. "If you're trying to make me cold, I don't think it will work. I'm an Ice elemental, you see. Ice and Stone, actually. I can create Ice cubes with my bare hands that are colder than you are. And if you're trying to scare me, well, you should know that I've spent a good part of my life being an assassin and killing people – bad, bad people. So I don't scare easy."

The mountain girl dropped her hand. She backed up a few steps, crossed her arms over her chest, and considered me, her silvery gaze taking in every little thing about me from my heavy fleece jacket to my chocolate-brown hair to my grey eyes that were almost as cold and pale as hers were. I stood there and let her stare. As an assassin, I was used to being patient, used to waiting for my targets to become vulnerable, no matter how long it took – minutes, hours, days, weeks. Or in Mab's case, years.

But even I couldn't compete with a haint. She had all the time in the world, and I had things to do, specifically a restaurant to run.

"Well," I said. "I hope you find what you're looking for. Peace, revenge, whatever. Maybe I'll see you the next time I come here to visit Fletcher."

The haint didn't speak, of course, and I didn't really expect her to. Still, the mountain girl stood next to Thomas's forgotten grave and watched me disappear into the darkening twilight.

"I think I'm being haunted," I said the next day.

Finnegan Lane, my foster brother and partner in murder, mayhem and mischief, arched an eyebrow. Amusement filled his bright-green eyes, which were the same color that Fletcher's, his father's, had been. "Really? Has one of your previous dark and dirty misdeeds came back to bite you in the ass?"

"Nothing as dramatic as that. I seem to have brought home a haint from the cemetery."

I jerked my head to the right. Finn stared at the spot, but he didn't see the mountain girl spinning around and around on the stool next to him, a small, silly smile on her face. I wasn't quite sure how she could spin like that and the stool not move, but then again, haints weren't my specialty. Killing people was. So I just sighed and leaned my elbows down onto the counter.

It was almost closing time at the Pork Pit, the barbecue restaurant I ran in downtown Ashland, and my gin joint was largely deserted. I'd already sent the wait staff home for the day, and the only people still inside were me, Finn and Sophia Deveraux, the dwarf who was the head cook.

Well, us plus the haint.

I'd first noticed the mountain girl when I'd opened up the restaurant this morning. I don't know how she'd tracked me from the cemetery to the Pork Pit, but she had. I'd found her wandering around inside, looking at the well-worn, but clean, vinyl booths, the peeling blue and pink pig tracks on the floor that led to the men's and women's restrooms, respectively, the long counter in the back of the restaurant, even the bloody, framed copy of *Where the Red Fern Grows* that decorated one of the walls.

She'd perked up when I'd come into the Pit, her ghostly figure pulsing a brighter silver. I'd tried to talk to her, to ask her what she was doing here and what she wanted, but all she did was stare at me with her big eyes that almost glowed with hope.

I had no idea why. I wasn't one to inspire hope in people – more like fear, followed quickly by terror, panic and death.

The mountain girl had hung out in the restaurant the rest of the day, always keeping me in sight. When I went over to a booth to take someone's order, she tagged along. When I went into the alley in the back of the restaurant to dump the day's trash, she stayed two steps behind me. She'd even followed me into the bathroom, until I shooed her away and told her that I liked to do my lady business in private.

But none of the folks who'd come into the Pork Pit had noticed her hovering over their shoulders, wistfully eyeing their thick, juicy barbecue beef and pork sandwiches, steak-cut fries and baked beans coated with Fletcher Lane's secret barbecue sauce. Apparently, I was the only one who could see her.

Well, me and Sophia.

I supposed it made sense. Sophia was an Air elemental, which meant that she could create, control and manipulate all the natural gases in the air the same way that I could in the stone around me. No doubt she sensed the psychic vibrations the ghost was giving off. Not that Sophia would say anything about it, since she didn't talk much. Still, every once in a while, the dwarf would stare at the mountain girl out of the corner of her eye.

And the mountain girl stared right back at her. That's because Sophia wasn't just a dwarf – she also happened to be a goth. Sophia wore black from the bottoms of her heavy boots to her thick jeans to her T-shirt, which featured a grinning pirate skull and crossbones. A matching silverstone skull dangled off the black leather collar that ringed her neck. Her hair and eyes were black too, although her lips were a bright, glossy pink in her pale face.

Sophia's clothes stood out in stark contrast to Finn's slick, designer, Fiona Fine suit and the simple long-sleeved T-shirt and jeans that I wore.

"And why do you suppose this particular haint has decided to haunt you?" Finn asked, taking a sip of the chicory coffee he favored. "You didn't kill her, did you? Or someone she cared about?"

"No," I said. "According to the gravestone she was floating around, she probably died long before I was even born."

Finn perked up. "Gravestone, eh? What was the name on it?"

In addition to being an investment banker, Finn also had a network of spies throughout Ashland and beyond. To him, digging up dirt on other people was an amusing hobby, as was seducing whatever woman happened to be strolling by at the time. I'd never been able to decide what Finn liked best – money, secrets or women. But his unashamed pursuit of all three was one of the many things I loved about him.

This time, I raised my eyebrow. "You really want to research this for me? It's just a ghost."

"A ghost who's haunting you," Finn pointed out. "She's got to have a reason, right? Otherwise, why not just stay in the cemetery and hang out for another hundred years?"

He had a point. Truth be told, I was kind of curious myself why she'd latched on to me. Oh, I could tell the haint wanted *something* – I just didn't know what it was or why she thought that I could give it to her. As a semi-retired assassin, I wasn't known for my kind and generous nature. Quite the opposite, in fact.

"All right," I said. "See what you can find out."

Finn toasted me with his coffee mug, downed the rest of his brew, and left to get started on his mission. On his way out the front door, Finn passed someone coming into the Pork Pit.

Owen Grayson.

A smile creased my face at the sight of the sexy businessman, and all sorts of warm feelings flooded my veins – feelings that I didn't want to examine too closely. Owen and I had been lovers for several weeks now, and it always surprised me how much I'd come to care about him in such a short time.

But the really crazy thing was that he seemed to care about me just as much.

Owen knew all about my violent, bloody past, present and future as the Spider, but it hadn't made him run screaming in the other direction – yet. He never shied away or ignored who I was and what I did as an assassin, mainly because he'd done his own share of dirty deeds over the years to keep his younger sister, Eva, safe. Owen's complete acceptance of me was one of the things I liked most about him, along with the fact that he always gave me the time and space I needed, whether I was stalking a target or trying to come to grips with our blossoming relationship.

Still, despite all we'd been through, some small, cynical part of me couldn't help but wonder when it would end. When Owen would get tired of the danger that I put myself in and all the nights that I came over to his house with blood spattered on my clothes. When he'd tell me that we were through. Sure, Owen cared about me, but I didn't know that we were meant to last for ever.

I wanted us to, though – more than I should have.

As Gin Blanco, my deepening feelings for Owen were unsettling enough, since I'd never been the type to wear my heart on my sleeve. As the assassin the Spider, they were downright disturbing, since I knew just how very easily someone could take Owen away from me for ever. I'd already lost so many people – my mom, Eira, my older sister, Annabella, Fletcher. I didn't want to lose Owen too. Not now, not ever.

I smoothed my features and kept the troubling turmoil out of my eyes. "Hey there, handsome," I drawled.

"Hey there, yourself," Owen rumbled.

He leaned across the counter and gave me a quick kiss that made me wish we could skip the dinner reservations he'd made and go straight back to his house for dessert.

He drew back, and I realized that the mountain girl had stopped her spinning and was staring at him. No surprise there. Oh, Owen wasn't as handsome as Finn was, since few men could compete with my foster brother's perfect features and smarmy smile, but there was something in Owen's face that had attracted me right from the start. I'd never been able to figure out if it was the slightly crooked tilt of his nose or the thin scar that slashed underneath his chin. Or maybe it was his piercing violet eyes, which were further set off by his blue-black hair. Either way, once you looked at Owen, you didn't want to stop. At least, I didn't want to stop.

"You ready?" Owen asked. "Our reservation's at eight. I figured we'd swing by my place first so you could shower and change."

I arched an eyebrow. "Shower, eh? You know, I never end up showering alone at your house. Why do you think that is?"

A devilish grin spread across his face, and heat sparked in his violet gaze. "Well," he said, matching my earlier drawl, "I wouldn't want you to get lonely in there. Besides, you need someone to wash your back, and I'm more than happy to volunteer for *that* particular job."

I laughed. "Well, how can a gal refuse such a generous offer? Just let me close up for the night and get my bag."

Owen made a low, formal bow. "As you command, my lady. Now and always."

His voice dropped to a raspy murmur on the last word. The intense look in his eyes made my heart quiver with longing, but I pushed the wistful feeling aside. For what seemed like the thousandth time, I told myself not to care too much for Owen Grayson, even if I knew it was already too late.

Sophia helped me turn off all the appliances before grabbing her own things and leaving through the swinging doors that led to the back of the restaurant. The goth dwarf would close up behind her, which left me to lock up the storefront.

I was so busy laughing and talking with Owen that I forgot about the mountain girl until I stepped outside and turned to pull the front door shut behind me. She stood there in the doorway and I hesitated, wondering how rude it would be of me to reach through her translucent body to grab the knob.

The mountain girl's silvery eyes flicked to Owen, then to me. An aching sadness filled her face for a moment before her mouth flattened out into that determined line again. She reached over and touched the brick that lined the door of the restaurant, pressing her ghostly fingers into the stone as best she could. Then, she looked at me once more, raising her eyebrows in a silent question.

I frowned, then reached over and put my hand on top of hers, so that we were both touching the brick.

As always, my Stone elemental magic let me hear the clogged, contented murmurs of the brick – the ones that matched the stomachs and arteries of so many of my customers after eating at the Pork Pit. But there was something else in the brick now, some other faint emotion mixed in with the usual pleasure. I closed my eyes and concentrated, focusing on that sound, pulling it out of the stone and trying to make some kind of sense of it . . .

Help him, a soft voice whispered in my mind. *Please*.

Startled, I dropped my hand from the brick. My eyes snapped open, and I found the mountain girl staring at me once more. Who was *him*? Thomas? And why did she want me to help him? Thomas was dead and buried in the cemetery, just like Fletcher was. There was nothing I could do for either one of them now. I killed people – I didn't bring them peace after the fact.

"Gin?" Owen asked. "Is something wrong?"

"No," I said, plastering a smile on my face. "Everything's just fine."

Her ominous plea delivered, the mountain girl stepped back inside the restaurant. I hesitated a moment, then leaned forward, grabbed the knob and pulled the door shut.

My hand trembled the faintest bit as I slid the key into the lock and turned the deadbolt. I looked inside at the haint once more. The mountain girl's sad silver eyes were the last thing I saw before Owen put his arm around me and pulled me away from her for the night.

"She's definitely a haint all right," Jo-Jo said two days later. "Definitely a haint and not a ghost."

"What's the difference?" Bria asked.

I was curious about that myself. Fletcher had always used the words "haint" and "ghost" like they were interchangeable, and so had I.

"Well," Jo-Jo said, bending over to put another coat of magenta polish on Bria's nails. "For the most part, ghosts are just troublemakers. Mean old souls who like to scare the living. They rattle chains, they moan and groan, they break mirrors, and they generally make pests out of themselves. But haints, now haints have a specific purpose. A mission, if you will. They're clinging to this life for a reason, and they can't or won't let go until that mission is completed, no matter how long it takes."

Well, that told me the mountain girl wanted something from me, but it still didn't tell me what that something was.

"And why do you think I can see her?" I asked. "I thought only Air elementals like you and Sophia could see haints or ghosts. Not someone like me, with Ice and Stone magic."

Jo-Jo stared at me. "It might be because you're supposed to help her with her mission. It happens like that sometimes, no matter what kind of elemental magic you have or even if you have none at all."

I looked to my left. The haint was here today, of course, pacing back and forth across the room. She'd been shadowing

me for three days now. Every time I turned around she was there
– including when I'd been in the shower with Owen two nights
ago. I would have knifed her for that little intrusion if I could
have. She must have seen the murderous glint in my eyes,
though, because she'd backed off a little after that. I hadn't seen
her again until the next morning when I'd opened Owen's
bedroom door and found her slumped against the wall outside.
Since then, though, she'd been my constant, silent companion.

Now, the three of us – well four, if you counted the haint –
were in Jo-Jo's beauty salon, located in the back of her large
antebellum house. Jolene "Jo-Jo" Deveraux made her living as a
self-proclaimed *drama mama*. In addition to healing wounds,
Air elemental magic was great for fighting the ravages of time,
and Jo-Jo used her power to do everything from smooth out
crow's feet to get rid of pesky sunspots to put various body parts
back up where they had been ten years and twenty pounds ago.

Scissors, combs, tweezers, blow-dryers, curling irons and
every other tool that could be used to cut, wax, pluck or exfoliate
could be found in Jo-Jo's salon, along with cherry-red chairs,
stacks of beauty magazines and dozens of bottles of pink nail
polish. Rosco, Jo-Jo's pudgy basset hound, snoozed in a wicker
basket in the corner.

Like her sister Sophia, Jo-Jo was a dwarf, although she was
pink and sugary sweet as cotton candy compared to Sophia's
darker gothic nature. Jo-Jo's white-blonde curls were perfectly
arranged on top of her head, and she wore a pink dress covered
with enormous daisies. A string of pearls dangled from her neck.
Even though it was January and the salon floor was cool to the
touch, Jo-Jo's feet were bare.

Mountain girls, I thought and smiled.

Jo-Jo had offered to give Bria and me manicures and pedi-
cures so we could spend some time together. Bria Coolidge
might be my long-lost baby sister, but she was also a detective
for the Ashland Police Department – one of the few honest cops
on the force. A few weeks ago, Bria had found out that not only
was I, Gin Blanco, really her big sister Genevieve Snow, but
she'd also discovered that I was the assassin the Spider.

Needless to say, Bria had more than a few problems with my
former profession and occasional pro bono deeds for the good
citizens of Ashland. Still, we were trying to have some kind of

relationship, trying to get to know each other again, and it was more than I'd ever hoped for.

Jo-Jo had already finished my nails and was now working on Bria's. I wasn't much for manicures. As an assassin, I'd always kept my nails short, since it made getting rid of the blood that settled underneath them that much easier. But Bria had always loved playing with our mother's make-up when we were kids, so I'd come to the salon and sat through Jo-Jo's ministrations. The dwarf had also trimmed Bria's blonde hair while she was at it, forming it into a bob that was sleek and tousled at the same time.

"I heard of a few haints when I was living down in Savannah," Bria said. "But nothing like what Gin's describing. What do you think this one wants? What do you think her mission is?"

I shrugged. I hadn't told anyone about the whispered words the haint had sent me through the brick of the Pork Pit, but they'd echoed in my head ever since.

Help him. Please.

"Well, I don't know exactly what she wants, but I know who she is," Finn called out from the doorway.

My foster brother swaggered into the salon, a cup of steaming chicory coffee in one hand and a thick manila folder in the other. He pulled up a chair so that he was sitting between me and Bria, then turned and gave my sister his most charming smile.

"Love the new 'do, detective," Finn murmured. "It really brings out your bone structure."

Bria snorted, but a spark of interest shimmered in her blue eyes. Finn had laid a very public, very passionate kiss on my baby sister a few weeks ago during a Christmas party at Owen's house. Ever since then, the two of them had been engaged in their own sort of mating dance, with Finn running after Bria the way he did any beautiful woman who crossed his line of sight, and Bria just as easily resisting him.

I didn't know what the final outcome would be, but so far, it had been entertaining to watch their battle of wills.

After another moment of ogling Bria, Finn turned his attention to me and held up the file.

"You know, I didn't expect this to be quite the challenge that it was," he said. "I actually had to go over to the newspaper office and bribe one of my sources to let me into their morgue."

"Poor baby," I murmured with false sympathy.

Bria snickered at my tone. Finn glared at her a second before turning his attention back to me.

"Seriously, Gin, do you know what a pain in the ass it is to go through microfilm? It took me *hours* to find the information. Hours I could have spent in the arms of a good woman – like sweet Bria here."

Bria rolled her eyes, and this time, Jo-Jo snickered.

"You were the one who volunteered," I said and plucked the folder from his hand. "So lay it out for me."

Finn batted his eyes at my sister one more time. "The guy who's planted in the cemetery is one Thomas P. Kirkwood."

"I knew that already."

I opened the folder and found a black-and-white picture on top of a stack of papers. Thomas Kirkwood had been a handsome man. Thick curly hair, kind eyes, a nice smile. Even a couple of dimples in his cheeks. I could see why the haint had been drawn to him. Most women would have been.

The mountain girl floated over to me. She bit her lip and stretched out her fingers, caressing Thomas's face, even though it was only a photo. A silver tear slid out of the corner of her eye, streaking down her face like a falling star.

"Yes," Finn said in a smug tone. "But you don't know how he died. You don't know how he was *murdered*."

"Murdered?" Bria asked, bristling. "When?"

"Relax, detective," Finn said. "This was back in the twenties, well before you were a twinkle in anyone's eye. Apparently, there was something of a feud going on between Thomas and another man, Homer Graves."

Jo-Jo stiffened at the name.

"Do you know him?" I asked.

The dwarf looked at me with her clear, almost colorless eyes and nodded. "I do. He's a vampire. Probably around three hundred years old or so. Lives up on top of one of the ridges not too far from Warren Fox's store, Country Daze."

Her words were innocent enough, but concern filled her middle-aged face. Whoever Graves was, he was a bad person – bad enough to worry even Jo-Jo, who was one of the strongest elementals around.

"Anyway," Finn continued, "Thomas was in love with a girl

named Tess Darville. By all accounts, she was in love with him too, but her parents wanted her to marry Graves instead. "

My eyes flicked over to the haint. She looked at me and nodded. *Tess*, I could almost hear her say. *My name is Tess.*

"So what happened?" Bria asked.

"Well, everyone thought that Tess and Thomas just up and ran off together." Finn hesitated. "Until their bodies were found two weeks later. They'd both been tortured. Mutilated, really, with their throats slashed from ear to ear. But the worst part was that their, um, hearts were cut out of their chests and never found. Of course, Homer Graves was the prime suspect, but the cops could never prove anything. They just didn't have the forensic science back then that they do now. It's all there in the newspaper clippings."

Bria frowned. "Their hearts were cut out of their chests? Where were the bodies found?"

Finn looked at her. "Out near the old Ashland Rock Quarry. Why?"

Bria's face tightened. "Because I got called out to a body dump there three days ago. Two victims, a young couple, both eighteen. They'd been missing for almost two weeks."

"And let me guess – their hearts were cut out of their chests," I finished.

Bria nodded. "I need to call in about this. See if Graves has any connection to my two victims."

Bria barely waited until her nails were dry before getting to her feet. She pulled out her cell phone and called Xavier, the giant who was her partner on the force, filling him in. Finn trailed my sister out of the salon, insisting that he was going with her, that he could tell her even more.

I waited until I heard the front door of the house shut behind them before I turned to Jo-Jo. "What else do you know? I saw how you tensed up when Finn said Graves's name. He's rotten, isn't he, Jo-Jo? Rotten to the core."

She hesitated. "There was some other talk about Graves as well. Not only that he murdered that poor couple way back when, but about how he did it."

My eyes narrowed. "What kind of talk?"

"That he was an Air elemental in addition to being a vampire," Jo-Jo said in a low voice. The dwarf raised her clear eyes to mine.

"That he . . . that he actually *ate* their hearts. Fried them up like hamburgers, put them on a bun and everything. Supposedly, cutting out their hearts helped him suck their souls out of their bodies. Eating them, well, I think he did that just for fun."

I'd seen a lot of bad things in my time as the Spider, and I'd done more than my fair share of dark deeds myself, but that turned even *my* stomach.

"Can you . . . can you even *do* that with Air magic?" I asked. "Tear someone's soul out of their body?"

Jo-Jo slowly nodded.

I rubbed my chest, which was suddenly aching, and glanced over at Tess Darville. The mountain girl floated over and took Bria's chair. For a moment, her features blurred, and she looked exhausted. Just . . . exhausted.

I had no doubt that Graves had murdered her and Thomas Kirkwood out of jealousy or spite or both. But I still had so many questions. Had the Air elemental vampire really sucked out Tess's soul? Was that what I was looking at right now? And where was Thomas? Where was his soul or spirit or whatever? If he'd loved Tess as much as she did him, then why wasn't he here with her right now, even if they both had been murdered?

Tess stared at me, and I could tell exactly what she was thinking. *See? This is why I've been haunting you. Because you're the only one who can help me. Because you're the only one strong enough to do what needs to be done.*

Suddenly, I knew what Tess wanted and why she'd latched on to me that day in the cemetery. It was my own fault really, for telling her who I was and what I did. I should have known better than to open my mouth, even to a haint. Fletcher had taught me that. But the old man had also taught me that it was OK to help folks who couldn't help themselves, and that sometimes, the only way to do that was with the edge of one of my knives.

I stared at the mountain girl. After a few seconds, I nodded. Tess blinked at me in surprise for a moment before she nodded back.

"Gin?" Jo-Jo asked, looking first at the haint, then at me. Since Jo-Jo was an Air elemental, she could see Tess just like her sister Sophia could. "What are you going to do?"

"I'm going to do what I do best," I said. "What I've done so many times before as the Spider. I'm going to kill that murderous son of a bitch Graves so Tess here can finally rest in peace."

Jo-Jo gave me directions to Homer Graves's place. I grabbed a bag of tools that I kept stashed in her house for just these sorts of situation, got into my car, and headed out. Normally, I would have been more cautious, would have waited to do some recon at the very least before going in knives slashing. But there was no time. Not with Bria sniffing around. She'd do the right thing, the cop thing, and go get a warrant before she went to question Graves. I already knew Graves was a murderer who liked to torture his victims. I didn't want my baby sister anywhere near him – especially if he was the soul sucker that Jo-Jo thought he was.

Besides, Tess had waited so long already. I figured she was anxious to get on with things. Even a haint could only be so patient.

I got as close to Graves's rugged, remote property as I could, then pulled my car off the side of the road, shouldered my bag of supplies, and hiked the rest of the way in on foot. Tess floated beside me the whole time, her face tight with worry, her hands fisting in the ghostly folds of her gingham dress. I didn't know why. I was the one sticking my neck out here – hers had already been cut long ago by Graves. Still, her concern touched me.

According to Jo-Jo, Graves lived at the top of a holler in the mountains above Ashland. I followed her directions up a faint hiking trail, then stopped when I crested a forested ridge and spotted Graves's house through a screen of trees. Above me, the bare skeleton branches creaked and cracked back and forth as the wind tangled through them. The faint whispers almost seemed to be warning me. *Stay away . . . stay away . . . stay away . . .*

I pushed my unease aside and used the binoculars I'd brought along to peer at the house in front of me. It could have been a replica of a hundred others I'd seen in hollers like this one – cheap white clapboard that had long ago turned dingy with age, a porch with warped, weathered, sagging boards and a dull tin roof dotted here and there with black mold. Charming.

Whatever else he was, Graves definitely didn't care what kind of disrepair his property fell into. Still, his neglect would make my job easier. It was only about three in the afternoon, and he would have easily seen me creeping through his yard if the grass hadn't been as high as my waist and choked with winter weeds and black briars.

Once again, that feeling of unease crept up on me. Maybe it was because the area was so completely lifeless. No birds fluttered in the trees, no rabbits scurried through the fallen leaves, nothing moved at all but the wind with its relentless whistle of cold air.

"OK, Tess," I whispered, turning to the haint. "Time to earn my pro bono services as the Spider. Where's Graves most likely to be? I want to do this quick and quiet-like, before he even knows I'm here."

Tess bit her lip, then pointed to the left side of the house. Still keeping inside the tree line, I put my binoculars back into my bag and skulked in that direction.

A small shack was attached to the backside of the house, made out of the same dingy clapboard as the main structure. I got down on my belly and left the trees behind, crawling through the grass and masking my furtive movements with the gusts of wind that blew across the overgrown yard.

Five minutes later, I reached the side of the shack and eased back up into a standing position. I peered in through one of the windows, but an inch of grime covered the glass. All I could see inside was a faint glow, like someone had left a bare bulb burning.

The windows were too small for me to go through, so I dropped my bag on the ground, palmed one of my silverstone knives, and tiptoed over to the door.

And then I waited, counting off the seconds in my head. *Five . . . ten . . . fifteen . . .*

Five minutes later, I was still waiting, and I hadn't heard a peep from inside the shack. No rustles of clothing, no soft footsteps, no whispers of movement. Graves wasn't here.

"All right, Tess," I said in a low voice, "he's obviously not in there. So where to now? The main house?"

The haint shook her head and pointed at the door. I sighed and started to move away, but she darted in front of me, stomped her bare foot into the ground, and stabbed her finger at the door again. Whatever was in there, Tess wanted me to see it.

"Getting bossed around by a haint," I muttered. "Finn will never let me live this down."

I hesitated a moment, then reached out and tried the door-knob. To my surprise, it turned, so I eased it open and slipped inside. I thought it would take a few seconds for my eyes to adjust to the semi-darkness, since the windows were smeared with dirt, but there was plenty of light in the shack.

Hundreds of lights, actually – all trapped in glass snowglobes.

The globes sat on shelves that covered all four walls of the shack from floor to ceiling. A large stone table was set into the middle of the packed dirt floor. Even from here, I could see that the table was crusted with dried, black blood, and I could hear the harsh, ragged screams that raged through the stone.

Bad things had happened on that table, some very bad things indeed.

This was where Graves had tortured Tess and Thomas and who knew how many other people over the years, including the two bodies that the cops had discovered in the rock quarry. This was where he'd cut out their hearts.

This was where Graves had stolen their souls.

I'd never given much thought to my immortal soul before. As an assassin, I figured I'd already booked a front-row seat on the express bus to Hell a long time ago. But somehow I knew that was what was in the globes – their souls. It was the only explanation that made sense. The lights were the same pale silver that Tess was, that same pale, translucent silver that I'd never seen anywhere else. Two of the lights bounced around inside their globes like ping-pong balls, as if they could somehow knock the globe off the shelf, break the glass and free themselves. But the others – all the others – had sunk down into the bottom of the globe, and they barely glowed at all.

My mother had collected snowglobes before she died. It was bone-chilling to see something so harmless used in such an evil way.

It was one of the most disturbing things I'd ever seen.

"Graves brought you here and he hurt you, didn't he?" I asked Tess. "Because you didn't love him like he loved you. Graves kidnapped you and tortured you and Thomas because you two were in love. You and Thomas both died, but somehow, you kept Graves from getting your soul. But Thomas is trapped here somewhere, isn't he? In one of the globes. That's why you needed my help. To kill Graves. To free Thomas . . . and the others."

Tess gave me a haunted look and slowly nodded her head. She floated over to the back wall and hovered there in front of a globe. Judging from the hobwebs wrapped around it, this snowglobe had been in the shack longer than all the others. For a moment, the light inside perked up and glowed at Tess's appearance. Then, it settled back down into the bottom of the globe and winked out like a firefly. Tess wrapped her fingers around the globe, trying to pick it up, but of course she couldn't. She might be able to brush away a few leaves, but something this heavy was beyond the haint's abilities.

The longer I stood in the room looking at all those trapped souls, at all the people that Graves had murdered over the years, the angrier I got, until my rage matched what I'd felt when I'd touched Thomas's gravestone.

"That soul-sucking son of a bitch—"

That was all that I got out before I noticed Tess waving frantically. I heard footsteps behind me and immediately whirled around, but I was already too late. I turned my head just in time for someone to smash me in the face with a shovel.

I was out cold before I even hit the dirt floor.

When I came to, I was strapped down on the stone table that I'd seen when I'd first come into the shack. Thick ropes lashed my legs and feet, while two more held out my arms as if I were crucified. Not too far-fetched an idea, given what I knew about Homer Graves.

"You're finally awake," a smooth voice said. "Excellent."

Footsteps sounded, and a man came into view. Homer Graves was not what I'd imagined. Given the decrepit state of his house and yard, I'd expected a run-down hillbilly who wasn't too big on personal hygiene. But Graves's black hair was carefully styled and slicked back from his high forehead, and he'd just shaved because I could smell the lemon-scented aftershave he used. A fitted black suit draped over his tall, thin body, and a silver tie had been artfully knotted at his skinny neck.

All together, he looked like an undertaker – mine, if I wasn't careful.

"So you're the big, bad, Air elemental vampire who gets his kicks by cutting out people's hearts and stealing their souls. I thought you'd be taller."

I made the words as light and mocking as I could, considering how hard my head was pounding. Graves had whacked me good with that shovel, and I felt scattered and hollow inside, like a piece of me was already missing. I slowly moved my jaw and blinked my eyes. My vision was OK, but I could taste hot, salty blood in my mouth. I wasn't in the best shape of my life, but I was still a long ways from dead.

Graves regarded me a moment, then held up something where I could see it – one of my knives. I bit back a curse. Of course, he'd searched me while I'd been unconscious and found them. The two up my sleeves, the one in the small of my back and the two more tucked into the sides of my boots. The bastard probably thought he was going to carve me up with my own blades, but I'd be damned if I let that happen.

Instead of responding to my taunt, Graves smiled at me, revealing two gleaming white fangs. Then he leaned forward and drew one knife across my stomach. The swift strike wasn't deep enough to kill me, but it definitely got my attention. Blood immediately soaked into my shirt and jeans. Underneath me, the stone of the table started to wail. It knew what was coming next – more cuts, more blood, more pain. So much more pain.

I ignored the stone's cries, sucked in a breath, and focused on pushing the burning fire of the cut away.

The vampire cocked his head. "So you're not a screamer then. Well, that's disappointing. Before I kill you, though, I suppose I should ask the basic questions. Who are you? And why did you come here?"

Despite my precarious position, Graves wasn't going to be breathing much longer, so I saw no reason not to tell him the truth. Besides, I wanted to rattle the bastard's cage a bit. Rattled people made mistakes, and I needed the vamp to make one right now, so I could cut myself free before he started in on me with my own knife again.

"Tess sent me. Tess Darville, the woman you murdered almost a hundred years ago."

For a moment, Graves's hazel eyes widened, and he looked as shocked as he could, what with that hangdog face of his. Then his features smoothed out into a pleasant mask once more.

"Tess? Tess sent you? Is she . . . is she here now?" He licked his lips and looked around the shack.

Suddenly, I knew what he wanted – what he'd always wanted. Tess's soul, trapped in one of those damn snowglobes along with all the others.

"That's why you killed all those other couples, isn't it?" I whispered. "Because Tess somehow got away from you."

Graves shrugged, but he kept staring around the shack, a sharp, sick, hungry look in his eyes now. Since I was tied down I couldn't see if Tess was here, but I hoped that she wasn't. I didn't want Graves to trap her too.

"I'd already killed Kirkwood," Graves said. "I left the shack just for a few minutes to go put on a clean suit. I wanted to look my best for Tess before I took her soul. She was special, you see. So special to me. The first woman I loved, the first woman I killed. But I came back, and she was gone. She'd somehow cut herself free. She didn't get far, though. I found her just inside the trees, but she was already dead, and her soul was already gone . . ."

His voice trailed off, and I could tell that he was lost in his memories. A lot of vamps were like that. They lived so long that the past and present often blurred together for them. After a moment, Graves came back to himself. He looked at me and smiled.

"You know, I never could lure Tess back in here, not even when I used Kirkwood's soul as bait. But I'm sure she'll come for you, since she sent you here in the first place. I'm sure when she hears you screaming she'll come running, and then my collection will finally be complete."

Graves stepped closer and tightened his grip on my knife. "Tell me, where would you like me to make the first incision? I used to be a doctor during the Civil War, so I always give my patients a choice about where I cut them first."

He'd been a doc during the Civil War? OK, this was getting creepier by the second. I supposed that explained why Graves liked to butcher people, though, since surgery was quite barbaric back then. Well, that and the fact that he was just a sick son of a bitch.

Graves brought the knife up once more. He gently drew the bloody blade down my cheek, then my neck, before finally stopping the knife right over my heart. He pressed down, and the blade pierced my shirt and nicked my skin. I felt the hot blood well up over the knife, roll over my breast, and start trickling down my side.

"I think I'll start with your heart," he murmured. "Everyone screams during that. It's sure to bring Tess flying straight to you."

Graves drew back, and I tensed myself for what was to come. I'd only get one shot to take him down, and I had to make it count—

"You're not going to do a damn thing to her," a loud voice boomed.

Graves whirled around just like I had minutes before.

Owen stepped into the shack, threw himself forward, and crashed into the vampire.

The two men fell to the dirt floor, punching, kicking and grunting.

"Owen," I whispered.

Soft wonder warmed my heart at the fact that he'd come for me without my even asking him for help. I let myself revel in the emotion and its heady power for a sweet, sweet second before I pushed my lover out of my mind. Owen had given me the opening I'd needed to free myself – something I had to do or we were both dead.

Graves had taken away my silverstone knives, but that didn't mean I was helpless. Far from it. I was an elemental, after all, so I immediately reached for my Ice magic. A cold silver light flickered in my palm, centered on the spider rune scar there, and, a second later, I was holding a jagged Ice knife. I had to bend my wrist at an awkward angle, but I managed to slice through the rope that tied one hand down. I used the Ice knife to cut the rest of the ropes and sat up. The wound in my stomach stung with every movement, but I hissed through the pain and used my magic to make a second Ice knife. They weren't as strong as my regular blades, but they'd do the job.

I'd make sure of that.

By that point, Owen was on top of Graves. He drew his fist back to punch the vamp, but Graves brought up his hand. Graves's eyes flashed like topaz in his face, and a blast of wind exploded from his palm and blew Owen off him. Owen flew through the air, crashed into the doorjamb, and fell to the ground. The globes on the shelves closest to him rattled like dry bones at the vibration and the lights brightened, shocked out of their slumber by the sudden bout of violence.

The spider rune scars branded into my palms itched and burned at the influx of the vamp's elemental magic, but I forced the sensation aside, hopped off the table, and put myself between Graves and Owen, who was groaning and struggling to get to his feet.

The vamp saw my weapons and let out a polite, cultured laugh. "Ice knives? Really? Do you really think those pitiful blades will beat me? Silverstone is so much better, so much sharper."

I smiled. "That's the thing about me, Graves. I always make do with what's available."

This time, I was the one who sent out a burst of magic with my hand, but not Ice. I was the rarest of elementals in that I was gifted in not one but two areas and, this time, I put my fingers down on the edge of Graves's butcher's block and used my Stone magic to shatter the table into a thousand pieces.

Chunks of bloody rubble blew back onto Graves, who lost his footing and went down on the floor.

I was on him a second later.

I cut and cut and cut him, making Ice knife after Ice knife as they broke and shattered in my hands, but the bastard just wouldn't die. Hell, he wasn't even *bleeding*, no matter where or how deep I cut him, and I couldn't figure out why. All that appeared on his skin were these thin silver lines, like I'd dipped my fingers into a bucket of moonlight and had decided to paint stripes all over him.

I let out a low growl of frustration, and Graves just laughed in my face.

"Let me know when you get tired," he said. "I'll be happy to kill you then."

A ghostly hand waved at me, and I turned my head to see Tess standing in the middle of the shack, right where the table had been. Tess held her hands out wide and whirled around and around, the faint shimmer of her body reflecting like moonlight off the snowglobes. It took me a second to realize what she was trying to tell me.

"The souls," I whispered.

Somehow, Graves was drawing his power from the trapped

souls. That's why I couldn't kill him, because he couldn't *be* killed until they were free.

Graves saw me hesitate, then used his Air magic to blast me off him the same way he had Owen. I let him. I crashed into one of the shelves, then slumped down onto the floor and stayed there.

Graves got up, straightened his tie, and stepped toward me. "And now I think it's time for you to die, my dear."

I ignored him. Being smug was a quick way to get dead in my experience. Instead, I stretched up a hand, reaching for the closest globe. It only took a second for me to use my magic to make it Ice over. I kept concentrating, and the elemental Ice quickly spread from one globe to the next. In seconds, the Ice had coated all of them, and the inside of the shack looked like a snowstorm had suddenly erupted inside.

"What are you . . . what are you doing?" Graves asked, but it was already too late.

I sent out a final, brilliant burst of Ice magic and shattered each and every one of those damn snowglobes.

For a second, nothing happened. Then, one by one, the globes erupted like mini volcanoes, until the smashing symphony of glass was all that I could hear.

Well, that, and Graves's screams.

As the globes broke, all the trapped souls spilled out. One by one, they woke from their long slumber and winked back to life, until the whole shack pulsed with their bright, beautiful lights.

And then, they went after Graves.

It was like watching a swarm of killer bees attack a wounded animal. One after another, the lights – the souls – slammed into Graves until they covered his entire body. The vampire screamed and screamed, but the souls only attacked. He fell to his knees and then onto his back, but the souls kept on with their psychic swarm, feasting on him the way the vamp had once feasted on them. I couldn't really see what was happening, but I got the impression that the souls were taking back whatever pieces of them Graves had stolen in the first place.

It seemed to go on and on, although it couldn't have lasted much more than a minute, two tops. Finally, the souls started to peel off. In ones and twos, they flew out of the shack, escaping

up into the atmosphere – to Heaven, to Hell, or maybe some-
place else entirely. Either way, they were finally free.

And when it was over, and the last of the silvery souls had
faded away, I got to my feet, dug one of my knives out of the
rubble, and walked over to where Graves lay spreadeagled on
the floor.

The vampire was a mere husk of his slick self, literally.
However he'd used his Air elemental magic to trap the souls in
the first place, however they'd been sustaining his existence over
the years, all that power was gone now, and him along with it.
His skin was dry, splotchy and shriveled, like he was severely
dehydrated. His black hair slid out of his scalp in clumps, and
his formerly white fangs were now brown and brittle-looking.

I'd seen photos before of vampires who'd been starved, who'd
been denied the blood they needed to survive. That's what
Graves looked like. It was nothing less than he deserved and far
kinder than what he'd inflicted on his victims.

Soft whimpers rasped out of the vampire's throat, and he
looked like he was about a minute away from dying. As the Spider,
I was good at judging things like that. His desperate eyes fixed on
me, and I leaned over him just like he'd done to me earlier.

"You know what the difference is between you and me, Graves?
I don't give people a choice about where I cut them," I said. "I
know it's not very sporting, but one slice is usually all I need."

Then I leaned over a little more and cut the bastard's throat,
just to be sure.

This time, he bled, and his blood was just as red as mine.

Once I was sure that Graves was dead, I helped Owen to his feet,
and the two of us stumbled out of the shack and into the yard.
We found a rickety iron bench half hidden in the weeds, and the
two of us sat down until we could get our breath back. Owen
picked glass and other debris out of his hair, while I lifted up my
shirt and looked at the wound on my stomach. Still bleeding,
but I'd be all right until I got to Jo-Jo and she healed me.

I turned to Owen. "Jo-Jo called you, didn't she? And told you
where I was going?"

Owen winced. "She said she had a feeling you might need
help and sent me after you. Are you mad at her? Or . . . me? For
coming after you? I know you like to . . . work alone."

I might have been angry before, back when I'd been the Spider full-time and still killing people for money. But since then, I'd learned that it was OK to rely on other people – sometimes, anyway. If anything, today proved that Owen's feelings for me were real, and so were mine for him. Owen had come after me when I'd needed him to, and I'd known that if I didn't find a way to kill Graves, that the vamp would have sucked out Owen's soul and stuck it in one of those eerie snowglobes. And that upset me more than anything had in a long, long time.

"I don't want to crowd you, Gin," Owen said, taking my silence for disapproval. "But I'm always going to come for you, no matter how much danger you're in, no matter how much danger it puts me in. I hope you know that. I hope you know just how much you mean to me. You're just . . . everything."

The intensity burning in his violet eyes took my breath away. I reached over and squeezed his hand in mine, trying to put all my feelings into that one simple gesture. Owen squeezed back, telling me that he understood – and that he always would.

"I know that," I said in a soft voice. "And I feel the same way about you. I'm glad that Jo-Jo told you what I was doing. Believe me, I was happy you showed up when you did."

Owen grinned. "You know, we make a pretty good team. I come in as the distraction, and then you take care of the clean-up. Or something like that."

I shook my head and laughed. We sat there, holding hands and resting for a few more minutes. I was just about to suggest that we hike down the holler to my car, when a shimmering light caught my eye and Tess strolled out of the shack.

This time, though, she wasn't alone.

The mountain girl was holding hands with a man who was just as pale and translucent as she was. Thomas Kirkwood. I recognized him from the photo Finn had shown me at Jo-Jo's salon. The two of them drifted a little way from the shack, then stopped. Thomas stared down at Tess, and she beamed right back at him.

"Wow," Owen whispered.

I eyed him. "You can see them?"

"I can," Owen said in a low voice. "They look so . . . happy. So . . . in love."

And they did. Thomas brushed a strand of Tess's hair back

over her shoulder, his fingers lingering there like he couldn't believe she was real, like he couldn't believe they were finally together again after all these long years apart. Tess clamped her hands over her mouth like she was trying not to cry, then threw her arms around Thomas's neck. She rained kisses on her lover's face, and a silver star exploded with each press of her lips against his skin. Thomas turned his head and caught Tess's lips in his, and a whole shower of stars flickered and danced around them.

"Wow," I whispered, echoing Owen.

We sat there and watched the two lovers. Finally, Owen spoke again. "Do you think that'll be us in a hundred years?"

I arched an eyebrow. "You mean will we finally be reunited after you've spent almost a century being a soul-sucking vampire's power source and lightning bug? I sincerely hope not."

Owen bumped me with his shoulder. "You know that's not what I mean."

"I know," I said, laughing.

I turned my attention back to Thomas and Tess. They had their arms wrapped around each other. Somehow I knew they'd never be apart again. Tess saw me staring and gave me a happy wave. Her smile was so wide and bright that I thought she'd never stop glowing. Maybe she never would, in whatever after-life she was headed to now that she'd been reunited with her long-lost love.

"I don't know if that will be us or not," I said, my voice thick with all sorts of emotions that I didn't want to think about too much right now. "But it's a nice thing to hope for, isn't it?"

Owen slipped his arm around my shoulder and pulled me close. I wrapped my arms around his waist and rested my head on his shoulder.

Quiet, still, bruised and bloody, we sat there on the bench until the sun set and Tess and Thomas finally faded away for good. Finally at peace and with each other as they belonged, as they were always meant to be – and as they'd always stay from now on.

Always.

Hat-Trick

Gwyn Cready

APT FOR RENT: 2 BR, 1½ BATHS, GAS FP, BUILT-IN
BREAKFAST NOOK, PARKING SPACE, PET-FRIENDLY BUILDING,
CLOSE TO TRAIN, AFFABLE GHOST

"Seriously?"

Cass pointed a finger at the last part of the ad and thrust the folded newspaper in the direction of the rental agent, who shrugged.

"Seriously. I don't know what to make of it, but the last tenant swore he had run-ins – well, 'run-ins' probably isn't the right word. He said the guy was very nice. But the law says we have to disclose it, and you never know," the woman added with a nervous laugh, "some people might actually like that sort of thing."

Cass made a private eye-roll and reminded herself some people also liked butterscotch and Gordon Ramsay. She gazed fondly at the small but adorable fireplace, the perfect antidote to a broken heart in the middle of a Pittsburgh winter, and weighed that against what she imagined to be the infinitesimally small possibility of running into a ghost, friendly or otherwise.

"I'll take it."

She took the last sip of coffee, put down the crossword puzzle and stood. Then she turned the key at the side of the hearth. The fire died with a *whoosh*. The final clue – "Macbeth laundry nemesis", ten letters – had proved beyond her capabilities this morning, and in any case if she didn't leave now, she was going to be late for work.

In the weeks since she'd moved in, she had grown to love the little Tudor apartment building, as much for its steeply pitched roof, diamond-paned windows and half-timbered facade as for the independence it represented to her. "Broken heart" had been an exaggeration, especially a year after her break-up with Brian, though Cass still felt an involuntary stab of longing each time she saw him. However, she had to admit the ability to move out of the house they'd shared had brought a sense of much-needed closure to her. This place was hers. Her life once again was hers. Things were starting anew, like the grape hyacinths in the pot on the windowsill, happily thrusting their tendrils into the room's warmth in anticipation of spring, or the unexpected bubbles that had raced through her veins when she ran into the broad-shouldered and utterly too young MBA student who lived on the first floor, across from Mrs Cantor.

As she slipped on her boots and donned her coat, she heard the muffled *thump* of the third-floor tenant's cat, Misty, jumping to the floor. She hadn't met all of her neighbors yet, but she liked the sense of them she'd gotten so far.

She spotted the box sitting beside the door and felt an odd charge go through her chest. The box held stuff of Brian's she'd found while moving. She was planning to leave it at his office the next time she was downtown, and while part of her reaction was irritation at finding herself *still* cleaning up for him after all this time, another part of it was fueled by a seemingly unkillable hope that she might run into him when she was there. She had also written the note – about a zillion times in her head – she might or might not leave with the box.

Ugh. She wished this unattractive phase of broken-heartedness would end soon, as had the anger, the crying and finally the depression. To be still wrestling with feelings of attraction left her feeling vulnerable and more than a little ridiculous. Brian had been one part shy of being a perfect guy, but the part he'd been missing – fidelity – had been a damned important one.

The box was big and clumsy, and Cass shoved it over the threshold with her foot so she could lock the door behind her. The December sun had not risen yet, and the hall was inky black.

Once the door was secured, she picked up the box and started down the staircase, when her foot came down on something illogically uneven. In a harrowing nanosecond, she knew she would fall. She convulsed with the horror of this inevitability before something caught her, setting her upright on the landing. Misty, a black, angular thing with pumpkin eyes and an alarming habit of appearing when you least expected it, ran hissing down the stairs.

"*My God!*" Cass's heart thumped in relief. "That was close."

"The landlord needs to put in a light. Are you OK?"

The man, swaddled in a blur of grey wool and cashmere, gazed at her with concern. His eyes, the only spots of color in the darkened hall, shone a friendly blue. Though his features were in shadow, he exuded that air of attractiveness possessed by certain good-humored men just north of forty. A slightly less handsome Gerard Butler came to mind . . . er, a considerably less handsome Gerard Butler, but still a very pleasant face.

"Yes." She mentally checked her ankle, which seemed fine. "Thank you."

He said nothing, just smiled, and Cass, suddenly warm, murmured, "I guess I'd better be on my way," before starting down the stairs again, this time more carefully. She could feel his eyes upon her, and she tried to walk in a manner that showed she was generally capable, if occasionally clumsy. She also tried to recall how he had caught her and whether he'd been ascending or descending the stairs, but even though a small charge ran through her arm where he'd presumably caught her, she had no physical memory of his touch.

"It's a damned spot for a cat," he added.

Damned spot! The answer to the crossword clue!

She turned at the landing to thank him, but he was gone.

Tired after the long day, Cass made her way back up the walk that led through the snow-covered garden in the apartment building's small courtyard. According to her rental agent, it was – or would be if spring ever arrived – "typically English". Cass grinned at the pink glints of setting sun that sparkled on the snow's surface.

She slipped the ancient-looking key into the front lock, pushed the knob and discovered the MBA student rifling his mailbox in the entryway.

He'd been jogging, for his cheeks were flushed and he wore a clingy red runner's suit, which set off his trim hips and muscular thighs. He smiled when he saw her, and his tousled blond waves, brushed away from his face, shone in the glow of the overhead light.

"You look happy," he said. "Big plans for tonight?"

"Only if you call a feta and tomato omelet big plans."

He grabbed one Saucony-covered foot and pulled, setting off an awe-inspiring ripple of muscle. "I have to tell you, this kind of weather really puts the 'wind' in 'wind sprints'."

A small derisive noise came from the stairway.

She turned. Her morning rescuer reclined on the stairs, leaning back on his elbows, mild disgust on his face. As far as jokes went, the student's observation had been on the lame side, and she had little doubt the muscle rippling had been as much for his benefit as hers, but still . . .

She scanned the student's face, looking for signs of irritation but found none. Evidently he hadn't heard.

"I admire anyone who runs on a day like this," she said pointedly. "I give up if it looks like there might be a *cloud* – and that's in May."

The MBA student laughed. "I'm actually thinking of inventing an app that encourages people to run," he said, "you know, like a personal coach. I'm very entrepreneurial, actually. The trouble is, I'm in finance – the money thing is a real interest of mine – so I don't have all that much time to execute."

Her rescuer snorted. Loudly.

"Look," she said to the student, "if this is bothering you . . ." She gave the seated man a sharp glance.

"No, no, I love to talk," he replied, running a few steps in place.

"Gee, there's a surprise."

Cass turned pointedly away from her rescuer, hoping to silence any further comments from him. "I am *very* pleased to meet you. I'm Cass Oakes. I moved in a month ago."

"Greg Wilder."

His hand was large in comparison to hers, and Cass suddenly wondered what the relative ratio of other key extremities might be. *You sly old predator. He can't be more than twenty-five.* Not that there's that much difference between twenty-five and thirty-six, she reminded herself. And she was an extremely good-looking thirty-six, if she said so herself – but more to the curvy, soft end of things than the ripped and trim.

"I guess I'll be seeing you around." He picked up a scraper, and she saw he was heading out to clear his car. She waved him out the door.

She gathered her mail, which included three magazines and an oversized box of free dryer sheets, hoping that when she turned the other man would be gone. He was, and she decided as she climbed the stairs he must be the new tenant Mrs Cantor said was moving into the third floor.

"I don't think he's right for you."

"*Jesus*." She nearly dropped her mail. How had he appeared on a landing she'd been certain was empty? "Not that it's any of your business." She fumbled for her key.

"Well, not technically." He took the mail from her arms.

"Well, not at all." Now that she was closer, she could see he wasn't wearing a scarf or a coat. It was simply that the edge of his outline was blurry, like she'd forgotten to put on her glasses. Only she didn't wear glasses.

"He's not smart enough for you."

"He's going to graduate school."

"For an MBA."

She squeezed her eyes tight, like she was removing ocular sludge, and reopened them, but it didn't help. Her rescuer had an attractive face – wide cheekbones, a strong jaw and the sort of full, quirked lips that usually made her dizzy with longing – but the rest was a blur.

"And, of course, there is the other issue," he added under his breath.

"Look, I don't know who you are, but I'm entirely capable of handling my . . . What other issue?" She narrowed her eyes.

He coughed into his fist. "It would be ungentlemanly of me to mention it."

"And we wouldn't want you to be ungentlemanly, would we?" Good Lord, why was she engaging him in this? She flung open the door, grabbed the mail from his hands and kicked the door closed. *So, if the lips are capable of making me weak-kneed, why is my only instinct to actually knee him?*

As she tossed the armload of mail on the chair, he knocked.

"Go away."

The door made a funny shimmer, like steam coming off glass, and he stepped through, as if the wood were no more than air.

"It's not quite that easy," he said, unperturbed. "I live here."

She clutched her chest, biting back a moaning shriek. "I know who you are," she said, pointing. "You're that . . . that . . ."

"'Affable ghost'. Yeah, I'm going to be honest. I'm not really loving that title. How about the 'Incredible Wraith' or 'Ghost Invader' or something like that? 'Affable Ghost' sounds like a kids show." He slipped off his scarf and hung it on her coat rack.

"I . . . I . . ." She didn't know what to say. She took a step back and swallowed. "Do you come in peace?"

"Do I come in *peace*?" He shook his head, incredulous. "Good Lord, I wish I were still alive. The ghost world could use a good PR agent."

She clutched the back of the couch. "Is that what you were?"

"Yes. For athletes."

He didn't look any more dangerous than he had in the hallway, just equally irritating. She felt her shoulders relax a degree. "How did you . . . you know?"

"Die? I was on my way to meet with a whiney client who'd called right in the middle of a freakin' Pens game, saying we had to talk immediately. You know, until you spend time with professional athletes, you can't imagine how completely self-centered a person can be. They're like two-year-olds with handguns and Lamborghinis. Whatever happened to a plain old love of the sport? Anyway, I was just crossing the street to hop the train when a snowplow hit me. I don't think it was planned – by the powers that be, that is, not the plow driver. At least I'm pretty sure the plow driver didn't plan it. Though now that you mention it, he *was* driving the wrong way down a one-way street, and I'm pretty sure I heard 'Weapon of Choice' playing before I went down."

Cass winced. "Did it hurt?"

"For a second or two. But then this sort of euphoria came over me, and I was standing on the side of the road again, looking at everything that was going on. All I could think about was that I didn't have to go to that stupid meeting – or any stupid meetings ever again. I felt *wonderful*! Then I heard a cheer go up in this building. I knew the Pens must have scored. I walked toward the cheer – well, floated would be a better word – through the entry hall, up the steps and into this place. Richard – that's the guy who lived here before you – was standing right where you are now, beer in hand, jumping up and down, playing air guitar to that Gary Glitter song. And I knew I was home. No hassles, no deadlines, no complaining clients." He made a happy sigh.

"So that's what heaven is like, huh? Gary Glitter and beer?" *If I hadn't been agnostic-leaning before, that would have been all I needed to hear.* "Well, I'm terribly sorry, but you can't stay here."

"Look, I'm not sure how much you know about ghosts, but there isn't a lot of choice. You go to a place when you die, and that's it."

"But you haven't been here for the last month."

There was an odd silence. Then it hit her. "Oh, my God! You *have* been here for the last month!" Her mind raced over all the baths she'd taken, the time she brought home an angel food cake and ate the whole thing, and the underpants dance she did every time that Kesha song came on. Her jaw fell open and she swung around. "You . . . !"

He held up his palms. "Don't say you weren't warned. I heard the rental agent say it myself. Just because I'm dead doesn't mean I'm not breathing."

"That's why you said, 'damned spot'. You knew!"

"Oh, that." He grinned. "You're good. I thought I was good, but you're really good. I hated to see you get so close without finishing."

The cock of his brow when he said it made her remember with a rush of embarrassment what else she had done in her apartment in the last month. "I. Always. Finish." She felt the smoke start to build in her ears.

He held up his palms. "Whoa. Calm down. It's only a crossword puzzle. I'm just saying, it goes faster when you have someone to help. I'm Danny, by the way. And, of course, I know you're Cass."

She was speechless. All this and she hadn't even taken her coat off yet. "So I take it invisibility is one of the joys of the afterlife?"

Danny winked out of sight with a soft *click* then reappeared with a flourish. "Harry Potter has nothing on me."

Cass rubbed her forehead. "This is definitely not going to work."

"Did I hear something about a feta and tomato omelet?"

★   ★   ★

Day freakin' ten.

Cass felt like she was on some strange version of *Lost*, where instead of a deserted island it was an apartment-turned-sports bar that showed hockey 24/7, and while you could go home anytime, you never really wanted to.

"C'mon, c'mon, c'mon, c'mon, c'mon! They shoot! They *score!*" Danny jumped off the couch, corn chip in mouth, and pumped his fist in the air. "Woo-hoo! Man, you gotta love an offense like that."

Cass picked the crumbs off her book and slid her wine glass out of the line of fire. "You do."

"What? You're not a hockey fan?"

She gave him a forced smile. "I'm certainly learning to be."

He sunk onto the couch, abashed. "Well, what would you be watching now if you were alone?" He held the remote out to her half-heartedly.

"Oh, I don't know. Maybe a cooking show or the latest on *Masterpiece Theatre*."

He grimaced. "*Jeez.*" Withdrawing the remote, he said gently, "Maybe the problem is you don't know enough about hockey."

"Maybe the problem is you don't know enough about culture."

"Oh, I know about culture." He leaned back and shoveled another handful of chips into his mouth.

"Clearly."

"Just so you know, my girlfriend was all over that stuff. NPR, Colin Firth, cloth napkins – she did it all."

Cass bit her lip. She'd never considered the fact Danny must have had loved ones. "She must have been devastated when you died."

He downed a gulp of beer. "Doubtful. We broke up eight years ago. Uh-oh! Couch wave!"

He leaped up, flung his hands in the air and sat down. "Aw, c'mon," he cried when she didn't move. "You gotta love a wave."

She smiled politely and stretched her feet toward the fire.

"Seriously," he said, sitting down, "let me teach you about hockey."

He looked so earnest, she couldn't say no. She closed her book. "All right. You can try. My ex-husband said I was hopeless."

"Hopeless?" Danny hit the mute button and looked at her.

"That's sort of a jerky thing to say. I hope you reamed him for a load of alimony. No one's 'hopeless'. That's the sort of talk that keeps women from enjoying hockey – and orgasms, for that matter."

She laughed. "And you're the perfect teacher, I suppose?"

He gave her a sly look. "Depends what we're talking about. They do say when the student is ready, the teacher arrives."

Eyeing him dubiously, she said, "Really?"

"OK, first," he said, clearing a space on the coffee table, "scoring is the object of the game."

"Are we talking hockey or orgasms?"

"Both. But it's harder in hockey."

She rolled her eyes.

"Next, the rink is divided into three zones—"

"Now, that," she said, "I've actually been looking at. It looks like there are some rules governing movement across the lines that teams have to watch out for."

"*Exactly*." He gave her a concerned look. "You're not hopeless. Seriously, why would he say that?"

"Oh, he was pretty full of himself sometimes. Frankly, I think he just wanted to watch the game without any interruptions. Hopefully, the year he's had since I found out he was sleeping with his admin has given him all the alone time he needed."

Danny's brows knitted. "Ouch."

"Yeah, it sucked." She paused, remembering the whole horrible time. "You know, it's funny. I was so furious when it happened. I ordered him out of the house. I filed for divorce the next day. I was like some sort of superhero – a Terminator Ice Princess or something. I just assumed my fury would carry me forever. But then the anger wore off, and life carried on, and I know I did the right thing – totally sure of that – but it's been hard. Harder than I expected." She traced her finger over the base of her wine glass, struggling against the rising vulnerability. "I need the Terminator Ice Princess back."

"And there's your hockey team name." He reached out to pat her, but his hand went right through her skin, leaving a strange, warm tingle in its wake.

"That was weird." She met his eyes and saw his cheeks had reddened. "What?"

"I keep forgetting," he said. "No mass."

"What do you mean? You can hold a beer can. You eat. You drink. What gives?"

He sighed. "For whatever reason, the lords of the afterlife have decided we ghosts can handle inanimate objects, but not living, breathing ones."

She thought of her near fall. "Is that why it felt so weird when you caught me on the stairs the other day?"

"Yes. I had to jam myself in front of the box in your arms."

"Interesting. By the way, *your* team name? Lord of the Afterlife. Put out your hand."

He did it with obvious reluctance.

She swiped her hand through his once then twice. Each time the same magnetic pulse fluttered through her. It was almost like the feeling you get when you're on a good date and sitting close enough to feel the electricity that comes from anticipating what's next. She wondered if he was getting the same feeling. She couldn't tell by his eyes, which seemed to be unexpectedly guarded.

"Tell me," she said, gaze flicking to the screen, "what's a hat-trick?"

He jerked his head toward the TV, where a plethora of hats lay strewn across the ice. "Oh, crap! Did I miss Crosby's hat-trick?"

She unmuted the sound for him. "Well, you missed something, and the word 'hat-trick' was definitely on the screen."

He watched the replay, face glowing with excitement. "God, what a player."

"It's kind of funny they do that," she said, indicating the tossing of the hats. "What is a hat-trick exactly?"

"Three goals in a single game by one player." He seemed to realize he'd abandoned his teaching and hit the mute button again. "It doesn't happen all that often. I think the phrase originated in cricket. Now they talk about it in a lot of sports and it's come to stand for a bunch of different things, but usually a trio of noteworthy achievements. For example, when Gordie Howe played—" He stopped. "You know Gordie Howe?"

"Four letters. Detroit's high sticker."

"Excellent. Well, they called it a Gordie Howe hat-trick when a player scored a goal, an assist and got in a fight, all in the same game."

"Ha!"

"It's unofficial, of course. Still." His eyes twinkled blue. "I've always sort of wondered what my hat-trick would be."

"What do you mean?"

"Well, you need three good things that sort of define you, like the fighting and the scoring for Gordie Howe. I've got two. I had a great life. Truly. And I've certainly been having a kick-ass death. I've just got to find that one last thing. Then trademark the name, of course."

"The Affable Ghost Hat-trick?"

He groaned.

"By the way, is there any other weird stuff I should know?" she asked. "I think I've figured out that I'm the only one who can see you. Took me a while, but when you wandered around in your boxers when I was talking to Mrs Cantor and the only thing she talked about was Misty's latest round of tapeworm treatments, that pretty much settled it for me."

"Could mean I need to up the ante on loungewear a bit."

A cheer rose from the TV, and Danny jumped up, knocking the wine glass to the floor, where it broke, and scattering corn chips from one end of the hearth to the other.

Yes, she thought, because what I need is a ghost in a pair of lurid low-rise striped briefs.

"Listen," she said, over the blare of the game, "I think I'm going to be hitting the hay. Do you think you can—"

"Teach you tomorrow? Sure. No prob. Watch out for the glass."

"Thanks."

Hand cupped over her ear, the woman pressed her eyes closed with an intensity that suggested she was listening to the transmission of the final Enigma codes. The sign on the door read, "Chateau Monica – Astrological Readings, Energy Stones and Potions", but Cass felt like she had entered a remote outpost of a mental hospital.

Monica pointed her finger slowly in the direction of her customer. "You have come to me today for a love potion."

"Couldn't be more wrong."

"Oh." She opened her eyes and settled onto the Aeron chair draped with a brown Buddha head throw and an Elmo bed sheet. "Why don't you tell me why you're here, then?"

"I've got a ghost I need to get rid of."

"Friendly or unfriendly?"

"Affable. A little too affable. Like the guy who won't leave your party, even though you've changed into your pajamas and started doing the dishes."

"Got it." Monica eyed her wares, which to Cass looked a lot like a Tupperware container filled with baggies, and pulled out something that appeared to be black and orange confetti. "The thing about the ghosts we see is they're stuck. They can only move on by transferring to a corporeal host."

"A corporeal host?"

"A body. A living body. But that's death for them. Their own personality is subsumed within the new owner's. Parts will remain, but for all practical purposes, the person is gone."

"This guy will never go for it. He likes being here. Near as I can tell, he spends all day sitting on my couch, watching TV."

"And at night?"

"What do you mean 'at night'?" Cass asked carefully. "I certainly haven't given him any reason to find my apartment attractive at night. At least not voluntarily." She sat up straighter. "Oh, God, I hope you're not suggesting he bury himself in me."

An innuendo-laden silence filled the space between them.

"That's not what I meant," Cass said hotly. The idea was laughable. But even as the thought entered her head, she recalled the odd, warm tingle as her hand passed through his, and the look in his eyes after. She touched her palm automatically.

"Of course not." Monica smiled but her eyes lingered on Cass. "Now, this ghost—"

"Danny."

"Danny, yes. Is he attracted to you?"

"I . . . I . . ." Heat rushed across Cass's cheeks.

"Let's assume 'yes'. You're attractive. You seem like you have a good head on your shoulders. It's a safe bet."

Sure, Cass thought. Because so many people with good heads on their shoulders find themselves discussing ghosts with Monica, the potion-making astrologer.

"So what we need is . . ." Monica's fingers fluttered at her lips like a spider spinning a web. Then she stopped. "Do you have a man friend of some sort? Not a great friend, of course, since the idea is to lasso our ghost in then get rid of him, but an acquaintance. The sort you'd be just as happy to kick to the curb."

She thought of blond-haired Greg. "Maybe. Why?"

"Well, it's a little on the femme fatale side, but I think you should get Danny to move into him."

"I'm pretty sure Danny wouldn't think *that* was a good idea." Dumb jock blond meets cranky couch potato. There'd probably be hailstorms where the two spiritual fronts met. Though, she had to admit, it was a rather delicious thought.

"That's where the femme fatale part comes in."

"How's that?"

"You have to make the male friend seem like the only place in the world Danny would want to be."

"How would I do that?"

"Well, let's see. The friend would have to be doing something Danny himself would give anything to do. What would that be?" Monica stroked her chin and peeked at Cass from the corner of her eye.

Cass frowned, confused. Suddenly, the horror of what Monica was suggesting became clear. "Oh, no! No, no, no, no! I'm not going to . . . Is that even legal?"

"I'm not suggesting you go all the way," Monica said. "That wouldn't be proper. Just make it, er, interesting."

"Interesting?"

"You know, some . . ." Monica waved a hand in the direction of her voluminous bosom. "And maybe a hand down . . ." A bejeweled finger pointed south.

"Oh, I see. So stripping in front of a man I hardly know and letting him get to third base while a ghost watches, that's considered proper?"

"I didn't say it was going to be easy."

Cass harrumphed. She considered her options, which seemed to consist of a quick brush with pro bono prostitution or a lifetime of couch waves and a rubber wine-glass.

"I'll do it."

"I just don't understand." Danny chewed a mouthful of chocolate chip cookie and downed the last of his milk. "I thought you didn't like Greg?"

This was the third time Danny had voiced this particular

concern, in varying states of agitation, since she'd broken the news she had invited Greg over for dinner earlier that afternoon.

"I never said *I* didn't like him. That was you." Cass bent over the table, lighting the candles. There was something about knowing you were wearing red lace underwear that made even the most mundane task feel sexy. She'd been wearing Gap cotton panties way too long.

"That must be what I remember. What on earth will you two have to talk about? One suggestion: don't tackle the crossword."

"Who said we were going to talk?" She pointed at him. "Ah, ah, ah. If you're done with that mug, put it in the sink."

"Normally, I wouldn't mind. 'I'm very entrepreneurial, actually. The trouble is, I'm in finance –the money thing is a real interest of mine – so I don't have all that much time to execute.'"

"Hilarious."

He carried the mug to the kitchen.

Cass jumped on the opportunity to grab the remote and turn off the TV. When Danny returned, she gave him a pointed look.

"What?" he said. "I certainly hope you don't expect me to leave."

"I do."

"Well, I won't."

"Suit yourself." Or unsuit yourself. She smiled.

The doorbell rang.

"Remember the good old days, when men used to wait at doors to be invited in?" she said.

Danny settled on a bar stool at the counter in front of the kitchen.

She shrugged off her cardigan, revealing the low-cut swing top that grazed all the right places. Before Danny could voice the comment forming on his lips, she opened the door.

Greg broke into a big grin. He was dressed in dark trousers and a brown V-neck cashmere sweater that matched his eyes. "Whoa! You said casual, right? You look like a movie star – like Pamela Anderson or Kim Kardashian or something."

Danny said, "By 'movie', I see we mean 'sex tape'."

Cass ignored this. There was something sort of sweet in Greg's eyes. She regretted having to do this to him. She hoped the potential of a free grope would be enough to offset the punishment of having Danny grafted to him.

After she hung up Greg's coat, she inclined her head toward the fire. "Should we sit down for a bit before dinner?"

"Sounds great."

Greg took a step toward the narrow passage between the chair and the couch at the same time she did, and they stopped. Greg laughed. He waved her ahead. "I have to admit I'm a little nervous."

"Really?"

"I can't believe you invited me up."

"Wow," Danny said. "Any more toe-in-the-sand, and we'll be picking beach glass out of our teeth."

"Can I ask you something?" Greg took a seat on the couch.

Danny said, "Do you know all the words?"

"Of course. What?" Cass placed herself as close to Greg as she could.

"Do you mind if I kiss you right now?"

"Jesus, he's smooth," Danny said.

"I really want to enjoy our dinner," Greg added, "and I figure if I can get our goodnight kiss out of the way, I can relax and just really get to know you."

"That's so sweet," Cass said.

"Yeah, right." Danny walked to the coat rack and began rifling in Greg's jacket. "It's so hard to reconcile such sweetness with the, let's see, one, two, three, four condoms in his pocket." He held up the length of foil and waved it at her. "Looks like someone's going to be needing a sitz bath later."

"I . . . I . . ." Cass gasped as Greg tilted her expertly against the back of the couch and found her mouth. His tongue was thorough, conjuring a wave of hungry desire like someone flipping on a light switch, but his lips were thin and soulless.

"That was nice," Greg said a moment later, but Cass found herself thinking more about Danny's faltering breathing than about the kiss.

"Yes," she admitted.

"More?"

"Yes."

"Cass, I'm serious." Danny said. "You're like six times smarter than he is and twenty times more interesting. You'll be bored before the soup course is over. I understand you need to get back on the horse, but seriously, is this the saddle you want to get back on?"

It wasn't. She'd had more than enough dates like this before she met Brian to know where it was leading. But she also wanted her life back.

Greg lowered her onto the couch. On a primal level, he was pushing all the right buttons. Her body responded like a racing car that had been up on blocks, but the feeling didn't go anywhere near her heart.

Letting out a happy "Mmm," Greg drew a hand down her hip and clasped her ass.

She thrilled to the touch, but she wished it was someone else's hand – Danny's, she realized with a shock.

The moment the thought of Danny entered her head, the racing car jumped to life, roaring from the tips of her toes to the roots of her hair. She could feel the vibration in every cell.

Greg's hand snaked up her blouse, and she closed her eyes.

C'mon, Danny. This is it. Your big chance. Show me what it's like to be in your thrall, to feel those warm, questing hands on me and kiss those full, quirked lips.

Was Danny watching? She couldn't see him, but she could feel him, the power of his supernatural energy filling the room, palpable bursts of anger and desire that shook her bodily.

Greg brushed her nipple with his thumb. But it was still Greg. Even with her eyes closed, she could tell that. What was it going to take to jerk Danny out of his paranormal bindings?

"Cass, you're being a fool."

She growled. The fantasy Danny was much easier to deal with than the real one. "Stuff it, pal."

Greg flinched.

"Sorry," she said quickly. "I didn't mean you. It's just something I do sometimes."

"It is?"

"My therapist is working on it."

Greg gazed at her uncertainly, and she brought her mouth to his to jump-start things. It took a few seconds, but pretty soon he picked up where he'd left off and so did her imagination. Danny's hands, Danny's mouth, Danny's hard, flexing hips. She had one move left, but Greg anticipated her, lifting her so she straddled his lap and then pulling her blouse off slowly.

The room made a *whoosh* as if the air had been sucked out of it.

Her back was to Danny, but she knew what he saw, knew what he was thinking. Her breasts weren't large but they were perfect – soft and erotic with dark-pink nipples that Brian had said played a part in every dirty dream he'd had since the first time he saw her naked.

She heard Danny's breathing clearly now and felt his gaze like a laser, tracing the outline of her body. Her blood beat like a tympano in her ears.

Now, Danny, now.

Greg caressed her breasts, laying them out in his palms like ripe exotic fruits and drawing the nipples between his thumbs and forefingers until the flesh tightened.

The coat rack hit the floor with a crash, and when Cass wheeled around the door shimmered red and Danny was gone.

Danny swung at the building's half-timbered facade, happy when his palm met resistance. Why could he feel the cold and the roughness of the wood and the sting of scraped flesh when he couldn't feel her? Why could he smell the scent of pears and spice on her hair and not wrap the silky tresses around his fist? Was the burning jealousy that smoldered like a pool of molten metal in his chest the closest he would ever get to love?

He was nothing to her – couldn't be. Not when he lacked substance to do as much as curl a single finger around hers. Greg was wrong for her. Danny knew she knew it. Greg, with his smooth talk and empty, avaricious head. Of course, the only moments Danny could share with her would be the sort of moments they'd already shared, talking about hockey or arguing over the remote.

He winced.

Technically, that last bit wasn't entirely true. Unlike Cass, he knew there was another way. He could lose himself in another person. Like diving off a cliff in the dark, he could let go of everything and pray some meaningful part of him would still be left when he surfaced. It was both death and the chance for a life, and he'd felt the opportunity with each passing stranger, almost as you would the hum of static electricity on a dry night, though it had never been more than a minuscule pull. That is, until tonight.

God, how he'd had felt the pull. It was as if Greg's body had been a massive magnet and Danny had been an iron filing. How easy it would have been to let go, lose himself and get to feel her arms, the warmth of those legs, the scant weight of her breasts in his palms.

But it would have been death – worse than death – for he knew with absolute certainty Greg would not be allowed to stay in her life. No matter what she thought tonight while she was dizzy with his kisses, she would have tired of the fool, and then where would Danny be? Imprisoned in a dumbass. Sentenced to watch her come and go, knowing he'd never be anything to her. Real death would be easier. Real death *had* been easier.

Danny felt an uneasy prickle and turned.

A late-model Lexus pulled up to a stop. A man in a Burberry trench sat behind the wheel, talking animatedly on the phone. He was fortyish and attractive with sandy hair cut closely enough to reveal the first signs of a lengthening forehead. He wore a red print tie Danny would have picked for himself and, when he laughed, he fingered the knot.

The man scanned the front of the building as he talked, counting the floors with his eyes as he made responsive nods to whoever was at the other end of the call. It wasn't the man's interest in the building that had triggered Danny's unease, though. It was the overriding sense that he represented a threat. Not a physical threat. The man didn't look dangerous. Something else. Something that rattled Danny more deeply.

When the man finally stowed the phone and exited the car, Danny stepped into the shadows – unnecessarily, he realized, but old habits die hard. The man approached the building with interest, taking in every detail. A muffled ring broke the night's silence. The man pulled the phone out of his pocket, looked at the display and broke into a smile.

"Don't tell me," he said, laughing. "You've changed your mind." He listened for a moment, grinning. "It's been almost a whole minute since you agreed. For all I know, that's all it takes for Julie Wilson to get cold feet." He laughed. "Right. So we're on for Saturday at seven. I'll see you there. I'll be the slightly balding man clutching a lottery ticket because that day is obviously his lucky day." He laughed again, said goodbye more formally and exited the call.

Julie, eh?

Danny didn't like it. He didn't like it at all.

Cass wrapped her fingers around Greg's wrists and slowly pushed him away.

"I don't think so." She gathered her blouse and, with some effort, smiled apologetically. She felt like a fool and rightfully so.

"You want me to stop?" Greg looked like a kid who'd just lost at checkers to his four-year-old sister.

"'Fraid so." She slipped the silk over her head and unseated herself from his lap.

"But—"

"And as long as we're skipping dessert, as it were, I hope you don't mind if we just skip dinner, too."

He got to his feet, dazed. "What happened?"

She sighed. "It's nothing personal, Greg. Really. You seem nice enough. I'm just . . . not ready."

"Sometimes it takes a while for women to get ready. Do you have any tequila?"

She opened the door. "I do," she said, righting the coat rack and handing him his jacket. "And I promise I will have some just as soon as you go."

He exited reluctantly, leaving Cass feeling both used and a user.

That, she thought guiltily, was a failed experiment – that is, unless testing my aversion to airheads was the idea.

For the first time since she'd moved in, the apartment felt empty.

"Danny?" she called tentatively. "Danny?"

Diverted by a psychic tug, like the feeling of the sun's rays on a cloudy day, Danny turned, expecting to see Cass. Instead, Greg stalked out of the apartment building, scowling, and made his way to the street.

Another tug and Danny let himself go into the drift, finding himself whisked upward and back into Cass's living room.

She was dressed again – thank God – and her face changed to a fretful smile the instant she saw him.

"I'm so sorry," she said. "That was terrible."

"Well, it sort of depends on your perspective. Perhaps if you'd turned just a little." He had hoped for a laugh, but abandoned the effort when he saw the tears forming in her eyes.

"C'mon, Cass," he said gently. "Forget it." He reached to comfort her, but his arms went through her like fog through fog. God, he was useless.

She swiped at her eyes. "I guess we should chalk it up to idiocy."

"His?"

She laughed despite herself. "I wish."

"Hey, it played a part."

Danny held out his hands, and she placed hers on top, letting them hover just over where normal touch would occur. He could feel her body heat.

"What does it feel like to you?" he asked.

"A sort of thickness in the air. Like a cloud, I guess. Not that I've ever felt one. And warm. A sunny cloud."

"I like that." He smiled.

"What would it be like, do you think, if we kissed?"

He almost stepped back, the ache of shame at his inability to give her what she wanted as painful as a blow, but managed to stand his ground. "Not much to talk about, I'm afraid."

"Let me be the judge."

He stood still, letting her position herself with her hands on his shoulders and her body so close he could feel his own body heat surge.

"I just go through you," she said, moving a little closer and watching her elbows sink into his mist.

"You do." Eyes shut, he allowed himself to remember what it was like, shuddering with the rawness of the feeling.

She lifted her mouth to his.

Her lips were there, just beyond the border of his senses. If he let himself, he could feel the life in them. He bent. His lips burned with the closeness, and the rest of his body with desire. She was everywhere around him yet untouchable, unknowable, unpossessable.

When she pulled away, he felt as if he'd been unplugged. Could he even summon the strength to move? She looked so beautiful, so full of joy.

"I'm ready," he said. "To go. Permanently."

"What?" she cried, immediately on the alert. "No. Why? Because of the kiss?"

"No. Not at all. It was wonderful. Truly."

Her eyes turned clear. "But?"

"It wasn't enough."

She tried to argue but he could see she came up empty.

"That doesn't mean you have to leave," she said, finally.

"Doesn't it?"

"No. Who would I learn about hockey from? A girl's life shouldn't be only *Masterpiece Theatre* and cooking shows."

He smiled. "I thought I annoyed you."

"You do. But I think I can smooth out the rough edges."

He wouldn't mind losing his edges if it meant he could smell that hypnotizing mixture of pears and spice for the rest of his life. But there was still that ache. "Let me think about it—"

He was interrupted by the buzzer, whose unholy rattle filled the apartment until she pressed the speaker button.

"Yes?"

"Hey."

It was the voice of the man from outside, and that "hey" had carried with it a lifetime's worth of intimacy. Danny felt nauseous. It had to be her ex-husband. If Danny hadn't recognized the relationship in the man's tone, he would have in Cass's body language, which showed a tense yearning Danny experienced almost as a shove.

"What are you doing here?" She gave Danny a fleeting, apologetic glance that made him want to grab the man and throw him bodily back in his Lexus.

"I got your note. That was really nice. Can I come up?"

Come up? The man who'd just finalized plans for a rendezvous with Julie?

Danny almost left, but the worried flush on Cass's face kept him anchored in place.

"Yeah, sure. I mean, I guess." She pressed the buzzer then looked at Danny with obvious anxiety. It was like one word from this guy had taken her self-possession and scrambled it like a raw egg.

"I'm going to go," Danny said.

He didn't wait for an answer. He let himself disappear into

invisibility and slipped into the hall, but when he saw the man saunter into the apartment, he couldn't help but follow.

"Brian," she said.

Danny could feel her turmoil. It hung in the room like a storm only he could see, and it made his own stomach roil.

"You look great," Brian said. "Of course, you always look great."

Unlike Greg, Brian's words had the ring of honesty to them. That was something, at least.

"Thank you," she said.

"I came because of the note."

Flustered, she brushed a spot of dirt off the pot of flowers on the table. Danny noticed she had already taken away Greg's place setting.

"Yeah, that was probably a mistake."

"Why?" Brian tossed his coat over the back of the couch as if he were already certain he would be staying. "You just said you want to be friends. I do, too."

Danny could feel the layers of protection Cass had built up over the last year torn from her body. The storm was raging, blowing her this way and that, even though she stood perfectly still.

Brian held out his hand. Danny knew if she touched it, even once, everything she'd worked for would be gone. The visions flew through his head at a dizzying speed. A shared dinner. A kiss. The careless seduction. Cass exuberantly happy and then utterly destroyed. He gasped at the last, her tears so despairing.

He'd die before he'd let that happen. He'd die. He'd absolutely . . .

He jerked his gaze to Cass, just beginning to extend her hand. Then he relaxed his hold on this world and was gone.

Cass's hand came to rest in Brian's. "This," she said, nodding to the interlacing of their fingers, "really is a mistake."

"It's not, Cass," Danny said carefully. "I promise you, it's not."

Ghost of Blackstone Manor

Donna Fletcher

Amanda Steele paced in front of the large bow window. Where was he? He told her he'd be there by four at the latest. It was ten after and there was no sign of him. It would be dark within the hour and she didn't want to spend another night alone in the house.

She gazed out at the long driveway, praying a car would come into view, but her prayer went unanswered. The wind suddenly picked up, swirling the autumn leaves across the circular driveway around the three-tier fountain, settling them on the parcel of grass.

Amanda shivered, staring at the gargoyle that sat atop the fountain and spewed water from its mouth in the spring and summer months. By October it sat silent and ever watchful – a guardian of Blackstone Manor.

She smiled, recalling the first time she had seen the house as a child. The three-story stone structure with ivy creeping up along one side, numerous shuttered windows that kept prying eyes from seeing in and a wide veranda where white wood rockers would rock on their own, had frightened and delighted her. She had loved exploring the twenty-odd rooms in the mansion, and though the attic scared the wits out of her, she would gather what courage she could and go explore the many trunks and boxes stored there.

Her grandmother, Sophia Barnes, a renowned Broadway actress, had claimed to have bought Blackstone Manor on a whim, insisting it was the perfect getaway place for the family.

Tucked away in upstate New York along with other mansions built in the late nineteenth century, and not far from the quaint village of Meldrick, it was the gathering place for the rich and famous of her grandmother's day.

Besides, no one had wanted the old place. It had fallen into disrepair, and that – Amanda suspected – was what had drawn her grandmother to Blackstone Manor. Sophia Barnes had felt a kindred spirit with the place. It had still retained a modicum of splendor and character, just like she had. But having grown old – a death toll for a Broadway star where parts for older women were few, if any, even with several Tony Awards to her credit – she had found herself no longer relevant to her profession.

So she worked on restoring the mansion, and when it was completed, she never left the place. She insisted it needed her as much as she needed it, and so she threw fabulous parties for friends and relatives and held family gatherings that everyone loved to attend.

Amanda loved the house as much as her grandmother did, and so when Sophia passed a couple of months ago no one was surprised to learn that she had left Blackstone Manor, and the money to maintain it, to her granddaughter, Amanda.

Amanda had been thrilled and eager to spend some time there. That was, until two weeks ago when, only a couple of days after arriving, strange things had begun to happen. Doors opened on their own, lights went on and off without being touched, and while she wanted to believe it was her grandmother's spirit lingering, unable to leave the home she loved, it was what happened the past few nights that had forced her to call Mitch Connell.

The crunch of tires on the stone driveway had her relieved to see a car pulling up in front of the house. She didn't waste a moment. She ran to the foyer and, thanks to her daily yoga routine, she had no trouble pulling the heavy door open.

She watched Mitch Connell slip out of his car; he was tall, broad-shouldered and ruggedly handsome, with shoulder-length black hair. The few scars on his face proved that he was a man who didn't shy away from a brawl, and they made him all the more appealing. He was like a warrior of old who wore his scars like badges of courage, and who you could count on to fight to the death when needed. And she needed a warrior right now.

Even his confident swagger told her he was a man used to winning.

"You made it," she said, extending her hand.

He gripped her hand firmly, then quickly placed his other hand over their clenched ones, as if to let her know she needn't worry any longer. "It's good to finally meet you, Amanda."

The warmth and strength of his hands turned her skin to gooseflesh and sent a slight shiver racing through her. Though rough, handsome men usually didn't appeal to her, his touch sparked her interest, but she ignored it. She needed his specialized skills for a more important matter.

"I know how busy and in demand you are, and I so appreciate you seeing to my problem so quickly. I don't know what I would have done if you—" She froze, trying to deny what she heard behind her, but as the squeak grew ever louder she couldn't deny it.

The front door was slowly closing on its own.

She couldn't help but tremble. The door was simply too heavy to move all on its own.

Mitch kept firm hold of her hand while he tucked a secure arm around her waist and yanked her close against his side. He walked forward with determined strides, taking her along with him. When they reached the door, his arm left her waist and his hand shot out, shoving the partially closed door wide open, and entering the house with her close at his side.

That he impressed her was an understatement. Her grandmother had had the door designed from a piece of thick, solid oak. She had joked that no one would be able to shove their way in. Mitch had just proven her wrong.

They stood in the sizeable foyer, Mitch casting a quick glance around, his arm once again wrapped around her waist. She didn't mind his touch; it eased her worries. It was obvious that he was a man capable of protecting her, though would he be able to protect her from . . . a ghost?

"I don't know about you but I'm hungry," he said. "Why don't you get your coat and we'll go have a bite to eat in the village."

The door swung shut with such force that the framed paintings on the gold damask wallpaper quivered.

Amanda nodded and grabbed her red jacket from the hall

closet, slipping it on over her grey knit sweater that matched her pencil skirt. She quickly swiped her large black leather purse from the hall table and hurried to open the front door.

It wouldn't budge. No matter how many times she tried to turn the handle, it wouldn't move. It was almost as if a ghostly hand kept her from turning it.

She shut her eyes against the stark image and jumped when a warm hand covered hers.

"Let me," Mitch whispered in her ear and stepped closer, his body pressing against hers as he eased her hand off the knob and with a quick jerk turned it. The door popped open and with a firm hand to her lower back he ushered her out the door.

It closed with a sharp snap behind them.

"I would ask you if you remembered your keys," he said directing her to his car, "but it isn't necessary. The house wants you back and so the door will always open for you."

They were seated at a corner table in the Chowder House. It was frequented by locals during the week, since on weekends tourists mobbed the place and a table couldn't be had. Each one of their chowders was better than the next, as were their sandwiches and salads.

Their wine list wasn't bad either, and she was relieved when Mitch ordered a Sauvignon Blanc. They both decided on the seafood chowder and home-made corn bread.

After several sips of wine – her nerves a bit calmer, though not totally – she was ready to ask what he had meant by "the house wants you back", when the waitress appeared with their bread.

"You're that ghost-hunter fellow, and you're Sophia Barnes's granddaughter." The older woman smiled. "You're the image of your beautiful grandmother; even have her famous sapphire-blue eyes and long black hair." She turned to Mitch. "You're handsomer in person than you are on TV." She kept chattering, not giving them a chance to reply. "I guess you're here to finally get rid of that ghost at Blackstone Manor. You'd think he would have left that place by now."

"Susie, some help please," another waitress called, struggling with a full tray.

Without another word, Susie took off to help her.

"No matter how many times I explain that I'm not a ghost

hunter . . ." Mitch shook his head. "I don't hunt ghosts or chase after them nor am I out to confirm their existence, though I could easily do that. I help ghosts move on and it isn't always easy."

She leaned forward, cupping her wine glass with both hands. "I hope the one at Blackstone Manor will not prove difficult to move on."

"Tell me about the ghost," he said.

Amanda was grateful that at that moment a different waitress approached with their chowders. It gave her time, if only briefly, to collect herself and think of how to tell him what she had been experiencing. But would he believe her?

He reached out and took hold of her hand. "Trust me."

His words didn't help, having heard exactly this phrase from men who, in the end, weren't at all trustworthy. But then this wasn't that type of relationship, so there was no need to worry that he would disappoint her. He had an excellent business reputation and if she needed to trust him in order for him to help her then so be it.

"At first I thought my grandmother haunted the house," she said. "Doors opened and closed, lights flickered, electronic devices gave me trouble. I assumed my grandmother was letting me know how pleased she was that I was staying in the house for a while."

"You don't intend to live there?"

"I'm not sure what I intend to do with the place. It's awfully big for one person."

"When did you realize the ghost wasn't your grandmother?"

Amanda took a sip of wine and realized that this wasn't the place to discuss this. "Do you mind if I reserve that answer for later?"

"Not at all," he said. "Tell me about yourself."

While Amanda was grateful for the change of subject, she wasn't comfortable talking about herself. Her life wasn't very exciting, her job in human resources restrictive and boring. She had thought by now she'd have advanced further in her job and been married, perhaps even have one child, but neither had happened and it wasn't making her feel too confident about the future. So she switched the subject and regaled him with stories of the famous Sophia Barnes.

★   ★   ★

When they got in the car after dinner, Mitch waited and didn't start it. He looked over at her and said, "I believe it would be best if you answered my question now before we return to the house. When did you know the ghost wasn't your grandmother?"

Amanda didn't hesitate; she wanted to get this over with. "When he touched me."

Mitch didn't appear shocked by her answer, so she continued, "At first I thought I was dreaming. I drifted between sleep and wakefulness . . . when I felt—" her hand drifted inside her open jacket and rested beneath her breast "—the hand lingered there for a moment and then it stroked my breast, so feather light that goosebumps ran down my arms. It moved, exploring my other breast, squeezing ever so lightly while his thumb played with —" She paused and took a deep breath, her hand moving down along her midriff and across her stomach before moving even further down . . .

She gasped and her hand stilled. Her eyes startled wide when she realized that her hand rested between her legs.

Now Mitch would know what she hadn't intended on telling anyone – the ghost had aroused her.

She was too embarrassed to turn and face him. She remained staring out the front window of the car.

"Has this happened every night?"

Did she dare tell him that she wished it had? She had never been so aroused in her life and it wasn't for lack of attentive lovers, or at least she had thought they had been attentive.

She shook her head. "No. After the first time, it didn't happen again until two days later and then every other night until finally . . ."

"It's been every night now?"

She nodded, growing wet at the thought that her ghostly lover would visit tonight.

"More often than not a logical explanation can be found."

She was mortified. Did he think that she aroused *herself*? That this was nothing more than her wishful imaginings? "You don't believe me?"

"That's not what I'm saying at all," he said. "The world between sleep and wakefulness is hard to define. It is a place of lucid dreams and an opening for spirits to slip through. It can also be nothing more than nonsense, which is why science has such a difficult time explaining and defining it. There are no set rules in that unique world and one must approach it with caution if you want proof."

She still didn't turn and look at him. "What you're saying is that it's possible that I could simply be crazy."

She jumped, startled, when his fingers took firm hold of her chin and forced her to turn her head and look at him. It wasn't his rough good looks that sent her heart beating madly; it was the sincerity in his dark eyes and the confidence of his words.

"You're not crazy. I'll take care of this for you. I promise."

His hand dropped away and he started the car. They sped down the road toward Blackstone Manor, Amanda eager and fearful to be returning home.

They spent the remainder of the evening in conversation, Mitch declining any more wine, though eager for a cup of hot tea. She joined him and added gingersnap cookies to the tray she brought into the living room.

"What made you take up this line of work?" Amanda asked, tired of the discussion being only about her. She wanted to learn more about him than just what she had read in his books.

"My grandfather raised me, not because I didn't have any parents, but because they were never around. They're scientists and travel extensively around the world." Surprisingly, he didn't say it with bitterness but rather with sadness. "Though my parents had left me behind, my grandfather made sure I didn't miss a thing. He gave me the most wonderful childhood, and when he died—" he shook his head "—it devastated me. That was fourteen years ago when I was twenty, and my life changed completely."

Mitch continued. "My grandfather came to me right after his funeral. He told me there was work to be done and I needed to be ready. It took several years of study and trusting that I wasn't nuts, but finally I accepted the gift my grandfather had given me. I had the ability to detect ghosts and help them move on and, as they say, the rest is history."

She was about to ask what his scientist parents thought of his profession when the lights in the room flickered off then on then off and then on again.

"Does this usually happen the same time each night?" Mitch asked, not at all perturbed.

"I've noticed no pattern, and I did have an electrician check for any problems. He found none."

"Did your grandmother ever make mention of a ghost while she occupied the house?"

"No, Grams was very happy here," Amanda said, thinking back to the time that she had spent here. "She wore a constant smile and laughed often and friends and family visited frequently. She didn't spend much time alone."

"And not once did she ever make mention of a ghost?"

"No, whenever my wild imagination would take flight, she'd take time to calm me and make me see reason," Amanda said.

"It doesn't make any sense."

"What doesn't?" she asked, curious and a bit apprehensive.

"Do you recall what our waitress said tonight about the ghost?"

"Not the exact words."

He repeated the waitress's words. "'I guess you're here to finally get rid of that ghost at Blackstone Manor.'" He rubbed at his chin. "That would lead me to believe that the ghost has been around for a while."

Could it be possible? Could the ghost have been the reason her grandmother had stayed and never left? Had it been her secret all these years?

"You said there were old trunks and boxes in the attic. Were they left by the previous owner?"

She nodded. "A lot was left by the previous owner. My grandmother had much of the furniture refinished, and simply left the old steamer trunks stored in the attic."

"Then that's where we'll start our investigation tomorrow . . . the attic."

It had been years since she had ventured up there, her youthful imaginings having faded completely. She found the attic now nothing more than a chore. Only a few months ago, Grams had asked her to help sort through the collected mess and discard what wasn't necessary.

Could her grandmother have had something else in mind? Was there something there she had wanted her to find?

"It's getting late," he said. "We better get some sleep. We have a busy day tomorrow."

She conceded with a nod, though she really didn't want to go to bed, at least not alone.

She led the way to the second floor where her grandmother's suite was located along with two other bedrooms. Mitch carried a small suitcase. Earlier, he'd informed her he would probably need to stay a few days, and that had been fine with her. He could stay as long as he wanted.

She intended to show him to the bedroom next to the suite, but that was before she spotted her door slowly opening. She didn't recall closing it.

Mitch grabbed hold of her hand and marched straight for the room. The door slammed in his face before he could enter.

"Whoever it is either doesn't want me in there or wants my attention." He shoved open the door.

She entered the room along with him, not letting go of his hand. It was empty. No ghostly apparitions or cold spots. It was a lovely room decorated in a long bygone, opulent era. It had suited her grandmother perfectly, though not Amanda, but she didn't have the heart to change it.

Mitch released her hand and explored the room. Amanda wondered how she could get him to sleep with her . . . actually *sleep* with her, so she wouldn't be afraid of the ghost.

The warm, soft whispered breath on her neck was enough to make her run to him. She grabbed hold of Mitch's hand, pleading, "Please sleep with me tonight."

He smiled and ran a gentle finger down along her cheek. "I never turn down a chance to sleep with a beautiful woman."

His innocent touch teased her senses and she was surprised by her instant response. Or perhaps she had thought her hormones dormant for so long that they had just withered and died. She couldn't honestly recall the last time a man's touch had excited her.

She figured she'd better clarify. "I didn't mean—"

"I know what you meant," he said. "You're hoping my presence will discourage the ghost from visiting you."

"It was a thought."

"A good one," he said. "Let's see if it works."

She went into the bathroom to change into her most comfy pajamas – pink and purple polka-dotted knit bottoms that rested on her hips. A plain pink T-shirt that didn't quite cover her midriff matched the bottoms, but she didn't feel comfortable wearing it to bed with Mitch beside her, so she threw on a large white T-shirt, the hem almost reaching to her knees.

"Sexy," he said with an amused grin when she walked out of the bathroom.

He certainly filled that word out quite nicely. He was stretched out on the bed wearing black pajama bottoms and no top. He had a broad, muscled chest that would make women salivate and fill men with envy. And damn if she didn't want to touch it.

She wondered which was worse, being aroused by a ghost or sleeping beside a sexy man and not taking advantage of it.

She got into bed and reached up to turn off the light – when it shut off by itself. Without hesitation she moved closer to Mitch. Not close enough that their bodies touched, but close enough so that she could feel him there beside her.

When the bedroom door slammed forcefully shut she nearly crawled on top of him.

"It's never closed like that before," she whispered in his face and realized that her breasts were plastered to his chest and her leg was wrapped tightly around his. She reluctantly eased herself off him, and he didn't stop her. And foolishly enough, it disappointed her.

"At least we know he's not happy with my presence," Mitch said.

"Have you ever known a ghost to do harm?"

He turned on his side to face her in the half-light and she noticed that he kept both hands tucked beneath his pillow. Didn't he trust himself not to touch her? It was a crazy thought she had no business thinking, though she did recall reading in one of his books that he wasn't in a relationship. He had claimed his work made it difficult to find a woman who didn't mind that ghosts visited him at odd hours of the day and night.

"I've never come across one," he said. "It's the fear that ghosts instill that causes the biggest problems, though if your grandmother had seen the ghost he certainly hadn't frightened her."

Amanda smiled. "Grams once told me that after being on Broadway for years there wasn't anything that could frighten her."

"I would have liked to have met her," he said, "though perhaps I still will."

The thought of seeing Grams as a ghost made her want to move closer to Mitch again, though not for protection – for comfort. He struck her as a man who wouldn't mind consoling her, but she had never been with a man who offered to console without wanting something in return. Somehow she thought Mitch would offer her comfort without strings attached.

They exchanged a few more words before drifting off to sleep.

Amanda didn't want to leave the dream. And it *had* to be a dream, for she had never felt such an all-consuming passion. Sex had never swept her away to the point where nothing else mattered, where nothing else existed and you surrendered everything, every bit of yourself to his touch, to his kisses and to a climax that built to such a fever pitch that you screamed out his name over and over until . . .

Amanda woke breathless and naked with Mitch rising over her ready to . . .

She let out a yell and he jumped off her with a shake of his head. She did the same, shaking her head, trying to get rid of the fuzziness.

Mitch paced the floor beside the bed, running his fingers repeatedly through his hair.

She quickly reached for her clothes and grabbed his bottoms along with hers. She tossed them to him, needing him to cover up, for the more she looked at him naked the more she wanted him.

"Hurry and dress," he said as he did the same, all the while avoiding looking at her.

If the lights hadn't been on the task would have been easier, their arousals less evident, though the scent of sex was heavy in the air.

When had the lights gone on and who had turned them on? Amanda shook her head again. She wasn't thinking straight. She should be demanding to know why he had touched her, but then she had invited him into her bed. But hadn't he asked her to trust him and hadn't she done just that?

She stared at him, not sure what to say.

His hands went up to defend himself. "I thought it was a dream."

"I thought the same."

"Your scream jarred me awake."

What had woken her? A clap of thunder sounded and she realized then what had snapped her out of the dream. Thunder.

She shivered and he stepped forward, as if ready to comfort her, then pulled back. She was disappointed. She would have liked his arms around her at that moment, though it probably wasn't a good idea. She still throbbed with passion, and from the size of him he hadn't exactly lost his desire.

"I should sleep in another room."

"No," she said, not wanting him to leave, though why she wasn't sure. Was it her fear of the ghost or her fear that she wouldn't experience his touch again?

"I'm sorry. I don't know what happened. I felt your touch and . . ." He shook his head.

"I touched you first?"

"In my dream you did, and I couldn't help but respond."

He couldn't help it. Didn't that mean he was attracted to her? She wanted to smile but she didn't, though her stomach fluttered.

"Unless . . ." He stared off into space for a moment. "I've never experienced it before, though I've read about ghostly possession."

Was he suggesting what she thought? "You can't mean that . . ."

"It would explain why we both woke shocked."

She didn't want to think that it wasn't him that had been touching her so intimately, or whose kisses had spiked her passion like never before. She didn't want to believe that it was a ghost who had aroused her like no other man had ever done, for how could she ever find a man who could compete with a ghost?

They sat in relative silence the next morning sharing breakfast, if you can call a slice of toast breakfast. It seemed that neither of them had an appetite. The weather didn't help any either – torrential rain falling with a rumble of thunder now and again.

Neither of them made mention of last night's incident and that was fine with her, though it certainly lingered on her mind. When she had finally fallen asleep it had been restless, and she had woken alone in bed.

"Are you ready to start investigating?" he asked.

She stood. "Do I look ready?"

He smiled. "Like I said last night – sexy."

She grinned at his teasing, since grey yoga pants, an oversized, red knit top and her long black hair pulled back in a ponytail didn't exactly fit sexy. Why then did she detect a glint of interest in his eyes? While she hadn't dated recently she still could tell when a man was interested and Mitch Connell was definitely interested.

They made their way to the attic. It was a bit creepy, like most attics. After all it was similar to a graveyard: pictures, objects and, definitely, memories were brought here and forgotten.

"Where shall we start?" she asked.

"Let me have a look around and see if anything speaks to me."

"Speaks to you?"

He nodded as he began exploring. "Ghosts that linger are usually attached to certain things. It could be as simple as a picture that gives me a clue to the identity of the ghost. Once I make the connection the ghost usually appears."

"But ghosts do appear without you doing anything."

He turned and smiled. "You read my book."

She liked his smile; it made her smile. "All four of them, and enjoyed each one."

"Then you know that some ghosts can be stubborn. The most stubborn ones are the ones with issues to settle, and they can be more of a challenge."

"My ghost is a challenge."

"Not for long."

As soon as his hand touched an old steamer trunk he said, "Let's start here."

Amanda joined him, patiently waiting while he cleared some space around the trunk, taking the time to admire his firm, round backside that looked so good in his black jeans. Though recalling last night, she preferred seeing it naked.

She cringed at her thought. This wasn't the time or place, but then when was a good time or place to admire a man's backside? She should just be glad that she finally found one that she did admire, whether the time proved right or not.

Her logical reasoning allowed her to keep watching him without guilt; though she did pay a price – she got aroused. Damn if it didn't please and annoy her all at once. It continued to prove that her dormant hormones had finally been roused.

"Ready?"

She had to grin; she definitely was ready. She nodded.

He eased the trunk open and the attic flooded with the musty scent that develops when something has been shut away for years. There were men's clothes and an Army uniform from World War II, and, wrapped in a man's white silk scarf, which had yellowed with the years, were old black and white pictures.

"Do you think the things in this trunk belong to our ghost?" Amanda asked.

"I think something in here connects with him," he said, and sat in front of the trunk. He patted the spot beside him for her to join him.

She didn't hesitate. She sat down, though much closer to him than she had intended – or had she? She had to stop thinking about him sexually. He was here to help her; perhaps afterward . . . she felt a brush of hot breath along the back of her neck.

Her hand clamped down on Mitch's arm and she whispered, "He's here."

The breath grew heavier and she wondered if the ghost's touch would follow. She scooted closer to Mitch and his arm went around her, tucking her against him.

"How can we help you?" Mitch asked calmly.

She listened, as if expecting to hear a reply, but was met with only silence.

The hot breath on her neck suddenly vanished and she turned to Mitch and whispered, "He's gone."

She hadn't realized how temptingly close their lips were, or how much closer she wanted them to be. She began to turn away from him when, suddenly, his hand cupped the back of her head and swiftly brought her lips to meet his.

He kissed her like a man who knew what he was doing. He didn't hesitate or hold back. He kissed her hard and decisively and sent a tingle rushing through her body that left her shuddering.

She didn't know how or when it happened but she found herself on her back with Mitch nearly covering her. And she didn't care. His kisses were too intoxicating to give a damn about anything. She wanted only to lose herself in the moment and make memories.

His hands began to explore her body, touching places she had never paid mind to but that he made come alive. Who would have thought that the stroke and squeeze of her shoulder could send her hormones into frenzy?

Her hands rushed beneath his grey sweatshirt, eager to touch his naked chest. His hard muscles felt ever so good. They rolled around on the dusty attic floor, mopping up cobwebs along the way but not caring, so lost in the need for each other. Until Mitch abruptly stopped.

"Did you hear that?" he asked with a whisper.

She started to ask what when he shook his head.

She listened but couldn't hear anything. And then she heard it . . . a faint chuckle.

They both lay perfectly still, though it wasn't easy with his hard arousal digging into her side. She would have much preferred it digging in where it belonged . . .

Belonged? Where had that thought come from?

When the chuckle wasn't heard again, Mitch jumped up and began pacing in front of the trunk, just as he had paced last night in her bedroom.

"Something's not right," he said with annoyance. "I can't keep my hands off you."

"Am I that repulsive?" she asked, hurt by what sounded like an accusation.

He stopped pacing and shook his head. "No, you're beautiful, but I never allow anything to interfere with business."

"You're attracted to me?"

"I'm not sure."

Again his words hurt and so she was blunt. "Then why kiss me as if you never want to stop, or touch me like you want to make love?"

"Because the need to do both came after you felt the presence of the ghost. And so it makes me wonder if . . ."

"It was the ghost who wanted me and not you."

"Exactly."

"Does that mean I want the ghost and not you?" The very idea upset her.

He looked upset himself, and it gave her small comfort to think that the thought might have actually disappointed him.

He went straight for the photos and scooped them up where

they lay scattered on the floor. "We need to find out who this ghost is and get him to move on."

She wanted to ask what happens afterward, but she didn't think she was ready to hear the answer. This growing attraction, this lusty need for each other wasn't something she wanted to let go of just yet – or maybe never, if she were honest with herself.

Her previous relationships hadn't come anywhere near to being as passionate and exciting as what little she had shared with Mitch so far. And if this were just the beginning, she wouldn't mind finding out what would happen if they spent more time together . . . without the interference of the ghost.

"This man had an exciting life," Mitch said, as they sat at the kitchen table looking over the photos.

Amanda had to agree with him. There was one man that appeared in almost all the pictures. He was a good-looking guy, and she couldn't help but think of her grandmother. "Gram would have referred to him as debonair, like some of the movie stars of the forties."

"I can see that," Mitch agreed. "He looks the confident and charming sort. He was also a world traveler. Look at the different locales in these pictures." He pushed a few toward her. "I believe this is Cairo, another is London and I'm certain one is Cuba as well. He certainly got around."

"I wonder who he is," Amanda said. "It really is a shame that people don't put names, dates and places on the backs of pictures."

"Let's see what we can find out on the internet about this house," Mitch suggested. "We may get lucky and come across a picture of him."

"That's a good idea." Amanda stood to go get her laptop from her bedroom when thunder sounded as if it rent the sky in two. The lights flickered and she wasn't sure if it was caused by the storm or the ghost. She remained where she was and looked at Mitch.

"I'll go with you."

She grinned, glad that she didn't have to ask.

She switched on the hall lights and, as they climbed the stairs, the lights flickered on and off again.

This time Amanda chalked it up to the storm rather than the

ghost, since thunder rumbled loudly outside, and headed to the bedroom, the door open just as they had left it. She approached it without trepidation and, as she turned to enter the room, the lights went out, plunging them into dusky darkness.

"A lot of good the computer will do us now," she said, turning her head to look at Mitch as she entered.

His focused stare warned her that there was something in the room she might not want to see. As much as she didn't want to turn around, she did. In the far corner floated an apparition that slowly formed into the full-fledged ghost of the man in the pictures. He was transparent, though his identity was quite clear. He stood there staring at them, as if letting them know he purposely allowed them to see him, and then stretched his hand out, pointing to Amanda, and smiled.

Mitch stepped in front of her protectively. "Let me help you move on."

The ghost nodded and then vanished.

"He's gone, that's it. It's over?" Amanda asked.

"No, it's just beginning," Mitch said and, to her surprise and delight, he wound his arm around her, yanked her up against him and kissed her like a man claiming his territory.

A few minutes later they found themselves rolling around on the bed together, his shirt and her top quickly discarded along with sound reason. It got hot and heavy fast, his kisses driving her insane.

The man was a virtual Casanova in bed; she simply could not resist him.

The thought was like a splash of cold water in her face. Was it Mitch or the ghost making love to her?

She pushed at Mitch, though he didn't respond at first. Only shouting his name got him to stop. It made her think that perhaps he was possessed, and not just with a hungry need for her.

He bolted off the bed, grabbing his shirt, and disappeared into the bathroom, slamming the door behind him.

She quickly slipped her top on and readjusted her ponytail. She couldn't help but feel a sudden loss. Her heart ached, as if she had just lost a loved one. This was driving her mad. She had always dreamed of falling in love – young foolish dreams, though Grams had always encouraged them.

"Don't settle," she would say. "Wait for the man that makes your heart beat madly and who can't keep his hands off you. Wait even if it takes a lifetime, and then you'll never have any regrets."

Amanda had always accused her grandmother of being a romantic, and her grandmother would laugh and agree. "Romance is everything, my darling. It's an indication of whether a man loves you more than he loves himself."

Mitch hadn't hesitated to step in when the ghost had reached out to her. He had held her close when they had entered the house and had immediately taken her out when he had seen how upset she was. He was tender, kind and attentive to her.

Why wouldn't he be? You hired him, you idiot.

She shook her head, trying to get rid of the sensible thought. She didn't want to think sensibly; she wanted this to be real between her and Mitch. She wanted the lusty passion, the quick, heart-stopping attraction and the undeniable craziness of taking that first step off a cliff and falling into love.

He came out of the bathroom and she noticed that his hair was damp around his face. Cold water had definitely been necessary for him. She could use a shot of it herself to ease the heat that continued to pulse through her body and torment all those intimate nooks and crannies.

"Grab your laptop and let's go downstairs. We need to find out who this guy is and get him out of here before . . ." He shook his head and marched out of the room.

Amanda quickly followed, the laptop tucked under her arm.

The house had an interesting history. Blackstone Manor was built at the turn of the century by the Blackstone family. Thomas Blackstone, grandson of the Blackstone patriarch Henry, followed in his grandfather's footsteps, amassing even more wealth through various businesses and investments. Thomas, when in residence, threw lavish parties for friends and relatives at the manor. He traveled extensively for business and pleasure, often taking the youngest of his five grandchildren, Michael, who also lived with him.

And in no time the two of them sat silently staring at a picture of their ghost on the screen.

"Michael was a good-looking man," Amanda said, though

that was an understatement. The man was drop-dead gorgeous. "I bet many a woman lost her heart to him."

"He sure looked like he had it all," Mitch said.

"You think?" she asked, staring at the man who looked happy enough in the photo. "I wonder if he ever found love."

"Did you hear that?" Mitch asked, quickly scanning the room.

Amanda remained silent and listened.

"I could have sworn I heard that chuckle again."

They listened for a few minutes more but heard nothing.

Mitch scratched his shaking head. "Let's see if we can find out more about Michael Blackstone."

A half-hour later they both sat staring at the computer screen.

"How sad," Amanda said, "for him and his grandfather."

"It would seem that after Michael died in World War II, his grandfather lost all interest in life and just locked himself away in the house."

Amanda cast a glance around the living room; a fire crackled in the fireplace and soft lighting added to the peaceful ambience. But no matter how lovely, she couldn't imagine shutting herself away here for years on end.

"He lived twenty-five years secluded in this house mourning the loss of his grandson," Amanda said.

"*Or* he spent twenty-five happy years here sharing the place with his grandson's ghost."

"You think that's what kept him here . . . his grandson's ghost?"

"That waitress did mention something about thinking the ghost should have been gone by now."

"That's right," Amanda said, "the ghost would have left with his grandfather's passing."

"Something else keeps him here." Mitch stretched his arms above his head and she couldn't help but admire his flexing muscles and the way he groaned as he worked the tension out of his back.

She was attracted to him still, and the ghost wasn't around.

But she spoke too soon, the hot breath once again suddenly at the back of her neck. She jumped up, annoyed. "Damn it, what do you want from me?"

Suddenly Michael Blackstone materialized in a shadowy corner.

Mitch was already standing, his arm reaching out for Amanda and drawing her close.

Amanda asked again. "What do you want from me?"

He pointed at her.

"You can't have me," she said. "Tell me how I can help you."

He continued pointing at her until he finally drifted away like a puff of smoke.

Mitch immediately stepped away, leaving a chill to run through her. She stared longingly at him.

"I can't," he said. "I can't come near you right now. I want to kiss you and not stop kissing you."

She wanted the same, though she wanted more than kisses from him.

"We're going out to eat; get dressed," he ordered.

She didn't argue; they needed time away from the house, or perhaps a safe distance from each other. She hurried out of the room and upstairs to her bedroom. She would have liked for him to come with her but that would have been tempting fate. And, at the moment, she feared the consequences of being alone in the bedroom with him more than she feared facing the ghost.

Within a few minutes, she had changed into a red sweater and jeans and black heeled boots. She freed her hair, giving it a good brushing, and left it to fall free. She glanced at the portrait of Gram over the bed and smiled.

People insisted that she resembled her grandmother, but Amanda was nowhere near as beautiful or as elegant as her. Gram had had a grace about her that Amanda lacked. Perhaps it was all those years on stage, her every movement flowing like a lovely melody that captured the attention of the endless audiences she had played to.

When Gram entered a room everyone took notice.

"I miss you," she said to the portrait, and then fled the room, tears brimming in her eyes.

Mitch waited at the bottom of the staircase. She stopped at the top when she saw him and attempted to collect her fluctuating emotions.

"Damn, but you're gorgeous," he said.

He said it with such conviction that her tears spilled over her cheeks. She flew down the stairs and into his arms.

Mitch held her tight, as if he never intended to let her go. "What's wrong?"

"I miss Gram."

He kissed her then, a gentle, consoling kiss that soothed her. He kept his arm around her as they walked to the front door, which he opened without incident. Neither of them heard the chuckle that followed them.

They returned to the Chowder House. Susie was working, and they were seated in her section. It was a quiet night, the place almost empty due to the storm, so Susie could linger talking with them.

"The Blackstone family was well known around here. If it hadn't been for Thomas Blackstone this town would have died years ago. He got a lot of the businesses going. I remember meeting him when I was young, a big jovial man, always smiling. That is until his grandson died. No one saw him much after that.

"Everyone here was really happy when your grandmother moved in. Businesses began thriving again from all the work your grandmother sent their way." Susie shook her head. "The only thing no one in town could figure out was why Thomas Blackstone had left the place to her. Why do you leave a mansion to somebody you never knew?"

"My grandmother inherited Blackstone Manor?" Amanda asked, shocked at the news.

"You didn't know that, honey? Your grandmother didn't tell you?"

Amanda was relieved when Susie got called to pick up an order. "Why did Gram lead everyone to believe she bought the place?"

Mitch reached out and took hold of her hand. "I don't know, but I do know that people don't leave valuable property to strangers. There's a connection there somewhere and we need to find it."

They finished their meal and returned home, going straight to the computer, but found nothing that connected Sophia Barnes with Thomas Blackstone. They continued their hunt well past midnight, until finally their continuous yawns drove them toward the bed.

They both changed their clothes – in separate rooms – then stood staring down at the bed.

"I have to say something before we get into bed together," Mitch said.

Amanda waited.

"I'm attracted to you, have been since I first saw you standing outside when I pulled up in my car. I've had the urge to kiss you long before that damn ghost got in the way." He shook his head. "I can't get the thought of making love to you out of mind. It haunts me as much as the ghost haunts this house. I've never felt like this before and . . ." He took a fortifying breath. "I want to make sure it's real because, if it is, I don't think I'm ever going to be able to let you go."

Amanda couldn't help it; she was so thrilled that she chuckled.

His eyes turned wide. "Do that again."

"What?"

"That little laugh."

She found it easy to do again, still delighted with the turn of events.

"That's the chuckle I've been hearing."

"But I haven't done it before." She gasped. "I've been told repeatedly that I sound just like Gram when I do it."

"I should have known," Mitch said. "The signs were obvious. There isn't one ghost here, there are two."

"Grams is here?"

"No doubt she's the one affecting the lights. New ghosts have a tendency to do that, whereas older ghosts can materialize easily. I wonder why she remains here."

The ghost of Michael Blackstone appeared so suddenly that they both jumped – startled. Mitch didn't hesitate. He skittered across the bed and wrapped an arm around Amanda.

"Where's Gram? I want to see her."

Blackstone pointed at Amanda once again.

"I don't know what you want," she cried out to him. "Please, I want to see Grams."

He disappeared as fast as he had materialized.

"I don't understand," Amanda said, close to tears.

"I think I do." Mitch took hold of her shoulders and turned her around. "He wasn't pointing at you. He was pointing at the portrait of your grandmother."

Amanda and Mitch scrambled up onto the bed and felt along the edges of the picture frame. Mitch found a latch, and the portrait slowly moved away from the wall to reveal a wall safe. There was a note attached to it.

Amanda read Gram's message.

The combination is hidden where you spent hours of play as a young child.

Amanda ran to Gram's vanity dresser with the triple mirror. She remembered sitting on the floor when she was a girl, watching her grandmother get ready for parties or dinner guests.

She opened the bottom drawer on the right side of the vanity, took out a floral cloth-covered box and opened it. It was full of the costume jewelry her grandmother had given her to play with. Tucked among the mound of jewelry was a folded piece of paper.

Amanda smiled and hurried to the wall safe, quickly feeding in the combination. The door popped open to reveal a brown leather journal. She took it out and hugged it to her chest.

Mitch closed the safe and clicked the portrait back into position.

The two sat on the bed, Mitch's arm around her waist.

She snuggled against him, glad he was there to share this moment with her. When she opened the journal, a letter fell out. They both read it silently.

My dearest Amanda,

This letter will briefly explain everything, and my journal tells the rest of the story. Let the world know if you want, for it is a grand romance. Since you're reading this, Michael has succeeded in helping you find it. Please don't mourn me. My time has come to an end and I must journey on. But I could not leave you, my granddaughter, the love of my life, without explaining everything.

Many years ago when I was young and just starting my acting career, I volunteered my time with the USO. I danced with many soldiers, handed out food and listened to their stories. One night I danced with an army officer. As soon as he took me in his arms, I knew we were meant to be. That officer was Michael Blackstone.

We had one glorious night together. When he left the next day, he promised me he'd be back and we'd be together for ever. But he never came back. I feared the worst since I knew in my heart he loved me and meant to return. It took almost a year to find out what happened to him. His death devastated me. I never found a love like that again, never found a man who could melt my heart with a simple touch or make my body quiver with just one kiss. Instead, I went from marriage to marriage until I finally gave up.

When I found out that I had inherited Blackstone Manor I was shocked. No one in the Blackstone family had ever contacted me. Even the lawyer wondered why the house was left to me.

I found out why on my first night in the house, when Michael came to me. In dreams he explained everything.

Oh my darling, Amanda, I had never been so happy to see Michael and feel his touch again after all those years. It may seem crazy to you but the years spent in this house with him were some of the best years of my life. I felt alive again and, even more startling, I didn't fear death, for I knew Michael would be there to greet me and we would finally be truly together.

Know that I am happy and that I love you dearly.

One last important thing. In your dreams, you'll find the truth. It is there that your yearning desires will conjure up the man of your dreams and bring him to you, though I think I've given you a bit of a nudge in the right direction. You have talents you're just beginning to discover, but then perhaps Mitch Connell can help you develop them.

Kisses and hugs, my darling. Live and love well!

Gram

P.S. How appropriate it would be if Blackstone Manor became a center dedicated to gathering data on ghosts and teaching those who have a talent for seeing them. You could call it the Sophia Barnes Center for Ghostly Phenomenon.

Amanda jumped off the bed and hurried to the table next to the pink velvet chaise lounge. She ran her finger along the stack of books piled there and eased one out, flipping through the pages.

She stopped at a picture of Mitch speaking before a large audience. Tucked between the pages was a picture of Amanda taken about a year ago.

"I remember now. One day when I was young, I had told Grams that I had seen a ghost looking out one of the windows while I was in the backyard. She told me it was nonsense and, after a heated debate, I told her that it was easy to see ghosts and I didn't know what all the fuss was about. I told her that one day I would prove it to everyone." Amanda shook her head. "But all my thoughts of ghosts faded over the years, until I had completely forgotten it all."

"No, you tucked the ghosts away until the time was right and you were ready."

Amanda smiled. "Gram left the books where she knew I would find them; her chaise is my favorite spot for reading. And she placed you in my thoughts before any of these strange activities started."

"I like your grandmother."

Gram's chuckle sounded loud and clear, and they both smiled.

"I think she likes you too."

Amanda wasn't surprised to see Michael Blackstone materialize in his favorite corner. He smiled and nodded at them.

"Take good care of Grams and give her a kiss for me."

Blackstone nodded and waved. Just when Amanda thought he would vanish, her grandmother suddenly appeared. She was younger-looking – so very beautiful – and wore the happiest smile. She blew Amanda a kiss, and then Michael slipped his arm around her and together they vanished.

Amanda ran to the spot where her grandmother had stood. "It's over," she said with a touch of sorrow.

"No, it's not," Mitch said advancing on her. "It's just beginning."

A shot of desire hit her like Cupid's arrow and spread like wildfire.

"You do realize that it was me you conjured in your dreams, me who touched you, me who you desired."

"It makes sense—" she shook her head "—and then it doesn't. I had been reading your book before I fell asleep and had seen my picture next to yours, so I suppose one could say it was a subliminal suggestion that conjured the dream."

He scooped her up. "You have a special gift, Amanda. You travel the dream world and bring people into it. I could use a business partner with your unique talents, but first . . . it's time that dream became a reality."

"I always believed that dreams could come true."

"Tonight, Amanda, I'm going to make all your dreams come true."

As he lowered her to the bed, the lights went out.

Seventeen Coppers

Jeannie Holmes

Day 10, Season of the Sun
53rd Octavian Cycle

"I want you to steal my husband."

Ro Vargas choked on her honey water. Coughing, she set the earthenware mug on the table with a loud *thump*. She dabbed moisture from the corners of her mouth with the back of her hand and leveled her gaze on the well-dressed woman sitting across from her. "I beg your pardon?"

Lady Helena Duffy straightened her spine. "I want you to steal my husband," she repeated softly.

"I don't know what you were told about me, but if you and your husband are looking for a little excitement in the bedchamber, you've come to the wrong woman."

Confusion cloaked Lady Helena's face until the shock of Ro's words sank in. "Stars preserve us," she whispered, her shoulders rounding in defeat. "I've made a right mess of things, haven't I?"

Ro sipped her honey water and waited for the woman to gather her composure. Looking around the open-air tavern, she was certain they made one of the stranger pairings. Lady Duffy was an aristocrat in fine silks, with flawless porcelain skin and her thick hair swept into a tidy chignon. No doubt she would be seen by others as the perfect example of a high-born woman. By contrast, Ro was an armed half-Fae bastard wearing a tattered short coat, faded breeches and scuffed boots – a Dreg.

And yet no one glanced more than once in their direction.

Ithe, the capital city of Asthega, was the first stop along the country's northern and western trade routes. The harbor brought merchant ships laden with textiles, spices and other goods from overseas. Anything that didn't find its way to the Queen's Market was sent out of the city on great steam-driven cargo engines or by airships.

Inevitably where legitimate trade prospered, smugglers and black markets thrived. However, most native Ithians turned blind eyes to the shadow economy that kept so many of them alive. Ro, with her bastard birth and Dreg status, was largely ignored by all Ithians, which only heightened her impatience to learn why a noble woman had purposely sought her out.

"Miss Vargas," Lady Helena began, "you misunderstand my intentions." She glanced around at the neighboring tables. "I have it on good authority that you're a woman skilled in the – shall we say – acquiring arts, and I wish to retain your services."

Only a high-born woman could call someone a thief and make it sound like a compliment. Despite the instincts screaming for her to leave, Ro leaned forward. "I'm curious. What *exactly* do you want me to do, my lady?"

"My husband, Everett, was stolen."

"He was kidnapped?"

"No, not exactly." Lady Helena plucked at the tasseled draw-string of her velvet purse. "A foreign man named Dacat murdered Everett, and then stole him before I was able to transport his ecto-impression to the Well of Souls."

"I see." Ro frowned. She'd heard of the Well of Souls and the practice of transferring ecto-impressions – the life force left behind when a person died – to the Well, but she'd never met anyone who could afford to do it.

The poor simply hung black flags over doorways and entrusted the remains of their loved ones to the Ithian Government for interment in paupers' graves. Numerous superstitions regarding ecto-impressions had taken root among the lower classes as a result. Ro, however, placed little faith in those superstitions.

"Why would Dacat kill your husband?"

"Everett owed Dacat a great deal of money, and when he couldn't pay, Dacat killed him."

"Not an uncommon practice. I assume Dacat is planning to sell the orb."

Lady Duffy nodded.

Ro sighed. Rumors had spread throughout Ithe of pirates in eastern Asthega retrofitting airships to run off the residual energy present in ecto-orbs. Airships powered by these orbs were supposedly faster and more maneuverable than their traditional steam-driven counterparts. However, siphoning off an orb's energy destroyed the trapped ecto-impression. It was a slow death for the dead.

Lady Helena sniffed and produced an embroidered handkerchief to blot away the moisture gathering in her eyes. "I want the orb returned. I need to know my husband is at peace, Miss Vargas."

Ro felt a stab of sympathy. "Where can I find Dacat, my lady?"

"He's here in Ithe. I've learned he's to leave tomorrow but will pass through the market after the sun's zenith."

Ro stared into the depths of her honey water, weighing the risks of pilfering something as valuable as an ecto-orb in daylight and in full view of a crowded market.

Lady Helena drew a deep breath and squared her thin shoulders. "Naturally, I'll compensate you for your efforts and any losses you may incur. A mourning ship, the *Kresa*, is leaving for the Well at dawn the day after tomorrow."

"That doesn't leave me much time to prepare, my lady."

"I used nearly all the money left to me to have Everett's ecto-impression entombed until I could see him safely to the Well. But if you bring my husband's orb to me before the ship leaves, twenty coppers shall be your reward."

Ro fought to contain her excitement. Twenty coppers was more money than she could acquire in an entire season of picking pockets in the market. "Give me half now, and it's a deal."

"I don't have that much presently." Lady Helena tugged open her velvet purse and retrieved three shiny copper coins. "I can give you these as a retainer and the rest upon delivery of the orb."

Ro held out her hand and grinned as the coins clinked in her palm. "I'll see you at dawn the day after tomorrow."

As the sun reached its apex the following day, shadows shriveled to narrow strips near merchant stalls, and the tips of Ro's delicately pointed ears felt as though they were on fire. Despite her discomfort, she stifled a smile as she surveyed one of the market's main thoroughfares. Brightly colored banners and flags sprouted from the tops of the trade stalls lining the street. Merchants called to shoppers, hawked their wares and insulted the quality of their neighbors' offerings.

The annual airship festival was held in Ithe to commemorate Queen Octavia's coronation as the country's sovereign ruler – not that her reign warranted celebration, in Ro's mind. But the festival had two primary benefits for which Ro did find cause to rejoice: the increased number of people jamming the open-air marketplace and the purses they carried, heavy with coppers and the occasional gem. The thought of being surrounded by that much wealth made her fingers itch in anticipation.

She rubbed the raised scar on the palm of her hand. A slick ridge of flesh, the scar's twin puckered the skin along the back of her hand. The result of a broken dagger thrust through her hand as a child. She'd been caught stealing food, and the merchant used the dagger to pin her in place until the Peacemakers arrived.

Her skills for pilfering what she needed to survive had much improved.

Nearby, a goodwife with three young children in tow dropped half a dozen coppers into the gloved hand of a merchant as he, in turn, passed a heavily wrapped package to her. The goodwife returned the small cloth pouch to a pocket in her skirts. It would be so easy for Ro to follow the woman and bump into her when the crowd naturally slowed and congested. She'd lift the pouch and escape into that same crowd without the woman ever knowing.

But she forced herself to take a deep breath and exhale. Her instructions were clear and lifting a purse or two would only jeopardize the task before her. Additionally, she made it a point to never steal from children.

Then again, the goodwife's casual attitude and lackadaisical security would make the picking easy, and go far to alleviate the hunger pains in her belly. She'd used the coppers Lady Helena gave her to purchase supplies for the assignment. There hadn't been much left for food.

Her fingertip pressed into the hardened scar tissue. No, her reward waited at the *Kresa* and—

Warm breath tickled her ear as a body pressed close to her back. "I wouldn't do that if I were you."

Ro pulled back from the voice, reaching for the pepperbox revolver at her side.

A firm hand wrapped around her wrist as she spun to face her accuser. Light hazel eyes sparkled with deadly amusement. "Is that any way to treat an old friend?"

Ro eased her stance. "Mason Beck," she said, as the man who held her smiled. "I thought you were in prison."

His smile widened to a grin and he inched closer. "I decided an early release was in my best interest."

"Hmm, I suppose self-release is a subject with which you are quite intimate."

Mason chuckled. His hand slid from her wrist to her shoulder, making her shiver despite the day's repressive heat. "My sweet Rosalind." His roughened fingertips stroked the flesh exposed by her shirt's collar. His distinctive southern Asthegan drawl colored his words with visions of verdant forests and balmy nights. "That wit of yours will be the key to your undoing."

Ro retreated a few steps, anxious to slow her racing heart. "Perhaps, but you, sir, won't be the one doing the undoing."

Mason followed her until she bumped into the rough-hewn edge of a market stall. He placed one palm on the wall beside her head. Sun-lightened brown hair pooled on his shoulders in soft waves as he leaned forward. His breath made her already warmed cheek all the hotter when he whispered in her ear. "Are you certain of that?"

Ro swallowed the lump in her throat to reply a little too breathlessly, "Quite certain."

He examined her face. A languid smile tugged at his full lips. He swept a lock of her golden curls over her shoulder and a wicked gleam sparked in his eyes. "A pity, love."

"Why are you here?" she asked.

His smile remained firmly in place, but his expression grew guarded.

"You wouldn't risk coming to Ithe without good reason," she continued.

"Isn't your company reason enough?"

"For you, no." She'd known Mason since they were both adolescents living on the streets. Both outcasts, but Mason's charm and pleasing features had made him a favored inamorato for many high-born women while Ro had fought to simply stay out of the brothels. However, it was Mason's inclination toward theft and piracy that had landed him in prison. "Thinking of stealing another airship? Maybe even Queen Octavia's crown?"

"Nothing as lofty as that, my sweet. My goals are far more humble and . . . personal."

Curiosity gnawed at her. She leaned close and lowered her voice. "What are you after, Mason?"

"Would you believe there's a price on my head and I aim to have it removed?"

"The bounty or your head?"

He laughed and his gaze shifted to the street. He stepped back, took her hand in his and kissed the scar in the center of her palm before turning away. "Always a pleasure, Ro," he said over his shoulder. "I do enjoy our spirited conversations."

She watched him depart and took deep breaths, willing her heart to cease its mad pounding. Heat from his lips lingered on her scar and made her skin tingle. Until today, her last encounter with Mason had been when he'd stolen the airship from the Merchant's Guild. He'd wanted her to leave Ithe with him, but she'd refused, scared of the motives she'd sensed behind his request. Now she wondered what his reasons were for returning.

Mason was a thief, a liar and a scoundrel, but he wasn't stupid or insane. She replayed their conversation in her mind. Dawning realization spread over her like the annual rains swept over the mountains.

"*Spirited* conversations," she repeated his parting words.

Only one thing could draw him to the festival to risk a meeting with the Peacemakers while tagged with a bounty – and it wasn't her.

"The orb."

Anger replaced her worry. She and Mason were both thieves, but unlike him, she had principles where he had few. She was under contract to produce the orb and return it to its rightful owner. Mason would undoubtedly sell the orb to the highest bidder and use the resulting profit to pay off his bounty.

She balanced on the balls of her feet and scanned the crowd. Like a phantom, Mason had disappeared. Stars above, why had she let him simply walk away?

Silently berating herself, she drew in a deep breath, savoring the zesty sweetness of fruits, spices and roasting meat. Her stomach rumbled its dissatisfaction. She pushed aside thoughts of Mason and food and focused on the task at hand.

Lady Helena had said that Dacat, the man who stole her husband's ecto-orb, would pass through this section of the market on his way to the airship port. Ro checked the vertical sundial on the tower in the center of the market. She studied the tightly packed street. He had to be here. Somewhere.

A man wearing foreign robes and standing a head taller than most of the native Ithians jamming the streets drew her attention. His dusky skin and knotted hair garnered more than a few stares as he strode through the crowd. Based on the description she'd been given, the foreigner had to be Dacat.

Ro settled a pair of smoked-lens goggles over her eyes to protect them from the burning sun, and stepped out of the lean shadows. Mingling with the throng, she angled her path to intercept Dacat. She could no longer see him or much of anything beyond the torsos of the people around her. Her small height and slender frame made slipping through crowds and tight spaces to escape the Peacemakers easier, but it often worked against her when she tracked a specific target.

Trusting her instincts, she diverted her path around a small group arguing beside an overturned cart and its spilled cargo of apples. Without breaking her stride, she scooped up a couple of the shiny red fruits and pocketed them for later.

The crowd thinned and she spotted her mark still advancing in her direction.

Ro sucked in a breath and slowed her steps. Mason Beck and two obviously intoxicated revelers swayed up the street behind Dacat. Mason's sober eyes met hers. He winked then doubled over in peals of laughter at something one of the other men said.

Her moment's hesitation cost her. The crowd swelled, cutting off her view as Mason closed the distance between himself and her target.

Stars burn him. He was going to reach the orb before her.

She pushed her way through the crowd. Raised voices admonishing her for her rudeness trailed in her wake. She hurled half-hearted apologies over her shoulder and continued to forge ahead. She had to reach—

A foot hooked her ankle and sent her stumbling forward. Her momentum knocked both her and the person in front of her to the ground.

"Blazes, woman!" A deep voice rumbled as vicelike hands grabbed her arms. "Get off me!"

"I beg your pardon, sir," Ro countered, feeling heat rise in her cheeks. She tossed a mass of tangled pale curls from her face. "Truly, I don't know—"

Ro's apology died as Dacat's furious gaze bored up into her as he lay trapped beneath her.

Another pair of hands grabbed Ro and hauled her to her feet. Mason stepped between her and Dacat, offering his hand to the downed man. "Need a lift, mate?"

Ro could only watch as the stranger accepted Mason's hand and was dragged to his feet.

Mason swatted dust from the man's robes, sending small plumes of the fine red powder into the air. "There we are. No harm done."

"I'm sorry, sir," Ro said, trying to insinuate herself between Mason and Dacat. "I hope I haven't injured you in my carelessness." The crowd around them had stopped to watch the spectacle. Peacemakers would be coming to investigate soon. She had to grab the orb. Quickly. "Please, allow me to—"

"Hands off, love." Mason swatted her hands. "You've done quite enough, I think. Now shove off and ply your wiles elsewhere."

"Ply my wiles?" she spat between clenched teeth. "Just what kind of a woman do you take me for, sir?"

Mason paid her no heed. He turned to Dacat, blocking her access with his body. "'Tis a shame a gentleman such as yourself should fall prey to a wanton harlot's uncouth behavior."

Ro's mouth opened and closed like a gasping fish.

"You know this woman?" Dacat asked, nodding in her direction.

"Ah, Stars above, no," Mason said with a laugh. He glanced at Ro. "But I've seen her type before." He leaned closer to the other man. "No doubt a paid concubine."

Ro's voice returned. "Now see here—"

Mason grabbed her arm and spoke over her. "Your protestations fall on deaf ears, woman. Save it for the Peacemakers."

Her eyes widened when a low rumble sounded from the end of the street. The crowd in that direction parted as though something large moved through the market, heading toward them.

Mason saw it too, and bowed to Dacat. "I'm certain you have business to attend, good sir." He nudged Ro in the direction of the thinning crowd. "I'll see that she's dealt with properly."

"Let me go," Ro hissed. "The Peacemakers are coming, you idiot."

As if summoned, four men encased in heavy steel suits appeared among the crowd. Steam belched from their armored joints as they plodded toward Ro and Mason. An amplified voice issued from the lead Peacemaker. "You two! Halt in the name of Her Majesty!"

"Run!" Mason shoved Ro to the left side of the street.

She didn't argue. They pushed through the crowd, ducking under brightly colored banners and dodging would-be attempts by merchants to block their escape. The steady pounding of the earth behind them warned her that at least two Peacemakers were in pursuit. Once the armored suits gained their top speed, they would be nearly impossible to outrun. Their only hope was to go to ground until the Peacemakers abandoned their search.

Mason tugged on her sleeve. "This way," he ordered, correcting her course.

She trailed behind him and dashed into a merchant's deserted stall in time to see Mason's head disappearing over the back wall. Without slowing, Ro hopped onto a derelict crate, and leaped for the top of the wall. One hand caught the rough-hewn wood edge but the other slipped off, splinters gouging her palm. Her face slammed into the vertical surface before the rest of her body. Stars burst before her eyes but her grip on the wall held.

The salty-copper taste of blood trickled into her mouth. She cursed Mason and her own stupidity as she grabbed the top of the wall with her free hand. Using all of her strength and scrambling over with her feet, she managed to heave her body up and almost over.

But steel-encased fingers grabbed her leg before she could pull it up.

"C'mere," the amplified voice of the Peacemaker growled. He tugged on her ankle and nearly unseated her. "You're not getting away so easy."

Ro kicked and struggled to free herself. The Peacemaker could snap her bones as effortlessly as a zeppelin sliced the air. Once a Peacemaker had a grip, little could be done to loosen it.

He tugged again, almost toppling her. She pitched forward and wrapped an arm around a nearby flagpole to maintain her precarious perch. Using her free hand, she searched the pockets of her coat and pulled out one of the apples she'd pilfered earlier. She aimed it at the clear glass visor that was the Peacemaker's only view on the world.

The fruit hit and splattered the glass with a dark mass of pulp and seeds. The Peacemaker snarled and tried to wipe at the mess but didn't release her.

Her perch swayed with sudden added weight. Mason's face appeared inches from hers. He let out a piercing whistle that made Ro's ears ring, and lobbed a smoking clay sphere into the stall.

The Peacemaker shouted a curse, released Ro, and dived for the street.

Ro swung her body over the edge of the wall and dropped safely into the narrow alley along with Mason. The leg that the Peacemaker had crushed protested, and she groaned.

Mason grabbed her hand, pulling her roughly along behind him. "Don't you dare stop now."

His order summoned up a memory of their first meeting. She'd stolen a loaf of bread from a merchant's stall. As she ran from the market, she and Mason had collided, knocking the bread from her hands, but he'd caught it before it hit the ground. With the merchant screaming for the Peacemakers, and the husband of the woman Mason had recently bedded rounding a corner, Mason had grabbed Ro's hand and led her through the streets, commanding her not to stop, despite her pleas.

Now, she and Mason launched into a sprint down the alley. They'd evaded the Peacemakers for the moment, but they would double back soon and come after them again. "What did you—"

Mason shoved her against a building, covering her with his body as an explosion shredded the air. Bits of shattered pottery pelted the market alley. Wisps of black and red smoke curled around the building, carrying a stench unlike any Ro had experienced.

"By the Stars, what *was* that?" She gagged and pulled a hand-kerchief from her pocket to cover her nose and mouth.

"Stink mortar," Mason coughed. Keeping a grip on her hand, he retreated into a lane until it dead-ended. "Something I learned to make during my holiday in Dismia."

Ro wondered what else he'd learned while in prison, but didn't dare ask. As the stink from the market intensified, she wondered if the remaining seventeen coppers owed to her were worth suffering Mason's intrusion.

A small iron grate at the end of the street drained into a network of tunnels beneath the city. Mason grunted as he moved the grate aside. Ro sat on the edge of the opening, pushed her goggles to the top of her head, and dropped onto a small ladder.

Mason followed, and moments passed while he maneuvered the grate back into place. When it settled into its resting clamps, they both heaved sighs of relief. Even if the Peacemakers tracked them to the tunnels, they wouldn't be able to follow in their armor.

They slipped into the darkness and down the ladder, beyond the sun's reach. Pausing at the bottom, Ro rummaged through her pockets and produced a Y-shaped copper frame attached to a wooden handle. A glass tube, with thin copper mesh lacing its exterior, lay nestled between the tapered prongs. Two disks – one made of thick leather and the other of flat copper – capped the tube's ends. When Ro moved the tube and the copper disk touched the frame, a gas trapped in the glass sparked and radiated a soft bluish-white light.

"Impressive," Mason said, nodding to her glow-rod and adjusting goggles to cover his eyes. He twisted a small knob attached to the side of the goggles and two tubes similar to Ro's flickered to life. He smirked. "But not as impressive as mine."

Ignoring his comment, she ran her free hand over his waist-coat and shirt. "Where is it? I know you have it."

"Looking for something, love?" he asked, laughing.

"The orb. I know you have it."

"As a matter of fact, I have two." He grabbed her wrist and guided it to his crotch.

Ro yanked her hand. "You cad!"

He cocked his head, giving her the impression of a predatory insect studying its next meal. "Are you blushing?"

Warmth spread from her neck to her cheeks.

"By the Stars, you *are*." Mason grinned and stepped forward as she retreated. He raised his goggles to his forehead. "Could it be that my sweet Rosalind has never known the touch of a man?"

The heat in her face intensified and stoked her anger. She threw and landed a solid punch to his jaw.

He blocked her second blow and slammed her back against the tunnel wall. "How many times have I told you, love? *Never in the face.*"

"I'll be certain to aim for your precious orbs next time," she huffed. "Now release me."

"Your threat hardly gives me incentive to let you go. In fact, I feel inclined to teach you a proper lesson in etiquette."

"You wouldn't dare."

"Wouldn't I?" He smacked her bottom with his hand, forcing a yelp out of her.

She loosed a string of curses when his hand lingered. "Mason Beck, by the Stars, I swear I'm going to—"

The unexpectedness of his kiss startled her. She tried to break away, wanting to run. He pressed close, enveloping her petite frame with his taller form. Her protest melted with the heat of his advance.

Crudely formed bricks dug into her back as she returned his kiss. Fire raged beneath her skin, reducing her mind to cinders. She tugged at his coat and shirt, knowing only his touch could restore her sanity.

He shrugged out of his long coat without breaking contact. Something heavy within the inside pocket thumped and clinked against the tunnel floor.

Ro dropped the light in her hand and slipped her arms around his waist. Her fingers traced the muscular curves of his lower back. She hesitated for a moment and then slipped her hands down the tight contours of his buttocks.

A small growl rumbled in Mason's chest and he molded his body to hers; the evidence of his arousal intensified her own. His lips trailed from her mouth to her neck.

Chills prickled her flesh and made her gasp. The light from his goggles seemed to pulse an eerie green along the tunnel. Cold seeped slowly over Ro from the passage leading up to the street.

She glanced at the ladder. Her breath solidified in her lungs. She froze and her eyes widened.

Mason leaned back to look at her, his voice a husky whisper. "What's wrong?"

Ro couldn't speak but nodded toward the ladder.

He followed her gaze.

A man dressed in a faded brown suit and bowler hat seemed to float at the bottom of the ladder, his lower legs lost in a swirling mist of greenish-blue light. He studied his surroundings, confusion evident on his pale face.

"Where am I?" he asked in a hollow voice. "What is this place?"

"By the Stars," Mason breathed. "Are you seeing what I believe I'm seeing?"

"Yes," Ro answered.

He relinquished his hold on her and moved closer to the hovering specter.

Her knees quivered and she locked them in an effort to remain standing. A fresh wave of chilled air washed over her. She wanted to call Mason back, to wrap herself in his warmth again, but the sudden coolness seemed to break the fever that had taken hold of her senses. Realization of what she'd nearly done slammed into her and brought the sting of tears to her eyes.

"I'd heard it was possible," Mason muttered, examining the apparition. "But I've never actually seen an ecto-impression. It must have been triggered when the orb hit the ground."

Seemingly aware of Mason's inspection, the largely transparent man squared his shoulders and glared. "Young man, it is *most* impolite to stare."

Mason jerked away, his boots tangled in his discarded coat and he sat down heavily, shock and wonder filling his face.

Ro laughed, but she clamped a hand over her mouth as the phantom focused its dull eyes on her.

"Hello, my dear." Something in the lines of the man's face softened when he looked at her. "Would you mind telling where I am?"

She slid forward, unsure about moving closer. "You're in the tunnels beneath Ithe, sir."

"Ah," he exclaimed, reexamining the passages. "That would explain the chill."

"Do you remember who you are?"

"Of course, I do! What a silly question." He puffed out his chest and tipped his hat. "Lord Everett Duffy, at your service, Miss . . ."

"Vargas." She smiled in quiet triumph. "Rosalind Vargas."

"Enchanted, Miss Vargas," Lord Duffy said. He shifted his focus to Mason. "And you, sir?"

"No one with whom you need concern yourself," he grumbled, regaining his feet.

"There's no need to be rude," Duffy retorted.

"I beg your pardon, but Ro and I were—"

"Mason," Ro hissed his name in a warning. Heat bloomed across her cheeks. "That's enough."

He grumbled an oath and picked up his coat, shaking it free of clinging debris.

"My lord," Ro said, focusing on the phantom. "I was hired by your wife to—"

"My wife? Where is she? Is she well?"

"Yes, she's fine. She's waiting for you at the *Kresa*. I was hired—"

"The *Kresa*," Duffy interrupted, scratching his bearded chin. "But that's a mourning ship. Why would Helena be on board a mourning ship?"

"Poor bastard doesn't know he's dead," Mason muttered.

"Dead!" the specter exclaimed. "I most certainly am not, sir! Why I'm . . ." He levitated on a cloud of green and blue mist. "I'm . . ." He frowned and looked at the swirling vapor that comprised his lower legs. "Stars preserve us. I remember . . ."

Ro brushed past Mason. "What do you remember, my lord?"

"Dacat . . ." Duffy grabbed his chest as if in pain and shook his head. "It doesn't matter, my dear. Helena is my only concern. She must be worried if she hired both of you to find me."

Mason stepped in front of her. "Your lady is *very* worried, sir. Perhaps we should take you to her straight away."

Ro shoved him aside. "*We* aren't going anywhere, you rascal. Lady Helena didn't hire *you*. She hired *me*. And we can't leave yet. Not after you set off that stink mortar. The market will be filled with Peacemakers."

"Not up to the challenge, love?"

She sighed. "We'll have to find a safe place to stay the night, then go to Lady Helena in the morning."

"You want to stay here?" Mason scoffed. "In the tunnels?"

"It won't be the first time," she retorted, searching the ground near Duffy.

"What are you looking for, my dear?" the specter asked.

The dark glass orb reflected the light of the churning haze around him. Ro scooped up the fist-sized sphere and Duffy's apparition wavered. "I'm looking for this."

Mason snatched it from her hand. "That belongs to me, love."

"No, it doesn't." Ro reached for the orb. "It belongs to Lady Helena."

He juggled it between his hands, keeping her off balance. "I don't see her name on it."

Duffy shuddered. "Be careful with that!"

"Give it back, Mason, or I'll—"

"You'll what?" He dropped it into his pocket and grinned. "Run to the Peacemakers and tell them I filched something you were hired to pinch? Unlikely."

What would she do? What *could* she do? Fighting him for the orb wasn't an option. Mason stood more than a full head taller and outweighed her. She needed to distract him and take the orb without his knowledge.

Ro grabbed the lapels of his coat and kissed him.

His shock lasted seconds and then his arms wrapped around her waist, threatening to crush her.

Duffy cleared his throat and muttered, "Highly inappropriate behavior."

The fire that had previously consumed her mind flared to life. She fought to control it, to keep Mason distracted, but her desire eroded her focus.

By the Stars, she could still feel his excitement and it set her thoughts into a confusing jumble.

Lady Helena was counting on her . . .

Mason had never kissed her before despite his flirtations because . . .

Ro hooked a leg around Mason's and his hand slid from her waist, over her bottom and down her thigh. She slipped one hand to his neck and the other into his pocket.

. . . to return her husband's soul in exchange for . . .

. . . she was a Dreg, nothing could change that, not even . . .

The smooth surface of the ecto-orb cooled her fingertips.

. . . she was just a Dreg . . .

. . . to return the orb for . . .

She pulled the orb from Mason's pocket and transferred it to her own.

. . . seventeen coppers.

She broke the kiss, startled by her own overlapping thoughts.

Mason sucked in a quivering breath. "Do that again, love, and you may not leave these tunnels with your virtue intact."

"Give me the orb," she whispered, her own voice shaky with emotion.

He smiled and smoothed a lock of her curly hair behind her pointed ear. "Nice try but the answer is still no."

She lowered her leg and stepped back. Heat scalded her face. She hoped he would mistake her blush for anger, and not for the confusing mixture of excitement and sorrow she now felt.

Ro scooped up her fallen glow-rod. "If you're not going to return the orb, then I suggest we find a safe place to stay for the night."

Mason watched her for a moment as though he'd encountered an unexpected obstacle, and then settled his goggles over his eyes. He drew a breath and blew it out in an explosive puff. "We can always go to the Furnace Room."

Ro cringed. While she often used the tunnels beneath Ithe as a safe haven, she usually avoided the informal tavern and black market outpost that had sprung up in the cellar of one of the burned-out buildings.

"Sunset isn't for another few hours," Mason said, seeing her reluctance. "We're going to need food and drink eventually. We can find both there."

"You're right." She sighed, and gestured for him to lead the way.

Holding her glow-rod aloft to illuminate the tunnel, she picked her way through the debris piles left behind by the storm run-off. Her steps landed lightly on the tunnel's brick floor and made no noise as she passed from one passageway to the next, following a series of symbols carved into the walls that shone in the light.

A chill, sweeping along behind, alerted her that Lord Duffy's ecto-impression still trailed them. The spirit had fallen silent after her and Mason's overly affectionate display.

She wasn't proud of herself, but pilfering the orb, by any means possible, had been necessary.

Now the memory of his body pressed to hers quickened her pulse. Her thoughts drifted to her earlier encounter with him in the market, when he'd jokingly implied her company was the reason for his return. An unexpected rush of excitement made her skin tingle.

She would admit she found Mason attractive, but despite his often bawdy banter, she'd never seen him look at her the way he did other women. She'd never seen the same heat in his eyes or the piercing stare that stole other women's breath. She'd never had the sense that he saw her as anything other than a rival or the occasional criminal companion.

But what did she know of men? No honorable man in Ithe would touch her because of her bastard birth. How many times had she seen Mason diving out of a window when a woman's husband or lover returned home? It would be easier to count the Stars above . . . and yet he *did* come back and save her from the Peacemakers.

And the way he'd held her . . .

Ro gritted her teeth. By the Stars, she would *not* allow herself to develop actual feelings for him.

When they paused at an intersection, she couldn't prevent herself from opening her mouth. "You never did tell me the real reason you came back to Ithe."

His spine straightened and he looked sidelong at her.

"You weren't lying, were you? You *do* have a bounty on your head."

Light from her glow-rod highlighted his profile as he nodded. "How much?"

"It doesn't matter."

"It does to me."

He looked away.

"You're planning to use the ecto-orb as a bartering chip."

His eyes were hidden behind his lighted goggles, but she felt his gaze skip from her to Lord Duffy and back.

"You would so willingly trade another man's life for your own?"

Mason's face twisted in anger. "He's dead, Ro!" He jabbed a finger at Duffy. "He has no life. I do."

"He has a right to be at peace in the Well of Souls."

"And I have no right to freedom?"

"You can't barter another's soul for your own, Mason!"

He punched the wall, making Ro jump.

"There's no honor in such an act, and you know it," she whispered.

Mason braced his palms against the tunnel wall, his chin lowered. "You and your Stars-cursed principles," he growled. Sighing, he set off down an adjacent tunnel.

"Where are you going?" Ro called after him. "The Furnace Room is the other direction."

He didn't respond.

"Mason?" She watched as the brightness of his lighted goggles reflecting on the walls disappeared around a bend.

An eternity filled only by the sound of her anxious breath seemed to pass before Lord Duffy spoke. "He cares for you, Miss Vargas."

She glared at the ecto-impression. "Mason Beck cares for no one but Mason Beck." With a final quick look after Mason, she headed up the opposite passage. "He just proved that," she murmured.

Duffy floated along beside her. "His actions may seem selfish, but a man's heart is a complicated creature and is often at odds with his head."

"You'll forgive me, my lord, if I disagree."

"You only see one side of him, my dear, but my gaze penetrates much deeper." He fixed his dull eyes on her. "Like all men, your Mister Beck must resolve the incongruity between his heart and head. I wager when he returns it'll be with a much different outlook."

"Mason doesn't change his mind easily."

"Not even for you?"

"Especially not for me." Her own words echoed back to her, cutting more deeply than she'd believed possible.

Duffy seemed to ponder this for a moment. "He is your betrothed, no?"

She laughed, sharp and bitter.

"Forgive me, but I thought, with the—"

"I'm nothing to Mason aside from a rival thief."

"But you and he—"

"A game of one-upmanship, my lord. He and I want the same thing – your ecto-orb – and we're both willing to do what we have to do to get it." Ro shook her head. "Besides, Mason is human. I'm half Fae. Even if Mason were marriage-minded, it's forbidden for Dregs like me to marry, and I won't consider a common pair-bonding."

Duffy offered no further observations, and they continued on in silence, allowing Ro to reconcile her newest misery.

They passed through several more tunnel intersections before reaching a section that had been boarded over. Standing before the patchwork of planks, Ro knocked once, paused again, knocked once more, paused, and then rapidly three times.

An answering two knocks came from the other side of the barrier and a panel slid open. A pair of dark eyes peered at her through the opening for a moment before disappearing. The panel shut and, a few heartbeats later, a series of locks tumbled and clicked, and a hidden door swung open on silent hinges.

Ro stepped into a makeshift alcove. What had once been another tunnel had been sealed off after a minor collapse several years prior. Now the guard's bulk consumed most of the space, and the scent of stale bread and sour whiskey made her stomach churn. Glowing glass tubes, similar to the one she held, were suspended from wires strung along the ceiling of the entry and along an adjacent corridor.

The guard closed the door and slid a massive bolt into place. Hidden gears clanked, and the *thump* of locks turning echoed up the passage. The guard waved her through the entry, seemingly unaware of Lord Duffy's ecto-impression hovering behind her, and settled his sizeable bulk onto a steel-reinforced bench.

Ro entered a narrow earthen channel and soon reached a set of spiraling stone stairs. Climbing the steps, she emerged in what had been a spacious basement beneath a warehouse. When the building had burned and collapsed, the entrance to the basement from the street level had been blocked. The darker side of Ithe's population quickly seized the abandoned space, permanently cutting off access to the basement except through the underground network of tunnels, and established a thriving tavern and black market.

Conversations ended and heads turned in her direction. Anyone entering the tavern was bound to an oath of neutrality and non-violence so as not to attract the Peacemakers. However, this didn't prevent the Furnace Room's patrons from looking at her with suspicion or whispering insults under their rank breath.

She ordered a mug of honey water and some bread from the barkeep and handed over a few brass mites, remainders of the coppers Lady Helena had given her. Ignoring the glares directed at her, she sat at a small corner table opposite the doorway.

Lord Duffy's specter bobbed and dipped and finally settled in a chair beside her. "Do you always receive such a warm welcome here?"

Ro glanced at the occupied tables over her mug as she sipped the sweetened and spiced water. No one noticed Duffy's question or returned her gaze. "Not only here," she muttered. "It's all of Asthega."

"Because you're half Fae?"

She nodded as she chewed a bite of bread.

Duffy sat mute for several minutes while Ro finished the last of her meager meal. "Have you ever thought of leaving Ithe, even Asthega? Perhaps going somewhere that is more tolerant of your people?"

Ro sighed and raised her mug to hide her moving lips from the other patrons. "Ithians *are* my people, my lord. I've never met a Fae, nor do I wish to."

"Surely your life would be better somewhere else."

"My life is what I make it."

"Don't you tire of always being alone?"

"I don't need anyone's company or approval to be happy." She sipped her honey water.

"Not even Mister Beck's?"

Anguish pricked her and drew her anger. She didn't want to desire Mason. She certainly didn't want to miss him. Her gaze drifted to the empty doorway.

Stars burn it all. Ro cursed herself for allowing Duffy's questions – and Mason's departure – to unnerve her. She gulped the last of her honey water and stood. Striding for the exit, she didn't wait to see if Duffy was following, and part of her hoped he wasn't.

The scrape of shoe leather on stone pulled Ro from her sleep.

After leaving the Furnace Room, she and Duffy had navigated the tunnels and ended up at a section known as the

Narrows, which ran beneath Ithe's aristocratic neighbor-hoods. Here the tunnels constricted so that you were forced to travel in single file. The area also offered a host of niches and a variety of chambers that could be used by the high-born citizenry to escape the occasional sandstorm that assaulted the city.

Now, she forced her breathing to remain steady. She opened her eyes a crack to locate the source of the noise.

Flickering candlelight illuminated the entrance to the small chamber in which she'd taken shelter for the night. A dark shadow lingered behind the flame. A malevolent gaze raked over her huddled form, assessing and calculating.

Ro quietly slipped her hand to the curved wooden grip of her pepperbox revolver. She had been sleeping with her back to the wall, her knees drawn to her chest and her short coat draped over her like a blanket. Whoever blocked her only exit from the chamber was too short and bulky to be Mason. Lord Duffy's ecto-impression was nowhere to be seen.

The shadow stepped into the chamber.

She repressed the urge to pull her revolver. If she missed, she wouldn't have time to twist the multiple barrels by hand in order to fire a second shot before the stranger reached her.

Leather scuffed along the stone floor as the shadow slid forward. It stopped a few strides from her and eased into a crouch, setting down the candle stub it held.

She could see more details now: a bearded face, tattered clothing and piercing black eyes. A vagrant using the tunnels for shelter. Just like her.

He stayed in his crouch, studying her, and when he did spring forward, it was with more agility and speed than Ro anticipated. His hands were on her shoulders, pushing her to the floor before she could raise her revolver.

She landed an awkward punch on his jaw.

He grunted and pulled back, surprised.

Ro pulled her revolver. The drifter knocked her hand aside as she squeezed the trigger. The booming crack of the shot deafened her. Her attacker cried out and reared up. She kicked him in the stomach and scrambled to her feet.

A heavy weight crashed into her spine and carried her to the floor. Twisting, she landed on her back with her attacker on top of her. She lost her grip on the revolver, and it skipped over the stone and out of the chamber.

Rank breath washed over her and made her gag. "'Ere, now," the man's low voice rumbled in her ear. "Dark tunnels be no place f'sumpin so lov'ly 'nd sweet."

Ro screeched as he grabbed her hair and yanked, pulling her head back at a sharp angle. Dry and cracking lips pressed against hers, and she tasted the sour remnants of ancient whiskey. She bucked and kicked to free herself, landing ineffective blows against his larger frame.

The man cackled and pawed at her clothing. The bodice of her shirt ripped, exposing her flesh to the cool air. "'At's 'it – I likes it rough!"

Terror settled into Ro's core. She fought to reach the dagger hidden in the top of her boot. If she could only—

Light flooded the chamber and her attacker froze. The silhouette of another man appeared in the entrance. "Oi," a familiar voice drawled. The light and the silhouette bobbed as Mason Beck moved into the room. "In the mind to share, mate?"

The vagrant stared at Mason, blinking against the bright light, and then chuckled. "Sure, mate. Lots o' life in 'is one."

Ro shrieked again as he cupped her breast and squeezed.

The light shifted and Mason towered over them. His lighted goggles covered his eyes, and he pointed a long-barreled pistol at her attacker's head. "Aye," he snarled, "and I aim to keep it that way." The distinct *click-clack* as the pistol's hammer locked into firing position echoed along the tunnel. "Now let her go."

The drifter slowly backed away and rose to his knees, arms pointed skyward to show he had no weapons.

Mason stooped, keeping his eyes and pistol trained on the man, and helped Ro to her feet. He gently guided her faltering steps so she stood behind him.

The vagrant's voice took on a pleading tremor. "Please, sir, thought she be a harlot." His lips parted in a leering smile to reveal blackened and missing teeth. "No 'arm meant."

"No harm? I'll show you the meaning of no harm." Mason struck the man across the temple with the pistol.

The man crumpled, and Mason dropped to his knees, striking him again with both his fist and his pistol.

"Stop!" Ro grabbed Mason's arm and tugged. "Leave him – he isn't worth it!"

Mason jerked away and pushed to his feet. Breathing heavily, he spat on the unmoving man and holstered his revolver. He turned to Ro and pushed his goggles to his forehead so the light illuminated the chamber but didn't blind her.

Ro tried to cover herself with the tattered remains of her shirt. Her hands trembled like the ground beneath running Peacemakers. "I . . . I . . ." Words lodged behind her teeth and refused to move.

Mason took off his long coat and draped it around her shoulders. The hem brushed her ankles as he worked to close it. "Where's your jacket?"

"I'm not certain," Ro whispered, not looking at him. She threaded her arms into his coat's sleeves, seeking the warmth he'd left in the garment.

He looked around and the light moved with him, casting odd shadows on the walls. He stepped around the now groaning vagabond and picked up a mass of torn dark fabric. "I don't think you'll want to keep the coat, but if you have anything of value in the pockets, you'll want to retrieve it."

While Mason used a length of twine to tie the drifter's hands behind his back, Ro rummaged through the remnants of her ruined coat. She retrieved Lord Duffy's ecto-orb first. Green and blue light pulsed in its depths as she slipped it into her pocket. Goggles, her glow-rod and a pouch containing a set of brass lock-picking tools were the last items she retrieved.

She pulled her goggles over her head to hold her hopelessly tangled curls away from her face. Mason joined her as she tossed the tattered coat into a corner.

His hand brushed her cheek. Dark emotions swam in his eyes. "I shouldn't have left you."

Ro felt the sting of gathering tears and looked away.

His hand searched for hers, which was hidden within the folds of his coat. Finding it and holding it tightly, he led her out of the chamber. "Let's get you out of here."

They paused long enough for her to pick up her revolver, and then she allowed him to guide her through the Narrows and into the broader tunnels until they reached a ladder.

"I'll move the grate." He peeled off his lighted goggles and handed them to her. "Wait here until I give you the signal."

She nodded.

Mason hesitated for a moment before swinging onto the ladder. His rapid ascent soon took him out of the reach of her light.

Anxiety gnawed at Ro. Had Mason come looking for her because he discovered the orb was missing? Or had he come in search of her for other reasons? How had he found her? Where was Lord Duffy's ecto-impression? More questions rampaged through her mind, distracting her, so that she nearly dropped Mason's goggles when the grate scraped along its resting clamps above her.

"All clear," Mason called.

Ro held the strap of the goggles between her teeth and scaled the ladder. The length of Mason's borrowed coat made finding her footing on the rungs difficult, but she kept a steady pace. Soon she felt Mason's hands on her upper arms, helping her out of the hole.

Gas lamps lining the streets still flickered in the monotone greyness of the pre-morning hours. Dawn hadn't yet painted the buildings in shades of rose, violet and gold, deepening some of the vibrant colors that made Ithe the country's crowning jewel.

Ro glanced at the surroundings, trying to gain her bearings. Their escape from the tunnel had placed them in a small courtyard surrounded by squat single-story buildings. She waited with her back to a wall, which still retained the coolness of the night's air, while Mason replaced the grate. She handed his goggles over when he came to stand in front of her.

He switched off the lights and pocketed the goggles. "Did he—" He choked on the question. "Are you injured?"

She shook her head. The memory of the vagabond's hands pawing at her made her shiver. Tears slipped down her cheeks.

Mason pulled her into his arms, and she melted into his embrace. He held her while her shoulders shook with muted sobs.

Once her tears eased, she listened to the steady rhythm of his heart. Perhaps she was wrong when she told Lord Duffy she didn't need anyone to be happy.

Mason understood what it meant to be outcast. Perhaps he and she . . .

Her eyes slipped shut against the threat of more tears. No, she was a Dreg. Her existence on the fringes of Ithian society wasn't something she could share without guilt.

Not even with someone like Mason. He deserved better. He deserved to be free.

"Thank you," she finally mumbled against his chest. She craned her neck to see his face. "For coming to my rescue."

"I have a confession." He eased away from her. "I knew when you kissed me in the tunnels that you were stealing the orb."

She gasped. "Why didn't you stop me?"

A lopsided smile lifted one corner of his mouth. "To be completely honest, I was enjoying it."

Ro groaned.

"And I knew I could get it back. But then we argued, and like an idiot I left." He sighed and his smile vanished. "I was halfway out of the tunnels, on my way to sell the orb, before I remembered you had it."

"Mason—"

"I went to the Furnace Room, looking for you," he continued. "The guard told me you'd come and gone. I had no idea where you might be so I wandered the tunnels, thinking about why I'd been so stupid to let you take the orb. The only answer I could give myself was that I wanted your kiss more than I wanted the orb."

A knot cinched deep inside Ro's gut.

"Once I realized that, I thought of why I came back to Ithe."

"The bounty."

He shook his head. "I've had other prices on my head, and I've never tempted fate as I have this time."

Ro slumped against the courtyard wall, her head swimming and stomach churning. "Mason, don't do this. Please."

"When I admitted to myself that I'd come back to Ithe because of you and not the bounty, I stopped wandering the tunnels and started searching for you in earnest." His voice dropped in pitch. "That's when Duffy came to me and said you were in danger."

She stared at him, not certain she'd heard correctly.

"He told me you were in the Narrows," Mason whispered. "He told me about the bastard stalking you, and it—" He drew a deep breath before continuing in a rush, "It frightened me. The thought of someone hurting you because I'd abandoned you was more than I could bear."

Ro hung her head and wrapped her arms tight around herself. She didn't want to care for Mason. She didn't want him to want her. She didn't want to *need* him.

And yet when he gently cupped her chin and coaxed her to look at him, need was precisely what she felt.

"I won't leave you again," he murmured, dipping his head toward her. "My sweet Rosalind."

"Stop." She braced her hand against his chest. Guilt stabbed Ro's heart. "I can't do this, Mason. I'm sorry."

"I don't understand. I thought . . ."

"Take this." She pulled Lord Duffy's ecto-orb from her pocket. It pulsed with light, an indication of the impression's presence within. "Take it and go. Sell it."

"Ro—"

"Pay off your bounty." She dropped the orb into his hands. "And then leave Ithe."

He stared at the glass sphere. Green and blue mist swirled and churned in its depths. "You don't mean that."

"Yes, I do." She shoved him. "Be free. It's what you want."

"Not anymore."

Her heart shattered. "*I* don't want you here."

Mason looked from her to the orb to the eastern horizon. His jaw clenched. Anger and a steely determination shone in his eyes when he focused on her again. "No, I won't allow you to push me away, Ro. Not when you give me the means to keep you."

His hand seized the back of her head before she could respond. He kissed her hard until her legs threatened to buckle and her lungs screamed for air. Then he was gone, running toward the Queen's Market.

The shock of his absence slammed into her. She gulped in breaths of air. Shifting hues of violet, crimson and orange brightened the eastern sky as the sun began its slow climb out of darkness.

"Dawn," she whispered. "Lady Helena."

She hiked up the hem of Mason's long coat to her thighs and galloped after him. Her chances of stopping him before he reached the *Kresa* were slim. But she couldn't allow him to throw away his life just to be a part of hers.

Ro dashed through the streets, puffs of fine red dust rising with each strike of her boots. She rounded a corner and the brightly colored flags and banners of the Queen's Market rose before her.

Airships were tethered to moorings along the western wall on the other side of the market. The *Kresa* would be among them, boarding passengers and a cargo of ecto-orbs to deliver to the Well of Souls.

She caught the flash of a white shirt darting among the silent stalls. "Mason!"

A shadow detached from the deeper gloom. Metal glinted in the weak dawn light as the figure darted after Mason.

Fear spurred her fading strength. The market's colors blended into a rainbow of confusion as she ran. Her heart drummed in her chest. Her mind emptied of all thoughts but reaching Mason before he returned the orb.

Bursting from the market, Ro saw the outlines of airships bobbing and swaying over their moorings. The rising sun painted the white gas-filled balloons of the larger cargo dirigibles pink and yellow. Smaller brightly colored zeppelins remained dull ghosts of themselves in the shadow of the merchant vessels. But only one dirigible sported black canvases.

The *Kresa*.

Ro slowed as she neared. Crews were already readying their ships for the day. Men called out orders and used large steam-driven carts to move heavy pallets of cargo from the warehouses opposite the docks.

She scanned the gated entrance leading to the *Kresa*, searching for either Mason or Lady Helena. Neither was among the few crewmen assisting passengers into the lift that would take them up to the ship. "Stars burn it all," she mumbled and retraced her steps toward the market.

In the narrow space between two warehouses, a swirling green and blue mist formed beside her as she walked, taking the form of Lord Everett Duffy. "Miss Vargas," he said, once fully visible. "You must hurry. Helena is in danger, as is your Mr Beck."

"Where are they?"

A clang of metal against metal and a pained cry answered.

Ro reversed course, heading back toward the airships, with Duffy keeping pace. They exited the alley as a body crashed through the side entrance of one of the warehouses and landed in the dust in front of them. She recognized Mason's white shirt as he struggled to regain his feet.

A dusky-skinned man wearing foreign robes followed him out. He had a firm grip on Lady Helena's arm. The tip of a curved scimitar's blade pointed at her throat.

"Dacat," Ro sighed and ducked into the dark shadows beside the warehouse.

Duffy remained at her side, his dull eyes wide. "You must help Helena," he whispered.

Ro motioned for him to be quiet.

"Where is the orb?" Dacat demanded. "I know you stole it – you and that Fae-bastard woman."

"Sold it," Mason huffed, raising his cutlass.

Guilt sliced through Ro.

"You're lying. If you sold it, why were you running here to meet this woman?" Dacat pressed the scimitar point into Helena's flesh so she whimpered.

Mason grinned. "I have to catch an airship, mate. Even a Dreg expects certain matrimonial *accommodations* in exchange for her virtue." He gestured to Lady Helena. "And I've never seen this woman before."

Ro winced. Even though she knew her place, hearing the common Ithian insult from Mason's lips sliced her. She steeled herself against the hurt and shrugged out of his borrowed coat. It was too cumbersome. She would soon need to move quickly.

"I saw you the two of you speaking," Dacat snapped. "If you don't know her, why—"

Mason laughed. "I'm a thief, you ninny. Unless I want to steal an airship, passage aboard one isn't free. I see a high-born woman, unaccompanied on the docks, I see an easy mark."

While Dacat seemed to be weighing Mason's explanation, Ro eased forward on silent feet, keeping to the darker shadows, and slipped the dagger from her boot. If she could sneak up behind him without drawing his attention, perhaps she could—

Her foot kicked a discarded bit of metal hidden beneath the fine powder dust on the ground. The fragment skipped across the ground, bounced, and thumped against Dacat's boot heel.

The foreigner looked to the ground and then over his shoulder at Ro.

Stars abandon us.

"You!" Dacat shouted at her, and shoved Lady Helena to the ground. Mason lunged for him. The two men brawled their way out of the alley.

Ro rushed to Lady Helena's side. "Are you harmed?"

The old woman's face was a frozen mask of terror. Her entire body quivered. She made weak mewling noises when Ro laid a gentle hand on her shoulder.

"My lady?"

Lady Helena offered no response or recognition that Ro had spoken.

"She's in shock," Lord Duffy said as he appeared beside his stricken wife. He reached for her. His hand dissolved as it passed through her in a haze of blue and green mist only to reappear on the other side of her body. He looked at his arm in surprise. Sad grey eyes focused on his wife. "Dearest Helena . . ."

Ro's guilt crushed her. What had she been thinking? How *could* she have given the orb to Mason, told him to trade Duffy's life for his own? Duffy belonged with Lady Helena.

Alarm bells clanged in succession along the docks, summoning the Peacemakers and demanding Ro's attention. Airship crewmen scurried to secure gated entrances as Mason and Dacat continued to fight their way over the docks. Early morning light flashed off sword blades and they lunged and parried.

"Remain here, my lord," she said to Duffy, who nodded. "I have to help Mason."

As she hurried to join the melee, she saw Dacat block a sword thrust and punch Mason in the face. The thief staggered back and fell to one knee.

"Mason!"

Dacat whirled, his robes trailing like a banner behind him. He slashed at her.

She dropped to the ground and rolled. The foreigner's blade sliced the air recently occupied by her head. Regaining her feet, she thrust her dagger upward, aiming for his heart.

But he twisted and the blade pierced his side.

Dacat's fist slammed into her jaw and sent her sprawling. Pain radiated down her neck and her head felt as though it would explode.

Sunlight flashed off Dacat's sword as he loomed over her, preparing to deliver a final blow.

Then the tip of a cutlass pushed through Dacat's chest. He screamed. Mason's face appeared over the foreigner's shoulder, a thin line of blood seeping from the corner of his mouth. He wrapped his arm around Dacat's throat, and then kicked him between the shoulder blades, sending him sprawling forward. The cutlass slid out of the man's lifeless body, trailing blood.

As Dacat toppled into the dust, Mason turned back to Ro and swiped at the blood on his chin. "Never in the face," he spat.

Ro couldn't help smiling at the absurdity.

He returned her smile and jammed his cutlass into the ground. He offered her a hand. "Need a lift?"

She clapped her hand in his and groaned as he pulled her to her feet. "Stars burn it all, that hurt."

"Let's see it." He gently tilted her head to examine her jaw. "You'll bruise nicely but I don't think you'll suffer any permanent damage."

Her fingers stroked his already swelling cheek where Dacat had struck him. "Nor will you."

"Praise the Stars," he mumbled. His strong arms crushed her against him and his lips captured hers.

Despite the pain in her jaw, Ro returned his kiss. Sweat slicked his skin and soaked his shirt but she didn't care.

He was safe and whole.

Dacat was dead.

Duffy had been reunited with—

"Lady Helena," she gasped, breaking the kiss and pulling away from Mason.

"Wait." He held on to her hand and reached into his pocket. Lord Duffy's ecto-orb glittered blue and green in the morning sunlight. "Give her this." He dropped the orb into her hand.

She met his unwavering stare. "Are you certain?"

He nodded.

Ro balanced on the balls of her feet to kiss his cheek, and the guilt twisting inside her eased. "You're an honorable man, Mason Beck, whether you want to acknowledge it or not."

"Only because you leave me little choice." The emotion swirling in his eyes made her heart ache.

"Mason . . ."

He released his hold. "Go."

She backed away slowly, fixing him in her memory, and then ran to Lady Helena without looking back.

The woman still sat in the dust but now her face was buried in her hands and her shoulders shook.

"My lady?"

"Lost," she sobbed as the first low rumblings announced the approach of a Peacemaker squadron. "My dear Everett is lost."

Ro glanced at Lord Duffy hovering at his wife's side. "No, he isn't."

Lady Helena lowered her hands. She gasped. "Is that . . ."

Ro handed the ecto-orb to her.

"Everett, my love," she murmured and cradled the orb to her.

"Dearest Helena." Lord Duffy's whisper was barely audible as a squadron of Peacemakers in heavy steel suits fanned across the docks. "I am so sorry for leaving you."

"You didn't leave me. You were taken." Lady Helena focused on the specter at her side. "Twice."

Duffy dropped his gaze.

"My lady," Ro said, and continued when Lady Helena looked at her. "Forgive me, but . . . you can see him?"

She smiled. "Of course. It's the magic of the orb. Anyone who holds it may communicate with the ecto-impression contained within. But only the impression may choose to leave the orb and be at peace in the Well of Souls."

"And I've changed my mind," Duffy announced. "I don't want to travel to the Well."

"Everett, please . . ."

Duffy extended his hand as if to cradle his wife's cheek. "I wish to remain with you, Helena."

Captured tears glittered in Lady Helena's eyes. "And I wish for you to stay."

A lump formed in Ro's throat and she looked away.

Peacemakers strode toward them. More surrounded Dacat's body, and two loomed over the kneeling Mason. One held the thief's bloodied cutlass in its metal-encased hand. The other clamped heavy shackles around Mason's wrists and hauled him to his feet.

Fear sliced through Ro. She darted forward. "Mason!"

A Peacemaker caught her and kept her just out of reach.

"Let him go," she pleaded.

They ignored her, and the two Peacemakers tramped back toward the Queen's Market with Mason in irons between them.

"Where are you taking him?" she shouted.

"He'll be shipped to Dismia colony," one answered.

"No! Mason!"

He glanced over his shoulder, winked, and shouted, "Always a pleasure, love."

She continued to scream his name until she could no longer speak through her tears. The Peacemaker holding her released her once Mason and the others had disappeared. She fell to her knees in the dust, sobbing.

Dacat's body was taken away, and the Peacemakers left after speaking with Lady Helena and several of the airship crews.

Ro's tears finally dried, but still she remained slumped on the ground.

Lady Helena knelt beside her and draped Mason's long coat over her shoulders. "Thank you, Miss Vargas, for giving me back my husband."

Ro closed her eyes against the stab of loss she felt for Mason.

"I'm sorry about your companion. I wish I could do more." Lady Helena placed a pouch in Ro's hand. "Seventeen coppers, the remainder of your fee, as agreed."

Ro opened her eyes and stared at the small velvet purse she clutched.

Lady Helena rose in a swirl of silk skirts.

"I don't want this," Ro said hoarsely, her throat raw.

Lord Duffy appeared before her. "But you earned it, my dear."

"I don't *want* it," she repeated through tightly clamped teeth.

Lady Duffy frowned. "We agreed on the price."

"That was before I knew how much stealing your husband back would truly cost."

"I don't understand."

Feeling drained and hollow, Ro stumbled to her feet and dropped the pouch in the dust at Lady Duffy's feet. "Keep your coppers, my lady. I have no use for them."

Turning away, she pulled Mason's coat closed around her. She hugged herself in a futile effort to stave off the growing void within, wishing it were his arms that held her instead of her own. She headed for the market.

★   ★   ★

Shadows crept across the Queen's Market like hungry locusts, devouring the merchant's stalls and stealing their vibrant colors. The sun had dipped below the towering mountain ridges to the west of Ithe. Most of the city's residents had made their way home, but those who had nowhere to go still wandered the streets or huddled over tables in open-air taverns.

Ro stared into the depths of her honey water. A plate filled with a thick root-vegetable stew sat in the center of the table. The feast represented the final brass mites she'd had left from the three coppers Lady Helena had given her. It was meant to be a celebration, a way to alleviate the sorrow that weighed on her.

But it was a hollow gesture.

She'd refused Lady Helena's payment, which meant she would be forced to return to stealing after tonight.

Mason was arrested by the Peacemakers and awaiting transport back to Dismia Prison Colony.

Once again, Ro was outcast and alone.

A pair of merchants entered the tavern talking loudly, their laughter like gunshots in her ears. She glared at them. Their dark eyes swept over her as though she were as transparent as Duffy's ecto-impression had been.

Watching them over the rim of her mug, she noted how each carried several pouches – no doubt filled with the day's take – tucked into his belt. She set down her mug and rubbed the scar on the back of her hand. It would be easy to pass them and slip away with one of the pouches. She could be out of the tavern and into the tunnels before either noticed.

Warmth pressed against her back and a familiar accented voice drawled, "I wouldn't do that if I were you."

Ro froze. Her heart stammered and then galloped within her chest.

Mason Beck dropped into the chair next to her. An ugly blue and purple bruise marred the strong line of his jaw.

"You wouldn't do what, sir?" she asked softly, her voice quivering.

He leaned closer, gently tilting her head to view a matching bruise along her jaw. "Go for the pouches." His gaze flicked to the merchants and back to her. "Wait until they've had their drink and their heads are swimming."

"How did you know I was—"

"Your scar." He clasped her hand in his and traced the outline of the wound with his fingers. "You always massage it when you're thinking *improper* thoughts, love."

His touch made her breath catch.

"This morning I killed a man and was arrested by the Peacemakers. I was on my way back to Dismia Prison Colony." His fingers trailed from her hand to her elbow and back. "And yet, by sundown, I'm a free man sitting in a tavern." Hazel eyes pinned her. "Strange, don't you think?"

"Quite," Ro squeaked.

"Naturally, I was curious when the Peacemakers released me." Mason smiled and returned to caressing her hand. "Imagine my surprise when I saw Lady Helena and Lord Duffy waiting for me."

She sucked in a deep breath and attempted to withdraw her hand.

He tightened his grip but not enough to hurt. His smile faded. "Why did you do it, Ro?"

"I don't know what you're—"

"Lady Helena told me you refused to take the coppers. Why?"

Ro dropped her gaze to the table and shrugged. "I didn't want them."

"My sweet Rosalind," he sighed. "You and your Stars-cursed principles—"

"Are the reason you're a free man," she interjected, focusing on him.

It was his turn to look away.

Moments passed as they sat in silence, lost in their own thoughts.

"You're free to follow your heart now." Ro broke the silence. "Where will you go?"

He tucked a pale curl behind her pointed ear. "My heart lies in Ithe, love."

Heat blossomed in her cheeks and her heart raced.

He stood, kissed the scar on the palm of her hand, and then bent forward to whisper in her ear. "I abandoned my heart once in the tunnels and nearly lost it. I won't do it again."

"Your heart will be your undoing."

"It already has been."

She searched his eyes for traces of subterfuge and found none.

Mason kissed her cheek and smiled, releasing her hand. "You should've taken the coppers, love."

Ro rubbed the scar on her palm as he stretched out his hand for her to follow.

A smile touched her lips as she took his hand. He pulled her into his arms, and she couldn't help but wonder if seventeen coppers would be her own undoing.

Yours in Eternity

C. T. Adams

One

I dragged my wheeled suitcase up a brick path lined with fragrant pink roses. Inhaling deeply, I basked in the familiar scent and feeling of homecoming. I hadn't been to my mother's house in two years. When she'd gotten ill a neighbor's son asked if he could rent it furnished. We needed the money for her care, and I couldn't bear to sell the place. So, he'd rented. I'd thought maybe, eventually, he'd buy it. Instead he married a woman from up north and moved away. With my mother dead, it was time to clear the place out and sell, or move in and stay: to fish or cut bait as Tomas would have said. Ah Tomas, love of my life.

I turned the key in the lock. Even after such a short time empty the place smelled musty, and the houseplants were wilting from lack of water. With a sigh I brought the suitcase over the threshold and closed the door. I'd best water the plants first, before I forgot. Then I'd go upstairs and unpack before fixing myself some lunch.

It was impossible not to think about Tomas in this house. He'd picked me up at that front door for our first date. I'd gotten my first kiss on the balcony outside my bedroom.

My parents hadn't approved, of course. We were from the north, from money with a capital "M". Daddy had brought us down when he'd been promoted to regional vice-president.

Tomas's family was from "the wrong side of the tracks" as my mother put it. I couldn't have cared less.

I'd met Tomas Petitjean my first day at Lafayette Junior High. He'd been tall, gangly, with skin like caramel, liquid brown eyes and a ready smile that showed off deep dimples and naturally straight white teeth. My heart lurched in my chest the minute I set eyes on him, and I knew . . . this was the one. He'd ignored his big brother Hector (who was in the same class, having been kept back in grade school) and ambled over to sit next to me instead.

"I'm Tomas."

"Lola." I smiled back at him, and he took the empty seat beside me.

"Where you be from?" He said it in a soft Cajun accent that made me shiver.

"Chicago. We just moved here two weeks ago."

"Lucky for me."

Lucky for me, too. Because not only was he handsome and charming, he didn't think I was crazy.

From early childhood I've been able to see and talk to ghosts. My mother called them my "imaginary friends". But there was nothing imaginary about them. And while they tried to smile and pretend everything was normal, my parents were very much afraid I was insane.

Tomas never questioned it. He'd been raised to accept that magic was a part of life. Spirits of the dead not only existed, they looked in on and after the living.

To him I wasn't a freak. I was special. We became practically inseparable – and Hector hated me for it.

I shook my head. I didn't want to think about Hector Petitjean. It would just upset me. So I crossed the living room and turned on the stereo, tuning the radio to one of the local music stations.

With musical accompaniment I went from room to room, opening all the windows to let in some fresh air.

I wasn't really comfortable moving into my parents' former bedroom, so I went to my old room instead. Nothing had changed. Not having any use for a frilly girl's room my tenant had kept it shut tight. Dust coated everything. I'd have to clean. I was also going to have to go up in the attic and get fresh linens, or I'd be sneezing my head off.

The stairs to the attic were narrow and cramped. The attic itself was crammed full with boxes containing personal items, clothing and the various things I hadn't wanted the tenant to have access to. I knew I'd stored the linens in my mother's old hope chest, but the chest was buried under a pile of boxes.

I lifted the lid on the first dusty box. Sitting on top of the photo album was a small black velvet box. I opened it, sliding the gold band with its ivy pattern and tiny diamond chips onto my finger. My wedding ring. Inside it was engraved with three letters: YIE – yours in eternity. Tears stung my eyes as I looked down at my hand. *Oh Tomas. If only . . .*

"He didn't leave you, you know. Not by choice."

I turned at the sound of a woman's voice, and saw the sparkling blue glitter of energy that marked a ghost taking shape.

"Yes. He did. We argued and he left." And never came back, not even as a ghost. I didn't say that last out loud.

"He never came back because he couldn't."

Ghosts are people. Dead and incorporeal, but people. People lie. There was no reason for me to believe this spirit – other than the fact that I wanted to. I've found that just like live people, when a ghost tells you what you want to hear, they're looking for something from you.

"Why are you coming to me now? What do you want from me?"

"I was following the magic, looking for the woman wearing Tomas Petitjean's ring. If you are her, I need your help. By helping me you can help yourself . . . and Tomas."

Two

Taking a deep breath, I lifted my hand to knock on Mrs Petitjean's door. I felt quite uncomfortable coming here. For one thing the neighborhood wasn't great. My little sports car stuck out like a diamond on a dung heap. It made me sad to see how far the place had gone downhill since the last time I'd seen it. What had once been a tidy little white house with green shutters, tucked behind a wrought-iron fence, now looked forlorn. It badly needed to be repainted, and the yard was so overgrown I worried about snakes. A pair of men's muddy boots had been kicked off and left near the metal rocker on the porch. I sighed. Apparently Hector was still living with his mama.

Ah well, it was after one o'clock. I could only hope that Hector had hauled himself out of bed by now and gone off to do whatever it was he did to pass his days. Not work. Unlike his brother, Hector had never been able to hold a job for more than a week or two. He preferred to skirt the law and make his money "under the table" to avoid paying taxes and child support liens. Then again, the boots lying on the porch weren't a good sign.

Steeling myself, I brought my knuckles down on the rough wood door. Whether or not I wanted to see my brother-in-law, I needed to see Mama Petitjean. For one thing, she'd expect to see me if I was in town. She'd be hurt and offended if I didn't stop by. For another, Tomas had gotten his magic from her side of the family. She could tell me if what the ghost had said was possible. If she would.

The door opened, and I came face to face with Hector. He was unshaven and unbathed, his sleeveless undershirt stained and sticking to his chest. A battered cane supported his vast bulk. Were the tales I'd heard true then? Had he really had his kneecaps broken for failure to pay gambling debts?

"Watchu doin' here, Lola?" He didn't step aside or show any sign of letting me past him. In fact, his words were almost a hiss. Hector obviously hadn't missed me any more than I'd missed him.

Before I could answer, Mama Petitjean's voice called from the kitchen. Her accent was even thicker than I remembered it, and I found myself smiling in spite of everything. "Hector, who dat knockin' at da do'?"

I shouted a greeting before Hector could lie and say I was a salesman or something. "'Heya, Mama, it's me, Lola."

I heard her gasp and start bustling her way to the living room from the kitchen. "Lola! Dat really you?" She appeared in the doorway, drying her hands with a checkered dishcloth, her face alight with pleasure.

"It's really me."

"Step 'side, Hector, let dat girl in." She shook a finger in his direction. "An' you go an' get cleaned up. We got comp'ny."

Grumbling and giving me a dark look, he stepped aside. I

ignored him, stepping forward to claim the hug my mother-in-law was offering me. "Not company surely? I'm family."

She waited until Hector was down the hall and out of earshot before whispering to me. "Chere, if'n it'll get dat man clean . . ."

I laughed. I couldn't help it.

I looked around and smiled. The outside of the house might have deteriorated. Inside nothing had changed. A braided rug in shades of blue covered the wood floor. The same couch, worn but comfortable, sat facing an old television. Pictures of the Petitjean family from three generations back to the present were proudly arrayed atop the family piano, including more than a few of Tomas and me. Without even thinking about it, my hand stretched out to touch the frame of our wedding picture.

Mama Petitjean hadn't changed much either. She was still small and dark, with bright button eyes, her grey hair pulled up in a tight bun; still wore a faded housedress that was ironed and starched so crisp it might well stand up without her.

"It's good to see you, Chere. You come in da kitchen an' have you somtin'. Den you can tell Mama whats eatin' at you."

Three

It had been hard to find the words to explain to Mama Petitjean what the spirit had told me. I knew Tomas had told her of my talent. I didn't know whether she believed in it.

I needn't have worried. She listened attentively, her expression growing more and more concerned. "You tink dat ghost be lying?"

"I don't know, Mama. Maybe. But Tomas never came back to me. Never came and said goodbye."

She sat in silence for a long moment. "Chere, my boy loved you wit' all his heart."

"I know, Mama."

"He woulda come."

"I thought so too."

She rose from her chair and began rummaging around the kitchen. "You gotta do dis ting, you gonna do it right. I'll make the pound cake for da offerin'. You get the candles outa dat closet an' you put it wit your prayer to da lady."

The lady was Marie Laveau, voodoo priestess and possible saint, a powerful figure in the religious beliefs of the Petitjean clan.

The pound cake was still warm from the oven when I put it at the foot of the statue of St Expedite. I'm not a big believer in voodoo, but Mama Petitjean was, and I wasn't taking any chances. It wouldn't hurt a thing to leave the cake, or the candle and flowers with my request to Marie Laveau. If Mama Petitjean was wrong, no harm done. If she was right, these actions might just make the difference between success and failure. I wanted every advantage I could get.

It was full dark by the time I made it back to my mother's house to start the ceremony.

I used my mother's piano bench as an altar. Candles on each end were the only light in the room, casting flickering shadows on the wall. Fragrant incense hung heavy in the air, making me a little light-headed. I sat cross-legged in front of the altar, holding a small cloth doll filled with herbs. Pinned to it was a picture of Tomas taken at our wedding. Just looking at that smile, my heart caught in my chest.

I was afraid. Truly terrified. I might have lived with my talent my whole life, but this, this was something else entirely. I had no experience in this sort of thing. I'd never attempted magic before. I wasn't even sure I believed in magic. But if there was any chance, any chance at all that the ghost had told the truth – that Tomas's soul had been trapped by an evil sorcerer – then I had to at least try to free him.

Chanting the prayers as I'd been instructed, I grabbed the hatpin that was sitting on the altar and jabbed it into my finger, drawing blood. I set the doll on the altar and squeezed the injury until a drop of my blood fell onto the photograph.

It happened in an instant. In my mind I was wearing my wedding gown, running through a darkened maze, the only light coming from the candle in my hand. I called my husband's name, but there was no answer from him, only mocking male laughter that came from nowhere and everywhere.

"Tomas? Is that you?" I was sure it wasn't. I'd heard his laughter a million times and it had never sounded so smug, self-satisfied . . . evil.

"Go home, little girl. You have no business here."

I stopped, holding the light up so I could peer further into the blackness. "Where is my husband? What have you done with him?"

"Last chance, girlie. You're dabbling in things you don't understand."

"I'm not leaving without Tomas."

"Then you won't be leaving at all."

Four

The light rose slowly, and I found myself standing in front of a polished mahogany table. Behind it, in one of those burgundy leather chairs with brass studs you see in lawyers' offices, was a distinguished man of middle age. I recognized him immediately. His name was Jean LeClaire. A well-known figure in the city, he was alleged to have Mob connections. The prosecution's case had fallen apart when the key witnesses, his wife and her lover, had disappeared.

LeClaire's black suit and matching tie were no darker than his hair, his red shirt the exact shade of the ruby in his pinky ring. On the table in front of him were two crystal balls, both the size of my fist. Inside each was the flickering blue glitter of a trapped soul.

"So, little girl, you really think you want to challenge me, like your husband before you?" He leaned back in his chair looking most pleased with himself, a sly smile pulling at the corner of his sensuous lips.

"You will release Tomas. Now."

He raised his eyebrows, looking amused. But I stood my ground, glaring across the distance that separated us.

He shook his head with mock sorrow. "Oh no, girlie. He lost the challenge – fair and square." LeClaire's hazel eyes locked with mine, and his smile returned, wide enough to show sharp white teeth. "Of course, if you're absolutely determined to do this – we could play. If you'd care to gamble. If you win, Tomas and the boy who helped cuckold me go free."

"If I lose?" I was fairly sure I knew the answer, but I had to ask.

"You're mine." With a wave of his hand a chair appeared on my side of the table.

"Shall we play?"

My mouth was too dry to speak. So I simply nodded and took my seat.

"As the challenged, it is my right to choose the game. I believe I'm in the mood for blackjack, or twenty-one as you might call it."

I might as well have been mute. My voice was gone. My heart was pounding in terror. I kept twisting the ring on my finger, round and round, as I prayed silently.

"Bring us a deck," he called into the darkness. I heard a series of thumps followed by dragging footsteps.

I suppose I shouldn't have been surprised when Hector stepped into the light, but I was. At my gasp LeClaire chuckled. "I see you recognize my employee."

Hector was clean and clean-shaven, dressed in black jeans and a matching black T-shirt. Face drawn with pain, he made his way slowly forward, the cane in his hand shaking under the pressure of his massive weight. He leaned against the table for a long moment, gasping for air and wiping the sweat that had begun trickling from his brow.

After taking a moment to recover, he reached into the pocket of his jeans to withdraw a sealed deck of cards. He handed them first to my opponent. LeClaire examined them carefully, declared himself satisfied and returned them to Hector, who then passed them to me.

I checked the seal. It didn't appear to have been tampered with. Apparently I would have a fair chance. Not that it made me feel any better. But when my courage began to fail I looked at the crystal balls with their imprisoned souls, and thought of Tomas, trapped for eternity. It gave me the strength to continue.

Hector ripped the plastic from the deck. Setting aside the jokers, he began to shuffle the cards, his movements practiced and sure. He presented the deck to be cut, but I shook my head. Let it stand.

He began to deal.

To me, the queen of hearts. I blinked and stared at it for a long moment, for the face on the card was the smiling face of Marie Laveau.

To LeClaire, the king of spades.

My second card was the king of hearts, and he was portrayed by St Peter, or Papa Limba. In his hands were the keys to the kingdom of heaven. I gasped, feeling hope surge in my breast. I wasn't much for signs, but surely this was a good omen. And twenty, twenty would be hard for him to beat.

LeClaire was dealt the four of clubs.

I gestured that I would hold at twenty. Everything now depended on my opponent's next card. I held my breath. In the corner of my eye I saw a ghost begin to materialize, but I paid it no attention. My whole focus was on the card that Hector was placing on the table in front of my opponent: the nine of diamonds.

LeClaire leaped to his feet. Upending the table with one hand, with the other he drew a Derringer he'd had hidden. He aimed it at me. I tried to dive out of the way, knowing I would be too late.

Neither of us had counted on Hector. He swung his cane with all his might in a vicious arc aimed directly at LeClaire's head. LeClaire dodged the blow, but it cost him his aim. His first shot went wide, missing me completely. But Hector wasn't finished. Off balance from the swing, his movements painful and awkward, still he staggered forward, throwing his bulk into my attacker. LeClaire fired his second shot as the pair fell to the ground, and I saw Hector's body jerk, heard his grunt of pain. Still, he pinned the other man with his great weight, his huge hands closing inexorably around LeClaire's throat.

LeClaire fought, clawing and struggling, as his face turned red, then purple. But Hector held on and LeClaire stopped struggling, passing into unconsciousness.

I rushed forward to roll Hector over. Stripping off my shirt, I held it tight against the bleeding wound in his chest. "Oh God. Hector. Hang on. Don't die."

"Tomas?" Hector's eyes widened as he stared over my shoulder.

"I'm here, brother." I turned at the sound of that familiar voice. Tomas was here. Pale, and haggard, but he was here. He knelt down beside me, his hands joining mine to put pressure on his brother's terrible wound.

"I'm sorry. Please . . . say you forgive me." Hector was gasping raggedly for air, bloody froth coming from his lips.

Tomas leaned forward, setting his forehead against his brother's. "Of course I forgive you."

Hector turned to me. "Lola?"

"You saved my life, Hector."

"You wouldn't have been in danger if it weren't for me." His voice was weak, thready. I could tell his strength was fading fast, the makeshift bandage had soaked through, both my hands and Tomas's were red with his brother's blood. Hector's eyes closed. I could barely hear him whisper, "It was my fault."

"I forgive you."

He drew one or two more shuddering breaths and then he was gone. His body and LeClaire's both shimmered for a moment and disappeared. The ghost and her lover, too, were gone.

Tomas and I knelt alone on the floor of a place that both was, and wasn't. I knew it was not real, but it felt real. His hand was so warm holding mine. I stared into the endless depths of his dark eyes for the first time in so long and there were no words in the English language that would be enough to express what I was feeling.

Tomas smiled, but it was a sad smile. He reached up, brushing a stray hair from my forehead. "I love you, Chere. But you have to go. Your body, it's wearin' thin."

"I don't want to leave. You just got here!"

"I know, Chere, but you gotta go. Someone needs to take care of mama now that Hector's gone."

"But . . ." I started to protest, but he set a single warm finger against my lips.

"It's not your time. Not yet." He moved his finger away. Leaning forward, he gave me a tender, lingering kiss. "You go on back. I'll wait. And when it's your time . . ."

"We'll be together." I wanted him to promise.

He nodded, smiled and said, "In eternity. I promise."

The Lovers

Julia London

York, 1898

Agnes Whitstone admired herself from all angles in the mirror. She was wearing a gown her father had commissioned for her to wear to the York Spring Cotillion Ball, and she'd never seen a more beautiful garment. It was gold, with dark-green trim. The décolletage was enticingly low, which had alarmed her mother, but thrilled Agnes.

Her father was determined that his daughters would be the most fashionably turned out at the Cotillion Ball. It was his belief that in addition to a young lady's usual accomplishments and impeccable manners, if she looked to come from means, her prospects for marriage were that much improved.

But Agnes had already accepted an offer of marriage. And this was the gown that she would wear to her wedding. Which would occur sometime tomorrow. And for the next eight hours, she had only to pretend that all was quite ordinary.

But she was busting with excitement.

John Parker, her beloved, had said she must not confess to *anyone* what they intended to do. John said that if she told as much as one sister, her father would hear of it and find a way to keep them from their hearts' desires. "Be patient, my love," he'd said that afternoon, when they'd met secretly in the potter's shed behind the apple orchard, "do as I ask and we shall be man and wife by this time tomorrow."

At seventeen, it was very difficult for Agnes to be patient. She and John Parker had been in love for what seemed ages. They'd been introduced to one another after church services one day. She'd felt an instant attraction sweep her up and wrap its arms tightly around her. John had sent her a letter very soon afterward in which he'd proclaimed his esteem as well, and now, they stood on the cusp of lifelong conjugal happiness.

"I can scarcely look at my sisters, for I fear I will burst with the news!" Agnes had moaned when John had warned her to keep their secret.

"Not a word, Agnes," John had said, and he'd kissed her silent, his mouth on her bosom, his hand beneath her skirts, roaming to spots that had never been touched by another person, places that made her swell and stir and yearn desperately for more.

"Make love to me," she whispered into his neck.

"Hush," he said, his voice drifting over her like a silken drape as he pressed the palm of his hand against her breast. "I can scarcely contain my desire as it is without such enticements from you." He kissed her lips.

"We are leaving today. Why must we wait?" Agnes complained, and caught a breath in her throat as his hand drifted up her ankle, to the inside of her thigh.

"We have survived this long." He kissed her cheek. "The anticipation will make our coupling that much sweeter."

Agnes shivered and closed her eyes, lifting her face to him. His lips singed her, made her roast with desire. She had heard tales of the marriage bed, of the duty of a woman to her husband, as if it were something to be feared. But if it were anything like this, she thought, as John's hand cupped her breast, she would as soon live in her marriage bed as in the world. There was no feeling quite like it, nothing that made her heart fill to bursting as her love for him made her feel – dizzy, weightless. Adored.

"Agnes," he whispered against the hollow of her throat, then down further still, to the mound of her breast.

Agnes let her head fall back, relishing the thrill of his hands and mouth on her body. He freed her breast, then took it into his mouth.

Agnes gasped wildly and pressed against him as he drove her to madness. She was wet with desire, aroused like a sleeping dragon. Her hands flitted across his temples, his shoulders, his neck. She thrust her fingers in his hair, squeezed her legs around him and fought the abandon inside her.

John responded with desire as hard and heavy as hers. He ravaged her, teething the rigid nipple while his hand danced around to the apex of her legs, then slid into the damp folds. Agnes thought she might expire from pleasure when John, dear John, suddenly stopped.

"God help me, but I cannot resist you," he said roughly. He rose up, caressed her hair, and looked into her eyes before kissing her once more. "But resist you I must, for a few hours more. Then you will be my wife, Agnes, and I will have you as a husband ought to have his wife." With that, he sat up, pulling her up with him. "Go," he said. "Go and ready for tonight."

Agnes reluctantly did as he asked. Her body was still burning, her heart still throbbing. She saw such desire in his eyes that she could not suppress a shiver. But he smiled and smoothed her hair. "I love you, lass," he said. "I love you more than I can possibly express."

Agnes smiled and leaned up to kiss him. "I love you, John. You are my heart."

They had left the shed, walking into air that was warm and moist. They did not notice that the winds had picked up and the smell of rain was in the air. As they walked, John gripped Agnes's hand and made her review their plans again. At the stroke of midnight, when Agnes could be certain everyone was abed, she would meet John at the potter's shed. He had a horse, which they would ride to York. From York, they would board a train to Scotland and Gretna Green, where they would marry at once. They had agreed that no matter the weather, they would make their escape.

She had only to wait a few hours more.

With a sigh, Agnes removed her gown and returned to her simple green day gown. She folded the gown she would wear to her wedding very carefully.

When John had asked for her hand, she'd wanted to go to her father straightaway, but John had cautioned her against it. He'd suspected her father would not approve, and he'd been right.

"John Parker?" her father had boomed when Agnes, egged on by her sister Aurora, had announced one evening that she esteemed him. "You will take your esteem elsewhere, Agnes Whitstone. John Parker is not of a station to marry my daughter."

"Whatever do you mean?" Agnes had cried, deeply offended that anyone would find John less than perfect.

"He is the son of a carpenter. *You* are the daughter of a man who owns the county's largest mercantile," her father had boomed. "These are two occupations that do not suit in business, in pleasure, and certainly not in marriage." He'd lifted his newspaper to thwart any argument. "You will set your sights on someone of a proper caliber, or I shall do it for you."

Her father's opinion of John had not improved with time, and Agnes had become increasingly agitated. It was John's suggestion that they elope. Oh, but Agnes longed to tell her sister Esme, who was closest to her in age and demeanor. But it would have been no use – Esme could scarcely think of anything else than the spring ball.

Agnes wrapped her wedding gown and a pair of embroidered slippers in a cloth, bundled it, and slipped it under her bed. When she was satisfied it was well hidden, she glanced out of the window at the early spring day. The weather was cool and blustery, but otherwise a perfect day to elope.

She did not notice the gathering of clouds to the west.

Her bundle ready, Agnes sat down to her last task as an unmarried woman. She wrote a letter to her parents, which she intended to leave on her bed.

Dearest Mother and Father,

Please do not be cross when you find this letter and understand what I have done. I do not mean to cause you pain, but I love John Parker with all my heart and cannot bear to be without him. We are quite determined we shall not be kept apart. Do not come for me, for by the time you read this, we will have crossed into Scotland and will have pledged our lifelong devotion to one another. We intend to reside in York, where John has arranged the let of a small house on Queen Street. Esme will want my chamber, and I am pleased that she should have it.

Your devoted daughter, Agnes.

The rain began just after eight that evening. The family was gathered in the drawing room, where Father liked to read from the Scriptures. Agnes's eyes were trained on the mullioned windows, watching the rivulets of rain on the panes of glass. A gust of wind rattled one window that was not entirely closed; Mrs Whitstone hurried to latch it shut. "Good heavens, it will be quite a storm," she said, shivering.

As her father droned on from the Gospel of Mark, Agnes fretted. She reasoned that the storm would surely pass by midnight. But the storm did not pass. The deluge continued with great sheets of rain, long after the family had retired. Agnes prepared nonetheless; she retrieved the letter she'd written to her family and gathered her bundle. She dressed in a sturdy traveling gown and cloak, and boots. When the clock struck midnight, Agnes looked out of the window and winced. It was still raining, and the wind was blowing quite strongly. But it seemed that the lightning had moved to the east. Agnes blew out her candle, picked up her bundle and opened the door.

She made her way carefully along the darkened corridor. As she reached the top of the stairs, she saw something below that looked like the flicker of a candle. Agnes froze. She peered into the dark, straining to see.

There it was again – someone was moving about downstairs, carrying a single candle. Agnes jumped back, her heart racing. Who was it, her mother? God help her, but she'd heard her mother complain there were nights she could not sleep. Agnes hurried back to her room and shut the door. She stood with her back to the door in that darkened room, desperate to know what to do, imagining John at the potter's shed, waiting for her.

Agnes whirled around and pressed her ear to the door, but it was impossible to hear anything with the storm raging outside. She looked at the window; a thought occurred to her, and she rushed to the window and opened it. Rain lashed her face and cloak; Agnes reared back and quickly pulled her hood over her blonde hair, then leaned out again.

The drop to the ground was quite a long way, but she tossed her bundle out all the same. Directly next to her window was a tree with an overhanging limb. There was a time she had excelled at tree climbing, and had managed this limb more than once. It scraped against the house, and she could stand on the window ledge and catch it, then swing down to a spot on the tree where she could stand. She'd done it dozens of times.

Agnes looked down. There was her bundle on the ground

below her, getting soaked by the rain. Her beautiful gown – it would be ruined! She pushed the window up higher and maneuvered one leg out. Then the other. Using the edge of the window recess, she managed to inch her way up to her feet.

The rain seemed to fall harder, and the branch danced before Agnes. She drew a breath, thought of John, and jumped. But the wind gusted at the moment she jumped, pushing the branch just out of her reach.

Agnes's last conscious thought as the ground rushed up to greet her was that John would think she hadn't come.

In the years that followed, people would say it was the worst storm they'd seen in a generation. Agnes was not found until the following afternoon. Agnes's mother thought she'd done her daughter a kindness by allowing her to sleep while the wretched rain fell, but by mid-morning, there were too many chores to do to allow the girl to sleep the day away. When Agnes's mother found the note, and saw the open window, she screamed for her husband. She did not look out the window; she assumed Agnes was well on her way to Scotland.

The groundskeeper found Agnes's body while friends searched for the young lovers. She was a bit waterlogged, and her neck was bent at an odd angle. Her hair had come undone and was strewn across her blue face like gold seaweed.

John Parker was found in the apple orchard near an old potter's shed the following day. He'd died by his own hand, his fingers still curled around the gun. He'd left a note, full of the anguish of guilt and loss of his beloved.

There were those in the villages around Whitstone House who privately hoped the young lovers would be united in the hereafter.

Matthew and Hillary Sparks rocked down a pitted road in a rented car so small that one might have sworn it had previously housed two servings of peas. They came to a dead stop where the road met a circular drive and both leaned forward, peering through the bug-splattered front window of the car.

"That's it?" Hillary asked.

"I guess so," Matthew said. He turned off the car and climbed out.

Hillary reluctantly did the same. She was not exactly thrilled with this latest development in their lives. When Matthew's mother had died last year, he'd discovered that he and his two siblings had inherited an old house in England. *England*! It was the first the three of them had heard of any house in England that any of them could recall, and they were shocked to discover that their mother had inherited it from a distant relative fifteen years prior. She'd never mentioned it, but then again, his mother had been suffering from a form of dementia. Perhaps she never understood she'd been willed a whole house.

Matthew was astounded and especially curious about the place. Of all of the siblings, he could afford to be – he'd been laid off from work when the recession hit. In some ways, Hillary believed this house had become a substitute for a job.

One day, when Hillary came home from work, Matthew told her they were going to England. "Neither Craig nor Elaine can go right now," he'd explained, referring to his siblings. "So we need to."

"I can't go," Hillary had said quickly, shocked that he would think that she could. She had a thriving real estate business in the Hudson Valley, specializing in high-end properties. How could she go to England? Had he forgotten that she was the sole source of their income?

But he'd said, somewhat dismissively, "You can go. I talked to your mom and she said she'd be happy to have the twins for a couple of weeks this summer."

"You talked to my mother before you talked to *me*?" Hillary's blood pressure had begun to rise, but that was par for the course these last few months. Their marriage was on shaky ground, and, apparently, he'd decided they would take their troubled marriage and go to England, right in the middle of the house-buying season in the States, to see some old house that his mother hadn't even mentioned. Hillary could picture it: a dump, some crumbling little cottage where cows walked in and out, feasting on the thatched roof. It would be more work than it was worth. And for that, she was supposed to take time away from the job that kept a roof over their heads.

Matthew no longer spoke to her – he informed her of decisions he had no right to decide, like some king on a throne.

It had been like this between them since Matthew had lost his corporate job at a national mortgage company. The housing industry had turned belly up like some diseased whale, and it was a miracle that Hillary had managed to hang on to her business. But then again, she'd spent ten years cultivating her clients, and she was dealing in properties that were recession-proof.

But Matthew seemed to grow more distant the more apparent it became that she could provide them with a good living and he couldn't find a job.

At the beginning, he'd believed he'd find another job very quickly. "I've got some major experience," he'd said confidently when the pink slip had come. "I'm not worried. I don't want you to worry, either."

She didn't worry. In the first couple of months, Matthew had papered banks and mortgage companies and financial institutions with his stellar résumé. He had been upbeat when he'd called his contacts. Several people promised him he had a leg up.

But the weeks dragged by and nothing came of it.

"The economy sucks right now, bro," his friend, a banker at a national bank, told him. "No one's hiring. You might have to ride it out."

Hillary knew that men tended to be defined by their jobs and their incomes, and without them, they could feel emasculated. Matthew was not the sort of guy who could ride things out. He needed to be doing, to be moving and shaking, and it had become clear that when he wasn't doing those things, he didn't quite know what to do. Six months after the pink slip came, Matthew was starting each day in his pajamas, in front of ESPN Sportscenter. He snapped when Hillary asked him what his plans were. He grew impatient with their six-year-old twins, Mickey and Mallory. Hillary and Matthew's sex life took a long vacation.

Hillary tried to talk to him about it. "I feel like we aren't . . . connecting," she'd said one day when he'd met her for lunch. They weren't connecting emotionally, sexually, or even casually.

But the moment she'd said it out loud, Matthew had looked down at his plate and sighed. "Hillary, come on," he'd said. "I'm going through a hard time. Can you just . . . let it go for now?"

She had let it go, not because he asked but because she honestly didn't know how to proceed with him. Was she supposed to be the patient wife and wait it out? Was she supposed to prod him along? And really, how long was she supposed to wait for her husband to come back to her?

These were the questions swirling about her head when his mother's estate had been probated and the mysterious house in England had been discovered.

Hillary hadn't paid much attention to all of the chatter between the siblings about the England house. She had enough on her plate trying to be a top-producing realtor, a mom, and wife to a man who was clearly mired in a major depression. She was too busy cooking dinner after working all day, then picking up around the house after a day of Matthew. She remembered looking at him as he'd talked about that damn house, wondering if they were ever going to make love again, or if she was going to be stuck in one of those loveless, sexless marriages. She missed Matthew. She missed the guy she'd met twelve years ago who'd made her laugh and sent her roses for no reason. The guy who never started a day without a smile, who could not keep his hands off her.

And then he'd announce they were going to England, and he'd already arranged it, and they had a huge argument in which they'd both hurled words that were probably better left unsaid. At the end of it, Hillary had pleaded with him. "I can't go on like this," she'd said. "Our marriage is falling apart."

"Just do this one thing for me, Hillary," he'd said. "Just this. Please."

Hillary had caved. And now, here she was in England, gazing up at the house that was so important to Matthew. It was bigger than most of the houses they'd passed on the way up from London, but it looked old and dilapidated. Matthew had told her it was manor house – it looked more to Hillary like an over-grown cottage. Even with her professional realtor's eye, she couldn't see much potential.

The west end of the house was covered with thick, leafy green ivy, but where stone was exposed, it looked dirty and crumbling. It was a two-story structure, with two rows of eight windows across the top and bottom, several of them broken. There were four chimneys, a weathered double door and small round stoop.

"Wow," Matthew said. He was grinning. "This is *great*."

"It looks kind of run-down to me," Hillary said skeptically.

"Are you kidding? It will look like a palace once we get it cleaned up."

For this house to in any way resemble a palace would take much longer than the two weeks they planned to be in England, which she wanted to point out to Matthew, but he was already on the stoop, trying to fit the key into the door.

Hillary followed him inside.

"This is spectacular," Matthew said.

To Hillary, the house did not improve on the inside. There were no furnishings save a table in the foyer and a single chair beside it. On the table was a cardboard box full of candles, which Hillary did not see as a fortuitous sign. She understood that the house had been without an inhabitant for several years and had been looked after by an occasional caretaker, but the dirt and grime and general ramshackle appearance was overwhelming.

"Look at this woodwork," Matthew was saying, his fingers running along the molding around the door frame. "And these windows. Do you know how much windows like this cost these days?"

"No clue," Hillary said, looking up. There was a lighting fixture hanging from the ceiling, in the center of a papier-mâché medallion. The walls were covered in dark wallpaper, the floors a dull, pitted wood.

"Come on," Matthew said, and disappeared into a dark corridor.

They walked through the ground floor. There was a large room with an enormous fireplace, which Matthew said was likely the drawing room. Next to it, a dining room, which he guessed from the wainscoting. Hillary had no idea when he'd become an expert on old English manor houses, but he seemed to know a lot about them.

There was another room with a smaller stone fireplace that he guessed would have served as a sitting room. "Where the ladies practiced their piano and needlework."

"Who are you?" Hillary asked, and Matthew laughed. He looked happier than she'd seen him in some time.

The kitchen looked positively medieval, with a wooden table in the middle of a stone floor, an old industrial sink and a gas stove that she doubted would actually fire. There was also an old-fashioned icebox, complete with an ancient refrigeration unit on top. "Oh my God," Hillary groaned.

"Hey; if it works, who cares what it looks like?" Matthew asked. "Hillary, please try to enjoy this. We're in England, stomping around an old house. Can you try? It's important to me."

"Why?" Hillary asked. "Why is this so important?"

He pushed his fingers through his dark hair. "I don't know. It just is. I've felt drawn to this house since I saw the words printed on the probate papers." He didn't say more than that, but turned his back on her, as was his practice these days, and walked down the corridor ahead of her, his shoes clapping loudly on the wood floors and kicking up dust, which made her sneeze.

"Look at this staircase," he said, pausing at the bottom. It curved up to the landing. The steps were covered in what Hillary guessed was red carpet underneath all the grime.

The upstairs was a series of bedrooms, two smaller rooms that had been turned into baths, and a large family area. There was something about the emptiness of the house, about the dusty drapes and floors, that felt strange to Hillary. Something just not quite right, although Hillary had no clue what it was. She wandered over to look out of the window. The grounds were, predictably, overgrown. There was a faded barn and a clothes-line that stretched across the garden. She could see a small pile of trash, as if someone had quickly tidied up the grounds before they'd arrived.

There it was, that feeling again, a sense that the energy in this house was a little off.

After an hour of looking around, Hillary was tired and hungry and still suffering from jet lag. "Shouldn't we go find a hotel?" she asked, checking her watch. "I am dying for a hot bath, and I really need to make a few calls."

"A hotel?" Matthew said. "We're staying here."

Hillary looked up. She looked around the empty landing. "Are you kidding?"

"No."

"*Here*?" she cried. "There is no *here*! This house has been closed up for years – we can't stay here, Matthew. That's insane."

"We'll open some windows and air it out," he said quickly. "We've got time to clean a room tonight."

"And what, sleep on the floor?" she exclaimed. Not only was he suggesting they stay there, he wanted her to *clean*? "Not to mention there is no food or cleaning supplies."

"All easily resolved," he said. "We'll go into the village to the pub and have dinner, stop in at the market and stock up for a couple of days. We can get some bedding and some sleeping bags and camp out."

"Be reasonable," Hillary pleaded. "We can come back first thing in the morning – we don't even know if there is water or electricity."

"There is water," he said. "I checked. And the toilets work," he added quickly before she could mention it. "And there should be electricity. I spoke to the estate agent about it last week."

She groaned. "And if there is no electricity?"

"Then there is a basket of candles in the front hall."

"Oh Jesus."

"Hillary." He tried to smile. "Where's your sense of adventure?"

"This isn't adventure; this is you trying to make me miserable."

Matthew sighed. He shrugged. "I really don't have to try this hard, do I? I mean, you're miserable all the time."

"What do you expect?" Hillary demanded. "You don't consult me about anything, you just announce your decisions." God, she did not want to do this now. She just wanted to take a hot bath. She just wanted things to go back to the way they'd been before Matthew was laid off. Back when they'd loved each other's company, when he didn't cling to some rustic, run-down old English house like it was his lifeline. But he had seemed so excited, and she hadn't seen him excited in a long time, and really, where *was* her sense of adventure? "Matthew, I—"

"Look, I am staying here," he said curtly. "You can get a hotel if you want."

Just like that, he pushed her into a corner again. "Fine," she said irritably. "Far be it from me to interfere with whatever this is," she said, gesturing to him and the empty space around him.

He looked annoyed. "I'm going to get the luggage."

Hillary watched him troop down the stairs. When she heard him go out, she looked around the landing once more. Why did she feel so uneasy? As if she were invading someone's space. She didn't like the feeling at all, and hurried downstairs to help Matthew.

They made a trip into the village of Tadcaster, picked up some supplies, a few groceries that they could stuff into two coolers, and some sleeping bags until they could arrange for a bed.

It was early evening when they arrived back at Whitstone House. As they pulled into the drive, Hillary squinted at the door. "Did you leave it open?" she asked Matthew.

He looked, too. "I didn't think I did. The latch is probably rusty," he said. "I'll have a look."

They hauled in their purchases, and dragged the coolers into the kitchen area. Hillary dumped ice on top of them while Matthew checked the door. He came back to the kitchen and told her nothing was wrong with the latch. "It's fine. I guess I left it open."

"What about electricity?"

"Got a little problem there," he said apologetically. "I can't find the breaker box. I'll have to call the caretaker tomorrow."

"Great," she said.

"I'm going to go sweep out a room for us," he said, and left her to finish up in the kitchen. When Hillary was done, she went upstairs to help. They went around opening windows, airing out the house, trying to get rid of the musty smell.

When dusk fell, Hillary opened a bottle of wine while Matthew lit candles. He showed Hillary an old concave mirror on the wall in the main drawing room. He explained how those mirrors were intended to reflect light to provide more of it.

"Seriously, how do you know these things, like the history of light?" Hillary asked curiously.

Matthew grinned. "I've been reading," he said. In the candlelight, she noticed that he looked boyishly handsome, like the guy she'd fallen in love with twelve years ago. They'd met at an engagement party for one of Hillary's co-workers. Hillary had just sold her first house, and Matthew had brokered the mortgage. He'd said hello at the party, asked if she had any other sales. Hillary remembered that great smile, the shining blue eyes under a mop of dark hair. He used to tell people he couldn't look away from her brown eyes, that they reminded him of pools of honey.

Whatever had clicked between them that night, Matthew had

left with her number, and over the several weeks that followed, they fell in love.

God, how hard they fell! They loved the same movies, the same sports, the same books. Their lovemaking had been out of this world. Hillary still got a tiny little shiver just thinking about those days. She'd had a little loft apartment above a coffee shop and, on weekends, they'd lie in her bed all day, making love, taking little breaks to run downstairs for coffee and pastries. It had been a perfect existence, a perfect love.

After a couple of years of dating, they'd married, and the twins had come along eighteen months after that. They'd been delighted with their babies, and so much in love, and Hillary had believed, truly believed, that it would always be like that. And it was. For years. Until Matthew lost his job.

"I'm going to build a small fire and see if this main chimney is working," Matthew announced, drawing Hillary back to the present. "I saw some wood down by the shed. I'll be back in a few."

Hillary decided it was getting a little chilly, and took a candle upstairs to close some of the windows. They had chosen the room at the end of the upstairs hall to use as a bedroom. It had windows on two walls and a fireplace with a carved stone mantle, which, Hillary had grudgingly admitted, was pretty cool.

As she moved down the hallway, a cold draft caught her flame and extinguished it. "Damn," she muttered. There was still enough twilight filtering in that she could make her way. The light in the room at the end of the hall was better, and Hillary relit her candle before putting it aside. She closed the windows on the east side, then those on the west side. When she turned back to the room, something caught her eye, and Hillary's heart plummeted to her toes with fright. Someone, a woman, a face, was staring at her through the window. The woman's hair was wet and hung well past her shoulders.

Hillary's heart was beating wildly; she whirled around, thinking it was a reflection, that there was a woman standing behind her, not at the window, but there was no one there. And when she jerked around again to the window, the woman, the face, was gone. Hillary rushed to the window and opened it, leaning onto the sill to look out. There was nothing there. There couldn't possibly be anything or anyone there, for it was straight drop to the ground, and there was nothing on which the woman could have been standing.

Impossible! She slammed the window shut and fell back from it. She tried to make sense of it – it had to have been a shadow, some trick of the light. Yet she had seen a face as clearly as if the woman had walked up to her and shook her hand.

"Hillary?"

The sound of Matthew's voice below was a welcome relief. "Up here!" she shouted, and hugged herself tightly, trying to rid herself of that awful strange feeling.

"Why are you in the dark?" Matthew asked a few moments later as he walked into the room with an armful of wood.

She hadn't even noticed the candle had gone out again. "A draft, I guess." She was shaking, she realized.

Matthew noticed it, too. "Cold? Well, I've got a surprise for you," he said. "The heat is on, which means . . . hot water."

"Great," she said, and risked another look at the window. Nothing. Her imagination, that was the culprit.

As for the bath, it took some doing, with the pipes groaning and shuddering, but after a couple of blasts of junk, hot water flowed out of the pipes and into an ancient claw-footed tub.

Matthew lit the bathroom with a dozen candles.

"This is great!" Hillary exclaimed, truly delighted. She looked at her husband and felt a sudden rush of longing. "The tub looks big enough for two . . . want to join me?"

"Ah . . . you go ahead. I need to make sure we're locked up." He smiled a little absently and went out. Deflated, Hillary undressed and sank into the warmth of the bath. In fact, she didn't come out until Matthew assured her he'd made a suitable pallet on which they could sleep.

The jet lag had caught up to both of them. Hillary found the sleeping bag surprisingly bearable and, as she drifted into welcome sleep, she thought she heard the faint sound of a woman crying. But the need for sleep was too great and pushed her under before she could think much more about it.

Hillary awoke from a dreamless, deep sleep the next morning to find Matthew's bag empty. She sat up and looked around. Bright sunlight was streaming into the room and, in the morning light, the house looked entirely different. Warm. Almost inviting. She did not feel that weird, unsettled feeling she'd felt all day yesterday. She wandered downstairs and found Matthew sitting on the back steps, eating cold cereal.

"What time is it?" she asked sleepily.

"Ten," Matthew said, and smiled up at her. "You were really sawing the Zs, so I didn't wake you. Cereal?"

"Please," she said, and sat next to him. "This could be gorgeous," she said, looking out at the vista before them. The grounds swept down to a narrow river. Mature trees rose up on either side of the grounds, enclosing the property.

"There's an orchard of some sort down that road," Matthew said, pointing to a two-track road that ran along the river. "I went for a run this morning and found it. I think they are apple trees."

"How quaint," Hillary said. "And really lovely, in an agrarian way." She laughed.

"I saw a guy at the far end of the orchard," Matthew said. "I thought he must be the orchard keeper or whatever you call it, so I detoured to ask him about it, but he disappeared over a hill. I guess that means there are more houses on the other side of the orchard. I'm really not sure how big this property is."

"Want me to check it out when I go to the village to do something about beds?" Hillary asked.

"What, you don't like roughing it?" Matthew asked, nudging her with his shoulder.

She laughed. "Have you met me?"

He looked at her, his blue eyes shining with amusement. "Fortunately for me . . . yes," he said, and kissed her. It was more than he'd done in weeks. In fact, Hillary thought, as he went to get milk for her, she couldn't remember the last time they'd really kissed.

They puttered around after breakfast, making a list of things she needed to get. As she picked up the keys to leave, Matthew said, "Thanks, Hill."

She paused. "For what?"

"For this," Matthew said, gesturing to the house. "For being a sport. I just want to do some work and get it ready to sell. It gives me . . . it gives me something useful to do," he admitted sheepishly.

Hillary smiled and lovingly touched his cheek. "I'll see you later."

Matthew turned his face into her hand and kissed her palm. "Be careful. Remember to look right, and that they drive on the wrong side of the road."

Hillary laughed. She went up on her toes and kissed Matthew's mouth, lingering there and feeling, for a moment, like she could wrap herself into him like she used to do.

In the village, Hillary found a little housing goods shop which happened to have a double bed in stock, as well as a couple of used armchairs. "Can have that delivered today if you'd like," the man behind the counter said. His nametag read "Stan".

"Thank God," Hillary said with a laugh. "Do you know the Whitstone House?"

"Sure I do. Are you staying near there, then?"

"We're actually at the Whitstone House."

Stan stopped writing the invoice and looked up. "Do you mean you've let it?"

"Actually, my husband inherited it," Hillary said. "Just like that, out of the blue." She laughed at Stan's astonishment. "He didn't know his mother had it or was even connected to the Whitstones. Talk about a surprise."

"I can see that it would be." Stan looked down at his invoice once again. "Been years since anyone's lived there."

"Right. Why is that, do you think? Is it too far from Tadcaster?"

"Oh, perhaps. But, you know, they say it's haunted. That might have something to do with it. People round here can be bloody superstitious."

Hillary's gaze locked on the shopkeeper. "Excuse me?"

He looked up. "You haven't heard it, then? Oh, pay me no mind, miss. They say that about all the old houses round here. This one or that one died, and therefore it's haunted." He grinned at her. "I wouldn't fret too much about it."

Hillary would have laughed along with him had she not seen that face in the window last night. "How would I find out about the house? I mean, about who lived there before?"

"Now I've gone and scared you. I'm sorry for that, it was not my intent. But you can ask the librarian. She keeps a room of local records. Now then, I can have the bed and the two chairs delivered by four o'clock if that suits?"

"Perfectly," Hillary said. She didn't believe in ghosts. She wasn't going to let what he said rattle her in the least. What she'd seen in the window was some sort of weird shadow and light thing, it was not a *ghost* for heaven's sake. And the fact that there was even a tiny niggle of doubt in her mind told her that she had watched far too much late-night cable TV.

At the library, Hillary met Mrs Browning, the librarian, who, she quickly realized, also happened to be Matthew's estate agent. "Not a lot of buying and selling here," she explained with an infectious laugh. "One needs an occupation outside of it." She was a cheerful woman who wore a thick cable-knit sweater in spite of the mild summer temperatures. She wore her grey-streaked hair in a ponytail.

"Ah, the Whitstone House. How did you find it? One of the treasures in this county, isn't it? The original structure was built in the 1700s, although it's been added to over the years."

"What can you tell me about the previous owners?" Hillary asked.

"Miss Esme Whitstone was the last of them. My mother knew her quite well, actually. Here now, here is the file," she said, placing a box between them. It was labeled "Whitstone". Mrs Browning put her glasses on her nose and opened the box. "I know there were four siblings, three girls and a boy. The boy married an American, which is how you've come to have it," she explained. "Poor Esme never married and lived out her days in the very house in which she was born." Mrs Browning picked up a yellowed newspaper clipping. "Ah, that's it, I recall now," she said nodding. "This is Esme's obituary. Her older sister Aurora married a London boy and lived there until her death."

"What of the other sister?" Hillary asked.

"Oh dear, that would be Agnes." Mrs Browning put the yellowed newsprint aside and sifted through the papers, picking up another one. "This is the late Mr Riggin's work. He fancied himself the local historian and wrote little papers about all the old houses and esteemed families round here. Agnes is the one who died so young. Only seventeen years, can you imagine it?"

"She died?" Hillary said. "How?"

"Oh, a nasty fall," Mrs Browning said, wrinkling her nose. "Broke her neck. Now, depending on what story you choose to believe, she either jumped to her death when her father wouldn't allow her to marry her beau, or she fell out of a window trying to escape. Either way, a tragedy." She clucked her tongue. "The note the poor girl left for her parents is in the box. It was in Esme's things when she passed."

Hillary gaped at Mrs Browning. "Agnes died at Whitstone House?"

"Indeed she did," Mrs Browning said, nodding enthusiastically.

"What . . . what happened to the boy?"

"Well now, that's the worst part of it. When he found that Agnes was gone, he took his own life. Very Romeo and Juliet, isn't it?"

"Very," Hillary agreed.

"It's all in here. You are welcome to check out the file if you'd like, for a small surety," Mrs Browning offered.

"Thank you. I believe I will," Hillary said.

The bed and chairs were delivered at four o'clock as promised, and with the linens and the small area rug Hillary had purchased, the room at the end of the hall was suddenly very cosy. Hillary's vision of what the house could be was improving. She could imagine a pair of chairs by the hearth, a nice wardrobe as well. She was beginning to see the potential in the resale value of the house. She was beginning to believe that Matthew was right – that with a couple of weeks of hard work, it would be an outstanding property.

She said as much to Matthew over dinner.

He looked at her with surprise. "Wow. That's a sudden change of heart."

"Maybe," she said with a sheepish shrug. "But I've had a few days to decompress since we left New York and . . . and I guess I am starting to see what you see."

"Really?" he said, grinning now. "I think we can do it. I've lined up all the labor we need. If you and I tackle the cleaning and painting, I think in a couple of weeks, we might have a gold mine on our hands. So you're in?" he asked, lifting his wine glass.

"I'm in," she agreed, and clinked her glass to his. "Hey, I stopped in at the library today and got some history on the house." She told him about the Whitstones, as well as some other things she had read in the file about the construction of the house. She showed him some grainy pictures too, of people standing next to Model T cars in early twentieth-century dress. In those pictures, the house looked really very grand. They looked at an old bill of sale for tallow. And they found the note from Agnes Whitstone. Hillary told him what Mrs Browning had told her about Agnes's death.

Matthew read the note again. He shifted, uncomfortable.

"What is it?" Hillary asked.

"I don't know. I just had this strange feeling," he said, shaking his head, and looked at Hillary. "I know what that feels like, that desperation to be with someone."

Hillary gazed back at him. She felt something flow between them – something she hadn't felt in years.

"Look at that," Matthew said, breaking the spell and pointing at the picture. "They had a butler."

"I want a butler," Hillary said, dreamily.

"You have one," Matthew said, and kissed the top of her head as he stood to clear the kitchen table of paper plates and the empty pizza box.

That evening, they worked on the kitchen. Matthew took measurements for some new cabinetry while Hillary scrubbed the tiled surfaces of the workspaces. Hillary was, oddly, almost hyper-aware of her husband's physical presence. Without looking at him, she could feel him moving around the kitchen. She kept looking at him, at his hands and hips, the breadth of his back. She wanted him. She wanted him to take her right here, in the kitchen. And she couldn't remember the last time she'd felt so . . . *randy*.

"It's cooling off," Matthew said. "I'm going to get some wood." He picked up a flashlight. "Back in a bit."

Hillary finished up in the kitchen and walked down the hall to the foyer. She was digging around for some trash bags, and heard Matthew come in the kitchen, clomping about doing God knew what. "Hey," she called out to him, "will you bring the rest of the wine?"

Matthew didn't answer. Hillary stood up and looked in the direction of the kitchen. A strange sensation washed over her, making her feel slightly off balance, and the hair stood up on the back of her neck. She started for the kitchen, but the front door suddenly opened. Startled, she whirled around with a shriek as Matthew walked in with his arms full of wood.

"What?" he said.

"What are you doing?"

"Wood, remember?" he said, nodding at his arms.

"No – I heard you in the kitchen," she said, pointing away from them. Matthew looked at her curiously. Hillary's heart began to pound. "Someone is in the kitchen, Matthew." As if to prove it, there was the sound again, of someone walking around.

Matthew frowned. He put the wood on the chair and strode for the kitchen with Hillary at his back.

Matthew paused at the threshold and flipped on the light. They both saw the cat jump off the counter and disappear behind the stove. Matthew dived after it, leaning up over the stove, peering behind it. "A huge hole," he said. He turned around and smiled at Hillary. "That's what you heard, baby. Just a cat."

"Right." But Hillary was shivering. The kitchen was ice cold and she couldn't believe a cat could make the sounds she'd heard. Someone had been in here.

"Come on, let's go light a fire," Matthew said, and took her hand in his.

Hillary debated saying anything. Was she crazy? Or was something going on in this house?

After he'd built a fire in their room, Matthew sat cross-legged on their new bed and went through the file box. Hillary crawled into bed beside him and nestled closely to him. Matthew put his arm around her, but he did not put the file down. He kept reading Agnes's note to her parents.

Somewhere in the night, Matthew put his arm across her and pulled her to him. It was as close as they had been in weeks.

For the next two days, nothing happened at the Whitstone House, and Hillary decided her imagination had gotten the best of her. The strange incidents of the first couple of days were all but forgotten, and she focused on renewing a relationship with her husband. She felt remarkably free without her BlackBerry constantly chirping at her, and she felt remarkably attracted to her husband. The man was *hot*. Had she forgotten that? It was strange; it was as if she'd only just met him and was drawn to him, craving his attention.

She wondered if Matthew felt the same way. She caught him looking at her, his expression different than what she'd grown used to in the last few months. He looked at her with interest, with desire. But he did not act on it. It felt almost as if he was intentionally holding himself back.

The next day, a crew arrived to repair any plumbing or electrical problems. Another crew arrived to buff and shine the wood floors. And yet another pair of elderly gentlemen began work on the yard. Hillary realized she hadn't thought of her work in over a week. Honestly, she didn't even know where her BlackBerry was.

One afternoon, Mrs Browning came to the house to have a look at the progress. She and Hillary walked through the rooms together, Mrs Browning exclaiming at the moldings and the crystal doorknobs, the original wood floors and the carved mantles. "It's a beautiful old house. It will be brilliant when you've finished, won't it?"

"I hope so," Hillary said. They were standing in the room at the end of the hall where Matthew and Hillary had been sleeping. Hillary walked to the window on the east wall. "Come see this huge old tree," she said. "How old do you suppose that is?"

Mrs Browning joined her at the window and looked out. The oak tree had long, twisting limbs, but it looked as if it had been harshly pruned away from the house. "I'd wager it is three hundred years old," Mrs Browning said sagely.

"Really?"

"Certainly!" she said with much authority. "Such a wonderful setting for this old house." She turned away from the window and moved toward the door. "Oh," she said, stopping abruptly.

Hillary glanced at her. "Is something wrong?"

Mrs Browning looked up and around the ceiling. "There's a draft, isn't there? It's very cold just here." Hillary walked to where Mrs Browning stood. She felt it, too. They looked around the room, but could find no vents, no open windows. As they looked, they were surprised by a *thud*, and both turned toward the mantle. The file box had fallen, its contents scattered across the floor.

"These old houses," Mrs Browning said with a laugh as she bent to help Hillary pick it up. "So full of drafts and what not."

But Hillary thought that was an odd thing to have happened.

When she mentioned the cold and the falling box to Matthew later, he explained to her that he'd had chimney sweeps out, and they'd felt the air from the hearth. "Probably knocked the box off, too."

Perhaps. Hillary supposed that made sense. Sort of.

Over dinner that night, Hillary and Matthew talked together like they hadn't done in months. They discussed plans for selling the house. They chatted about the origins of the place and the Whitstone family. "Isn't it tragic," Hillary said as they drank wine by the fire, "that the girl lost her life?"

Something came over Matthew's face. He looked at Hillary strangely. "She died because she loved completely," he said.

Hillary laughed. "What a strange thing to say, Mr Sparks."

"She died because she loved completely," he said again.

Hillary's smile faded. "OK . . . are you all right?"

Matthew blinked. "Who, me?" He grinned and stood up, gathering the plates. "I'm great."

"It's just that you are usually not that sentimental. Or flowery."

Matthew's gaze riveted on her. "I'm not?"

She was surprised by his reaction. She smiled nervously. "No . . . I mean, you don't think you are, do you?"

He looked puzzled. He put down the plates and put his hands on his hips. "I think I'm a lot of things that you don't understand. That *I* don't understand."

Hillary sat back. "What does that mean?"

He shrugged.

"You know . . . we've been having a great week, Matthew," she said, sensing a strange change in him. "I don't want to mess that up. I want to keep it, and try to get back to what we were because I . . . I really miss you."

"I miss you, too, Hill. I . . . I miss you so much." His voice quivered with emotion.

Hillary's heart went out to him. He sounded lost, as if he had lost her irrevocably. Sometimes, she felt that way, too. She stood up and wrapped her arms around him. "How do we get back to what we were?" she asked softly.

Matthew shook his head, as if the question confused him. "I am trying." He kissed her tenderly. And then he left her.

Hillary watched him walk out of the kitchen with questions

and desire raging through her. What kept them from each other? Why couldn't they just reach for each other and fall into bed as they used to be able to do? What had happened to them?

The rain started the next morning. It was slow and steady, drenching the world around them, forming a curtain between Whitstone House and the world.

Hillary felt as if she were getting a cold – she was light-headed, off balance. She worked in the kitchen, painting the old cabinetry while Matthew replaced some light fixtures throughout the house. She stood up to stretch and happened to look out of the window. A man stood in the front drive, seemingly oblivious to the rain. He was dressed oddly, his coat to his knees. Thinking he must be one of the workers Matthew had hired, Hillary walked to the front door to let him in. But when she opened the door, no one was there.

"What's up?" Matthew asked, walking into the hall behind her.

"There was a man standing on the drive," she said. "I saw him out of the window. And now he's gone."

"What man?"

"I don't know. Some guy in a coat," she said absently.

Matt looked at her. "To his knees?"

"Yes! Who is that?"

Matt grimaced. "I don't know, but I've seen him a couple of times now. He's always walking around, looking. And then he just disappears."

"Is he looking for work?"

"I don't think so," Matthew said. He looked down at Hillary. "This will sound crazy, but have you seen a woman wandering around?"

Hillary's eyes widened. "I . . . I saw a face," she admitted reluctantly. "In the window, looking in. But it was upstairs. I . . . I didn't tell you because it sounded crazy."

Matthew didn't look surprised. "I've seen her, too," he said grimly. "Outside, around that old oak tree."

"When?"

"A couple of times when I've been out working. She stands there looking out to the orchard."

"Matthew . . ." Hillary grabbed his hand. "You don't believe in ghosts, do you?"

"Ghosts?" He chuckled. "No, baby," he said, and put his arms around her. "I believe it's more likely some locals wanting us gone for whatever reason. They are trying to scare us."

"Scare us? But why?"

"Who knows? Anti-American, maybe."

Hillary wanted to believe that, too. But, as the day progressed, she felt as if someone were breathing down her neck. Matthew seemed oddly out of sorts too, and, more than once, Hillary saw him staring at her as if he wanted to devour her.

That night, the rain worsened. It was coming down in great sheets, filling the drive and the yard with huge pools of water. Hillary and Matthew had hardly spoken since the afternoon. Hillary felt exhausted, unable to even carry on a conversation. She made sandwiches for them and, as they sat down at the table to eat, something brushed against her leg.

"That cat again," she said.

"What?"

"That cat. I felt it against my—" Something or someone grabbed Hillary's leg and she cried out, jumping up from the table.

"Hillary, what is it?" Matthew demanded, but her reply was lost in the flickering of the lights. Outside, a blinding flash of lightning hit the old oak tree. Even as it was happening, Hillary knew there was something terribly wrong – the lights had flickered before the lightning struck.

And in the next moment, the house was plunged into darkness.

"Here's a flashlight," Matthew said, finding her and thrusting it into her hand. "I'll go look at the breakers."

"Matthew, wait—"

But he'd already gone. Unsteadily, Hillary started for the hallway. She made it as far as the foyer, her whole body trembling with an unearthly fear. "Matthew?" she called out, but the rain made it too hard to hear.

She heard a noise at the door and jerked toward it. The front door flew open, banging against the wall. At the same moment, something brushed past her. Hillary jumped back, knocking against the wall.

She saw her then, the apparition of a woman with wet hair, rushing up the stairs. Hillary screamed.

"Hillary!" Matthew shouted. She saw the light of his flashlight rushing from the opposite end of the house toward her. But she heard footsteps behind her too, and bolted for her husband.

"I saw her! I saw her, Matthew. She went up!"

Matthew looked up the stairs. He let Hillary go and raced up, taking the steps two at a time. Hillary ran after him. Matthew marched down the hall to the room at the end and threw the door open just as another bolt of lightning hit and illuminated the room. Hillary saw what Matthew saw then – the woman hovering above their bed.

She screamed and grabbed his arm; a rush of icy cold hit her squarely in the face, and a sour smell permeated the room. The rain sounded louder, and Hillary looked to the windows. "Look!" she cried, pointing. The windows were open.

Matthew started for the window, but, as he moved, an icy cold invaded Hillary's body, passing through her. She gasped at the sensation; in the next moment, she suddenly felt on fire. Matthew whirled around and looked at her. His chest was heaving with his breath. His ravenous gaze raked over her and that thing, that hot, lusting thing, was swirling through Hillary, and she held out her hand to her husband. He dropped his flashlight and walked to her in the dark, taking her face in his hands, kissing her hard on the lips.

He lifted his head and pressed his forehead to hers. "I want you," he said, his voice deep. "Now. This moment. Say that you want me, Hillary. Say it."

"I want you. Desperately." She looked at his mouth, his lips. He was a powerfully magnetic, desirable man. "Make love to me, Matthew," she moaned.

Matthew grabbed her up in his arms. His lips found hers as he stooped to pick her up, then he moved to the bed and deposited her there.

The apparition had disappeared, but Hillary could still feel her cold energy flowing about the room, in and out of her, in and around them. The ghosts, the storm, the lights – everything ceased to be of importance. Nothing mattered but this – knowing her husband again.

Matthew crushed her to him as if he were afraid she would fly away if he let go. Hillary didn't recognize them – the passion, so absent from their marriage in the last months, flared and erupted between them. The touch of his lips jolted her every bone. She was scorching with need and grabbed for him, filling her hands with his flesh. They quickly removed their clothing, desperate to feel each other's skin, clinging to the warmth of their lips.

The staccato of the rain seemed to grow; it thrashed the house as hunger thrashed between Hillary and Matthew, all coming together in a perfect storm of sensation.

Hillary's heart pumped furiously; she eagerly explored his mouth with hers, his body with her hands, as if she'd never known it, her fingers dragging through his hair, stroking his face, cupping his chin.

Matthew's mouth moved over her, exploring, as his hands caressed her. His body moved lower, his lips searing her skin in their wake. He took her breast in his mouth and a white-hot shiver of anticipation shimmered down her spine. His hand swept the swell of her hips, and he pushed the hard ridge of his erection against her.

Hillary's breath grew ragged.

Matthew's hand slid down her leg, to her ankle. He lifted her leg and put it on his shoulder, kissing the inside of her knee. With his other hand, he caressed the soft flesh of her inner thigh, then sank his fingers into her folds and began to stroke her, driving Hillary to a madness she'd never felt before.

She fought for breath as Matthew transported her from Whitstone House, from the rain, from everything but the carnal pleasure he was giving her. She could feel the excitement building in her, groaning with the intensity of it. His strokes grew fevered, his eyes intent on hers as he watched her succumb to his touch.

"*Matthew*," she said, her voice rough and hoarse and strange to her own ears.

He whispered something, words she couldn't grasp, as he moved his hand so intimately between her legs. And just as her body began to shatter, he thrust into her. Hillary cried out with the exquisite sensation, arching into him. She felt the waves of pleasure spilling over her, through her, until Matthew cried out, too, his body shuddering into hers.

In that moment, she knew what it meant to be one, to be loved by her husband. All her doubts about their marriage evaporated. Their lovemaking was surreal, ethereal and powerful. It was, quite simply, the best lovemaking of her life. She stroked Matthew's head at her breast as they both sought their breath, slowly swimming to the surface of some very deep emotions.

Matthew lifted his head and looked at her. Something swam between them, something intoxicating and uniting. "That was different," she whispered.

"That was of some other plane, baby," he agreed, and kissed her.

The rain continued to fall, lashing at the windows and stirring the trees wild with it, but Hillary and Matthew slept in each other's arms, oblivious. They didn't fear the apparitions. They both knew, in that way of knowing those things, that the ghosts were gone.

Matthew and Hillary never saw the man or woman, or felt the strangely unsettling energy in the house again. They finished their work on the house and headed back to the States, their marriage revitalized.

Two months later, Mrs Browning sold Whitstone House for two million pounds.

Matthew had enjoyed the work on the house so much that he opened a renovation business and left banking behind. He began to renovate houses that Hillary would sell. Every once in a while, Hillary and Matthew talked about what had happened the night of the storm, and the feeling of being inhabited by something unworldly. They privately joked about their ghosts, yet they never mentioned what had happened in England to anyone else.

But every time it stormed, they would look at one another and smile, and make love with the energy of two lovers who had waited a hundred years for that very moment.

A Single Girl's Guide to Getting Ahead

Liz Maverick

"Your replacement ghost has arrived," the deliveryman said, pulling a clipboard and pen from his messenger bag. "Sign on the dotted line."

I looked down at the box at his feet.

"Let me." He hoisted it up with a grunt and lugged it over my threshold.

"It's so much bigger than the first one," I said.

He shrugged. "You ordered 'extra scary'." Noting my hesitation he added, "You can borrow my box cutter, but I'm not allowed to open it for you. It's an insurance thing."

I sighed. Stupid insurance. He was going to have to walk me through the summoning process again anyway. I sliced open the box and began emptying the contents on the dining-room table.

The deliveryman balanced his clipboard against his stomach, checking off the inventory as I lined it up. "What was wrong with the first ghost?"

"He didn't get the job done. My ex-boyfriend is still here."

"Touchdown!" the announcer screamed from the television in the adjoining room where my ex was cheering madly. If I never saw the back of Freddie's head against the glow of the television again, it would be too soon. Every time I passed the sofa on my way to the bedroom or the front door, there was Freddie's head. I could not stare at Freddie's head for the rest of my days. I wanted him gone before the summer was over and I had to go back to law school, and it was already well into August.

"That's it. Ready for the summoning when you are."

"I'm ready. Although . . . why are there so many candles this time?"

"Probably because you ordered 'extra scary'," he repeated. He rummaged in his messenger bag. "Since it's my first day, I'm going to read straight from the manual. It's better not to take any chances."

"Splendid," I said.

"OK. Here goes. Place the candles in a circle."

I did.

"Light them."

I did.

"Dip your finger in a pinch of lavender powder from the – no, the *lavender* powder, that's right – and now right into the teal . . ."

Even a little flustered, I still managed to follow his instructions correctly.

"'Whisk your powder-laden finger across the flame'," he read robotically off the page.

I did.

"Repeat after me: 'Leatrize, leatrize, cumlaudebacuss, hauntum quantum mechanico localda semanaca'."

"Leatrize, leatrize, cumlaudebacuss, hauntum quantum mechanico localda semanaca."

"Wait a minute." His finger moved to another section of the page. "Oh. 'Localsum diamanaca'."

"Is there a problem? Should we start over?"

"I . . ." He looked a little nervous for a minute and then glanced at his watch. "Uh, no, I'm sure it'll be fine. It's the same ghost. You'll get the same result. If there's a problem, you can contact the home office."

"What?"

"Just go ahead and blow out the candles while ringing the bell."

I felt a little off balance as I finished the summoning, but the result seemed the same as the first time. A whooshing sound accompanied a flash of light; the frame of my replacement ghost pulsed into sight and a human shape began to form in the glow. I'd never been so annoyed in my life when I finally saw enough to know what he looked like. "This is 'extra scary'?" I asked, hands on hips.

The deliveryman looked at the ghost and then looked at me like I was insane. "Lady, *this one hasn't got a head*."

The ghost was, indeed, headless, but as his body continued to materialize, I saw that he was muscular and nicely proportioned. He was wearing a fitted suit in a flattering European cut and would have made a suitable date for a cocktail party. Under different circumstances, of course. And if he'd had a head.

I frowned. "I don't think he's going to be able to do the job. I assumed 'extra scary' meant grotesque and unpleasant and this ghost doesn't seem unpleasant in the least. He's wearing a collared shirt and a tie! And is that a Rolex? The last ghost couldn't get the job done and he wasn't half as attractive as this one. Well, you know what I mean – this one's got quite a nice body."

The deliveryman folded my invoice in crisp thirds and handed it over. "You'll have to take it up with the home office."

Freddie called for a beer from the living room and belched loudly enough for the sound to carry. "Wouldn't it be simpler and cheaper to just break up with him?" the deliveryman asked.

I sighed. "I did. It doesn't seem to have registered. We broke up months ago and he won't leave. I just want him out."

The deliveryman looked sympathetic. "You'd like to get on with your life. Date again."

"I'd like to get on with my life, but I'm not planning to date again. I'm done with men. I just want to be alone."

"At some point you'll change your mind. I'm always hearing girls gripe about how hard it is to meet guys in the city."

What was that supposed to mean? That we should settle?

"All I'm saying," he continued, "is that maybe there's a reason why the first ghost failed. Maybe it was meant to be and—"

"It's not hard to meet guys," I said bristling at the insinuation that the blob on my sofa otherwise known as Freddie might actually be my soulmate. "It's hard to meet guys *worth dating*. My friend and I wrote this fake, impossible profile and put it on an online dating site, and guys answered as if they actually met the criteria! 'Meant to be', my ass!"

The deliveryman was not appropriately outraged. He checked his watch again. "I've got to run. Good luck."

Still fuming, I closed the door behind him and turned to the shimmering ghost. The headless, shimmering ghost.

You are Miss Shelby Robbins?

"I am. Could we just get on—"

Call me Joe. It's a pleasure to meet you.

"Likewise," I said, without enthusiasm. Add polite and gentlemanly to his list of flaws. I couldn't help fixating on the way his suit sculpted his shoulders, all nice and fitted around his glowing, muscular torso. None of this boded particularly well for scaring off Freddie. "Do you mind if we get started?"

Of course.

"So, we should take a moment to strategize here," I said. "I'm thinking it will take maybe three or four hauntings. One *now*, and we'll see if it takes. Then maybe we save the rest for when it's darker in a couple of hours. Night can be so effective. Maybe if I'd just had the last one focus on evening sessions, things would have—"

Exactly what sort of result are you looking for?

A feeling of dread swept through me. He wasn't paying attention! "No offense, but I filled out quite a lengthy form when I ordered the first ghost. I'm sure it's in the computer."

Sorry, I'd just like to clarify that you don't expect me to kill him.

I gasped. "No! Just scare him away for ever. Don't kill him. He's not that bad."

Joe's glow moved toward the living room. Freddie scratched his balls and took a swig of beer. The inertia surrounding the guy was palpable. *He looks bad*, Joe said.

"Listen, Joe, I'm serious. I ordered a permanent scare, nothing more. Now, if you don't mind, I'd like to finish discussing the strategy. I understand that this process will likely go quite late, and I'm prepared for that. But if we could just lay out the steps, I'm happy to go out and purchase any props or supplies that you—"

Do you mind looking the other way? Joe asked.

I looked the other way. "What are you doing?" I felt Joe leave my side and then Freddie was off his couch for what seemed like the first time in months unless you counted bathroom breaks, and he was running around yelling his head off, picking up his belongings, stuffing them in an enormous Macy's shopping bag and before I knew it he was out the front door screaming about how this place was haunted and he was never coming back.

The door slammed shut. Joe turned off the television. I heard silence in my own home for the first time in way too long. I turned toward Joe's shimmering. "Thank you," I said, caring nothing about the tears in my eyes. "Thank you for that."

It was my pleasure, he said. *I hope you can be happy now.*

I would have been deliciously, deliriously happy had it not been for Joe settling himself on the couch exactly where Freddie had been.

"There's really no need to stay," I said. "I was looking forward to a little peace and quiet, some personal time. I don't mind paying for the whole day. I mean, you were astoundingly efficient. You're a real pro. But don't hang around just because you think you have to."

I do have to, Joe said with a sigh. *You summoned me for a week.*

"But I only paid for a day," I said.

You summoned me for a week. You can't return a ghost prematurely. It's an inventory issue. Did you read the FAQ?

"It was the mechanico part! I had a feeling it didn't sound right. The delivery guy knew what went wrong and he said it would be fine. Damn it! Can't you just go back to the home office and explain you finished early?"

I can't separate myself from the summoning, he said.

"You're going to be in my house for a week?"

I don't mind.

"But I hired you because I wanted to be alone!"

I'm not particularly loud.

And he has a sense of humor, I thought grimly. Why weren't there any real men in the world with these qualities?

The doorbell rang again.

Shall I get that for you?

"No! That's probably Lillian. Do you mind going into the bedroom? I don't want you to scare her."

He projected the sense of quirking his eyebrow at me and faded. Interesting that I could sense his emotions and detect the expressions he would have had, had he been a complete package and actually arrived with a head. Part of me wished I'd ordered him with a head, but then I remembered I didn't order him specifically headless, I ordered him specifically 'extra scary'. And in fact, Lillian was the one who handled all the online crap for the replacement since I was busy hiding in the bedroom, overcome by the twin insults of the fumes from Freddie's dirty laundry and the fact that the first ghost was less effective than somebody trying to scold an adorable puppy for chewing a slipper.

"I know you're in there!" Lillian yelled from the other side of my door. "Has Freddie left yet?"

I opened the door. Lillian didn't look hopeful. I think asking about Freddie was sort of second-hand now, like, "Good morning." Or "How's it going?"

"Is Freddie gone?" she repeated.

Suddenly, in spite of my new ghost problem, it hit me. Freddie was finally gone. I burst into tears of relief.

"Oh!" Lillian said, looking horrified as she put her arm around my shoulders. "Don't worry. The replacement ghost arrives today, yes? It will be OK. I promise."

"He's here."

"I know he's here. He's been here for months. We'll think of something else."

"No, the replacement ghost is here. Freddie is gone."

Lillian looked stunned. She looked like she'd seen a . . . "Ghost here? Freddie gone?" She ran to the kitchen.

"Where are you going?"

"This is cause for celebration!" The champagne had been in the refrigerator forever, waiting for this moment. We had some chocolates too, but Freddie discovered them and ate them around the two-month mark. She grabbed the champagne, got out two flutes and then noticed that I wasn't quite as celebratory as I ought to have been. "Oh, my God. Did you kill him?"

"Of course not." I glanced toward the back room. "The replacement ghost is still here. He won't leave."

Lillian's eyes narrowed. "What do you mean he won't leave? The job was a scare, and then it was supposed to be well-deserved peace and quiet for Shelby. I'm the one who ordered it. I know exactly what I ordered." She put down the champagne flutes and literally rolled up her shirtsleeves. "I'll take care of this."

Before I could stop her, Lillian marched out of the kitchen and into the back bedroom. I popped the cork on the champagne, poured two flutes and waited for some shouting.

There wasn't any. I waited for thirty seconds. Nothing.

I started to get nervous. I forgot to mention to Lillian that the ghost had arrived *sans noggin*. Maybe she didn't know that either. What if he'd just scared her to death? My heart pounding, I headed for the back room. "Lillian?" I could see her standing just inside my room, but it was dark in there.

Lillian suddenly turned and cleared her throat. Her eyes were a bit wide, but she wasn't scared. She was . . . a bit sweaty, a smidge more tousled than when she'd arrived . . . and she had a sort of angelic smile on her face.

"Are you OK?" I asked.

She walked past me. "Gotta go. I have that computer class in fifteen minutes. We're discussing that pesky copy and paste function I've been struggling with, and it's one class I don't think I should miss."

"If I'm looking at you like you might have just gone insane it's because I think you might have just gone insane. What just happened? What did he say to you?"

"Sorry, Shelby, no time for chatter. I'll see you at drinks tonight. Congratulations on the Freddie exorcism." She grabbed her purse and slammed the door behind her.

I swung around to find Joe leaning against the doorway with a distinct air of satisfaction.

I blinked. I looked at my watch. "Did I miss something?"

I don't think so, Joe said.

"Would you like a glass of champagne?" I asked, paling the instant I said it. "I'm sorry, I wasn't thinking."

His silence was edged with a kind of sadness. "If I'm very near to it, I can taste and smell anything I once had in real life. I'd love a glass of champagne."

I went into the kitchen with Joe following behind. I raised my glass and Joe engulfed his in his glow. We clinked glasses. I took a swig. Goodbye, Freddie, I thought. Goodbye to the past. It's just me now, at last.

You really want to be alone.

"Yes. I mean, I don't know about for ever. I just know that I want to be alone now."

I felt a sudden rush of well-being, but it vanished as quickly as it had arrived. Joe stood quietly with his ghostly hand around the stem of his glass, but I had the sensation that he'd meant to do or say something else.

You can try to reverse the summons, Joe said. *I should have told you before, but . . .* He shrugged.

"Well, you told me now. Let's try." I put down the champagne flute.

Joe followed me to the table. *Do you remember the steps?*

"I'll have a go," I said with a sigh. I began arranging the props to the best of my memory. "What do you get out of this, anyway? The job. The service."

Joe thought for a bit before he answered. *As a ghost, when you finally understand that you have died, the first thing you realize is that you don't know what to do with yourself. There's a sense of displacement. You need something to focus on, something to occupy your time, something to give you a sense of purpose until you find a new "home". And when I say "home" I'm not talking about a literal thing. I'm talking about that intangible something that makes you feel like you have a place you want to be and sense of being at rest. If you can find what you were missing in real life now that you're a ghost, you'll be as close as you can ever hope to be to peace. I suppose that sounds too* woo-woo?

I couldn't tell if he was joking that time. "So you're working for the delivery service until you find 'home'."

I am. Until I find home. Ready to try the reversal?

For two hours we tried, me uttering every possible permutation of the summoning ritual I could think of until my brain was a muddle of leatrixes, cumladebacles, hauntum squantums and maniacal lofaldo secaldacas. By the end of the second hour, teal and lavender powder covered my face, I'd set the dining room tablecloth on fire not once but twice, and candle wax was stuck in blobs all over my sweater.

I tried calling the home office but apparently the ghost business is pretty dead on Friday afternoons and nobody answered.

I scoured the internet for similar complaints and accompanying solutions, but it was slow going. Lillian had a habit of muddling up all the settings on my computer, and I was not rewarded for my perseverance in putting it straight – all I could find were links to the Better Business Bureau which reported that the ghost service I'd used had, overall, an excellent rating.

In a blink of the eye, it seemed, the dining room had gone dark with the loss of the sun and there was the doorbell ringing again. I asked Joe to hide, just in case, but it was only Lillian arriving for drinks.

"You are so not ready," she said. "The secret to being a good wingman is to look good enough to reel in men but bad enough to lose their interest when they see me."

I didn't have to look at myself in the mirror to know that I was a mess. "We've been trying to reverse the summoning all afternoon," I said, pouring myself a glass of warm champagne.

Lillian looked around rather hopefully. "Joe is still here?"

"Yes," I said wearily. "He's still here."

"I don't see him."

"He's in my bedroom."

Her eyes widened. "Pretty incredible, eh?" she said, adding a lot of nudge, nudge, wink, wink. "For having no head."

I put down the empty champagne glass. "What are you talking about?"

Genuinely surprised, Lillian stared at me for a moment and then tried to fold her expression into something more nonchalant. "Nothing." And then after an indecipherable pause added, "He's just a very unusual ghost."

I shook my head and sighed. "I suppose. Joe!"

Joe materialized instantly.

"We're going out. I'll see you . . . later."

Lillian walked right up to him in a total violation of personal space and just stood there as if she were waiting for something.

Joe emoted a smile.

"OK, kids," I said, still unsure what I'd missed. "Lillian, I'm doing this for you, so let's get on with it."

Lillian went into the hall, and I closed the door and started for the elevator.

"We should have invited Joe," she said, just as the unmistakable essence of Joe's presence made itself known.

I stopped in my tracks and put my hands on my hips. "Apparently, we did." I wheeled around, spitting mad. "You said you couldn't go back to the home office because you couldn't separate yourself from the summoning. Well, the summoning was back in my apartment, so I find it very strange you are here with me now."

Joe folded his ghostly arms across his chest. *If you think I want to go and hang out with a bunch of Freddies in a bar while they hit on you and your friend, you're out of your head as much as I am. You are the conduit for the summoning, not your apartment. When I said I couldn't separate from the summoning, I meant I couldn't separate myself from you. So, for the next week – which I suspect will turn out to be one of the longest in my entire unlife – I'm forced by contract to go where you go, within a reasonable distance.*

"What's a reasonable distance?"

Well, as you may have noted, I was in the bedroom while you were at the door. Approximately that distance.

I looked at Lillian. She shrugged.

"I'm calling the home office again first thing in the morning," I said.

Call them again right now. The graveyard shift should be starting soon, Joe snapped. *Nobody wants to be forced into somebody else's company.*

Something tugged at me then. Joe didn't have a say in the matter. And he was right: nobody except a Freddie wants to be where he isn't wanted.

"Joe . . ."

Yes?

"I'm so sorry. I never considered your feelings in all of this. I am truly, truly sorry."

Something happened then. In a way, I wish I could have seen the look on Joe's face. I mean, I didn't have to, but I think I would have seen something touching and wonderful there.

He cleared his throat and said in a husky voice, *That's the nicest thing anybody has said to me since I died.*

"I guess nobody really thinks about a ghost's feelings." A wave of bittersweet softness swept over me like a breeze. I stared into Joe's glow and it was like he was looking back into my eyes in some otherworldly sense. For a second I wished we were alone. Even though Lillian had been my best friend since forever, this moment with Joe was something I wish I could have had just for me.

The elevator started beeping – Lillian had been holding it open too long. "Let's all get a drink," she said. "Joe's probably a better wingman than you, anyway."

Joe turned himself invisible once we were in the elevator, and only Lillian and I knew he was there. Well, actually Lillian didn't seem quite as attuned to his coordinates and sometimes she'd start talking thinking he was on one side of her when he'd moved to the other side. For some reason, Joe and I never lost our connection. Maybe it was the summoning link, but part of me thought it might be his choice. In the same way that he was able to reveal what he was saying and thinking and feeling to me while technically headless, when he faded himself out in public I still knew exactly where he was.

The bar was just down the street from my apartment. It was one of those overpriced wine and cheese numbers, but Lillian and I agreed we should try to stay in more upscale circles when we looked for potential boyfriends for her.

Things started out normal. But then after a short period of time, things seemed somewhat . . . less . . . normal. Joe *was* a good wingman. In fact, too good. He seemed to be generating ghostly charisma even while invisible. The bar patrons were subconsciously moving toward our side of the bar. And that wasn't all. There was something particularly strange about the behavior of the women . . .

"Joe?" I asked suspiciously. "What are you doing?"

What do you mean? he asked, too innocently.

"Why are all the girls in the bar hot and sweaty?"

I'm able to give them an orgasm by mere proximity.

My jaw dropped.

"Close your mouth," Lillian whispered. "And stop talking to an empty bar stool."

"I'm talking to Joe," I said.

"Well, talk to him without talking," she said and went off to flirt.

Can I do that? Talk to you without talking? I asked Joe.

Joe projected a broad smile. *Apparently, you can.*

An orgasm by mere proximity? Why was that phrasing so familiar? I looked around the bar. It was standing room only now, and I couldn't deny there were pheromones wreaking havoc on the place. Everyone looked like they were having the time of their life and that they had no idea why.

That's quite a skill, I said. *Lillian and I used to joke that the perfect . . .*

Yes?

I looked over at Lillian who was now flirting her way back from the other side of the room. I glanced back at the non-space where Joe stood. I narrowed my eyes. *That's* why it was familiar. Lillian and I made that joke once before – that the perfect guy could give you "an orgasm by mere proximity".

That's quite a coincidence, Joe said when I told him.

Yes, it is, I said, suddenly in ill humor.

What's the matter? Joe asked.

I wasn't sure what the matter was. Was it the fact that I don't believe in coincidence? Or was it the fact that I seemed to be the one person in the bar who wasn't the beneficiary of ghost-proximity pleasure?

I was trying to decide whether or not to interrogate him on that score when Lillian grabbed a vacant bar stool and began making eyes at the general area where Joe sat.

"He's not your ghost," I whispered testily in her ear. "Not to mention that he's altered the gravitational pull of this bar just for you, and I think you should take advantage of it."

She looked at me with dreamy eyes. "I think he's lovely, but you know I'd never compete with you for a guy. We both know he's *your* ghost."

"I'm not competing," I said, wondering just how much of this conversation Joe was catching. "I just . . . It's just . . ." What was wrong with me? "Listen, do you mind if we call it an early night? I've had a hell of a day."

"If Joe will walk you home, I think I'll stay. Jody and Peter just walked in so I know people." Her dreamy expression morphed into concern. "Are you mad at me?"

"Of course not. I'll see you tomorrow."

I pushed my way through the crowd and stepped outside, beelining for home.

You're mad at me, Joe said, predictably on my heels.

I'm mad at me, I answered, forgetting to answer out loud. "I shouldn't care one little whit. I'm not looking for a relationship anyway. It's just that . . . It's just . . ."

It's just what?

"Why did you do that for every single person in there except for me?"

Joe stopped in his tracks. He didn't answer. It was as if he couldn't find the words or was surprised by my frankness or didn't want to say. *Because . . .*

"Because?" I prompted.

Good God. Good God. A swell of mixed-up emotions burst forth from the shimmering area of his presence.

It hit me smack in the chest. I took a breath, a little overwhelmed, and a little excited in a way that was hard to process. Joe hadn't appeared the least bit out of control until now. Could you have an existential crisis if you didn't exist? "Joe, you're actually scaring me a little."

A beat of silence passed between us. *You ordered "extra scary",* he said softly.

We both laughed. "What's happening here?" I asked.

I don't know.

Suddenly, I lost my sense of where he was standing. A soft wave of air brushed across my skin, sinking into my lips like a divine potion.

"Joe?" I said uncertainly when I was finally able to speak.

He didn't answer.

I turned slowly and finished the walk home. I knew he'd moved next to me, but neither of us spoke. Once inside my apartment I felt suddenly nervous, as if we were at the end of a date and I didn't know what might happen next.

Nothing happened next. *I'll stay on the Freddie couch,* he said.

Oddly bereft, I smiled and nodded. Then I retreated to my bedroom and proceeded to sleep the sleep of the dead until the doorbell rang the next day around noon.

Disoriented and only half-remembering all the events of the previous day, I opened the door to find the deliveryman waiting, clipboard in hand. The other half of yesterday came right back to me.

"I shoulda had you do it over," he said, shaking his head. "I figured you were getting more than you paid for so it wouldn't be a problem. Sign here, and we'll start the reverse summoning process."

"Um . . ." I wheeled around, my eyes searching for Joe. He must have slipped into the bedroom at the doorbell since I'd always asked him to before.

"He doesn't need to be right here. We can do the procedure as long as he's within a reasonable distance."

"Er . . ."

The deliveryman began to reorganize the mess on the dining-room table from the failed reverse summoning attempt. Still no sign of Joe. I glanced back into the bedroom. "He already left," I blurted.

The deliveryman looked up. "That's not possible."

"Well, he's not here, is he?" I said with excessive perkiness.

The deliveryman's brow furrowed quite deep.

I began to panic. I didn't want Joe to leave without saying goodbye. I didn't want Joe to leave like this. We'd had a moment last night and, for some damned reason, I wanted it to mean something. I at least wanted Joe to know that I wasn't just another job. I wanted him to know I cared and that I hoped he'd find *home*. It suddenly seemed so sad. I began to weep. It wasn't a strategy; it was this incredible amount of suppressed emotion all wrapped up in the endless string of Freddie feelings and stuff to do with how different things were with Joe.

"Is there any possible way ... any *possible* way," I said in a tremulous voice, "that you could come back a little later? It's just not—" I emitted an enormous snotty snuffling sound "—a good time."

The deliveryman looked as if he was reconsidering his career track. "I'll leave the materials right where they are, and I'll come back in an hour." He backed out the door with the air of a man eager to put some serious distance between himself and an over-wrought female.

Come here, Joe said from somewhere behind me. I turned, tears streaming down my face. He took me in his arms and kissed me.

Or so it seemed. In my mind, I stood in the middle of my living room as Joe's lips took mine. A divine shiver ran down my spine. I closed my eyes against the blinding shimmer that surrounded us. Joe's kiss was soft and greedy, his tongue playing with mine. He was with me in a way that I could never explain though his mouth never actually touched me.

I didn't give you an orgasm by proximity because, with you, I would rather have it be a real one. It's not that I mind leaving, Shelby. It's just that I want more time with you.

I have no idea how long we stood together in that state, but finally the sound of Lillian's voice penetrated the fog in my brain. "Shelby, I'm coming in. You're making me nervous."

I heard the key in the door, and Joe let go of me. I fell limply into a chair as Lillian entered the apartment.

"Is Joe still here? You look weird. What's wrong? Did something bad happen?"

Joe decided to materialize for her. I saw Lillian look over my shoulder and then back at me. This happened a couple of times. And then she sat down on the couch next to me and likewise slumped back. "Oh, I see where we are. You don't want to part and he has to go. This is tragic."

"What are we are going to do?"

There's nothing we can do, Joe said. *I'm under contract for twenty-five years.*

"I could order you every day," I said, knowing that the money and the summoning energy required for that would be a bit of a problem.

"Why on earth would you sign a contract for twenty-five years?" Lillian asked.

The alternative was going straight to Hell.

The doorbell rang. "Oh, no!" I wailed. I opened the door, my face blotchy and gross, defeat written across my slumping shoulders. "Just give me another hour. Just one hour. I'm beggin—"

The deliveryman looked sympathetic but he shook his head. "I can't be late on the return. I'm new."

"I love him!" I blurted.

Lillian let out a low whistle. Oddly, I sensed no reaction from Joe.

The deliveryman's sympathy vanished so abruptly, I thought he might have seized up. He did a double take toward the screen of his barcode scanner, and his expression changed first to one of confusion and then of pure horror. "What am I supposed to tell the home office?"

"That they need some sort of a release clause?" I said bitterly.

"What did you *do*?" he asked.

"I didn't do anything. There's nothing I *can* do. Except wait twenty-five years for his contract to run out."

"On my third day? In my first week?" he babbled. He held out what I had mistaken for a barcode scanning device, and I saw it was an emanations meter. The digital readout said "0.00".

"It must be broken," Lillian said, tapping the plastic with her finger.

"It's not broken. There's just no ghost around," he said, the pitch of voice rising. "This has a range of thirty feet. There is no ghost around for thirty feet."

"Joe?"

Nothing. We all looked at each other. "What does it mean?" I asked, starting to panic. "I never got to say goodbye! Not like this!"

"It means . . . it means . . . give me a sec . . ." The deliveryman pulled the manual from his messenger bag and flipped to the back part where I could see it was labeled "Troubleshooting". "It could mean one of several things. He may have switched to the Negative Reinforcement division." He flipped the page and scanned the lines.

"Negative Reinforcement?" Lillian asked, since my head was already in my hands after assuming the worst.

"Yep. NR focuses on working as a force for evil. You know, haunting good people and causing citizens to step in the way of buses before it's meant to be their time, stuff like that. There's no wait on transferring to that department and it allows you to break your contract with any other division with no penalty."

Lillian and I gasped.

The deliveryman ran his finger along the fine print. "Or he may have combusted into antimatter. Which means, as Joe, he no longer exists . . ."

Lillian and I gasped louder.

"Or it's possible he left service while under contract, which means he may have already been relocated to Hell."

Lillian and I clutched at each other in horror. The deliveryman looked up and perhaps realized a more tempered explanation would be in order. "But there's always Other. He may have done something under the auspices of Other."

"Other? What sorts of possibilities fall under Other?" I asked.

"I don't know," he said, starting to crack. "It's anything in the fine print of the contract specific to the individual ghost. Jay-sus, did you hear what I said? *This is my third day on the job.*"

I turned back to my living room. "Joe? Joe, are you here? Is everything OK?"

He didn't answer, and I didn't feel any of his emotions.

"What am I saying? Of course, it's not OK," I blubbered. "If he turned evil, our relationship is over. If he's antimatter, our relationship doesn't exist. And if he's been relocated to Hell, we can't have a relationship because I refuse to live in that neighborhood."

Lillian put her arms around my shoulders. "He's probably just ghosting about somewhere with a broken heart. He knows he'll have to come out eventually."

Shaking his head, the deliveryman said, "He couldn't separate so far from the summoner, and my meter can detect ghostly presence a bit further than the dimensions of this apartment. It doesn't make any sense . . ." The deliveryman had started shifting his weight from one foot to the other, his eyes bugging out. "They didn't mention any of this stuff in the training," he muttered. He rummaged about in his messenger bag and pulled a wad of legalese from the accordion file therein. "This is all the paperwork associated with this case. If there's an Other, it has to do with the fine print in the contract. My God, I need a drink."

I took the contract. "Lillian, take him down to the bar."

"I don't want to leave you," she said.

"Please. Just . . . take him to the bar."

Lillian took me by the shoulders and looked me square in the eyes. "Find the loophole, Shelby. You can do it."

We hugged and she shepherded the nearly catatonic deliveryman into the hall and closed the door behind her.

I went to the sofa with the contract and sat down. I waited for a moment in the silence, hoping Joe had just been hiding and that, with the deliveryman gone, he'd come out and crack a joke. He didn't. It was silent and still.

I blew my nose and wiped my eyes and started going through the section titled "Other" in Joe's contract.

The legalese was enough to kill the hardiest of lawyers but I plowed through, desperate to find something. Only after quite a long time of careful reading did Subsection A, Section 4, Part II stand out: "The Supernatural Party in question may be released from this contract without reservation for any one of the pre-selected following circumstances . . ."

Possible circumstances and examples were provided: Honor, Fate, Religious Reasons, Stupidity, Loyalty . . . and finally there it was. One word at the very bottom of the third page.

Love.

I held my breath as I turned the page to read more of the fine print. At least let me find something about visitation or haunting rights, perhaps once a month, bi-weekly if we were lucky, something, anything that would allow me to date Joe, to *love* Joe—

Shelby.

"Joe?"

I'm right here, he said.

I clapped my hand to my heart. I could sense him somewhere behind me. I couldn't make myself turn and look at him. I didn't want him to see my face if he had bad news. "There's a possible loophole here. It might be very small and very limited."

I know.

"Then just say yes or no. Can you stay a little longer?"

Yes.

I took a deep breath. "When do you have to leave?"

I'm not leaving until you ask me to – and if you do, I swear you won't have to pull a Freddie exorcism.

"I don't want you to leave! But how . . ."

When I signed my contract, I specified "Love" in the twenty-five year escape clause. So, every day, I'd look at the orders coming in to see if there was someone I thought I could love – who I thought could love me back. Your reorder got quite a lot of attention from the guys in my department with the same escape clause – it was right up our alley.

"Huh. 'Get-rid-of-ex' doesn't seem like that unusual a request to me. In any case, you got the job."

The guys in the Fright department didn't have all the other skills and requirements you'd asked for. Being from the Department of Lonely Hearts, I did. Well, with one exception, which is why I had to remove my head.

"You removed your head specifically for this job? Why?"

It was the only way to become "extra scary".

A ball of light exploded just above Joe's torso and his head began to materialize. He was insanely handsome. Not extra scary at all. Not even a little scary. "Oh my God," I said, trying to not act like I'd never seen a guy with looks like that before. "I see the problem . . . but I liked you even without your head. How did you scare Freddie?"

Oh, I just told him I'd kick his ass every day for the rest of his life if he didn't leave you alone.

I had to laugh. "But I still don't understand why my order stood out so vividly for you."

Joe shook his head. *If I'd known Lillian was so bad with computers, I might not be here.* He flipped to the end of the contract where the order form was stapled.

When Lillian had provided an explanation of the first ghost debacle as justification for a new ghost, she'd apparently accidentally copied and pasted something that didn't belong. Submitted as part of her demand for a highly skilled replacement was the fake, impossible profile we'd jokingly uploaded to her dating site.

Looking For The Following Qualifications:

- The face of a movie star and the body of a superhero
- Able to give orgasms by mere proximity
- Inertia unwelcome. Proactively finds solutions to problems; not afraid of taking the steps necessary to get ahead.

So, a word of caution. The next time you order a ghost— Joe began.

"There isn't going to be a next time. I'm a one-ghost girl." I snuggled against his superhero chest and gazed adoringly up at his movie-star face, quite visible since he'd gotten a head. "Now about that second bullet point . . ."

Jonquils in the Snow

Annette Blair

One

Amishman Caleb Skylar shifted the sleepy six-year-old in his arms and stepped from the empty house to the porch that ran full around it, wondering if the ghost that led him to this place would disturb his peace as much as the one he'd left behind.

His people did not believe in ghosts, and yet no footstep marred the veneer of snow that covered Dovecrest Farm like a pall. Flanked by rich fields and lush pastures, it appeared as if the farm's inhabitants had all passed reluctantly on, leaving their uneasy spirits behind.

He'd read the sign in the window: FARM FOR SALE. SEEK HANNAH PEACHY WITHIN. But the house stood empty. "This seems as good a place as any to make a new start," he said aloud, as if to prove that he was still alive. "What say you, Susiekins?"

"No." With a pout, Susie rubbed her big doe eyes to keep them from closing. "Mommy cannot watch over me from heaven if we hide on this faraway hill. She will not know where to find me."

Caleb glanced beyond silver skies and clouds heavy with snow. "Naomi," he said. *If you are up there . . .* "Our Susie lives two hundred miles to the west at the top of the rise."

A good farm, this – though he supposed it would have been better if a spirit had not led him here. The specter, an Amish woman with wispy sunshine curls that escaped her *kapp*, and a dimpled smile that eased his troubled heart, had twirled in the farm's driveway on arrival, as if she'd come home.

Dancing was forbidden to their people, but in heaven, maybe not.

After he'd packed up Susie for a quick escape, and set aimlessly off, the spirit of the unknown woman appeared, as if from nowhere, skipping in front of his buggy.

Allowing himself to be led by joy – rather than sorrow – for a change, Caleb found himself helpless to do anything but follow. Assuming she'd been sent by a higher power, he'd acted on blind faith. Hard to believe he had any of that left. And as his matched bays clip-clopped behind the dancing spirit, she reminded him of his need to live, not mourn, and make Susie laugh again.

He sighed. "How can we buy this farm?" he muttered. "If no one is here to sell it to us?"

That joyful spirit reappeared and motioned for him to come. He followed once more – she, walking backward, maintaining her distance, without so much as a footstep in the snow to show for her guiding presence.

Caleb finally saw a woman across the narrow dirt road – a living breathing woman, her back to him as she knelt in the *grabhoff*, the Amish graveyard, her black winter bonnet and shawl stark against the snow. "She must be freezing," he said to himself.

The mourner drew him to her in a way he could no more explain than resist – in the way the specter had drawn him – and though Caleb hesitated, the spirit indicated that he should proceed, hurry even. So he did.

Iced blades of grass crisped beneath his feet as he gave less thought to the specter's reason for bringing him here, than to his for doing her bidding. Desperate times, he supposed. Besides, the mourner might know where he could buy the abandoned farm.

Moving forward had become his only hope, for his sake as well as his daughter's. No going back to that place where Naomi's life had ended and Susie's nightmares began.

A nudge on the graveyard's wooden gate made it swing open fast and wide, the wail and clatter of it as it hit the fence alerting the mourner to his presence. Kneeling in the middle of the head-stones, she stiffened. Fear, he thought it was called.

Meanwhile, his specter waved him over. Engraved on the tablet: "Anyah Peachy, beloved sister, best friend". She had died at the age of twenty-three.

A deep sense of sorrow overtook him.

The spirit indicated the middle stone. "Baby Grace Barkman, beloved daughter". Grace left this earth the day she arrived, the same day Anyah died.

On another near gravestone: "Gideon Barkman, husband, father". Same date of death. The word "beloved" markedly missing – a feeding frenzy for the gossips.

Caleb stopped close beside the trembling woman and waited patiently until she had no choice but to look up at him.

His heart raced when she did. He thought never to see another such as her. As ethereal up close as from a distance, her dimpled smile tugged at the cold hidden part of him. He fought the pull, shivered and pushed the quilt closer around Susie, asleep, finally.

"How old is your little one?" she asked, her dulcet voice soothing as she turned to set another bulb in the frosty earth.

"Susie is six," he said with forbidden pride.

"She must be heavy."

"Ya," Caleb said. "But I like the weight of her, especially her little head on my shoulder. Makes me feel safe."

While Anyah faded, her twin sat back on her heels, assessing, nodding. "It is good that you know what you have. My little one sleeps here beneath the snow. I felt safe when I held her, too. But winter – it lives in my heart all the time now." She patted the snow-cloaked earth, as if to make her little one more comfortable.

Caleb slipped his gaze back to the gravestones. Her babe had died two years ago. Still, her pain must be as tangible as the warmth of Susie's breath on his neck.

Caleb started to speak but was forced to clear his throat first. "I do not think your Grace would want you to live so long in winter," he said, reminding *himself* not to shun such wisdom. "Spring can be beautiful," he added, meaning it for the first time in months.

"Winter has its own beauty," she replied, and Caleb believed it, because this woman with the winter heart must be one of God's most beautiful creations.

She turned to the grave on her left and began, again, to dig. Gideon had been twenty-nine.

"Your husband?" Caleb asked, regretting the seemingly casual question the minute it passed his lips.

The woman's jagged half-nod, her demeanor, alert and strained, no longer revealed a serene acceptance. Guilt, he saw darken the gold of her eyes, raw and unbearable.

He knew it well. "I am sorry," he said, as if she might understand the yoke of self-blame he regretted for both their sakes.

"A buggy accident," she said, looking into a painful past, her deer-in-lantern-light expression proving that she did not understand his burden any more than her own. "It happened so fast," she whispered. "Gideon died instantly. I was thrown and . . . Gracie was born, there, on the side of the road."

"Anyah?" Caleb asked. The specter was behind her, this time with a babe in her arms.

"Anyah was thrown too, but she crawled to me, helped me hold the babe, and after . . . after . . . Anyah promised that she and Gracie would walk together with God."

Caleb cleared his throat, and ignored the sheen hazing his vision. "So you lost all three, your husband, your child and your twin."

"No, you are mistaken. I lost everything. Myself even."

Two

The young widow stood and gazed beyond Caleb's shoulder toward the horizon. "I have yearned for two years to join Anyah and Grace." The woman shrugged and regarded him with acceptance. "But I am still here."

Acceptance, duty: they were everything in the Amish faith, or they were supposed to be, but Caleb had come to the rebellious conclusion that they were not enough. "I understand," he said.

If not for Susie, he might leave the faith altogether. Unable to say more, because the knot in his throat and heart made words useless and impossible, Caleb shook his head in apology.

The woman understood; he saw it in her eyes. And she smiled, as if, inside him, she had seen something . . . worthy, and suddenly, all around him, a lingering darkness began to recede.

As grateful as he was shaken, Caleb experienced a heart-jolt, foreign and disorienting, like the ground had just dropped from beneath him.

How odd that guilt and sorrow had driven him from home, and somewhere along his lost way, he'd entered this confusing, compelling realm of crystalline perception, where he and a stranger saw into each other's souls.

The resulting face-warming discomfort was almost enough to make him want his understandable, if unstable, world back. Almost.

The widow seemed to agree, because with a swipe of her muddy hands down her white apron, she brought him back to reality with a jolt, the color contrast as jarring as black wool on snow . . . or flower bulbs in a frozen earth.

"Are you lost?" she asked, the mundane question further settling him. And for someone like him with a winter heart, her smile could surely bring the sun.

"My name is Caleb Skylar, Mrs Barkman. I seek Hannah Peachy so I may purchase Dovecrest Farm." Facing this woman, he felt . . . resurrected. God help him.

"I am Hannah Peachy."

He checked her husband's name.

"Yes, I went back to my maiden name. I like to keep the gossips busy. Come, I will show you the property. Would you like me to carry Susie for a bit?"

Surprised at her offer, Caleb stopped and, when he did, he caught in her expression a longing he suspected Hannah Peachy would want no one to see.

"I would not mind," she said, pleading in her own way.

Caleb did not want to deny her, and yet . . . "It is just— Susie would scream if she woke in your arms. She is afraid of every-one, except me."

Shoulders lowering the barest measure, Hannah Peachy nodded and walked on, while reciting a litany of the farm's good and bad points, from orchards, fields, farm equipment, to barn. "The *daudyhaus* is through the kitchen," she said.

"I have no ageing parents or in-laws to live there," Caleb said, "but I suppose friends could stay there as they pass through town."

"Anyah lived in ours." Hannah's smile grew wistful.

"I already like the house," Caleb said, stepping in behind her. "Susie and I took a tour when we first looked for you. Though it is bigger than a bachelor with one child needs—"

"I am offering it with furniture and linens, dishes and pans. Furnishing a place so large would be your biggest concern, and that is not necessary."

"I left everything of our old life behind, it is true," he said, "and your banked-barn will be a luxury on a farm the size I can manage alone, but your thresher and manure-spreader sold me."

He counted out $200 in cash, and Hannah accepted it, hands trembling, and tucked it into her apron pocket as if it could save her soul. And though she had already washed the mud off her hands, she swiped them down her apron again. "I will be out in an hour," she said, posture and expression relaxing as if she'd shed a great burden.

"I did not intend to put you out tonight," Caleb said, confused by her eagerness. "Where will you go?"

Hannah led him around the house and pointed to the small home on the next property halfway between Dovecrest Farm and Dove Hollow. "There is my new house, ready to move in."

"At twenty-five, you will live alone?"

She firmed her lips and raised her chin. "Yes. I can barely wait to move out," she said. "I no longer wish to eat from the dishes our friends gave us with hopes for a long and happy life, or to sleep alone beneath my wedding quilt."

Her last words came out wrong; they both knew it. Hannah firmed her lips, but the implication lingered. With anyone else, a tease would have been in order, but Caleb understood that Hannah mourned not so much a *long* wedded life as a *happy* one, and more than that, she mourned the loss of her babe, for which there were no words.

Blushing despite herself, he rather suspected, Hannah raised her chin. "I have to go now, Mr Skylar."

"We are neighbors," he said. "I will call you Hannah and you will call me Caleb, please. And you will come to eat supper in the kitchen of my new house tonight. And maybe when you do, you can tell me where to find the pots and pans I need to cook Susie's dinner? At noon, we ate the last of the provisions my Pennsylvania neighbors made for our journey. I am desperate."

Her unexpected laugh rang as pure and refreshing as a dipper of spring water on a hot summer day. "I will come, only if you and Susie share *my* supper. Seems I never lost the habit of making enough food for— I cook too much. I will see you at six?"

"I thought you would never offer," Caleb said, bringing her near-smile.

At six that night, with an efficiency of movement and knowledge of her surroundings, Hannah Peachy took a battered blue enamel coffee pot from the bottom of an old oak corner cupboard, and shut the door with her hip. "When will Susie awaken from her nap?" she asked, scooping coffee from a jar in the pantry. "I cannot wait to meet her. Does she always nap during the day?"

"She sleeps when it is light. Rarely in the dark. Do not be in such a hurry; she will blister your ears with her crying when she claps eyes on you. You will not take it personally, please. She has been this way ever since—" *She found her mother's body floating in the pond*, he could not say.

Caleb gave a half-nod, hating that he could still tear up. "We both have our ghosts and our regrets, you and I, Hannah, but for Susie's sake, if not our own, we will not let them get us down, yes?"

"No. Yes? I am hoping she will awaken soon. I want to meet her."

He sighed. "And the longer she sleeps now, the less sleep I will get tonight," Caleb said, looking for movement on the kitchen's daybed. He got up to take matters into his own hands.

Hannah watched her new neighbor lift his daughter into his arms and kiss the shell of her ear peeking just beneath her tiny prayer *kapp*, amazed at the rare surge of anticipation she experienced, almost as if she'd come alive again, despite her hopes to the contrary.

In a twinkling, life could change, she remembered. *Sometimes . . .* for the better.

Caleb and Susie had dragged her too easily onto a plane of existence where lack of feeling was not allowed; a place less comfortable, perhaps, but more expectant. More painful in some ways, but far less grim.

While Hannah pondered it, the remarkable mix of brawn and

gentleness that was Caleb Skylar crooned to his daughter in Penn Dutch. He called her his *liebchen*, his little love.

At such gentleness, emotion, untamed and all encompassing, swamped Hannah. It clogged her nose, blocked her throat and threatened to spill onto her lashes.

To keep her new neighbor from noticing, she turned to fill the pot from the pump at the zinc-lined dry sink while she took several deep, calming breaths.

How could so simple a thing as a man's tenderness do this to her?

Because she had been proved unworthy of receiving and incapable of giving love by her father *and* her husband. Because with the parents Gracie would have had, Hannah feared her babe fared better with Anyah in heaven.

Suddenly grief stung her eyes, and tightened her chest, the surge threatening to overwhelm her.

Then Caleb crooned *her* name, one brawny arm turning her into him, her face pressed against his broadfall jacket, keeping her there when she would pull away, saying without words that life must go on whether we want it to or not.

She never cried. She had never cried for Anyah and Gracie. Now a stranger comforted her, and her sobs hurt, they grew so harsh. When a small, stroking hand touched her *kapp*, Hannah stepped back, afraid to frighten the child.

Grief passed that fast, because it must, but the battle against Caleb's embrace and Susie's touch left her weak, battered.

If she were not careful, Caleb Skylar and his little Susie would destroy the peace she had worked so hard to attain. She ran her hands down her apron, pushed longing aside. When she stepped back, she came face to face with a pair of big brown eyes, as bright, inquisitive and all-seeing as Caleb's.

"Hello there, Susie-Q," Hannah said in Penn Dutch, her arms aching to hold the sleep-warm child to her heart. "You want some *goot schnitz* pie for dessert?"

Caleb stiffened as if for the worst, but Susie failed to cry. She nodded instead. "Yes please." Then she reached out and caught the tear on Hannah's cheek, her touch like a blessing.

Caleb regarded his daughter with wide, amazed eyes.

Hannah was sure she did the same. "Life changes in a blink," she said, "and we seem never to be prepared, good or bad."

Three

Hannah could not draw Susie out during supper, but neither did Susie scream as Caleb had predicted. She did, however, sit quietly in his lap throughout.

Hannah poured Caleb a second cup of coffee to go with his second piece of pie. She liked his hearty appetite, his warm appreciation for her cooking. She liked the way his long hair waved away from his square jaw, the red lights in his beard, twinkling almost as bright as the mischief in his wise brown eyes. She liked that within that large, capable body beat a good and gentle heart.

She'd liked him on sight, the way he cuddled Susie. A man who could love a child and still act the man – something new to her, a wonder. "What did you intend to do, Caleb, if I had not been willing to move right out?" Hannah asked. "Had you a place to stay tonight?"

"I would have gone back to New Philadelphia to stay with friends until I could move in."

Because she could not bear not to connect with Susie, Hannah tapped the child's pert little nose. "Sugarcreek to New Philadelphia is a long trek. Ohio is not as civilized as where you came from. Some places are more like wide rutty paths than roads. Besides, you seem to have everything you own in your buggy."

"I cannot say I did not hope to stay," he admitted, his sheepish grin warming a heart she would prefer to keep frozen.

"It is good for a change," she said, "to fulfill a man's hope."

The words hung between them, and she stood so fast, she knocked over her chair. "I will accept your offer and leave you with the dishes," she said, bending to kiss Susie's cheek. "Bye Susie-Q. Goodbye, Caleb. The leftovers are yours."

"Goodnight," he said, rising and extending his hand. "Neighbor."

Hannah stared at his big clumsy hand for so long, Caleb wanted to reclaim it, until she finally slipped her hand into his, and then reclaimed it as fast. Only once before had he felt shock at first touch – with Naomi, the woman he loved . . . until he did something unforgivable, and now she was dead.

But life was for the living, he must remember. For Susie, if not for him.

After a quick bath, Susie's head cleared the neck of her white cotton nightgown. "She smells like a just-for-pretty garden, Datt."

Caleb did not need to ask who. Half an hour later and Hannah remained on his mind as well, gentle and frightened, sad and sweet, gardening in the snow and tucking her dead child into the earth for a good sleep. "You like her then?" he asked, caring more than he should about his daughter's answer.

He pulled Susie's hair from the neck of her gown as she swiped it from her face "No."

Always a "no" since her mother died.

He knelt beside her at the side of her new bed while she blessed Mommy in heaven – and the "flower lady", Hannah, too. Then he kissed his daughter's nose, her ears, her elbows, and by the time he kissed her toes, he'd reduced her to giggles of the finest kind.

He cleared his throat when she kissed his lips. Then she huffed and rubbed her chin. "Your beard, it tickles. I always itch myself there."

His eyes twinkled as he tucked her in. "You will marry a man whose beard tickles."

"The boys I like don't have beards."

"That will change, and so will you, but you will stay cuddling size for a while, please."

"Yes, Datt. Datt?"

"Yes, Susiekins?"

"The flower lady's goodnight kiss made me feel as nice as purring kittens – a shivery, all-over kind of heart-soft and easy-sleeping nice."

"Ach, she makes me feel that way, too." God help him.

His perceptive daughter sighed and snuggled beneath the quilt Hannah had probably made. Even Hannah's name slipped heart-soft and sweet off the tongue.

Smoothing the quilt's fabric, Susie closed her eyes and sighed. Caleb dared hope for a good night's sleep for them both.

Before going to bed, he went outside to sit on the porch and enjoy a pipe. Maybe the ghosts of Dovecrest Farm would rest now that Hannah had moved on. He glanced at the stately cedars across the road marking the entrance to the *grabhoff*, and wondered how he could help Hannah get on with her life.

One day in her company and such thoughts should have him running for the hills. So why did the notion not frighten him?

Caleb walked around his house until, from out back, he could see Hannah's cottage, halfway down to the Hollow, one window bright with the light from a kerosene lamp.

"'Night, Hannah Peachy," he said. "Dream happy."

Four

Hannah liked the newborn hope of early morning, the way the air crackled with possibilities, her heart beating apace, as she made her weekday trek down Juniper Hill.

She liked the smell of chalk dust and her students' freckled faces. Teaching gave her life purpose; well, her students did. They were not hers to love, so they were not hers to lose or fail.

In the one-room schoolhouse, she lit the pot-bellied stove and passed letter-practice slates for grades one, two and three. Multiplication tables went to grades four and five. Grade six got geography books, seven, history, and eight, *The Martyr's Mirror* for High German lessons.

The children's running feet erased thoughts of her neighbor, thoughts she was pleased and loath to shed.

After the children hung hats, bonnets, frock coats and capes on the double row of pegs around the room, they stood for prayer. They'd barely started when a rare sound brought all heads up.

A knock on the schoolhouse door?

The children tittered as she called, "Come in?"

Caleb felt foolish. Late for school, like the old days. He'd barely slept when Susie came screaming into his room. It took more than an hour to calm her. Then, as he predicted, she wanted to play when he wanted to sleep. A fear of her dreams kept her going; dreams she would not share. She slept around four, as did he, and they overslept. Good thing no cows, heavy with milk, suffered for his laziness.

Hat in hand, Susie by the other, he entered, prepared to face a ham-fisted, sour-faced spinster. But the woman who occupied a good many of his thoughts smiled a true welcome. "She did not sleep well, after all, did she? Neither you, I think."

Caleb sighed. "Neither me."

"First grade?"

"Yah, first day of first grade . . . with everything going on."

"Shame on you!"

"Want to rap my knuckles?"

"Later," Hannah promised, sending a shot of anticipation through him.

"Susie, you may take this empty seat up front."

To Caleb's surprise, Susie sat, so he grabbed his hat and turned to go.

Susie started screaming.

Caleb turned back to Hannah. "Ear-blistering, like I said."

Susie quieted.

Hannah smiled like a friend who shared such things. He might like having her for a friend. He enjoyed sharing his thoughts with her – except for the as-yet-unspoken-of guilt and sorrow they also shared.

At the same time, a friendship with a woman, any woman, unnerved him. "I will take her home," he said, when he realized the class watched him as he watched their teacher.

"You most certainly will not. Not one more day of school will Susie miss." Hannah pointed toward the back of the room. "Take that empty seat in the last row, Caleb, where Susie can see you."

And like a ten-year-old, Caleb squeezed his six-foot-two frame behind a desk built for nurslings, because Hannah was suddenly all teacher, pushy and in charge. And despite his foolish offer, he did not want to get his knuckles rapped.

Going back to childhood, he was. Good place for such nonsense, with twenty or so children, half white-*kapped*, the others hatless, watching.

Susie, three rows up, regarded him, too. In her, he saw the anxiety of new beginnings. To put them both at ease, he winked and, when he did, she let out the breath he did not know she held. She stood to come to him.

"No," Hannah said stopping her mid-stride. "You will return to your seat and stay there. Your *datt* will stay too."

But his stubborn daughter hesitated.

"If you do not do as I say, Susie, I will make your *Datt* leave until school is over. It would not bother any of us to hear you scream all day, though it might hurt your throat some."

Wide-eyed, his daughter regarded her teacher and returned to her seat, almost docile, though she sneaked a peek at him. "Datt?" she called in a whisper, as if no one else could hear. "Her flowers have thorns in them this morning."

Caleb covered his mouth and wiped away his smile.

At recess, the boys played corner ball, him too. Suze watched his every move, the only one who did *not* laugh when Junior Elam Yoder bounced a ball off his head, though Hannah laughed harder than anyone.

At noon, Hannah offered to share her lunch with him and, when she saw the mess he'd made of slicing last night's bread and ham for Susie's lunch, she shared with Susie too.

"What?" Caleb asked. "It is still tasty." He ate a mangled clump of both and rubbed his middle. "*Goot.*" He did not know, then, whose eyes twinkled more, Susie's or Teacher's, but it brought out Hannah's dimples. He fell into a little bit of trouble then, because of how much he liked seeing Hannah happy. She weakened his vow to avoid the kind of kinship that could cause pain.

Hannah Peachy's smile was that dangerous.

"Where is her mother?" Hannah asked, suddenly beside him, while Susie washed her hands at the pump.

His scowl made her step back. "I am sorry," she said. "I did not mean to pry."

"I will tell you, maybe, another time. But her mother is gone. Right now, it is Suze I am worried about."

"Gone," Hannah whispered. "What does that mean, exactly?"

"It means, I need to protect her," Caleb said.

"From what?"

"Everything."

Five

During his second week of first grade, second time around, Caleb wanted to attend the livestock auction in Mount Hope come Monday, rather than attend school.

Interrupting his reverie, Hannah placed a picture to paint on the desk before him. "We need to talk about Susie's dependence on you," she whispered.

Ignoring the skittering inside him that this woman's nearness caused, Caleb glanced at the picture then up at her, one speaking brow raised. "I forgot my paints."

A twinkle lit Hannah's eyes. "For today, you may use mine. Come for supper tonight," she said, more and less of an invitation than he wanted. "So Susie can get to know me better. Maybe when she sleeps, we can talk."

"When she sleeps, I will sleep," he said, to diffuse his anticipation. But he nodded, ignoring the skip of his heart at her smile.

What harm could it do to have Hannah's company for another meal?

That night, she made pretzel soup and *schnitz un knepp*, and Susie became more relaxed in her presence.

"Do you like it, Susie?" Hannah asked, as Susie gathered bits of ham and apple in her plate with her last bite of dumpling.

She nodded. "Datt's bratwurst catches fire and from noodles he makes mush."

With a belly laugh, Caleb pulled Susie's *kapp* string. "Don't tell my secrets, Susiekins."

His daughter patted his face. "I like Teacher's cookin' Datt, but I love you more."

Caleb regarded Hannah. "She intended no slight."

"I understand. She does not really know me. I loved my *grossdaudy* more than anybody," she told his daughter.

"Is your *grossdaudy* here?" Susie asked. "Can I say hello to him?"

"No, *liebchen*. He has gone to walk with God."

"Did he drown in a pond like Mommy? Do you see his blue face coming for you in the night? Are you afraid, though you loved him, that he will pull you into that water with him then beneath the dirt in the *grabhoff*?"

Caleb took his daughter's revelation like a knife to the chest.

"Oh. Oh, no, sweetheart," Hannah said. "He was old and ready to go."

"Mommy was ready. She told me so when she came to say goodbye."

Caleb blanched and grasped his daughter's arms. "You did not tell me that. What did Mommy say?"

Susie swallowed hard. "That she would . . ." His daughter's words trailed to nothing. Tears filled her eyes.

"Easy, Caleb," Hannah said, covering his hand on Susie's arm, her touch getting through to him.

He relaxed his grip and brought his daughter close. "What did Mommy say, Susiekins?"

"That she would watch over me from heaven."

Hannah jumped when Caleb stood, knocking his chair to the floor. He pushed Susie into Hannah's arms, ignoring his daughter's sobs, and made for the door. "I have to—" His voice broke. "I need to . . . walk."

Hannah thought he should have said "run". Panic, she read in him. Horror. Fury.

Before she had a chance to respond, he was gone.

Hannah understood. She did not even mind that Susie's weeping got louder.

"It is all right, Susie. Your *datt* just needs . . . a minute. He will be back." But Susie did not calm. Her screams escalated instead, as did Hannah's worry for her and her father. She wanted to go outside and look for Caleb, but Susie's wailing would only make him feel guiltier. He needed time to absorb what he had just learned.

His wife drowned but said goodbye first?

Lord, what must he be feeling?

Hannah rocked and held Susie tight while promising the child that she would see nothing but bunnies and kittens in her sleep, until her crying stopped and she slept. By then, an hour had passed and Hannah worried about Caleb. She placed Susie on her bed and left the bedroom door open, and then she went out to her small yard.

In the moonlight, she could see Caleb clearly – no coat or hat – about twenty yards distant, standing beside the fish pond, just staring at the water.

Could he imagine his wife floating lifelessly there?

Did he believe himself as responsible for the death of another, as Hannah believed herself responsible for so many? "It is not your fault," she said when she reached him, mostly because that is what other people told her, though she did not believe it, and neither would he. Still, she had to try.

"Where is Susie?" he asked.

"Asleep on my bed."

"What?" he shouted, turning on her. "She will be scared to death when she wakes."

"No, no, she will be fine. She already knows my room. Earlier she examined it from—"

He bumped her shoulder as he passed, unaware of her losing her balance and barely regaining it. "Caleb, come back. It will do you good to talk."

"My daughter needs me."

"You cannot hide behind her small skirts forever," Hannah said, regretting it instantly.

Caleb stopped but did not turn to look at her. "If that is what you think is going on here," he said, his words clipped, "then you would be no kind of mother."

He must have heard her gasp, because he turned to see her step back, as if he had struck her a physical blow. "Hannah, I did not mean—"

"You did mean." She took some satisfaction now in passing him by, going inside, and letting the door shut in his face.

No matter the wound, Hannah gathered Susie in her arms and held her close, taking comfort in her heartbeat, if only for a moment. When Caleb entered the room, she placed Susie in his arms. "You are right, she will be safer now. Even *your* mothering instincts must be better than mine."

Caleb set Susie back on the bed and covered her with the bright quilt.

In the hazy light from the kerosene lamp, the quilt's "sunshine" squares seemed sunnier somehow with Susie's beautiful head of cinnamon curls peeking from beneath them.

Caleb took her hand and tugged. "Come," he said, but she did not move. His touch felt so good, she knew it must be wrong.

"Hannah," he begged. "Forgive me. Please. I am so sorry."

Her legs began to move, finally, but all she could feel was the touch of his hand warming her. Despite his earlier display of temper, he stopped and placed her shawl around her shoulders.

On her small porch, she sat on the new swing Old Abe Hershberger had made for her.

The wind whistling up the valley sounded like a cautioning wail as Caleb sat beside her and took her hand in his. She looked into the void of the past and she saw . . . winter.

When the silence stretched, she turned to Caleb. "For Susie's sake, if not for your own," she said, "tell me what happened to her mother."

Six

"I do not know what happened to Naomi," Caleb said. "One day she was sick, the next she was dead."

Relief surged through Hannah. "Dead from her illness, then."

Caleb shook his head, leaned forward, elbows on knees, and covered his face with his hands. "I wish to God I knew what happened that night."

Despite his muffled voice, Hannah caught both prayer and irreverence in his words, and her icy heart began to thaw. "Tell me what you do know, from the beginning," she said. "Share your burden, lighten it. No one will treat it more gently than I."

Caleb sighed but remained silent and, when Hannah prepared to give up and check on Susie, he sat back and cleared his throat. For a few silent minutes, he ran his thumb over her blunt, broken fingernails, and Hannah wished she had not defied the laws of nature to dig in the winter earth. How prideful to care about jagged fingernails at such a time.

"Naomi had been unhappy for a long while," Caleb finally said. "Since before our marriage, worse after it, but worse still after Susie turned a year old, because there were no more babies. Not that I kept from—" He cleared his throat. "I mean, there should . . . could have been. I . . . loved her, you know?"

"I understand," Hannah said. "You did not keep from her."

He nodded. "Yes, no, I did not . . . keep from her."

"How sad your wife must have been, if she chose to leave a man who loved her so much he could tell a stranger so."

Caleb faced her. "Funny, I met you yesterday, but I do not think of you as a stranger."

She squeezed his hand. "*Danke*," she said. "Thank you."

"A year ago, we thought she was carrying, maybe six months gone, but she was in pain, and she grew too big too fast."

"Cancer," Hannah whispered and saw the surprise in his eyes, wishing the moon was not so bright, because she could also see the tears he tried to blink away. "My mother," she explained.

She read his sympathy. "Naomi died the night of the day we found out," he said. "My fault."

"No, that cannot be. She said goodbye to Susie. You did not know until just now in my kitchen. How could it be your fault? She did it herself."

He raised an angry hand to stop her from speaking the vile word. *Suicide*. The only explanation possible, and yet she knew he would not accept it, not even to free himself of blame. "I knew she was afraid after we saw the doctor. I knew. And still, after she slept – or so I thought – I went to the barn to check on a mare about to foal and I stayed to deliver her."

"Any responsible farmer would have done as much."

"A good farmer maybe, but a selfish man for certain. I wanted to think about anything but the fact that my wife was dying. I wanted to pretend life was normal, not filled with the dread of a slow and painful death. Naomi was young and beautiful. She should not have died that way. She should still be alive and—"

Wishing she had married another man, Caleb nearly said.

Was that why he had let Naomi down? Because the only thing she ever felt for him was disappointment because he was not someone else?

He looked full at Hannah then. "Someday Susie is going to figure out that her mother . . . that Naomi seems to have chosen . . ." He covered his face again and rubbed briskly, as if he could wash the truth away. "What will I tell her?"

"You could tell her that her mother's pain might have driven her beyond rational thought. That God forgives. He forgave you, Caleb, if absolution was your due, though I suspect it was not. Now you must forgive yourself."

With a hand to her face, Caleb turned Hannah so he could see her better. "I think I am not the only one who needs to forgive myself."

She must know that her blush spoke volumes, because she tried to pull away. So he would not read her? Or because she did not care for his touch? He wished he knew.

"Want to tell me about it?" he asked. "You know my worst secret." He used to think his biggest secret was the fact that he had married a woman who did not love him, who was forced by her father to marry him. But it was not so simple as that. He had been certain he would fill Naomi so full of love that she would not be able to help loving him in return. He paid dearly and daily for being that young and foolish.

Hannah shook her head and slipped from his grasp. "We should go in before Susie wakes."

"Someday, you will share your pain with me," Caleb said. "It does lessen it, as you said. *Danke*. You are a good neighbor."

"And a better cook than you, I hear."

As she intended, he chuckled. "Ach, that too." They rose together, but he stopped, caught by the bench. When he tried to free himself, something ripped loudly.

"I am sorry," Hannah said. "Abe doesn't do carpentry so well anymore. His eyes are going. What was it?"

"Are you as good at mending torn britches as you are at cooking?"

"I am. Are you still decently covered?"

"Near enough. Why did you want to know?"

She stopped, and Caleb accidently walked into her. To keep them balanced, he grasped her waist from behind. After a minute, during which he savored the feel of her beneath his palms, she opened the door, and his hands slipped away as she stepped inside.

"I asked because I thought you might want to wait outside while I got Susie," she said.

"Oh. Too bad."

Hannah shook her head but kept walking. "I darn socks too, big and little ones. I miss such chores. You would not have some for me, would you? It would be a great comfort, if you did."

Caleb caught her hand. "I am rich with socks to darn." He squeezed the hand and let go before they reached her room. "I will take my sometimes noisy little girl and go home now. See you at school tomorrow."

"Ya, see you," she said, tucking her quilt around Susie in his arms. "Do not forget your paints," she said following them.

Outside, Hannah smiled when Caleb charged his horse Indigo to "fly like the wind". As she watched his buggy disappear into the barn at the top of the rise, she could still feel his big strong hands warm at her waist. She pulled her shawl tight and sat on the hickory swing until Caleb emerged from the barn carrying Susie. He waved before going into his house.

For the first time in four years, Hannah almost wished she still lived there. What would it be like to sit with Caleb in harmony of an evening, or to step with him into a shared bedroom at the end of a day?

She did not think he would be sullen or turn on his side, away from her, in the bed. She already knew he did not eat in aching silence, ignoring her good food. Ignoring her.

"Foolishness," she said aloud. "What makes you think you would be a better wife to anyone than you were to Gideon?" There must have been a reason he was so unhappy, that his last words were a scold.

Caleb might complain less than Gideon, she thought, but he would likely be as miserable, if he were so foolish as to consider marrying her.

She turned to go inside, but before she did, she looked up the hill one last time.

Was that Caleb or a shadow in the window facing her way?

She noted the next morning that Caleb arrived with mischief in his eyes. "Turns out we have only one set of paints between us," he said. "Suze and I will have to share."

Hannah took his hat off his head, because it seemed natural to do so, then she blushed at the familiarity, as if she'd been doing it for ever.

Her ease in his presence could be dangerous to her peace.

It would all end soon, anyway, she told herself, as soon as Susie could stay at school without him. Then everything would go safely back to normal . . . but she would always hold these days dear.

Before Caleb went to his seat, he regarded her, seeming to ask if he should test Susie by trying to leave this morning. She shook her head imperceptibly and he nodded.

How had they done that, Hannah wondered, spoken without words? She did not remember having the ability with Gideon. But they agreed; Susie was to have an easy and quiet day. Them too.

When school ended, Caleb stopped beside her desk. "How would you feel about having supper at my place tonight? I think Susie could use another evening or two in your company and then she should be fine here. What do you say?"

"Fine," she said. "What were you thinking of cooking?"

Caleb looked taken aback, but then his eyes began almost to dance. "Bratwurst," he said. "And noodles."

They laughed like when the boys jumped him at recess, a squealing pig pile, just because he asked the girls to play corner ball with them.

"How about roast and slaw with cherry pie for dessert?" Hannah asked. "Can you cook that?"

Caleb paled.

Hannah rapped his knuckles with her ruler, lightly, just for fun. He yelped, loud.

She shook her head. "You are as bad as the little ones. I will do the cooking, and I will help you wash Susie's hair."

"I washed it last night."

"Ya, I can tell; you left too much soap in. That's why it is more like hay than hair this morning. Six o'clock," she said as another parent came in, a woman known to gossip, and plenty. Lord, it would be all over the district tomorrow that Caleb hung around the school.

Seven

"Teacher does it nice, Datt," Susie said, from a washtub in their new kitchen before a roaring fire. She pushed her father's big hard-scrubbing hands aside and pulled Hannah's gentle ones back to her hair. "And she doesn't get soap in my eyes."

Hannah raised a brow Caleb's way before she went back to tending his daughter. Then she bent and whispered something in Susie's ear.

Distracted by their conspiring giggles, Caleb did not expect his daughter's cupped hands to become a ladle for throwing water his way, until it was too late.

The shock of it made him jump back, and slip in the puddle on the floor. Grabbing Hannah for support, he toppled them both, him on his back, her on top of him.

Susie, in the washtub beside them, shrieked when he started falling, as did Hannah, but now they were all stunned silent. Noting the tears in Susie's eyes, he winked to reassure her. He grunted and removed Hannah's knee from between his legs, grateful nothing important got bruised, and then he lifted her face from his chest. "Teacher likes to play, I see."

He plotted retribution as he tried not to tumble headlong into the bottomless depths of her wide sky-blue eyes.

Hannah knelt beside him. "I—Oh, Caleb, I—" Her sobs came fast and from so deep inside. Then he was rocking and shushing her while juggling his slippery daughter in a towel as she joined Hannah in his arms. All three on the floor.

Together they tried to calm Hannah and, while she accepted hugs and kisses, even his, absolution she would not accept.

There on the kitchen floor in a cool puddle of soapy water, the confession of Hannah's "flighty" ways came tumbling out. "I laugh and play too much," she said. "I sing at all the wrong times. My behavior is unseemly, disgraceful."

Caleb's rage at Gideon Barkman grew. "Whoever convinced you of this had no more right to stifle you than a nightingale," Caleb declared. "Your joy in life is as God-given and beautiful as any creature's song."

"Not joy, frivolity, Caleb. I almost killed you with it. I did kill Gideon and Gracie."

"You most certainly did not!"

Hannah nodded, her eyes overflowing. "I distracted Gideon with my singing and when he turned to scold me, the horse slipped on the ice and he could not—" Sobbing, she returned to his embrace.

He might like having her in his embrace, if the reason were not so sad and regrettable. If it did not make him so angry. "Sounds like his temper did the damage," Caleb said, stroking her back, "but until you see it, no good will come of my saying so. I would drive better with you singing beside me," he said. "I could do anything better that way." And to prove it, Caleb sang as he rocked her in his arms, a song about forgiveness and love.

He liked having her there so much he sang it twice.

After a while, he gave her his *schnoopduff*, his handkerchief, and when she dried her eyes, they found his singing had put Susie to sleep.

"Did you hurt yourself?" Hannah asked him, seeming as loath to rise from his embrace as he was to have her leave, no matter their foolish spot on the floor.

"We nearly bruised my . . . dignity."

That incited a smile from her as they rose from the floor.

Susie got tucked in and never even woke for supper. She needed sleep more.

Alone together, the kitchen warm and cosy, dinner conversation flowed, pleasant and relaxing, until he asked the question uppermost on his mind. "Do you think you will marry again?"

Hannah rose to clear the dishes. "Why do you ask?"

"Because you are young and pretty."

She blushed. "Goodness. No one has ever said such a thing."

"That you are pretty? How could they not?"

She shrugged. "We are Amish. Looks do not count with us, or have you forgotten?"

"A man notices. It is in his nature to do so, no matter his upbringing. He sees what is on the outside before he decides whether to look at the inside."

"You are looking for another wife, then?"

Caleb groaned. "Frankly, I cannot bear to fail another."

"I feel the same," she said.

Did she mean that she did not want to fail again, either? If not, it might be better, he thought, if they stopped having supper together, better for both of them. On the other hand, if she did not care to remarry, he was safe with her.

"Ah," Hannah said, raising her chin. "Here he is, come to prove my lie." Then she hid her emotions. "The bishop will not allow me to remain single. I have two months of freedom left, and I intend to enjoy it."

"What happens after two months?"

She stepped out to the porch, and Caleb followed. "I marry Enos Miller. Bishop's orders. Down the road, he comes now. Enos, not the bishop."

A yellow buggy pulled into Dovecrest Farm, its driver using the horsewhip more than Caleb approved. "He's eighty if a day!"

Hannah shook her head. "Seventy-three."

Anger filled Caleb. "You love *him*?"

"Of course not. But I will not die inside when he dies, which must be soon. I could not bear the pain when I lost Grace and Anyah."

No mention of Gideon, Caleb noticed.

"Hannah!" Enos Miller called, as he tied the horse to the post. "You are not at your small house at such an hour, yet I find you here with this stranger!" And the louder he talked, the higher Hannah raised her shoulders and the lower she bent her head.

"Did the bishop choose Gideon for you?" Caleb whispered so Enos would not hear.

"Yes," Hannah whispered. Her submissive reaction looked natural, in an unnatural sort of way.

"Enos is Gideon all over again, is he not?"

She forgot to cower when she looked up at him, her surprise genuine.

"Notice that you do not shrink in *my* presence," he snapped. And his heart came to life with a vengeance, for the first time in years. "We will see who you marry in two months' time," he said, before he turned to go back in the house and shut the door behind him.

He had all but dismissed them both. Caleb was appalled, at himself, at Hannah, at all of it. Who was this harsh bishop?

The following day, a warmish spring-is-coming Saturday, Caleb played checkers on the country store porch while Susie slept in the buggy at the hitching post. There, Caleb learned that Hannah's farm money went to pay the largest of Gideon Barkman's debts. He learned also that Enos Miller was some big mad, because he'd expected Hannah to bring the proceeds of Dovecrest Farm to their marriage.

Instead, she would carry a bouquet of small Barkman debts.

Caleb quit the checker game when he saw Hannah heading toward the store. He met her, apologized for his anger the night before and offered to carry her packages.

His public attention flustered her but she did not cower.

"Hannah, what kind of bulbs did you plant that first day?" he asked as they walked.

"Jonquils, for forgiveness," she said. "They are like tiny daffodils. But they will not flower. They never do."

He regarded her quizzically. "Forgiveness?"

"I could not bear to work the farm after I lost them," she whispered, looking earnestly up at him. "I am not even a good *widow*."

In the wake of the indiscreet revelation, Hannah raised her chin, reclaiming her dignity and giving him a glimpse of her stubbornness, which he liked. He appreciated her honest emotions with him.

Unfortunately, she firmly believed in her uselessness as a wife – because her husband had told her so.

Yes, those checker players, those old men with the wise-looking pipes, and white beards, had had much to say. In fact, they'd taken great pleasure in bringing him up to date on the business of his neighbors.

There are many sins the Amish avoid. Gossip is not one of them. It is, in fact, their greatest entertainment.

Normally, he would not listen to it, but this was Hannah Peachy, and whether either of them wanted the connection or not, she had worked her way to a place very near his heart.

Eight

The next morning at school, after another bit of silent conversation, he and Hannah agreed that Caleb would try to leave.

He kissed Susie's little nose. "This is it, Susiekins. I am going to buy a plow for the farm today while you stay in school and learn many new things. Before long you will read to me of an evening."

A tear slid down his daughter's china cheek, but she did not make a fuss. Caleb's throat tightened as he closed the schoolhouse door behind him. After he climbed into his buggy and took up the reins, he stayed there, watching, waiting for the moment he would be called upon to rescue her – foolish him – until Hannah came to the window.

She looked both sorry and reassuring, but she made a shooing motion to tell him to go away and leave everything to her; Susie would be fine. His heart expanded as he got Sparky moving, lazy horse, and made his way toward Mt Hope and the day's farm equipment auction. Afterward, he would go to Sugarcreek to check on the track-laying, then to the brick factory so he could build a smokehouse.

In Sugarcreek, he met Old Abe Hershberger, whose wife, Ida, asked him to supper. She was friendly and honestly seemed to want his company, so he said he would be there. One of the older schoolgirls, who Susie liked, had offered to sit with Susie if he ever needed her, and he would accept her offer.

Ida's invitation reminded him of the Pennsylvania matchmakers, but he was so new, this couldn't be the same thing.

No matter how many errands he had to run, Caleb couldn't

wait to get back to Dove Hollow to see how Susie had managed. He supposed he should be glad they were not all eating together again tonight. It would be best if they did not become so easy that Susie would come to expect it, as if they were a family, only to have Hannah leave them for Enos. The thought rankled him, though it was probably best.

His daughter did not need to be kicked by life again and *he* did not need to fail anyone else.

Every morning for the next two weeks, Susie went quietly, if listlessly, into school alone. By the third day, Hannah stopped coming to the window to wave him off. That day, he waited outside to collect Susie. Everything back to normal. *Goot.* He did not like surprises.

Yes, he missed adult conversation. Yes, Susie missed Hannah's attention, especially hair washing, but they were fine, the two of them. They did not need a woman to change things, not even Hannah.

Hannah – he should not think of her in so intimate a way. She should not be the first person he thought about upon opening his eyes, nor the last when he pulled her dratted quilt up to his chin and closed them. He should not be dreaming of her.

He should put her quilt away and never think of her sharing it with Gideon. He especially hated imagining her sharing a quilt with Enos. He did not want to think of her *at all*, except that he did nothing but since he stopped seeing her.

Hannah missed Caleb. And though she saw Susie every day, she missed mothering her and fixing her hair. She wanted to teach her to stitch a sampler and bake cookies.

She needed to stop yearning for what she could not have.

More than a month had gone by, and Caleb, she imagined, had forgotten about her as she would forget him in time. It was best.

She went to the Hershbergers for dinner that night because she missed adult company. With her promised to Enos, there would be no danger of matchmaking.

As in most Amish parlors, an assortment of rockers with footstools circled the room for *goot* talk. In a glass-fronted china cabinet made by Abe Hershberger, Ida displayed her beautiful but useful dishes and serving pieces, likely wedding gifts purchased at local glass factories.

But the focus of Hannah's attention was the man who rose from the far rocker. "Caleb. Good evening." They were trying to match her with Caleb? Why? "Where is Enos?" she asked, and Caleb scowled. He was disappointed to see her paired with him, then?

"I apologize, Miss Peachy, for being a disappointment," Caleb said, claiming her emotion. Why did he think she would be disappointed?

During dinner, she fidgeted beneath his discomfort, and her own. Abe and Ida Hershberger were the most uncomfortable.

Their silence called for an early evening. Abe offered to hitch up his buggy and take Hannah home.

"Nonsense," Caleb said. "I am going to the same place, or as near to as makes no difference. I will take Hannah. Thank you for dinner."

"Yes, thank you," Hannah said. The minute they drove away, she lit into him. "You did not even ask if I wanted a ride home?"

"You would rather walk? I could let you out?"

"Do not be smart with me."

"You would rather I be stupid?"

"Ca-leb!" She stretched out his name in exasperation.

"Han-nah!"

They looked at each other and tried not to laugh.

"Hannah, I apologize. I wanted out of there. Fast. That was awful."

"I am sorry if having dinner with me was so difficult," Hannah said. "I do not know why I should be surprised. Gideon used to feel the same."

"What are you saying?" He slowed the horses. "You are wonderful company."

"Then why were you so miserable?" she asked.

"Because you wished I was Enos."

"I am promised to Enos. Seeing you confused me."

"No," Caleb said. "I saw how much you disliked being paired with me."

"Caleb, I love having dinner with you and Susie. Though I like it better without the Hershbergers. I was relieved Enos was not there, believe me, but I was embarrassed to put you in that position."

Caleb slowed the buggy. "You know, Hannah, it strikes me that there might be a way to stop this nonsense."

"What particular nonsense?"

"Matchmaking *and* your marriage to Enos."

She tilted her head, one *kapp* string curling around a breast. "How?"

"Marry me."

Nine

"Marry you?"

Caleb forged on while Hannah's laughter charmed and worried him.

"Stay at Dovecrest Farm and wait for spring. We can watch the jonquils bloom together – you, me and Susie. Work beside me through every season of our lives. Being apart from you for so long was torture."

"The jonquils never come up, Caleb. And spring is always such a disappointment. I had rather not wait for it, if you do not mind."

"I do mind. You do not give a seed pod for Enos."

Hannah nodded her agreement. "Exactly why I *can* marry him. Losing him will not break me."

"Suppose you marry Enos and, the week after that, I am killed in a buggy accident?"

Hannah slapped his arm. "Do not say such things even in passing."

"Would you mourn my loss?"

"I would . . . die a little more inside, like I did when Anyah and Grace died."

"What will your Enos think about you mourning another man?"

"Caleb!"

"Could you pretend you did not care?"

"No, of course not. That is foolishness, Caleb."

"You think so? Think on this, then, Hannah Peachy. If I did die, I would want you, and no one else, to raise my Susie. I have no family, and she loves you already. It must be you. What would Enos say to that? To the expense of another mouth to feed? What would he think about you giving my daughter the love you could not give him?"

Hannah held a hand to her heart. "Susie? If something happens to you, you want me to be Susie's mother, to teach her what all little Amish girls should know?"

"Never mind if something happens to me. I want you to be her mother, period. I want you as my wife. I have been smitten since— No, let me go further back than that. I believe Anyah chose me for you to marry."

Hannah scooted back from him, whether to see him better or to get away, he could not tell. Then she tugged the lap rug off him to wrap around herself. "That Anyah brought us together is a cruel thing to say."

He stopped the buggy in the middle of the snow-capped field they cut through. "Almost from the moment I left Pennsylvania," he said, "a joyful young girl, filled with life, skipped in front of my buggy. She led me here, Hannah. And, when we arrived, she twirled in your driveway as if she had come home."

Hannah covered her mouth with a hand, her eyes filling. "Our Anyah, she liked always to twirl, Caleb. Made the bishop plenty mad." She wiped her eyes, though her tears continued.

Caleb took her in his arms and kissed her wet cheeks. "Cry, Hannah. Give in to the tears you have bottled up. Two years worth, maybe more." He soothed her, wiped her eyes and gave her his handkerchief. "She is a treasure, your Anyah, and she loves your baby girl."

Hannah buried her face against his chest and slipped both her arms around his waist.

Taking that as a sort of permission, he spread a hand against her bodice, beneath her breasts, claiming her, to his mind.

"Anyah wanted for us to leave Gideon," Hannah whispered. "She wanted to make a new start in Pennsylvania. Spinster sisters, she called us. And then Gracie was coming, and we never went."

"If Anyah had not died, would you have left Gideon?"

"I am a coward when it comes to escaping, especially for my own sake," Hannah confessed. "But I would have done it for Anyah."

"Then do it for me and Susie. Escape *to* me. Let me help you."

Hannah sighed, fear filling her expression.

"Anyah got her escape," Caleb whispered against her ear.

"She is happy, Hannah. She would see you happy, too. She has the ways you call 'flighty' but I love that in you. Yes, you laugh and play, but not too much," he said. "I have heard your laugh, and I cannot imagine a wrong time for you to be happy, unless of course if you broke into laughter while I tried to love you."

Hannah shoved his arm, but she chuckled. "My behavior can be disgraceful. I would embarrass you." She tried to remain serious.

"Please be disgraceful and flighty with me," he begged. "Sing with Susie. Laugh and play with her, with both of us. Bring us back to life, Hannah. Only you can." He nuzzled her neck, her ear. "And if you sing while we make love, I will only want you more."

Hannah folded her hands in her lap, her cheeks pink. Caleb thought that maybe she prayed for guidance, or sanity. He decided to pray as well, for a "yes".

"I could do this for Susie," she whispered after a minute, "but not for myself."

"Could you not do it for me?"

"No man has ever wanted me before."

"Not even your father?"

"Especially not him."

"You should know that I can already buy farms for our children, as is the Amish way, even if we have a dozen. I also have the means to pay off Gideon's debts, and never will it come between us," Caleb said.

Her head came up fast. "You want more children?"

"*Half* a dozen?" he asked, amending his request so as not to scare her off.

"How about a baker's dozen?" she countered.

"Thirteen it is." He jumped from the buggy and lifted her down, took her in his arms and twirled her, shouting his joy.

"Caleb, Caleb, this is—"

"Fun?"

"Flighty."

"Then let us be flighty together, shall we?" he asked, but as if censure could not wait, a carriage approached.

"The bishop!" Hannah whispered pushing him hard away from her.

"The same bishop who wants you to marry Enos?"

"Yes. He is stubborn. He will not approve of us."

"Leave it to me." Caleb stepped forward, claimed her and squeezed her waist. "Promise?"

Hannah gave a quick nod and trembled beneath his hand as they turned to face the buggy pulling up beside them, its wheels cutting through the frozen field with crushing reproach.

"Vat's iss?" The bishop asked. Anyah, the ghost, sitting on the wagon seat beside him. Had Hannah's twin led the bishop here?

"A celebration," Caleb said.

"Bishop," Hannah said, "this is Caleb Skylar, a new member of our community."

"I have just asked Hannah to marry me," Caleb confessed.

"Is this true, daughter?" the bishop thundered.

Caleb wished he knew about their family connection. Strong measures would be called for to make a father go back on his choice of son-in-law.

"Yes, it is true." Hannah shrank deeper into herself, and Caleb wanted to tell her to stand straight, but then he would be no better than every man who'd bruised her with such orders.

The bishop grumped. "She is *promised* to Enos Miller."

Caleb cleared his throat. "I think Enos will not like his bride to give birth to my child eight months after his wedding."

Anyah clapped in delight. Hannah squeaked and gave a whole body shudder.

Caleb slipped off his broadfall jacket and put it over Hannah's caped shoulders. She was not the kind of girl would stand in a frosty field lying.

At the intimacy, the bishop stood, towering over them from his buggy. "Hannah?" The single word held a threat. "Is this true?"

Anyah stood beside her father, somewhat aglow of a sudden, and Hannah gasped. She could see the spirit of her twin now, Caleb thought, because Anyah signaled with several enthusiastic nods that Hannah should say yes.

Hannah squeezed his hand. "Yes," she whispered and raised her chin. "Yes, Father. I carry his child."

"We must be wed *this* church Sunday," Caleb said.

The bishop grunted and urged his horses forward. "Tomorrow is church Sunday. Be ready."

Ready? Ready for what? Caleb wondered. It had been his experience that a lie never had the desired effect.

Hannah wilted against him as her father's buggy disappeared, and he could feel her trembling. "I lied to my father." Her guilt changed to joy. "I saw Anyah, Caleb, and she does look happy."

"Only because you will be when you marry me."

"You will not blame yourself, please, when I get sad. I do not know how to be happy."

"Oh, you do, it is in you. Be yourself. Susie and I want the real you."

When she opened her mouth to argue, he opened his over it with a hungry kiss. That fast, passion rose between them, cocooned in the dark of night, the stars winking down in approval. He learned her with his hands and, more important, she dared to learn him. A happy surprise, her eagerness.

"I want to take you to my bed, now, tonight," he whispered against her lips. "Does that frighten you, *liebchen*?"

Hannah toyed with the broadfall flap of his pants, at his waist, bold girl. "What frightens me," she said, "is that I want to let you."

Ten

Were they really going to do this? As Caleb helped her into the buggy the next morning, Hannah marveled at the possibility of a union inspired by a lie. Where her anticipation came from, she did not know. She settled falsely prim between Caleb and Susie and smoothed her skirts. She should worry about a marriage begun in such a way.

Along the way, Hannah dared clutch Caleb's arm. She liked his wink, the light in his big brown eyes. "A wedding, Caleb. Ida will think she worked a miracle last night."

"She will tell the world how she did it."

"May I teach Susie to bake and stitch? I so missed having a little girl of my own." She took Susie onto her lap so she could sleep more comfortably in her arms.

"Soon, she will belong to both of us," Caleb said. "You may claim her any time you want, especially when she screams."

When the three of them walked into Andy Byler's barn for

service that morning, everybody stopped talking, and soon enough Zeb Shotz, the new preacher came in, the signal for everyone to sit.

As was the custom, the men sat on one side, facing the women on the opposite, with babes in arms and children at their feet. On the rough-hewn barn wall, men's hats hung on nails in a crazy quilt pattern.

For the first time, Hannah did not feel her lack of children as a failure. Susie had come in with a hand in Caleb's and one in hers, to everyone's interest. Then the shy child looked from the men to the women, and reached for her skirt. That small gesture brought such a rush of joy.

Hannah felt . . . prideful, for perhaps the first time in her life, but sin reaped its own harvest. Her father's arrival put period to pride.

An hour into the service, her father excused Preacher Shotz and stood before them. A confession he called for – from her and Caleb, of course. All bishop, no father.

Everyone hushed.

"Hannah Barkman," he said, with no claim for her as his daughter. "Will you confess your sin before these your brothers and sisters?"

Caleb shot to his feet to argue, but he caught her warning glance. His look said he was there for her, that he *cared* for her.

Imagine, being brought to her knees before the district, and feeling cherished, which she did not deserve. Utter foolishness, and yet, she could do this.

She knelt before her father, her stern bishop, praying Susie would sleep throughout.

Their high holy leader rocked on his heels, until shame rolled off her in waves. "Do you, Hannah Barkman, confess to sinning with the newcomer, Caleb Skylar, and to conceiving his child?" Had her father's voice ever been louder?

The newcomer, who had been there three months, already.

"I do confess it," she said, voice soft, a lie to save Susie, in the event something happened to Caleb. And yes, a lie to save herself, as well. And what did that make her?

She glanced at Caleb and his answer came to mind. *Human*, it made her. A forgivable sin, humanity.

While the crowd murmured in whispers, her father combed

his beard with his fingers. Disgust she saw in his eyes, and something else. Speculation? Suppose, as her punishment, he did not make her marry Caleb?

Now she prayed, she prayed hard. For her punishment, she asked for Caleb, a man she did not really know – except that she did, she believed.

Did she? Some men changed the minute you married them. She knew.

"For your punishment, you will go from among us and . . ." His words hung in the air. Shunned? Was she shunned? No, oh no! "Sin no more," her cruel father added, finally finishing his sentence. Maybe. Not shunned then?

"And . . ." her father intoned, so loud, the birds in the rafters took to fast and noisy flight. And this bishop, with no compassion for his daughter, let the threat sit so long, spots danced before her eyes.

"No marriage celebration. No corner table for you," he said.

Torture, he doled out, and torture she took, though this was the worst. "Your sin will not be spoken of again," the bishop said. "Go back to your seat."

Hannah did not know – was her punishment not to marry Caleb? To bear her child – hah, what child? – in shame?

She rose and went back to her bench, saw understanding on some faces, condemnation in others.

"Caleb Skylar, kneel before me."

He obeyed but humility did not suit him. His tight fists and stiff shoulders came hard. But he echoed her.

"Are you sorry for this sin?" her father asked him.

"Not sorry to love Hannah," Caleb said.

Ach, another lie, Hannah thought.

"Not sorry to have another babe," Caleb added. "Sorry if I displeased the Lord in this."

"You did. Your punishment Caleb Skylar will bring His forgiveness. Stand please. Hannah Barkman, you will stand beside him. Abe and Ida Hershberger, you will stand witness."

Hannah's head came up, the blood drained from her face. A wedding after all? Was she to be rewarded for her lie, then? She obeyed, breathed deeply when she stood beside Caleb, let her heart slow to steady. Then she nearly smiled when Anyah appeared beside her, the witness she would have chosen, pushing Ida back a step, though Ida seemed confused as to how she stumbled.

A gift for punishment – little did her bishop know. She did not need pretty glass dishes and a day of singing. She did not need to sit at the *Eck*, the corner table, where all brides and bridegrooms sat for a day of celebration.

She wanted only Caleb and Susie and their life on Dovecrest Farm to erase the memories of her previous life there. And after her lie of a confession, she wanted more than ever for the jonquils of forgiveness to bloom next spring.

After the bishop pronounced them man and wife, Caleb wanted out.

He went to collect Susie, still sleeping on the bench in the women's section. Then, he took his bride's arm, and they left service early.

Hannah liked to feed the gossips, Caleb remembered, and he found he enjoyed it as well.

He wanted to tell Hannah to raise her head as they left, but all he had to do was look at her, and she did raise it, her eyes sparkling.

Her father followed them. Caleb did not speak to the high holy man until he put Hannah and Susie in the buggy and hitched the horses. Then he let the bishop draw him aside.

"I am a zebra who cannot change my stripes," the bishop said. "It is either black or white for me . . . most days, but I know my girl. You will make truth of that lie you two just told, or I will know the reason why."

Ach, and this father-in-law of his was human after all. Caleb did not dare smile. Besides, he heard talk that Enos was trying to make the bishop pay Gideon's debts, or he would refuse to marry Hannah. So, his father-in-law was not only stern but cheap.

Caleb did not care; he got Hannah, though she might have preferred her freedom to marrying him. No, that did not wash; her father would never let her have her freedom. He, Caleb, was the lesser of evils. Good enough.

"Daughter," the bishop said with a nod as Caleb drove the buggy from the yard.

"Father," she replied with the same lack of affection, and Caleb wanted to whoop he was so proud of her.

They rode in silence for some time, her staring ahead, chewing her lip with nervous energy. She finally turned his way. "How do you feel about wedding nights?" she asked.

Caleb bit his own lip to tamp down his enthusiasm. "You may as well ask how I feel about breathing, Hannah. I was drawn to you from the first. I am *for* wedding nights, and *every* night, come to that, if you get my meaning?"

Hannah's face grew pink. She got it.

"About the wedding night . . ."

"Yes?" he asked. Here it came. She would now tell him that their marriage would be in name only. Caleb closed his eyes to await the horrific verdict.

"I hate the lie, so I would like—" She cleared her throat. "I would like for the lie not to be."

"Behold your confused bridegroom."

His bride huffed. "I want to make it true, what we told my *datt*, what we confessed. I have to get with child and fast, starting tonight."

He stopped the buggy, carried Susie to the back and covered her warm with blankets. Then he climbed to the seat and looked into his bride's eyes. "Starting now," he promised, then he opened his mouth over hers, showing his willingness, his hunger for her, and she did not stiffen or pull away.

His Hannah – yes, *his* now, and after tonight, his in every way possible – sat closer, her body moving in rhythm with his kiss. Mutual hunger, happy need; a mating of minds and bodies. Caleb pulled away first, caught his breath. "I am not sure I can wait for tonight."

"Yah, I can tell. But a man's body is not under his control, is it? How do you feel in your mind? In your heart? Willing? Or grumbly unwilling?"

"I feel, Hannah mine, as if I have just been given the greatest gift of all."

"But love is the greatest— What are you saying? I do not understand your jest, Caleb."

"Well, let me be clear. Loving you *will* be a burden—"

The color left her face.

"No, no! Another jest, *liebchen*. I thought you would know by my kisses." He slipped his hands up her body, cupped her breasts and tested their weight. "I am very willing. *Eager*. As a matter of fact, we should wake Susie and keep her very busy today, get her so tired she cries for sleep. Yes?"

Hannah's eyes brightened. "You do not *seem* as though you would turn from me," she said, almost to herself. "It will not be a burden for you to get me with child?"

"A burden? You are quoting Gideon again. I, your husband, want you something wonderful, every night. With or without the task of begetting. While you are big with our children, I will want you. I fear, in time, that you will run from me, Hannah Skylar."

"I could not run, because I will want you to catch me, Caleb Skylar."

Eleven

Caleb tweaked Hannah's rosy cheeks after what she admitted. "Pink cheeks mean a big temper or an embarrassed bride," he said.

"Pink cheeks mean a nip in the air."

"Nip, nip. Nip, nip, nip," Susie said, from behind them, making a pinch-bug with her thumb and forefinger, nipping at Hannah's cheeks, then Caleb's.

Hannah nipped Susie back, making her grin. Then his bride made to nip at him, but he anticipated her and caught her fingers in his teeth.

Hannah shrieked and tried to pull back, but Caleb acted like a pup who would not relinquish his bone.

Susie laughed, a rolling sound from somewhere deep in her belly, a sound of pure joy that Caleb had not heard from her for a long, long time.

He placed his hand on either side of Susie's face and kissed her nose. "*Ich liebe dich*," he said. "I love you." Then he did the same with Hannah, kissing her nose and looking deep into her eyes, sensing that she was not ready to hear that he loved her, too. "The both of you make me very happy," he said, and then he started the buggy again.

He peeked at his bride. "You do not believe you are lovable, do you? Every time I compliment you, you color up, as if you could not possibly believe me, or you are sorry I am such a liar."

Hannah shrugged.

At Dovecrest Farm, he carried Hannah inside to Susie's delight. When he set her down, he said, "I like you, Hannah Skylar." Then he took her into his arms and kissed her. "You are good and kind and loving." He kissed her again. "I . . . *more than* . . . like you, but I am afraid just now to say so."

Her eyes widened.

"What? You do not like my kisses?" he asked.

She tilted her head, considering. "I . . . *more than* . . . like them."

Caleb ran an impatient hand through his hair. "How do we make Susie tired enough to sleep deep tonight?" he whispered.

Hannah's eyes brightened with a new twinkle. "I will teach her first to bake cookies, change the beds, clean the kitchen. Then she can help make our wedding supper, all the trimmings, like Christmas. She will learn to help clean up after, too."

She took his shoulders, which Caleb liked, and turned him toward the door. "Go. Work our farm. Your presence is requested at 5.30, not before." She laughed without reason.

Caleb turned back to her. "What is so funny?"

"I made a good Amish deal. I sold you this farm for two hundred dollars and now I have it back. Shrewd, I am."

For that, he kissed her again, and left the house thinking night would never come.

Hannah worked beside Susie and worried. She feared that just punishment for lying about bearing a child would be that she could never bear a child again.

Other than that, she enjoyed working and laughing with Susie's lessons, and looking out the window to see Caleb working the farm. It seemed so real, as if she deserved it.

During dinner, she could barely look at Caleb without a shiver of expectation. When their fingers touched, even to pass a dish, pinpricks ran from that touch to all parts of her body. Her breasts became achy and tender, her woman's center, ready, like never in her life.

Embarrassed, she was, and aching for her husband.

Caleb would be appalled if he knew.

Twelve

Welcome to my wedding night, Caleb thought.

Hannah lay in their bed, arms at her sides, stiff as butchered beef. But her nightgown told a different story. It revealed swollen, ready breasts, budding nipples aching for his touch.

God, let her want him as much as he wanted her.

Seeing her concern – the way she bit at that lip – he crawled beneath the quilt in his nightshirt, and placed his arms around her. He would gentle her like a skittish colt, and pray he could last.

Already, he could not seem to get enough air. Or enough Hannah.

The flare of her hips beckoned, so he tested them with the palms of his hands. As he did, the air in the room thinned, and he became less patient, more ready. "Hannah," he whispered, a plea for her to join the exploration.

She rubbed her face against his, her parted lips at his ear, breathing warmth there and everywhere. She combed her fingers through his beard and, God help him, he found even that arousing.

"Having you whisker my skin feels nice, Caleb."

"Susie hates getting whiskered."

"A woman will change her mind with a man as gentle and kind as you."

"Love, it is called, Hannah."

She hid her face against him, her body trembling, her tears soon forming a trail down his neck, branding him.

He waited patiently, his body cooling, praise be, and eventually Hannah looked up at him. He kissed her tears and wiped them away with his fingertips.

She sighed. "We tried . . . sometimes . . . for children," she confided, "but he never looked at me, or held me. I have never been kissed, but for you. 'Too flighty', not a proper Amish wife."

"Then he never made love to you? You have a treat in store, if I do say, and I am humbled – no *proud*, blast it – to be your first."

Caleb stood and offered his hand. "Come to the bed in the *daudyhaus*; tomorrow we will switch them. I want no past memories in our bed, just us, Hannah. I say goodbye to Naomi at this moment. Say your goodbyes."

"I did that a long time ago, Caleb."

"To the man, maybe, not the scars. Them, you will send to perdition. You are *my* wife. Grab the quilt, though, because I want to do the things I dreamed of doing to you beneath it."

"This is a new quilt," she said taking it. "I washed the old one and gave it to the needy."

"It is not your original wedding quilt?"

"Susie sleeps beneath that. It never deserved to be put on my former marriage bed."

Caleb lifted her in his arms, carried her to the addition used for ageing in-laws, and lay her on the bed. He donned the quilt like a cape, and lowered himself over her, pulling the quilt over them both.

"You are mine, Hannah, and flighty is my favorite way for us to be."

"I don't need false compliments, Caleb."

"I never lie, er, except to marry the woman I love."

Hannah bit her lip. "I should not smile at a lie."

"We will make it true, starting now, yes?"

"Yes, please."

"Then, it's off with the nightclothes for us." He rose to straddle her and remove her hands from the tie at her neck. "Let me."

She rose on her elbows. "You will let me remove your nightshirt?"

His body rose to attention. "I thought you would never ask."

He could barely keep up with his bride's eagerness. "Your breasts, Hannah, they are so beautiful, rosy, tight, and standing as if calling to my hands." He demonstrated how that would work.

She raised her chin, her whole body, so his sex touched her center, and closed her eyes in ecstasy. If she were half as ready as him, nothing they did tonight would take long, not the first few times, anyway. "I want your breasts against my bare chest," he said, and that quickly – skin against skin – they were, her breasts crushed gloriously against him, her bare foot stroking his bare legs.

He kissed his way to her nipples, while she held her breath. When he closed his mouth around one, she gasped and let her hands learn him, everywhere.

She shocked him when she took his length in her hand, and he knew that not only did he have the bride God intended for him, but a lifemate, the kind every man dreams of, but rarely gets.

"I never knew," she whispered against his ear. "You do wonderful good things to me, Caleb. Outside and deep in. Maybe I should not talk of such things."

"With me, your husband who loves you, sweet Hannah, you will speak of these things. In our marriage bed, we will be wonderful good, naked and frisky as spring lambs. Flighty and full of life, we can talk and laugh, close as honeybees in spring. No words barred. Everything said. Even of the most intimate things – like the growing length of my rod in your hand, and the warm, wet center of you – we will speak. Because such is good between a husband and wife, yes?"

She hid her face for a warm blushing minute, then she moved her body so as to accommodate his length at her center.

Caleb pulled her into his arms, opening his mouth over hers like a man starved. This kissing with the mouth open was new to her, but Hannah followed Caleb's lead to learn what he liked.

And learn she did.

She learned his hard muscle against her eager lips caused them both shuddering pleasure. She learned to make him shout with need, while he begged her to stop, and go, and more, and, "Again, Hannah. Do it again!"

She learned to feel more than she thought she could, and that he would let her rest and make her ready again.

She acquired a taste for his flesh against her tongue.

Caleb groaned. "I do not know for certain who gentled who this night."

"Either way," she admitted, "we both win."

Her husband laughed. A blessed beginning to their life together.

Closing her eyes, Hannah savored every touch. With hands and heart and body, she memorized Caleb. Here, his sun-rough face, his wire-soft beard, a warm mouth that knew how to smile and laugh, cool lips, all pleasure-pulling and dear.

She stroked his neck and downward, and he shuddered as she parted chest hairs and budded a hidden nipple.

He whispered love words while she made her downward descent, one hand testing, stroking, pleasuring. At the same time, she held his manhood, moved it to his bidding, tried a few moves of her own. Hard inside; soft silk outside. She learned sinew and bone, and hard throbbing man. She found in Caleb a shelter from storms, a mate made of flesh and caring, eager and ready.

Her husband. Hers, to cherish. To . . . love. Did she dare?

He took a breast in his mouth, suckled her, as he found her center, and unfolded her like petals coming to flower. Soft. Wet. Ready. She should be embarrassed but she was not. He brought her to life, burst pleasure inside her. Waves and waves of it.

Thunder roared. Hot. Loud. In her head. In her heart. Instead of hiding, she looked straight at him, and saw the fire in his eyes. The caring. Hunger too. A manly hunger that would be sated. "I am as hungry for you," she admitted.

He groaned. "I planned to love you slowly and tenderly," he said. "Your body is ready, but if you are not, for whatever reason, you will stop me, please, and be frank, brutally frank, loud even, because I am losing myself in you, I do not quibble to admit."

She raised her arms in welcome and sighed in utter, unapologetic contentment as her bridegroom slid finally inside her. No pain, she felt, no bruising, no worry, no need to pretend indifference.

Pleasure bright and alive she welcomed. A wonder of pressure, like a volcano, built inside her, though she fought the eruption.

"*Ich liebe dich*," Caleb said against her lips. "I love you. Let it happen. Let yourself go. Feel the pleasure. It will come again and again if you let it. Give me the gift of your release. I will give you mine."

He was, indeed, loving her, Hannah thought. Sweet, heart-whole lovemaking, this was. The way it was meant to be.

God help her, she loved this new husband of hers, the way he loved her, though she dare not tell him so. Not yet.

With each thrust, each riotous stroke and bliss-making kiss, and with each vow to cherish, Caleb loved her and, in doing so, he brought her higher than the moon, in a place brighter than the sun.

Heaven on earth, with nothing to mourn and everything to celebrate.

Afterward, he lowered himself to her side and pulled her against him. No moment had ever seemed so ordained.

Thirteen

Nine months later, a veneer of snow blanketing the earth, his love made true the lie they told her father.

With Anyah at her side, and Ida Hershberger to help, Hannah gave birth to not one baby, but two – twins, like her and Anyah, with one difference. Boys, the both of them, squeaking, and squirming, and looking around like they'd been waiting for ever to see all this.

"They are so loved," Caleb said, kissing Hannah's lips, stroking her hair, "I ache with it. With love for Susie, and for them, and especially for their mother."

"Shush, not in front of Ida."

"And in front of your *datt*. Turn your head."

Hannah squeaked at her father bending toward her. For what, she wondered. But she knew soon enough. He kissed each baby boy on the head.

Yes, well – *boys*. He would.

Then he did something wonderful rare. He kissed her brow, too. "Thank you," he said. "For my grandbabies."

Hannah had lost her voice, but her tears stayed at the ready.

Caleb gave one baby to Ida and one to their *grossdaudy*, then he wrapped Hannah in the quilt and lifted her into his arms.

"Caleb, where are you taking me?"

"I have a surprise for you."

"What? Outside, already? It is winter, still."

"Spring. I watched you planting bulbs a year ago today."

He kicked open the kitchen door and took her to the porch. "Look, across the way, at the *grabhoff*."

Life had not only been stirring inside Hannah, but forgiveness as well. "I think every bulb you ever planted grew a hundred blossoms."

"Jonquils, Caleb? They are everywhere. In patches of snow, even."

"As far as the eye can see. The neighbors have been driving by since you went into labor, just to see the blossoms. Never so many jonquils has anyone seen in one place, and so early in the season."

"Oh," Hannah said, her eyes bright.

Anyah appeared at the base of the steps then, with that glow she got when she wanted Hannah to see her. This time, she carried baby Grace, raising the babe to show Hannah. Gracie wiggled as if with a wave goodbye.

"Oh," his wife said again. Not too good with words today.

With a nod, Anyah Peachy, sister, best friend, aunt, smiled and skipped down the road to disappear into the mist.

"We will never stop loving them," Caleb said.

Hannah cupped his face. "*Ich liebe dich*," she said, actually telling him for the first time. "I love you, Caleb."

"It's about time."

"You knew," she said.

"Aye, I did. You show me your love all the time. Still, it's nice to hear the words."

She winced. "Maybe I learned the silence from my father. Sorry. I guess we are both growing, though."

"Praise be."

"He likes the babies, Caleb. You know, if we have them two at a time, we might get that baker's dozen. We've already got Susie."

Laughter overtook him. *The kind of wife every man wants but hardly ever gets.*

He thought of Anyah.

Danke. Thank you.

The Heart Thief

Cindy Miles

One

North Eastern Scotland, on the North Sea, near Cruden Bay – late August

"Right. Lubbly jubbly! All you lambs and woolies – here's your home for the next two nights," Miley, the tour guide, a sandy-haired girl from Australia, said joyfully. "Gather your bags and rucksacks from the overhead, your suitcases from the back of the coach and meet me in the lobby. Chip-chop! Supper's in an hour and I'm famished!"

Dari St James stood but was immediately pushed back down as the horde of passengers of Wilde Ride Coach Tours scrambled to exit. With a sigh she sat and waited as everyone else rushed to get out of the coach. She literally lacked the energy to fight anymore, and the last thing she wanted to do was waste what little energy she did have shoving and shouldering her way to the coach's front door.

She mentally cursed her sister and best friend for convincing her to go on a chartered tour of "Magical Scotland". Alone. And with a group of eighteen- to thirty-year-olds. Most of them being closer to eighteen.

Dari being closer to thirty.

And, to the horror of her sister and best friend, still single.

Needless to say she was, hands down, the matronly portion of the group, and the others sort of stuck together. Dari didn't care. She'd agreed to go on the tour for the sole purpose of acquiring spectacular material and photos of Scotland for the company. With her sister Becca, and best friend, Samantha, they together ran Dream Vacations Travel Outfit out of Charleston, SC, and Dari had taken some fantastic photographs of Scotland so far for their in-house travel magazine. Even if she did have to suffer being the old lady outcast of a party-hardy tour group. Bah humbug.

"Er, you're coming along then, right?"

Dari glanced up at the only person left in the aisle and on the tour who seemed to notice or care she existed: Malphus MacPhee. At twenty-two years old, Malphus was a tall, rail-thin computer programmer from Dublin, with a long sharp nose, brown hair and perpetual allergies. He'd come on the tour in hopes of finding "someone special" – at least that's what he'd told her the first day they'd been on the road. He'd also told her he fancied Americans. And that he liked her hair (nothing special – it was shoulder-length, wavy, blonde with highlights/lowlights).

Dari had a suspicion Malphus wanted her to be that someone special.

She was pretty positive she didn't want to be.

"Sure," she said, rose from her seat and grabbed her camera bag from the overhead. She offered Malphus a quick smile and moved into the aisle ahead of him. "Thanks."

"Absolutely," he said. He moved closer behind her. "Er, what are you doing later? Fancy a drink at the pub?"

Dari squeezed her eyes closed for a second then took a deep breath. "Um, I'm actually doing some work," she said, giving a light-hearted chuckle. A long hank of bangs escaped her ponytail holder, and she blew it out of her face. "Boring, I know, but that's why I'm here." She glanced over her shoulder and shrugged. "Work— whoa!"

Dari's hiking boot caught against the rubber mat and sent her sprawling. Lucky for her, the metal handrail at the front of the bus stopped her from hitting the floor.

Unfortunately, it used her noggin to cushion the fall.

"Are you all right?" asked Malphus, pulling her back by her shoulders.

Dari held her forehead and inwardly cringed. "Yes, I'm fine – no worries," she lied. It throbbed, but no way would she let Malphus doctor her. The pain would eventually stop. She pasted on a smile. "I fall all the time. *Seriously*. I'm totally used to it," she said, and that wasn't a lie. She had to be the clumsiest person she knew. With another reassuring smile, she climbed from the coach and threw him a wave. "See ya, Malphus." She hurriedly walked to the back of the bus and gathered her single rolling suitcase. Malphus, now engaged in conversation with Miley, was sidetracked. Relieved, Dari glanced around.

She sucked in a breath of surprise.

So distracted by Malphus and smacking her noodle on the handrail, she hadn't paid attention to their surroundings. The beauty of it shook her and she stood in the car park, drinking it in. The wind was decidedly stronger, and it whipped her pony-tail, making her squint against the briskness of it. She almost didn't notice, so taken she was with the sight before her.

Across the single-track lane wound a graveled road leading to an aged stone two-story dwelling with weathered black shutters. It sat dramatically upon an ancient shelf of rock, surrounded by gorse and clumps of purple heather, and looked out over the North Sea; a faded white-and-black painted sign swayed on rusty hinges in the wind over the entrance and read THE CLACHAN, EST. 1620. Shouldering her camera bag, Dari grasped the handle of her rolling suitcase and began to move toward the inn. A prickle of excitement coursed through her, and, all at once, despite the rest of Scotland's beauty, *this* particular place spoke to her. She thought she'd never seen anything more rugged and beautiful in her entire life.

"Are you all right, love?" Miley, the bubbly tour guide said as she and Malphus passed her.

Dari hadn't even realized she'd stopped. She gave a quick smile and adjusted her camera bag. "Oh yeah, no prob. Just . . . looking around."

"Gorgeous little nugget, yeah?" Miley said, and turned back to her conversation with Malphus.

"Yeah," Dari said quietly, more to herself. "It sure is."

A sudden movement on the inn's rooftop caught Dari's attention, and she peered into the fading sunlight. She blinked.

A man stood, propped casually against the chimney stack. He

seemed to be staring directly at her. She couldn't make him out completely, but he looked strong-bodied, young, wearing a white billowy shirt and dark pants, and—

In the next blink, he was gone.

Dari rubbed her eyes with her fist, and then looked again. Nope. Nothing there.

"I'm losing my mind," she muttered, drew a deep breath, then headed inside to check in. Must have been a carpenter, repairing something on the roof. In the morning, she'd set out early for sunrise photos. Anticipation gave her a spring in her step she hadn't experienced since boarding the Wilde Ride Coach Tours bus.

She could hardly wait for morning.

Two

Justin Catesby watched the girl below bound into the front office.

She'd seen him. He was sure of it. She'd trained her gaze directly on him.

Not an easy feat for a mortal when faced with a spirit for the first time.

Scratching his chin, he leaned over the edge of the roof, bracing his weightless self against his thighs. He watched her ponytail swing, and her backside, err, well he watched her sashay straight into the office, dragging that rolling monster behind her.

"For shame, lad. You're all but pawing her from afar. A rogue voyeur. A shameless pirate."

Justin grinned. "Jealous, Godfrey?"

"Damn right I am," Godfrey said, sighing. He eased closer to the rooftop's edge and peered down. "I don't see her, boy."

"She's inside," Justin said.

"Did she see you?"

Justin stood and met his old friend's gaze. "Aye."

Godfrey, wearing that ridiculous plumed hat he fancied, scratched his forehead in thought. "And had you made yourself visible to the lass?"

"Nay."

"Interesting," Godfrey replied. He moved away from the edge and regarded him. "So she's . . . sensitive?"

"That's the only thing I can surmise," Justin said, then grinned. "And to think I wasna even goin' to stop by the old place. Flat glad I did."

"Did you get a good look at the lass?" Godfrey offered.

Justin shook his head. "Nay." He glanced at his friend. "But I will. Tonight."

"Let's go then, lad, and make you ready!" Godfrey began to disappear.

"Right behind you," Justin said, and glanced at the inn's entrance once more. Something struck him about the girl. He had no clue what that something was, but he was damn happy to find out. Easing into his invisible state, he joined Godfrey.

He could hardly wait for the night.

Dinner at the inn was an event.

Especially when sitting beside Malphus. He continuously stared at her. She could see him out of her peripheral vision.

When he cleared his throat she knew she was in big trouble.

"Um, yes. Dari?"

Dari popped a chip in her mouth, chewed and swallowed. "Yes?"

Malphus broke out into a cold sweat across his forehead; he mopped it with his napkin. "Would you care to go on a walk with me? After supper?"

Eesh! She smiled, hopefully concealing her strong desire not to go for a walk with him. "Well, thank you, Malphus, for the invite. I'm really beat though – was going to stay in and do some work before bed. You know?"

Malphus hung his head. "Right – of course. You're on a working holiday."

She smiled. "Yeah. I am."

"What about in the morning?"

Well, gotta give him a point for persistence. And guts.

Oh go on and tell the lad yes, for saint's sake.

Dari glanced over her shoulder, then back to Malphus. "Did you say something?"

Malphus turned beet red. "No, never mind."

A chuckle, male, strong, and *so* not Malphus's, sounded behind her. Dari turned quickly to look. Nothing. No one stood there. It had sounded *right* in her ear.

"Did you just laugh?" she asked Malphus.

He merely shook his head. "No, it wasn't me. Goodnight, then."

"Yeah," Dari said. "Goodnight."

Malphus rose and left the dining room.

Dari inspected the other diners, all from her tour. They were all engrossed in their own conversations, no one paying the first bit of attention to her. Malphus had been the closest and she knew the sounds hadn't come from him.

Who then?

With a head shake, she drained her glass of soda, rose, dropped two pounds on the table, and wandered upstairs to her room. On the top floor, down the hall and to the right, she stopped at her door, unlocked it and went inside.

That laugh, that voice, stayed in her head all night long. Even when she pulled out her laptop to work on the travel brochure, the voice sounded in her head. And even when she went to sleep.

She tossed and turned all dang night. Or at least until she woke with a start.

Dari had no idea what startled her, but she bolted up and looked around the room.

A man stood over her. And for a split second – a split *second* – terror gripped her. She could do nothing more than stare. Tall. White billowy shirt, leather vest. Dark pants. Long hair.

With a gasp, she clapped her hand over her mouth and squeezed her eyes tightly shut. With her heart slamming against her ribs, she tried to breathe in, out, catch herself before she hyperventilated. She lifted one eyelid slightly open. Then, opened it all the way. Then both.

No one was there.

Dari nearly fell out of bed reaching across the mattress to the side table to click on the lamp. Quickly, she gazed around the room. Nothing; nobody. Hanging over the edge of the mattress, she slowly lifted the bed skirt, then jerked it up. Her eyes roved beneath. She saw nothing. Just clean, wooden floorboards.

In only her knickers and T-shirt, she squirmed and wiggled until she was back on the bed. She sat there on her knees, glancing about.

What the heck was going on? She sighed, scooted back to the headboard, pulled the covers up to her waist, and waited.

Nothing happened. "Well, I'm for damn sure not going to turn the lights out and go to sleep," she muttered to herself. Maybe it was an old inn. Scotland was filled with magical lore and stories, and they'd told her plenty on the tour. Maybe her head had just heard enough. Now she was waking to finding billowy-shirted men staring down at her?

She was a freak to the nth degree for sure.

Tomorrow had to be better. She'd planned on taking an early morning photography hike out to Slains Castle – rumored to be the inspiration for Bram Stoker's *Dracula*. She'd read it – again – on the transatlantic flight. Maybe that's what her problem was – a little too much Bram?

Soon, she yawned, stretched; exhaustion claimed her, and Dari closed her eyes.

Three

Captain Justin Catesby stood, just outside the girl's chamber, his head against the door. He could, of course, slip back inside, but whereas his invisible ghostly state worked with most mortals, it apparently did not do so with Dari St James.

He'd checked her name at the inn's registry.

She'd bloody caught him staring at her whilst she slumbered. He hadn't meant to stay so long, but damn, she was fetchin'. There was something more than just her lithe body, her lovely hair and her bonny face. 'Twas more tae do with the way she'd scrunched her nose up at supper when that oaf Malphus had persisted to ask her for a walk. 'Twas certainly more tae do with the way she'd insisted she'd heard something. For the most part, she'd caught his attention when she'd tossed her backside to the air with nothin' more than the slightest sliver of bloomers to cover it, all to check beneath the bed.

He'd fancied it.

Nay, no' just the sight of her in her knickers, but the way she'd behaved when alone. Endearing. True.

And she did have the cutest little bum.

Justin turned and nearly ran straight into Godfrey.

"You cannot just watch the lass whilst she doesn't know it, boy," he accused. "Have you been inside her quarters then?"

Justin frowned. "Aye."

Godfrey gasped like a wee girl. Even covered his lips with his fingers.

Justin scoffed in disgust. "Damn, man, stop that. 'Twasna like she was naked. She wore . . . things."

Godfrey frowned now. "What things, lad? We've been around modern lasses, you and I, and we know just what sort of things they have these days."

"Knickers and a T-shirt then," Justin said. And when Godfrey frowned deeper, he sighed and pinched the bridge of his nose. "I didna go in there to catch her in her knickers, fool," Justin said. "I . . . just wanted to watch her slumber."

"Well, you mind your manners," Godfrey said. Then, he grinned. "Or at least bloody wait for me to join you next time."

Justin smiled and shook his head. "Daft."

Godfrey patted his shoulder. "Maybe, my boy. How 'bout a game of knucklebones, aye? Take your mind off yon lassie?"

Justin draped an arm over his old friend's shoulder and started up the corridor. "Do you ever grow weary of that game, then?"

As they disappeared through the wall, Godfrey chuckled. "Never, young Catesby. Never."

Justin threw a glance at Dari's door before he disappeared. He'd follow her tomorrow, just to see what she'd be up to.

Dari woke with a major crick in her neck.

She'd slept against the headboard all night long.

With her vision still sleep-hazy, she peered at the clock: 5.20 a.m. Easing off the bed, Dari made her way to the en suite bathroom, took a quick shower, dried her hair and dabbed on a little make-up. After brushing her teeth, she pulled on some worn, faded jeans, a pair of old brown hikers, an under-tank and a long, over-sized cream sweater; then gathered her hair into a ponytail. She grabbed her camera equipment and set out. It was almost 6 a.m. and she wanted to get an early start, possibly a few sunrise pictures. Those would look wicked in a brochure. Nearly forgetting about the night's strange incident, Dari set off downstairs.

Bruno, the desk man, was already awake and at his post. Of course, he lived there, and it was just what Bruno did. He was an older gentleman, cheerful, with a head full of thick, wavy silver hair.

"Morning, Bruno," Dari said. She pulled out a rough map of the A975 that ran along the coast and pushed it beneath Bruno's gaze. "Can you point me in the general direction of Slains?"

"Aye, aye." He used his thumb to press against the map. "Just here ya go," he said, then leaned over the desk. "'Tis just up the road there, about a couple of kilometers. Be careful, though, lass – 'tis quite treacherous to the untrained."

"Thanks, Bruno. I'll be careful," she said, and headed out into the early Highland air. The moment she stepped out, the unique scent of clover and heather assaulted her and, as she walked to the road, she noted the yellow gorse and purple heather in bushes and clumps. Still too dark for great pictures, she decided just to get to the ruins and find a place to set up her tripod for sunrise shots. Walking along the A975, she managed the hike in a handful of minutes with some brisk walking and crossed the road, toward the ruins. The sun was just peeking over the North Sea, and Dari hurried. She was just in time.

A burst of yellow and orange and red glowed over the water, and the angle she'd chosen, with Slains in the foreground, took her breath away. She managed several shots as the sun rose, the old stone of the ruin at first looking black, then slowly taking on color.

She wanted another angle.

She gauged the climb and the fact she'd have to haul along her camera equipment.

It would certainly make for some fantastic shots.

Shouldering her equipment, Dari made it to the open ruins and inside to what once was the courtyard. Picking her way through the rooms full of vegetation – sometimes shin-high – she marveled at the structure, wondered at the souls who could have wandered through. Especially Bram Stoker, who'd been inspired by the ruins.

She should have been looking where she was going – she knew that right off. But something up above – not a puffin, or a kitti-wake, or a razorbill – something . . . else. The sun peaked, casting a bright beam of light through one of the chambers, and Dari shaded her eyes with her hand and stared at the stone ledge above.

And just before she stepped, just before she gasped, just before her eyes focused on what she thought she saw, she stumbled. Fell. Busted into and dropped through an old rotted doorway covered with growth. She fell downward, and she had a fleeting thought, just before she hit her head, that it was a cellar. She landed with a thud, her head whirled, and blackness formed behind her eyes, and claimed her.

Four

If Justin had a pair of lungs, he would have lost his bloody breath.

Dari had just disappeared beneath the sod!

Justin listened for a moment; he heard the very faintest sound of breathing. It was even, calm, non-pained. She must have fallen into a bloody underground larder. He peered into the gaping hole; it was dark, and he couldna tell how deep she was. Moving himself, he appeared in the darkness beside her. The space was a small chamber, and several meters deep; only a weak shaft of light shot through from the hole above. Justin wanted to make sure she hadn't broken anything, or landed on her head, so he drew a breath – just for the sake of it, since he had no lungs to breathe with – cleared his throat and spoke.

And prayed he wouldn't do more damage than good.

"Ms St James? Are you hurt? Can you move?"

The voice, seemingly far away, grew closer. Dari opened her eyes but saw only darkness. "Hello?" she responded. "Who's there?" She tried to move but her head swam. "Ouch."

"Oi," the voice said. "Dunna move, lass. Just lie still, aye?"

Heavily accented with a sexy Scottish brogue, Dari thought she recognized the voice but couldn't place it. Not at all. "Who . . . are you?" she asked hesitantly. "Where am I?"

"Right," the voice said hestitantly. "I'm, err, Justin, and you seem tae have fallen into an old food cellar at the ruins."

"The ruins?"

"Aye," Justin answered. "Slains."

He had a really nice accent; voice not too deep-pitched, not too high-pitched either. Spoke with calm, soothing tones. Of course, a Scottish brogue was sexy no matter how you sliced it. "I was here for sunrise pictures. Have we met, Justin?"

"I . . . dunna believe so, ma'am."

Dari tried to sit up once more, and her head swam again. "OK, I'll just lie right here," she said. Justin had sounded as though he didn't want to tell her his name. "How did you know I was here?" she asked. "I was all alone – except I could have sworn I saw a man standing on the ledge above me. He wore a . . . hat of sorts. That's when I stepped . . . and fell."

"I, err, was out walkin' along the lane there and saw you fall," Justin offered. "'Tis treacherous out here, lass. Many holes and gillyways and such, hidden in the grass."

"So I've been told," Dari answered, although she had no clue what a *gillyway* was. "Well, Justin," she said. "Thank you for coming to see to me. It's . . . sort of embarrassing— oh. My camera bag! I have a flashlight in it. Can you help me find it? I . . . feel like I'm sitting in damp dirt, and I want to make sure there aren't any spiders or gross things crawling near me." She patted around, not really noticing that Justin hadn't responded. "Oh, here it is."

"Right, err, hold on there lass, you dunna want tae be—"

"Got it," Dari said, grasped the light by the handle and pushed up the switch. She swept the beam across the small cavern – and directly over, rather *through*, the body of a man. *Through him.* His body was not solid.

He looked as mortified as she felt. He looked familiar.

Wearing a leather hat, billowy white shirt, long leather overcoat, dark pants.

"Whoa!" she said, and was so surprised that she dropped the light. Her heart slammed into her ribs, and her insides seized. "Who are you?" she managed, all the while feeling for the flashlight's handle. She found it and searched for him again in the shaft of light. She found him, crouched not three feet away. "How did you get in here?" she stuttered, her insides growing numb with fear, her mind a web of confusion. She had no idea who this guy was or what his deal was, but he'd been in her room the night before; she recognized his voice from dinner and he'd been standing above her, on the ledge, just before she fell. He was stalking her. She knew that now. *And he wasn't frickin frackin solid! Had she really seen what she thought she'd seen?*

"Err, Dari, please," he began. "Dunna get so frantic—"

"*Frantic?*" Dari half-hollered. "You're stalking me, you . . .

weirdo! You're see-through! You're— Just . . . get out and leave me alone!" She forced herself to rise again; her head spun and a wave of nausea hit her. "Oh, hell," she said, crumpling back to her original position. She wasn't going anywhere just yet. "Please," she muttered, her voice meek, her strength leaving her. She barely had enough left to hold the flashlight as a weapon. She'd thought of whacking him with it but had a sneaky suspicion a weapon wouldn't do her any good. She wasn't sure what she was seeing, but she didn't think for a second that it was normal. *Wasn't natural.* "I don't know who you are, or . . . or *what* you are, or why the light shoots straight through you. But please. Don't hurt me."

Justin Catesby pulled his tricorn off, shoved his hand through his hair and stared, helpless, at Dari St James. He hated that she was so afraid of him but what else could he expect? He was a bloody spirit for saint's sake! He'd made some poor choices in his day but this was probably the poorest.

Besides the one that took his life – whatever that was.

He had to help her. At least make things right. He settled his tricorn back on his head.

"Ah, Dari?" he said, softly, so no' to frighten her. "I willna hurt you. I vow it." He sighed. "No' that I could anyway."

"Who *are* you?" she asked again, her voice steadier this time.

He sighed again, and glanced at where she lay. "Why dunna you put your torch on and set it beside you, lass," he advised. "That way you can see a little."

Several seconds went by in silence, then a small *click* resonated in the cellar as she flipped on the torch. It lay beside her, and the beam was just enough to illuminate the area. He, of course, could see in the dark, but he wanted Dari to see him.

The faster she did, the faster she'd accept him.

He hoped anyway.

Justin Catesby didn't know what to expect from this unexpected event, but at least it had thrown him and Dari together. He only hoped she could grasp what he was.

A ghost. One that had walked the earth for hundreds of years.

He cleared his throat. She glanced at him hesitantly, her eyes wide as she inspected him. "My name is Captain Justin Catesby, lass. Originally from Aberdeen. Lately of Sealladh na Mara." He tipped his hat and gave a nod. When he looked, she was still staring, speechless. Several seconds passed. She opened her mouth, closed it; opened and closed it again.

Finally, she spoke. "Am I supposed to believe you're . . . dead?"

Justin met her dubious gaze. "Aye. That's exactly what I'm tellin' you."

Five

Dari stared, almost disbelieving. *Almost.*

Without another thought, she picked up the flashlight and flung it at him.

It passed straight through him and hit the earthen wall.

The corners of Justin Catesby's mouth tipped upward in a crooked smile. "I confess, I wasna expectin' that."

Because of the way the flashlight now lay, Captain Justin Catesby was completely illuminated. Openly studying the form before her, Dari let her eyes travel the whole of his body. Still crouched, he wore a leather hat similar to that of a pirate, a long leather overcoat, leather vest beneath, a white shirt with billowy sleeves, and dark pants tucked into leather boots that rose to mid-calf.

Her stalker was . . . a pirate?

A laugh emanated from Justin Catesby. "Nay, no' truly a pirate. A sea captain, if you will."

An icy film covered her insides. "You just read my mind."

Justin's sexy mouth widened in a full smile. "Bein' dead does have a perk or two, lass."

Dari blinked. "I'm not having this conversation. You're not real." She put a hand to her forehead. "I'm not here, in a hole beneath castle ruins, talking to a dead guy."

"Aye," Justin said matter-of-factly. "You are, in truth. Now can you move?"

"Why?" Dari asked, still completely stunned.

Justin laughed. "So you can hoist yourself out o' here, gel."

"Oh," she mumbled. At least if she were imagining a conversation with a ghost, he seemed to have a little sense.

He chuckled again.

Taking a deep breath, Dari slowly sat up.

"Now stay like that for a handful of seconds," Justin said. "Get your bearings."

She did and, after a few moments, her head stopped spinning so much. "OK."

"Now," he said. "You're goin' tae have tae pull and crawl your way out o' here." He rose on his haunches and shuffled to the wall. "See you here? Use these roots and such as steps."

For the time being, Dari was simply going to put it out of her head that a pirate ghost was helping her out of a hole in the ground. "All right," she agreed, and slowly stood. "I'm going to get my flashlight first, so don't . . . let me walk into you."

"Of course," Justin said, and moved away.

Dari, glad her head no longer swam, lifted her camera bag and tripod case, grasped the flashlight, and shouldered it all. She found the roots, dug her toes into the hard-packed sod and, in moments, she was out of the hole.

Captain Justin Catesby was standing there, waiting. He looked even more amazing in the daylight.

"Whoa!" she exclaimed, and stepped back. "Don't do that!"

Justin grinned. "Dunna do what, gel? Simply stand here? I'm doin' nothin' more than makin' sure you're out o' harm's way."

Dari stood in the courtyard of Slains Castle and stared at a pirate ghost.

"Sea captain," Justin corrected. "There is a difference."

Dari found a large stone, walked to it and sat. First, she checked her camera. It had fallen in the case and, luckily, remained intact. She slipped it over her shoulder, zipped the case up and breathed. Then she turned to Justin. She couldn't take her eyes off of him. She could actually see fine detail in the light; although he was just the slightest bit transparent, he still looked . . . mostly solid. Weird. She regarded him closely. Tall – at least six foot; his brown wavy hair, all one length, rested against the top of his shoulders, and soft brown eyes rimmed with thick lashes looked back at her. His smile was wide, his lips full, and never had she seen a more gorgeous man.

He took her breath away.

"Well," she said out loud. "If I'm going to bonk my head and dream up a dead guy, at least he's gorgeous."

Justin again chuckled.

Then, Dari noticed something else. Upon his left forefinger, a ring; the design contained a half-moon with a fang in the center. Fascinating, the details she conjured after hitting her noggin.

With a slight glance around, then at her watch, Dari sighed. "Well, Justin Catesby, once of Aberdeen, lately of . . . that other place." She couldn't remember how to pronounce it. She stood. "It's been great dreaming you up. I have to say this forced tour was well worth its early torture." She smiled. "See ya."

Dari simply nodded her head and walked away.

Justin smiled, shook his head and fell in step behind her.

He took the freedom to study her in full daylight.

A head shorter than he, she walked straight and purposefully, her soft blonde ponytail swinging with each step. Her woolen jumper looked at least a size too large, but her trousers fit snugly against a fetchin' bottom—

"You're staring at my ass."

Justin blinked, then chuckled. "Aye, I am."

Dari looked at him as she walked, then turned and faced forward again, shaking her head. "Great. I conjure up a make-believe hot pirate guy and he's a perv."

"I'm no' a perv, lass," Justin countered. "I appreciate fine things. Art, jewelry, scenery." He grinned. "And women, by the by."

Dari glanced at him. "Gee. I wouldn't have guessed that about you."

Justin shrugged a shoulder and smiled.

As they walked, Dari took in the scenery; it was hard not to. They were on the east coast of Scotland, the North Sea. Clumps of purple heather and bushes of yellow gorse colored the bleak stones and tumultuous seascape, and Dari couldn't pass up a shot despite walking down the A975 with a flirtatious deceased sea captain. She stopped and took several shots of the roadside, with the North Sea to the side.

"If you turn round you can get a right nice shot of the ruins with your flowers," Justin said. Dari looked at him, and he grinned and pointed. "See there?"

She turned and almost gasped, the sight was so breathtaking. Almost as breathtaking as the sight standing right beside her. She really hated that he wasn't real.

After quickly setting up her tripod, she photographed Slains Castle from the direction of the spirit.

Six

Justin thought Dari St James rather funny.

'Twas in fact too bad she didn't actually believe he existed.

He'd made his mind up to make her believe.

Watching her face as she photographed his country, Justin could tell she had the same passion for its beauty as he. Mayhap she hadn't known Scotland for as long, but she had that fiery sparkle in her green eyes when her gaze lighted on something she fancied.

Like the ruins, for example.

She stood alongside the road now, taking pictures with her digital.

"You're staring at me again," Dari said, still looking through the camera's eyepiece. "If you were real, I'd throw something at you."

"You did throw something at me," Justin reminded her.

Dari rose, and turned to him. She studied him for some time. "Are you just in my head?" she asked. "Is it because of the fall I'm seeing you?"

Justin held her gaze with his. "Nay, lass. You saw me before you fell in yon hole." He held up his hand. "Once, when you first arrived."

Her eyes widened. "That was you on the roof."

Justin smiled. "Twice. In your room."

Dari frowned. "You saw me in my knickers."

Justin forced himself not to laugh. "Thrice. On the ledge above you, just before you fell." He lowered his hand and gave her a low bow. "And again, now." He rose and walked a bit closer. "As you can see, gel," he said, boring his gaze into her lovely green one. "I am as real as you are."

She studied him for several seconds. "How do I know you're not just a figment of my imagination? Can others see you?"

Justin shrugged. "Some can, others canna. Depends on if they're sensitive."

She cocked her head, and he at once thought it an endearing gesture. "Sensitive?"

He nodded. "Aye. Like, now, for instance," he said, and pointed up the road. "Flag down that lorry there and we'll put it tae the test." He grinned, proud of himself. "We'll stop, say, three vehicles."

She frowned. "And say what, exactly?"

Justin rubbed his chin. "Merely ask if they see anyone else standing at the roadside besides yourself." He winked. "Scots are rather helpful folk, Ms St James. You'll be surprised."

Dari turned, studied the lorry and narrowed her eyes at Justin. "OK. I'll do it." She waited for the lorry to approach, then stepped near the side of the road and threw up a hand. She waved, and the lorry slowed.

A middle-aged man with a shock of ginger hair pulled up beside her and lowered the window. "Aye, love. You needin' somethin'?"

Dari smiled wide. "Um, sort of." She scratched her forehead, suddenly embarrassed. "Do . . . you see anyone here besides me?" *Oh my God, I feel like a nut job.*

Justin smiled at that, and then looked at the man.

He could instantly tell he had a true Scotsman on his side. Luck was wi' him this day.

The lorry driver looked dead at Justin. "Och, o' course I do, lass. You've got a young pirate fellow wi' you, I see." He nodded to Justin. "Good morn, lad."

Justin nodded in return. "An' to you, good sir."

The ginger-haired lorry-driver smiled wide at Dari, revealing a gap between his two front teeth. "You'll be needin' anything else, love?" he asked.

Dari slowly shook her head. "I don't think so. Thank you."

"Aye." He nodded. "Good morn tae ya, then."

And with that, he drove off.

Dari stood with her back to him, and Justin used extreme control not to peer inside her lovely head and read her thoughts. He'd wait patiently. She was bloody well worth it.

When finally, moments later, she turned, dusky green eyes sought his. She stared at him for so long, he wondered if she'd fallen asleep, just standin' there. Then, she spoke.

"I've got to go now," she said, then promptly turned and started back up the A975.

The brisk wind blowing off the North Sea whipped at her pony-tail, carrying with it the heady brine scent of the ocean, the sweet scent of clover and heather, and something else undecidedly, simply Scotland. With a deep breath, Dari pulled it into her lungs, savored it and banked it to memory.

The ghost of a sea captain walked beside her.

The lorry driver had seen him.

That was indisputable evidence.

"Ms St James, what's the matter?"

Dari chanced a peek at Justin Catesby. "I just discovered ghosts really do exist, Captain. Please. Give me a moment to let my brain wrap around the notion."

He chuckled. "Aye."

She breathed. In, and out. In, and out. She stared at the small worn footpath alongside the road. She glanced at the sea, and then behind her at the ruins. Then again at Justin Catesby. "You're really walking beside me."

"Aye."

Dari noticed the Clachan up ahead. "We're walking together, toward the inn."

"Aye."

She slowly shook her head. "It's really, really hard to believe." She glanced at him and stopped. "Do you live here?"

Justin crossed his arms over his chest. "I live wherever," he said. "Mostly on the opposite coast, in a wee village called Sealladh na Mara."

She nodded. "And where else, if not there?"

He pointed. "Along the coast, in the North of England, Dreadmoor Castle and Castle Grimm. I've friends in both."

She again nodded. "And where else?"

He pointed. "West, close to Inverness, the Munro clan. A fine lot o' lads, and the laird's wife is a fine, fine woman."

Dari stared at him for several moments, clapped her hand over her forehead, and started back up the road. "This is crazy." She walked until the Clachan's gravel path came into view. "So, what do you do? Find hapless people and stalk them until they finally admit they believe you exist?"

He blinked. "Nay."

She narrowed her eyes. "Then why me?"

"Well," he said, drawing close, his accent thick, "there's just somethin' about you, I suppose."

Seven

Dari bore her gaze into his ghostly one. She shuddered.

He really did have a way with words.

"Shall I walk you to your room?" Justin asked politely.

She narrowed her gaze. "No, I'll be just fine, thanks." She began up the path, then stopped and turned back. Justin stood in the same place. "We leave in the morning," she said. "We stay in Edinburgh for one day then fly home."

Justin nodded. "I would very much like tae accompany you."

Why she'd hoped he'd say that, she didn't know. But she was glad. She could do nothing more than accept her fate: she'd encountered a spirit. She believed.

"OK," she agreed, then narrowed her gaze once more. "But no sneaking around and peeking at me in my room and in my knickers," she said, slightly mortified that he'd seen her half-naked. "Ask if you want to come in."

He gave a low bow. "I'll take that as an invitation, then," he said, then smiled. "Until."

And with that, he faded away.

"Wait!" Dari called.

"Aye?" Justin said, reappearing just as fast.

"Where are you going?"

A slow smile pulled at Justin's mouth. "Are you saying you'd rather no' be rid o' me just yet?"

"Well," Dari said, looking around. "I don't exactly have anything scheduled."

Captain Justin Catesby smiled. He inclined his head to the sea. "Care for a walk along the shoreline?"

Dari grinned. "Sure."

So together, they walked.

Dari discovered her mind was easily convinced. Ghosts really did exist. Not all can see, and not all spirits can make themselves known. Just her luck she ran into a certain circumstance. It had a name.

Captain Justin Catesby.

The wind off the North Sea swept over the sand and pebbles and rock; it whipped Dari's ponytail and made her squint. It smelled crisp, salty, and it added to the fact that she was in the magical Highlands walking with a miracle.

★　★　★

"And from where do you hail, Ms St James?"

Dari rolled her eyes. "Dari. Call me Dari. And I hail from Charleston, South Carolina, on the south-east coast of the United States."

Justin grinned. "Ah, that accounts for your fetchin' speech then, Dari."

She blushed.

"And do you have kin?" he asked. He found he wanted to know all about her.

"I do. A mother, father, two brothers and a sister." She looked at him. "You?"

A somber feeling washed over Justin; it hadn't happened in some time and for the life of him, rather *un*life, he couldna figure out why it washed over him now. "Nay. Only my surrogate kin."

They talked for nearly two hours; the sun warmed overhead, making the water sparkle. The seabirds caused quite a ruckus, but Dari was thrilled with them and she took several photos.

"Do you always wear that?" she asked, giving his attire a glance. "I think it's wicked sexy, but, you know . . . Walking around with a sea captain may cause people to talk."

Justin laughed. "I'll surprise you."

They walked, they talked; he learned of her family, her job as a travel agent and photographer. She learned a little of his home in Sealladh na Mara, of his surrogate family, Gabe, Allie and young Jake; of his friends at Castle Grimm, at Dreadmoor, at the Munro estate. She even met old Godfrey.

Well, he'd just sort of shown up as they sat close to the shore on a pile of rocks.

"God's knees, lass," Godfrey said as he simply materialized before her. "You're more fetchin' up close for a certainty!"

"Whoa!" Dari hollered, jumping down. "*Another* one?"

Justin laughed. "Let me introduce a good friend: Sir Godfrey of Battersby."

Godfrey, the fop, made a big production of bowing, that ridiculous plume flopping all over.

"'Tis wondrous to meet you, lady. I hope the boy here is minding his manners?"

Dari glanced at him, and her eyes softened.

At that point, so did his heart.

"Yes, he is," she said. Then, shook her head. "I wish I'd met you at the beginning of this tour. It seems the time is flying by now. Soon—" she looked deep into Justin's eyes "—I'll have to leave."

They'd connected; Justin felt it.

He didna want her to go.

"We'll make the verra most of it, lass," he said. "I vow it."

Dari lay in bed that night, restless. She could hardly sleep. Didn't want to sleep.

She'd not only encountered a ghost, and come to accept they actually share the same plane of existence as mortals, but she'd found she really, really liked Justin.

Enough so that when she left day after tomorrow she'd miss him.

A lot.

The night finally passed, Dari got a little sleep and, when she emerged from her room to meet the tour group downstairs, Justin stood in the corridor. He grinned and gave her a low bow.

"I shall meet you at the Mercat Cross in Edinburgh," he said, grinning. "We'll have a day of it, and I'll show you my Edinburgh."

Dari smiled widely. "You're on, pirate man."

Justin burst out laughing.

It was the longest bus ride she'd ever taken.

Her insides were a nervous cluster of butterflies.

She was meeting a centuries-old, hot pirate in Edinburgh.

A smile crept across her face and stayed there until the Wilde Ride Coach Tours bus pulled into the city.

"Oh, Ms St James!" cried Malphus. "Shall I assist you with your bags?"

"No thanks, Mal!" she cried back. "I've got it. Nice meeting you!"

She didn't even wait for him to respond. Pulling her rolling suitcase over the cobbles, Dari checked in to her hotel as fast as possible, found her room, threw her stuff on the bed and changed into her comfy worn jeans slung low on her hip, a long-sleeved black T-shirt and hiking boots. She'd let her hair hang free today, so there was no need to worry about it. After a quick look in the mirror, she dashed out.

At the front desk she asked directions to the Mercat Cross.

"Lass, 'tis in the center of Parliament Square," the desk clerk said. He reached below and grabbed a city map. "Here you go."

"Thanks!" Dari said. She ran out, glanced at the map, got her bearings and hurried up the street.

As she weaved through the crowd on the Royal Mile, she could hardly believe the changes she'd seen, just since yesterday after falling into a hole. She'd met a man. He'd died centuries before.

He had no idea how.

And somehow, that had kept him here.

She was awfully glad.

At Parliament Square she found the Mercat Cross, ran to it and waited. People, tourists, were all around. She saw no sign of Justin.

Her heart dropped.

She wasn't quite sure when she became so enamored with him.

"Excuse me?"

Dari whipped around at the familiar voice. The figure before her was not so familiar. Her jaw slid open, just a fraction. She couldn't help it.

Justin Catesby stood, in totally modern clothes, wearing faded jeans, a cream-colored sweater and hiking boots. His long bangs were pulled back and gathered at the nape of his neck; the rest of his wavy brown hair hung loose.

She almost melted. "Good God," she muttered, openly gaping at him.

Justin laughed and inclined his head. "Sorry – I was waiting at the *old* Mercat Cross." He pointed to the ground a few yards away. "'Tis the site of the original." He grinned down at her. "I watched you run up here at full speed."

Dari frowned. "I did *not* run."

Justin just smiled. "Right. Let's see the city, aye?"

And they did.

The day went by way too fast for Dari.

Justin showed her everything; they explored the castle, Greyfriars cemetery, every inch of the Royal Mile and several of the closes. He told her of the disease and death that had once

plagued the city. Looking around at the bleak grey stone buildings of the old town, she could easily imagine it.

Soon, the sun began to sink.

Dari's heart began to sink with it.

Damnation, he'd never wished a day to last longer.

Justin watched Dari openly; she sat on the bench eating fish
and chips with gusto.

"Um," she said between mouthfuls. "This is the best, Justin.
Honestly."

Justin grinned. "It seems tae be."

She grinned. It was the most beautiful thing he'd ever seen.

She'd be leaving in hours.

They walked and talked the day away; he'd had to dodge
several people. The last time he was out in the public and a
passer-by passed through him, they'd nearly died on the spot.
He didna want anything like that to happen, so he kept on his
toes.

It didna matter; it made Dari laugh, and he'd do just about
anything to hear that pleasing sound over and over.

By the time the sun began to set, they'd walked to the gardens
at the castle, found a secluded bench and sat. She watched him;
he watched her.

Justin knew they thought the same thing because he went
inside her thoughts and peeked.

Neither wanted to say goodbye.

"I know it sounds ridiculous," Dari said, looking at him with
sincerity. "I've only known you for a couple of days." She
glanced over the gardens, then back to him. "I've had the best
two days of my life, Justin." She shook her head. "I don't want
it to end."

Justin's heart leaped. "Nor do I, lass."

They sat close; he moved closer, dropped his head to catch
her downcast gaze. "I wonder if it would have been simpler to
have left you alone?"

Dari's head snapped up. "Why?"

"Because I was content before, sort of," he said. Then, he
looked at her hard. Her green eyes pools of confusion. "But
now? Knowing you exist? Thinking of you yet not having you to
myself?" He shook his head. "Bloody torturous, Ms St James."

Dari leaned her head against the back of the bench, keeping her soft gaze trained on his. Her eyes filled with tears. "You'll be the best memory I've ever had."

It was then, Justin knew, he'd never be the same again.

Together they shared dreams, secrets, late into the night. Dari didn't want it to end. She didn't want to leave. Never before had a man touched her the way Justin did, and not just because he was so gorgeous. He had a kind soul. They connected.

"What are you thinking?" he asked.

She slid him a look. "You're asking? Usually you just go in and see for yourself."

A twinkle of devilment shone in his brown eyes.

She knew then she was in trouble.

"I feel the same way," he said after several moments. They walked along Princes Street, the lights casting long shadows over the walkway. "Mayhap you can visit again?"

Dari nodded. "I'd love that."

Before she knew it, they were standing at the entrance of her hotel. She turned and gazed up at him. He looked so real, so tangible. Her hand moved without conscious thought to his jaw. Her fingertips tingled as they grew close to the lines of his form.

"Would you permit me one thing?" Justin asked, his voice low, his accent deep.

Dari nodded. "Yes."

His eyes trained on hers, the muscles flexing in his jaw, he sighed. "Be verra still."

Eight

Dari's heart beat a thousand times per minute.

Justin slowly lowered his head, hovering his mouth over hers.

They stood there, beneath the lamplight in Edinburgh, and kissed the only way a live soul and a restless one could. Their essences melded in that one kiss, where his lips barely grazed hers, and tingles shot through her mouth, her skin, and clear to her heart.

"I'd give anythin' for it tae be real," he said against her, sending more shock waves across her nerve endings. He pulled back slightly and stared into her eyes. "I've ne'er met another like you, Dari St James."

Tears burned beneath her eyes. She felt stupid; she'd only known Justin for two days, and she was crying? How could that be?

"Soulmates, mayhap?" Justin offered. He grinned. "Sorry. 'Tis just too tempting."

Dari smiled at him. "Will you stay with me until I fall asleep?"

He returned the smile; longing and passion shone brightly in his gaze, and it saddened her to think she'd never get to fully experience Justin Catesby.

She'd take what she could, though.

He stayed with her the whole night.

As she lay there in bed, he sat beside her, stretched out and looking just as mortal as anyone. They talked until sleep claimed her. Just as she slipped into slumber, she heard his voice; his deep, sexy brogue speaking a language unknown to her. It soothed her, comforted her and made her want him all the more.

When her alarm went off at 5 a.m., Justin Catesby was gone.

A hole began to tear, unravel a little more inside her heart.

It was the longest transatlantic flight she'd ever experienced.

Her sister Becca was at the airport to meet her.

She immediately knew something was up.

"What?" Becca protested. "Something happened, I can tell. Spill da beans, woman." Then her eyes stretched wide. "Oh. My. God. You met a guy and had to leave him there. Didn't you?"

Sometimes it really sucked that her sister knew her so well. "Sort of."

"Sort of? What does sort of mean?" Becca demanded. "I want details and I want them now."

Dari smiled. "Let's do it tomorrow, OK? I am so tired."

Becca stared, then blinked. Then, she hugged her. "I'm sorry, Dar. It'll be OK. Let's go home."

Becca drove through Charleston, and Dari stared out of the window silently. Justin lay heavily on her mind, and she highly doubted he'd ever leave it. She'd found someone and gained a broken heart, all in two days.

It'd take a lifetime to get over it.

"Are you sure you don't want me to stay the night?" Becca asked.

Dari smiled. "No, Bec. I'll be fine. Pinky promise." She blew her a kiss. "I'll call you in the morning. K?"

"Love you," Becca said.

"Love you back," Dari said. With a sigh, she turned and walked up the steps to her house. It faced the Atlantic, a small beach cottage she'd gotten for a steal from a satisfied travel client. That was her perk, she guessed.

She walked in, dropped her belongings, and went straight to the double glass doors leading out to the deck. The moment the brine washed over her and the sea breeze caught in her hair, memories of another sea, another wind, crashed over her.

"About bloody time you got here."

Dari nearly jumped out of her skin. But as fast as she turned, her brain registered the voice faster. Justin Catesby sat, reclined in an Adirondack chair, in the corner of her deck.

With a wicked smile on his face.

She grinned and fought not to launch herself at him. "Justin!" She hurried to him. "What are you doing here? How did you find my house?"

Justin stood, still wearing the beguiling modern clothes she'd last seen him in. "I've been around a long time, lass," he said, and winked. "I've got people."

Dari laughed. "Well. Welcome to South Carolina." She'd never been so happy to see another person in her life.

"Well, I fancy you feel the same way as I do, lass," Justin said. "Now, I've one question for you." He drew closer, dropped his head a bit, his eyes boring into hers.

"What's that?" Dari said, breathless from his closeness, and the incredible urge to kiss him.

A smile stretched over his handsome face. "I know 'tisna fair to ask you tae give your heart to a spirit. 'Twouldna be right."

Confusion clouded her mind. "Go on."

He lifted a hand, and where his knuckle trailed close to her jaw, her skin tingled. "How far would you be willin' tae go to help me reverse whatever curse has kept me here, as a spirit?"

Dari blinked. "I didn't know you were cursed."

Justin grinned. "I didna either. But if there was a way to mayhap reverse it, would you want that?" He leaned closer.

"Would you want me? Because I bloody hell want you, Dari St James."

Dari felt breathless and full of life at the same time. "I'd do anything." She lifted a hand and grazed his bottom lip. Her finger tingled. She couldn't help but smile as she looked into his eyes. "And yes, Captain Justin Catesby," she said. "I bloody want you, too."

They stood there for a while, wrapped in one another's essence, and Dari's heart soared. Justin had a plan. He knew people.

He knew *white witches* in Wales.

And you can bet Dari would do anything to give him another chance at life.

"Nay," Justin said, drawing his lips close to hers. "Another chance at life wi' you."

"You stole my heart in two days," she accused, smiling at him.

"I suppose that makes me the heart thief," he said sexily.

And so their story begins.

Ghost in the Machine

Dru Pagliassotti

Thunder crashed and the wire-caged electrical lights that dangled down from the manufactory's high ceiling flickered. Constante's hands jerked, spattering ink across the letter she was writing.

She blotted the flecks of black and decided they weren't bad enough to require a rewrite. With a deep sense of weariness, she signed her name at the bottom of the page.

"*. . . attempt to fill your order as soon as we possibly can. With the deepest regret for your inconvenience, Constante Wicketsmith, Wicketsmith's Wondrous Automata.*"

The letter was a formality, but their prestigious clients expected it. Most of them would have already read about Ambrose Wicketsmith's murder; a letter would reassure them that, despite the shock, his children still had the business well in hand.

Constante folded the letter and sealed it with a gummed Wicketsmith label.

Ambrose Wicketsmith had always insisted on professionalism. He would have been the first to urge his children to stop wasting precious time mourning and get back to work.

Which they would . . . soon. But until the funeral was over, neither Constante nor her brother were quite ready to start up operations again. And with Stephen . . .

No, she didn't want to think about Stephen.

She picked up one of the Pneumatic Dispatch Company's tubes, slid the letter inside, and sealed it. Outside, a gust of wind blew rain against the manufactory's tall windows with a sound like nails thrown against the glass panes.

"Scrapes, deliver."

The wire-haired terrier drowsing by her slippered feet stood, wagging his stubby tail, and took the cylinder in his jaws. His nails clicked on the wooden floor as he trotted across the vast, shadowed manufactory to the dispatch tube by the front door.

"Connie? What in the name of heaven are you doing down there at this time of night?"

Her younger brother Davenport stood on the rickety metal stairs that coiled up to their small living chambers on the top floor of the manufactory. His round face was still puffy with sleep as he squinted through his spectacles and belted his brightly dyed paisley dressing gown.

"I couldn't sleep." She looked down at the pile of stationery. "I thought I'd finally get a start on our correspondence. It seemed a more useful thing to do than tossing and turning in bed all night."

On the other side of the warehouse, the tin dispatch door clicked as Scrapes pawed it open and dropped the mail tube inside. Constante glanced over at him, feeling a pang of loss. Her father had taught Scrapes the delivery trick.

Tail still wagging, the terrier nosed the button that started the pneumatic pumps.

"Don't be ridiculous." Davenport began walking down the stairs. "Tomorrow's going to be—"

A flash of light turned the windows white. A millisecond later, thunder boomed and the overhead lights flickered and went out. Scrapes gave a frightened yelp, and something clattered to the floor as the terrier dived for cover.

Davenport swore, his voice floating through the darkness over the pounding rain.

"Don't move," Constante said, leaping to her feet. "The lightning must have knocked out the public works tower again. That's the third time this month."

"I read that they're working on better insulation," Davenport remarked as the metal stairway creaked. "The problem should be fixed soon."

"*I* think the city should go back to using a nice, clean energy source, like coal." She pulled the lace-trimmed skirt of her nightgown close with one hand and held the other in front of her as she walked.

"Don't be ridiculous!" said Davenport. "*Nobody's* going to be using coal in a few more years! Why in the world would you want people to grub in the dirt hacking their lungs out when we can depend on nice, clean aetheric energy, instead?"

Constante cautiously slid her slippered feet across the manufactory floor. The wide open space was criss-crossed by tables covered with half-built automata, soldering stoves, lathes, aetheric batteries, a diamagnetic generation chamber, standing blackboards covered with her father's and Steph—no, she wasn't going to think about him – her *father's* notes, and rows upon rows of oak filing cabinets.

It was a veritable maze, and only the fact that she'd grown up in it enabled her to negotiate through in the dark.

"Aetheric energy's dangerous," she said, more to distract herself than because she thought she could change Davenport's mind. "The more I study it, the more I dislike it. It attracts too many other forms of energy."

"Which is precisely why I love it," her brother added cheerfully.

"Oh, shut up, Davie. That's not energy; that's superstition."

Outside, lightning flashed and thunder rumbled. Constante was grateful when her fingers touched the smooth metal of the emergency generator's master control panel. Working from memory, she flipped the levers that would activate the heavy-duty battery banks which powered the generator.

The generator clicked and hummed, the crystalline jars on top of its battery banks sparking and crackling as they released their stored energy.

She flipped the next set of levers, breaking the connection between Civic Public Power and the manufactory's electrical grid and connecting to the generator instead.

In the middle of the warehouse floor, the diamagnetic chamber gave a loud series of crackles before settling down into a steady buzz. The electrical lights overhead began to glow with a yellowish, half-power radiance that did little to illuminate the manufactory floor.

"The battery banks are low," Constante observed as her brother continued down the stairs. "Have you been letting your friends hold their meetings in here again?"

Her brother liked to run the aetheric generator during his spiritualist society's gatherings, so that he and the rest of his friends could, as he put it, "thin the veil" between the worlds. Constante had objected when she'd lived with the rest of the family, but she'd been boarding in the Young Ladies' Dormitory of University College for the last year.

"No." Davenport hesitated, glancing at the buzzing metal walls of the diamagnetic chamber. "But Father and Stephen had been running the generator that night, for another test of your gyroscopic stabilizer . . ."

"Oh."

Stephen.

Her fingers crept up to the brass key suspended by a cord around her neck. But she pulled her hand back down. For two days she'd been struggling with herself over whether to take the key off, delaying the inevitable as she'd hoped against hope that the city constabulary would find her father's missing employee.

And that he would have a very good excuse for having vanished on the same night her father was murdered.

"I turned the generator off the next day," Davenport continued, uncomfortably. "After the constables came. As soon as I remembered."

"Of course."

Despite herself, Constante's eyes moved to the desk where her father had been found, sprawled on the floor in a puddle of his own blood.

Ambrose Wicketsmith been shot in the back, and the drawer in the desk that had held their confidential plans for the gyroscopic stabilizing mechanism – an invention that promised to make Wicketsmith's automata capable of a much wider range of movements than any others could achieve at this point – had been empty.

As had been the box that had held their prototype.

The investigators had been quick to suspect Stephen DeVry, her father's missing assistant. They hadn't believed her when she'd told them he couldn't have done it, that he'd been all but a part of the family.

That someday she'd hoped he'd really *be* part of the family.

"Here, now." Davenport walked up and put a gentle hand on

her shoulder. "I told you – we can still find out what happened to Father."

She took a deep breath, squaring her shoulders. "I'm *not* going to allow you to conduct a seance."

"Father's spirit will be far more helpful than the city constabulary."

"Father's spirit is long gone."

Something groaned by the door. They both spun around, then nervously laughed as their eyes fell on the pneumatic dispatch tube shuddering in its metal bindings.

"It must be jammed." Constante mustered a weak smile, grateful for the distraction. "So much for getting a start on our correspondence tonight."

"There's really no need for it," Davenport said, solicitously patting her arm. "I'm sure we'll see most of our clientele at the funeral tomorrow. Which, I might add, is going to be long and tiring, so we should both do our best to get some sleep."

"I can't. Not . . . not when there are so many questions left unanswered."

Her brother gave her a knowing look. She blushed and refused to meet his eyes.

"And yet you refuse to ask the one person who can offer any answers," he said, gently.

"You know how I feel about spiritualism."

"Then you think I'm a charlatan?" he asked, his eyes widening as he assumed a hurt expression.

She rolled her eyes. Her brother could be shamelessly melodramatic, although it didn't keep her from feeling the guilt he intended.

"Of course not! You know better than that. But I think you and your friends are mistaking rattling pipes for spiritual messages, or experiencing some sort of mass hallucination – I don't know." Constante hated discussing spiritualism with her brother. "I'm certain you're *sincere*, Davie. I just think you're *wrong*."

He looked disappointed. "Well, that doesn't change the fact that we have a busy day ahead of us. If you can't sleep, sit up and read, but either way, do it in bed. You'll catch a cold if you sit down here wearing nothing but your nightgown."

"I suppose you're right." She picked up the hand-held torch

near the generator. It ran on a smaller version of the aetheric batteries that powered the mechanicals that Wicketsmith manufactured for the government and a few high-end private purchasers.

She snapped it on and played the beam around the shadows.

Another burst of rain hammered against the manufactory windows. Scrapes began to whine and snarl. She swung the torch's beam toward him and saw the small dog staring at a point in mid-air, his ears upright and his teeth flashing as he alternately threatened and hesitated.

"What's wrong, boy?"

"He must be sensing something," Davenport said, his voice dropping. "I'll wager there's a spirit here with us. Canines are *much* more sensitive to the spiritual plane than humans."

"Davie, stop it!"

"We're not automata, Connie." Her brother indicated the mechanical dolls around them, each in a different stage of completion. "Our vitalic force doesn't wear out like the charge in an automaton's battery. The human spirit is eternal and omnipresent."

"Rats are eternal and omnipresent, too," she shot back, "and a lot more likely to be here than a ghost."

Scrapes suddenly sat back on his haunches, giving a startled bark.

Constante patted her leg. The terrier's intensity was making her skin crawl. It was almost as if he *did* see something she couldn't. "Come here, boy."

Scrapes cocked his head, his gaze moving as though he was watching something in motion. Constante followed his line of sight and recoiled. Something was moving under the desk where her father had been killed.

"It *is* a rat! Scrapes, get it! Get it!"

The terrier cocked its head, one ear twitching.

"It's not a rat – it's a ghost!"

"It's a rat."

"If it were a rat, then—" Her brother's voice trailed off as the terrier stood up, whined again, and then slowly walked forward, his tail moving in an uncertain back-and-forth. Then the dog stopped again, his head rising with half-closed eyes, as if he were enjoying a head scratch.

"It's a ghost," Davenport said with conviction.

Thunder cracked and Constante's heart skipped a beat.

The thing under the desk moved again, and this time Scrapes approached, angling himself sideways to paw and bite at the object until he'd dragged a corner out.

A leather-bound book.

"Father's calendar!" Forgetting her disgust at the thought of rats, Constante hurried forward and grabbed it. The book seemed stuck to something, and for a moment she tugged on it – and then it was released and slid into her hands, almost as though something behind it had given it a push. She sat back and lifted it, her eyes widening as she saw the dried blood all over the cover.

With a cry of anguish, she let it fall back to the floor. Scrapes jumped out of the way, giving her a surprised look.

Her father's blood.

"What's wrong?" Davenport hiked up the hem of his dressing gown as he crouched next to her. "Oh, dear. Come here, Scrapes." He pulled the terrier close. "I suppose it must have fallen off the desk when Father was shot."

"How horrible." Constante raised the cover with one finger squeamishly and let it fall open. Blood had seeped onto the pages, over her father's name handwritten on the front. A lump rose in her throat.

The pages began to turn, one by one.

She snatched her fingers back as Scrapes gave a protesting yelp. Davenport loosened his grip on the terrier with a muttered apology.

Flip, flip, flip, flip, flip.

Mustering her courage, Constante forced herself to hold her hand out again, hoping to feel a gust of air – a breeze through a cracked window, a vent, a gap in the masonry, anything – but even though a lightning storm raged outside, the manufactory's cold air remained still.

The bloodstained pages stopped moving on last Wednesday's date.

The day her father had been murdered.

The page was covered with scribbled notes and appointments. Constante picked up her torch and held its beam on the page to give them more light than the dim overhead lamps were providing. Davenport's head moved next to hers as they inspected the entries together.

"Meriwether . . ." They both saw the name at the same time.

"Why in the world would Father have been meeting Meriwether?" Constante demanded.

Davenport frowned. "Come to think of it, he did mention that Meriwether had approached him a few weeks ago, wanting to discuss some sort of joint business venture."

"*Henry* Meriwether?" The grasping owner of Meriwether's Mechanicals was no friend of theirs.

"Caught wind of your new invention, most like, and was hoping to ferret out a bit more information. Father and I laughed it off, but . . ." His voice trailed off and he looked around, blinking rapidly behind his spectacles. "Father? Is that you? Do you have a message for us?"

"Davie!"

One of the overhead light bulbs popped and went out with a hiss and a puff of smoke.

"Ah." Davenport swallowed. "I'll take that as a 'yes'."

"No!"

"Connie, you *aren't* going to tell me those pages moved by themselves."

Constante shivered. That's exactly what she wanted to tell him. Except she didn't believe it herself.

The problem with having a scientifically trained mind was that it was very difficult to deny the evidence of one's own senses.

How many people, exactly, did it take to experience a mass hallucination?

"I think we should give the calendar to the constables and let them deal with it," she ventured. "They can go question Meriwether about what happened."

Another light popped overhead.

"Was that a 'yes' or a 'no'?" Constante asked, nervously.

"I couldn't say." Davenport stood, setting Scrapes down. "But it seems quite clear that Father's spirit wants to communicate with us. I'm going upstairs to get my planchette."

Constante groaned.

"You stay down here and turn on every aetheric battery you can," he directed, smoothing the front of his paisley dressing gown. "All the torches, all the automata; everything. With only the two of us, and you a skeptic, we'll need to thin the veil between the worlds as much as possible."

"Using that much aetheric energy in the middle of a lightning storm could get us both electrocuted."

"Then let's hope the communication goes swiftly." He picked up another torch and headed up the wobbly metal stairs to his room.

Constante stood, giving the calendar on the floor a wary look. "Is that really you, Father?"

The book slammed shut.

She gasped, jumping back and bumping into the work table behind her. Scrapes barked, his tail wagging and his eyes fixed on an empty spot in the air.

Heart pounding, Constante decided not to question any more inanimate objects.

She hurried to the nearest work table and reached for the half-built automaton lying on it. A metal panel fancifully engraved with a heart around the keyhole adorned the torso of every Wicketsmith automaton, securing its battery chamber. It had been her mother's idea, back when the manufactory was first starting out. The panel was only there to keep the battery from jarring loose, and all the locks were identical, but the design was a Wicketsmith signature. Even after his wife's death, Ambrose Wicketsmith had fastened the decorative plates on all of his creations.

Constante ran a hand over the table, scattering pliers and coils of wire and screwdrivers and wrenches as she hunted for the key. Wind and rain rattled the windowpanes, making her imagine someone trying to get in.

All right, so maybe her brother was correct, she thought as she searched. Maybe there really were . . . *things* out there. Davenport was the dreamer of the family, ruining his eyes reading philosophical tomes, writing spiritualist tracts and punching cards for Wicketsmith's complex automaton-control routines. Constante preferred to keep herself firmly grounded in the material world, her interest primarily on making mechanical improvements to the family's automata.

The gyroscopic stabilizing mechanism had been her idea, although her father and Stephen had run most of the tests while she'd attended classes.

Lightning flashed and something tickled her neck.

Constante reached up to slap at it – hoping it wasn't a spider – just as her necklace's knot slipped open. Cord and key started to slip down the front of her nightgown. She grabbed them both. Then, with a sense of trepidation, she opened her hand to look at the key clearly for the first time since her father's body had been found.

"Wait," her father's assistant, Stephen, had said. He'd straightened and held out the small, shiny brass key. "We left a key out of one of the crates."

"Can't be – I double-checked them all," Davenport had objected, looking down at his packing list. "It must be a spare."

"All the automata had their keys around their necks when I packed them yesterday," Ambrose had agreed.

"It might have fallen out of one of the new supply crates," Constante had volunteered, looking up from her textbooks. She'd just passed the entrance exam to University College, and she hadn't hesitated to leap into her studies before the term began.

Stephen had given the key a quizzical look, shrugged, and walked over to her desk.

"Then keep it as a good-luck talisman, Miss Wicketsmith," he'd said, presenting it to her with a playful smile. "May it open the door to success in everything you do."

Constante had blushed as she'd taken it. Stephen was two years older than she was, and she hoped with all her heart that he'd never noticed that his employer's daughter enjoyed watching him work while she was pretending to study.

"May it get back in the box where it belongs," her father had retorted, dryly. But behind Ambrose's back, Davenport had winked.

Her brother noticed everything.

"Thank you, Mr DeVry," she'd said, avoiding his gaze and casually setting the key on top of one of her books.

Half an hour later, when nobody was looking, she'd slipped it into her purse.

If anybody had ever realized that one of the crates was short by a key, they'd never mentioned it to her.

A year of being absently rubbed as she'd studied – or, some-times, daydreamed – had worn down the key's decorative markings. Now, as she studied it, Constante wondered if she'd been secretly cherishing a murderer's gift all that time.

No matter. It would come in useful tonight. Giving up on her search of the table, Constante used her own key to unlock the automaton's chest panel. She reached in and flipped the switch. The crystalline battery sparked and grew radiant.

Leaving the chest plate open for the extra light it offered, Constante moved through the warehouse following her brother's advice. Wicketsmith's Wondrous Automata had fourteen automata close enough to completion to have their batteries installed. Four were hulking, multi-armed iron soldiers destined to be shipped off to the Punjab; their mechanisms had been painstakingly insulated and plated to protect them from grit. One was completely assembled and the other three were nearly finished, just waiting for their final wiring.

Two of the automata were incomplete iron horses commissioned by the city, which meant they were ugly and strong rather than finely crafted aristocrats' toys. Five more were labor-class automata for mines or trench digging or some other form of repetitive, dirty work, all lined up and ready to be shipped. The last three were private commissions, two mechanical maids and a mechanical butler, all elegantly shaped with smooth metal faces that could be covered, if the owner so desired, with realistic rubber masks. The private commissions cost the most, but they were the pinnacle of Wicketsmith's artistry and the focus of their work to make automata as realistic as possible.

They had been experimenting with the gyroscopic stabilizer on the butler automaton, hoping a smoother gait and better balance would allow it to carry and pour drinks more precisely, an improvement the libation-loving earl ordering it would be happy to pay extra for. It wasn't Constante's ultimate goal for the stabilizer, but innovation cost money, so performance enhancements for aristocratic toys came first and practical applications could be developed later.

Soon all of the automata were gently crackling and buzzing, their aetheric batteries sending coronas of light dancing inside their well-insulated torsos. The air on the manufactory floor began to take on the freshly charged feeling that indicated a build-up of aetheric energy. Constante turned from the last mechanical and glanced at the windows, swallowing.

As if in response to her fears, lightning flashed and was followed by a sharp roll of thunder directly overhead. Scrapes whimpered and Constante started so hard that the key slipped from her fingers.

"Connie! Are you all right?" Her brother's worried voice floated down from upstairs.

Constante froze, staring at the key which hovered inches from the floor. Something pale was wrapped around it – something pale and shaped like a hand. She could almost see the faint outline of fingers as they knotted the silk cord again.

"Connie?" Davenport shouted again.

"Are—" Her voice cracked. She cleared her throat, her eyes still fixed on the floating key and the ghostly hand. "Are you coming back soon?"

"Yes, in a minute."

"Hurry."

"All right, all right."

The key rose, slowly, its silk cord dangling.

Constante strained to see what – *who* – held it.

"Who are you?" she whispered. "Father?"

The key's slow rise halted. Was that a "no"?

The hand didn't look like a woman's, but . . .

"Mother?"

No movement. She hadn't expected any. Her mother had died a long time ago.

There was only one other Wicketsmith employee who was missing.

She had to fight to get the name out. "Stephen?"

The key bobbed up, then slid forward, hovering next to her, slightly above waist level.

Constante reached forward, her fingers trembling, and took the key. The well-worn brass felt ice cold.

"Stephen? But—"

The spectral hand faded. She fell silent, fear gripping her heart.

It couldn't have been Stephen.

Stephen was *missing*, not dead.

"Davie!" Her voice shook. "Where are you?"

"Here." The stairs clanged as Davenport hurried down them, his arms full. He dropped his bundle on the work table closest to the spot where their father's body had been found. "Sorry; I stopped to get your robe from your room."

Constante hesitantly slid the silken cord of her necklace back around her neck, shivering as the cold key touched her flesh.

"Here," her brother said, holding out her robe. "You look chilled to the bone."

"Thank you." She pulled on the robe and knotted its belt around her waist. The extra layer of flower-printed cotton made her feel more secure. "Davie . . ."

"Hmm?" He cleared a space on the table.

"Why do you think aetheric energy summons the dead?"

"The decay of the radiant matter inside the battery attracts them." He screwed a graphite pencil into place in a hole in the heart-shaped planchette. "When radiant matter is converted into aetheric energy, the disruption of the quintessential field creates empty spaces that need to be filled. Nature abhors a vacuum, you know. So energy is drawn into the *lacunae*, and lightning strikes the Civic Power Plant or spirits show up at an aetherically lit seance."

"So ghosts are a kind of energy?"

"I prefer the term 'spirits', but yes. They're pure vitalic energy released from their earthly shell."

"Do they *have* to be 'released'?" She touched the key through the fabric of her nightgown. "Could a ghost come from someone who's still alive?"

Davenport gave her an interested glance as he set the planchette on top of a blank sheet of paper. "Astral projection *has* been considered a form of vitalic transmission," he said. "But it requires a great deal of training – only the most powerful fakirs and swamis can separate their vitalic force from their flesh. Why?"

Constante didn't want to tell him about the hand. Putting it into words might make it real.

"I . . . I'm just trying to understand how this works. University College doesn't teach spiritualism."

"Someday it will." Davenport pulled up two chairs. Outside, another burst of wind and rain pounded against the manufactory walls.

"What about . . . table-tapping and ghostly trumpets and all that? How can vitalic energy do any of that?"

"The same way magnetism moves things: by sending ripples through the aether. Or, sometimes, by transforming back into material form, or ectoplasm, in order to manipulate the material world. When you see or hear a ghost, you're witnessing an ecto-plasmic manifestation."

Constante wanted desperately to be skeptical. Everybody knew that matter could be transformed into energy, but she'd never heard of it working the other way around.

Still, she couldn't quite convince herself that she hadn't seen a hand around the key.

She gestured to the planchette. "So, why do you need this?"

"It takes less effort for a spirit to nudge a planchette on casters than to pick up a pencil and write." Davenport touched the small wooden contraption, which rolled forward. "Sit down and put your fingers on top. Just a light touch, and don't fight the planchette's movement when it starts to shift."

She warily rested her fingertips on top of the wooden plank. Her brother settled into his own chair and put his fingers on the other side, across from hers.

Lightning flashed through the windows, close. Thunder followed at once, loud enough to momentarily drown out the crackling and humming of the aetheric generator and the buzz-ing of the diamagnetic chamber.

"Father?" Davenport asked, closing his eyes. "Father, we're ready for your message now."

Constante wondered if she was supposed to close her eyes, too.

Scrapes suddenly barked, sitting straight up by her feet, and the planchette quivered under her fingertips.

She shot her gaze at Davenport, but he was keeping his eyes shut, concentrating. The planchette slid to one side and Constante looked at it, feeling her fingers growing cold.

Was that . . . another set of fingers, close enough to hers to be felt?

The planchette jerked back and forth and she struggled to keep her touch light and steady.

danger mer—

A burst of white light filled the windows at the same moment that something slammed into the manufactory's metal roof and thunder deafened them.

Constante and Davenport both jumped back and Scrapes gave a long haunting howl as the aetheric generator shot off a curtain of sparks. The overhead lights that hadn't already popped exploded in a series of firecracker pops, sending shards of clear glass tumbling through the wire mesh that covered the now broken bulbs. The manufactory was plunged into a darkness alleviated only by the cold blue glow given off by the aetheric batteries on the generator and in the automatas' chests, and the dancing voltaic arcs that leaped back and forth across the metal walls of the diamagnetic chamber.

Constante glanced down at the table and saw the planchette still moving.

—iwether is here get ou—

"Look!" Davenport gasped, pointing.

The electromagnetic coils built into the diamagnetic chamber's metal walls were glowing and sparking, and a pungent burning smell began to fill the air as something spun between them.

"It's the stabilizer," she said, filled with joyful relief. "Stephen didn't steal it, after all!"

"Connie, wait!" Davenport grabbed her arm as she stood. She shot him an irritated look. "Where did it *come* from?"

She glanced from him to the floating metallic sphere.

That was a good question. The stabilizer hadn't been there before, not when the chamber had been quiet and not after it had reactivated when she'd turned on the generator. But now it spun weightlessly in the chamber's repulsion field, as if some magician had pulled it from a rabbit hole in space – or perhaps one of those quintessential lacunae Davenport had been talking about.

And, for that matter, she didn't remember a pistol lying next to the diamagnetic chamber, either.

Had it been hidden in the same place as her gyroscopic stabilizer?

Scrapes began to growl, his ears flattening as he stared at the chamber. The burning smell grew stronger.

Next to them, the planchette spun off the table. Constante had a second to absorb the scrawl on the sheet of paper . . .

—t he kil—

. . . before something pale and ghostly danced over the surface of the one completed iron soldier, a steel-plated military automaton with four arms, which began to twitch. For a moment Constante saw Henry Meriwether's wizened face transposed over the iron soldier's glowing eyes, turning its expressionless features into a mask of malign glee.

Scrapes's growling grew louder.

The automaton rose. One primary hand snapped its chest plate shut and the other reached out toward them while its secondary hands grasped the closest objects – a chair and a workbench.

"Come. Here." The voice was an iron growl and a mechanical impossibility. Iron soldiers didn't have mouths. They didn't need to speak.

The workbench in the soldier's secondary hand tilted as the behemoth lifted it, sending tools and machine parts clattering to the ground.

"Look out!" Davenport yelped, ducking under the table where he'd set up the planchette. "That isn't Father!"

The soldier hoisted the bench over its head and hurled it at them.

Constante dropped, using an oath that would have gotten her kicked out of the Young Ladies' Dormitory if the headmistress had overheard her. The bench flew over their heads and crashed into an oak filing cabinet behind them, knocking it over. Files spilled over the floor.

"It's Meriwether!" she cried out as the iron soldier took a ponderous step forward, lifting the chair. "Make him go away!"

Davenport gave her a panicked look from his hiding place. "I'm a spiritualist, not an exorcist!"

The chair flew toward them, more accurately this time. Constante threw her arms over her head, wincing in anticipation of the impact, but a pale figure materialized in front of her, knocking the chair aside. The chair bounced off Davenport's table and skittered across the floor, knocking fallen tools right and left.

Constante lowered her arms, staring, as the spirit turned to make sure she was all right.

"Oh, dear," Davenport muttered, from behind them, spying the ghost. "Now, that's truly unfortunate."

The spirit was, without question, Stephen DeVry, looking like a calotype negative of himself – his flesh was pale and glowing instead of darkened to a nut brown by the sun, and his hair and irises were white instead of black. Still, Constante recognized him, from his strong, handsome face and broad-shouldered physique to his rolled-up sleeves, worn leather braces and scuffed work boots.

She'd certainly studied that physique often enough over the barrier of her textbooks.

Which meant—

"You're dead?" she choked, her throat tightening.

He gave her a regretful nod.

"Look out!" Davenport shouted.

Something rumbled, and this time it wasn't thunder. Constante and Stephen both looked toward the Henry-Meriwether-possessed automaton. The giant steel-plated humanoid was using its two left arms to shove aside a heavy filing cabinet that stood between it and them, groping for something else to throw with its two right arms.

Her brother scuttled to one side, keeping low and using the work tables and benches for cover as he angled toward the front of the manufactory.

"Connie, come on!" He gestured frantically toward the front door.

"We can't!" she protested, looking around for a weapon. Henry's automaton would have no trouble following them out into the rain. Wicketsmith's metal soldiers were designed to function in all sorts of weather. They needed to stop him, not escape him. "Alert the police!"

"The alarm box isn't linked to the generator!"

Constante grimaced. He was right. It wasn't. She made a mental note to correct that significant flaw in the design as soon as she had some time.

Scrapes feinted toward the automaton, nipping at its metal heels. The heavy metal-plated head swung to one side. A terrier should be too small for the machine to register as a threat, but it seemed that Henry's ghost brought its supernatural perception as well as its voice to the machine's primitive senses.

A giant arm swung down, missing the dog. Scrapes growled and darted forward again, his teeth sliding harmlessly off the automaton's steel-plated ankle.

"Scrapes! Scrapes, heel!" Davenport's voice quaked as he edged out from beneath his desk. "Come here, boy! Heel!"

Stephen looked alarmed as he raised a ghostly hand to his mouth and gave an apparently noiseless whistle.

"Damn dog." The deep, inhuman resonance of Henry's spirit voice made the hair on Constante's neck rise. The metal soldier swept a table aside with one arm as its others grabbed for the terrier. With an angry snarl, Scrapes darted under a wooden chair, his entire body quivering.

"Scrapes!" Davenport stayed low as he worked his way forward again, holding a hand out for the dog. "Scrapes, come here!"

Stephen ran forward, his insubstantial form passing through the workbenches and shelves as if they weren't there. For a moment Constante thought he was going to grapple with Henry, but to her disappointment, he ran past the giant automaton and into the shadows.

Henry grabbed the chair and lifted it. Scrapes yelped and dashed between the soldier's legs toward Davenport. As he passed, Henry swept the chair around in a giant arc.

Scrapes gave a sharp, high-pitched bark of pain as one of the chair's legs hit him.

"I say—" Davenport leaped to his feet, outraged, just as Henry released the chair. Her brother barely had time to raise an arm over his face to protect himself before the chair smashed into him.

Constante heard a sickening crack. Davenport staggered back and sat down, heavily, on the floor.

"Davie!" Constante leaped forward, ducking around the table to kneel by her brother's side. The automaton took another step forward. Scrapes whined, spinning and bravely shielding them from it.

Behind Henry, one of the metal laborers took a self-propelled step, reaching out with a three-fingered hand to grab one of the large, heavy steel punches they used for their industrial riveting jobs.

"Meriwether!"

The voice was recognizably Stephen's, even though, like Henry's, it echoed as though it were being spoken in a space larger and emptier than the Wicketsmith manufactory. The fact

that the laboring automata also had blank metal face masks and
no lungs for breath seemed irrelevant; the voices, like the spirits,
defied every law of nature Constante had ever studied.

Henry paused and turned toward the new enemy. "You again?
Between you and that damn dog . . ."

Constante dragged her eyes away from the metal combatants
as they closed in on each other. Davenport gave her a sick look,
holding his arm close to his stomach. His face was as colorless as
the ghosts'.

"I think it's broken," he said, his voice strained.

"You need to get out of here." She winced as metal struck
metal behind them. "Can you move?"

He tried to force a game smile and failed. "I suppose I don't
have any choice, do I?"

"Not really." She crouched and slid an arm around his waist,
awkwardly bracing him as he stood. She winced at his whimper
of pain. "Easy."

The emergency police call box by the door would be dead,
as Davenport had pointed out. That meant they had to go out
to get help. But Wicketsmith's manufactory stood on the
outskirts of the city, in the middle of a sprawling industrial
neighborhood of walled manufactories and warehouses. They
didn't have any neighbors to run to for assistance. Still, some
of the buildings had night guards who might open the gates for
Davenport while she—

Blinding white light burst through the windows and a deafening crack of thunder echoed around the building.

Sparks flew from the aetheric generator and overhead lights,
and lightning danced down the bare metal water and gas pipes
which criss-crossed the manufactory walls. An electrical arc
leaped to her hand from the door handle Constante had been
about to grab, making her gasp and jerk back into her brother,
who drew in a sharp, pained breath. More electricity flew from
the tin dispatch door to the glass pneumatic postal tube, shattering it. Constante and Davenport cringed as razor-sharp shards
and loose paper burst into the air around them.

Metal shrieked and the strange burning smell from the
diamagnetic chamber grew stronger.

Constante blinked rapidly to clear the spots from her eyes.
Broken glass sprinkled down from her robe as she moved.

Davenport's eyes were wide and frightened behind his round spectacles; an eerie, pale light leached the color from the bright paisley print of his dressing gown and made him look nearly as ghostly as Stephen. One of the flying shards of glass had cut his cheek, and dark blood trickled down the washed-out white of his flesh.

"What was that?" Constante looked past Davenport, searching for the source of the unnatural light. Her brother, leaning on her, twisted to do the same.

The light was radiating out from the diamagnetic chamber, where her gyroscopic stabilizing device now seemed to be spinning in a portal to the void.

Several yards away, Henry gripped Stephen in his lower two arms and brutally ripped off his head with his other two.

The labor automata collapsed on the ground, twitching. Stephen's ghost stood where the metal man had been, looking clearer than ever, his fists clenching with frustration.

Henry Meriwether gave him a cruel, victorious smile. His ghost, too, seemed to have gained strength. His stolen, four-armed metal body was now covered with ectoplasmic flesh and fabric, turning it into a realistic but monstrous version of himself, attired in his usual natty suit, vest and bowler hat. Although Meriwether had been a slight, greying man in his sixties while living, his ghostly body now reflected the broad-chested strength of the military automaton he inhabited.

The steel punch jutting out from his neck was a jarring note, however. Stephen had gotten in at least one good stab.

"Do you surrender?" Henry demanded, reaching up and grabbing the punch. He began working it back and forth, pulling it from his metal neck.

"Never," Stephen shot back, turning and stepping into the next of the waiting metal laborers.

"It's the chamber," Davenport breathed. "The lightning – it's not just affecting the magnetic dipole moment anymore, it's creating some sort of aetheric flux . . . an inversion . . ."

"You think the ghosts and the chamber are linked?" Constante pressed.

"They seem to be getting stronger as the chamber gets stronger."

"All right. Go outside and get help." She released him. "I'll pull the plug."

"Be careful."

"Always." She gave him a quick smile and turned, drawing her robe closely around her and cinching its belt with a determined tug.

Stephen had succeeded in possessing the second laborer automaton. It stepped forward, but just as it was lowering its foot, Henry gave the mechanical man a sharp push.

Constante winced, knowing what would happen. Stephen threw his arms out in a vain attempt to steady himself, but the automaton couldn't regain its balance. It crashed to the floor.

Constante slipped between the tables and got closer to the glowing diamagnetic chamber while Stephen struggled back to his feet.

She froze when her eyes fell on the gyroscopic stabilizer. If she pulled the chamber's plug, her invention might vanish again.

She needed to retrieve it so that all of this wouldn't be in vain.

Angling around to the front of the chamber, she stole a glance at the two battling automata. To her consternation, Henry was leaning over Stephen's prone metal body. With a twist of one metal hand, the rival inventor plucked out Stephen's aetheric battery from his open chest plate.

The automaton froze, going dark.

Stephen's ghost rolled away from it, standing, as Henry turned and methodically began doing the same thing to the rest of the line of labor-class automata, yanking out their batteries as though pulling out hearts.

Constante darted to the front of the chamber. She was running out of time. Meriwether was smart, and he'd possessed the strongest automaton in the manufactory. If they didn't do something soon, he'd be unstoppable.

Her foot hit the pistol on the ground and she crouched, picking it up. She didn't want it to vanish when she pulled the plug, either. Not if it could be used as evidence.

Stephen might be dead, but at least she could clear his name.

Slipping the pistol into the pocket of her robe, she gazed into the abyss that stretched within the diamagnetic chamber.

The glowing void was filled with tiny points of light, like sparks or stars, swirling on invisible aetheric currents. Their movement was slow, measured, and hypnotic. The lace-trimmed skirt of her nightgown fluttered against her legs and the edges of her robe stirred, as though drawn toward the emptiness.

The void smelled like burning wiring. Or was that just the machine?

She stepped forward and grabbed the magnetically levitating stabilizer.

The mechanism should have slid smoothly toward her on its level magnetic field, but instead, she felt *herself* moving toward *it*. With a gasp, she clutched the metal door frame with her free hand, feeling dizzy. The void spun around her, pulling her forward more insistently, a living magnetic field drawing her inside. Her fingers slipped from the metal frame . . .

Hands closed around her wrist and waist, steadying her and drawing her back. She stubbornly kept a tight grip on the stabilizer and, after another second of resistance, it snapped loose from its field. She stumbled backward, into her rescuer.

"Thank you," she breathed, leaning on him for a moment while her pounding heartbeat slowed down. Then she looked up. "Stephen!"

Behind them, Henry was destroying the last of the labor automata.

"You don't want to fall in there, Miss Wicketsmith," Stephen said, his voice sounding almost normal now. "It's not a nice place."

"Were you in there?" She studied him, horror and fascination fighting for precedence. He was in his ectoplasmic form, but his touch was cool now rather than cold, and his hands felt solid. If it weren't for his strange, ghostly coloring, she would have thought he was alive.

"I was trying to keep Meriwether from taking the stabilizer when, abruptly, the power surged. That place suddenly appeared, and we fell inside." He glanced over his shoulder. "Is . . . did your father—"

"He's dead." Constante felt a fresh wave of loss.

"I'm sorry." Stephen seemed to remember himself, releasing her and drawing back. Constante flushed and smoothed her nightrobe, wishing he hadn't. "Your father wasn't in there with us. I'm sure he's already gone on to a better place."

Her throat tightened as she looked at him. Somehow, hearing him speak and feeling his touch was worse than just seeing him.

Stephen was *here*. He wasn't *alive*, exactly, but he was *here*, and the magnitude of what she was about to do to him struck her like a blow.

"I . . . I'm sorry," she whispered with dismay. "I need to shut this down."

I need to kill you again.

"I understand." He turned away. "I'll keep Meriwether busy."

"Steph—"

He was already gone, running toward the next set of auto-mata, again heedless of solid objects. Henry laughed and strode after him, slower than Stephen but using his powerful arms to sweep aside everything that stood in his path.

Constante knelt and grabbed the power cord for the diamag-netic chamber.

If this works, Stephen will be sent away, too.

To a better place, like her father? Or back into that glowing void, trapped for eternity with Henry and who knows how many other hapless souls?

She wished she'd said the words that had been lingering on the tip of her tongue. That he hadn't turned to leave before she could muster the courage to get them out.

But then again, maybe it was for the best. What good would knowing how she felt do him once he was trapped in that strange void again?

She didn't want to send him back.

But she didn't have a choice.

"I'm sorry," she whispered, giving the plug the hardest yank she could. Wires began to stretch. She yanked it again, and a third time, until the wiring tore away with a sparking *pop* and burst of short-lived flame.

The chamber crackled and went dark, the glowing void vanishing.

Constante turned to see if it had worked, bracing herself.

"Thank you, my dear."

She gave a very unladylike curse, staring at Henry's automa-ton. Its ghostly features had faded, but they were still faintly visible over the iron.

"I was loath to reach inside that machine myself. Losing my body once was more than enough." He held out one of his four massive hands. "Give me the stabilizer and I'll leave."

Her hand tightened on the metal orb. If Henry was still here, where was Stephen?

She couldn't have sent one away and not the other, could she?

Would it have mattered if one were possessing an automaton when the field vanished, and not the other?

Maybe, she realized with horror. Maybe, if the decaying radiant matter inside the automata's batteries *did* attract other forms of energy . . .

"Give it to me!" Henry insisted.

"No!" she shot back. "You killed my father. I'm not going to give you *anything*."

"I'll kill you and your brother, too, unless you give me what I want."

She backed away, and he followed.

"Why? What good will it do you now?" She bumped into a work table and reached out with her free hand, groping for a weapon. "You're dead."

"Dead?" Henry sounded amused, clenching one fist and rotating it. "On the contrary: I'm *immortal*. No more ageing. No more death. Just one new body after another. And that little invention of yours will be much more useful to me now than it would have been while I was still flesh."

Constante shivered, imagining a future in which Meriwether's Mechanicals drove all the other manufactories out of business, its ruthless and immortal owner doing anything necessary to monopolize the business. And how long would it take before he decided to expand into other areas, as well? Manufacturing, mining . . .

Government?

She reached into her pocket for the pistol, trying to remember where the metal soldier's most vulnerable spots were, when another automaton came hurtling out of the shadows, swinging a pipe. With a loud clang, the pipe struck Henry and knocked him forward a step.

Constante felt a moment's overwhelming relief. Stephen wasn't gone after all.

The iron soldier ponderously stabilized itself and turned as the small butler automaton moved in front of Constante, swinging the pipe again and again. Scuffs marred Henry's metal finish, visible beneath its ghostly flesh.

But Henry didn't seem worried by the furious assault. He laughed, grabbing the pipe with his upper arms. Stephen tried to pull it back, but the military mechanism effortlessly tore it from his slender metal hands.

"You're running out of bodies," Henry mocked, transferring the pipe to his two right arms. Stephen backed away. Henry swung, and the pipe slammed into Stephen's metal torso.

Constante jumped aside as Stephen's automaton was knocked past her and slammed into the table. The table collapsed and the butler fell on its back.

Henry took a step forward, raising the pipe over its head.

Constante brandished her pistol. "Stay back!"

Next to her, Stephen's automaton rolled onto its side and awkwardly pushed itself into a sitting position.

Henry chuckled. "That's a single-shot pistol, my dear, and I've already fired it."

Her finger tightened on the trigger. Nothing happened.

"*This* isn't single-shot, Mr Meriwether."

Constante's eyes widened.

Davenport had returned, holding an arc disrupter in his good hand. He'd used his paisley belt as a sling for his broken arm. His dressing gown hung open, revealing a rumpled nightshirt and felt slippers, and his normally cheerful round face was taut with pain.

Henry growled, a low sound like grinding gears. "You don't have the range."

"Get away from my sister." Davenport's voice had lost all trace of humor. "Or I promise you'll find out."

Constante dropped to her knees next to Stephen. Henry Meriwether was right – the arc disrupter didn't have enough range or power to disable a military-grade battery at anything less than point-blank range. But Davenport's bluff seemed to be making Henry nervous, and at least it would buy her a little time.

"Sit still," she hissed, as Stephen tried again to get to his feet. She yanked his dented chest plate wider and pulled out the leads for the mechanical butler's experimental balance-compensation system.

When he realized what she was doing, Stephen reached out his metal hands to hold the wires for her. Her fingers flew as she connected the wiring and tightened the terminal screws to hold it in place.

"His automaton is still stronger than mine," Stephen warned her. A table clattered and they both glanced up to see Henry angrily shoving the obstacle aside, glaring at Davenport. Constante's hands shook as she thrust the stabilizer into place.

"I know. Take this." She pulled the key and cord from around her neck and dropped it into his metal palm. "You can move faster than he can, as long as you keep your balance. Get in close, unfasten his plate and pull his battery, just like he did to you."

Stephen tried to pick up the small brass key, but it slipped between his fingers, falling on the ground. He reached for it, the butler's metal fingers sliding uselessly across the wooden planks as he sought to scoop it up.

"Not enough fine-motor action," he said, sounding frustrated. "I can't grip it, Miss Wicketsmith. I'm sorry. I just keep failing you, over and over."

She grabbed the key and handed it to him. "You *haven't* failed us, Stephen. You're protecting us, and I can't even begin to tell you how grateful I am to have you back again."

He looked up, startled, and the key slipped from his fingers again. Whatever he was about to say in response was lost in the crackling buzz of the arc disrupter as it was activated.

Constante looked up. Davenport was thumbing the "on" switch and backing away as Henry advanced. The disrupter's crackling arc played uselessly over the military automaton's iron shielding.

"I'll try to think of something then." Stephen gave up trying to pick up the key and stood, more smoothly than he'd been able to before as the mercury-filled stabilizer and feedback wiring registered every shift of weight and warned his mechanisms to compensate.

Constante swept up the key and got to her feet, slamming Stephen's chest plate shut. For a moment, her hand lingered over the engraved heart as more words caught in her throat, strangled as she realized how ridiculous it would be to say them to a ghost.

Stephen gave her a faint, rueful smile, then turned and ran forward, grabbing a broken table leg as he went. The adjusted wiring her father and Stephen had developed made a perceptible difference. She hoped it would be enough.

Stephen thrust the table leg between Henry's ankles as the soldier took another step. The military automaton swayed a moment, four arms stretching out for balance. For one moment Constante thought it would fall, but then the table leg snapped and Henry's foot came down with a loud, stable thud.

Wicketsmith didn't build its metal soldiers to be so easily unbalanced.

Behind them, Davenport sagged against a fallen filing cabinet, looking pale. Constante hurried to him while Henry was distracted by Stephen hauling a work table between them, sending sheet metal and loose rivets and screws tumbling all over the floor.

"The spirits weren't directly linked to the aetheric inversion," Davenport surmised, leaning on her as she reached him. She felt him shaking.

"I think the batteries are helping them stay here without it," she said, gently leading him toward the front door.

He took a deep breath, straightening and trying to act normal. "Ah. Yes, that would make sense. No reason to go away once they're here, not as long as they have a source of energy."

"Why are *you* still here? You were supposed to get to safety."

"Go out in this dreadful weather? Are you out of your mind?"

She squeezed his good arm. "Idiot."

Behind them, the work table was thrown aside with a crash that made them both wince.

"Besides," her brother continued, "there was always a chance the disrupter would work."

"On a *Wicketsmith* soldier?"

"Yes, well. I'm afraid I'm running out of ideas," Davenport admitted, releasing her as they reached the door. Scrapes was there, nervously darting back and forth through loose papers and broken mail cylinders, seeking in vain to deliver them to the now non-existent drop door of the Pneumatic Dispatch Company.

Constante opened her hand and looked down at the key. "I have one left."

Davenport followed her gaze and his eyes widened behind his spectacles. "You can't approach Meriwether yourself! He'll tear you apart! Let Stephen do it for you."

"The key's too small for him to grip while he's an automaton, and I don't think he can hold Meriwether still while he's a ghost."

"But—"

"I don't think we have any choice." Constante gave her brother a quick kiss on the forehead and turned before he could argue with her anymore.

It was clear that Stephen couldn't physically harm Henry, although he was keeping the larger and slower automaton busy working its way around furniture and over broken machine parts. But each time Henry swung one of his four arms, the tinier, slighter automaton was in peril. Stephen had already taken some damage in the fight; his left leg was hitching slightly, and beneath his faded spiritual skin, his metal torso was battered by the blows he had taken.

Henry's metal fingers curled around one of the standing blackboards and hoisted it. The blackboard splintered into broken halves as it struck Stephen across the head, rocking him backward.

Constante reached out and grabbed Stephen's shoulders, steadying him before he could overbalance farther than the stabilizer could handle. Stephen shot her an anxious look.

"Miss Wicketsmith! Get out of here – I can't hold him off much longer!"

Henry laughed and stepped forward, wielding the two broken parts of the blackboard like clubs. Constante and Stephen ducked as the boards whistled through the air.

"You know what I want!" the metal soldier declared. "Stop wasting my time!"

"Blind him," Constante breathed, squirming out of her flower-printed robe and handing it to Stephen. "Just for a minute."

Stephen's metal fist closed around the fabric as he stared with shock at her lace-trimmed nightgown. "But you—"

"Now!" she cried out, as Henry swung again.

The blackboard's pieces slashed through the air. Stephen grabbed her robe in both hands, ducked under Henry's arms, and threw it over the metal soldier's head.

The flower-printed cotton covered Henry's face. Stephen pulled it tight, darting behind the iron soldier as its two lower arms groped blindly for him.

"Damn you!" Henry roared, dropping the broken blackboard and raising his two upper arms to tear the robe free.

In that brief opening, Constante darted forward and jammed the small brass key into the automaton's chest plate. With a twist, the lock disengaged and the plate sprang open.

Fabric ripped as Henry's metal fingers tore her robe in half. His eyes met hers, and an arm whipped forward to grab her around the throat.

Constante plunged her hand into Henry's chest, her fingers closing around the warm, crackling aetheric battery. She ripped it from its housing.

The eyes went dark, and the automaton froze.

Constante jerked away from its grip, letting the battery and the key fall to the floor as she rubbed her throat and shuddered.

Then, with a snarl, Henry's ghost tore himself from his metal shell, glaring at her. She drew back, and Stephen leaped out of his own automaton, his ghostly hands clutching Henry's collar.

Henry staggered, clawing for escape as the younger engineer's fist slammed into his face.

"Connie!"

Constante turned and Davenport kicked the arc disrupter across the floor to her.

"Take out the generator! If you're right, we need to cut off as much aetheric energy as we can!"

Constante reached down and picked it up, her heart quailing.

Not again.

"Stephen!" she shouted, turning. "Get back into the butler!"

Stephen's ghost looked up and Henry kicked him in the knee. As insubstantial as the ghosts seemed to be, it must have hurt; Stephen winced, his grip loosening.

Henry tore himself away and sprinted toward the automaton.

"No!" Constante gasped, appalled. Stephen recovered and hurled himself forward, dashing through the tables and half-finished automata as easily as his foe. With a silent shout, he reached out and grabbed Meriwether's ectoplasmic coat tail, yanking him backward. Meriwether stumbled and fell, inches away from the butler automaton. Stephen jumped over him, disappearing into the machine.

Constante spun and activated the disrupter, playing its energy-dispersing arc over the generator.

The aetheric batteries, already depleted, went dark as their charges were dissipated. The generator's engine gave a death rattle and fell silent.

The only light came from the chests of the remaining half-completed automata, and the only sound was the rain pounding against the roof.

Constante held her breath, watching the butler automaton. His metal body was no longer clothed in spiritual substance; it looked like a regular, metal mechanical again.

Then it knelt, one metal hand touching the floor where Henry had been. Its fingers trailed across the wood and hooked through the silk cord of her necklace, lifting it.

She let out her breath with a relieved gasp.

"Stephen?" Her voice shook. "Is that you?"

"Miss Wicketsmith." His voice was a mere whisper.

She dropped the disrupter and hurried to him, kneeling.

"Is he gone?" she asked, reaching forward to touch the smooth metal features of his expressionless face.

It tilted toward her. "I think so. What happened?"

"Meriwether wasn't close enough to a battery," Davenport said, appearing out of the shadows with a rolled-up sheaf of papers in his good hand. Scrapes sniffed curiously at Stephen's metal legs. "Your proximity to radiant matter is giving you the energy to remain intact."

Stephen looked down, touching his heart-decorated chest plate.

Davenport turned and handed the papers to Constante. "Look at what Scrapes was trying to put back into the dispatch tube."

Constante unrolled the pages and saw the plans for her gyroscopic stabilizer, a line of new but smeared notations in her father's handwriting running along one edge. She turned the plans over. Her smile faded as she saw the bloody handprint on the back.

"The plans must have caused the jam," Davenport continued. He still looked weak and pale, his broken arm bound to his chest. "Can't imagine how they got there, though."

"Your father gave them to Scrapes," Stephen said, his voice still faint. "Meriwether tried to catch him, but I got in his way."

"Thank you." Constante set the plans to one side. "Thank you for everything."

"Indeed," Davenport agreed, his gaze moving thoughtfully from one to the other. "I'd say we're quite indebted to you."

"I'm glad I could help." Stephen held out his hand, from which the key dangled from its silken cord. "I hope you'll remember me, Miss Wicketsmith."

The necklace fell into her palm. She closed her hand around it, giving him an alarmed look. He wasn't leaving, was he? Not after she'd tried so hard to figure out how he could stay!

"You can't go!" she exclaimed.

"Certainly not," Davenport agreed, closing his eyes. He sounded pained. "At least not until you've fixed the alert box. If I don't get a physician soon, I'm going to do something very unmanly, like cry. Or scream. Or both."

Constante leaped to her feet, appalled by her own thoughtlessness. "Davie! I'm so sorry!"

Stephen stood. "We can wire the box to a battery long enough to send a signal to the nearest station."

"We'll need wire, and pliers, and a screwdriver—"

"I'll bring everything, Miss Wicketsmith," Stephen assured her. She subsided, chagrined. Of course he knew what they needed.

The automaton walked off, Scrapes cheerfully following at his heels.

"I still like him," Davenport observed as she walked with him to the alarm box on the wall. "Although it's a bit difficult to imagine him as a brother-in-law at this point."

She blushed, slipping the necklace back around her neck. "Davie, shut up."

"I said *difficult*; not *impossible*. Vitalic force and rats aren't the *only* things that are eternal and omnipresent."

"But he doesn't want to stay." The words hurt to say.

"Perhaps he just needs some encouragement." He sat in the nearest chair. "He's a spirit, Connie, not a mind-reader."

She bit off her reply as Stephen returned with the tools they needed. She quickly took a screwdriver and turned to the alarm box. Scrapes sat down by her feet to watch as she unfastened the cover plate.

"We're prepared to honor your employment contract, Stephen," Davenport announced.

The automaton whipped its blank face toward him, everything about its posture registering surprise. "But I'm dead."

"No you're not," Constante said fiercely, scowling at the alert box as she pulled out wires and began attaching them to the aetheric battery. "You're a soul inside a body. That's the definition of living."

"This isn't my body, Miss Wicketsmith."

"No, it isn't," Davenport agreed, "but I imagine we could build you one of your own."

"Of *course* we can," Constante exclaimed, brightening. "We can build a body with a whole array of batteries, enough to provide you with sufficient energy to look like yourself again whenever you want." Her mind was already racing, thinking through what would need to be done to build a new, improved mechanical man – a mechanical man designed for a ghost.

"Besides, having someone who can test our automata from the inside out would give us quite a manufacturing advantage," her brother added. "Enough to offset the expense of your maintenance, I imagine."

Stephen sounded unconvinced. "It wouldn't be right for something like me to stay in this world."

"Wouldn't be *right*?" Davenport pursed his lips. "It would hardly be right for you to abandon us in our hour of need, either."

The automaton cocked its head.

"Look at the mess you and Meriwether have made," her brother continued, waving his good hand around them. "Wicketsmith's Wondrous Automata is already behind on its orders, and repairing this wreckage is going to cause even more delays, not to mention use up most of our savings. Moreover, I'll be of little help making repairs until my arm mends. Do you really intend to leave my sister to run this manufactory on her own in the midst of her grief and destitution?"

Constante glanced at her brother as she tightened the last screw. The light over the alert box went green.

Grief and destitution? Davenport was such a shameless manipulator.

Although right now she loved him for it.

She flipped the lever. The bulb turned red, indicating that an alarm was going out to the nearest constable's station at last.

"I—" Stephen looked from Davenport to Constante. She quickly turned her gaze back on the box, blushing.

"We *can* rely on you, can't we?" Davenport insisted. "Constante and I? Connie, if you would please *stop* pretending to be engrossed in your work . . ."

"I'm sorry." Mustering all her courage, she forced herself to turn away from the wall.

This whole situation was ridiculous – impossible. She knew that. The ghost of the man she loved inhabiting a mechanical man? What was the point?

Except she'd *felt* his touch when he'd had the strength to manifest. She'd felt his hands and heard his voice. He was *real*.

One way or the other he was real.

"I know this must seem strange," she said, hesitantly. "But Davenport's right. We can build you another body, and you could stay here with us." She drew in a deep breath and took his hand, wondering if the ghostly form inside the mechanical man could feel her touch. "With *me*. Please."

It was impossible, of course, but she could have sworn the glow in Stephen's mechanical eyes suddenly grew brighter.

"If you want me to stay, Miss Wicketsmith—"

"Constante," she said, shooting a nervous glance at Davenport. Her brother gave her an encouraging nod. She looked back up at the automaton, enheartened. "Please call me Constante."

Stephen's fingers curled protectively around hers, metal over flesh. "Then I will stay with you as long I can be of any use, Constante."

Below them, Scrapes's stubby tail began wagging furiously with approval.

Three Little Words

Christie Ridgway

One

Dusk was beginning to fall as Jemma Scott's best friend pulled her close for a hug. "Weddings aren't the right time for holding back the truth," the bride said, her gaze sliding toward her new husband and the man to whom he was saying goodbye.

Jemma didn't look in that direction herself. The image of Troy Maxwell, who had played best man to her maid of honor, had been burned into her brain two years ago, when he'd moved into the condo above hers. Instead, Jemma glanced behind her at the fifteen-bedroom example of American Gothic architecture that had served as the locale for the small destination wedding of her two friends. "Some people would say that weddings aren't the right time for haunted houses," she pointed out.

The bride, Vicky, beamed as she slipped into the jacket of her going-away suit. "Unless they met on Halloween like me and my new hubby. Wasn't the weekend fabulous? Didn't I pick the most perfect place to get married?"

Jemma glanced behind her again. Now that all the other guests had left, the house was kind of creeping her out. It was isolated on a long gravel driveway that led to a lone country road over an hour from the nearest town. Until now, she'd been so busy with nuptial duties and celebratory hoopla that she'd not really taken time to notice exactly how spooky the place looked with its cadaver-grey clapboard exterior and pointed arched windows surrounded by funereal black trim.

A cold fingertip seemed to brush the back of her neck. "Yeah. Perfect. The only thing it's missing is a sign that says 'Lizzie Borden lived here'."

A low laugh sounded. "Don't tell me you're superstitious, Jemma," the best man said.

She managed to smile in Troy's direction, but kept her gaze from meeting his. He had beautiful hazel eyes. She'd noticed them the first day they'd come face to face on the path that led from the mailroom at their sprawling complex of condominium units, ponds and lush vegetation. He'd held out his hand, recognizing her as his downstairs neighbor. At that moment, when their palms touched, she'd had this eerie certainty that her life had turned a new corner. So, superstitious? Yeah, she supposed she was.

"Uh-oh, Jem," the groom, Michael, said. "You better not be getting the heebie-jeebies. That would make it a long night ahead for you with only my man Troy here for company."

Don't remind me, Jemma wanted to say. She pasted on another perfunctory smile. "I plan on a relaxing evening propped up on pillows with the company of a good book. I'll likely fall asleep before nine. So Troy's on his own." *Like I was, after he took that consulting job in Argentina six months ago.* Yes, neither of them had ever put any permanent spin on the dating-and-bedding relationship they'd had before he left, but they'd been tacitly exclusive. And they'd been about more than shared lasagne and lust. They'd talked about their jobs, his at an engineering firm, and her increasing responsibilities at the custom dressmaking shop which belonged to her aunt.

One day he'd been going on about a new project on the local waterfront. The next he'd informed her he was leaving at the end of the week to work in the Southern Hemisphere. He'd departed so abruptly he hadn't cancelled his Beer-of-the-Month subscription. She had cases of the stuff now stored in her small second bedroom.

Jemma was frowning over how she was going to get them to him now that he was moving back upstairs as Vicky drew her away, toward the sole car in the small lot. The trunk was open and it was filled with suitcases for the honeymoon trip. "Are you sure you're going to be all right? I know how you feel about Troy—"

"We're not talking about that," Jemma interjected. *I'm not thinking about that. Do not say the words!*

Vicky let out a little sigh. "Jemma, it's going to eat at you. Maybe if you discussed with him why he left—"

"He left because it was a good opportunity, I suppose. Case open, case closed. He didn't owe me anything. He *doesn't* owe me anything. I went on with my life—" *my lonely, Troy-less life* "—and it's been full, so full, with preparations for your wedding and the making of your gown and . . ."

Vicky was looking at her with sad eyes, which was the signal for Jemma to stop babbling. "You loved your bridal gown, didn't you?" she asked, hoping to subvert her friend's pity.

"I can answer that question," Michael said, as he and his best man strolled forward to join the women. "When she walked up the aisle I thought that besotted expression on her face was because she was so happy to be marrying my stellar self, but she has informed me it was because she looked in the mirror and never saw a more beautiful bride in a more beautiful bridal gown."

"The dress is incredible, Vicky," Troy put in. "When I saw Jemma wearing the mock-up she made of it, even a dedicated bachelor like me had to catch his breath."

This time, Jemma couldn't stop herself from looking at him. Staring, really. "You . . . you saw me in Vicky's dress?" She'd made a prototype of the design she and the bride had decided on out of some inexpensive fabric. She and her friend were of like size, and so she'd tried it on a time or two herself, making adjustments here and there. She'd had it at her house a while before taking it to the dressmaking shop where she worked on what would become the actual gown. "When was that?"

Troy's gaze slid away from her. "I don't really remember." Then he slapped his hands together. "Isn't it about time you two lovebirds went on your way?"

Michael grinned at his buddy. "Troy's convinced we should enjoy the hell out of our bliss, Vicky, since he's assured me it's only temporary."

The best man looked chagrined. "Hey, nothing against Vicky or you, Mike."

The groom slid his arm around his new wife and drew her close to kiss the top of her head. "And nothing against you either, my friend, but you don't know what you're talking about. I get that you're not a leap-of-faith type – that's what happens when you study structural engineering, you're all about how things can break apart – but me and my lady have a love situation going on here and we're pretty convinced the circumstance will last."

"Love," Troy repeated.

"That's right," Michael said, grinning. "Can't see it, can't measure it, won't find the details on a blueprint. It's the unexplainable that you just gotta believe in, even though it seems impossible."

The best man's doubtful expression was starting to make Jemma angry. This was Vicky and Michael's big day and Troy was turning it into a big dud. She went on tiptoe to kiss the groom's cheek. "Well your best man is right about one thing . . . you and Vicky have a flight to catch and some sun, fun and umbrella drinks in your near future."

"And sex," Michael added, with an exaggerated leer at his new wife. "We're going to have a seven-day-long rollicking private party in the bedroom."

Troy pretended to frown. "Come on, you're embarrassing Jemma."

Vicky scoffed. "As if she doesn't know about rollicking private parties."

Heat crawled over Jemma's body. She was still in her bridesmaid's dress, another of her own creations, which had a figure-hugging fit and a wide, U-shaped neckline. The apricot color probably clashed with the blush working its way over her throat and toward her face. When she thought of private parties in the bedroom, there was only one man who came to mind.

She could feel Troy's gaze on her. "Really? What has our Jemma been up to while I've been gone?"

Vicky donned a little cat smile, but her eyes narrowed. "As you said, you've been gone."

Suppressing her groan, Jemma dragged her best friend toward the car's passenger side door. "Time for all the good brides and grooms to get on their way." Under her breath, she murmured for Vicky's ears only, "Please don't bait Troy like that. He'll guess something's up."

"Something *is* up," Vicky whispered back. "You and I both know that you've been pining these past six months. You and I both know that you should have told him your feelings before he left. You should have come right out and said—"

"*No.*" Jemma wasn't going to ever think or say such a thing. She had only this one night to get through alone with Troy – and without making any kind of rash confession – and then she'd steer clear of him forever after. She raised her voice. "OK, I have everything under control. I'll gather up anything that shouldn't be left behind—"

"And you'll have to make do with the leftovers in the fridge," Vicky said, sliding into her seat and shutting the door. Then she unrolled the window. "You're stuck here until tomorrow."

When one of the other wedding guests had a business emergency before the ceremony, they'd had to shuffle transportation, leaving the best man and the maid of honor car-less until that friend returned to retrieve them. "Eric promised to be here before ten," Jemma said.

"And before that," Troy added, "we'll hand over the house keys to the undertaker."

Michael snickered as he ducked into the driver's side.

Jemma rolled her eyes. "Caretaker," she corrected.

"Unless the reported ghost of the house drives us screaming into the night," Troy added.

Vicky craned her head out the car window. "Oh, don't worry about that. Didn't you listen to the legend? Once it's full dark, the spirit locks you inside and then there's no escape. The ghost forces you to confess all your sins and all your secrets – unless you're scared to death first."

In the waning light, Jemma's gaze jumped to Troy's. Her secrets are what scared her. How she'd fallen for the lean, hazel-eyed man of logic. How his defection to Argentina had left her devastated.

Only one night, she reminded herself. That was all. She had to get through only this one night keeping everything she felt to herself.

*   *   *

With the honeymooners on their way, Jemma re-entered the house first, Troy behind. When the front door clapped shut at their backs, she couldn't deny the nervous jolt of her heart. Ignoring it, she murmured something about changing her clothes and headed up the stairs to the room she'd shared over the weekend with another bridesmaid.

Now devoid of that woman's overabundance of baggage and belongings crowding the space, the surroundings struck Jemma as if for the first time. Narrow beds of dark wood were placed against two walls, their headboards decorated with intricate carvings of roses and thorns. A pale mauve wallpaper in subtle contrasting stripes adorned the walls, while a border ran near the ceiling. Its design, in the same grey and black of the home's exterior, was of Victorian-styled children's faces. Not "children" she realized. The border depicted image after image of twin girls – one illustrated as a haloed cherub, while the other wore an evil smile and from her tousled curls peeked a pair of devilish horns.

Jemma quickly averted her gaze, and it caught on an ornate frame above a wooden washstand, which held a ceramic pitcher and bowl. The frame held double images too, but they appeared to be two separate old-time photographs of the same beautiful young woman posed in a pale muslin dress. Drawn by the lovely design of lacy flounces and narrow pin-tucks, Jemma walked closer. How she'd love to see that garment in person. The beautiful handwork she found on gowns of other eras was always inspiring.

Once her own dress was removed and put away in her garment bag, Jemma slipped into jeans, a long-sleeved T-shirt and her cosy sheepskin boots. Then she reached for her book, prepared to settle in for that promised read. But those weird twins looking down on her from the wallpaper border made her nerves too jumpy for relaxation. Remembering her promise to Vicky, she decided to do a walk-through of the house to make sure nothing had been left behind.

In the bedroom beside hers she found an abandoned gauzy scarf on the dresser. In the next – her heart jumped. An amputated foot! No, she realized, forcing air into her strangled throat. Merely a lone male sock stretched out on the rug. "Oh, brother," she murmured to herself, bending to retrieve the thing with a trembling hand. "You're getting punchy."

Clamping down on her fanciful imagination, she turned the handle of the subsequent vacant room. As the door swung open, a figure spun toward her. She shrieked – then cut off the sound when she recognized Troy.

"Oh! I'm sorry, I . . ." Her mouth was dry, but she wasn't sure if it was because of her brief fright or because the man was standing in front of her, half-naked. "I didn't know anyone was in here."

He shrugged into an oxford-cloth shirt, not bothering with the buttons. Apparently he'd decided to get more comfortable too. Behind him, she saw his tuxedo hanging in the closet. Now he wore jeans and a pair of battered, moccasin-styled loafers. "I switched rooms," he explained, then gestured behind him. "Bigger bed."

Oh, he had to bring up beds. She felt a resurgence of heat rush over her flesh. They'd burned up the sheets – at least in her opinion – when they'd been together those months before he'd taken off for Argentina. Maybe the sex hadn't been as good as she thought? The temperature of her skin went up a couple more degrees in embarrassment. To get away from him, she started backing through the door.

"Don't go," Troy said, coming closer.

She could smell him. It was faint, but his signature citrus-and-soap scent. Post-orgasm, she'd adored the satisfied languor of afterglow as they spooned body to body. But almost as good was reliving the memory of what had gone before when she showered, the hot water releasing scent-of-Troy from her hair and skin.

After he'd left the country, she'd found a purloined T-shirt of his. Not that she'd ever admit it, but she'd rolled it into a ball and tucked it like a sachet under a stack of her lingerie. The memory made her feel even more foolish, and she shuffled back a few more steps.

"Don't go," Troy repeated.

"We've nothing to say," she said, trying to sound airy, though she was afraid it came out more breathless than anything else. Stupid swathe of naked man skin. Her hand gestured toward his bare chest. "You should cover that."

"Huh?" He glanced down, then looked back at her, his expression . . . flattered? Smug?

Jerk. "You don't want to catch cold your first week back in the States." He'd done nothing more than stash his suitcases in his condo before the wedding party had piled into cars to head toward the rural environs of Vicky and Michael's haunted house wedding.

"About that . . ." Troy started, then his voice trailed off. He rubbed his palm over his breastbone.

"What? You're already sick?"

He grimaced. "I haven't been feeling myself for a long time."

"Take two aspirin and I'll see you in the morning," Jemma advised.

As she turned to leave the room, he caught her arm. The touch sprinted along her skin. Her heart started punching against her ribs like the needle shaft of a sewing machine with a heavy foot on the pedal.

"We should talk," Troy said.

A post-mortem of their relationship? She didn't think she could take it. For the last six months, she'd done her own autopsy on a nearly nightly basis. Holding on to her dignity, Jemma stepped away from his restraining hand and thought of something innocuous to discuss. "It was a lovely wedding, wasn't it?" There, that should do it.

"But a little weird, Jem, let's admit it. A haunted house?"

"I think Vicky might blame that on us. We *are* the ones who introduced them at that Halloween party, after all."

A little smile kicked up the corner of Troy's mouth. "I was just trying to get rid of our two friends so I could take you into a dark corner and peel off that cat costume you were wearing."

"What are you talking about? You went as Bond, James Bond, and I was Pussy Galore."

"Exactly." There was now a gleam in his wicked eyes.

He was playing with her. Toying with memories that teased up images of the two of them together. That night he *had* taken her to a dark corner. She'd not been dressed as a cat. Her costume had been straight out of the movie *Goldfinger*, a to-the-knee pencil skirt, pointed-toe high heels, which could serve as ice picks, and a wrap-style satin blouse she'd sewn for the occasion. The skirt had been too tight for panties. Underneath the shiny top she'd worn a lacy vintage bra that had lifted and separated her breasts into prominent cone shapes. The outfit had been, she admitted, a little outrageous.

What he'd done with his hand beneath her skirt was even more so. In the middle of the party – OK, their corner had been *very* dark and nearly isolated – he'd inched up her skirt to thigh height and then kissed the protests out of her as his hand found the wetness between her legs. She could only clutch his shoulders and hide behind his broad chest while he slid two long fingers inside her. When he'd caressed her clitoris, she'd tumbled right over the edge.

"Troy," she whispered now, then cleared her throat to strengthen her voice. "That . . . that was in the past." Months before he'd left for Argentina. And in all the time he'd been out of the country, he hadn't sent a text, an email, or even a postcard.

The person with the wish-you-were-here thoughts had been Jemma and Jemma alone.

So they weren't going to be expressed aloud, no matter what Vicky counseled. The words would not cross Jemma's lips.

As if that last thought had telegraphed, Troy reached out and brushed his thumb along her mouth. Goosebumps tripped over Jemma's chin to run down her neck and tighten her nipples. "Pretty girl . . ." he said, his voice hoarse.

Her heart started pounding again.

"I missed you, Jem." His voice was as soft as that thumb caressing her lips. "I missed this and every other thing about you."

It was her desperate willingness to believe him that sent her running. She stumbled away from Troy's seductive touch and sprinted for her room. Inside, she braced her shoulders against the door and put her face in her hands.

You can't fall for that, she reminded herself. *He left you before, without you even seeing it coming, without you even getting a hint of things not going right. He left you. Without a backward glance.*

Without a text, an email, or a postcard during the following six months.

She clunked the back of her head against the wood and let her hands fall to her sides. She stared, unseeing, at the darkness outside her window as the truth welled up.

"But I still love him," she whispered, the words no longer containable. "I'm in love with him, but I have to let him go. He can never know how I feel."

The lights in the room snapped out. The temperature dropped from normal to icy. Suddenly, the solid surface at her back swung inward as the door flew open. Unbalanced, Jemma stumbled into the hall. On its own, the door moved again, slamming shut.

And terrified, Jemma screamed.

Two

At the sound of Jemma's blood-curdling yell, Troy leaped through his open doorway and into the hall. Her slender figure stood a few feet away, her body shaking, her arms wrapped in a tight self-hug. He couldn't see what had set her off.

"Jemma?"

She whirled toward him, then seemed to fly through the air and into his embrace, her slender body slamming against his torso. Scanning the area for evidence of rodent or insect, he folded his arms around her. "What is it?"

She was pressed so close he could feel her frantic heartbeat against his ribcage. "I . . ." Then she shook her head and buried her face in his shirt.

Troy stroked her dark blonde hair. For the wedding, she'd worn it in an elegant roll at the back of her neck, but it was free now, and he sifted his fingers through the silky, shoulder-length strands. Having her in his arms again was . . . well, it wasn't supposed to be like this. His buddy Michael was right. Troy was a structural engineer. Troy was experienced in what happened when things fell apart – both from a professional and personal point of view. It was why he'd grabbed at the chance to take over the project in Argentina.

He figured he'd spare both himself and Jemma the disaster that was certainly looming between them. Six months, he'd reasoned, would be enough time to dispel the chemistry that had propelled them into bed. Six months would dissolve what had been building between them – putting a less-painful end to their relationship, one that saved them both from the devastation of the inevitable, total structural collapse.

Idiot that he was, though, when he'd been alone with her only a few minutes, he hadn't been able stop himself from telling her the truth.

In those six months, he'd missed her.

He'd missed touching her . . . and he wanted to touch her some more.

But that was a bad idea – their bond was gone – or near to it, anyway. So now, when she shoved against him, apparently trying to break his hold, he was all about re-establishing their autonomy. His head was, anyway. Because damned if his arms didn't stay locked around her.

"Troy," she said, looking up at him.

Jemma had the sweetest face. Heart-shaped, with a pair of blue eyes that were almost as enticing as her small mouth with its full, lower lip. She wasn't beautiful in a look-at-me sort of way – except perhaps in her Pussy Galore get-up – but she caught a guy's eye and made him think . . .

Mine.

Oh, hell, that's what he was thinking. Yes. Now. Again.

Mine.

She licked that puffy bottom lip. "Troy."

He tried refocusing on practical matters. "What scared you, honey? Why'd you scream?"

"I . . ." She shook her head, looked away. "I'm going to sound crazy."

Some of that's been going around, he thought. Look at me, still entwined with the woman I tried so hard to forget. "Give it a try."

Jemma glanced over her shoulder. "This is hard to believe, but . . . someone, something, propelled me out of my bedroom and slammed the door shut in my face. When you showed up, I felt hands on my back, forcing me in your direction."

He remembered the crash of her body against his. "It was just your fear. You spooked yourself."

She shuddered, then took a deep breath. "Sure," she said, stepping out of his embrace. "Of course, you're right."

"Let me open your bedroom door for you," Troy said.

"No. I can do it. I can handle everything on my own."

Telling himself it was for the best, he watched her move away from him. Her fingers reached for the brass knob. He saw her wrist turn, but only the slightest bit.

She looked over her shoulder at him, her expression strained. "It's locked."

"Locked?" He frowned. "Let me." But it *was* locked. And so, weirdly enough, were the doors on either side of hers. All the others were too, they then discovered. Every single bedroom door on the second floor wouldn't budge. The lone exception was Troy's. It still stood open, the warm glow from the bedside lamps leaking into the hall.

They both looked at the inviting light and then at each other. "I'm going downstairs," Jemma said hastily. "I'm going to make some tea and then camp out on the couch in the parlor for the night."

"I can break the locks. Force open a door—"

"*No!* I mean, we shouldn't do any damage. In the morning, it will be up to the caretaker to get me back in my room for my things."

"Then I'll take the couch."

"Absolutely not." She was shaking her head. "I'm smaller. I'll be fine down there by myself."

Not that he believed in premonitions, but something cold and prickly cruised along his spine as he watched her hurry down the stairs. "Be careful," he heard himself call out as she reached the landing.

The staircase turn took her out of sight and swallowed any reply she might have made. Troy stood there for several more moments, torn between keeping his distance and the eerie urge to keep her safe. Surely they were both better off apart?

He scrubbed his face with his hands, then sighed, and turned toward his bedroom. As he neared the threshold, a cold breeze rushed past him. The door to his refuge slammed in his face, leaving him in the hall.

Three

Jemma had left her purse in the kitchen downstairs. Her hands were shaking as she rifled through it for her cell phone. Once she established the call to her best friend, she roamed the downstairs, turning on every light she could find. It wasn't that many, because she discovered that nearly all the doors on the first floor were locked as well. She had access to the kitchen, the smallish parlor, and the downstairs powder room.

It was a draft, or the weather, or some odd trick of the security system, she told herself, but as soon as Vicky picked up she blurted out an idea that was scaring the heck out of her. "There's a ghost here, Vick. I swear to God I think this place is really haunted!"

The line went quiet. They'd discovered over the course of the weekend that the cell phone coverage was sparse and sporadic. Had she already lost her best friend? "Vicky? Vicky?"

Her voice came through, tinny. "Haunted?"

Jemma pushed her hand through her hair. "That can't possibly be true, can it? Something has me unbalanced."

"Some*one*," her friend said. "You know it's Troy who has you messed up, not to mention those feelings for him that you're keeping bottled inside."

Jemma groaned. Troy again. But Vicky's assertion had some truth to it. She remembered saying she loved him out loud and the next thing she knew, she'd been tossed from her room – and then into his arms.

She wasn't going to think about that. His embrace had felt so warm, so right – no, she wasn't going to think about that at all. He was upstairs, she was down, and it was better that way. In the kitchen, she put on a kettle for tea. "I'm sorry I bothered you on your honeymoon, Vick."

"Oh, we're still miles from the airport." The connection was clearer now. "You could entertain me, if you want, by telling me what you think you saw."

"I didn't *see* anything. I just felt . . ." She thought of those creepy cherub/devil figures in her room. The roses and thorns on the headboards of the bed. "This place is creepy, Vick."

"Of course it is. That's why it has a reputation. And the ghost legend. Lovely Lily haunts the place because her jealous twin pushed her down the stairs."

Twins? Jemma's skin seemed to shrink against her bones. "I don't think I want to know any more."

"Didn't you listen the first night when I read the story? Oh, no, that's right, you were upstairs repairing the hem of my little sister's bridesmaid's dress."

"I think I'm glad I missed out."

"Well, you know most of it now," Vicky replied, cheerful, and Jemma figured it was because she was moving in the opposite direction of this hair-raising house.

Lovely Lily. Jemma swallowed, hard.

But then the kettle began to sing. The happy whistle somewhat eased her nerves. Nothing could be really terrible when there was a hot cup of tea in the offing, right? She sighed. "You might as well tell me the whole story."

"Two sisters, twins as I said, Lily and Rose, who lived in the house about 140 years ago."

Jemma thought of those matching photographs in the room upstairs. Two women in old-fashioned dresses. "Go on."

"Lily had a suitor, but Rose didn't want to lose her twin and was adamantly against the match. When the man came one last time to argue his suit, he was sent away. But Lily had second thoughts and made to go after him. Rose was so angry that she pushed Lily down the stairs and she broke her neck in the fall. It's said she haunts the house, forever waiting for her beau to return."

Lovely Lily, Jemma thought, watching steam rising from a thick white mug as she poured the boiling water over a tea bag, forever waiting.

But with the scent of cinnamon and cloves in the air, she was starting to believe she'd imagined the whole episode upstairs. Though the Lily–Rose story was both sad and a little scary, it was just a story. Surely those suddenly locked doors had some innocuous explanation. Why, she could probably head up there right now and discover the door unlocked and her room once again available.

But those weird angel–devil faces would be looking down at her. And then there was Troy. He was upstairs too, in tempting proximity. Safer to stay below, farther away from him.

Before she could wrap up her conversation with Vicky, the call dropped. With another sigh, Jemma flicked off her phone and set it down, then brought her tea to her nose. The relaxing scent eased more of the tension in her shoulders.

She'd been overreacting. Of course the house wasn't haunted. It was just a story.

Then movement caught her eye. Her spine snapped straight. Hot liquid sloshed over her fingers and a little bleat escaped her lips as a figure suddenly appeared in the doorway.

Oh. Troy.

That it was him didn't relieve the renewed jangling of her nerves. "W-what are you doing down here?"

His expression was grim. "It's cold as a witch's . . . nose up there. And it just so happens that now I'm locked out of my bedroom too."

"Um . . ."

"Yeah," he said, as if she'd replied with an articulate answer. "I'm afraid we'll be spending the night together, sweetheart."

Four

Troy built up the fire in the parlor, determined there'd be no need for them to huddle together to stay warm. They both avoided the subject of the locked doors – at the moment he had no reasonable explanation – as they made a meal of wedding reception leftovers.

Afterward, they sat side by side on the rug in front of the hearth, each staring into the flames. A few moments passed, with only the pop and hiss of the fire interrupting the quiet. Then Jemma cleared her throat.

Troy glanced over at her, and then continued staring, fascinated by the lines of her profile. "What?"

Her gaze cut his way, then shot forward again. "Maybe we could call a taxi. Find another place to stay for the night."

The idea had occurred to him as well, but then practicality had squashed it. "Even if we could find a driver willing, the ride here and back would take at least three hours. We'd have to turn around and do it all over again at dawn." He worked to insert a light, teasing note into his voice. "C'mon, are you that nervous about being alone with me?"

"We just don't . . ."

"What?"

"Have anything to say to each other. Not anymore."

He shouldn't deny it. "Sure we do. We haven't seen each other in six months. Lots to catch up on."

She drew her knees to her chest. "Oh, sure. I can't wait to hear about all the pretty girls in bikinis you spent time with at Ipanema."

"Brazil has the famous Ipanema Beach. And I didn't date while I was in Argentina. I had . . . other things on my mind. What about you? Vicky hinted about some, uh, private parties that you had?" It was stupid to see red and feel green when he thought about them, about her with anyone else, but there it was.

"I was too busy working to do any . . . private partying."

He shouldn't feel so relieved. "Lots of dresses to make?"

"Mm. And my aunt is cutting back on her hours and giving me more responsibility." She made a sucking-on-lemons face. "I'm actually using my business degree, emphasis on accounting."

He smiled, because she always said it that way, as if the words tasted bad in her mouth. *Business degree, emphasis on accounting.* "You like the design and dressmaking best, though."

"We have that in common – the creating of things." She was silent a moment. "How about you? Was it all work, work, work, or did you take some time off to explore? Did you see penguins? The famous waterfalls?"

Huh. If she knew about the penguins and the waterfalls, then he figured she'd been blowing smoke with that Ipanema remark . . . An offhand way to find out if he'd been seeing other women? "So, you've been reading up on Argentina?" Over the last six months, had she been thinking about him too?

"I have the internet, I can spell."

He'd never once emailed her. A thousand times he'd considered it, but he'd wanted a clean break. A painless one. He settled back on his elbows instead of grabbing her in his arms like he wanted to, reminding himself of all the reasons they shouldn't be together again. "My youngest half-brother came to visit me for a few weeks. We toured around then."

She looked at him now. "You have a half-brother?"

"Step-siblings too, actually."

Pivoting on her cute little ass, she turned to face him, her back now to the fire. "You said your mom and dad were divorced, that you weren't close."

"They are. We're not. It's sort of hard to keep the connections tight when they both moved on to other spouses, other kids, more divorces. The latest victim of the fallout is twenty-year-old Evan. Poor kid took a leave of absence from college to get away from our mom's most recent debacle. She goes into marriage like a lamb and gets out like a lion. Lots of carnage."

"Carnage?" Jemma shivered.

He laughed a little, the sound not really amusement. "No actual body parts. But she used Evan's SUV to run over her husband's golf cart – though her spouse wasn't in it at the time."

"That's . . . awful."

"Yeah. Puts my own loss into a little perspective. I was eleven when she divorced my dad. She went after the model of the Golden Gate Bridge the two of us had been working on for nearly a year. One thwack with a baseball bat and all I had left were a couple of buckets of toothpicks and a robust aversion to marriage."

She scooted closer. "Oh, Troy." Her hand touched his thigh and her voice lowered. "No wonder you worry about how things will break apart."

Her words didn't sink into his consciousness. All he was aware of was those small fingers of hers, just inches from his groin. Blood rushed to meet them, getting waylaid at his cock. It went hard, and all his other muscles tensed, trying to restrain the urge to yank her on top of him. Jesus, he wanted inside of her, just like that. Inside of Jemma.

Now.

"Troy . . ." She shook her head.

"What?" He nearly groaned the word. If she didn't do something soon, move away, move back, distract him, damn it, he was going strip her naked and take all night to slake his desire for her body.

"Talk to me, Jem." About thread or fabric. Better yet, ice and snow. His pulse was pounding. Demanding. "Tell me what's on your mind."

"I . . . I . . ." She looked down. "I can't. I promised myself I wouldn't."

"Please, Jemma." Troy jackknifed up, his fingers curling into fists to stop himself from grabbing for her. He was supposed to be keeping his distance! "If you don't—"

"Kiss me," she commanded, her head coming up. "I don't want to talk anymore about anything. I just want you."

There was no thought of refusal. In a crash of torso and mouths, they grasped each other. Lips fused, arms entwined, they tumbled together onto the rug. Troy shifted, rolling on top of her and using his hips to make a place for himself between her legs. Her pelvis pressed upward, into his, and she moaned.

He tilted his head and thrust his tongue deeper into her mouth. She tasted like cloves and cinnamon and the sweetness of something too long denied. "Jemma," he said against her lips. "God, this is so good."

One hand found its way beneath her stretchy T-shirt. Her midriff was silky and warm and he splayed his hand over her bare skin, just absorbing the pleasure of her flesh beneath his palm. She squirmed, her lower body abrading his cock, and a rush of hot chills dashed up his spine.

His hand slid toward her breast. She arched into his touch and moaned again as his thumb scraped over the nipple he could feel beneath her bra. "Tell me what you're feeling."

She ignored this order to tug at the tails of his shirt. He grabbed the fabric between his shoulder blades to yank it up and off, feeling the pop of buttons giving way. One pinged as it hit the floor, and she laughed, the sound giddy.

Bare chested, he stared down at the stunning sight of her. Firelight turned her blonde hair to reddish-gold and illuminated the flush of arousal on her face. Her mouth was wet from his kisses, her features bearing the soft stamp of need. "Troy . . ."

"Tell me what you're feeling," he whispered, sliding his hands beneath her T-shirt and letting his wrists draw up the hem as his fingers caressed her warm skin. Lifting his palms to avoid touching her breasts, he peeled away the fabric and threw it to the side. "You're with me, aren't you?"

He wanted to hear that she was as turned on as he was. It was only fair. For six damn long months he'd tossed and turned and thought of all the things he wanted to do to her creamy flesh.

She made an inarticulate sound as he unfastened the front hook of her bra. Then, careful not to touch her himself, he lifted the cups from her skin. The heat of the fire caressed her now, and he imagined how hot her flesh would feel against his tongue once he took one of the tightly budded nipples between his lips.

Then he couldn't wait another second. He bent toward her breast, and sucked the tip, hard, rubbing his tongue around it and pushing it against the roof of his mouth. Her eyes closed, her fingers slid into his hair, and he played with the rhythm, hard, soft, fast flicks, long pulls. Her nails bit into his scalp and he lifted his head to blow cool air on the tortured nipple.

She moaned again, and he went to work on the other, his

pulse pounding faster, his lust ratcheting higher. When she called his name he took her mouth again and worked one hand between them to strip away her jeans and panties. She kicked free of her boots and then all the rest, leaving her naked to his gaze.

His heart slammed against his breastbone, the power of his lust paralysing him. Then he was moving again, his gaze running over her curves as he undressed. As she watched him through half-closed eyes, one small foot crept up, opening her thighs so he could see the glint of arousal on the petaled flesh between her legs.

His balls drew up, and he was ready, too ready. Clearly she was eager too, but he needed to slow this down or he'd be on her like an animal. With deep breaths, he fumbled with the condom from his wallet and rolled it into place. Then he drew the back of his forefinger from the notch at her throat to the soft curls at her cleft.

"Tell me what you feel," he asked again.

She shook her head, her lips pressing together as if to keep to herself some great secret.

"Silly Jemma," he said. "You know you can't hide from me." His fingers slid lower, into her slick wetness.

Her breath caught as he toyed with her. "Troy. Troy, please."

God, that little plea in her voice turned him on. The first time they'd had sex she'd floored him with it – that almost hiccup of sound that was the epitome of vulnerable femininity.

It had made him want to drag her back to his cave, which he'd done, in a manner of speaking. They'd been at her place, but right there and then he'd insisted on a change of venue. Only taking time to bundle her in a quilt, he'd carried her to his condo upstairs. When they'd both climaxed, it had been in *his* bed.

They'd spent the weekend at *his* place.

Monday morning, as she went through his front door to get ready for work, he'd been so bereft he'd known they were heading for trouble. But he'd been so besotted he hadn't cared.

Until that afternoon months later when he'd come home from work early. Thinking he'd surprise her, he stepped onto her little patio that he could access from the walkway. Peering through the sliding glass door, he'd glimpsed her in that mock-up of her best friend's wedding dress.

And started thinking about marriage. A week later he'd left the country.

"Troy. *Troy.*"

She was calling his name in that needy way again. He shoved away the old memories and focused on the moment. Jemma, her hips twisting as she tried to get more of his touch. He slid two fingers inside her and her muscles clamped down, the grip causing another round of chills to race over his skin.

"*Troy.*"

Restraint was over. He slid free of her flesh, heard her reluctant cry, and then lowered himself over her again. Her sleek thighs lifted, rubbing against his hips. The tip of him found her wet, swollen notch. Her hips tilted and he thrust forward.

Seeking home.

His mouth found a nipple again, giving her the edge of his teeth as he drove forward again. And again. And again.

He let her flesh pop free of his mouth. He sat back on his heels, spreading her open with his thighs, her legs draped over his. It was an incredible view, Jemma accepting his flesh, receiving his driving shaft, taking him in, and in, and in.

She lifted one hand to press against her nipple while the other gripped his knee. He was close, so close.

"Jemma," he said, his voice urgent. Was she with him? Almost there? He took her clitoris between his thumb and forefinger. "Tell me what you feel."

The stubborn girl moaned.

"Tell me what you feel," he ordered again, rubbing the sides of that button of flesh. His orgasm was ready to launch. In her quivering muscles, he felt hers gathering. But he needed to be sure. He worked her clitoris with a more demanding touch. "Jemma, tell me what you feel."

Her hips rose. Her inner muscles pulled his cock deeper. Heated bliss shot up his shaft. She convulsed and he dropped back over her body, thrusting home once more, twice, as she finally acquiesced to what he'd asked, using words that built a bridge between them all over again.

"I love you," Jemma said, still coming. "I love you."

Five

Stupid, Jemma admonished herself. Stupid, stupid woman. She'd left Troy asleep in front of the fire and now, back in her clothes, she was heading up the staircase, no longer concerned about locked doors or otherworldly hauntings.

Not when the very real and very dangerous ghost was out – the echo of those words she'd let slip as he propelled her toward paradise. *I love you.* How could she have allowed herself to say the one thing she'd promised herself she wouldn't?

Of course he'd said nothing in response to her awkward, awful confession. She could only hope he'd continue pretending he'd never heard those fateful three words. It wasn't as if *she* were going to bring them up a second time. What if you slip again? a little voice inside her asked.

Over my dead body!

She'd reached her bedroom. It didn't surprise her that the doorknob turned easily. She only felt relief, as her plan was to get into bed and pull the covers over her head and hide beneath them until morning. At first light she'd be waiting on the front porch with her suitcase, and hope that her ride back to civilization and sanity came early.

"When I get home," she murmured to herself, pushing open the door, "I'll move out of my condo and never see that man again."

Her feet turned in the direction of the bed, then stuttered to a halt. As the door behind her shut with a definitive click, she stared at the stranger seated on the dainty coverlet.

Jemma's hand crept to her throat. "Who are you?"

"In this case, your guardian angel," the woman said. Not that she had wings or a halo. Her dark hair was pulled back in a bun, and she wore lace-up, low-heeled shoes with her white nightgown.

Not nightgown . . . *dress*. Jemma's gaze traveled from the person on the bed to the photographs on the other side of the room. She must be dreaming, because those flounces and pintucks the twins were wearing in the pictures were of the same design that this . . . guest was wearing right now.

She blinked, then made another detail-by-detail comparison, her eyes taking in the identical ruffles, the identical button placement. "Is that a . . . a vintage gown you have on?"

"Who cares about clothes at a time like this?" the stranger said, clearly disgruntled.

Jemma put her hand to her head. "I'm a dress designer."

"I don't care if you're President Grant's personal tailor."

"Grant?" Oh, this was a really weird dream.

"Ulysses S., of course. Favorite of my father, though *I* wouldn't have voted for him, even if women had such a right."

Jemma just stared at the stranger, fixated by that dress . . . or oh, God, the fact that she could see *through* the dress. Her mouth went dry as her knees buckled and she sank to the floor. "Lily?" she croaked out. *Lovely Lily, forever waiting.*

The figure in white threw up her hands. "Why does everyone think of her first? They liked her best and it was always that way. Lily this, Lily that. Lily, won't you dance with me? Lily, here are some flowers. Lily, I brought you chocolates."

"R-rose?" Jemma scooted back on her butt. Was this Rose, the one who'd tossed her sister down the stairs in a fit of jealous rage?

"Don't look at me like that," the woman snapped out. "Why should you be afraid of a ghost? I should be afraid that you're going to ruin my chance at redemption."

OK, Jemma had had enough of this dizzying conversation. Clearly she was still asleep. "Troy?" She called his name, though it didn't come out much louder than a whisper. "Troy, please wake me up." She edged back some more, until her rump met the solid wood of the door.

Whoever, *whatever*, was sitting on the bed let out a gusty sigh and rolled her eyes. "You won't get away that easily, missy."

Jemma's throat tightened. "Troy," she croaked. "*Please* wake me up." She'd take the embarrassment of facing him over this creepy dream confrontation with the bad seed twin any day.

"Let's talk about him," the ghost said. "This Troy fellow."

He'd been Jemma's lover, then he'd gone away. Tonight, he'd become her lover again, but it wasn't going to last this time either, she knew that, because the practical, logical, science-minded man he was would never believe in something as ephemeral as love. He'd talked of his parents' nasty divorce. *All I had left were a couple of buckets of toothpicks and a robust aversion to marriage.* Apparently their next marriages hadn't gone much better either, cementing his conviction that love and commitment weren't worthy of his trust.

"You mustn't let him get away," the woman on the bed said. "The two of you belong together."

Jemma's head was reeling. "You really think so?"

The woman rolled her eyes again. "I'm a restless spirit, not a fortune-teller. I can only hope you're meant to be together because if I'm instrumental in your happy ending I have high hopes I can finally leave this house and move on."

"Redemption," Jemma said, the pieces finally fitting. The woman had said that word. "Lily isn't the one who stayed behind after her death, but you, for your part in it."

"Which I didn't exactly cause, contrary to rumor," Rose said. "She always was the clumsy twin. But I'm unable to leave here because I shouldn't have meddled. The fact is, I pretended I was Lily when her suitor came to propose marriage and it was I who rejected him. When she discovered the truth, she tripped over her own two feet as she ran to catch him."

"Poor Lily," Jemma murmured.

"Poor Lily?" Rose echoed. "How about poor me? This place got a reputation for hauntings and I've waited forever for some lovers to arrive who need my intervention. This is not a romantic destination, as you probably guess."

"Until Vicky and Michael, who met on Halloween."

"Just so." The ghost waved her hand. "Now go tell that Troy person you love him and let him return the sentiment and everyone gets what they want."

"I did tell him I love him," Jemma said.

The air in the room chilled. "What?" Rose seemed to waver where she sat. "Then what did he do?"

"He pretended he didn't hear. After that he went to sleep."

"Men!" Rose scowled, then made another little shooing gesture. "Well, go on. Go tell him again," she ordered. "Insist he love you back."

Jemma shook her head.

In a blink, Rose came off the bed, rage written all over her face. "Don't thwart me," she said, hovering in place, her old-fashioned shoes six inches off the floor. Her eyes widened and the iris and sclera went black. "You'll do as I say, you hear me?"

Again Jemma shook her head, even as the temperature in the room turned icy and her body started to shake. "I-it won't work."

"It *will* work," Rose said, her voice filled with a foreboding as dark as her eyes. "*It must work.* This is how to lay my spirit to rest. Don't you believe in me?"

Though Jemma's heart started pumping in panic – the creature looked devilish now – she remained in place. "Oh, yes, you've made me believe in ghosts, Rose."

"Then—"

"But you can't convince me that Troy will allow himself to believe in love."

Six

In Troy's dream he was striding down the walkway at his condo complex, aware of the smile on his face, anticipating the pleased surprise on Jemma's when she saw him. He'd thought a meeting would keep him from their regular Tuesday dinner date, but a last-minute cancellation had freed him to spend the evening with his favorite neighbor.

The beautiful woman who'd been sharing his bed for longer than any woman before her.

Jemma amazed him. She was bright, creative, loyal to family and friends . . . and undemanding when it came to him. He could hardly believe how easy she was about their relationship. She had never asked where they were headed. Never hinted at wanting to put a label on what they were to each other.

The thought of that made him so damn happy that he took a shortcut to her place. Rather than walking the long way around to her front door, he cut through a break in the vegetation surrounding her small patio. He knew she was working at home.

Glimpsing her figure through the sliding glass doors, he lifted his hand to knock, then went suddenly still. She was in front of a long mirror, her sewing supplies set out on the dining-room table nearby. White fabric clung like a lover to her breasts and hips, then fell in soft folds to the ground. As he watched, she picked up a length of gauzy material and in a flash fashioned a veil which she pinned to the crown of her head.

Jemma – dressed as a bride.

And just like that, he wanted Jemma as *his* bride.

It scared the living daylights out of him, wanting marriage with her. Marriages broke apart. Marriages broke people.

And beyond that, Jemma had never once given him the impression she couldn't live without him. She'd never once hinted that she might want to be his wife.

Worried that his desire for permanence with her would only grow, and hers stay dormant, as her so-casual attitude seemed to imply, Troy made a phone call to his boss and volunteered for the Argentina job.

The truth was, he hadn't left to spare them both the pain of a failed relationship, but to spare *himself*. Once he'd started thinking of wanting to build something real and lasting with her, he'd run because he wasn't convinced she felt the same.

Troy started awake, the dream fresh in his mind, the admission fresh in his heart. Argentina had been his bolthole from his own fears.

And tonight, after a six-month absence, Jemma had told him she loved him.

He rolled his head to where he expected to find her, only to discover she wasn't under the quilt he'd pulled over them after making love. An event during which she'd revealed her feelings and he'd responded with a stunned silence.

Troy groaned aloud. "What should I do now?"

"Tell the woman you love her, ask her to marry you, and get on with the rest of your lives," a voice said.

Startled, he shot to a sitting position. The blanket pooled at his lap, and he was glad that some time before falling asleep he'd pulled on his jeans for warmth. His head whipped around, his gaze catching on a woman wearing a long dress and weird shoes standing by the parlor entrance. "How did you get here?" he demanded.

"I never left."

She was a wedding guest? It had been a very small group, though, and he didn't remember meeting her.

"Now let's get down to business," the stranger said, drifting closer.

Troy blinked, stared, blinked, then stared again. "Drifting" was the operative word. The woman's feet didn't touch the floor. She was *floating* toward him.

"Who? How?" He rubbed a hand over his face. "What the hell is going on?"

"I'm Rose," the odd lady said.

"Rose?"

The floater sighed. "As in Lily and Rose, the source of the house's legend?"

"Rose? The evil twin Rose?" he asked, harking back to the ghost story Vicky had shared on their arrival. Was this some history re-enactor who had got the wedding date wrong?

A gust of cold air disturbed the smoldering fire. Sparks flew. "I am *not* the evil twin! Most people liked my sister more than me, true, but that just confirmed my opinion that most people are lacking adequate wit."

Or more than adequate judgement of character, Troy thought, rubbing his hand over his face again. Then he squinted, trying to sharpen his vision. In the dim room, lit only by the low flames of the fire, the stranger still appeared to be floating off the floor. "Where's Jemma?" he asked.

"She wouldn't do as she was told." The lady frowned. "Lily was like that. Stubborn."

A shiver rolled down Troy's spine. In the legend, Rose pushed her sister down the stairs. He shot to his feet. "Jemma?" he yelled. "Jemma?"

When he didn't get a response, his stomach roiled. "Where is she? What have you done to her?" He stepped toward the stranger and reached for her arm, determined to get an answer.

His fingers slid through her pale flesh. His heart froze, as he realized the figure in front of him wasn't solid.

She wasn't real.

He stumbled back, rubbing his clammy hand on his thigh. "I'm dreaming."

"She said you'd be hard to convince."

"I'm still asleep." He took another step back.

"Pinch yourself," the strange woman suggested. "That's supposed to be the test."

"I don't need to pinch myself," Troy said. "I'm asleep. I'm dreaming. There's no such thing as ghosts."

"His name was Roger Willow. And the fact is, I think he should be haunting this forsaken place too, because he was at least a little bit responsible for my sister's death. When I turned down his marriage proposal, posing as Lily, why did he walk away?"

Troy wondered if he'd remember all this in the morning. He usually didn't recall his dreams upon waking, but this one was a doozy. Skirting the white-clad woman, he stepped toward the nest of blankets in front of the fire.

The dream-ghost was still talking. "Wouldn't any man worth his salt, who really cared for a woman, at least stick around a while?"

Troy stilled. He'd set into motion his plans to leave the very night he realized his feelings for Jemma. Seven days later he'd been gone. "Maybe he couldn't believe she'd really love him back."

"Maybe he was a coward."

That too. "Marriages break apart," Troy said. "Marriages break people."

The ghost gave him a malevolent smile. "Bones break too, when a person takes a nasty spill on the stairs."

Troy's blood iced over. "Where's Jemma?" He knew he was addressing this dream figure, shouting at it, actually, but he didn't feel asleep any longer. He felt terrified for the sweetheart he'd stupidly left behind six months ago. "*Where is Jemma?*"

Shrugging, the spirit just smiled again.

In the distance, Troy heard banging. Upstairs. Someone knocking on a bedroom door as if trying to get out. "Jem!" he yelled, running from the parlor and toward the staircase.

He heard her muffled shout.

"I'm coming, Jem!" Troy took the stairs two at a time. As he reached the landing, he pivoted for the next flight, his eyes on the room she'd been assigned. His foot was on the first tread when her door burst open. He halted as she came flying through.

Relief poured through his system, followed quickly by horror. *Bones break too, when a person takes a nasty spill on the stairs.* He barked out a caution. "Slow down!"

But it was too late. One of Jemma's feet seemed to tangle with the other and she started to tumble.

Troy's heart went with her.

Seven

Jemma opened her eyes. She was in the parlor, in front of the fire, cradled in Troy's arms. Looking up, she met his gaze. Heat rushed across her skin and she swallowed to lubricate her voice. "I had the weirdest dream."

"Yeah?"

Her gaze dropped to his bare chest. "Oh." Heat flashed over her face again. "I guess that part really happened."

He laughed. "Felt pretty real to me."

But maybe she'd dreamed the embarrassing admission. Except then he tipped up her chin with the back of his hand and looked her once again in the eyes. "You love me, Jemma?"

"I . . ."

"Because you can't measure it, you know."

She sighed. "I know."

"Doesn't weigh anything."

"You're right."

"Something that ephemeral could just . . . blow away."

She narrowed her eyes at him. "Or take off to Argentina for six months."

He gave her a sheepish smile. "I deserve that. And I'm not sure I deserve your love."

"Me neither," Jemma groused. "So let's just forget I said those three little words."

"Nah. I'm not going to forget anything that happened tonight."

She went to push her hair away from her face. "Ouch." Her fingers found a lump above her temple. "What happened here?"

"You bumped your head on the banister."

Memory came back. Being locked inside her room. Troy calling her name, his voice panicked. The door finally opening, her sprint for the stairs, her loss of balance at the top, a sharp pain, then . . .

"You made sure I didn't fall down the stairs," she said.

Troy hesitated. "Someone made sure you didn't fall down the stairs."

"Huh?"

With a little sigh, his arms tightened on her. "Jemma, I don't know how to begin . . ."

Another thought occurred. Pulling free of Troy's embrace,

she sat up and looked around the room. There was no ghostly presence lurking in the parlor.

"Jem?"

She scrambled to her feet, Troy following suit. He put his arm around her when she wobbled a little. "Sweetheart," he said. "What is it?"

Without answering, she explored the first floor. As the early morning sun lit the windows, she discovered that all the rooms were now accessible. At the bottom of the stairs, she looked up and could see that the bedroom doors on the second floor were standing open.

The ambient temperature was pleasant. Outside, she could hear birds chirping.

"She's gone," Jemma said to Troy. She didn't know exactly how she was certain, but she was. Rose no longer haunted the house. Then she smiled into the eyes of the logical, practical, science-minded man who held her heart. "You love me, don't you?"

"Hey!" He pasted on a mock-frown. "You took those three little words right out of my mouth."

"You can't measure it," she reminded him, giddy. He loved her! "It doesn't weigh anything."

"But I believe in it," Troy said, taking her into his arms. "I believe in you and me and happy ever after."

"What changed your mind?"

"When Rose saved your life . . . and so saved mine as well."

Jemma raised her brows. "Rose?" She couldn't wait to hear her structural engineer explain the reality of a restless spirit.

He kissed her forehead, her nose and then her mouth. "It's a long story," he said against her lips. "It's going to take a while to tell it."

"How much time is that, exactly?" Jemma asked, pressing her cheek against his heart and holding him tight.

"Sixty years? Longer, with a good diet and exercise."

She giggled. "Let's have tofu for breakfast then, followed by a brisk walk."

He pushed her away just enough to look into her face. "I love you so much, Jemma Scott."

"I'm convinced of it," Jemma said. As he led her toward the kitchen, Jemma sent her gaze skyward. *Thanks, Rose*, she mouthed. *For an evil twin, you weren't so bad after all.*

Ghost of a Chance

Caridad Piñeiro

One

Tracy Gomez had heard her share of contest prizes that were too good to be true, but it was hard to ignore this one.

From the personal delivery of the invitation via bonded courier to the name of the very reputable New York law firm on the return address, everything about this contest seemed genuine.

A one million dollar prize to anyone who could solve the mystery of the Ryan deaths, which had occurred nearly eighty years earlier. An infamous case involving a politician, his actress wife and their daughter. It was a winner-take-all challenge set to take place at the former Ryan mansion, now a historic site in Sea Girt, New Jersey.

As a local true crime writer, Tracy had some familiarity with the basics of the case. Francis "Skippy" Ryan had been an up-and-coming state senator. His wife, Anna Dolan, had made a name for herself in an assortment of small roles on Broadway and attracted the eye of the handsome senator.

Romance ensued and soon the two were an item, making the rounds of the nightclubs and local hang-outs. Surprising everyone with their unlikely marriage and the child that followed barely nine months after. Although tongues were wagging about the precipitous birth, the marriage seemed blissful.

Until one morning, when Skippy Ryan had been found hanging from the parlor-room chandelier in his mansion. His wife and daughter were nowhere to be found and judging from the blood and trashed state of the room, it was assumed Skippy had done them in and disposed of his wife and child in the waters near the oceanfront mansion. Their bodies had never been recovered and, with no other motive available, the commonly held belief was that it had been a simple case of murder–suicide. It had also spawned a host of legends about the former Ryan mansion being haunted.

But clearly someone believed otherwise given the prize, Tracy thought, as she turned the expensive invitation over and over again, debating the merits of participating in the competition. Wondering who else had gotten an invite.

An icy draft shivered along the floor, creating a reciprocal shudder in her body.

Reason one to participate: money to fix the run-down inn she had inherited from her grandmother. It had been in the family for nearly four generations and Tracy didn't want to sell it, but repairing and maintaining the building required major bucks.

Reason number two: a boost to her flagging writing career. The numbers on her last book had been middling, hence the lack of bucks to fix the inn. If she were able to solve the mystery and win the contest, it would help drive sales for a new book.

If she could win, which made Tracy wonder again who else would be participating.

Dialing her cell phone, she called the Manhattan lawyer who had sent her the invitation. His assistant answered, but as soon as she identified herself, Tracy was transferred to the attorney.

"Peter Angelo," he said when he picked up, his voice a deep sonorous baritone that rumbled across the phone line and made her wonder what he looked like.

"Mr Angelo, this is Tracy Gomez. I'm calling about—"

"The invitation. I hope this means that you're accepting."

She tamped down the flare of irritation at his interruption. "Actually, I had a few questions. I hope you have the time to answer."

"Of course, Ms Gomez. I apologize for being presumptuous. It's just that I hoped you'd be on-board."

His apology mollified her somewhat, but made her wonder why her attendance mattered. "I appreciate the vote of confidence, Mr Angelo."

"Peter, please. Your reputation precedes you. That book you did on the Sylvester serial killer case was quite well done."

And had been her biggest bestseller, Tracy thought. "May I ask who else has been invited?"

"I'm not at liberty to say. In fact, anyone who participates will be asked to sign a confidentiality agreement," the attorney replied and a chill note filtered into his voice.

Tracy thought of all the research time she would need to prepare for the contest. So much work with the possibility of zero reward if someone else beat her to solving the case, since a confidentiality agreement would preclude her from using any of the work for a new book. "I'll have to give this some thought, Mr Angelo. I'm not sure it would be the right kind of project for me."

A surprised silence came across the line before the attorney said, "I hope you reconsider, Ms Gomez. A million dollars is a lot of money."

Tracy had no doubt about that. A million dollars would take care of fixing the inn and set her up quite nicely while she worked on her next project. But she was cautious by nature and wasn't about to change her spots for this case, even with the huge prize. Before she considered it further, there was one other thing she had to know.

"You seem to be quite determined about this contest. May I ask why?"

An amused chuckle was followed by, "I guess it's hard to deny I'd like you to participate."

Annoyance flared up that he hadn't really answered her question, so she repeated it. "Why is that so important to you, Mr Angelo?"

Silence came once more, followed by a heartfelt sigh before the attorney said, "My father believes he is Skippy Ryan's grandson. He also thinks you're the only one who can prove it."

Two

The black-and-white photograph on his law firm website didn't do justice to Peter Angelo, she thought as he stood at the front of the room.

He was strikingly attractive with black Irish looks, which

might make many a woman's head turn. Dark, nearly black hair, which might have been wavy if it wasn't ruthlessly styled into place, framed a face that was all chiseled lines. Piercing blue eyes were keen with intelligence and didn't miss a beat as they traveled over the half a dozen people gathered around the dining room table in the supposedly haunted Ryan mansion.

"Please sit," he said, although it was more command than invitation.

Tracy hadn't even taken a step when someone elbowed past her, eager to take a place near the head of the table where Mr Angelo would presumably take a spot.

Nancy Finch, Tracy thought, the name of the flamboyant psychic popping into her head as the redhead plopped her curvaceous ass into the chair, crossed her legs and assumed a pose obviously intended to show off her more than ample assets.

From beside Tracy came a solicitous, "After you."

She glanced at the man, recognizing yet another familiar face: Hank Jenkins, a television personality with a show on all things Jersey Shore on one of the local cable channels.

"Thanks." She sat and shot a quick glance to the opposite side of the table and the three other contestants. She didn't recognize any of them, but assumed Mr Angelo would soon remedy that situation.

As for their host, he continued to stand at the head of the table, his hands resting on the ornately carved wood of a dining-room chair until everyone was seated. Then he motioned to a young man who briskly closed the door, picked up a stack of packets and efficiently laid one folder in front of each of them before resuming his post by the door. Peter Angelo gestured to the packets with an elegant swipe of his finger. "You have all signed confidentiality agreements prior to coming here. Any and all documents in these portfolios and any information that you learn over this weekend is considered confidential and governed by those agreements."

"Can we skip all the legalese and get to the point of this?" said one of the men seated across from her. He had a thick New York accent and a liberally salted buzz cut. His dark suit was shiny from age and rather ill fitting. Judging from the bulge beneath one armpit, he was armed and hopefully on the right side of the law.

"Just getting there, Detective Daly," Angelo replied with the kind of indulgent tone that said he was used to dealing with law enforcement types.

"Inside the packets is basic information about the mansion and nearby grounds. Also some details from the original police investigation, as well as material that no one has seen before."

With an almost theatrical flourish, he flipped open his packet and removed a sheaf of papers from inside.

Tracy opened her folder and did the same, fascinated by what appeared to be a decades-old journal.

Peter Angelo skimmed his gaze over the various individuals he had assembled at the behest of his father. Each one was arguably a specialist, if not an expert in their particular field, but the one person that kept on drawing his attention was Tracy Gomez.

She looked younger than the photo on her book jacket, but then again, he supposed that was the purpose of those professional headshots. Make the author look suitably studious and authoritative.

Tracy was much more eye-catching than her photo, with an expressive heart-shaped face which was currently registering surprise as she read over the contents of the pages he had provided. Her eyes widened as she set the papers down and met his stare. Almond-shaped eyes in a rich shade of chocolate narrowed as she considered him. They were filled with questions. She raised her hand and after he had acknowledged her, asked, "Are you sure about the provenance of these pages?"

"The journal was found in a trunk which supposedly belonged to my great-grandmother. Unfortunately it was water damaged by leaks in the attic."

She nodded, but resumed reviewing the pages as he continued. "To win the prize you must determine if then Senator Ryan did in fact murder his wife and daughter, and if it is possible for my father to be his grandson. You have access to this mansion for the weekend. If you require any other assistance you may ask me or my assistant, Mr Parker," he said and motioned to the young man by the door.

"What about my seance?" blurted Nancy Finch, the psychic who had been busier eyeing him than the papers she had been given.

"Ah, yes, the seance. Ms Finch has requested the assistance of all of us—"

"Except the cop. I can feel his negative vibes all the way from here," she said with a practiced wrinkle of her nose and flip of her hand in the detective's direction.

"Damn straight, lady. I don't buy into cheap movie tricks," Detective Daly replied with a growly snarl.

And this was getting to be just like one of those low-budget horror flicks, Peter thought. Put six people together in an old and supposedly haunted mansion, make them want to kill each other with a prize they can't refuse and let the mayhem begin. If his father weren't gravely ill, he would never have agreed to this whole fiasco. But this crazy quest was the one thing that his father had requested and that seemed to be keeping him alive.

"Ms Finch wishes to channel the spirits in this home. We will be holding a seance tonight after dinner for anyone who wishes to participate," Peter said and eyeballed everyone around the table.

"And what if she claims to hear ol' Skippy and gets his confession? Is this entire gig done?" asked the detective.

Peter shook his head. "I want definitive proof. If Ms Finch somehow communicates with the departed Senator Ryan or his wife Anna, Ms Finch will have to elicit from them some other detail which can be corroborated and that was previously unknown."

"Something which is in this journal, I presume?" said the older gentleman sitting beside the detective.

By process of elimination, since the young star of a ghost hunting show was at the far end of the table, Peter assumed this was none other than John Marcovic, the bestselling mystery author. The man had to be at least eighty, which meant that the headshot on his book jackets was nearly thirty years old.

"Yes, Mr Marcovic. There are pages in the journal that contain a surprising bit of information. We've withheld it for the obvious reasons."

At the mention of the author's name, Tracy's eyes widened as she considered him, obviously as surprised as Peter about the author's age.

Hank Jenkins jumped into the discussion. "What about an

exhumation and DNA test? Wouldn't that accomplish what you want?"

Tracy nodded and her expressive face conveyed not only her obvious agreement with the local reporter, but her skepticism about the proceedings. He had clearly sensed that during his telephone conversation with her, and yet here she was, ready to participate. It made him think that spending the weekend with Tracy Gomez might prove to be quite interesting – they seemed to be of a like mind about some things. He, too, was skeptical about these proceedings.

"We lack the proof necessary for an exhumation. In addition, my father does not wish to disturb the grave. Besides, that won't solve the mystery of whether Senator Ryan murdered his wife and infant daughter."

"Can I bring my crew to the seance?" asked Tommy Smith, the young ghost hunter.

Peter inclined his head in the direction of Ms Finch, who immediately said, "I'm not a fake. I welcome anything that will confirm and document my abilities."

"Wicked," said Tommy gleefully and rubbed his hands together.

"Wonderful. We'll reconvene here for dinner at eight," Peter said and watched the crew of characters his father had requested file out the door. He had to give his dad credit. He had really put together a fascinating group, but Peter was doubtful they could accomplish his father's goal.

Except for maybe the captivating Tracy Gomez, he thought as she sauntered out, her keen-eyed gaze flitting over the portraits on the wall before shooting him a curious glance.

He smiled at her, but she quickly averted her gaze and continued on her way.

Interesting, he thought again, but he had little time to linger. His father was comfortably settled in one of the upstairs bedrooms and awaiting his report.

Peter hoped that by the time the weekend was done, his father might have the answers that would give him peace in what could possibly be his final days.

Three

The nice-sized room was well appointed, with views of the manicured lawns and gardens from French doors along one wall. The bright new green of early spring grass offset the darker mulch the park service gardeners had laid down around freshly planted flower beds.

The early afternoon sun blazed through the glass, but did nothing to dispel the chill in Tracy's body. She rubbed at her arms before opening her suitcase to unpack, though it did little to quell a classic case of the willies. Since stepping into the room she had felt as if she were not alone.

Not that she gave much credence to the various tales that the mansion was haunted by the spirits of the deceased Ryan family. In doing her prep work for this weekend's contest, she had come across more than one mention of witnesses who saw spirits wandering the mansion and nearby grounds. There were even a few visitors who had claimed to hear either a baby or woman crying late at night.

No way, she thought. It was just a case of people's imaginations running away with them since the case was unsolved and the bodies of Anna and her baby Francesca had never been found.

That one aspect had been troubling her during the course of her investigations. If Skippy Ryan had tossed his family's bodies into the ocean, they should have turned up, given the currents in the area, even if he had weighted them down somehow. And in light of the supposed chronology of events related by witnesses who had overheard a fight on the night of the murders and said they had seen him out on a boat, Ryan would not have had time for prepping the bodies with weights. They should have therefore washed ashore fairly quickly.

Which meant that it was possible that Anna and baby Francesca might not have died that night. And if they had survived, it was conceivable that Peter Angelo's father might be Skippy's grandson.

Another chill skittered across her body and, for a moment, almost seemed to wrap itself around her in an embrace. She shuddered, tossing off her apprehension. Craziness, she thought.

She walked to the French doors and threw them open,

allowing the warm spring breeze into the room. It was just a case
of a drafty old house, much like her family's inn. She lingered by
the doors, lifting her face up to the bright sunshine until the chill
in her body disappeared. Then she returned to her suitcase and
unpacked her notes and assorted research materials. She took
them to the simple mahogany desk at one side of the room and
laid them out. As she did so, she quickly reviewed the notes. She
remained convinced that she was on the right trail to prove what
had actually happened that night.

She hoped that over the weekend she'd find the last little bits
of information she needed to realize the truth about Francis
Ryan, determine if Peter's dad could be his descendant and, of
course, win the prize.

His lawyer son would definitely not approve, but Frank could
not resist watching his assorted guests on the laptop in his
bedroom. Although as Nancy Finch began to undress, he quickly
flipped away.

Frank Angelo was more a student of human nature than an
actual voyeur. It was why he had decided to assemble such a
diverse cast of characters to solve the mystery of the Ryan
family.

His family, he reminded himself as he laid his hand on the old
leather journal beside him on the bed. Its cover had the rich
patina of having been held often, but was warped from the water
that had damaged it. A goodly portion of the pages were curled
and hopelessly stuck together, but those that remained hinted at
quite a different story than the one that was publicly known
about Skippy Ryan.

In fact, if the writer of the diary was to be believed, Anna
Dolan Ryan and baby Francesca had left the mansion alive and
well that night and gone into hiding to await a reunion with
Skippy. A reunion that, sadly, had never occurred.

Anna had assumed another name to protect her family and
eventually remarried a local Italian laborer who had adopted
little Francesca as his own.

Frank had been named after his mother Francesca, Peter's
grandmother. Francesca Angelo was long since gone and if she
had known her history, she'd never said a word. Frank was
determined to find out the truth if it was the last thing he did.

Which it might be, he thought, as pressure gripped his chest and made breathing difficult. The congestive heart failure grew worse each day and none of his medicines were working to stem its progress.

The pressure increased, worrying him that he would not last to see the results of the contest. But then a gentle hand passed over his face and down to the center of his chest. "Rest, my child," he heard a voice say and, as if by magic, the weight stifling his life lifted slightly.

When the knock came at the door, he was able to muster a "Come in", but fumbled with clumsy hands to close the laptop.

His son entered and was immediately at his side, concern obvious on his handsome face. From his initial investigations, Frank had discovered that his son's face was very much like Skippy Ryan's.

"Are you OK, Dad?" Peter grasped his hand.

"Fine. Excited," he said, unable to manage more than single words as his breath failed him and his heart drummed rapidly in his chest. Once again a gentle pass of an invisible hand across his face brought calm and some relief.

Peter smiled indulgently and nodded. "I know, Dad. I hope you're not disappointed."

"Tracy. Win," he said, more convinced than ever that the young writer would be the one to solve the mystery. Months earlier, he had heard her give a workshop at a local library and had been impressed. Something about her determination had reminded him of what little he remembered of his grandmother.

The smile on his son's face brightened and spread up into his eyes at the mention of the young writer. "Yeah, I think she might have what it takes."

Frank suspected the comment wasn't solely about the contest, and inside of him something lightened, releasing the vicious hold illness had on his heart.

"Go. Visit," he prompted with a strong squeeze of Peter's hand.

His son chuckled. "Playing matchmaker? Really, Dad?"

"Want babies." He wished to see his son happily married and with children before he died. For some inexplicable reason, Tracy Gomez seemed like the kind of woman who could handle his sometimes obstinate and workaholic son. There had been something about her that Frank had connected with from the moment he had first laid eyes on her.

"Ms Gomez is pretty, I'll give you that."

"Smart," Frank added.

Peter shrugged and rose from the chair beside Frank's bed. "Get some rest, Dad. And let me have the laptop while you're at it. I'd hate for you to get all worked up watching the seance."

Caught red-handed, he thought, but he reached out and feebly passed the computer in his son's direction. In reality, he was feeling too tired to imagine staying up for the outcome of the seance anyhow. Plus, he didn't think it would accomplish much.

He'd been in the mansion for well on a week now, thanks to the strings he'd pulled, and, in all that time, there had been nothing to support the idea that the mansion was haunted. Well, nothing except what had happened just moments before. That alone wasn't enough to convince him, however.

"No ghosts," he said, but Peter only shook his head and chuckled once more.

"Finally something we can agree on."

Four

Tracy could safely say that she had never seen anything quite like the bedlam that had overwhelmed the gracefully elegant parlor room.

Tommy Smith darted from one piece of equipment to the next to make sure everything was in order to film the big metaphysical event. Cables and wires slithered along the floor like snakes as his crew connected them to a number of different cameras and monitors.

"This new puppy here is a tri-axial EMF meter to record any disruptions in the electromagnetic forces in the room," he said as he shot a glance at her over his shoulder.

"I suppose you'll take baseline readings," Tracy replied, creating an instant flurry of activity in Tommy who rushed over to one of his three technicians to give a spate of orders, including one for a reference point.

"Cruel," Peter said from beside her, causing her heartbeat to jump in both surprise and awareness of the non-existent distance between them.

"Just analytical," she answered, glancing at him from the corner of her eye.

He had changed out of the formal suit and tie into a pale-blue polo shirt and faded denim. The color only intensified his eyes and brought out blue-black highlights in his dark hair. The short sleeves on the shirt exposed wickedly ripped arms, which he crossed, shifting her attention to the equally sculpted muscles of his broad chest. She couldn't avoid the temptation to look downward past his flat midsection to where the soft fabric of his jeans hugged long, lean legs.

"Done analysing?" he said with a sinful chuckle and arch of his brow.

She was spared from answering as Nancy Finch chose that moment to make her entrance, the diaphanous fabric of her low-cut gown floating around her. Trailing her like little lapdogs were Hank Jenkins, Detective Daly and John Marcovic.

It surprised Tracy that during the course of their earlier dinner the men seemed to have become so taken with the psychic, especially the gruff NYPD detective.

Peter leaned close and said, "She seems to have them tamed. It will make her little show that much easier."

Tracy was slightly taken aback and peered at him. "So you don't believe in her abilities?"

He shoved the tips of his fingers in the pockets of his jeans, rocked back on his heels a moment and then shrugged. "Let's just say that in my world I'm used to dealing in facts. And you?"

"My stock-in-trade is facts. Not this." She waved her hand in the direction of the circus occurring before her eyes. Tommy and his crew had gathered, with an assortment of equipment, at the far side of the room before what looked like a control panel. Nancy had assumed a spot at the head of a small table, which had been placed in the center of the room. The three men jockeyed for spots around her and finally settled down, leaving empty seats for Tracy, Peter and Tommy.

Nancy glanced her way, lifted an artfully waxed brow and fluttered her hand, beckoning to them with perfectly manicured fingers. "Come. It's time to get started."

Tommy raced to a seat at the table, but Tracy and Peter

proceeded more slowly. As they took seats beside one another, Nancy glanced toward Peter's assistant, who stood by the door. At her nod, he lowered the lights, bathing them in the warm glow of the candles Nancy had insisted be placed at strategic locations around the room.

Tracy had to give it to the psychic. The lighting created an immediate sense of intimacy given their close proximity around the small table.

"Please reach out to your neighbors and grasp their hand."

Hold Peter's hand. She should have seen it coming, but suddenly found herself scrubbing her wet palm against her jeans before grasping Tommy's hand and then Peter's.

Warmth. Strength. An unexpected tingle that snared her attention and had her shooting him a half-glance.

His attention was likewise diverted, his gaze on her instead of Nancy. The psychic pressed forward, calling on the spirits in the room to show themselves. Asking for some sign that they were there.

Nothing happened with the ghosts, but Tracy was definitely getting signs from Peter. His blue eyes were bright with interest as he examined her face, and that tingle where she was holding his hand grew steadily until . . .

A chill snaked around her ankles, but in a mansion as old as this one, that wasn't unexpected. Then a low, almost masculine moan erupted from Nancy as her eyes rolled back in her head.

"Oh man, the EMF meter is going wild," one of Tommy's technicians murmured and clapped his hands gleefully.

Nancy's head lolled against the back of the dining chair and the two men on either side of her released her hands to come to her assistance, but she shook her head. "No, hold on," Nancy warned. "Someone is here. They are trying to reach us."

The chill, which had seemed like nothing more than a draft, grew bolder, traveling upward and wrapping around Tracy's legs. Insistent. Her heartbeat raced in her chest and pressure built inside her skull. She shook her head, trying to drive away the sensation overtaking her.

"Tracy. Tracy, are you OK?" she heard from beside her. But it came as if from a distance and echoed within her brain.

The cold had now embraced her entire body. She tried to

speak, but nothing came out of her mouth. A hand brushed the side of her face. Lovingly. Somehow grounding her as she struggled to free herself of the consciousness taking control of her body.

Peter ran his hand along her cheek and met her gaze, but the vibrant and intelligent gleam in her eyes had changed somehow. Her eyes were blank, dark, lifeless orbs staring back at him. The edges of her lips moved. Barely. And as he examined her face more carefully, it was almost as if the blurry image of someone else had been superimposed on her features.

A beautiful woman, he thought, and inside of him, awareness flared brightly. Warmth blazed more intensely, especially where he held Tracy's hand.

"They're here," Nancy said in an eerie sing-song, mimicking the famous movie line.

He looked around the table and realized all eyes were on him and Tracy.

"No," he said, but wasn't sure whether anyone had heard him, not even Tracy, since at that moment she broke contact with Tommy, raised her hand and laid it on Peter's cheek.

Her touch was electric, racing through him so powerfully that he jumped.

"Francis," she said, the name filled with such longing that it hurt his heart.

"Anna," he replied and jerked back again.

Anna? Not Anna. Tracy, he thought, battling the weird almost out-of-body sensation gripping him. It was as if someone else had dominion over his being and he was just a visitor, watching what was happening from the sidelines.

"I miss you, Francis," Tracy said and ran her thumb across his lips. "Come home to me."

Peter was pulled toward her, but something held him back. Kept him immobile. Fear, he realized. Gut-wrenching, heart-pounding fear.

Death. Death was near, he thought, his gut clenching. A cold sweat erupted on his body.

"Can't," he replied, shaking his head. He ripped away from her touch and something popped free inside of him.

Like a soap bubble bursting, whatever had taken hold of

Tracy disappeared. Awareness rippled across her face of where she was and what was happening. She shook her body like a dog tossing water from wet fur, forcing away the last of whatever had gripped her.

Tommy burst from his chair. "That was amazing. Did you get that?" he shouted at his technicians.

"Don't know," the crew member replied.

"Tracy? Are you OK?" Peter asked, his hand shaking as he brought it to her face and gently stroked the smoothness of her cheek.

"I think so." She glanced away from him to the others gathered around the table.

"That was something," said Hank Jenkins and wrapped his arm around Nancy's shoulders as she sagged into her chair.

"But what was it?" questioned Daly. He rose and jammed his hands in the pockets of his suit jacket, something he did often judging from the way they bulged even when empty.

He walked over to where Tommy stood with his technicians, who were busily playing with the equipment. Judging from the puzzled looks on their faces, something was not working as it should have been.

"Well, Tommy?" the detective pressed.

"We're working on it," Tommy replied with irritation.

"Technical difficulties. Not unexpected, given what we're dealing with," said Marcovic, his tone almost condescending.

"What we're dealing with?" Peter challenged and scooted his chair closer to Tracy, who still seemed a little shaken. When she leaned her head against his shoulder, he wrapped his arm around her, offering his support.

"Ghosts," said Marcovic.

"Ghosts?" Tracy replied weakly and rubbed her hands along her arms.

"They were here. I could feel them. Feel their pain," Nancy replied and glanced at Hank. "You saw them, right?"

"Them?" Peter asked, quickly replaying in his brain what he had seen, but recalling only the change in Tracy.

"You don't realize, do you?" Hank said, his gaze focusing on Peter and Tracy.

"Realize what?" Peter asked.

"You were him," said Detective Daly as he waved dismissively at Tommy and his people, who still appeared to be having problems with their equipment.

"Him? Who?"

"You were Francis," said Tracy, glancing up at him as if seeing him with new eyes.

Not possible, Peter thought, shaking his head. "How do you know?"

"Because I was Anna," Tracy replied.

Five

Tracy couldn't shake the chill that had gripped her earlier nor the lingering presence within her. It was if she was no longer alone. As if someone else was with her. Tucked into her heart.

Peter, she thought, only *not*. The connection she had experienced in the parlor room hadn't been with Peter. It had been with someone else.

Francis Ryan.

Except that was impossible, Tracy thought, as she paced back and forth in front of the French doors leading to the garden, before stopping to appreciate the beauty outside. The night was bright, the moonlight bathing everything with cold hoary light. Beyond the gardens, the ocean's wash shimmered along the shore as bright whitecaps broke the dark of the water's surface.

In her mind's eye the image changed. Darkened.

It had been a moonless night. Perfect for running rum. Perfect for running away.

She knew that now. Anna had been escaping with her baby that night.

But Tracy also knew something else – Anna hadn't been fleeing her husband. She had loved him. Deeply. Leaving him had cost her . . .

A knock came at her door, and although the last thing she wanted was company, she sensed he was there.

Peter.

She walked to the door and opened it. He waited, looking a bit sheepish. His hands jammed into the pockets of those well-worn jeans. She knew from the look on his face that he still didn't believe, but then again, she wasn't quite sure she did either.

"May I come in?"

She stepped aside and motioned him in.

He stood in the middle of the space, clearly uneasy. As if searching for something to do, he walked to the desk where she had laid out her research notes.

"May I?" he asked and, at her nod, leaned one hand on the edge of the desk as he flipped through the papers.

"Fascinating," he said when he finished, turned and leaned his butt on the edge of the desk.

"Not as interesting as what happened before," she said, crossing her arms and coming to stand in front of him.

"What did happen before?" he asked, mimicking her pose, both of them obviously in defensive mode.

"I was hoping you could tell me. Did Tommy and his people get anything?"

"Nothing visible on the videotape. But he did get some drastic changes in temperature and wild EMF readings."

"All of which means . . ."

Peter shrugged and the action pulled the fabric of his shirt across the broad muscles of his shoulders. "I wish I knew, Tracy."

But she did know something, even if she couldn't explain the why of it. "Anna loved her husband. She was afraid that night, but not of him."

Peter nodded, but it was reluctant. "If I believe that I tapped into something from the beyond . . . I felt fear. Deadly fear."

"I think I may know why," she said and brushed past him to the surface of her desk. Shuffling the papers around as he had earlier, she dug up some notes and photocopies.

"Did you know nearly 40 per cent of all the illegal alcohol that came into the United States during Prohibition came through Newark, Skippy's hometown?"

He turned, grazing her back with his chest as he examined the papers from over her shoulder. "Is that him?" he said, pointing to a grainy photo from one of the newspapers.

"That's Skippy. Before Prohibition, Newark had a number of local breweries and saloons."

"So there was a significant economic impact when those businesses had to shut down," Peter surmised.

"Definitely, and Skippy's area took a direct hit." She motioned to the photo and circled a face near Francis Ryan. "This man is Izzy Merlman, one of Newark's bootleg kingpins. His runners would bring big ships with whiskey and rum to just outside the twelve-mile limit we had back then. Smaller skiffs would meet up with them and bring the liquor ashore."

"So you're saying good ol' Skippy was involved with the bootlegging?"

"Or maybe competing with Izzy," Tracy said and placed her notes back on the desktop.

"They used to bring alcohol into Newark Bay and Long Branch mostly, but they also brought it through the Shark River Inlet. When we used to spend summers down the shore my grandmother would tell us stories about it," Peter added.

"But your grandmother would have been young during Prohibition."

"Six or seven. Her father told her the stories. She used to say that her mother would ask him to stop," he said as if suddenly remembering it. He moved, sitting back on the edge of the desk as she faced him. His thigh skimmed her legs, awakening the connection she had experienced before in the parlor.

Needing a little space, she moved away from him. "If your great-grandmother was Anna Dolan, and if the bootlegging had caused her to lose her husband, that could explain why she wouldn't want to glamorize the rum-running."

"Sounds plausible, but how do we prove it?" he asked.

Tracy smiled. "Not *we*. Me. Remember the contest?"

With his proximity to Tracy, he had forgotten about a lot, including the contest. He supposed that was exactly what his father had wanted, and something inside of him rebelled for a moment, but only for a moment. It would have been foolish to ignore what he was feeling on account of his father's manipulation. But, if anything, the contest had made the situation a little more difficult. "I suppose that I should go so that the other contestants don't feel slighted somehow."

"I suppose," she said, but it was half-hearted.

"The rest of them are in the parlor, arguing about Tommy's data and what it means." Which was what he supposed they should be doing and so he said, "We could join them."

Tracy considered returning to the parlor and experienced a

chill again at the thought of the spirits that still might be in the room. "Or we could go for walk around the grounds since our time in the mansion is limited."

His smile broadened and spread up to his eyes, which glittered a bright blue. "Seems like a much better use of our time here." He pushed off the edge of the desk and offered her his arm.

"Shall we?"

Six

Tracy slipped her arm through his. Awareness of him awoke again. How could it not? He was a handsome and seemingly caring man. What she was experiencing was due to that and not to any lingering effects from what had happened in the parlor.

If *anything* had actually occurred there, she thought. The logical and practical side of her refused to believe that Nancy the psychic had somehow managed to channel a spirit or two. Especially one who had managed to take over Tracy's body for only the space of a few heartbeats and yet left behind emotions she was finding it hard to forget.

Instead of heading out the bedroom door, Peter walked her to the French doors and tossed them open. They strolled through the gardens and down to the water's edge. The wind had kicked up the surf, washing up small jellyfish which glittered like diamonds from the moonbeams.

"It was dark the night it happened. Anna was afraid," Tracy said, and wrapped her arms around herself, slightly cold from the strong breeze.

Peter, who had been walking beside her with his hands in his pockets and his shoulders hunched against the nip of the wind, slipped one arm around her and pulled her close. The warmth of him abated the cold instantly. "Francis was afraid also. I remember that feeling from the parlor. He was very, very fearful."

"A local fisherman had been beaten to death about a week before. He used to deliver fish to the mansion. Maybe he brought more than that to the back door," she said.

"If Izzy killed the Ryans—"

"I think the dead fisherman was a warning to Skippy to stop, but Izzy might not have been happy to stop there," Tracy said as they neared a jetty that marked the end of the mansion's property. She stopped and looked back toward the house, noticed the boathouse about ten feet away from where the jetty ended and a wall of rocks rose up. Sand turned to grass as the property sloped upward toward the boathouse.

Peering up at Peter, she pointed to the boathouse. "Can we look inside?"

"We have the run of the entire property for the weekend, so hopefully that's open as well."

Together, they ambled to the door of the building. A shiny new padlock hung from a rusty latch hasp, but it was unlocked. They removed it and swung open the heavy doors to reveal the equipment within. An assortment of old chains, ropes, oars and life preservers adorned the walls. In the center of the space, a wooden rowboat lay upside down across two sawhorses. Beside it on a small boat lift was a sixteen-foot skiff painted a dark grey and sporting an outboard engine.

Peter and Tracy walked around the skiff and, as they did so, Tracy wondered aloud, "It's the right age and color for a rum-runners' skiff."

Peter climbed up on a cinder block beside the boat and examined a brownish stain along the top edge. "Could be blood or rust. Seems like your theory is coming together."

Tracy scooted up onto the block and peered at the large blotch also. "I'm surprised it's been there all that time and no one ever wondered what it was."

"Doubting yourself now?" he said. She lost her balance briefly and he eased his arm around her waist to keep her steady. The action brought her flush to him.

His body was all lean muscle and totally tempting. Too tempting. Considering what had happened earlier in the parlor, her emotions were a jumble. Was what she was feeling her own desire? Or was it truly possible that the ghosts of Anna and Francis had dropped by for a visit, leaving behind the attraction between them?

Slowly stepping back down to the floor of the boathouse, she said, "Sometimes you need to step back and re-analyse to see if what's before your eyes is actually real."

*   *   *

Peter would have to be a fool not to realize the double meaning behind her words. He had the same hesitation about what he was feeling for her, although in retrospect, he had been drawn to her even before the possible visitation by their ghostly visitors. Taking a step closer, he bent his head until his lips were barely an inch from hers.

"This seems all too real to me," he whispered.

Her lips were soft and slightly cold from the earlier breeze. They warmed quickly beneath his and, as her eyes drifted down, she appeared to lose her earlier reluctance. Her mouth was fluid against his as she met his kiss, opened her mouth to taste him.

He groaned at that touch of her tongue along his lips, and slipped his hands to her waist. Grasping the slim lines there, he drew her near, loving the brush of her ample breasts against the wall of his chest. Feeling himself harden as her softness cradled him.

It feels so right, Tracy thought as she kissed him, opening her mouth to his. She danced her tongue along the perfect edge of his lips as he tightened his hold on her and brought her body to rest against him. There was no missing his desire and she rubbed her hips along his in invitation.

When he raised his hand and cradled her breast, she sighed with pleasure at his tender caress.

The loud clang of something metallic broke them apart just moments before a strong gust of wind whirled around them. Peter drew her tighter and tucked her head close to his chest against the cold blast of air. The breeze was powerful enough to rattle the metal chains and knock one of the oars to the ground. As it stirred around them for one last whirl, it whipped Tracy's hair up into his face.

And then, just as quickly as it had kicked up, the wind died down.

Peter smoothed Tracy's hair as she looked up at him. "That was weird."

It was, he thought, and, for a moment, a vision of auburn hair flashed through his mind.

"Are you OK?" she asked and reached up, ran her hand through his hair to smooth out the wind-blown locks. As she did so, she realized something. "Skippy Ryan had dark hair and blue eyes, just like you."

"But Anna was a redhead. A deep rich color." At her questioning glance, he explained, "I just saw it in my head. Right after the wind left."

"Another ghostly visit?" she said, her tones mirroring his own skepticism.

"If they are trying to tell us something, they're being rather obtuse," he said and, with Tracy tucked tight to his side, he urged her from the boathouse. After they had closed it up once more, they walked, arms wrapped around each other, back to the French doors to Tracy's room.

Inside they hesitated. "I'd ask you to stay for a bit—"

"But it wouldn't seem right, would it?" he finished for her.

"No, it wouldn't. If I can somehow solve the mystery—"

"Is winning that important to you?" he asked, cradling her cheek, making her wish that he would stay the night so they could explore the emotions growing between them. But there was something else that made his staying unwise.

"I could use the money," she confessed, but then quickly added, "But now, it's about more than that."

"And I somehow make it more difficult?"

To say that he was a distraction would be an understatement. "I need to keep my wits about me so your father can find peace and, crazily, so that these spirits can rest if they really do exist."

A very smug smile came to his mouth a second before he lowered his head and whispered against her lips, "All I can hope is that you solve this mystery quickly, because I'm a very impatient man."

And as if to prove his point, he kissed her once again, placing every ounce of emotion into the kiss, rekindling the fire that had threatened to blaze out of control in the boathouse before the resident spirit had doused it with its wind display.

When they broke apart, they were both breathless, and it took the greatest restraint not to forego common sense and spend the night together.

Tracy closed the door behind him and changed into her pajamas, although sleep was the furthest thing from her mind. She wanted to review her notes and outline the steps she would take tomorrow in her quest to solve the mystery. At the desk, someone had thoughtfully left a small tray with a tea service and a plate of cookies.

She sat down and poured herself a cup of tea, and ate some cookies, as she reviewed her notes. The discussion at dinner tonight had yielded little information since everyone seemed to be playing their cards close to the chest. The seance had offered just raw emotions, too confusing to understand just yet. At least the trip to the boathouse had moved her closer to a viable theory.

The few pages from Peter's great-grandmother's journal offered only some additional insight. It was clear that she had been a woman of great intelligence, offering her opinion on some of the problems of the times and her role as a woman. Here and there she made reference to "her other life" and how different it had been. Part of it had clearly been economic as many an entry on the pages referred to how she was struggling to get by. She also mentioned how lucky she was that someone would even want a woman in her condition.

Tracy pondered that comment, wondering if it was a reference to her poverty or to her being a woman alone with a child. Unfortunately, the pages stopped before providing enough information to decipher the meaning behind those words.

With her head drooping and her eyelids drifting closed, Tracy decided it was time to call it a night. She was too tired to learn much more this evening and she wanted to be fresh in the morning to continue with her investigations.

The linen sheets were cold and slick as she slipped beneath them and snapped off the reading light on the nightstand. Then she thought better of that and turned it back on.

She might not be fully convinced of the existence of ghosts in the mansion, but until she had a way to explain what had happened today in the parlor and then in the boathouse, she wasn't going to take any chances.

Seven

A rhythmic slap, slap and sway of the bed beneath her slowly roused her from sleep. Only when she opened her eyes, it was dark.

With her gaze slightly unfocused, she reached for the bedside lamp and flipped the switch several times, but the room remained pitch black. Well, not quite black since a multitude of stars illuminated the sky overhead.

Blinking, Tracy fought against the remnants of what must have been a dream and, as she did so, the sounds of voices raised in anger drifted into her consciousness. Was that Peter's voice? she thought a moment before fear overtook her, jolting her awake and providing her with the answer.

No, not Peter's voice. Skippy's, she guessed from the slight trace of brogue.

She had to go to him. Had to help him this time. Tracy's mind muddled as she tried to separate reality from the waking dream she could not shake.

Compelled to move, her body not her own, she left the bedroom and hurried toward the parlor along the dark corridors, part of her wondering what was happening while the other part only knew one thing: get to the parlor.

As she neared, she heard a shout followed by the crash of furniture. Her hurried pace became a run as silence reigned.

At the door to the parlor, Tracy hesitated until the voice in her head said, "Help him!"

She took hold of the heavy glass doorknob and turned it, then walked into the parlor room, which was blazing with light. It was as it had been before, with Tommy's equipment tucked into one corner and the small round table in the center. But all around the room there appeared to be evidence of a fight and blood. A trail of blood along the floor, except . . .

Tracy crouched down and ran a finger along the stain of blood, but the floor was dry. As she blinked several times to clear her vision, it was as if a film were playing, with the room around her acting as the screen.

With that thought came another from within her. *Where is Skippy?*

And, as if in answer, Peter rushed into the room by a doorway that led to the kitchen. He was bare-chested, his hair tousled from sleep. A confused not-quite-there look was stamped on his face.

Tracy understood, since she was feeling it as well. Not quite sure what was happening.

Peter took a step toward her, raised his hand and said, "Anna, I told you to stay away."

Overwhelmed by elation, she rushed forward into his arms, burying her head against his chest as she said, "I had to come back. I had to help you."

Peter's arms came around her, shaky and slightly uncoordinated. As she glanced up at him, the lines of his face wavered, grew unfocused. Softened, becoming those of someone else.

"Francis," she whispered and Peter wagged his head as if trying to dislodge whatever had commandeered his body.

"You need to go, Anna. It's the only way," he said and laid his hand on her belly. Her slightly rounded belly and suddenly it connected. The condition that the writer of the journal had mentioned.

Anna had been pregnant with their second child.

As Peter tenderly ran his hand across the slight swell, the fierceness of his love washed over her and, in that second, Tracy knew Francis could not have killed his wife, baby and unborn child. Somehow she pushed back the force that had overtaken her and asked, "What happened, Francis? Why did you kill yourself?"

Peter ripped away from her, raking his hands through his hair like a man possessed, which she guessed he was. He took a few sharp steps away from her, then whirled to face her, hands outstretched. His voice was pleading as he said, "It was the only way to protect you."

"Why?" she asked, approaching him and taking hold of his hands. As she did so, a wave of longing washed over her, so intense that her knees grew weak, but she hung on, fighting the emotions threatening her conscious being.

"Izzy sent one of his goons for the money."

'What money?' she wanted to ask him, but the voice inside her head answered before she could do so. *The bootlegging money.*

So Francis had been running rum as she had suspected.

"I told him it was gone. That I was giving it to the people in my ward who had lost their jobs," Peter continued, in obvious distress. Once again he shook his head, battling against whatever had taken hold, but Tracy reached up and smoothed her hand across his cheek.

"Let him explain, Peter. It will set him free."

She didn't know how she knew that, but she did. That was why they were here, caught up in this rerun of a long ago night.

"He said Izzy wouldn't like that and took out a gun." Once again the spirit controlling Peter took over, pulling away from her and pacing back and forth before finally facing her once again. Guilt and remorse were etched on his face.

"We fought and I killed him. There was blood everywhere and then I knew. I knew how to protect you."

This time Tracy was the one who lost command of her body as she went rushing across the floor into his arms. The spirit within her cried, "No, Skippy. I waited for you, but you never came."

Almost as if not hearing his wife's anguish, he said, "If Izzy thought you were dead, you'd be safe. And I was a dead man anyway."

"We could have fought him," she said, her throat tight with grief and her heart heavy at the realization of what her husband had sacrificed for her safety.

Peter calmed then, dropped his hand and covered her belly once more, a final gesture she realized. "I could not risk it. I left you a note. In our secret place," he said and motioned to a spot on the wall.

Tracy tracked the line of his arm and could see what looked like an oval frame hung there, only in reality it wasn't there. Only in the dream state that had overtaken them.

"Forgive me, love," he said, cupping her cheek and bending to brush a kiss across her lips.

"I forgive you," she whispered before returning his kiss. As their lips touched, something broke free, releasing them.

Peter stumbled back from her, looking around the room and seeing none of the blood and upturned furniture that had been there a moment before. The room was lit from the dull light of an emergency exit sign and Peter reached over to snap on the chandelier, which was swinging wildly.

Tracy squinted at the bright light, shielding her eyes with her hand. "Are you OK?"

Looking down at his body, he realized he was physically fine, but mentally . . . "What happened? What was that?"

Tracy walked toward him. She laid a hand on his chest, to prove to herself that he was real. "They were here. Francis and Anna. But now they're gone."

She did a slow turn around the room, as if searching for them, but he knew that she was right. Whatever he had been feeling before was gone, although scattered memories and emotions remained in his mind.

"He sacrificed himself to protect them," Peter said.

Tracy nodded and walked toward the spot where she had earlier seen the oval frame. "She was pregnant when she left with baby Francesca. That was the condition she mentioned in the journal, but your father didn't mention any aunts or uncles so . . ."

Pain washed over her, so powerfully she had to put her hand to her chest to press against the spot to ease the heartache. "She lost the baby."

"That's what the journal said. You couldn't have known that from any of the research that you did."

No, she knew it from Anna. From the pain her spirit had been carrying for so long. Looking toward the wall, she said, "Something is missing here. A picture frame."

Peter laid his hand on her shoulder and offered a reassuring squeeze. "Maybe it was moved to another room?"

She nodded. "Maybe. Can we look for it?"

He dipped his head in agreement and slipped his arm around her waist. As they walked out of the parlor, a bleary-eyed Tommy came down the stairs, dressed in sweats. A moment later his crew of techs followed.

"Thought I heard some noise. I was worried about the equipment."

Peter and Tracy shared a glance before Peter inclined his head in the direction of the parlor. "Equipment is fine, but if you've got anything motion activated, you may want to check it out."

Tommy and his crew scrambled down the hall, their animated voices carrying up the stairs, awakening most of the other inhabitants of the mansion. They came out of their rooms and hurried down the stairs, except for Hank.

"I can feel them around you," Nancy said, raising her hands and circling them before Peter and Tracy.

"Cut the theatrics, Nancy," the detective said gruffly, but Nancy only winked at him, dragging a blush to his features.

"Do you care to explain what happened?" asked Marcovic, his nose upturned in a superior kind of way.

Tracy was in no mood for the man's diffidence. "We're

looking for another clue." The final clue, she wanted to say, but bit that back. No sense having him hounding them.

Peter motioned toward the parlor. "Tommy and his gang are in there. I think his cameras might have caught something."

With that, Marcovic headed in their direction, but Nancy and the detective hung tight with Peter and Tracy.

The quartet walked along the halls, Tracy scouring each inch for something resembling the oval frame she had seen. At one point the detective asked, "Mind telling me what we're looking for?"

"A frame," she said, worried that with all the years that the mansion had been first uninhabited and then in the state's care, the object she sought might have disappeared.

She was losing hope when she rounded the corner and entered what had once been a large larder off the kitchen. A goodly number of the shelves that had once held food items for the mansion had been removed to create an exhibition area. Two long rows of glass-encased displays took up the space.

Tracy headed to the first exhibit case. Inside were various books and journals that had belonged to the Ryan family. "They probably put the more delicate items in these cases to preserve them."

Peter followed beside her as they looked over the first row and then the second. Dead center in the display was an oval frame and, as Tracy peered at it, she felt an immediate pull toward the object.

"That's it," she said.

Peter raised the glass on the display case. Gently, he lifted out the frame and held it for Tracy's examination. Nancy and Detective Daly stood behind her, also reviewing the object.

"He said there was a note in their secret place," Peter pointed out, trying to see how that was possible.

The detective spoke up. "The frame is kind of thick. Almost like it should open up." He mimicked the action with his hands.

Tracy flipped the frame to the side and, sure enough, there was a small space obscured by the fine filigree of the mahogany frame. With gentle pressure she pulled at it and the frame opened like an old-fashioned locket. Inside was a folded piece of paper, slightly yellowed, but well preserved by the almost airtight space between the two halves of the frame.

Peter took the note in his hands and carefully unfolded it, since it was a bit brittle. He read it and shook his head, sucked in a deep breath. "It's Skippy's suicide note. He killed Izzy's messenger and dumped his body out in the ocean."

"That explains the blood on the skiff," Tracy said.

"And the witnesses who heard a fight and saw Ryan rowing out to sea," Daly added.

Nancy held her hands out and Tracy gingerly handed over the frame. Bringing the frame close to her heart, Nancy closed her eyes and swayed for a moment before saying, "There's great emotion here. A connection to both of them. A physical connection."

She brought the frame back out where all could see it and traced what looked like an embroidered floral design in the frame. "The Victorians used to create ornate pictures and jewelry using human hair."

She handed the photo back to Tracy who scrutinized it more carefully. "There are red and black motifs here. Like Anna's and Skippy's hair."

"Which would give you the DNA proof you need. Right, Angelo?" the detective asked Peter.

"Right. I'll need to get permission from the State to take some samples, but I'm hoping they'll be cooperative considering the situation," he said and glanced at all of them. "I guess we have to determine who is the winner of the contest."

Tracy waved her hands. "Winners. I had the theory and found the frame, but we wouldn't have totally solved the mystery without Nancy's seance or the detective finding the hiding place."

Relief flooded through Peter at her words. As a lawyer, he was used to dealing with the bad side of human nature. It was nice to witness someone actually behaving like a human being. Looking to the psychic and the detective, he realized they were all in agreement.

"I guess that settles it. I'll advise the others and my father. Contact the State about getting samples of the hairs in that artwork."

Nancy and the detective immediately headed off, leaving Peter and Tracy alone in the room.

"So is that it?" she asked, but he knew she was referring to so much more than the contest.

He stepped close to her and slipped his arm around her waist. His body reacted immediately to her nearness, but it wasn't any lingering emotions from Skippy or Anna. It was him responding.

"What do you think?"

Tracy smiled knowingly and raised her hand, ran her fingers through the thick strands of his hair. "I think there's still a lot we need to learn about each other, but I'm game if you are."

"I'm game," he said with a grin before he swooped down and sealed the promise with a kiss that curled her toes.

When they pulled away with breathless anticipation, she took his hand in hers and said, "Then let's get started."

Eight

Tracy sat beside Peter as the closing credits ran on the documentary Tommy and his crew had produced with the help of all of the contestants except Hank, who, to their surprise, had been so freaked out by the ghosts that he had left the mansion. As had John Marcovic. Apparently, the project had been too lowbrow for the mystery writer's participation, even though it was tasteful enough for the cable television station that had chosen to buy the rights. In the end, Tommy and his crew had become winners as well when Peter's father had agreed to lift the confidentiality ban so Skippy's true story could be told. It had been icing on the cake when Tracy sold a novel about the ghostly encounter and the real story behind the Ryan family.

Peter squeezed Tracy's hand and rose. He grabbed a bottle of champagne that they had been keeping on ice to celebrate with everyone gathered in the inn, which he and Tracy had been lovingly restoring over the past several months.

His father sat in a wheelchair next to the sofa, his color and energy much improved since the night Peter had come to relay the information that the mystery had been solved. After that night, and the day weeks later when the DNA testing had proved that he was Skippy Ryan's grandson, his health had taken a decided turn for the better.

Nancy and Detective Daly sat side by side on a love seat, clearly taken with one another. Peter supposed the police officer had that worn and weathered look some women might find attractive.

Tommy's crew was in motion, as it always seemed to be, moving from in front of the large-screen television to the cameras off to the side for a short behind-the-scenes piece they planned on doing.

With Tracy assisting, Peter poured glasses of champagne for each of their guests and offered up a toast. "To Anna and Francis Ryan and their everlasting love."

Everyone around them chimed in with their wishes and Peter took a sip of his champagne, but noticed that Tracy wasn't having any of hers.

"Are you OK?" he asked.

She smiled, took hold of his free hand and brought it to rest on her belly. "Better than OK."

"I'm getting my babies," his father said joyously and, a second later, the lights in the room flashed on and off.

"I think Anna and Skippy approve," said Nancy, and the detective raised his glass in agreement.

Embracing his newly wed wife, Peter grinned. "I guess we're going to be expanding more than the master suite in this old place."

Tracy smiled and inched up on tiptoe to brush a kiss across his lips. "You know Francis can be either a boy or girl's name."

"Seems right to me," he said and once again the lights dimmed off and on, but neither Peter nor Tracy paid it much mind.

The tragedy of an unlikely pair of ghosts had brought them together. It seemed only fair that they hung around for the good times to come.

In His Hands

Sara Reinke

Can someone haunt you if they're not even dead?

Jack woke up naked and face down in his bed, the sheets kicked back in a rumpled heap at the foot of the king-sized mattress. He opened his eyes slowly, groggily, and, after a moment's disorientation, realized the sun was rising, a pale glow spilling through the panoramic windows that faced the eastern banks of Fallen Leaf Lake, just south of Lake Tahoe.

He groaned, closing his eyes, groped blindly for a pillow, which he then crammed over his head. After a moment spent in this cool, comfortable darkness, he remembered the night before and sat up abruptly, shoving the pillow aside.

"Hello?" His voice was a croak scraping loose from the back of his throat.

"Tell me your name," he'd pleaded with the woman, sweat-soaked and exhausted in the aftermath of lovemaking, lying beneath her as she straddled his hips and gazed down at him. Her blonde hair fell in a lazy tumble of loose waves down past her shoulders, mermaid-like as it draped over her breasts. They'd been at it for hours, non-stop, nearly relentless, as if she'd tapped into some hidden and heretofore unknown reservoir of stamina within him, some kind of primal lust that her touch, her kiss had unleashed.

"Please," he'd whispered, caressing her hips, tracing the long, lean contours of her thighs with his hands. "Tell me who you are."

But she'd only smiled and leaned over, her hair spilling around his face as she kissed him softly, her lips lighting across his.

He hadn't had more than a casual dinner date in the last year and a half, and he could count on two fingers the number of one-night stands he'd had in his entire life.

What the hell possessed me last night? he thought, although he knew.

The dress.

The bar had been crowded, standing room only, patrons shoulder to shoulder and flanking the pool tables. But even from a distance, across the smoke-filled breadth that had hung between them, he'd caught sight of her. It was the dead of winter, yet she'd worn a sleeveless dress, little more than a scrap of red silk and sequins suspended from her shoulders. He'd been dumbstruck, a cue stick in one hand and a half-empty glass in the other.

"Hello? You still here?" he called out in his bedroom, stumbling to his feet, squinting against the glare.

He hadn't had a condom on him, but somehow that hadn't even mattered. He remembered the young woman leading him toward the restroom at the back corner of the bar, slipping her fingers through his own and guiding him wordlessly, willingly in tow. He'd closed the door behind them and turned the lock home. They immediately fell together in a tangle of arms and legs, kissing fervently, furiously. Her hands fumbled between them, unzipping his fly, pushing his jeans down from his hips. Her lips were soft and velveteen, her tongue warm and sweet.

When he'd plunged into her, her fingernails dug into the meat of his shoulders. Again and again, he'd shoved her back against the bathroom wall, making the window above them rattle in its pane with every stroke. She'd cried out as she climaxed, tightening around him, and he'd shuddered with his own sudden, powerful release.

He'd just had sex with a complete stranger, a woman he'd met less than fifteen minutes earlier and, by all rights, his mind should have been racing, panicking as the trained physician in him rattled off a litany of risks he'd just foolishly, impulsively subjected himself to . . .

HIV . . . syphilis . . . herpes . . . hepatitis B . . .

By all rights, he should have been kicking himself, but instead, all he'd found himself doing was thinking about her, about how he'd probably just experienced the most incredible sex of his entire life, and how he was ready to do it again, hardening at just the thought.

"I live on the east shore," he'd whispered. "I've got a house up by Fallen Leaf Lake. We could—"

She'd nodded, cutting him off, her eyes hungry as they locked with his own. "Take me there," she'd breathed – the only words she'd said to him all night.

He called for her again as he padded down the stairs from the loft bedroom. "Hey! Are you still here?"

The rest of the house had an open floor plan; the better to showcase the expansive windows facing the lake, as his landlord had pointed out. There was no such thing as a lousy view in Jack's house, which was exactly why he'd rented it, and why, as soon as he hit the front foyer, he could see that he was alone.

Where did she go? he thought, bewildered. She couldn't have walked back to town. It's at least twenty miles. And it was freezing last night. Even if she hitchhiked, she couldn't have . . .

His thoughts trailed off and his eyes flew wide with realization. "Son of a bitch," he gasped, darting back to the foyer. Here, on a small entry table, as a rule, he'd toss his keys upon entering the house. That morning, the table was bare.

"Fuck," Jack said, rushing back up to his bedroom. Let me have forgotten, he thought. I was drunk last night. I must have forgotten, left them in my pocket, on the nightstand or my bureau . . .

But he hadn't and he knew it and he didn't need to make a frantic, frenzied search of the loft to prove it.

I drove her here last night. She saw where I put my car keys. Son of a bitch – she stole my car!

He nearly fell down the steps as he raced down again, recklessly taking them three at a time. The house was ringed by a wraparound deck; he pushed the patio door open and ran outside.

It was shockingly cold. Frost had crusted on the ground and his breath immediately fogged in the air, framing his face in a hazy halo.

"Hey!" he shouted, as if he had half a hope she would still be within earshot somehow, still sitting in the driveway behind the wheel of his Jeep Wrangler.

He rounded the corner of his deck and realized two things simultaneously – first, his Jeep was right where it was supposed to be, present and accounted for. Second, his next-door neighbor, a heavy-set, grey-haired blackjack dealer named Joann Limon was just getting home from her late shift on the Nevada side of the lake. As she climbed out of her car, she heard his shout and turned, her expression curious.

That was about the same time Jack remembered he was naked and froze like a deer pinned by oncoming high beams. Even though there was more than twenty feet between them, along with at least ten pine trees and a pair of wispy aspens, he saw Joann plainly through the low-hanging boughs. She saw him, too; her eyes were wide and surprised as she glanced down the length of him, taking into account his state of undress.

"Oh, uh . . ." Jack clapped his hands over his crotch and side-stepped clumsily. "Hey, Joann."

"Jack," she replied mildly, as if this was no more than an everyday occurrence, something to which she was completely and comfortably accustomed. "Everything all right?"

"Uh . . . yeah," he said, flipping her a quick wave – which left him mortifyingly re-exposed. He clamped his hand back between his legs. "Fine. Everything's fine. Thanks. Yeah."

To her credit, she didn't laugh at him, at least not to his face, and he managed to beat a hasty, if not immodest, retreat. Before he could scurry inside for the relative cover of his living room, however, he stumbled to a halt. There, in the patio door lock, glinting in the early morning sun, were his keys, dangling from the lock in the patio door.

Right where I left them last night, he realized.

"Goddamn it," he muttered.

As Jack pulled into the lot facing the sprawling hospital complex in South Lake Tahoe, California, he was surprised to find a local news channel's van parked in front of the main building. A relay mast and satellite dish had been mounted on top, and he could see someone setting up a camera and tripod on the sidewalk approaching the entrance. A blonde woman in a bright-red coat stood nearby in conversation with a man dressed in a wool overcoat.

"Here he is now," he heard the man say as he climbed out of the Jeep. Biting back a groan, Jack recognized his voice: Bill Rumpke, the hospital's chief of staff – his boss. "Jack? Over here. Jack!"

Perfect. Jack glanced at himself in the side-view mirror and winced at the visible shadows around his eyes, the scraggly growth of day-old, hungover beard stubble on his chin and cheeks. *Just perfect.*

"Uh, good morning, sir," he said as he hesitantly approached the entrance. Eyeing the news crew warily, he added, "What's all this?"

"KLVE-TV news." The blonde woman stepped forward, her toothy grin too dazzlingly white to be anything other than artificially tinted. She thrust her hand out to him. "It's a pleasure, Dr Harris."

"They're here to do a story on you," said Rumpke.

"Me?" Jack blinked in surprise.

"The thoracotomy yesterday," Rumpke elaborated. But before Jack could do more than sputter in protest, Rumpke glanced past his shoulder, smile widening. "Ah! Here come the Bennetts now."

Jack turned as a middle-aged couple walked through the sliding glass doors of the main entrance. He recognized them from the night before – the parents of an accident victim he'd worked on in the emergency room. Though bundled up against the winter chill, they were both clearly dressed in their Sunday best beneath. The woman carried a framed photograph in her hands. Both she and her husband had looked uncertain, somewhat hesitant, upon their exit from the hospital, but brightened visibly now to see the news van – and, more specifically, Jack.

"Dr Harris!" the woman exclaimed. When she drew close enough, she hugged him, enveloping him in a tight, sudden cloud of Chantilly perfume.

"Mrs Bennett," he managed somewhat breathlessly as her stranglehold momentarily choked him. "It's, uh, nice to see you again." Because her husband had his hand outstretched, dangling in mid-air, Jack reached for it, accepting the fervent clasp. "Mr Bennett."

"Dr Harris," Mr Bennett said, his eyes glossy. "We can't thank you enough for what you've done."

Jack always found it unnerving to see a grown man cry, especially one who was nearly the same age as his own father. In his line of work, he saw this entirely too often, but it never made the experience any less unsettling. "Like I said last night," he offered in clumsy reassurance. "Just, uh, doing my job."

Laura Bennett had been delivered by ambulance to the emergency room following a single-car crash in which she'd skidded off the road and struck a tree. The impact with the driver's side airbag had left her suffering from fractured ribs and the ragged edges of broken bone had punched past her lung into the thick muscle of her heart. With every beat, it hemorrhaged; with every contraction, it forced itself closer and closer to arrest.

"Give me one milligram atropine by IV push, stat," Jack had ordered, cutting a deep incision beneath her breast. Using a surgical expander, he'd spread the third and fourth ribs apart, allowing him unobstructed access. While another doctor, Pete Howard – his best friend since medical school – tilted her lung out of the chest cavity, Jack worked quickly to repair the damaged heart underneath.

"I need your finger—" with the tip of the scalpel, he'd guided a nearby trauma nurse "—right here. Put pressure on that wound."

The nurse, Margot Williams, quickly complied and, when she'd stepped beside him, he caught the distinctive whiff of patchouli. The residents liked to call her "Weirdo Williams" – though never to her face – because she liked to talk about alternative medicine and all things supernatural, like crystals, Ouija boards, divining rods and tarot cards.

On that night, though, Margot had been all business, and hadn't said a word as Jack had sutured the torn cardiac muscle closed. Just as he'd slipped the last thread into place, Laura's exposed heart had quivered and shuddered in the throes of arrest – then abruptly stopped. On the monitor, the spasmodic spike of her pulse rate abruptly flatlined.

"She's coding," Pete had shouted.

While around them the flurry of activity continued unabated and more frantic than ever, Jack had reacted on instinct, reaching into Laura's chest to cradle her heart against his palm. Using his other hand, he pressed against it, rhythmic and deliberate, gentle but firm.

Aloud, he'd called out, "I need one milligram, epinephrine, intracardiac, stat, then ten more of atropine by push, q-five."

In his mind, he kept count – one and two and three and four – as he'd pumped her heart, forcing blood to cycle through its inner chambers.

"You did great," Pete had told him later, as they sat together on a curb outside of the hospital. Within moments of beginning his cardiac compressions, Laura's heart had started to beat again on its own and she'd been carted off unceremoniously to an awaiting operating room. In the aftermath, as the rush of frenetic adrenaline had faded, Jack had felt exhausted, spent, like he'd just gone ten rounds, pay-per-view, with a heavyweight boxing champ.

"What say we kick out of here at shift change, head down to T. Bomb's?" Pete had asked.

"No thanks." Tom Bombadil's – or T. Bomb's as it had been affectionately dubbed – was a favorite after-shift gathering spot for the hospital's interns and residents.

"Come on," Pete had pressed. "I'll buy you a Jack and Coke. After that resuscitation, man, you deserve one. A double, even."

Despite his fatigue, and the inner voice of reason nagging at him in reminder that he had another lengthy shift to pull in less than twelve hours, Jack had agreed. And the rest, as they say, was history.

"Dr Harris, is this type of procedure common?" the TV reporter asked, thrusting a microphone at Jack as the light from the camera glared in his face.

"A thoracotomy? Uh, not too uncommon." Jack gave a wary glance to his boss. "It's used for a variety of purposes, both in emergency—"

"But it's the first time in our facility's twenty-two-year history in which one has been performed for resuscitation." Rumpke barged into both the conversation and the camera frame. "During the procedure, Dr Harris used his hands to pump the patient's heart. His heroic efforts saved her life."

"Heroic?" Embarrassed, Jack winced. "I don't know if I'd call it . . ."

"He's right," Mrs Bennett offered timidly.

The reporter turned and Mrs Bennett held the framed photo in her hands toward the camera. Clearing her throat, she said more loudly, "I said he's right. Dr Harris is a hero."

Jack glanced at the photograph, did a startled double-take, then jerked back as if he'd been slapped in the face. *What the hell?* he thought, blinking in bewildered shock at the image of Laura Bennett. He realized he'd seen her before. Last night as a matter of fact – only not in the emergency room because he hadn't noticed her face then. He'd been too busy with her heart.

I saw her after that, at T. Bomb's, he realized. *I took her home with me. She's the girl I had sex with last night!*

"Is everything alright, Dr Harris?"

After the interview, he'd gone up to the cardio-thoracic intensive care unit, where Laura Bennett had been admitted following surgeries that had lasted well into the early morning hours. She was resting now, surrounded by monitor screens, IV stands, automatic pumps and a tangle of tubes, cables and wires.

It can't be the same woman. With a frown, he shook his head. *There's no way.*

At the sound of Mr Bennett's hesitant voice from behind him, he turned in surprise.

"I'm sorry," the older man said. "I didn't mean to startle you. I just didn't expect to see you again so soon. Is everything all right?"

Jack cut one last glance back at Laura, then managed a smile. "Everything's fine, Mr Bennett. I just wanted to see how she's doing."

"They did some kind of scan on her, a CT, I think?" Mr Bennett walked into the room, dropping his coat onto a nearby chair. "Anyway, it didn't show any signs of brain injury, thank God. Her surgeon's optimistic about her chances of recovery. Said it could take days, weeks even, for her to come out of it, but he seemed to think she'd shake this off."

"That's good news," Jack said. "I'm glad to hear it, Mr Bennett."

"Call me Frank," the older man said, offering a smile. "My wife will be sorry she missed you. She's run down to the cafeteria to get some breakfast. You ask her, she'd say you hung the moon."

Jack smiled again, embarrassed. "I appreciate that."

"You know Laura's a singer?" Frank said, gazing at his sleeping daughter with a sorrowful, nearly wistful expression. "Like a little bird. I guess she started performing down at Harrah's about a month or so ago, three nights a week in the piano bar. It's not much, but she's sure been excited about it. Said it could be her big break."

He sounded momentarily choked and drew his hand to his mouth. Because he said nothing more, Jack took it as his cue to leave. Just as he stepped across the threshold, however, he stopped again. "Does Laura have any sisters?" he asked, adding in his mind, *Who happen to look exactly like her?*

Frank shook his head. "No. Claire, my wife, she'd have had a whole houseful of children if she could have, but the doctor told her when we were younger she'd probably never have babies. It took us five years of trying before we wound up with Laura. We always said after that we'd had more than our fair share of miracles, but . . ." His voice grew strained again. Then, quietly, hoarsely: "Looks like the Lord must've had at least one left in him for us last night."

"Hey, man!" Jack grimaced as Pete Howard clapped him heavily on the shoulder. "You're a real celebrity now. I saw the TV van outside. That's some shit, huh?"

"Yeah. Terrific," Jack grumbled as they stepped into a waiting elevator together. As the doors closed and they backed against the far wall, making room for other riders, he glanced at Pete. "You make it home OK last night?"

"Took a cab." Pete laughed. "Had to get up at the ass-crack of dawn to go back for my car. How about you?"

"Like you don't know."

Pete blinked at him. "Huh?"

Jack rolled his eyes. "Come on."

"No, seriously. What?"

Jack frowned. "The girl last night." Frankly, he was astonished and impressed that Pete had not only managed to keep mum about it to that point, but also looked genuinely bewildered at the mention. "Blonde hair. Red dress. Hot as hell. I left with her. Don't you remember?"

"I remember you coming up, saying something about hitting the road, but by that point it was late and we were both pretty fucked up."

Jack's frown deepened. "Whatever, man."

"Seriously, I have no clue what you're talking about," Pete insisted. "What was her name?"

"I don't know."

"She didn't tell you?"

"Of course she did. I think so, anyway. She must have." With a glance to make sure no one could overhear, he leaned toward Pete and added, "We fucked in the bathroom at T. Bomb's."

"*You*? No way."

Jack frowned. "What the hell's that supposed to mean?"

Pete laughed again. "It means you're the lamest guy I know."

"Thanks," Jack muttered.

"What? It's true. I mean, you hardly even date, for Christ's sake."

They reached their floor. As the doors slid open, Pete glanced at him, his brow raised. "You're serious, aren't you? You really banged some chick at the bar." When Jack nodded, annoyed, he laughed again and clapped him on the back. "Holy shit, man. There may be hope for you yet."

Thirteen hours later, with another completed shift under his belt, Jack returned home. Exhausted, he dropped his keys and wallet in their customary places and ducked into his kitchen.

God, I swear I can still taste the stale scum of Jack and Coke from last night, he thought with a wince. He could sure as hell still feel it rattling around inside his skull, a dim but tenacious ache.

Propping the refrigerator door open with his hip, he pulled out a carton of orange juice. Not bothering with a cup, he unscrewed the lid, drew the container to his mouth and tipped his head back. Just as he started to drink, he caught a glimpse of movement out of the corner of his eye, something outside on his patio.

It was fully dark now, the glow of the living room light reflected off the glass, and, with a curious frown, he put the juice away and approached the windows. He thought he saw a silhouetted figure standing out among the heavy shadows, but it wasn't until he reached the door, cupped his hands to the glass and peered out that he saw the wink of light off red sequins and realized.

"Laura," he gasped, startled. Grabbing for the handle, he threw the door open wide, even as he heard the soft, rapid-fire patter of her bare feet slapping the deck as she ran away. "Laura," he cried, taking off after her. "Laura, wait!"

Just as she reached the stairs, he caught up to her, grabbing her by the elbow. "Wait," he gasped as she struggled in his grasp. "Laura, stop. Stop it!"

Whether the sharpness in his voice startled her, or she'd simply exhausted herself, he didn't know, but she fell still, her breasts hitching up and down as she hiccupped for breath. It couldn't be her, and he knew it; the rational part of his mind understood that there was no way in hell Laura Bennett was standing on his patio, alert, conscious and walking of her own accord. And yet, somehow, impossibly, it *was*; her face that he caught sight of beneath the mess of her hair, her unmistakable brown eyes, the full curves of her mouth.

"Please help," she whispered. "She's after me."

Jack swept his gaze down the steps toward the driveway. He didn't see anything, no vehicles except his Jeep, no hint of headlights or the sound of a distant motor, maybe a taxi driving away.

"Who?" he asked, but she didn't respond. Her skin was like ice and he could hear her teeth chattering together. "Come on. Let's go inside, OK? It's freezing out here."

She still didn't speak, but offered no resistance as he guided her into the house. He led her to the sofa, and then knelt on the floor in front of her as she sat.

"Do you know where you are?" he asked. "Do you remember how you got here?"

"I was lost in the woods," she murmured. "I . . . I was cold and couldn't find my way."

He grabbed a blanket off the nearest sofa arm and wrapped it snugly around her, letting her clutch the folds of it closed beneath her chin.

"She's after me," she mumbled again, shivering. Her eyes darted nervously to the windows.

"Who is?" he asked, but again, she wouldn't elaborate. When she looked back in his direction, he said, "It's OK. You can talk to me." Because he didn't know if she'd remember or not, he added, "My name's Jack Harris."

She reached for him, brushing her fingertips against his face, tracing the line of his mouth. "Jack."

He nodded. "I'm a doctor," he said. "I can help—"

His voice cut short in surprise as she leaned forward and pressed her mouth against his with an unexpected passion. Immediately, her tongue slipped against the seam of his lips, then past.

"Wait," he said, trying to draw away. "Laura, stop."

She caught his face between her hands and pulled him back, kissing him again, fiercely, deeply. The blanket fell from her shoulders as she slipped down from the couch cushions to the floor, her thighs sliding to frame his hips as she straddled him.

No panties, he realized, biting back a groan as his hands fell against her thighs, tantalizingly revealed as the short hem of her red dress slid up. Just like last night.

Her lips trailed to his cheek, then his throat, settling against the delta of his jaw. He could feel his body responding to her; the crotch of his pants felt uncomfortably tight, the zipper digging into him as he swelled beneath it.

"Stop," he whispered, as he felt her reach between them, her fingers busy at his fly. But the truth was, he didn't want her to. In that moment, he was as overwhelmed with desire – an irrepressible, undeniable *need* for her – as he'd been the night before. When she pushed him back against the floor, he didn't resist, instead raising his hips so she could jerk the hem of his shirt loose, and then open the front of his pants.

She kissed him again, and he tangled his fingers in her hair, pulling her near. Within moments, he was inside her, spearing into her warmth, and she rocked against him, drawing him in more deeply. She sat up astride him, the motions of her hips growing faster, sharper, and he clasped her waist between his hands to urge her on. Arching his back, he matched her pace, driving himself into her, watching as she tilted her head back, her long hair spilling past her shoulders, her breasts bouncing beneath the sequined bodice of her dress with every forceful thrust.

"Jack," she gasped, shuddering with pleasure, bringing him to a sudden, crashing climax that left every muscle in his body rigid, straining, trembling with release.

"Jesus," he whispered as she crumpled against him. It occurred to him that he'd seen no wounds on her, no incisions at all on her torso, no bruises on her face, no cuts or scrapes anywhere at all.

Which isn't possible, he thought. She nearly died in a car crash. I cut her open myself, for Christ's sake. She shouldn't be here . . . she can't be. None of this can be real.

What the hell's going on?

Laura fell asleep within moments, spooned at his side. Moving slowly, he managed to lift her and gently reposition her on the couch. He reached for the fallen blanket and pulled it over her to keep her warm. As he did, he couldn't help but look at her again, head to toe, and note the glaring absence of any wounds on her body.

"This can't be right," he whispered, raking his fingers through his hair, bewildered.

He heard a soft *plink!* like something hitting one of the windows behind him. With a frown, he glanced toward the patio, but saw nothing except the reflected glow from the nearby lamp and impenetrable darkness beyond. Then he heard it again.

Plink!

Leaving Laura to rest on the couch, he rose to his feet, tugging his pants back into place and zipping his fly.

Plink!

He saw a wink of light off one of the windows and his frown deepened as he realized the source – a sliver-like crack that had formed in the glass.

What the hell? he thought, then – *plink-plink-PLINK!* – the crack grew right before his eyes, racing in a crooked, jagged diagonal toward the upper right and lower left corners of the pane.

"What the . . . ?" he whispered, reaching up, brushing his fingertips lightly against it. When the window abruptly shattered, sending in an explosive burst of splintered glass, he had less than a second to backpedal in startled alarm, jerking his arms reflexively up. He hit the floor, diving headlong against the hardwood, trying to keep his face covered as a sudden shower pelted him, thousands of shards tearing into his back and shoulders, shredding skin and shirt.

As he sat up, he felt blood streaming down his face from dozens of shallow cuts in his scalp. From the kitchen, he heard a sudden, noisy clattering and, when he looked, he saw all of his cupboard doors swinging open wide, then banging shut again, over and over, with a furious, deafening cadence.

"Holy shit," he gasped, and then all of the drawers suddenly shot out from the cabinets, literally rocketing from their recesses. They smashed into opposing walls, the stove, the base of his breakfast bar, and their contents – silverware, plastic containers, knives, spatulas – scattered in all directions.

He cried out as the cabinet doors on the living-room entertainment center flew open and DVDs began shooting out, the plastic jewel cases launching themselves as if out of a machine gun. Behind him, one by one, the windows framing his deck began to burst, sending fresh new showers of glass flying through the house. Scrambling to his feet, he dove for the sofa and found Laura crouched on the floor, her eyes flown wide with terror.

"Jack!" she screamed, ducking as a DVD whipped directly for her face. He threw himself on top of her, trying to use his body as a shield. From the kitchen and bathroom, he could hear banging, thudding, a thunderous din as cans, bottles and boxes shot out of cupboards and cabinets, flying through the air, smashing into walls.

A horrific screech ripped through the air, terrifying and inhuman, like metal scraping against metal. At the sound of it, Laura panicked beneath him. Her elbow rammed back into his gut, whoofing the breath momentarily from him, forcing him to loosen his grasp enough for her to break free.

"Laura," he gulped as she stumbled to her feet. He tried to grab her, but she darted frantically for the patio door.

"Laura!" he cried out, hoarse and breathless. Either she didn't hear him or she didn't care; that hideous shriek had pushed her over the edge from frightened alarm into full-blown hysteria, and she darted outside, into the darkness. Jack moved to follow her, made it halfway from the couch to the door when an airborne electric skillet – catapulted from the kitchen – connected solidly with the back of his head. The blow stunned the senses from him and knocked him to the ground – and out cold – instantly.

When he came to, he found himself on the floor, surrounded by broken glass. His head ached miserably, and he grimaced when he touched the tender spot at the base of his skull where the skillet had struck him, his fingertips coming away blood-smeared.

I need to go to the emergency room, he thought as he

staggered to his feet. Dazed, he surveyed the trashed remains of his house. In the kitchen, the refrigerator door listed open wide, a carton of milk lying on the floor in front of it, surrounded by a large, white puddle. Half-empty cartons of Chinese takeout had been violently hurled at the opposing wall, leaving splattered patterns of hoisin sauce and barbecued pork stains on the back-splash above the sink. Cans of green beans, tomato soup and French-fried onions had rolled into the far corners. A litter of plastic bowls, mismatched lids, potholders, dinner plates, soup bowls, flatware and a loose scatter of elbow macaroni covered the polished pine floor. Paintings and framed photographs that had once graced the walls were now smashed, shattered and strewn across the floor, along with overturned houseplants, scattered magazines and books.

It looks like a tornado hit this place.

He limped into the bathroom and groped for the light switch. The fixture cover had been knocked askew, and the fluorescent bulb above the mirror buzzed loudly, then blinked several times before coming to life.

"Jesus," he whispered, staring at his reflection – because he looked like he'd been thrown head first out of a plate-glass window from the top of a twelve-story building, and had lived to tell the tale.

His face and neck were smeared with blood, his shirt torn and stained. Glass shards glittered in his hair like stardust. When he touched the back of his head again, he felt a knot the size and consistency of a hard-boiled egg rising.

I need to go the emergency room, he thought again. *I don't know what the hell just happened here or what the fuck is going on, but I know that much for sure.*

Leaning over the sink, closing his eyes as a wave of vertigo washed over him, he did his best to rinse the blood from his face. He stumbled upstairs to his bedroom and found even more mess. Like those in his kitchen, the drawers to his bureau had flown open wide, as had the doors to his closet. His clothes lay tumbled and heaped haphazardly around the room. He found a clean shirt among the mess and, moving slowly, painstakingly, he put it on.

He limped back downstairs and went outside. Once behind the wheel of his Jeep, he sat for a long moment, struggling to clear his head. I think I have a concussion, he thought, pressing his fingertips to his brow. I probably need a CT scan.

But when he fired up the Jeep, he didn't head for the hospital. Instead, ignoring the nagging little voice of reason that recited a litany of possible dire complications – subarachnoid hemorrhage, subdural hematoma, cranial contusion – he followed the winding, two-lane highway that led around the outer edge of Lake Tahoe.

She started singing down at Harrah's about a month or so ago, Frank Bennett had told him of Laura. It stood to reason if she'd been there a while, then surely she'd made some friends along the way, a co-worker or two. Someone who might be able to help me, he thought. Someone who might know what the hell is going on.

Harrah's Casino was located in the heart of Stateline, Nevada on the south-western shore of the lake. Tourist season was underway and, upon Jack's arrival, he found the brightly lit resort filled to overflowing with guests.

"Excuse me," he said, having shoved his way through the boisterous crowd in the lobby to reach a young woman at the guest-services counter. "I'm trying to find out about one of your . . ."

His voice faltered as he caught sight of a flat-screen display near the desk. On it, he saw a promotional video for the casino's nightclub in which scantily clad women performed circus-like aerial acrobatics above the neon-illuminated dance floor.

He recognized one in particular. "That girl," he said, pointing to the screen as a close-up on Laura's face panned out to show her twirling slowly, upside down, on a trapeze. "Her name is Laura Bennett. Do you know her?"

"No," the woman replied. She studied him with undisguised wariness, and he knew despite the clean shirt he still looked like hell. Hesitantly, trying to be polite, she added, "But all the Vex Girls look alike in those dresses they wear."

"The what?"

"Vex Girls. They perform shows here during the week."

She told him how to get to the nightclub, and he worked his way back through the throng to reach it. Given his battered appearance, he half expected her to be on the phone to alert security the moment he turned around, but was pleasantly surprised to reach Vex without incident.

Like the lobby, it was packed, the lights dimmed low, which helped disguise the fact his face was cut and bruised. The enveloping darkness was broken only by the staccato pulsations of strobe lights and lasers set in time with music that blared, deafening, from all directions. More by luck than anything, he caught a waitress passing by and asked about the Vex Girls show.

"They don't start for another hour," she yelled over the din.

"How can I find out about one of them?" he shouted and, to make it worth her while, he gave her a twenty-dollar bill.

"Look for the cages. That's where they go when they're not in the air." She cocked her head, directing his gaze to a nearby stage, small and round, encircled with bars so it resembled a birdcage. Inside, a young black woman in an all-too familiar dress wiggled and gyrated. Red with spaghetti straps, trimmed in sequins, it looked exactly like the dress Laura had been wearing at T. Bomb's.

When Jack approached the cage, curling his fingers around the bars to look up at her, the woman shimmied in his direction. He tried calling up to her, but she just smiled and shook her head, cupping her hand to her ear as if to tell him there was no way she could hear him over the music. He shouted again and, this time, she must have caught the name "Laura Bennett", because, all at once, her smile faltered. She stopped dancing and crossed the narrow circumference of stage to squat down in front of him.

"Do you know Laura Bennett?" he asked again.

"Who's asking?"

"My name's Jack Harris. I'm a doctor. She was in a car crash last night."

"I know," the black woman said. "It was all over the news today. Is she going to be all right?"

"Yeah," Jack said, because it was easier than trying to go into a lengthy discussion of her diagnoses and prognosis over the pulsating din of the music. "Listen, I thought she was a singer here. In the piano bar, her dad said."

The dancer laughed. "Yeah, she told her folks that so they wouldn't freak. But a girl's got to make a living, you know? And record producers from LA come in here all the time. She's been hoping to meet one, slip them a demo tape, get her big break."

"You know if anyone was pissed off at her?" he asked, and the woman shook her head. "You sure? Maybe she was dating someone with a jealous ex?"

She's after me, Laura had told him more than once, never hinting as to who "she" might be.

"Laura? No way. She wasn't seeing anyone. She would've told me. Said she's waiting for her Prince Charming, or some such bullshit." The dancer said this with an eye roll. "You know, like in *Sleeping Beauty* or *Snow White.*"

Left with more questions than the answers he'd hoped to find, Jack went back to his Jeep and climbed inside. Again his head swam and he closed his eyes until the momentary dizziness passed, wondering if his next stop should be the ER. As he slipped the key into the ignition, he glanced up into the rearview mirror and yelped in surprise. A woman sat in the back seat, unmistakable despite the shadows.

"Laura?" he gasped and whirled around in the seat to face her. "Jesus Christ, where did you . . ."

"I'm cold," she whispered, and now he could see that her eyes were glossy, swimming with tears. She wore only the red slip dress again, her arms wrapped around her narrow frame as she trembled. "Please, I . . . I'm so cold."

"Here." Shifting his weight, he unzipped the front of his coat. He shrugged it off and leaned over the center console to tuck it around her shoulders. "Laura, listen to me." He smoothed her hair back and cupped his hand to her face, drawing her gaze. "How did you get in my car?"

She shook her head. "I don't know."

"Where did you come from?"

"I don't know," she whimpered again. "I can't remember." Then, with a hesitant glance over her shoulder out the back window, she said, "But she's after me again. She was chasing me."

"Who?" Jack pressed.

Her bottom lip drew in beneath the edge of her upper teeth. "I don't know," she whispered. "But she can fly."

"What?" Jack cocked his brow, dubious.

"I heard her," Laura insisted, her eyes round and urgent. "In the tree tops. She was flying through the trees, trying to find me. I heard her laughing." She blinked at him, mournfully. "You don't believe me." Covering her face with her hands, she began to cry.

"Hey." Leaning further in the seat, he touched her face again. "I didn't say—"

"Help me." She caught his hand between her own, clutching at him with a frantic sort of desperation. "Please," she whispered, her cheeks tear-streaked and glistening. "Help me."

The car stereo snapped on all at once, completely of its own accord, tuned to a sudden, ear-splitting volume. A shrieking guitar riff tore through the Jeep at what sounded like at least one hundred and eighty decibels.

"Shit," Jack exclaimed, reaching for the radio, pawing at the control as Laura shrank back in her seat, clapping her hands over her ears. No matter which direction he turned the knob, the volume only spiked higher, thrumming through the entire chassis. At the same time, all of the dashboard lights began flashing and blinking, manic and strobelike, while the dome light overhead burst into life. Its dim yellow glow grew progressively brighter and brighter, until the little bulb inside burst, shattering the plastic fixture cover, sending a spray of broken, jagged fragments flying.

Jack yelped. From the back seat, Laura uttered a shrill wail. He glanced up past the dash, beyond the windshield, just as something enormous came swooping down directly at them. He didn't get a good look at it, no more than a split-second glance, but he could have sworn it was a woman, her skin as alabaster as the surface of a glacier, her body nude, her lips pulled back in a gruesome snarl to reveal a mouthful of wickedly hooked teeth.

And she had wings.

"Shit!" He threw his arms up to protect his face as the winged woman crashed headlong into the windshield, shattering it in a sudden spray of high velocity glass shards.

The Jeep's alarm went off, the horn blatting out in a disharmonic din to accompany the blaring stereo. The headlights blinked and flashed, the wiper blades flopped crazily back and forth against the gaping maw where the windshield had once been and, all at once, the airbag deployed. It sounded like a shotgun blast leveled squarely at his face, and Jack's head snapped back as it knocked the breath from him, stunning him momentarily senseless.

Reaching blindly, he pawed for the door handle. He tumbled out of the Jeep, his ears ringing, his head swimming. As he staggered away, he looked around wildly for the winged woman who had struck his car. Somehow he'd lost sight of her after she hit the windshield, and there was no sign of her now – no body crumpled against the hood or roof of his Jeep, or on the pavement nearby. There was no blood, nothing except a small crowd gathering nearby to watch the spectacle with curious expressions.

"Where'd she go?" he cried to the nearest bystander. "The woman who hit my car! She just . . . Jesus Christ, she flew right into the windshield. Did you see her? Where did she go?"

The man shook his head, mute and dumbfounded, as he backed away nervously, as if Jack were foaming at the mouth. Laura hadn't gotten out of the Jeep yet, and he floundered back toward the truck.

"Laura?" To his surprise, he found the cab now conspicuously empty. Like the winged woman, Laura, too, had seemingly vanished.

"Laura?" Stupidly, he reached out, leaning past the driver's seat and patting his hands against the upholstery, as if he needed palpable evidence to be certain. Against the interior of the Jeep, he caught sight of a new batch of reflected lights flashing – red and blue. Biting back a groan, he turned to find a South Lake Tahoe police cruiser pulling in to the parking lot immediately behind him.

Oh shit, he thought, as a uniformed officer stepped out to face him.

"Step away from the vehicle, sir," the officer said, dropping his hand conspicuously toward his belt, where his pistol was holstered.

"It's all right," Jack said, holding up his hands. About that time, he felt the landscape side-slip like he'd just stepped foot on a gigantic Tilt-A-Whirl.

"I . . . I'm a doctor . . ." He'd hit his head hard too many times that evening and, with a groan, he crumpled, his eyes rolling back, the horizon within his line of sight listing at a dramatic but blessedly short-lived angle.

"Have you had anything to drink tonight?" Margot Williams asked as he sat before her in the emergency room.

It was a legitimate question, given the circumstances of his arrival, but he frowned anyway as she drew her penlight laterally inward, shining it briefly in his eyes. "No."

He'd tried to explain what had happened to the police officer and paramedic crew who had arrived at Harrah's. He'd been semi-lucid and dazed, rambling as they'd loaded him, strapped to a stretcher, into the back of an ambulance. By the time they'd reached the hospital, he'd regained his senses enough to realize he needed to keep his mouth shut, but by then, the damage had been done.

Margot nodded as if accepting his denial, but he still noticed that one of the blood samples she drew after that had infused into a phlebotomy tube with a royal-blue rubber top – which indicated it would be used for a toxicology screening. He would have ordered the same had he been presented with a patient in his condition.

They think I'm drunk, he thought dismally. Or crazy. Or both.

Most of the glass cuts on his chest and back had been shallow enough to not warrant stitches, but Margot sutured those that needed them, and dressed the others with small squares of white cotton gauze and paper tape. He'd been surprised that she hadn't offered to realign his chakra, manipulate his aura or do any of the other mystical bullshit he'd heard she was into in rumors from his fellow residents.

"Dr Howard said to sit tight for a while. He's going to order you a CT scan," Margot said as she turned to leave the curtained bay.

"I don't need a CT scan," Jack growled, even though again, he would have made the same call had he not been the patient.

"He wants to admit you." She paused, looking back at him. "At least for overnight observation."

"No, thanks. I'm fine." With a grimace, Jack eased himself off the examination table and reached for his shirt, shrugging it back over his shoulders. "Really. So if you could just ask Pete to sign that discharge form, I'll be on my way."

She studied him dubiously and turned again to leave.

"Margot, wait. Can I . . . ask you something?"

She stopped again, glancing over her shoulder at him. "Sure, Dr Harris."

I can't believe I'm doing this, he thought. "Do you believe in ghosts?" he asked, the words rushing out of him before he could stop them.

Margot looked at him for a moment, her expression cool, but otherwise unreadable. "Why do you ask?"

"I . . . I don't . . ." he began. Then, sighing heavily, he shook his head. "Never mind."

Still standing at the edge of the drapes that marked the boundary of the examination alcove, she tucked his chart beneath her arm. "I know what people think of me around here. What they say."

"What? I . . . I don't . . ." he stammered, feeling heat rise in his cheeks. "I mean, I've never . . ."

She smiled, but her eyes were sharp, stern and piercing. "I've seen more things in my nursing career than most of you residents probably have in your entire lives. Enough to convince me there's more at work in this universe than can be explained away by science. If you want to make fun of that, it's your business. I don't care."

"I'm not making fun of you," he said, pleading. "It's just . . ."

His voice trailed off, and a heavy silence hung between them. He didn't want to talk to her about this; didn't want to talk to *anyone*, because it sounded so damn crazy. But all at once, he held out some inkling of hope that Margot might believe him, might know what was happening. Because she was there, he thought. In the ER, when they brought Laura in. She saw her. She saw what happened.

He looked at her for a long moment, his head hurting. "I need your help," he whispered. "Please."

Jack had been cleared to leave the hospital over Pete's strenuous objections – as both his friend and attending physician – that Jack, had their roles been reversed, would have echoed. He'd gone home and had set about taping plastic garbage bags up in the ruined frames of his shattered windows. He'd need to call his landlord in the morning, because an insurance claim would have to be filed, but for the life of him, he couldn't figure out what in the hell he'd offer by way of plausible explanation.

Margot had promised to come by after her shift ended. He'd finished all but one of the windows by the time she made it – nearly midnight – but hadn't even touched the mess of broken glass and strewn debris littering the floor.

Her large eyes looked all the wider as she stepped lightly,

cautiously through the glass. "All of this happened in a matter of minutes, you said?"

He nodded. "Five or less." With a bitter laugh, he added, "And you should see what's left of my car."

Can someone haunt you if they're not even dead? He'd asked Margot this in the hospital, and then told her everything that had happened. Or almost everything. He hadn't mentioned the fact that he and Laura had been making love like a pair of jack-rabbits in heat – there were some things so crazy, he doubted even Margot would believe them.

"It sounds like poltergeist activity," Margot remarked, surveying the damage.

"What?"

"A poltergeist. Some believe they're invisible spirits that cause damage and destruction like this. They're like supernatural practical jokers."

Har-de-fucking-har-har, Jack thought. Some joke. "Spirits," he repeated, and she nodded. "So Laura's a ghost, then?"

"Yes and no," Margot said. "Many religions hold that you don't have to be dead in order for your spirit to leave your body and manifest itself. Laura flatlined in the ER last night. It's possible that her spirit left her body, but couldn't find its way back once you saved her. Now she's trapped in a limbo of some sort, her physical form comatose, her spirit unable to return."

"Why not?" Jack asked. The entire line of conversation was ridiculous to him; a part of him wanted to throw up his hands and simultaneously laugh and burst into exhausted, bewildered tears. Had he not been standing in the shambled midst of what had once been his living room, surrounded by broken glass, he might have felt more strongly inclined.

"I don't know." Margot looked thoughtful. "But some para-psychologists think poltergeist phenomena is actually spontaneous manifestations of psychokinetic powers."

"What does that mean?" he asked.

"It means Laura could be doing this," she said. "Or it could be something else, something that's following her, another spirit of some sort. You told me you saw something attack your car?"

He nodded. "A woman. At least, it sort of looked like a woman. With wings."

"It could have been an angel," Margot remarked thoughtfully.

I'm not so sure about that, Jack thought, recalling the momentary but horrifying glimpse of the shrieking, furious creature's face. "Whatever it is, how can I get rid of it? How do I stop this?" With his hands, he motioned desperately to his ruined home.

"I don't know," Margot admitted. "But if you have a computer I can use, I might be able to figure something out."

He didn't mean to doze off, not with his house still in shambles, and Margot at the breakfast bar with his laptop open in front of her. As she'd searched the internet, he'd started a fire in the fireplace, stacking wood haphazardly and pushing against the kindling with the tapered point of a cast-iron poker. He'd only meant to sit down for a moment, because his body was aching, his back and shoulders stiff and sore from his impact with the airbag. The moment he reclined on the sofa, however, tilting his head back and closing his eyes, letting the warmth radiating from the hearth wash over him, he was out like a light. The next thing he knew, Margot's voice, low and close by, startled him awake.

"What?" Eyes flying wide, he sat up, blinking stupidly at her. "What is it? What's wrong?"

"Nothing," she said, leaning down into his line of sight. "I hate to wake you up, but . . ."

"No, it's all right." He shook his head and shoved his hair back, wincing as he stumbled to his feet. "Did you find something?"

"I think so."

With a yawn, he followed her back to the computer. She'd left it open, the screen alight, and he was surprised to see an illustration posted to the browser window – one that looked eerily familiar. It showed a pale woman with sharp teeth, clawlike talons instead of hands and feet, and batlike wings sprouting from her shoulders.

"What the hell is that?" he asked.

"It's called a Ker," Margot said. With a pointed glance at him, she added, "I think it's what attacked your car tonight. They're sort of like the vultures of the underworld in ancient Greek mythology. They rip the souls of the newly dead from their bodies and drag them off to the afterlife."

Jack grimaced. "Lovely."

"Their job was very specific," Margot continued. "They could only claim the souls of those killed violently, like in battle. In a lot of ways, they're similar to Norse Valkyries, except they weren't portrayed as beautiful or noble. Instead, they were pretty terrifying."

Jack leaned closer to the computer, studying the image onscreen. "You said they only want souls if someone dies violently? What about in a car crash?"

"That seems like a pretty violent way to go to me," Margot admitted. "Laura wasn't dead for long. Maybe only time enough for something like this to grab her spirit, try to drag it to the underworld. Only you resuscitated her body, brought her back to life. From what I've read, a Ker is pretty vicious. She'd feel cheated out of her prize – Laura's soul. And she'd try her best to keep it."

"Is that why Laura's haunting me?" he asked. "Or whatever she's doing. Why she keeps finding me?"

"She knows who you are," Margot told him pointedly. "She must feel safe with you. From her perspective, you beat the Ker once when you saved her life."

"Yeah, but how do I stop it now? If this thing is, in fact, one of those . . . a Ker, did you call it? How do we get rid of it so Laura's spirit can go back to her body?"

"I don't know," she said. He stared at her stricken. "I couldn't find anything online that could tell me how to stop one of the Ker. The closest I found was . . . here." Brushing past him, she reached for the computer and scrolled down past the illustration. "According to Greek poems, no one mortal can escape them because we can't avoid death for ever. But here, listen: 'a Ker has yet no absolute power over the life of men, and even mortals may for a time prevent their attaining their object, or delay it by fighting them or fleeing'."

"Fight them with what?" Jack asked.

Margot shrugged. "The ancient Greeks probably would have used a sword."

"Terrific," Jack said. "Just what everyone has lying around the house."

"Look, you're exhausted," Margot said. "Why don't you try to get some sleep? I'll run home and check in a couple of other sources, come back first thing in the morning and we can go from there."

He started to argue, and then cut himself short. The truth was, she was right. He *was* exhausted. His nap on the sofa, however brief, had been dreamless and deep, and his mind and body ached at the sudden temptation of resuming it.

Margot shrugged her purse over her shoulder. "Will you be all right? It's cold in here. You could come back to my house. I've got an extra bedroom."

Jack shook his head. "I think I'll be OK. I'll just camp out here in front of the fireplace. Thanks, though." When she nodded once, then turned for the door, he added, "For everything. For believing me."

She smiled, letting herself out. "You're welcome."

Jack collapsed onto the couch and dragged a blanket over himself. The pervasive chill outside had seeped through the trash bags covering his windows and, although he faced the fireplace and his front half was toasty, his back remained cold.

I don't care, he thought. He'd tossed back a couple of extra-strength Tylenols and now closed his eyes, burrowed beneath the covers, letting his mind re-submerge into the comforting abyss of sleep.

The sound of Laura's soft, sob-choked gasps ripped him abruptly awake again. His eyes flew open and he jerked in surprise to find her kneeling directly in front of him, less than a foot away from his face.

"Jesus!" he gasped, sitting up with a start.

"She's after me," Laura pleaded, looking up at him, her eyes ringed with heavy shadows, her cheeks glistening with tears. Her hair was tangled, with brambles and leaves caught in the disheveled locks. There was dirt on her face, mud splattered and dried on her dress and legs, and something else – something that looked suspiciously like blood.

"What happened?" Jack asked, reaching for her. She crumpled into his arms, shuddering against the shelter of his chest, and he saw a ragged series of scratches, long and deep, gouged into her back. "Laura, who did this to you?"

"The woman in the woods," she whimpered. "She's out there, Jack. She was right behind me."

As if on cue, from somewhere outside, beyond the patio, they heard a sudden screech, animal-like and shrill.

"Oh God!" With a frightened cry, Laura cowered against him.

"It's all right." Taking her face between his hands, Jack forced her to look at him. "I won't let her hurt you again. I promise, Laura."

Her eyes widened in alarm as he rose to his feet. "Where are you going?"

"I'll be right back," he called as he hurried to his bedroom. "I'm going to get something from upstairs."

Squatting beside his headboard, he reached behind it, fingers fumbling, until he found the shaft of a Louisville Slugger he kept tucked there for security. Old enough to be an antique, its black varnish worn down to reveal the pale wood beneath in places, it would still pack a pretty decent punch if swung hard enough.

As he pulled the bat out, he felt the floorboards suddenly thrum beneath his feet. From his bedside table, a loose scattering of change began to jingle disharmonically, the coins bouncing together then dropping to the floor. From his bureau, a framed photograph of his parents began to skitter back and forth, the glass cracking loudly as it pitched to the floor. All around him, things began to vibrate and move – rumpled piles of clothes he'd yet to return to his closet, books and papers, discarded socks and shoes.

Laura could be doing this, Margot had told him – what she'd called "poltergeist" activity. *Or it could be something else, something that's following her, another spirit of some sort.*

"Damn," he whispered, turning toward the stairs. From the first floor, he heard the sudden sound of plastic and duct tape ripping loose as someone – or something – burst through one of the broken windows on the first floor. Laura gave a piteous, terrified shriek that was immediately drowned out by another one, even louder.

The Ker.

He raced down to the living room, his heart jackhammering. He could hear the leathery flapping of the creature's wings and the crashes and clatter as it plowed past, knocking over anything and everything in its path.

"*Jack!*" Laura screamed as he rushed into the room. She'd

pressed herself beside the creek-stone hearth, cowering on her knees, her arms thrown up to protect her face. Above her, hovering in mid-air, was the Ker. At Laura's cry, it whipped around to face him, and Jack skittered to a shocked, uncertain halt, the baseball bat drooping impotently in his hand.

Beneath the shocking white of her translucent skin, the Ker's nude form was strapped with muscles, the bony prominences in her collar, hips, shoulders and spine all apparent. Her fingers and toes were elongated, the tips capped with wickedly hooked claws. Her hair, a sickly, nearly jaundiced shade of blonde, framed her gaunt face in a wild, untamed mess. Her eyes, deeply sunken and red-rimmed, were black and featureless, like a shark's; her mouth was likewise predatory, filled with crooked fangs.

"Shit," he whispered. Then the Ker was on him, arcing her wings and diving directly at his face, her hands outstretched, her mouth open wide as she screeched.

Backpedaling in alarm, Jack reacted on panicked reflex, grasping the Louisville Slugger in both hands, and then swinging it sharply. The broad end connected solidly with the side of the Ker's skull as she swooped in attack. With a caw, she careened sideways, smashed into the wall and hit the floor.

Dancing back, Jack had less than a second to admire his handiwork before she was up again, moving impossibly fast, plowing into him headlong. Thrown off his feet, he toppled backwards, cracking the back of his head against the floor. The baseball bat was the only barrier between him and the Ker as she landed atop him, straddling him, and when she reared back, then lunged forward, those hideous teeth snapping at his face, he managed to push the bat higher, blocking her.

"Get off me," he yelled as her fangs sank into the wood; like a terrier on a ham bone, she shook her head furiously. Bucking his hips, he managed to force her off balance and twisted the bat loose.

"I said get off!" Jack smashed the bat's flared pommel into the monster's cheek, sending her sprawling sideways.

He stumbled to his feet and turned to Laura. "Run!" he shouted. That had been one of the solutions Margot had mentioned; something from an old Greek poem that said mortals could flee from a Ker. "Run into the woods. I'll hold her—"

His voice cut breathlessly short as the Ker attacked again, lungeing at him from behind and reaching over his shoulders to grab either end of the bat. She jerked against it hard, slamming him backwards into her, catching him brutally beneath the shelf of his chin with the ash shaft of the bat. She abruptly flew toward the ceiling again, dragging him with her, choking the breath from him. His feet pedaled in the open air and he gagged, pinned to her chest. He could hear her laughter, scraping and shrill, and, below him, saw Laura staring up, her face twisted with horror.

"*Jack!*" she screamed.

He couldn't breathe. Strangling, straining, his line of sight grew murky as his oxygen-starved consciousness waned. With all of the strength he could muster, he wedged his fingers between his throat and the bat. It wasn't much, but it gave him just enough room that his head slipped down through the narrow margin of space. With nothing left restraining him, Jack fell to the floor, landing hard against the coffee table, splintering it beneath him.

He felt Laura's hands against his shoulders, clutching at him, shaking him. With a groan, he tried to sit up.

"Come on," Laura pleaded, hooking an arm around him, supporting his weight as he stumbled to his feet. "Jack, please. We have to get out of here."

"No." Jack shook his head.

"But . . . but you said to run," she sputtered, wide-eyed and bewildered.

"I know what I said. I was wrong. If we run, she'll just come again. She's not going to stop." Jack pressed Laura back into the wall by the fireplace again, positioning himself protectively in front of her. Margot had also told him there was another way to stop a Ker; he hadn't considered it until that moment. *Fight.*

"It ends here. It ends now, tonight."

The Ker flapped her wings, rising clumsily back into the air again, marking a wary distance from Jack and Laura as the thing bared her teeth and snarled.

"Come on, you bitch!" Jack shouted hoarsely. "What the fuck are you waiting for? Come on!"

With a shriek, she dived at him. When he swung the bat,

aiming for her head, her hand whipped around, catching the
shaft. She was strong – incredibly, impossibly so – and damn
near wrestled the bat from his grasp. As he struggled, waltzing
clumsily while her wings beat down around him, her free hand
swung around, fingers splayed. He felt her talons swipe against
the front of his shirt, and then the side of his face stung like fire
as the nails tore through his skin, laying his cheek open. She
clawed at him again, those wicked nails coming straight for his
eyes, and he dropped to his knees. The move was unexpected; it
startled her enough to loosen her hold on the bat and he ripped
it free. Dragging the bat with him, he scrambled out of her path
and onto his feet.

He felt the whip of wind from her wings as she went airborne
again, following him. He drove the bat around in a broad,
sweeping arc, twisting his hips, putting all of his strength behind
the swing. The shaft smashed into the side of her head, knocking
her sideways in a messy, tangled sprawl of claws and wings. He
heard the crunch of splintering teeth and bone. When she hit the
floor, he didn't give her the chance to recover.

"You can't have her," he yelled, raising the bat high and driving it down onto the head of the fallen Ker. With a furious
screech, she tried to stumble to her feet, but he hit her again,
then again. "You hear me, you fucking bitch? I wouldn't let you
take her before, and I won't let you now!" With every word,
shouted breathlessly as he swung the bat, he struck the monster.
"You—" *whap!* "—can't—" *WHAP!* "—have her!"

When at last the Ker stopped moving, stopped even the last
feeble, scrabbling hints of protest and fell still, he staggered
back, gasping for breath, sweat-soaked and trembling from a
mixture of exertion and adrenaline. Shell-shocked, he blinked at
what was left of the thing.

It hadn't bled, not blood anyway. Something black and
glistening, viscous like warmed tar or oil had gushed from her
battered form, standing out in stark, ghoulish contrast to her
pale skin. The left side of her skull had been battered inward,
leaving a sunken, misshapen crater. Her eyes were open,
black, button-like and unblinking, fixed with unfocused
attention on a point against the wall somewhere past his
shoulder.

When she blinked once, he was startled and drew the bat over his shoulder to swing again, crushing her skull further, sending more of that ichor splattering in all directions. With a disgusted cry, he staggered away.

For a long moment, he stood there, gore-splashed and gasping, waiting for her to move again – damn near counting on it. When she didn't – when he'd counted to ten and back again in his mind and the Ker remained still – he let the bat drop from his fingers.

"I did it," he whispered. With a shaky laugh, he turned around. "Laura, I did . . ."

His voice faded. She was gone.

"Laura?" He hurried to the corner by the fireplace where he'd last seen her. "Laura!"

"Behind you!" he heard her scream and, as he whipped his head to follow the frantic sound of her voice, he saw the Ker springing at him.

Her outstretched claws grazed the front of his shirt, but then she gave a violent jerk. More of the ichor, hot and thick, slapped Jack in the face as the sharpened end of a wrought-iron fireplace poker suddenly thrust out through her chest, driven with murderous ferocity through the creature's heart. Behind the creature, he saw Laura, her brows furrowed, the poker handle clutched between her hands.

The Ker uttered a low, breathless croak. Her fingers slipped clumsily from Jack's shirt as she pitched to the floor, landing face down this time, the poker protruding from her back like a grisly place-marker.

Jack blinked at Laura in shock. For a long moment, neither of them moved; neither of them spoke. Then, at last, he reached for her.

"Oh God," she gasped as she rushed into his embrace. "Did we do it? Is it over?"

"I think so." Closing his eyes, Jack clutched her fiercely, kissing her ear through her hair. *Christ, I hope so.*

He didn't even get to say goodbye. One moment, he was holding her, her body pressed to his own, and then in the next, there was nothing in front of him but open air, nothing for his arms to encircle but empty space.

"Laura?" Startled, bewildered, he lowered his hands, looking around. "Laura?"

But she was gone. And so was the Ker. Of its crumpled body, the puddle of black that had pooled around it, there was no longer any sign. The trashed remnants of his house remained, but the causes of all the destruction had literally vanished in the blink of an eye.

"No." Dragging his hands through his hair, Jack ran frantically through the house. "No, no, no."

He threw open closet doors, looked vainly under tables, in corners, behind furniture, any place he could think of, anywhere she might be hiding. At last, with a frustrated, anguished cry, he threw his head back and shouted at the ceiling. "We stopped it! It's over now. She's supposed to be OK. She's supposed to . . ."

He fell silent, his eyes flying wide as he realized. If they'd defeated the Ker, if they'd destroyed it and saved Laura, then, according to Margot, that would mean her spirit was free to return to her body.

Her body! he thought, racing for the patio door. It wasn't until he'd charged outside into the dark, cold night that he remembered his Jeep was currently sitting in an impound lot somewhere, trashed beyond repair. For a wild, frantic moment, he didn't know what to do.

"Margot," he whispered, rushing back into the house.

By the time they reached the hospital, almost an hour had passed. Jack was out of his seat before Margot had even killed the engine. He hadn't put a coat on, or shoes, and sprinted barefooted across the icy parking lot, his breath huffing around his face in thick, pluming clouds of frost.

By the time he reached the cardio-thoracic intensive care unit, he was red-faced and out of breath from having taken the stairs up from the lobby at least two at a time. The staff at the nursing station jerked in simultaneous surprise as he burst through the unit doors, ragged and filthy, his clothes torn and stained with the Ker's blood.

"Dr Harris?" one of the nurses gasped after a long, stupefied moment's silence. When he said nothing in reply, simply tore off in the direction of Laura's ICU bay, they all sprang to their feet in bewildered alarm. "Dr Harris, wait! What are you—?"

Frank Bennett and his wife had fallen asleep at Laura's

bedside, sitting side by side in a pair of uncomfortable-looking chairs. As Jack burst through the curtains and into the small alcove room, they startled awake, both of them twisting in their seats and gasping for surprised breath.

"Dr Harris?" Frank asked, bleary and confused.

Ignoring him, Jack hurried to Laura's bed. Clinging to the side rail, he panted heavily for exhausted breath, his face glossed with sweat. "Laura," he gasped, reaching out, seizing her by the hand.

He didn't understand. She was still unresponsive, her eyes still closed.

But she can't be, he thought in dismay. We did what we were supposed to do. We stopped the Ker. She's supposed to be OK now. She's supposed to wake up!

"Dr Harris?" Frank asked again, on his feet now, alarmed by Jack's appearance. Laying his arm against the crook of Jack's elbow, he said, "What's going on?"

"Laura." With a frown, Jack shrugged loose of his grasp. He heard the rapid patter of approaching footsteps in the hall, and tried to shake Laura by the shoulder. "Laura, wake up."

"I said what's going on?" Frank said, but when he caught Jack by the arm again, Jack whirled on him, brows furrowed, fists bared.

"Get your goddamn hands off me," he snapped, and not only did Frank recoil, but so, too, did the trio of nurses who had suddenly appeared in the curtained doorway. They all stared at him in shock, eyes round, mouths agape.

"She's supposed to be awake," Jack said, turning back to the bed. Still clutching Laura's hand, he leaned over again, stroking her hair back from her face. "Laura, come on. You can wake up now. It's all right."

"What's wrong with him?" Mrs Bennett asked, her voice soft and frightened. "What is he doing?"

"What is this?" Frank demanded of the nurses. "What kind of outfit are you people running here?"

"Dr Harris, please . . ." one of the nurses began.

Jack ignored them all. Voice choked, eyes stinging with the dim heat of sudden tears, he said to Laura, "It's OK now. I promise. I won't let anything hurt you, never again. I promise, Laura. I swear to God."

And then he thought of something Laura's friend at Harrah's nightclub had told him earlier that night.

She's waiting for her Prince Charming, or some such bullshit. You know, like in Sleeping Beauty *or* Snow White.

Pulling away as Frank again tried to grab his sleeve, he leaned further over Laura's bed, lowering his face toward hers.

"Dr Harris, stop," the nurse said again, sharper now. "What are you—?"

When Jack kissed Laura, he heard her mother utter a horrified cry from behind him. A fluttering gasp of shock rippled through the nurses, and then Frank seized him roughly by the scruff of his collar, hauling him forcibly away from the bed.

"What the hell are you doing?" he demanded. He'd closed his free hand into a fist and drew it back now, ready to introduce Jack's teeth to the bridge of his knuckles. "You sick son of a—"

"Daddy . . . no," Laura said, her voice soft and frail. At the sound of it, Frank's fist froze, and his furious grip on Jack's shirt abruptly slackened. Eyes flown wide, he swung toward the bed, where the nurses, too, had now flocked in stunned disbelief.

"Don't . . . hurt him," Laura breathed, her eyes heavy-lidded but open. "Please."

Frank and his wife rushed to her, all but falling over the side rails to embrace her. "Laura," he cried. "Oh, my God!"

"It's . . . fine, Daddy," she murmured, hoarse and feeble. Blinking sleepily past her parents, she saw Jack.

He didn't know if she'd recognize him, remember what had happened. For one fleeting, horrifying moment, he worried that she'd have forgotten it all, that he'd be a stranger to her – but then she smiled.

"Jack." She reached for him, and this time, when he went to her, everyone stepped aside and let him pass. He felt her fingers twine weakly in his hair, pulling him toward her. In her physical form, she was injured still, her face battered and bruised, but she kissed him with the same passionate certainty he'd felt when she'd come to him as a ghost.

"Is it over?" she whispered as they drew apart. "Did we do it?"

In the doorway, he saw Margot, finally catching up to him after the long sprint from the parking lot. She blinked at Jack and Laura, then smiled. He didn't need to ask her; in that moment, he knew for sure.

"Yeah, Laura. It's over." As he gazed back down into her eyes, it occurred to him that there was something else he was sure of as well; something certain and true in his heart. Kissing her again, he whispered in promise: "Everything's going to be all right now."

Can You Hear Me Now?

Sharon Shinn

Stacey was on the phone with her father when he had the heart attack. She heard his gasp, his struggle for breath, the sound of his body falling to the floor. "Dad? Dad? *Dad*?" she cried, but there was no answer except the faraway tinkle of glass breaking 300 miles away.

They'd both been on their cell phones because he loved the notion of free long-distance in-network calling. She kept shouting into the cell phone while she leaped across the apartment to dial 911 on the landline. "I have an emergency in another state, I don't know what to do," she panted to the operator who answered. "I can tell you the area code, I can tell you the address—"

The operator was brisk and efficient, and paramedics were on the scene within twenty minutes. But it was too late. Stacey's father had already died.

It was two months after the funeral when the first call came.

The power had been flickering off and on all evening as a thunderstorm blew through the city. A lightning strike – which had to have hit the nearest street lamp – was followed by a roll of thunder that actually rattled the furnishings. Seconds later Stacey's cell phone churned out the opening bars of Blondie's "Call Me", the ringtone she'd chosen in more carefree days. No number came up on caller ID, but that wasn't unusual; three of her friends were lawyers who routinely blocked data on their outgoing lines. Stacey flipped open the phone.

"Hello?"

"Hey, sweetie, how've you been doing this week?"

She dropped to the couch because her legs folded beneath her. "*Dad*? But . . . how . . . where—"

"Have you enrolled in that whatchmacallit like you said you would? That Matchbox service?" His voice was rough and warm, a little froggy, like he might have caught a cold and was trying to conceal it from her.

Stacey was so confused she hardly knew whether to scream or sob. "I . . . what? Matchbox? Oh, you mean that online dating thing?"

She remembered now. The last time they'd been talking, right before the heart attack, he'd been quizzing her about her love life. *I don't have a love life, Dad. I haven't met a new guy in two years.* That's when he'd started asking her about computer dating. Had she ever tried that? What did it cost? He'd pay for it if it was too expensive. But she was such a pretty girl, such a nice girl, all a guy would have to do was meet her and he'd want to take her out.

"That's it, Matchbox," he said, sounding pleased. "Did you ever enroll?"

"No, I . . . I've been busy." *I've been distracted. I arranged your funeral. I attended your funeral. I cleared out your apartment and settled your debts and dealt with your insurance companies, and I grieved. I buried you, and now you're calling me on the phone.* "What's . . . what's been happening with you?"

"Oh, you know, same-old, same-old. Nothing much ever goes on with me."

It was a ghost – it had to be – but she'd never heard of a ghost that could make phone calls. She figured there was a strong possibility she was dreaming. Or crazy. But once her shock and bewilderment started to fade, she found herself flooded with happiness at the chance to hear his voice again.

"Your health?" she said, pressing a little. *What does it feel like to be a ghost?* "How's your knee?"

"Hasn't bothered me at all lately! And my back's been good, too. I'm having a little trouble remembering things, but I haven't forgotten anything important. Don't you worry."

"I . . . no, I wasn't worried. I was just . . . well, it's good to hear from you, that's all."

"So? This dating service? Have you signed up?"

Stacey couldn't restrain a slightly hysterical laugh. Even after death, her father was determined to see her married. She wondered if he planned to call her every week for the rest of her life until she finally tied the knot.

It was enough to make her consider remaining a spinster for ever. Though she supposed twenty-seven wasn't old enough to qualify for the word yet.

"I haven't," she said. "A couple days ago I talked to the guy next door, though."

"Guy next door? Who's that?"

She couldn't believe it. Her father was calling from beyond the grave and *this* was the topic they were stuck on. "Um, he said he was Nathan. He moved in about a month ago. He's really cute, but I don't know anything about him. I mean, we talked for five minutes."

"Is he tall? You're a tall girl."

She strangled a laugh. "Yeah. Yeah, he's tall. But, Dad, listen, let's talk about you for a minute. What are you—"

"Wait a second, honey." There was a muffled sound, as if he'd put his hand over the receiver, and then he came back on. "Listen, I've got to go. I'll call you later."

"But, Dad—"

Then he was gone.

Stacey was so stunned she sat there for five minutes, staring at the open phone in her hand. *That could not have just happened. Stress has finally warped your brain and you're hallucinating. Time to call a doctor.*

Or call somebody, anyway. She was mentally flipping through her address book, wondering who could offer both a soft pat of sympathy and a sharp dose of reality, when a sudden loud crashing in the hall made her jump to her feet and drop the phone. Running over to throw open the door, she found her neighbor Nathan in the hallway, kneeling on the floor in a welter of spilled groceries. Oranges and melons had rolled down the first two stairs; what looked like ketchup and grape juice made a gooey cocktail on the welcome mat right in front of Nathan's door.

"You want some paper towels?" Stacey asked.

He looked up, his face rueful. Still cute. He had wide cheekbones and a firm chin, hazel eyes and straight brown hair that badly needed cutting. "I was thinking maybe a bath mat. Sop the whole mess up and throw it away."

"I don't have a spare one of those. Oh, but I have a raggedy old beach towel I used to clean up my car when a friend of mine threw up in the back seat."

"Sounds perfect." He glanced at the mess again, his face even more rueful. That's when Stacey realized that the dark purple liquid was not, in fact, grape juice. "I'd offer you a glass of wine for your help but it seems like the wine is one of the items that did not survive the fall." He gestured at his door. "I've got some Jack Daniel's left over from a poker game the other night."

She laughed. "Let me get the towel."

It took them half an hour to clean up the mess and retrieve the salvageable foodstuffs. Nathan carried the welcome mat inside his apartment to dump it in the shower, leaving behind a purplish aureole of color around a pristine rectangle on the hall carpet. Stacey brought in the last of the supplies and laid them on the counter that separated the small kitchen from the living room. She couldn't resist taking a quick look around. His apartment was laid out like a mirror image of hers, so she guessed the two rooms she could see in the shadows off the hallway led to a cramped bathroom and a single bedroom. The open living area wasn't exactly spotless, but no worse than her own, with newspapers piled in corners and shoes kicked off beside the battered couch and a humongous plasma TV taking up all the space on the interior wall.

Nathan reappeared, drying his hands on his jeans. "I really appreciate your help. Can I get you something to drink? I just remembered, I've got a couple beers, too, if that sounds better. Or Coke, if you'd rather."

"I just got a phone call from my dad," Stacey said.

Something in the tone of her voice caused him to pause in the act of turning toward the kitchen. His eyebrows lifted. "Is that a good thing or a bad thing?"

"He's been dead for two months."

Nathan nodded and continued on toward the kitchen. "Right, then. Whiskey it is."

They sat on Nathan's couch and talked for the next two hours. Despite looking like a dispirited floor model from a run-down furniture factory, Nathan's fuzzy brown couch was surprisingly comfortable, and the Jack Daniel's was as smooth as honey. Both of them encouraged Stacey to confide.

"I loved my dad, but he would drive me crazy. He'd call me two or three times a day with something stupid he wanted to tell me – a joke, or the plotline of some made-for-cable movie that didn't make any sense. Sometimes I didn't answer the phone when he'd call because I couldn't fake the interest for another half-hour. Then after he died—" she pressed a hand to her heart "—I kept thinking, Oh, what wouldn't I give for one more call from Dad? And then tonight. When he *called*. I kept thinking I was hallucinating." She glanced around the apartment. "I still think I might be."

Nathan leaned back. He'd kicked his shoes off and stretched out, slouching down so his head rested on the back of the sofa and his butt was almost off the seat cushion. "Well, *I'm* not hallucinating. I think we're both very real. But I can't explain the phone call. I've never believed in ghosts."

"No, me either!" Stacey leaned forward. "This sounds so weird but I was talking to him on my cell phone when he had the heart attack. Do you think . . . Would it make sense . . . I mean, could his soul or his consciousness or whatever have imprinted on my phone? Like, gotten tangled up in its electronics some-how? I mean, when you think about it, how remarkable is it that we can transmit voices 300 miles? We aren't even sending sound through wires any more. Those voices are going through *air*, from one little handheld device to another. So why can't souls go through the air, too, and end up in a phone?"

Nathan spread his hands. "I can't answer questions like that. I'm not a science guy who can explain electricity and conductiv-ity and fiber optics. And I'm not a religious guy or a New Age guy, so I can't tell you what souls do and how spirits move through the vortex or whatever. I mean, I believe you, but I couldn't tell you why or how it happened."

Stacey took another sip of her whiskey. It was amazing how the alcohol smoothed away all the rough edges. The disembod-ied call no longer seemed so spooky or unnerving, and the sorrow she had carried around with her for the past eight weeks had loosened its grip on her ribcage. She couldn't imagine why she hadn't been drinking more or less continuously since her father's death. "Well, what kind of guy are you?" she asked.

"Software engineer guy."

Her response was half a laugh and half a hiccup. "Oh, because there's such a need for those here in Kansas City."

"Well, I wanted to get away from Silicon Valley. And . . . stuff there."

"What kind of stuff?"

"My wife died six months ago."

"Oh, I'm so sorry! That's terrible."

He took another swallow of amber liquid. "We'd been separated for a year. It's a long story."

"You don't have to tell me about it," she said. "But I'd listen if you feel like talking."

He was silent a moment, studying the liquor in his glass, then he shrugged. "We got married just out of college. Had all those early hardscrabble days that you're supposed to remember fondly when you're older and richer. Lived in an apartment smaller than this one with crazy neighbors upstairs and a drug dealer downstairs, or at least that's what we always assumed." He paused again, remembering, or maybe trying to edit the story down to its essentials. "We argued a lot. And it didn't get better once we both had jobs and could afford a bigger place. We just had more rooms to argue in. Finally we agreed to a separation."

He straightened up, poured himself another shot of whiskey, and sat there a moment, resting his forearms on his knees and gazing backward at his past. "We still called each other every week or two, but I knew she was seeing someone else. I tried to go out with other girls but I couldn't really get in the spirit of dating. One night she died in a car crash. One of our friends told me she'd been trying to get up the courage to ask for a divorce so she could get married again."

Stacey knocked back the last of her whiskey and held her glass out for more. "Well, that sucks rocks."

Nathan carefully poured another portion into her glass; she could tell he was rationing. He didn't seem miserly, so she figured that meant he realized she was drunker than she realized she was, and he was trying to spare her the effects of excessive inebriation.

"Yeah," he said. "That's what I always thought."

"So you left California to leave your memories behind," she said. "Is it working?"

"Not so far," he said. He looked surprised. "Except. Well. Talking to you tonight. I haven't thought about Mandy until I started telling you the story."

"I know. This is the first time I've felt kind of cheerful since my dad died." She looked at the glass in her hand. "Do you think it's the whiskey?"

He shook his head. "Probably not. I've had whiskey before and it hasn't helped this much. I think it's the company."

"Oh." She thought that over a moment, then smiled at him tentatively. "Well, I'll be happy to scare away your ghosts any time you're willing to hear me talk about mine. I don't know – did that sentence make any sense?"

"Enough sense for me to know what you meant," he said. He was smiling, too. "Let's have dinner tomorrow night and see if the magic lasts."

Stacey thought going out on a Wednesday was probably easier than going out on the traditional date nights of Friday or Saturday, but she was still nervous the next day as she looked over her wardrobe. She wanted to appear cute but not overtly sexy. She was literally the girl next door, and if the dinner didn't go well, she didn't want Nathan to mentally roll his eyes every time he encountered her for the next few months. *Oh yeah . . . there's the chick who was wearing the see-through black lace blouse when we went to Red Lobster for dinner.* So she picked a soft white sweater with just enough cling, blue jeans, boots and an art-glass necklace she'd bought at a street fair. She was relieved that she was having a good hair day, plenty of body still left in her shoulder-length brown curls. A quick sweep of the comb, a swift mist of spray, a deep breath, and she was ready.

Nathan was knocking on the stroke of seven. "I figured I had to be on time since I could hardly say I got stuck in traffic," he said with a grin as she opened the door.

She grinned back. "Are you usually late?"

"Well, I wouldn't say *usually*. It's been known to happen."

She angled her head back to study him. She liked that he was taller than she was; many men weren't. "Because you're disorganized, because you lose track of time, or because you think a deadline is more of a suggestion than a commitment?"

Now he was laughing out loud. "Oh, you're the kind of girl who likes to nail things down, are you?"

"Well, I like to understand the operating system."

They were still standing in her doorway, but now he motioned her forward, so she stepped out and locked the door behind them. They headed down the stairs at a leisurely pace.

"Mostly it's because I lose track of time," Nathan said. "I'm a pretty organized guy, so I tend not to forget appointments or misjudge how long it will take me to get somewhere. I say, 'OK, I'll work on this project for an hour and then drive to Joe's,' and when I look up again, two hours have passed and I'm officially late." He glanced down at Stacey. "I do *call*, though, when I realize I'm behind. That is, when I have your phone number."

That surprised a ripple of laughter out of her. "Oh, that was subtle, that was smooth!" she exclaimed. They were in the cramped lobby and pushing out through the main door onto the street. The scents and sights of a Midwestern spring instantly surrounded them – new grass, wet dirt, fluttering birds, a random sprinkling of purple and yellow flowers. "I'd be happy to give you my phone number."

"I mean, sometimes it might be impractical for me to just come knock on the door," he explained, touching her lightly on the back to steer her toward a car parked in front of their building. It looked like a Honda with more than a few miles on it – practical, reliable, comfortable and well put together. Stacey tried not to draw obvious parallels to its owner. "You might be in the shower—"

"In which case I'm not answering the door *or* the phone."

"Or entertaining romantic guests."

"Haven't been a lot of those lately."

"Or in your pajamas."

She smirked at him as he waited for her to settle into the passenger's seat before shutting her door. "Are you trying to find out what I wear to bed?"

He laughed, closed her door and circled the car to get in. "Well, I've seen what you wear down to the laundry room," he said, starting the engine. "I figured your night-time attire was a likely variant."

Now she was giggling, but also trying to remember. "Wait – when did you see me doing laundry?"

"Couple of weeks after I moved in. I was getting stuff from my storage locker in the basement, so I don't think you saw me." He had pulled easily into traffic. She liked that he seemed to be a careful driver, though not a nervous one. "You had on this green stretchy top and these black – I don't know – leggings or something. And I thought, Wow, there's a girl who doesn't give a damn what anyone else thinks of her." He glanced over. "I thought that was pretty cool, but I have to say I was *relieved* to see that you had other options in your wardrobe."

Now Stacey was slumped back in her seat, covering her face and strangling a groan. "Oh, my God, and when I think how I agonized over what to wear tonight! If only I'd realized you'd already seen me at my worst."

"Really? That's your worst? Well, that's something else that's good to know."

"My hair was probably a real mess, too, jammed on top of my head with one of those butterfly clips."

"It was," he said. "Looked like you hadn't washed it in a couple of days."

She heaved a dramatic sigh. "See, it's so unfair. Girls have to spend hours doing their hair and putting on make-up and choosing the right outfit or they look awful. But a guy can show up wearing a wrinkled T-shirt and baggy shorts, not even having combed his hair, and he looks sexy."

"Yeah, I don't think that's really when I look sexy," Nathan said.

She turned her head to gauge the strong profile, the tousled hair. She thought he was probably wrong in his self-assessment. "So when *do* you look sexy?" she asked.

"When I'm in a tuxedo. I look great."

"Really? And how many times have you worn one?"

"Mmmm. Three times. No, four. Been a best man three times and every time I rocked."

Unsaid went the explanation that his fourth outing in a tux had been at his own wedding, or so Stacey assumed.

"Wow, three times as best man?" she said. "I've been a bridesmaid four times, but only maid of honor once. You must be a great friend. Or have a lot of brothers."

"Only one brother, and he's not married yet," Nathan said. "So I guess I'm a great friend."

She would have asked about those friends, except he was already signaling to pull into a parking lot. "I guess we're here," she said. She kept her voice neutral, but part of her was thinking, Would have been nice to have some input into the decision about where to have dinner.

But it was hard to be annoyed when he cut the motor and turned to her with a slightly anxious look. "I hope you're OK with Italian food," he said. "The guy I work with is married to a woman who recently opened this restaurant, and I think it's struggling a little bit, and I thought it would be nice to give them a little extra business on a weeknight."

Right then she felt her heart melt. If this guy is for real, I am grabbing him and never letting go, she thought. "Love it," she said. "Hope you're OK with garlic."

"Love it. Let's go."

They were debating dessert after a truly fabulous meal when Stacey's cell phone rang. She made no move to dig it from her purse, but Nathan gestured. "Go ahead, get it, I don't mind," he said.

"I'll just see who it is," she said, but no data came up on caller ID. She felt a little tingle go down her back as she flipped open the phone. "Hello?"

"Hey, baby," said her father's voice, still a little gruffer than it used to be. "How you doing today?"

"Hi, Dad," she said, and watched Nathan straighten in his chair. "Good. I'm out on a date."

"Yeah?" He sounded pleased. "Who with?"

"The guy in the apartment next door. We got to talking last night and we had a good time, so we decided to go to dinner today." At her words, Nathan nodded emphatically.

"Yeah? Is he nice?"

"Seems to be."

"Good-looking?"

"*I* think so."

"Is he going to pay for the meal?"

She had to choke back a laugh. "We haven't gotten that far yet."

His voice took on a scolding note. "You shouldn't be all modern and insist on splitting the check. A man *likes* to take care of a woman."

"I'll keep that in mind. Hey, Dad, how are *you* doing? How are you feeling?"

"Great, couldn't be better. But I gotta go, honey. I'll call you next week."

He disconnected, and Stacey was left staring at a silent phone. She felt a curious mix of euphoria and unease that left her shaky and off balance.

"Kind of freaky, huh?" Nathan said in a soothing tone.

Stacey lifted her eyes to gaze at him. He was solid and sincere and as far from spectral as you could get. "Pretty freaky," she agreed. "On the one hand, wow, how great to hear his voice! On the other hand, it's really spooky. I feel kind of—" She let a tremor run down her back. "Shivery."

"Do you think he's going to call you every day?"

She stopped herself right before uttering an automatic *God, I hope not.* "I have no idea," she said. "That would certainly take some getting used to."

He nodded. "Well, there's really only one way to deal with events as unnerving as this." At her inquiring look, he said, "Double chocolate espresso cake."

She laughed, and the shivers went away.

He paid for dinner, too.

Even though the meal had gone so well, Stacey felt herself growing ridiculously tense as they drove back to the apartment and climbed the stairs. She'd never been the type to sleep with a guy on the first date, and there was still that how-weird-would-it-be-to-live-next-door-to-an-ex question knocking around inside her head. So the night's goodbye felt uncomfortable to her before they'd even arrived at their adjoining doors.

When she risked a look up at Nathan, he wore a thoughtful expression. "I can't decide if this is cool or awkward," he said. "Pretty easy to walk you home! But kind of strange to just wave and say goodnight."

She relaxed a little. "I keep looking ahead," she confessed. "You know, after we have the torrid affair, then we break up, and then we're always running into each other on the stairwell, and half the time you've got a new girlfriend with you – makes it hard to live in the moment."

He rubbed the back of his neck. "The torrid affair part sounds good, though," he said.

It surprised a laugh out of her. "Yeah, I haven't had torrid in a while."

Before she'd had time to brace for it, he leaned down and kissed her on the cheek. "But maybe we'll hold off on that for a few days," he said. "Till we get to know each other a little better."

She smiled up at him. "That sounds good."

"Not this weekend, though," he said, his voice regretful. "I have to work twelve-to-twelve both days. We're installing a new system and it's supposed to be up and running by Monday. It *won't* be, but the software guys are working around the clock to make it look like we're doing our part to get it going."

"OK, well, I'll blow you a kiss if I see you in the hallway," Stacey said. "Goodnight. Thanks. It was . . . I really had a great time."

"Me, too."

He stood there and watched her as she fumbled for her keys, which of course were at the very bottom of her purse under her wallet, her sunglasses, her make-up case, her comb. She was blushing when she finally unearthed them and unlocked the door. He was still watching her, so she paused and blew him a kiss before going in. Then she stood just inside her apartment and waited until she heard his door open and shut before she threw the lock and headed to her bedroom.

It was three in the morning Saturday night – or Sunday morning – when the next call came. Stacey was so disoriented that at first she didn't recognize the tinny, rhythmic music as being the sound of her cell phone ringing in the other room. She dragged herself out of bed, practically knocked over the lamp as she turned it on, and stumbled into the living room, groping for her purse. She was surprised that the phone was still ringing; it usually went to voicemail long before this.

"Hello," she said breathlessly, when she finally found the handset and pried it open. There had been no number listed on caller ID, so she half-expected to hear her father speaking in reply.

But she didn't. "Hello? Hello? Carina?" asked a woman in a rushed and frantic voice.

"No, wrong number," Stacey said wearily.

"Don't hang up! Please don't hang up!" the woman cried. "I've been trying for days – I can't get through – I don't know what's wrong with her phone—"

Stacey sank to the couch, one hand holding the phone to her ear, one hand shielding her eyes from the lights she'd turned on. "Maybe you could call the operator to assist you."

"I did! Of course I tried that! But the operator won't answer either. *No one* answers. I've tried every phone number I can think of. You're the first person I've been able to get through to."

Stacey felt a cold premonitory tickle send a live current down her spine. "Where are you calling from? Maybe there's some . . . cell tower down or something."

"I'm in New York. There are cell towers everywhere! Look, could you take a message for me?"

"I don't know—"

"Please. Call my mom. Tell her I'm fine. I'm working on the story, and it's going great."

"But I—"

"I'll give you her number. Do you have a pen and some paper?"

Stacey figured it would be easier to acquiesce, even if she never made the call. So she found a pencil and an empty envelope from the gas company and dutifully took down the number. "Who should I say you are?"

"Teresa Sanchez," the woman said, then laughed. "Well, of course you don't have to tell my *mother* my whole name. Just tell her Teresa called. Oh, and tell her it's a lot warmer than I thought it would be! I don't even need my coat."

That caught Stacey's attention. "You don't—"

But the connection had already been cut.

Stacey sat there a few more minutes, more awake with each passing second, and finally nerved herself to boot up her laptop. She went straight to Google and typed in Teresa Sanchez. And swallowed a squeak of terror when the first page to come up was a two-week-old news item on CNN.com: *Journalist Shot in Central Park.* "A thirty-four-year-old reporter in town to interview a source was found dead early this morning. Police speculate that Teresa Sanchez was killed by a man she had come to talk to as part of a story she was writing for the *San Francisco Chronicle* . . ."

"Jesus," Stacey whispered, rocking a little as she sat on the couch, the laptop on her knees. "Oh my God. Oh God."

Not even bothering to shut down the computer, she set it on the end table and came to her feet, unsteady enough she thought she might tip over. Her hands were shaking and she was cold to the bone. "Now what?" she said aloud, rubbing her fingers against her thighs. She was wearing an old KU T-shirt and plaid, Christmassy pajama bottoms; the flannel felt good against her fingertips, but the friction wasn't generating any warmth. "I go back to bed? What if the phone rings again? Oh God, oh God—"

She shouldn't do it. She scarcely knew him. He'd been working all night, had probably been asleep for barely two hours. But she grabbed her keys and ducked out into the hallway anyway. She knocked hard on Nathan's door and stood there shivering until he answered it. He looked sleepy and even more rumpled than she was, wearing boxers and an inside-out undershirt.

"I'm sorry. I got another call and it freaked me out – from a stranger this time, and she wants me to phone her mom, but she's *dead*. She was killed in New York City, but I don't think she knows she's dead and I . . . Nathan, I'm sorry but I—"

That was as far as she got before he reached out and pulled her against him in a hug. He was warm and solid and smelled like deodorant soap. "Leave your phone in your apartment and come stay here for the night," he said, his sentence split in the middle by a yawn. "No one will bother you."

Stacey woke to the smell of coffee and the feeling of acute embarrassment. She knew exactly where she was – in Nathan's apartment, in Nathan's *bed*, though all they'd shared during the night were blankets. Well, and a little human contact. He'd tucked her in like a child, and then stretched out beside her on the king-size futon, which took up almost the entire bedroom. He was far enough away that she could scarcely feel his body heat. But he'd turned on his side, facing her, and taken her hand in a comforting clasp.

"Go to sleep," he'd said, and instantly dropped off.

Stacey had been unable to comply, at least at first. She'd lain there for a good hour, alternately rigid and trembling, before sheer exhaustion had forced down her eyelids and she'd slept.

And now it was the morning after and she felt like a complete idiot. Nathan would think she was crazy. Would think she was needy. Would think she was selfish and stupid and careless of other people's privacy and heedless of their desire to sleep after a really long workday that she had been told about in advance. And what must she *look* like? She buried her face in the pillow. Maybe she could stay here and pretend to be asleep until he left for his second long shift.

But, no. She had to use the bathroom. And she had to be an adult about this, get up, face him, humbly apologize, swear she would never do this again.

Unless she got more scary phone calls in the night . . . but she refused to think about that right now.

She was able to get to the bathroom without him seeing her and uttered a muffled cry of dismay when she saw herself in the mirror. Hair a mass of tangles, face pale and puffy, sleeping ensemble too wretched to contemplate. She used hand soap to wash her face, her index finger and Nathan's toothpaste to clean her teeth, and a comb she found in the medicine cabinet to improve her hair, if only by a narrow margin. She took a deep breath and headed toward the kitchen where Nathan appeared to be making breakfast. He stood at the stove, his back to her; by the wonderful smell, she thought he was frying bacon and eggs.

For a moment, she studied what she could see of him. He'd thrown on a robe but didn't seem to have bothered with the comb. His body language was relaxed. In fact, she thought he might be humming.

She took another deep breath and said, "I am so, so sorry. I should never have come over and woken you up in the middle of the night—"

He'd turned at her very first words, a smile already on his face. "Not a problem," he said. "I'm glad I was here."

Nathan had to leave by half past eleven, so Stacey called Teresa's mother at eleven o'clock, because she wanted him there for moral support if it all went really badly. She sat on the fuzzy brown couch, while he settled in to the nearby chair, looking at ease as always.

The 510 area code must be California, Stacey thought; she wasn't surprised when the woman who answered had a strong Spanish accent. "Good morning, you don't know me, but I'm calling about your daughter, Teresa," Stacey said.

She heard the gasp on the other end. "Teresa? *Sí*? Are you with the police?"

"No, no – this is very strange, so I want you to hear me out instead of hanging up, OK? My father died a few months ago, but lately his . . . his spirit has been contacting me. Calling me. And last night your daughter called me."

"What? My daughter called you?" The incredulous words were followed by a spate of incomprehensible Spanish. Stacey tried twice to interrupt, but a few moments later, a new voice came on the phone.

"This is Diego, I'm Teresa's brother," he said in a voice that sounded faintly menacing, even over about 1,500 miles of open line. "What are you saying to my mother?"

"Listen. I don't understand it. I didn't ask for it to happen. But I've started getting phone calls from people who are dead." Stacey heard the words coming out of her mouth and almost wanted to laugh. Unbelievable. She would have hung up on anyone who called her with such nonsense. She glanced at Nathan and he gave her a reassuring smile and a thumbs-up. She continued, "Your sister called last night and asked me to get in touch with your mother. She wanted me to say that she was doing well; she was working on the story. She said she was so warm she didn't even have to wear her coat."

There was a moment's silence. "She was worried about her coat," Diego said. "She didn't have a heavy one to bring with her, you know? She had this green suede jacket. She kept saying, 'Do you think it will be warm enough?' I said, 'It's New York City, you can buy a coat,' but she thought it would be too expensive." There was a sound as if he were shaking his head. "But she didn't have time to shop. She was only there a day before she died."

"I'm so sorry," Stacey said.

"So she called you? Why did she call *you*? Why didn't she call *me*?"

"I don't know. But the past few days I've started getting calls on my cell. See, my dad and I were talking on cell phones when he died, and I keep thinking – I don't know – maybe that opened up some conduit to the otherworld or something—"

"Teresa was on her cell phone when she was shot," Diego said sharply. "She was talking to her editor. He heard the gunfire. He heard Teresa scream."

"Jesus," Stacey whispered.

"But you say she's OK now?" Diego asked, sounding for the first time like he accepted the news, like the news was *good*. "She's happy? She's not in any pain?"

"She said she was fine. She said she was warm. She sounded happy."

"*Bueno*," he said. "*Gracias*. You did a good thing to call *mi madre*."

"You're welcome," she said. Diego hung up before she could think of another thing to say.

Stacey closed the phone and stared at Nathan. "I think he actually believed me," she said.

He shrugged. "Good, since it's true."

"But *is* it? I mean, why do you believe me? If you were the one telling me you were hearing from ghosts – well – I wouldn't be going out to dinner with you and letting you in during the middle of the night. I'd be calling the cops and reporting you as a lunatic."

He tilted his head, considering her as if he were considering the question at the same time. "I don't know," he said at last. "I just do."

She took a shuddery breath. "And thank God you do. I'm not quite sure how I'd have gotten through this week without you."

"You realize this won't be the last one," he said.

"The last what?"

"Phone call. You realize if you really do have some . . . some conduit to the afterlife, you're going to get more calls."

She could feel her mouth go slack as her eyes went wide. "Hell. Will all of them be people who were on their cell phones when they died?"

Nathan looked interested. "Was Teresa Sanchez?"

"That's what her brother said. And my dad was."

"Well, that narrows the pool to a finite number," Nathan said. "Though not necessarily a small one."

Stacey groaned and put a hand to her forehead. "I think I need some coffee."

"Coming right up," Nathan said, getting to his feet. He paused to glance down at her. "And then maybe . . . a shower."

She was laughing so hard she couldn't aim straight; the pillow she threw at him landed a good three feet wide. That didn't matter. What mattered was that the laughter loosened some of the dread that had clamped around her heart. But maybe he was wrong. Maybe the phone wouldn't ring again.

Stacey got eight more calls on her cell phone in the next two weeks.

One was from a mountaineer who had completed a dangerous ascent. "We made the summit, but there was an avalanche as I was calling my wife. Could you let her know it will be a while before we dig out? But it's beautiful here. You cannot believe the view. I've never seen anything like it, not from Everest, not from K2."

Two were from girls who had been in car crashes, one of them rear-ended while she was on the phone with her boyfriend, one having lost control of her vehicle when she tried to text and drive.

Another caller was a man who had been electrocuted while he was trying to fix a wiring problem in his house. He'd been on the phone with his brother, getting instructions that were obviously incomplete. Another was a farmer who slowly bled out in a field two miles from his house after he got his arm tangled in a piece of equipment.

A day later she heard from a young man shot during what was clearly a drug deal. Stacey was nervous about phoning his mother, but this woman was the one person who most readily accepted what Stacey had to say. "He was a good boy," the woman repeated over and over. "He was a good boy. He's in a better place now, with better friends."

She was contacted by a woman who wanted to let the police know someone had broken into her house. She was hiding in the bedroom closet. That was the call that made Stacey sick to her stomach, but the woman herself sounded remarkably cheerful.

"Guess it was just the cat knocking something over in the kitchen," she said. "But I'm going to wait until tomorrow to go down and clean it up. You have no idea how comfortable a walk-in closet is! And it smells so good. I've been using this organic laundry detergent, and all the clothes smell like orange blossom. I think I'm going to start sleeping in here every night!"

The strangest call came from a woman who had dialed a number as she went skydiving for the first time. Stacey could only guess that the woman's chute had failed to open. "I'm trying to tell my friends that I did it," she complained to Stacey. "But no one will answer their phones. I'm seventy years old and I jumped out of an airplane! How cool is that?"

"Pretty cool," Stacey said. "I hope I'm as brave as you are when I'm your age."

She stopped being frightened every time the phone rang. She stopped needing to run to Nathan's when the calls came in the night, though she invariably told him about them the next day, since he invariably stopped by to ask. But the sad, hopeful, confused communications took their toll on her and she wished they would stop. She ordered a sleek new BlackBerry with a brand-new number, though she didn't trade in the old phone. But she no longer recharged it; she even took the battery pack out.

Even so, the calls still came in, and she still felt obliged to answer them. And obliged to take down messages and contact loved ones and pass on the implausible, inconceivable and desperately welcome news. *I talked to him this morning and he was at peace . . . She told me all the pain is gone . . . It's sunny there, it's safe, no need to be afraid . . .*

Her father phoned every few days, too. Those calls were more welcome, but wearying in their way. It was hard to entirely let go, to complete her mourning process, when he still seemed so alive and so interested in her life.

He always asked about Nathan. "So? You still seeing that kid next door?"

"He's hardly a kid, Dad. He's thirty-two."

"Why isn't he married if he's thirty-two?"

"He *was* married. It didn't work out."

"Well, you know, maybe he learned how to be a better man to his next wife. Of course, maybe she left him because he's a lazy slob. You want to make sure you find out before you get too attached to him."

"He doesn't seem lazy. Or slobby, either."

"What, you've been inside his apartment?"

I spent the night there once. "Sure. I've gotten a glimpse now and then. He seems neat enough."

"I hope he's not too neat. That means he's kind of a funny guy, if you know what I mean."

She couldn't help laughing. "He's just the right level of neat, Dad, but thanks for explaining it to me."

She told Nathan about those conversations, too. It seemed like she told him everything. What her ghostly callers had said. What her boss had done. What she'd had for lunch. What she'd majored in when she was in college. What she liked about the small Missouri town where she'd grown up. Everything.

His default mode was to listen rather than speak, but any time she prodded him with questions, he willingly answered. When he was a boy, he'd wanted to be a racecar driver. He rarely followed series television, but he could spend hours watching ESPN. The place he most wanted to visit was Alaska, followed by Norway. ("I want to see those Northern Lights.") When he bought his own house, the first thing he was going to get was a dog. ("Big one. Collie or shepherd or Lab. Maybe I'll get two.")

She could tell he liked her. She could see him watching her from time to time with that *look* she remembered from boyfriends in the past – the *look* that meant she was under his skin, on his mind. Occasionally he'd take her hand or put his arm around her shoulder, but he hadn't kissed her, even on the cheek, since that first date. She thought he was ready to fall in love again, but something was holding him back. It wasn't too hard to guess what that something was.

They'd known each other almost a month when she deliberately brought up Mandy's name. They were sitting in his apartment, having finished an entire pepperoni pizza that was supposed to feed four, and he'd said, "I think you're the easiest person to be with that I've ever met."

"Glad to hear it," she said. "I always got the idea that Mandy *wasn't* so easy. I have to say I'm a little curious about her. About the two of you."

"Yeah, I can see why you would be," he said. He thought it over for a moment. "Where we were good together," he said, "was in our energy. We both liked *doing* things – riding our bikes, rehabbing the house, doing an Outward Bound course. It was when we had to sit in a room and have a conversation that we started wearing on each other. Picking at each other. Finding faults."

Stacey raised her eyebrows. "Seems like there have to be a lot of conversations between two people who want to live together."

He nodded. "Yeah. If you can't get that right, you're already in trouble." He glanced at her. "That's one of the reasons I think you're so great. I can talk to you."

She felt her heart bound with excitement, but managed to respond coolly, even with a touch of warning. "Yeah, but I'm not a great doer. I don't ride bikes or go hiking through the mountains or play sand volleyball."

"Well," he said with a little smile, "not *yet*."

She smiled back, but briefly. She didn't think they were quite done with the topic of Mandy yet. "So it's been six months since she died—"

"Almost seven by now."

"And you'd been separated a while before the car accident. Where do you feel like you are in the grieving cycle? You know, rage, denial, bargaining, depression, acceptance?"

As always, he seemed to give serious consideration to her question. "I think the rage and denial burned out pretty quickly, but I spent a long time bouncing between bargaining and depression," he said. "I wish I could say I'm at acceptance, but I still keep thinking . . . if I'd had a chance to hear it from *her,* hear her *tell* me that she was going to marry this other guy, I think that would have made it more real for me, you know? I'd have found it a lot easier to let go."

Stacey nodded. "Makes sense to me."

They were sprawled on his fuzzy brown couch, but now he sat up with a brisk energy. "And I keep wondering, why doesn't *she* call? Why doesn't *she* leave somebody a message?"

For a moment, Stacey was bewildered. "Mandy? You want her to call you?" And then she realized. "You want her to call *me*."

He nodded. "I never mentioned it, but she was on her cell phone when she died. She and her boyfriend were driving to a party, and Mandy was texting one of her girlfriends when he took a turn too fast and went over an embankment. They were both killed."

He gave Stacey a look filled with such pain that she couldn't keep herself from reaching out and taking his hand. "I'm so sorry," she said.

"She was on her cell phone," he repeated. "Why hasn't she called?"

If there was ever a crucial time to give the right answer, it was now. If ever there was a way to help him get over his wife, this was it. Stacey said, "Maybe we could call her. Do you remember her number?"

He looked startled enough to dissipate some of the grief. "But would that work?"

"I don't know. Worth a try, don't you think?"

For a moment, his grip on her hand clamped tight enough to cause a spasm of pain, then he released her. "Worth a try."

Stacey retrieved the phone from her purse and handed it over, absurdly glad to see he had to pull out his own cell and check the list of contacts before punching in the number. When he hit the speaker button, she said, "You don't have to do that."

"I want to," he said.

They heard three rings – enough time for Stacey to wonder if the number had been reassigned – before a woman answered with a cheery greeting. Nathan's quick, hard intake of breath was all she needed to be sure this was his wife on the other end.

His voice was a lot steadier than Stacey thought her own would have been. "Hey, Mandy," he said. "I've been thinking about you."

"Nathan!" Mandy replied with unmistakable delight. "How've you been? God, it's great to hear your voice. It's been too long."

"It has been," he agreed. "I'm good. Took a job in Kansas City a few months ago, working with a start-up software company—"

"You're in the Midwest? No beaches, no mountains? That's hard to believe!"

"I know. But I like it. Lots of friendly people." He attempted to smile at Stacey, but she could see that his eyes were watering. She gave an encouraging nod in response.

"Well, you always were a people person," Mandy said.

"What about you? Anything new in your life?"

"Oh, Nate – I've been thinking I need to call you. I want to tell you something, but I can't bring myself to say the words."

Stacey saw Nathan swallow hard, as if clearing an obstruction from his throat. "What is it? You can tell me anything."

"You know I've been seeing someone for a while. Greg. He's really a good guy, we get along so well. Nate, we *never* argue, can you believe it? And I argue with everyone."

"That's the truth."

"And the other day, he said . . . he asked me to marry him. And I want to do it, Nathan. I want to marry him."

"Then I think you should do it."

Stacey thought Mandy might be crying, too. "Really? You're OK with that?"

"I'm OK with it," Nathan said. "I want you to be happy."

Now there was no doubt that Mandy was weeping. "And you. I want *you* to be happy. I love you, Nathan. I just . . . we just . . . we couldn't get it right."

"I love you too, Mand. Maybe we'll both get it right next time."

"Promise me you will. Promise me you'll start looking for a nice girl." Mandy sniffed and attempted a laugh. "Maybe one of those corn-fed farmer's daughters they seem to grow there in the Midwest. Maybe you could find one of those."

Nathan reached for Stacey's hand again, interlacing his fingers with hers. "Already working on it," he said.

"Good," Mandy said, her voice growing faint. "Listen, Nathan, I've got to go. I'm so glad you called. I feel better about everything."

"So do I. Bye, Mandy."

"Love you! Bye!"

Stacey barely waited until he'd snapped the phone shut before she flung herself across the short distance separating them. She kissed him, she wrapped her arms around his head; she kissed him again. She didn't know if she was comforting him or claiming him, chasing away his ghosts or asking to be let in. Maybe all of those things. It didn't really matter. The only thing that mattered was that his arms curled around her, too; he was kissing her back. He was holding on to her as tightly as she was holding on to him.

She only got one more call on the old cell phone. It came the morning after the first night she and Nathan made love.

"You say you're not much of a doer, but you do that pretty well," had been his judicious assessment, and she had giggled so long that she'd thought she might never fall asleep. She was still feeling pretty upbeat when she was back in her own apartment the next day, and she answered the phone with a breezy hello.

"Well, *you* sound happy," her dad said.

"I am. I had a wonderful date last night – with Nathan, thank you very much – and I'm feeling really optimistic about the long-term chances for this relationship."

"So you love him?"

"It's early days, so it's hard to be sure, but I think I do."

"That's awfully good to hear," he said. "That's all I wanted to know."

"So how are you doing?" she asked, but there was only empty static on the line. "Dad? Dad?"

Feeling a little unnerved, she shut the phone, and set it on the end table so she'd be sure to hear it if it rang again. But it never did. Not that day, not that week, not that month.

Not ever. Stacey imagined her father hanging up on his end of the line, satisfied and smiling. It seemed that once his spirit stopped animating the phone, all the magic was gone from that enchanted artefact; no other calls could come through.

Or maybe it wasn't magic. Maybe it was longing, pure and primal, that had opened and sustained this mystic portal for the past few weeks. It was love, after all, that powered so many miracles, and that made possible superhuman feats of strength and will. Stacey knew her father's love was what had caused him to cling to her, worry over her, haunt her, long after he should have moved on. She thought that knowing she had found another kind of love must have given him the strength to let her go.

The Storm

Linda Wisdom

One

Storms always put Zoe on edge. She ignored the rain pouring down, and tried not to trip over the three dark-grey fluffy kittens that were stubbornly underfoot.

"OK, girls, off to your kitty cave," she ordered them, as she filled her tumbler with coffee and grabbed an apple on her way out of the kitchen.

Tic, Tac and Toe refused to be dismissed, though, as they followed her into her office. A necessary sanctuary for a computer geek, it was filled with up-to-date computer equipment, a small flat-panel TV on the wall, and the kind of comfy chair she could sleep in if she felt like it.

Zoe loved designing offbeat websites. It helped that her clients liked the odd and unusual. She considered her work perfect for goths, with their love of the colors black and red, who want something that will stand out on the World Wide Web. It never mattered that the right design might take days and nights to create. It wasn't as if she had anything better to do.

Too bad today wasn't going to be one of her more productive days. Not when she had to tune out the major storm that she swore had been going on for days. She tensed when she saw flashes of lightning in the distance and heard the faint rumble of thunder on its heels.

She ignored the weather enemies who wanted to tear her

house apart, left the half-designed "Dating the Dead" site behind and moved around the house, pulling drapes closed and making sure the doors were locked up tight. Not that anyone would show up on her doorstep. The house was pretty much out in the middle of nowhere with only the woods for company. Zoe's closest neighbor was five miles away and he wasn't all that friendly to begin with. Her parents had desired their privacy and she was only too happy to continue the tradition.

Wanting sounds other than the thunder that was growing closer, Zoe set up her iPod and cranked the speakers. The idea of holing up in the family room with books and candles, well prepared for a power outage, was a good idea. Even the kittens showed up, acting subdued – not normal behavior for the playful felines. They climbed up the couch and clambered all over her.

"We'll be fine," she assured them, as she stretched out on the couch with her book and coffee. "It's not the first storm we've endured."

She regretted her reassurances when a burst of lightning lit up the house even with the drapes tightly closed and thunder shook the building like it was constructed of paper.

"Damn!" Zoe rolled off the couch and just missed crushing Tac before the kitty slid under the sofa to join the dust bunnies. Zoe covered her ears with her hands, but it didn't help. The thunder kept rolling on. She felt as if the storm were centered over the house, complete with light and sound effects – and now an even heavier downpour, judging from the dripping sound against the windows.

She got to her feet and peeked through the drapes. The rainfall was so heavy she couldn't see anything beyond the glass. "I might need to build us a boat," she told the kittens, who had each now found their own sanctuary. Zoe was ready to do the same.

Once upon a time she hadn't minded storms. She'd even run outside and danced in the rain. Then something happened to change her mind. Now they left her unsettled, and this one scared the hell out of her.

Zoe moved from one window to the next, double-checking to make sure they were secure. The addition of a sweatshirt kept her warmer, but she still felt cold inside.

"I know just how you feel," she told the kittens that cowered on the couch. "It's the season for storms, so why is this one bothering me? Maybe once it would be nice to have someone to hang on to when I feel scared. Not that I am." She didn't think it was odd to talk to the cats as if they could understand her. She figured it was better than talking to herself.

When the power cut out, she lit the candles and dug out her iPod to help drown out the sounds of the storm while she made another walkthrough to make sure the roof wasn't leaking.

Zoe stood in the upstairs hallway, her face uplifted as if she could sense something. She winced at the tiny pricks of Toe's claws digging into her bare foot as the kitten tried to climb up her jean-clad leg.

"Don't you feel it?" Zoe whispered. "It's like something's going to happen."

Two

Zoe shouldn't have been able to sleep during the storm. The thunder and lightning had continued to the point where she wondered if it would ever stop.

But working three days nonstop on a site design had worn her out enough that she finally crawled into bed and pulled the covers over her head while the kittens curled up around her.

Even after the strange stormy evening, she dreamed of sunshine, fluffy clouds and having something new in her life – something insubstantial in the distance that grew closer to her while she eagerly waited for it.

And bells ringing in the distance.

Zoe finally pushed her covers off and listened. The bells weren't in her dream, but downstairs. She could still see lightning flashing into the room, heard thunder booming overhead and rain pummeling the house.

How could she hear the doorbell over all that?

And who could be out there?

"Do serial killers come out in rainstorms?" she asked the kittens as she wrapped a robe around her pajamas.

Zoe ignored the flashbacks from every horror movie she'd ever seen and crept downstairs. Maybe it was her surly neighbor. He was in his eighties and might need some help.

"Who is it?" she called through the door.

"Please, my truck's stuck in a ditch down the road. It's impossible to go anywhere. Lady, I'm feeling like a drowned rat out here."

Telling herself that maniacal killers wouldn't come out in a storm like this, Zoe unlocked the door and pulled it open, losing her grip as the wind pushed it out of her hands.

A tall figure staggered inside her house and helped her push the front door shut against the wind.

"Sorry for waking you up," the man apologized, falling against the door. "This storm is a real bitch. I wouldn't even have found your house if it hadn't been for the light."

She shook her head, not able to make out his features in the gloom. "What light? The electricity has been off since this morning." She frowned. "I don't even know how the doorbell worked without power."

"I'm just glad it did." He peeled off a heavy rain slicker and looked around. "Um, I hate to drip all over your floor."

Zoe looked up at a sudden flash of lightning and felt her heart stop.

Handsome strangers weren't known for coming to her door. Come to think of it, neither were ugly ones.

Not that she'd call her visitor handsome. His features were too rough-hewn for that, but he had that strong masculinity that called out to her on an elemental level.

She was suddenly aware of her major case of bedhead, and her ratty – but warm – robe covering her pajamas.

"Come into the kitchen," Zoe said. "My stove is gas, so I can offer coffee. I couldn't get my generator to work." She gestured him to a chair and picked up the old-fashioned coffee pot on the stove.

"I'd be glad to take a look at it," he offered.

"Get warm first. I'm Zoe Daniels. You can put your slicker out there." She pointed toward the small mudroom by the back door.

"Jon Reynolds." He draped his slicker on a hook and returned to the table. "I appreciate you letting me in. I can assure you I'm safe. Not even a parking ticket to my name." He flashed a grin as he sat down and released a deep breath. "I feel like I've been wandering around out there in the rain for weeks." He started to comb his fingers through his hair then realized all he was doing was shaking water off onto the table.

"The storm only came up this morning," she said, pulling mugs out of a cabinet. She glanced at the wall clock and decided 4 a.m. wasn't too early for breakfast. Luckily, she had eggs in the refrigerator and she also found peppers, mushrooms and onions to add to the omelet fixings. When the omelet was almost ready, she dropped some bread in the toaster.

Jon grimaced at his soaked shirt. "Sure feels longer than that. How long have you lived out here?" He looked around the kitchen.

"All my life. It was my parents' house and I inherited it when they died." Zoe filled a bowl with dry cat food that brought her frisky felines running.

"You've got a regular herd of cats there." Jon laughed, watching them wrestle their way to the bowl.

"They're good company." She regretted the words the moment she said them. The last thing she wanted to do was admit she lived alone. Oh wait, she'd already done that.

"Tic has a white dot on her forehead, Tac has one on her tummy, and Toe—" she chuckled "—on her right paw. They're such kittens at heart that I don't think they'll ever grow up."

Jon leaned down and laughed as Toe tackled his fingers. When he straightened up, Zoe set a full coffee mug, alongside his omelet and toast on the table in front of him. She added a jam jar to the feast before fixing her own plate.

"This looks great, thanks." He dove into his food.

Zoe ate while covertly studying her company. Thanks to the stove, the kitchen was warm and cosy. She wondered if she could find something large enough for Jon to wear while his shirt dried. She knew she couldn't do anything with his jeans. At least the water heater was also gas, so she could offer him a hot shower.

She couldn't remember the last time she'd had someone over for a meal. Or even just for a visit. Or the last time she'd gone out with friends for an evening.

When was the last time a friend had called her wanting to talk? All her conversations lately were via email.

As Zoe looked at Jon and felt his presence she suddenly understood what the word "lonely" meant. It wasn't pleasant.

Three

"I couldn't even see the road," Jon explained after Zoe asked how his accident happened. "Next thing I knew my truck slid and I was upside down in a ditch." He rolled his shoulders as if they bothered him. "I didn't think I'd ever get out. Then, when I felt as if a ton of water had rained down on me, I wished I hadn't. I just started walking, hoping I'd find someone to help who had a phone so I could call roadside assistance."

"Phone's out until the electricity comes back on," Zoe said, getting up to check her phone. "And cell service always goes down during storms like this."

"I'm surprised you'd be willing to live in such an isolated area."

"I'm a website designer and graphic artist, so I can work from home. It doesn't bother me." She finished her omelet then picked up both dishes and carried them to the sink and rinsed them off. "Do you mind my asking what you were doing out in bad weather like this?" She topped off their mugs with fresh coffee. "The storm was strong all during yesterday and didn't let up throughout the night. You were lucky you weren't killed on the road."

"There wasn't any sign of a storm when I left my apartment. In fact, it was a nice day and that's why I thought I'd go for a drive." He wrapped his hands around the mug, allowing the heat to seep into his skin.

"What do you do?" she asked curiously, noting his hands had the look of a man who worked outdoors. The fleeting thought that those hands would also be gentle on a woman raced through her head. She realized it had been a long time since she'd had a man in her life, much less gone out on a date. But it wasn't something to think about right now. No matter what, she didn't know him.

"I'm a contractor. My company works on renovating old houses."

"No wonder you showed up here," Zoe laughed, looking around the kitchen that she knew was in serious need of work. "I'm surprised you didn't take one look and decide you were better off in the storm."

Jon followed her gaze. "At first glance the place looks sturdy.

A house built with care." He turned his face back to hers, looking at her with eyes that were warm with some indefinable emotion.

"You could see all that in a downpour?" she teased, ignoring the butterflies making war in the pit of her stomach. "And here I thought you'd tell me everything that was wrong with this old place."

He shook his head. "That's not my style. Right now, I'm grateful to be in out of the rain." He smiled and lifted his mug in a toast.

Zoe returned the gesture and used the moment to study him further. His shaggy black hair showed a light sprinkling of grey along the temples, and faint lines beside his eyes and mouth said that he was a man who was used to laughter. She even saw a hint of that amusement dancing in his navy-colored eyes now.

Zoe realized just how alone she'd been. While the kittens provided some diversion, they couldn't hold a conversation with her or hold her during the long nights.

She lowered her eyes before Jon might see her thoughts.

"How much property do you have?" he asked, seeming to sense her unease.

"Twenty acres, although most of the land is wooded. With the bad weather lately, I haven't been out back. I'm sure the grass resembles a jungle." She glanced toward the back door. "I guess all the dampness has done something to the door – it's been stuck for a while. Luckily, I don't need anything out there. The generator is accessible through the mudroom."

"Wood swells. If you like I can look at it for you." He laughed as he smothered a yawn. "Sorry about that."

"I should be the one to apologize. You must be exhausted." Zoe jumped up from her chair and gestured for Jon to follow her. "The guest room is always made up and I keep the room aired out." She led the way up the stairs. "You'll have hot water for a shower and I'll see if I can find something else for you to wear." She pointed out the bathroom, retrieved fresh towels for him and then showed him the guest room. She heard the water running while she looked through closets, finding a couple of large sweatshirts and a pair of her dad's sweatpants, as well as some heavy socks. She left them on the bed then retreated downstairs to the kitchen.

"You girls behave, OK?" she whispered to the kittens as they scampered around her ankles. She winced as needle-sharp claws buried themselves in her skin. "Enough." She pried Tic off her foot and held the kitten up to her face. "I am not your scratching post." She nuzzled the soft furry face and laughed as tiny paws batted her cheeks. The other two kittens soon clamored for their share of attention. Pretty soon, Zoe found herself on the floor laughing and rolling with her furry companions who climbed over her as if she were their personal gym.

"Now that's a cute picture."

Zoe froze and looked up at Jon who stood in the doorway. Her oversized sweatshirt fit him pretty well, while her dad's sweatpants were baggy, but that didn't hide an obviously well-honed body. For a woman who prided herself on keeping her hormones under control, she sure was feeling them today.

"They tend to demand a lot," she admitted, accepting his helping hand and getting to her feet.

"I just came down to say goodnight, or I guess I should say good morning, and thanks again for taking me in." He didn't release her hand and she didn't draw back. He smelled like the citrus body wash she kept in the shower and he looked warmer now. Delectable, even.

"I'm glad I was here. People have died in these storms." She started when lightning flashed and a large thunderclap followed, shaking the house.

Jon moved closer to comfort her. "That was a big one. You'd think the storm would have moved on by now." He rubbed his hands down her arms.

"It seems we've had a lot of them lately." She managed a brief smile. "Sometimes I wonder if winter will ever end."

He nodded, looking a bit awkward. "Well, I'm going to catch up on my sleep. Thanks again."

Zoe watched him walk up the stairs and heard the soft snick of the guest-room door closing.

For the first time, she didn't feel as alone. It was a good feeling.

Four

Jon thought he'd fall asleep the minute his head hit the pillow. Instead, he lay under the covers thinking of the woman downstairs.

He was surprised he wasn't feeling too many aches and pains after his accident. At the time, he'd felt as if he was on some kind of insane carnival ride.

He didn't even remember getting out of the truck. He had found himself on the road and had just started walking until he saw a light and discovered Zoe's house.

He wondered why someone so pretty would live out in the middle of nowhere. She intimated she could do her work anywhere, so why not in town where she'd be around people? Did this house mean that much to her? Deep down, he didn't think so.

Jon didn't believe in instant attraction. He didn't believe in fate either. But what else other than fate had him turning his truck left instead of right when he couldn't see his hand in front of his face because of the driving storm? He'd known his share of women and not once had he felt the kind of quick connection he felt with Zoe.

From the second he looked into her sweet, delicate face with the large brown eyes beneath her tousled golden-brown hair, he felt as if he were falling off a cliff. The wild sensation in his stomach was the same one he felt after he tried bungee jumping for the first time off the Sawyer Bridge last summer. At least this time he didn't indulge in projectile vomiting afterwards.

But he would like to take her in his arms and see if what he felt about her was true.

He settled on his back, his arms crossed behind his head as he stared up at the ceiling, watching the flashes of lightning steal between the split in the drapes and light up the room.

When was the last time he'd met a woman who fascinated him? Obviously so long ago he couldn't recall one name.

Conversation with Zoe was easy. He hadn't felt that comfortable with a woman in ages.

His last thought before sleep overtook him was the hope that the storm would last long enough to give him a chance to get to know her better.

*   *   *

Jon had no idea how long he slept. He only knew that the rain was still sheeting against the windows and the thunder was still rumbling overhead along with sporadic flickers of lightning.

The room was chilly with the dampness of the storm outside, but he was warm under the covers. He grabbed the sweatshirt hanging on the bedpost and pulled it over his head. A glance at the clock on the dresser didn't give him any idea of the time – it appeared the batteries were dead. Even his watch had stopped.

"So much for claiming to be waterproof."

He used the bathroom then cocked his head to one side, hearing music playing softly downstairs. The scent of sugar led him to the kitchen.

"Have a good sleep?" Zoe greeted him with a smile. She was busy pulling a tray of cookies out of the oven. "Stormy days always put me in a cooking mood. I hope you like oatmeal chocolate chip." She nodded toward the array on the table. "Coffee's fresh. Help yourself."

He noted she'd changed into a pair of black jeans and a pink v-necked sweater that looked as touchable as she must be. Strands of hair escaped her ponytail and drifted around her face, and if he wasn't mistaken she wore a hint of lipgloss. Was that effort for him?

He filled a mug and refilled hers before trying a cookie. He watched her drop spoonfuls of dough onto another cookie sheet.

"What kind of websites do you design?" he asked, wanting to know more about her. He leaned back in the chair, stretching his legs out in front of him. He smiled as the kittens deemed him worthy prey and climbed over his sock-clad feet.

She paused, looking upward. "Lately, it's been for those you might call 'odd and unusual'. The one I've been working on lately is called 'Dating the Dead'. It's goth-related, for vampire wannabes. A couple of years ago, I was hired to do some graphic design for an underground club and pretty soon I had other similar clients asking me to design sites or logos for business cards and flyers." She laughed softly. "They're all very strange, but at least they pay promptly. I even had a psychic contact me not long ago. I've been so busy with my work that I can't remember the last time I left the house."

"You must grocery shop." He nodded toward the large mixing bowl.

"I tend to lay in enough supplies to last for months. Winters are hard out this way either with rain or snow. But I'll probably need to go into town soon." Once the cookie sheet was in the oven, she sat down next to him.

"Well, let me know when you're there and I could take you out to dinner," he said.

Her smile warmed his heart. "I'd like that."

Jon leaned in closer. He hoped he wasn't making a big mistake, but he had to find out.

"I would, too," he whispered, cupping her cheek in one hand and leaning in that last distance to kiss her.

His first thought was that she tasted as good as she looked.

His second thought was that he didn't want this kiss to end.

Five

Zoe was frozen to her chair.

She shouldn't allow a man she barely knew to kiss her. But Jon's mouth felt so good against hers. Warm and firm. His other hand rested lightly on her shoulder, his fingers gently stroking.

She felt suspended in time as his mouth moved over hers, his tongue stroking the seam of her lips, silently asking for entrance. When she parted them she tasted chocolate and coffee, mixed with the masculine flavor that was all Jon.

And here she was, thinking her cookies were addictive! Nope, Jon was way more necessary.

She melted against him as she thrust her fingers through his hair, feeling the thick strands curl around the tips. She wasn't sure, but she thought she moaned his name.

The faint hint of citrus from his shower was still there, along with a darker earthier scent that she already associated with him.

A feeling of loss took over when Jon moved away. He kept his hand on her cheek, his thumb gently caressing her skin in a circular motion.

"Do I need to apologize?" he asked softly.

Zoe shook her head. "It seemed . . . right." She wished she could come up with another word. A description of how she felt. She was so lost in his gaze that she didn't notice that the storm

had kicked up a notch and was assaulting the house with apoca-
lyptic fervor.

"It did." His smile warmed her better than the heat from the
oven. "Zoe, I don't go around kissing women for the hell of it.
It's just that I look at you and—" he lightly stroked the soft skin
at the outer corner of her eye "—I feel this strong connection. I
know it sounds crazy since we just met, but it's like I've been
looking for you all my life."

Zoe covered his hand with hers. "When I woke up yesterday,
I had this feeling that I wanted more in my life. Maybe fate sent
you to me."

"I like the idea of that."

The *ding* of the oven timer wasn't loud enough to startle them.
Zoe pulled the cookies out, shut off the oven and set the tray on
top of the stove. She turned back to Jon and held out her hand.

Jon didn't hesitate. He took her hand and stood, allowing her
to lead him up the stairs.

Zoe was grateful that she'd cleaned her bedroom the other
day – there was no clothing scattered around and there were
clean sheets on the bed. Since the room was dark from the
storm, she lit the candles on her dresser and on the vanity table
at the other side of the room.

She didn't feel any embarrassment as she turned to stand in
front of Jon. She slowly raised her sweater over her head and
dropped it to the carpet, then slid out of her jeans.

'Wait." He stopped her before she unclasped her bra. He took
off his sweatshirt and pants then put his arms around her, using
his fingers to find the clasp. He bent his head, dropping a kiss on
the tip of each breast when the bra revealed them. "Beautiful,"
he breathed against her skin.

Zoe smiled and closed her eyes to better appreciate the sensations Jon was setting off inside her. If this happened when he was
merely touching her, what would happen when she felt all of him?

Not content with being the recipient of his touches, she placed
the flat of her hand against his chest, feeling the tanned skin
rough with crisp dark hair. She was right. He was muscular from
daily physical work and she felt perfectly safe in his arms.

"Zoe," he whispered as he backed her up to her bed.

They fell onto the covers, Zoe pulling off Jon's briefs while he
worked on her bikini panties.

"Beautiful," he repeated, placing a kiss in the middle of her abdomen before moving downward.

Zoe felt her body immediately tighten in reaction, but in a very good way. She trailed her fingers over his chest, noting scars.

"Construction isn't always a safe job," he murmured, brushing kisses across her legs while he performed his own sensual Braille.

"This makes it all real," she whispered back, reaching down and finding him erect. She wrapped her fingers around him, feeling skin silk over steel. She raised her hips in invitation, but he ignored her while he continued to drop kisses everywhere.

"We need to take it slow." He pulled her nipple into his mouth, rolling his tongue around the turgid tip.

Zoe moved restlessly, rotating her hips against Jon. How could he move so slowly when she was going insane with what he was doing to her? She could feel the tension in his body, so she knew he wasn't immune.

"I want this to last." It was as if he read her mind as he whispered the words against her lips.

"Make it last *next time*." And then she squeezed his penis just a little.

Jon's laughter was raw and shaky. It was enough to make him move into the cradle of her hips and thrust inside.

Zoe inhaled sharply, feeling a fullness she hadn't felt in a long time, if ever. It was as if he'd been created just for her.

"Open your eyes, Zoe."

She did and smiled up at him.

Jon moved his hips as Zoe tilted hers up, creating the ultimate friction. Their movements increased and Zoe tilted her head back, breathing deeply. She swore lights sparkled in front of her eyes and her body started to take over. She felt as if she were flying. No worries there – she could see that Jon was right there with her.

She opened her mouth, ready to admit the three words that she had no right saying. They remained on her tongue, not willing to leave, because while her heart wanted to say one thing, her brain was unwilling.

By the time she imploded with her orgasm and Jon had collapsed on top of her, Zoe felt about as perfect as could be.

Six

This wasn't sex. This was true love.

No, this had to be a dream. There was no way lovemaking could be this perfect. Jon felt in sync with Zoe from the first moment he touched her and it only grew stronger.

Still, he'd always been careful with his emotions. He didn't allow his penis to rule his head, no matter how pretty the face was. Now, less than twenty-four hours after a woman gave him shelter from a bad storm, he had made love to her. Jon hadn't felt this good in probably for ever.

He wrapped his arms around her and she snuggled closer to his chest.

"That was amazing," she murmured, rubbing her cheek against him.

He couldn't hold back his grin. "Thank you."

"Hey, don't let it go to your head." Her slap against his shoulder didn't do any damage. "Who needs a teddy bear when they can have you?"

Zoe couldn't keep her eyes open and she felt herself drift off to sleep. She had no idea that the smile curving her lips was mirrored on her lover's face.

For once, she didn't even care about the storm. Not when it meant Jon would stay here with her.

For a second her bliss was marred by the thought that the rainstorm was the only reason Jon was still here.

"I like having you in my arms," he whispered in her ear before resting his chin on top of her head.

Zoe felt the warmth of satisfaction sink down all the way to her bones.

Maybe the storm had finally done something right.

Zoe didn't want to open her eyes, not when she was so warm and comfortable in bed. She heard purring in stereo and sleepily realized the kittens were perched on her stomach. But it was the aroma of coffee that woke her up.

"Is madam ready for her breakfast?"

She dislodged the kittens and shot up in bed. She clutched the covers against her breasts as she stared at Jon at the end of the bed. He held a mug of heavenly smelling coffee in one hand, using the other to waft the lovely aroma in her direction.

She blushed and kept the comforter tight against her. While she knew he'd seen everything there was to be seen, she still felt a bit shy.

"Here." He handed her the mug then walked over to the closet. He returned with her robe and laid it across the bed. "I can't make fancy omelets like you, but I can scramble up some mean eggs." He leaned over to kiss her. What started out as a light kiss quickly deepened. He plucked the mug out of her hand and set it on the nightstand, while she shooed the kittens off the bed.

"You're right," Jon muttered, following her under the covers and shedding his clothes. "Breakfast can wait."

"I didn't say that." She kissed him again.

"I can read your thoughts." This time he rolled onto his back and drew her over him. "Umm, I like this." He raised his head to kiss her again. "I could do this for ever."

Zoe couldn't control the laugh that escaped. "If I remember my basic sex education, you require some downtime, so to speak," she snickered.

"OK, that's it!'

She shrieked as Jon started tickling her ribs.

"*No!*" She wailed and laughed at the same time as she tried to avoid him, but he cut her off each time. Then her laughter drifted off to soft moans as his tickling fingers turned to sensual strokes.

Zoe couldn't remember a time when sex included mirth; when she looked at her partner and felt as if they were on the same wavelength. And like before, she felt as though she were being shot out into the universe, with Jon right there beside her.

"If I didn't know better I'd think you were a dream come true," she said, collapsing back against the pillows, Jon cradling her in his arms.

"Don't tell me you've been rubbing old lamps or wishing on a star," he teased, pulling up the comforter a second before Tic and Toe pounced on him. Tac was playing with strands of Zoe's hair.

"No." She wondered if it was a good idea to tell him that there were days she felt as if she'd turn into one of the cranky, lonely old ladies the local kids made fun of. "But I woke up the other day wishing I had someone here with me. And that night, you showed up." She idly ran her fingertips down his arms, relishing the warmth of his body around her. She couldn't remember ever feeling this protected.

"Do you believe in destiny?" Jon asked quietly.

"I do now."

"Do you believe in love at first sight?"

She stilled, not daring to hope he was serious. "I never did before."

"But now you do." He shifted until she faced him. "I stumbled in here like some kind of drowned rat. Or maybe a horror-movie idea of a serial killer. But you weren't afraid."

Zoe touched his face, relishing the roughness of his skin. "Maybe I instinctively knew the storm brought you to me."

They were silent as they listened to the rain drumming on the roof.

"Do you mind that we're doing things backward?" he asked. "What I mean is, once the rain's over, I want you to come into town with me, we'll go out to dinner, maybe a movie. And later, when you feel you know me better . . ." His voice trailed off as if he didn't dare voice the words that rang loud and clear inside their heads.

Zoe felt a burst of happiness. "I already know you better and, yes, I do believe in love at first sight. But only where you're concerned."

Jon settled back against the pillows. "Once the rain has tapered off and the road is passable, I'll call for a tow truck." He studied her face. "You can do your work anywhere, right?" He looked hopeful. "We'll pack up whatever you need, kittens included, and I'll introduce you to town life."

She nodded, not daring to hope he meant what he said, but she saw the sincerity written on his face. Jon loved her. And she had to admit she loved him.

"Yes, when the rain stops. But for now . . ." She reached under the covers. "Hmm, I'd say you've had plenty of recovery time."

Moments later, they were so involved with each other they didn't hear the rain sheeting the windows or the thunder rumbling overhead. They knew they wouldn't be bored waiting for the storm to end.

Epilogue

"Poor guy. Between the wet road and all the rocks in this ditch, he didn't have a chance." The patrol officer peered through the broken truck window at the man slumped over the steering wheel. "Looks like his neck broke when the truck hit the bottom." He shook his head and pulled open the door to dig for the man's identification. "These winter storms always take victims. Remember last month when we found Zoe Daniels in her backyard? She was struck by lightning. A real shame. She was a nice lady. She shouldn't have died alone. Do you know that the kids around here claim they see her ghost inside the house sometimes? And the candles flickering? We even found pet food dishes in the kitchen, but she never had any pets." He rolled his eyes as he studied the contents of the wallet. "His ID says he's Jon Reynolds out of Crescent Hollow."

"Look at his face," his partner commented. "If I didn't know any better I'd say he's smiling."

The officer spoke into his shoulder mic and requested a tow truck and a coroner's wagon.

"Maybe he found something to make a senseless death worthwhile then."

>>>---4EVR--->

Holly Lisle

Mike looked out into the sea of faces staring up at him, took a deep breath and turned to the newlyweds. Time to wrap up his toast. "So, for you, my best friend, and your beautiful bride, I wish long life, great joy, and every day better than the day before." He looked straight at Brandon, added, "You've earned it," and tipped his glass.

Against the background of applause, the clinking of glasses all around the estate's reception hall, and the shouts of "Cheers!", the groom managed a weak smile. Mike watched his friend link arms with Lauren – truly one of the most beautiful women Mike had ever seen – and drank from his glass like it was the ocean that would rescue him from a terrifying shore.

Four years earlier, Brandon had weathered the tragedy of his first wife's death only weeks after they were married, and two years after that, the humiliation of abandonment by his second wife (along with her theft of more than $50,000) while they were on their honeymoon. Mike hoped with all his heart that Lauren would give Brandon happiness and love.

But he had grave doubts. Lauren seemed to him like a classic gold-digger, and Brandon, ever the hopeful romantic, had refused a prenup. Brandon had had no doubts – or at least he hadn't *before* the wedding.

So Mike kept his mouth shut. His own track record with love was a nightmare. He would have bet his life, his honor and everything he owned that TJ, the only woman he'd ever loved, had been the woman he would spend the rest of his life with.

Five years ago, he'd been proven wrong. He was still trying to understand what had happened.

At least Brandon had made it as far as marriage – and Brandon's first wife had really loved him. Maybe Lauren would, too.

But the past was the last place Mike wanted to revisit on what was supposed to be a happy occasion for his friend and, as the best man, he had work to do. After the dinner, filled with laughter and loud stories all along the wedding party's table, he watched bride and groom step out onto the dance floor for the first dance.

Then he headed outside to make sure the idiots with shoe polish and streamers hadn't defaced the antique Rolls-Royce Phantom that Brandon had chosen for the honeymoon getaway. Mike needed to find a way to snap out of his funk. Weddings were difficult. The three he'd been to since T. J. took off – all three Brandon's – just made him miss her more.

Out in the cold and quiet, Mike felt better.

The bright sun, the sharp bite of the icy air, his breath streaming away in clouds – all reminded him that life went on, and he did, too.

He trudged across the snow-glazed lawn to the estate's enormous garage, unlocked the side door to make sure the car was pristine, then locked up after himself when he was sure it was. Everything was fine.

Until he turned around to head back to the reception hall, and lost his breath.

TJ stood in the shadows at the side of the garage, watching him.

He couldn't believe it.

Five years. He'd tried to find her for five years, had waited for any message, any news, any explanation. Not a single word. Then suddenly there she was, leaning in the corner, dressed too lightly for the weather, with her arms wrapped tightly around herself.

He felt like someone had nailed his feet to the ground. He couldn't move toward her, and he couldn't move away. "TJ?"

"Could you take me home?" she asked.

He couldn't breathe. He wanted to race to her, pick her up and hold her close, kiss her, yell at her for running away.

But.

Five years.

The distance between the two of them couldn't be measured in feet and inches, and it couldn't be crossed by a few desperate steps.

He wasn't sure he could get past the abyss of pain and loss that lay between them.

But he could take her home. She looked half frozen.

"Decided not to crash the wedding?"

She shook her head. "I have to talk to you, Mike. But not here. Not *here*. Can you take me home?"

"Yes. Of course." According to her parents, she'd run off with some rich guy from Argentina. Mike had never believed that and, standing there looking at her, he still didn't believe it. But she'd dumped him without an explanation, without an apology, and the first words out of her mouth five years later were asking for a favor.

She looked scared. He was supposed to drive Brandon and Lauren to the airport, but this was TJ, and one of the other groomsmen could take them. *This was TJ*, and Brandon would understand.

"I'll get my coat and tell one of the groomsmen to take over for me, and we'll get out of here. C'mon with me, wait inside where it's warm. This will just take a second, and no one will mind if you crash the reception. Besides, Brandon will be relieved to know you're all right."

She gave him an odd look. "I . . . can't."

He sighed. She'd always been funny about going where she hadn't been invited. "I'll be right back. *Don't. Move.* Promise?"

She nodded.

He raced back to the reception hall, and nearly ran over Brandon, who looked pale and panicked. Brandon said, "I thought you'd ditched me, man. I need the car. Drive me to the airport, will you? Hell, let's both just swear off women. I have all the damn tickets with me. *We* can go to Aruba, drink ourselves stupid, and do things we'll both regret that don't involve getting married."

"I'm getting my coat now," Mike said. "What happened?"

"I walked in on Lauren screwing her mother's husband in the men's room."

"The twenty-year-old gigolo is that harpy's *husband*? Damn. If

you're ready to go right now, I'll take you as far as the airport."
He put on his coat.

Brandon's face fell. "You can't come?"

He shook his head. "Ten minutes ago I would have been grateful for the vacation. But TJ's back," Mike said. "She told me she has to talk to me. Has to tell me something important."

He caught the look of shock on Brandon's face, and nodded. "Yeah. You look like I feel."

Brandon slowly shook his head. "No. Not quite. I don't know what's going on out there. I don't know what you think she's going to tell you that's going to make everything all right. But I'm not the idiot who still keeps believing in that . . . that bitch. I'm the one who remembers the last five years. *TJ ditched you*, man. Left you to chase after her, and all this time she didn't spare a single minute to get a single word to you. She broke your heart. I've been watching you bleeding for her for five years. You *can't* take her back. She doesn't deserve you."

Mike set his jaw. "I'll go with you as far as the airport. TJ's riding with us."

He headed out the side door, ignoring the uproar from the wedding guests behind him.

Brandon didn't say anything else. He just followed.

Mike set a fast pace across the lawn, saw TJ standing in the corner and, at the same instant, heard Brandon yell, "Mike! Behind you. The Argentinian!"

And everything went dark.

Mike woke up to grey, bleak light angling into his bedroom from the wrong direction.

TJ, he thought, as he pushed his way out of the confusion of sleep. TJ. And the Argentinian.

And Brandon. Hell, poor Brandon. He could really pick them.

Mike got out of bed and dragged himself into the bathroom, trying to remember how he got home.

Had Brandon driven him?

No. He vaguely remembered driving himself home. But there had been things before that. Police cars all over the estate grounds, dogs searching, Brandon telling the police about the man who'd attacked his best friend, and about the girl who'd been with that man.

He stared at himself in the mirror, and for a moment the brilliance of the light almost blinded him. He blinked a few times, thinking about TJ and wondering what the hell she'd been up to, while he waited for the light to die down to manageable levels.

Concussion, he thought, and was rather proud of himself for figuring that out. But the horrific headache would probably have been a better clue.

He looked about like he felt.

So he took a shower, and stood under the warm water with his eyes tightly closed, just so the intermittent halos of impossibly brilliant light around his field of vision couldn't make his headache any worse. He followed the shower with an aspirin and acetaminophen chaser and some coffee, on the theory that enough caffeine could fix anything.

Because he had to find TJ.

She'd come to the reception to talk to him. She'd been scared, and no matter what Brandon told the police, there was no way she would ever try to hurt him, or help someone else hurt him.

Coffee downed, he went to get dressed.

It was while he was digging through his dresser drawers for socks and underwear that he discovered TJ had left him a message.

He'd drawn TJ on their first date. The picture was a sketch on a napkin, done quickly to capture that moment. Now it lay on top of his dresser, still in the sandwich bag he'd given her so she could save it without it getting ruined.

Knowing that she'd kept it, even after she ran off, gave him some comfort, but also raised a question he couldn't answer.

How had it come to be in his room?

He turned it over.

On the back of the napkin, which had been unmarked when he put it in the bag years before, he found a note pencilled in her unmistakable angular script

Waiting for you. Come find me.

TJ

+

MK

>>>--4EVR--->

He knew where she'd be waiting.

He pulled on his winter coat and heavy boots and ran out into the snow.

The cicadas droned. Even in the shade, the afternoon was breathlessly hot. TJ, nineteen, sprawled on the heavy blanket she'd brought for their picnic, her thin cotton blouse sticking to her skin, her blue-jean shorts showing off long tanned legs.

"I have the supermarket job just to keep money coming in while I get the band together," she told him.

He lay across from her on the blanket, hot and sticky in T-shirt and khaki shorts, feet bare after he'd shed sneakers and socks. He still couldn't believe she'd agreed to go out with him, and the fact that she'd packed the picnic for the two of them was a thrill.

They worked at the same grocery store. She cashiered; he bagged and stocked shelves. He'd had the job a year longer than she had, and he was doing it to afford canvases and paints and brushes and thinner. His folks – less than happy with his career path – were nonetheless letting him live in the room above the garage rent-free until he was making enough from his painting to rent his own place.

TJ wasn't so lucky. "My parents keep saying, 'If you don't go to college, you'll never amount to anything,'" TJ told him. "But I'm a good musician. I sing. I play acoustic and electric guitars like I was born to them. I write *good* songs. I can do this. If I fail, *then* I'll go to college. But not now. Not yet."

"I had to explain the same thing to my mom about painting. My folks aren't too bad," Mike told her. "My mom wants me to have something dependable, so she's still against me trying to make a living with my artwork. My dad built his own business, though, so he sort of understands. Not the art part of it, but about me needing to pursue my own dreams and be my own boss."

"You're lucky. I'm an embarrassment to my parents. My brother is in law school. One of my sisters just graduated med school and is starting her internship. My other sister is working on her MBA. All of them got scholarships, all of them went through school and college with insane grades. None of that ever mattered to me – I couldn't make myself care. And the careers they're going after would eat me alive." She rolled her eyes.

"I try to explain about the music to my mother and father, and it's like I'm walking around with FAILURE tattooed on my forehead. I want *music*. *Need* it, like I need to breathe. And all they can talk about is me being the one who's going to get into booze and drugs and end up pregnant and strung out and living on the street, whoring to survive. That isn't who I've ever been. Why would I become that in the future?"

"You wouldn't," he told her. He understood what drove her, because the same thing drove him. Passion. Imagination. The burning need to create so he could make what he loved real in the world, and so other people could see it, understand it, and believe it the way he believed it. The way she believed it. "That won't *ever* be you," he added. "You'll make it."

And he meant it. When he looked at her, he could see her standing in front of a hundred thousand screaming fans, singing her heart out.

That was when she smiled at him – the smile he'd never seen before, so pure and intense and fierce it was like looking straight into the sun. "Silver Obsession," she said, like these were the two most important words in the world.

He raised an eyebrow, uncertain what she meant, and her smile, impossibly, got brighter.

"That's what I want to call the band. I haven't told anyone yet."

But you told me, he thought, and held the moment in his heart.

He always had a pen or a pencil with him, but at that moment he didn't have any paper. They had napkins left over after their feast of peanut butter and jelly sandwiches, chips, store-bought cookies, grapes and soda, though, and he took one, spread it out on the lid of the cooler in which they'd brought the picnic and started to draw her.

He wanted to capture her smile. The confidence of it. The joy. The sheer exuberant desire.

In a few lines, he had her long hair curling around her shoulders, the gleam in her eyes, and that glorious smile.

"Let me see," she demanded as he bent over his work, and after he finished the sketch and scrawled his initials and the date at the bottom, he handed it over to her.

"That's *wonderful*," she whispered. "You're amazing."

And that, too, he held in his heart. The day, the time, the light, the smells of the world around them at the moment she said it.

And later, he kissed her for the first time. Then, with his penknife, the two of them took turns commemorating the kiss – and the many that followed – by carving their initials into the maple tree beneath which they'd had their picnic.

"Should we add a heart?" she asked him.

"The tree's too small. Cutting through the bark to do a heart would wrap most of the way around the tree and kill it."

"Oh, we can't do that!" She thought for a moment, then carved a little "4EVR", right underneath their initials.

And he realized she'd left him enough room to add an arrow to run through it. It wasn't traditional. But it was theirs.

Standing wrapped in his coat in the bitter cold, he shook off the memory of that summer afternoon, the joy he'd felt at finding the girl of his dreams and discovering the two of them shared so much.

That had been then. This was a different time – hollow and grim, with the snow again threatening.

He wanted to think she'd meant that 4EVR. He wanted to believe that he still mattered to her the way she mattered to him. But he didn't see any footprints leading through the snow to their spot in the woods. Had he misunderstood her note?

He didn't think so. He set off along the snow-covered path, watching for her through the gloom.

She might have come in by a different path. She might be waiting by their tree.

Some part of him wanted to think she'd be there with a picnic basket. Some part of him would have happily sat on the frozen ground eating peanut butter and jelly sandwiches and chips.

After five years of silence, Brandon was probably right about her. Mike was, perhaps, ridiculous in wanting to still believe in TJ.

But seeing her again the night before showed him this: he had never stopped loving her. Instead, he loved her more.

Have a good reason for having abandoned me, he thought, willing her to hear him. Have a good reason for breaking my heart. I'll forgive you anything, if only I know you didn't forget me.

The path down to their place was long, but he covered it without any awareness of the passage of time. Hope, he mused, shortened journeys well.

He saw the little clearing where they'd shared their first date and, in the dim light, that was all he saw . . . at least at first.

Then he realized someone had pinned a white square to the tree where they'd carved their initials.

When he was close enough, he saw the only well-known artwork he'd done of TJ, preserved in a bigger plastic bag.

It was the watercolor she'd used for the front of her first – and last – indie album cover.

He took it down.

Beneath it lay devastation, and he found himself shuddering.

TJ + MK >>>--4EVR---> had been hacked and slashed and burned. The damage was not recent; bark was growing in over the blackened, scarred wood.

Those scars spoke of rage.

Not *his* rage. And he couldn't imagine TJ ever doing that. Who had hated her? Or *them*?

Without warning, hairs on the back of his neck lifted, and he knew someone was watching him. He looked around slowly, not wanting to startle whomever it was.

On the side of the hill, across the stream, he saw TJ. And in the instant he spotted her, snow started to fall.

She was still dressed too lightly for the terrible weather. She looked . . . fragile.

He realized he'd never thought of TJ as fragile before.

She stared at him for an instant. Didn't wave. Didn't speak a word. Instead, she turned and fled.

"Wait!" he shouted, but the falling snow started coming down harder and muffled his voice. "Dammit, TJ, wait for me! I'll help you."

But she didn't wait, and he realized that he couldn't hope to get across the stream to catch her – the water was high and fast, snowmelt that flooded the stream with muddy, dangerous run-off.

The weather needed to get colder, he thought. Or warmer. With the temperature where it was, just above freezing, the conditions were right for a blizzard.

He held the watercolor, forcing himself to ignore the memories of the day he'd done it, and turned it over.

"He hid his secret here," she'd written, her long, heavy letters like scars on the paper.

And he looked back to their tree.

Hid a secret by their tree?

No. She'd brought him to the tree to show him the burns, the scars, their initials and their little arrow destroyed. And she'd used the *first* drawing to get him there. She would use the *second* drawing to take him to . . .

Oh, God.

. . . The barn.

Her father's barn.

He never wanted to face her parents again. He remembered standing on their doorstep the day after TJ went missing.

Her father had answered the door, recognized him, and said, "Get off my property before I shoot you."

"TJ's missing," Mike told him. "She disappeared from her tour bus yesterday. None of her band members saw her go, and none of them is sure where she might have left the bus. All of her belongings, including her guitars, were still on the bus when it got to Cincinnati. The bus made three stops, and no one saw her at any of them. Everyone assumed she was sleeping in the back."

"She's not missing," her father said.

"You know where she is? She's all right?"

The older man's face had turned a dull, dark red. "She hasn't been all right since she met you. But I know where she is. Theresa Jeanne sent her mother an email saying she met a rich Argentinian gentleman, and she was leaving her unhappy life to go be with him." He started to close the door.

"She'd never do that!" Mike said. "I love her and she loves me. She would never just take off without letting me know where she was going!"

TJ's father had glared at him. "What did you expect? You turned her into a whore, living with you without marrying you. You encouraged her to waste her life and her intelligence on music. You kept her away from college and the work she should have done, becoming a nurse like her mother and taking care of the sick." He stared dully at Mike. "You destroyed her. She was a good girl, and you turned her into trash like you." And with that he had closed the door in Mike's face.

During the long months after, when Mike gave up everything

to try to find her, neither of her parents would even acknowledge that he existed. They had no interest in her, either. Didn't search. Didn't question. Didn't even think it odd that she'd abandoned the guitars into which she'd poured her soul since she was a kid.

And now she was leading him back to her father's barn.

He closed his eyes.

He'd never believed the Argentina story. He'd never thought TJ's parents had made it up, though.

Now? Now he had doubts. *He hid his secret here*, she'd written.

What secret, Mike wondered. And who hid it?

TJ was twenty-one. She stood in the barn behind her parents' house. TJ and Mike had been living together for six months at that point, and Mike had come to the conclusion that heaven on earth was a real possibility.

Except for this moment of insanity. "You're *sure* you want to do this?"

"Of course I'm sure." TJ grinned at him, the smile that always took his breath away. "You know the album cover I like. That Melissa Etheridge one."

Mike held a pad of ten-by-ten sheets of watercolor paper, his portable easel, brushes, paints, pencils. He sighed. "Yeah, I know the one. Topless, back to the camera."

"Yeah. Only I want mine with the bales and the old barn boards on the sides, the hill over there where the sun comes up as the backdrop. I want more shadow and contrast, and a lot more color. And on the album back, I want the front view of me."

He looked at her and shook his head. "That's going to get the album banned."

"It's going to get the album covered in a brown paper wrapper, and that brown paper wrapper is going to send sales through the roof."

He sighed, and she laughed. "Look, half the world has 'em, and the other half wants to see 'em, and it isn't like you're doing some cheesy snapshot. Having your artwork on the cover and your name and studio in the credits should help *you*, too." She gave him a woebegone look. "Silver Obsession is good, dammit. But no one's listening. This topless cover? This is just a stunt, and I know that. But if they buy the album, most of them will listen to it at least once. And I think if we can get them to listen just once, we can keep them. I'll risk taking my shirt off for that."

Silver Obsession had been playing little bars for two years. And they were really good, but TJ wasn't patient, and wasn't willing to wait for someone with connections to wander into one of the lousy gigs they could get. Along with entering band battles and auditioning for better gigs, she was taking their music directly to listeners every way she could.

He suspected she was right about the impact a double-sided topless cover would have, too. God knows, *he* loved to look at her.

When her parents saw the album, though, and recognized his work on the cover, they were going to kill him. Kill her, *then* kill him. Hunt the two of them down like ravening wolves after a brace of plump, juicy rabbits.

TJ didn't share his worry. She assured him her folks were all bark and no bite. And she loved her parents' old barn. She wanted him to paint the picture *there*, not in his studio with fake boards and contrived lighting.

He set up, and she stripped off her shirt and turned her back to him. Held her guitar in her right hand, by the neck. Lifted her chin, tossed her long hair, and planted her feet, in their six-inch spike-heeled patent-leather pumps, shoulder-width apart.

Her jeans were tight, worn thin in places, her skin was gold blushed with peach as the sun came over the horizon, and his heart caught in his throat.

His, he thought. She was his. "More to the right, and lift your arm just a little," he told her.

She adjusted, and the full curve of her right breast, underlit by the dawn, came into clear, glorious view.

He did a few quick lines with pencil and started painting, catching the luminous, fleeting colors of the day's first light with desperate speed, marking out the shadows of her spine, the wild tangle of wavy, windblown, coffee-brown hair, the curve of her shoulder.

Mine. Mine. Forever mine.

In twenty minutes, he had enough of the picture – he'd be able to finish it back at the studio.

He dragged his easel in front of her and off to the side, and pinned the second ten-by-ten sheet beside the first.

"Don't move," he told her, and started drawing.

He'd captured her outlines, and the brighter, fiercer sunlight tossed across her exquisite curves when he heard the rhythmic crunch of footsteps on gravel coming down the path.

From the weight and the stride, it was going to be her father.

He stared into her eyes, and saw the defiance there . . . and he shook his head. *I have enough*, he mouthed, and pointed to her shirt lying on the bale of hay beside her. She frowned, but he wasn't going to be party to World War III. He dumped the paint water in the dirt, covered the watercolors, and folded up the easel with the paintings still pinned in place.

He could finish both paintings in the studio that was the other half of his two-room rental.

She pulled her shirt over her head; he sat on a bale and started sketching her into his sketchbook. Her father came around the path, sucked in air in surprise, and said, "What the hell are you two doing here?"

TJ said, "Hi, Dad. We're using the barn as the backdrop for my first album cover."

"You don't get to be here," her father said. "And you don't get to call me 'Dad'. I don't know you anymore. You spit on your family when you turned your back on everything we believe in, when you chased after this life of drugs and sex and sleaze. You gave up on us when you moved in with that bum. Leave. Now." He paused, gave her a long, sad look, and shook his head. "And don't ever come back."

She'd stood unblinking, unmoving beneath her father's onslaught. Mike could see she was shocked. Stunned. But when her father finished, she lifted her chin and smiled at him – the tight, wounded smile Mike only saw on her face when she talked about her parents.

"We're on our way. You'll never see me again."

Mike studied the man, half a foot taller than him, probably eighty pounds heavier, with muscle built from a lifetime of daily hard work.

If Mike hadn't loved TJ, he could have liked her father. Admired him. The old man had endured a life of hardship and struggle to free his children from the pre-dawn risings, back-breaking labor, and constant demands that defined his existence. He'd worked himself to the bone to give each of them security and comfort.

But the man was throwing away the one kid he had who didn't *want* to be secure. And that broke Mike's heart.

TJ's father couldn't – or wouldn't – see her talent. Her brilliance. Her fire. He refused to see that she was the kid most like him, the one stubbornly capable of carving her place in the world with her bare hands and her ferocious persistence – jamming her flag into the hard earth and calling that place her own.

Mike pulled into the drive now, wondering if TJ's father still wanted to shoot him.

The old farm looked grimmer in winter, Mike reflected. Skeletal, dry, bleak.

Mike peered through the worsening snowfall into the darkness. That was then, this is now.

The path that led to the barn was covered with packed, well-worn snow – even during storms, the animals still had to be fed and watered and tended. No lights were on at the house, but if no one was home right then, they would be soon. He needed to be quick. Get in, get out.

TJ had walked up that path with Mike after her father told her never to come back. Mike never saw her cry about it. He knew she did though because sometimes he'd catch her with her eyes swollen and red, and he'd realize it was her mother's birthday. Or her brother's, or one of her sisters'.

But she'd said she'd never go back and, as far as he knew, she never had.

She chose instead to fight *her* fight, to live *her* life, to build *her* empire. She'd wanted to make the world fit *her*.

Except that right as she was gaining traction, she vanished.

And now?

He wasn't sure she'd be waiting for him in the barn. He just knew the barn had something to tell him.

His secret, TJ had written.

Inside the barn, he smelled hay and manure, heard animals moving heavily against each other, breathing deeply, lowing softly. He was startled by how warm and familiar it all was.

This place had been TJ's childhood. Horses and cows, hard work and long hours.

She'd told him she loved it. Liked riding the horses through the woods, liked brushing them and cleaning their hooves and smelling the sweet feed when she poured it into their buckets. She liked watching the spring calves chasing each other around the fields. She'd loved the old structure, the stables and pens, the huge storage areas above.

She hadn't wanted to make farming her life, but of all her siblings, she was the only one who had loved the farm, and who hadn't been eager to get away.

When she was ten, she'd made a private corner up in the abandoned west side of the loft, hidden behind bales of hay. She'd kept books and a pillow and a sleeping bag up there. She'd shown Mike her hiding place once, well before the day her father told her never to come back. When she'd talked about her hide-away, Mike watched her eyes light up.

"Mom and Dad don't go up there because this side of the loft only has a rickety ladder, and the loft on the other side has stairs. In the summer, I used to drag my guitar up there, and take food and extra batteries for my flashlight, and I'd spend as many nights there as I could. It's the best place in the world for reading on rainy days. Best place to stretch out and do homework. Best place to hang out with the barn cats and play with the kittens."

He'd suggested another thing it might be the best place for, raising an eyebrow, grinning wickedly.

That was one of the few times she'd flat-out turned him down. "The loft is sacred," she'd said. "This is the place where I was a kid. Where I read every book I ever loved, and listened to the radio and practiced the guitar until my fingers bled. This is the place where I wrote my first songs, and where I dreamed big dreams."

If there was a message for him in the barn, he thought he'd find it up in her loft.

So he climbed up, noticing the ladder had gotten less sturdy. He walked carefully through the darkness, feeling his way along the wall. He wanted TJ to be sitting there waiting for him. He wanted to stop chasing after her – he was tired of being three steps behind.

She wanted to tell him whatever it was that had her so scared, and he wanted to figure out a way to fix it for her, but he couldn't understand why she wouldn't just stay put and wait for him to catch up.

He reached the bales she'd used to form her hideaway's wall. He felt along them for the break between the stacks and, when he found it, he worked his way through the little maze to her private space.

And all of a sudden he felt sick. Scared. Chilled clear through, even though the barn, warmed by the cows and horses below, had been cosy and comforting an instant before.

He crouched with his back against the bale wall and tried to see through the darkness. Something was wrong, though he didn't know what. His skin crawled, his gut knotted and he tasted ashes on his tongue. He fished around in his pocket, past the pocketknife to the little flashlight he kept for emergencies.

He played the flashlight over the place where TJ had kept her books and sleeping bag. In the tiny circle of light, he saw two pairs of handcuffs, open, one fixed to each angle of TJ's corner by ten-penny nails bent and hammered back into the wood to form makeshift rings. The handcuffs were stained black in places.

The books – always stacked in the corner – had been ripped apart, their pages scattered, their covers cut and slashed by a knife.

He couldn't find the sleeping bag. It was gone.

That fact made him shake.

He ran the flashlight carefully over every inch of the corner, noting blackened, dried blood and tangles of long dark hair.

Who had used the sleeping bag? And for what? To carry her out after . . .

After . . .

Had her father done this? *Could* her father have done this?

Mike considered the possibility.

Someone knew her well enough to know about her secret place, and burned with enough rage or envy or sick desire to do terrible things to her. Someone wanted to desecrate the place of her childhood happiness.

Or worse.

Her father had sent her away, though. He'd proven himself content never to see her again. Mike couldn't imagine him dragging her back, or doing what Mike thought had been done to her here.

The old man was five different kinds of bastard – but not that kind. Not a sick, twisted pervert, not a sadist, not a torturer.

Not a killer. He'd sent his own child away because she didn't live up to his standards. But he *had* standards. He wouldn't betray those standards.

Mike looked for a note.

There was no note.

But this blood-crusted mess was TJ's secret.

Something hissed, and he jumped and turned to find a barn cat staring at him, back arched, fur on end, ears flat back.

"Shoo," he whispered, realizing he was probably trespassing on its den.

But from the corner of his eye, he caught slight movement, and flicked the flashlight toward it.

A strip of photographs fluttered to the ground.

They hadn't been in the corner before. He'd already searched it. They couldn't have fallen from the sharply angled roof. Nothing had been up there. The only way they could be where they had not been an instant before was if TJ was in the barn.

"TJ?" He kept his voice low. "TJ? Are you here?"

Are you hiding in the shadows, watching me – still not dressed for the weather? Still pale and quiet and withdrawn, when previously you were the sunshine in any room?

Are you what I think you are?

Nothing answered him but silence. He picked up the ribbon of pictures and turned it over.

Written on the back: "Do you remember your promises?"

He did. And he remembered where that strip of photos came from.

The lights were on in the house when he headed up the hill to his car. He thought about stopping by the house to tell her parents what he'd found in the barn.

But no. He'd follow this thing through to the end, wherever that end might be. He'd find out the truth.

And then he'd make sure everyone knew it.

*　　*　　*

After a string of gorgeous spring days, April showers had arrived. Outside the mall, the rain came down in sheets.

TJ was too elated to care. She'd found *Dance Naked*, Silver Obsession's first album, in the rack at one of the mall's music stores, and was holding it up to show him.

"See? The cover is perfect." She flipped it around, and laughed gleefully. The packager she and the rest of the band had hired had added a little pull-away tab over her breasts, with CENSORED in big red letters across the black strip. "I'll bet half the guys who buy the album buy it just to pull the tab off when they get home."

Mike snorted. "Not a chance. *Ninety-five* per cent of the guys who buy the album buy it to pull that tab. And *none* of those tabs are still in place when your male buyers get home."

"C'mon . . ."

"I'm serious," Mike said. "I know my people. We do not wait to see hot breasts. We pay for our merchandise, we get it out of the store, we find the first corner where we can take a look in private, and we open the package."

"Your people, huh?" TJ laughed and hugged him. "I'm grateful for your people. According to the demographic tests we've been getting back, women hear the songs and *then* buy the album. But men, ages nineteen to twenty-eight, buy the album and then listen to the songs. And according to our packager, men in that age group don't generally buy music by women, and they don't generally buy first albums. So I'm reaching beyond my expected market." She hugged herself and bounced up and down just a little as the excitement of her first real success caught up with her.

He hooked an arm around her waist and pulled her close. "You're wonderful. And now everyone will know it." They walked out of the music store, past the giant aquarium and down toward the food court. "With a different cover, all those men would have written you off as a pretty face and figured you were just another pop singer. You bypassed that whole 'pretty face' issue with your record cover concept. Your male listeners don't even know you have a face."

She laughed again. "I love your sense of humor."

"And I love the fact you think I have one."

They got burgers and fries and shakes from one of the shops at the food court and sat down to enjoy their meal together.

All of a sudden TJ turned serious. "Our manager got us a string of good bookings on the strength of record sales."

Mike tried to bring the lightness back to the conversation. "And you're worried because your contract calls for you to do one of the numbers with no shirt on?"

The corner of TJ's mouth quirked in a smile. "Nothing quite that awful." But the smile faded and she leaned forward to look into his eyes. "But things are going to change for us. This first tour is ten weeks, Mike. Small venues, but not bars, so we'll have a chance to actually get some notice. Only . . . the band and I will be living between the bus and crummy motels, and the tour never comes near here, so I'm going to be gone the whole ten weeks." She paused and looked up at him, a little hope in her eyes. "I mean, unless you could come along . . . ?"

And there it was. "I wish I could. But you were right about the cover generating good publicity for me. I'm getting commissions for more than dog portraits and paintings of newborns taken from photographs. And I also need to hit my deadline for the little show I've been offered at the Westhill Gallery." He sighed. "It isn't a ten-week tour. But it's a start."

"I know. And I understand. We both have our hands on our dreams, and now is not the time for either of us to let go."

He nodded. This was the part of the two of them he didn't want to face, or to think about. "We won't have to do this for ever," he told her.

"I know. But while I'm gone, I want you to promise me . . ." She stopped and stared down at her hands on the table edge in front of her. Around them, the din of the mall roared on, but the two of them seemed to slip into a hole in the universe where everything hushed.

"What do you want to ask me?"

She looked up from staring at her hands, and he saw her swallow. "I want three promises from you before I go."

He waited.

She frowned. "You're not going to say 'all right'?"

"You're asking this seriously. I'll answer it seriously. If I agreed before I heard what you have to say, it would be because I was blowing you off, TJ. I won't do that. Tell me what you want, and I'll decide."

She considered that for a long moment. "Thank you."

He waited.

"One: promise you won't forget me."

He smiled and nodded. "I promise. I can't forget you. You're my gravity and my oxygen."

"Promise you'll wait for me."

"What? You think there's another one of you running around out there somewhere? TJ, I knew from our first date that you were the only woman I was ever going to love. I promise. I'll wait for you."

She nodded. Took a deep breath. "Promise you'll always find me."

He frowned and studied her, not certain what she meant by that. "I don't understand," he told her at last.

"I've had nightmares. That I get . . . lost. I can't explain it, but they scare me."

She shared his bed. He was with her every minute he could grab from every single day. When had she had nightmares? "You didn't tell me?"

"They're stupid, Mike. They're childish, ridiculous. I wake up shaking and you're right there next to me, where you belong, and I take a deep breath and let go of my fear because I know everything is all right. But when I'm out on the road, when I'm in bed by myself, I may wake up from the damn nightmares and think they're real. So I just want you to promise me, if I get lost, you'll find me."

He took her hand in his, and ran his thumb over the calluses on her fingertips. "Always, TJ. If I have to march into Hell to get you, I will always find you."

"OK," she said, and her radiant smile returned. "I'm sorry for the stupidity. I haven't had nightmares since I was a kid, but now I'm having them all the time."

They finished their meal and wandered through the mall.

In an electronics store, they bumped into Brandon, and TJ told him about her upcoming tour. Brandon, who privately worried to Mike that TJ was going to get famous and move on, breaking Mike's heart in the process, congratulated her with enthusiasm.

Brandon seemed genuinely happy for her. Mike took it as a good sign. He knew TJ was going to be with him for ever, and he wanted Brandon to accept her, just so he'd stop worrying about Mike getting hurt.

The three of them parted company on their way out of the mall, when TJ decided she wanted pictures of Mike and her to take with her on the road.

A photo booth sat next to the mall entryway, situated between a drinks machine and four coin-op kiddie horses.

"I want your face in my pocket," TJ said, and Mike asked, "Is that even legal in this state?"

"Depends on which pocket." She laughed and hugged him, and the two of them squeezed into the booth like a couple of teenagers on a first date.

She cuddled up against him and fed the machine enough dollars to get a strip of photographs for each of them.

Then they made faces into the mirror while the camera counted down, then clicked, counted down, then clicked.

He would have bought another round, but the voice on the intercom said the mall was closed.

So they climbed out of the booth, and he pulled the photographs out of the tray.

There was only one strip.

And Mike heard someone running away.

"Stupid machine," TJ said.

Mike stared back the way they had come, listening to the receding footsteps. "Idiot kids. They think it's funny to take something someone else paid for."

Mike studied the pictures and said, "You're gorgeous as ever," and handed the strip of pictures to her. "Keep them in your shirt pocket so I'll know you have me close to your heart."

He couldn't count the number of times in the years that followed that he wished he'd gone after the little shit who'd stolen the second strip.

He wished right then he had those photos.

The mall seemed run-down and tired now, the snow falling beneath the orange glow of the sodium vapor lamps looking dingy rather than enchanting.

Mike didn't think TJ was going to be there. He'd stopped hoping for a happy ending back at the barn. Now he just wanted an ending of any sort. The truth. A way to understand why his world came to an end five years earlier. He had the "what" of the secret, he thought. Now he needed the "who".

He shoved through the mall doors and found the photo booth still there. An OUT OF ORDER sign hung beside each curtained entry.

Naturally the damn thing would be out of order.

He stared at TJ's scrawl on the back of the photos.

He remembered his promises. He'd never forgotten her. He'd never stopped waiting for her.

And he'd tried every lead he could to find her. He'd killed his future as a fine artist looking for her and had never found her, not even a clue as to what had really happened to her. She'd been lost, and she'd stayed lost. He'd failed her.

The remembered pain of his desperate search washed over him again. Everything he tried was futile. Every resource he explored gave him nothing. He'd lost her, but was never able to let go of her.

After three years, wrung out and broken, he'd taken time off from his search.

His painting career was a shambles, and he no longer had any desire to bring it back to life. He'd picked up a camera instead, and started taking pictures rather than painting them, because photographs didn't pull his attention away from what mattered the way painting did.

He hated himself for staying behind to paint when TJ wanted him to go with her. He blamed himself for her disappearance.

If he'd been taking photos, he could have traveled with the band. Could have been with her when the truth behind her nightmares had stepped between the two of them and ripped them apart.

He could have stopped disaster from happening, and she would never have gotten lost, and he would never have been without her.

He turned the strip of pictures over again, and looked at the two of them, mugging for the camera. The content of the pictures was standard stuff. One was of the two of them grinning, then one was TJ with her fingers behind his head in a V. Then the two of them kissing like they just heard the world was ending. Another one like that, because they'd got sidetracked. And the last one showed him with his face buried in her neck and her winking at the camera.

They were . . . cute. What made them magnificent was *her*. She lit them up like a goddess among mud men.

"Where did you go?" he asked her winking image. "And why am I chasing you?"

He slid into the booth, and sat down. She'd wanted him to come *here*, and it didn't matter that the photo booth didn't work. He wasn't going to get his picture taken. He was here to get the next part of her message. At first he didn't see anything out of the ordinary. It was the same booth. The seat was a bit more worn. Kids had scratched more graffiti onto the painted metal walls.

He sighed, closed his eyes, and remembered TJ with him, the way her warm, soft body pressed up against his, the weight of her head on his shoulder.

He leaned back, feeling tears creeping to the corners of his eyes. He squeezed them away, swallowed hard a few times and, when he had himself under control, opened his eyes and found himself staring at the ceiling of the booth.

He was looking up at a photograph of his own face, staring straight at him, wearing a bereft expression.

The picture had been taken through a bus window, and he realized now when TJ had taken it – he'd been in the parking lot the band had left to go on tour. He'd never seen that picture before.

He took it down and studied it, trying to figure out why the image made him queasy. He looked like a wreck already. He didn't yet know she was about to vanish from his life. Knowing what that picture actually represented, though – that had to be the cause of his queasiness.

Except . . . there was something else. A tiny detail out of place that his subconscious mind had spotted but his conscious mind hadn't yet caught. He kept looking, mentally dividing the photograph into a grid, and going over each square in turn.

And there it was.

Brandon was in the parking lot, too.

Brandon, who didn't like TJ well enough to see her off, and who seemed to be keeping himself out of sight anyway.

He stood deep in the background, leaning on the back of a white sedan that looked like a rental car.

And Brandon wasn't looking at TJ. He was staring at Mike, and though his face in the picture was small, the image was clear. The expression on Brandon's face was one of fury. Despair. Pain.

Longing.

Longing?

Mike stopped and little pieces of his friendship rearranged themselves into a new pattern, and took on a different shape.

Brandon's words as he was getting ready to flee his third wedding rang through Mike's memory: "Hell, let's both just swear off women right now. I have all the damn tickets with me. *We* can go to Aruba, drink ourselves stupid, and do things we'll both regret that don't involve getting married."

Mike got out of the booth feeling like an old man, his knees weak and his heart racing. He leaned against the frame of the photo booth and looked down into the tray.

A strip of pictures lay there.

He pulled them out, noticing that they were muddied, stained and punctured. He turned them over. They were the missing second set of pictures.

The strip that was supposed to have been his.

In each picture, TJ's face had been stabbed repeatedly.

Penknife? Nail? Mike didn't know. Couldn't guess.

But he knew where he was going next.

Mike stood in the snow at the end of Brandon's steep driveway, unable to force his feet up the walk. He knew he had to talk to Brandon. Confront him.

He knew the answer to his questions, and maybe the end of his years-long search, lay at the top of that hill. But he was frozen at the foot of the drive, kept there by some barrier inside himself he couldn't cross.

The drive to Brandon's home curved from the street up the hill to the estate. The house hunkered at the top of the hill, blank-eyed and forbidding, a darker smear against the lead-grey sky.

No lights were on.

Brandon might have decided to take his honeymoon alone, Mike thought.

Or maybe, when Mike told him TJ was back, he'd decided to leave the country for good.

The answers were up the hill.

Mike kept standing at the bottom, shaking. He was going to lose the man who had been his best friend since he was ten. And he realized TJ wasn't coming back because she was dead. The two people Mike had loved most in his life were gone, and he couldn't find the strength to walk up the hill and find out whatever truth waited there.

I should have stayed in the car and driven up to the house, he thought, and then couldn't figure out why he hadn't done just that.

At that moment, though, he caught movement from the wooded lot behind the house.

Light. Faint, pale light.

Whatever force had nailed his feet to the ground released him, and he started walking toward that light, and then running, and then racing as if his life depended on it.

"TJ!" he shouted, but his voice disappeared into the darkness and the falling snow.

The light started moving toward him, toward him.

He slowed.

The light was TJ. Dressed in jeans and a Silver Obsession T-shirt, without sweater or coat or gloves or boots to keep her warm.

She watched him solemnly, and stopped as he drew close to her. Waiting.

Waiting in a place he never would have thought to look for her. The place she would never have come on her own.

He knew what he was seeing, and he knew why, but he didn't want to admit it. He wanted to think that when he reached for her, he would be able to touch her. That when he wrapped his arms around her, he'd be able to pull her close.

"You found me," she said when they were close enough to touch. "You promised you'd find me. And you found me."

He nodded. He couldn't speak. He couldn't find a way to force words to move past his tear-choked throat.

Why had she come to him during Brandon's wedding? If she'd been on Brandon's property all along, why hadn't she reached out to him sooner?

"I have things I have to tell you," she told him. He moved toward her, but she backed up a step and held up her hand to stop him. "Listen first. This is important."

"Brandon did this to you," he croaked.

She nodded. "He followed the bus, caught me when we

stopped for gas, told me you'd been hurt in an accident on your way home, said you were in the hospital and you were asking for me. He said he was afraid you wouldn't make it."

"And you went with him."

"Of course. I didn't get my things off the bus, didn't waste time letting anyone know I was going. I figured I'd catch up with them. But I would have gone with him if you'd scraped your knee and asked for me. I was missing you so much I couldn't think from the second I got on that bus."

"How long had he been after you?"

"After me?"

"Stalking you."

"He wasn't after me, Mike. Not the way you think, anyway. I think he snapped that day, when I left and he realized even with me gone, you still didn't see him the way he saw you."

"But he killed you."

She nodded. "He took me to my hiding place in the barn."

"I'd told him about it. I just thought you were so cool for making a place like that for yourself. I never, ever thought anyone would use it to hurt you." Mike closed his eyes and focused on breathing slowly, the only trick he'd ever learned to calm himself that actually worked. He'd given Brandon the tools to destroy her. He thought of those bloody handcuffs, imagined her up there, begging for mercy, and Brandon— "What did he do to you?"

"Not what you think. He gagged me, dragged me up there, handcuffed me to the wall so I had to listen to him, and offered me an ungodly amount of money to disappear from your life. He was calm at first. Fighting hard to sound reasonable, and to keep me from seeing how desperate he was. He offered to fund my career, get me meetings with the biggest guys in the music business. Offered to pay for production and distribution for every album I made if they wouldn't sign me. Promised no matter what it cost, he'd make sure I had the career I wanted – the career I'd fought so hard for. He told me he'd make sure I wouldn't have to do crummy tours. He kept pointing to all the things in my corner of the barn that were reminders of my dreams of singing and writing songs and being famous. He said that I was lucky. That I had a big dream, a magnificent dream. He told me I could have a wonderful life just having that dream come true.

"And then he told me you were the only big dream he'd ever had. He said all he'd ever wanted since you guys were boys was for you to look at him some day and see him the way he saw you. For you to love him back."

Mike said, "I didn't figure that out until today."

"He feared rejection by you more than anything else in the world. So he made sure you would never guess he was gay. That until you loved him, he wasn't going to let you know how he loved you."

"All the men in the world who would have loved him back, and he wanted someone who never would. Not that way, anyway."

"I understood how he felt. If I'd made my deal with him, I could have found anyone in the world to replace you. But to do that, I would have had to give you up. You. And he didn't understand that you were bigger than my music, or that I could want to go on crummy tours and have you not with me, as long as I knew you were making your dreams real, too. He didn't understand *us*."

"No," Mike agreed. "He could never figure out why I loved you."

TJ said, "I was stupid to refuse his offer, though. I could have walked away from the barn if I'd just been thinking. I didn't consider that with what he'd done, he couldn't just let me go back to my regular life. And he didn't consider, of course, that I wouldn't have a price – that he couldn't buy me." She sighed. "If I'd been smarter, I would have agreed, then found a way to get word to you, and given him his money back. But I wasn't smarter. And neither was he."

Mike's fists knotted into balls. "What did he do?"

"First, he started crying. Hard, scary crying. The kind of crying you do when you look at everything you ever wanted, and it's dead on the floor, burning, crushed, no way to save any of it. Then he got up and climbed down the ladder, and I could hear him still crying while he was digging around down there. He didn't say what he was going to do, but I knew. It wasn't until then that I realized I could have worked with him and saved myself, but I'd trapped him. So I fought to get away. He came back upstairs with my father's cattle gun."

She paused. "He'd stopped crying by then, but he still looked sick and scared. He told me, 'I'm sorry. You don't deserve this, but I can't let you go.' He held the stunner to my head. I was terrified. And then it was over."

She stopped, and stood there looking at him.

Mike thought through everything she'd told him, considered Brandon, considered everything Brandon had done. And he came to an ugly realization. "You couldn't have saved yourself."

"If I'd agreed to his plan, he would have let me go. You didn't see him. He was devastated."

"I believe he was. But not for the reason you think. If he'd truly believed he could buy you out, he would have met you in a restaurant with his checkbook. He wouldn't have dragged you to the barn where, I'm guessing, he already had the handcuffs nailed to the wall. He did, didn't he?"

She nodded slowly. She didn't say anything, so Mike continued. "So he'd already made the trip there before he took you there. Premeditation. He'd thought out his plan. And Brandon is the least spontaneous person I know. He never does anything he hasn't planned in at least six directions.

"He never believed you loved me, TJ. He always thought some day you were going to break my heart. And I think he wanted to fool himself into thinking he would give you a chance – that if you gave him what he wanted, he would let you go. Some part of him was pretending that he could live with you still out there, able to go back on your word and seek me out at any time. But from the moment he decided what he was going to do, some part of him knew that he wasn't going to be able to drag you into the barn and handcuff you to the walls and then let you walk out of there alive, no matter what you promised."

"Oh, God," she whispered.

"He knew what he was going to end up doing the moment you got into his car. If you'd agreed to take his bribe, he would have killed you without regret, because you would have proven to him you *could* be bought, and he would have told himself you weren't good enough for me. As it was, he knew he'd been wrong about you, and you *were* the person I'd always known you were. Which made you a bigger threat. He still couldn't set you free – and he didn't want to, because he had to know I'd always choose you."

TJ closed her eyes. "He didn't understand how true that was.

He killed me, stuffed me into my sleeping bag and dumped me in the abandoned well at the back of this property. Then he used my email account to tell my parents I'd gone to Argentina. But he lost you anyway, because you gave up everything that mattered to you, including your painting, and being his best friend, to look for me." She wrapped her arms around herself and shivered. "I felt so sad for him, for how desperate he was, and how much he hurt. Even when he killed his first wife—"

"He *what*!"

"Right. I knew about that because I saw him do it. I forget no one else knows. It looked like an accident, but it wasn't. He went through with the whole thing – dated her, pretended to be her perfect man so she'd fall in love with him, and then killed her – all so you would know that he'd had someone who loved him, and she'd died. He wanted you to think he'd lost even more than you had, because he'd lost a wife who died, while you just lost a girlfriend you thought dumped you. He did it so you'd stop searching for me and go to him."

"Did he kill the second one?"

"No. He thought maybe the reason you were still looking for me by that time was because I'd shamed you. He'd walk around his house muttering to himself about it. He thought if he had someone who did that to him, and he got over her and the humili-ation of what she did, he could convince you to get over me."

"And when I didn't?"

"That's when I got scared for you. Yesterday's wedding was an enormous, expensive charade. He hired the bride and her fake family and the pretend minister, and paid them to act out that whole terrible scene so he could talk you into taking off with him for a month to help him get over this latest humiliation."

"His whole purpose in that wedding was to get me to go on his honeymoon with him?"

"Yes. Only this time, *you* were in danger. The tickets weren't for Aruba. They were for Argentina. No extradition. He had a passport for you, a house there, well away from everyone and everything. He intended to make you love him. The way he tried to make me agree to leave you."

"Oh, hell."

"I had to warn you. It took everything I had to make myself visible to you. I was just lucky he left me on his own property.

Making myself visible to someone alive gets harder the further I am from my body."

"So you saved my life."

TJ walked over, her eyes sad. She wrapped her arms around him, and he was stunned that she was warm. That he could feel her. He pulled her close, knowing as he did that he was hallucinating or was wishing he felt something he couldn't feel. But for whatever time he could trick himself into believing this was all real, he would.

Her cheek on his neck was warm and soft. Exactly as he remembered it. Exactly as he dreamed it. Her hair smelled like sunshine, her body was full and firm.

She held him tightly, rocking slowly with him from side to side. "I want you to know that if you stay calm and just hold on to me now, you'll be able to make your choices when you understand what they are. If you panic, I'm going to lose you again."

"What choices?"

"There's a moment when you realize something is true, and no matter how bad it is, you're suddenly . . . free. I don't know a better way to describe it. You know it doesn't bind you anymore. You know you aren't chained to it anymore. This is going to be one of those moments – and you have to know that sometimes, for some people, choosing to be bound is better than choosing freedom."

"I'm not sure I understand."

"Are you cold, Mike?"

"Well, no, but I have a coat and a hat and boots and . . ."

"Do you?"

He let go of her, stepped back, and looked down at himself. He wasn't wearing a coat. Or boots. He was standing in the snow in a black tuxedo and a grey silk cummerbund, glossy black shoes and a starched white shirt.

TJ said, "Brandon had an accident yesterday. He panicked when you told him you'd seen me. He was going to knock you out and take you with him, to try to convince you that you loved him. Only he hit you too hard."

"The Argentinian—" Mike said, then stopped. "Brandon killed you five years ago and made up the story of you running off, so of course there was never an Argentinian. He just yelled that so I'd turn my back to him."

"Yes." TJ took his hands in hers and pulled him close to her again. "Brandon lost everything that mattered to him yesterday. I still might. You don't have to."

"Talk to me, TJ. Make sense."

"You know the truth now. You died yesterday. So any second there's going to be a bright light, and you're going to be able to step into it and leave here."

"So we'll step into the light together," Mike said, "and live happily ever after."

"It doesn't work that way. I turned away from the light when it came for me, because you didn't know what had happened to me, and I couldn't let you wonder. I knew someday I'd find a way to tell you what happened. And then, I realized maybe I could save your life – only that didn't work." She pulled back from him just enough to look up into his face. "I stayed, and now I can never leave. The light only comes for you once."

"Then when it comes, I won't go. I'll hold you until it gets here, and I'll tell it to go away."

They stood holding each other. The light didn't appear.

They held each other for a long time. The light still didn't appear.

TJ said, "Mike? I don't understand. Did you already *see* the light?"

Mike considered. "I was in the shower this morning, horrible headache, looked like death warmed over when I saw myself in the mirror. And I got these blinding concussion halos—"

"What were you doing when you got them?"

"Figuring out how to find you."

"Did you have any urge to relax and embrace the light?"

"No. I had the urge to take something for the headache to make it go away so it would stop distracting me, because I'd promised you I would find you, and for the first time in five years, I knew you were somewhere out there to be found."

"You promised, so you stayed." She laughed. "Mike, you're the only person in the world who would look at your invitation to the afterlife as a bother to be fixed with two aspirin, rather than as something glorious you were giving up."

"Not true. I'm the only person in the world who had a chance to find something more glorious than some shiny afterlife." He looked down at her and grinned, and saw her smile in return, that luminous smile he'd seen for the first time on their first date. "So. We both gave up Heaven. Or whatever was supposed to come next. Does that mean we get to spend eternity here?"

"If I have my way, it does. You kept your promises, Mike. You remembered me, you believed in me, and you found me. You didn't quite have to march into Hell to do it . . . but close enough. And I kept my promise, too."

He studied her intently. "I never asked you for a promise."

"I made one anyway. On our very first date, when I knew you were the one I wanted to be with."

He closed his eyes and pulled her close, and she was warm and round and soft in his arms. He nuzzled her hair, and she smelled of summer and sunlight. "What was your promise?"

And when he opened his eyes, they were in the middle of summer, in the hollow down by the stream, sitting on a blanket with a picnic basket between them, and she smiled at him like he was her hero, and she was the fire inside of the sun.

She walked to their tree, once again unscarred, and trailed her finger across the bark. In its wake, her promise glowed gold.

TJ
+
MK
>>>--4EVR--->

Author Biographies

C. T. Adams
C. T. Adams is a *USA Today* bestselling author and winner of the *RT Book Reviews* Career Achievement Award in Paranormal Romance. She frequently co-authors with Cathy L. Clamp and also publishes on her own under the pen name Cat Adams. Adams and Clamp have written the popular Blood Singer, Tales of the Sazi and Kate Reilly/Thrall series.
www.catadams.net

Annette Blair
Award-winning author Annette Blair owes her contemporary theme – Magic with Heart – to Salem, MA. Whether magic or destiny, this national bestselling writer pens single titles for Berkley Sensations and Vintage Magic Mysteries for Berkley Prime Crime. Her historical backlist can soon be found on an e-reader near you. She has published thirty books to date.
www.annetteblair.com

Anna Campbell
Multi-award winning Anna Campbell, voted Australia's favourite romance writer, authors passionate Regency-set romance for Avon. Anna lives in Australia and loves to travel, especially in the United Kingdom.
www.annacampbell.info

Carolyn Crane

Carolyn Crane is the author of the popular Justine Jones: Disillusionists trilogy (*Mind Games*, *Double Cross* and *Head Rush*). She lives in Minneapolis with her husband and cats.
www.authorcarolyncrane.com

Gwyn Cready

Gwyn Cready is the recipient of the 2009 RITA Award for Best Paranormal Romance and the author of *Tumbling Through Time*, *Seducing Mr. Darcy*, *Flirting with Forever*, *Aching for Always* and *A Novel Seduction*. She has been called "the master of time travel romance". *A Novel Seduction* is her first foray into contemporary romance, as well as men in kilts, and she found both eminently satisfying. She lives in Pittsburgh with her family.
www.cready.com

Jennifer Estep

New York Times and *USA Today* bestselling author Jennifer Estep writes the Elemental Assassin urban fantasy series (her story here takes place between books *Tangled Threads* and *Spider's Revenge*), for Pocket Books and the Mythos Academy young adult urban fantasy series for Kensington. She's also the author of the Bigtime paranormal romance series. Jennifer is forever prowling the streets of her imagination in search of her next fantasy idea.
www.jenniferestep.com

Donna Fletcher

USA Today bestselling author of over thirty Celtic historical romances and paranormals, including her popular Sinclare Brothers series and Wyrrd Witches series. Her books are sold worldwide.
www.donnafletcher.com

Jeannie Holmes

Jeannie fears spiders, large bodies of water and bad weather. Therefore, she moved from rural Mississippi to the Alabama Gulf Coast where all three are in abundance. She writes the Alexandra Sabian series when she isn't spending time with her husband and four neurotic cats.
www.jeannieholmes.com

Holly Lisle

Holly Lisle is a full-time novelist with more than thirty novels and many short stories published, and more than a million copies of her work in print. She's in the process of retiring from teaching to devote herself exclusively to fiction, with three courses yet to complete before she's done. She has a husband and three kids (two adult and one closing the gap entirely too quickly).
www.hollylisle.com

Julia London

Julia London is the *New York Times* and *USA Today* bestselling author of more than twenty romantic fiction novels. She is the author of the popular Desperate Debutante and Scandalous historical romance series, as well as *The Year of Living Scandalously*, the first novel in the Secrets of Hadley Green series. Julia is the recipient of the *RT* Bookclub Award for Best Historical Romance and a four-time finalist for the prestigious RITA award for excellence in romantic fiction. She lives in Round Rock, Texas, with her husband.
www.julialondon.com

Liz Maverick

Liz Maverick is the bestselling, award-winning author of thirteen romance novels. Maverick and her books have been featured in *USA Today*, *Cosmopolitan* magazine, *San Francisco Magazine*, the *Chicago Sun-Times*, the *Toronto Star* and more. Known for writing fast-paced, unique plots, she created the *USA Today* bestselling author continuity series Crimson City and wrote the *Cosmopolitan* magazine Book Club Pick *What a Girl Wants*. Her science fiction romance novel *Wired* won the PRISM award and was named a Top Book of 2009 by *Publishers Weekly*.
www.lizmaverick.com

Cindy Miles

Cindy Miles is a national bestselling author of romantic ghost stories.
www.cindy-miles.com

Dru Pagliassotti

Author of the award-winning steampunk romance *Clockwork Heart*, Dru Pagliassotti has also recently published a

contemporary horror novel, *An Agreement with Hell*. She runs the Harrow Press and is a professor of communication at California Lutheran University, where she researches Yaoi manga and male/male romance novels.
www.drupagliassotti.com

Caridad Piñeiro

New York Times and *USA Today* bestselling paranormal and romantic suspense author Caridad Piñeiro wrote her first novel in the fifth grade. Bitten by the writing bug, Caridad continued with her passion for the written word through high school, college and law school. Her first novel was released in 1999, and today she has twenty-nine published novels and novellas to her credit. When not writing, Caridad is an attorney, wife and mother to an aspiring writer and fashionista.
www.caridad.com

Sara Reinke

Romantic Times Book Reviews magazine describes Sara Reinke as "definitely an author to watch." *New York Times* bestselling author Karen Robards calls Reinke "a new paranormal star", and Love Romances and More hails her as "a fresh new voice".
www.sarareinke.com

Christie Ridgway

Christie Ridgway is the *USA Today* bestselling author of over thirty-five contemporary romances. A five-time RITA finalist and winner of *RT Book Reviews* Career Achievement Award, she is a native Californian known for her sun-drenched, sexy and emotional love stories.
www.christieridgway.com

Sharon Shinn

Sharon Shinn has published twenty novels, one collection and assorted pieces of short fiction since her first book came out in 1995. She has won the William C. Crawford Award for Outstanding New Fantasy Writer as well as a Reviewer's Choice Award from the Romantic Times, and two of her novels have been named to the ALA's lists of Best Books for Young Adults. She also won the 2010 *RT Book Reviews*

Career Achievement Award in the Science Fiction/Fantasy category.
www.sharonshinn.net

Linda Wisdom
Bestselling author Linda Wisdom writes paranormal and urban fantasy romances featuring witches with attitude. She's received a variety of awards over the years and her Hex series has been optioned for film and television.
www.lindawisdom.com